In Ballast to the White Sea

D1607925

led through a fra
o a clearing, then he lea
watched the Unsgaard, snuffin
f wood, the wood of good trees, wo
warmth and goodness of fire. Perha
at her, his own purpose would be
away from it he would see it, li
as moulded, as iron; he would n
now he had hours, hours more
driver still

SOURCE: RARE BOOKS AND SPECIAL COLLECTIONS, UNIVERSITY OF BRITISH COLUMBIA LIBRARY, AND ARE REPRODUCED BY PERMISSION OF PETER MATSON (OF STERLING LORD LITERISTIC) ON BEHALF OF THE ESTATE OF MALCOLM LOWRY.

In Ballast to the White Sea: A Scholarly Edition

---

by
MALCOLM LOWRY

Edited and with an Introduction by
PATRICK A. MCCARTHY

Annotations by
CHRIS ACKERLEY

Foreword by
VIK DOYEN, MIGUEL MOTA, &
PAUL TIESSEN

University of Ottawa Press | OTTAWA

The University of Ottawa Press acknowledges with gratitude the support extended to its publishing list by Heritage Canada through the Canada Book Fund, by the Canada Council for the Arts, by the Federation for the Humanities and Social Sciences through the Awards to Scholarly Publications Program and by the University of Ottawa. The University of Ottawa Press also acknowledges with gratitude financial and editorial support from Editing Modernism in Canada.

Copy editing: Lisa Hannaford-Wong
Proofreading: Joanne Muzak
Typesetting: Infographie CS
Cover design: Aline Corrêa de Souza and Édiscript enr.
Cover art: Lawren S. Harris, North Shore, Baffin Island II, c. 1931 © National Gallery of Canada
Interior Images: Weiyan Yan

Library and Archives Canada Cataloguing in Publication

Lowry, Malcolm, 1909-1957, author
In ballast to the White Sea : a scholarly edition / by Malcolm Lowry ;
edited, with introduction & textual notes, by Patrick A. McCarthy ;
annotations by Chris Ackerley ; foreword by Vik Doyen, Miguel Mota & Paul Tiessen.

Includes bibliographical references.
Issued in print and electronic formats.
ISBN 978-0-7766-2208-8 (pbk.).--ISBN 978-0-7766-2180-7 (pdf).--
ISBN 978-0-7766-2179-1 (epub)

I. Ackerley, Chris, 1947-, annotator II. McCarthy, Patrick A., 1945-, editor III. Title.

PS8523.O96I5 2014 C813'.52 C2014-905792-X
C2014-905793-8

Reprinted by permission of SLL/Sterling Lord Literistic, Inc.
Copyright by The Estate of Malcolm Lowry.

© University of Ottawa Press, 2014
Printed in Canada

For Jan Gabrial

Contents

General Editor's Note

This annotated edition of Malcolm Lowry's "lost" novel, *In Ballast to the White Sea*, is the second of three related Lowry projects undertaken by an international team of Lowry scholars: Chris Ackerley (University of Otago); Vik Doyen (Katholieke Universiteit Leuven); Patrick A. McCarthy (University of Miami); Miguel Mota (University of British Columbia); and Paul Tiessen (Wilfrid Laurier University). The other projects are Doyen's edition of the novella *Swinging the Maelstrom* (along with the distinct earlier version, *The Last Address*) and Mota and Tiessen's edition of the first complete manuscript of *Under the Volcano* (1940). Each edition is annotated by Ackerley. Together, the three editions will give scholars detailed evidence of Lowry's intentions and achievement during the period 1936–1944, a time of transition when he worked simultaneously on three books that he imagined as a Dantean trilogy: *Under the Volcano* as the *Inferno*; *Swinging the Maelstrom* as the *Purgatorio*; and *In Ballast to the White Sea* as the *Paradiso*.

For their invaluable assistance, advice, and support, the editors of these volumes would like to thank the University of Ottawa Press and Peter Matson. We would like to thank also the late Anne Yandle at the University of British Columbia Library's Rare Books and Special Collections, whose early encouragement and guidance was so crucial to all who have worked on this project. Production of these important editions has been made possible by the support of a grant from the Social Sciences and Humanities Research Council of Canada, through its Editing Modernism in Canada project. For his ongoing support and advice as director of EMiC, we owe special gratitude to Dean Irvine.

MIGUEL MOTA
University of British Columbia

Foreword

With the publication of *In Ballast to the White Sea*, Pat McCarthy and Chris Ackerley invite us to a rare and most pleasurable literary event. They unveil a portrait of Malcolm Lowry and his work that most of us have never imagined, revealing the restless literary energy, the play of mind, and the political sensibilities of a barely known Lowry. This is the Lowry of 1929–1936: the Lowry of undergraduate days at Cambridge and, if we take the period of writing, the Lowry up to and including his years in New York. With its emphasis on political commitment, labour unrest, and widespread economic depression that helped to define the 1930s, *In Ballast* underlines Lowry's direct and passionate political engagement during that decade.

In June 1931, Lowry wrote Conrad Aiken, the American novelist who had become his mentor: "my fixation on the sea is complete, & moreover I feel honestly I haven't extracted all the juices from it yet" (*CL* 2:932). A twenty-one-year-old undergraduate at Cambridge, Lowry was writing his first novel just then, based on his 1927 voyage as a deckhand on the cargo ship, SS *Pyrrhus*. *Ultramarine* would appear in London in June 1933. But he was also preparing to carry his passion further, with an August-to-September 1931 journey by sea to Norway in the offing. He would be in search not just of writing material this time, but of a writer, the Norwegian novelist Nordahl Grieg, whose *The Ship Sails On* had deeply affected him. This journey led to *In Ballast to the White Sea*, his sequel to *Ultramarine*. During 1934–1936, having left the London and Paris of his post-Cambridge years and settled in New York, he showed *In Ballast* to publishers, but did not gain a contract. During the next eight years—precisely while he was writing the drafts of *Under the Volcano*—he continued to actively think about and, especially during the latter years, modify *In Ballast*: in Mexico (1936–1938), Los Angeles (1938–1939), and most fully in Vancouver and Dollarton, British Columbia (1939–1944).

However, in 1944 a fire engulfed his cabin on Burrard Inlet, destroyed many of his manuscripts and ended his dream of rewriting *In Ballast*. Margerie, his second wife, carried his *Under the Volcano* manuscripts to safety on the beach below, while Malcolm fled the shack with some of her manuscripts and pieces of his own work, including his *Swinging the Maelstrom* project. Still inside were a thousand pages of *In Ballast*, by then his longest-standing novel-in-progress. Determined to rescue it, he "dashed back into the flames," according to his biographer Gordon Bowker, "and had to be dragged out when a burning beam crashed down across his back." In *Under the Volcano* (1947), in Yvonne's dying vision at the end of Chapter 11, he memorialized the loss of those thousand pages: "Geoffrey's old chair was burning, his desk, and now his book, his book was burning, the pages were burning, burning, burning, whirling up from the fire they were scattered, burning, along the beach."

From June 1944 onward, *In Ballast* would live in Lowry's mind as his great lost work, a marker of ambition and vision left undone. As late as May 1957, one month before his death, he restated that loss. Writing from his final home at the White Cottage in Ripe near Lewes, Sussex, to Canadian poet Ralph Gustafson, Lowry spoke of *In Ballast* as the *Paradiso* in his projected Dantean trilogy, *The Voyage That Never Ends*. In earlier letters, too, he referred to the disappearance of *In Ballast* and also to its supreme importance in his imagined corpus, sending plot details of the story to various correspondents: in 1950 to a book reviewer for the Canadian Broadcasting Corporation; and in 1951 to the German translator of *Under the Volcano* and to David Markson, then a twenty-four-year-old graduate student at Columbia University.

For over twenty years, from 1944 to 1965, the broader community knew virtually nothing of a lost Lowry novel. For readers, Lowry was the author of one great book, *Under the Volcano*, with a much earlier but little-known first novel (*Ultramarine*) to his name. It was only with the publication of *Selected Letters of Malcolm Lowry* in 1965 that word of *In Ballast*, its relation to a Dantean project, and its tragic loss surfaced widely for the first time. In fact, however, when he spoke in those letters about the absolute obliteration of such a novel, Lowry was deceiving his readers. Through those posthumously published letters, Lowry, whether deliberately or not, was in effect bamboozling the literary community, which seemed prepared to accept a romantic interpretation of Lowry as doomed artist. Quite simply, in the *Selected Letters*—and, for that matter, in *Sursum Corda!*, the two-volume *Collected Letters of Malcolm Lowry* published in 1995/1996—he was not telling the whole story.

The recent discovery of the 1936 manuscript of *In Ballast to the White Sea* sets us on a new path in reading Lowry, different from the one along which Lowry attempted to lead us. What we know now is that in 1936 Lowry deposited a carbon copy of his then-current version of *In Ballast*—what he had shown to New York publishers in 1934–1936—with the mother of his first wife, Jan Gabrial, when he and Jan left New York for Mexico. Jan Gabrial later retrieved this copy and—reclaiming the reader/editor role she had provided for Lowry during the mid-1930s—typed a clean copy in 1991. In 2003, two years after her death and in keeping with her intent, the overseer of her estate deposited the clean copy and related material in the Manuscripts and Archives Division of the Humanities and Social Sciences Library of the New York Public Library.

With the present volume, Professors McCarthy and Ackerley construct a new Lowry, productively active during a startlingly fertile period between the publication of *Ultramarine* and *Under the Volcano*. McCarthy, who has edited Lowry's *La Mordida*, responds to the material qualities of the manuscript and to its literary contexts. Ackerley—continuing his tradition of exemplary literary explanation—provides an encyclopedic range of scholarly annotation for *In Ballast*, based on his wide reading and on multiple visits to key sites of the novel. McCarthy and Ackerley have collaborated extensively in producing this volume; they uncover for us new ground that will become central to our understanding of Lowry's distinctive position and status within twentieth-century literary modernism.

As McCarthy points out in his introduction, in 1937, Aiken, when he saw a draft of it in Mexico, said that he found *In Ballast* "a joy to swim in." This novel, in its absence, provided Lowry with an infinite alibi of pursuing dreams of Paradise in an ever-deferred Dantean trilogy; today, in its presence, we savour the realities of Lowry's dream with a newness of immediacy, clarity, and admiration.

VIK DOYEN
Katholieke Universiteit Leuven

MIGUEL MOTA
University of British Columbia

PAUL TIESSEN
Wilfrid Laurier University

Acknowledgments

Various people in several countries (Australia, Belgium, Canada, France, New Zealand, Norway, the United Kingdom, the United States) have contributed to this book, but there would have been no book at all if it were not for Dean Irvine, who in 2006 invited me to participate as a collaborator in Editing Modernism in Canada (EMiC), suggesting, as a project, an edition of Malcolm Lowry's *In Ballast to the White Sea*. Without his encouragement and support, I probably would not have undertaken this edition, which turned out to be even more interesting (and far more complex) than I expected. I am also indebted to Jan Gabrial for preserving a novel that Lowry scholars had long thought lost, and to Peter Matson of Sterling Lord Literistic, representatives of the Estate of Malcolm Lowry, for his support of this edition and Lowry scholarship in general. For access to the manuscripts and notebooks on which I have based this edition I am grateful to the Division of Manuscripts and Archives, New York Public Library (for the Jan Gabrial Papers), and to Special Collections at the University of British Columbia (for other materials, including notebooks for *In Ballast*). At this point I should thank the inventors of the Internet, without which the collaborative long-distance scholarship this book required would have taken far longer, if it were possible at all. On a regular, and often a daily, basis I have relied on Chris Ackerley not only for his remarkable annotations but for advice on editorial questions. He and the other members of our EMiC Lowry support group—Vik Doyen, Miguel Mota, Paul Tiessen—made innumerable suggestions that have led to improvements in the edition; they also sent me files that broadened the range of my research, and Paul even managed to hire a typist to help with the early preparation of the text. I am deeply indebted to all of them. Special thanks to Sherrill Grace and to Stephen W. Kramer (Jan Gabrial's attorney) for answers to my questions about Jan and the typescripts of *In Ballast*, and to the two anonymous reviewers of the manuscript for their detailed evaluations of the manuscript and their suggestions for revision. The University of Miami provided essential support in the form of a travel grant that enabled me to spend time at the New York Public Library and a year-long sabbatical leave that gave me time to write. Among my Miami colleagues there are three whose contributions to the book have been especially important: Phyllis G. Robarts (Otto G. Richter

Library) for resources; John Kirby (Department of Classics) for invaluable help with Lowry's Greek; and Frank Stringfellow (Department of English) for many matters, especially in connection with German writings. I am also indebted to Kay Voss-Hoynes (Orange High School, Pepper Pike, Ohio) for her commentary on Lowry's unreliable Norwegian. Finally, thanks to my wife Yolanda for her patience, love, and support.

Below, Chris has described the important contributions to this edition made by Colin Dilnot and David Large. Here, I add my thanks to his.

PATRICK A. MCCARTHY
University of Miami

I am grateful to my colleagues of the Editing Modernism in Canada editorial team: Pat McCarthy was an ideal collaborator, while (as Pat notes, above) Miguel Mota, Paul Tiessen, and Vik Doyen were unwavering in their support and hospitality. The Royal Society of New Zealand, through the generosity of the Marsden fund, provided both time and funding; the University of Otago and two Heads of my Department, Lyn Tribble and Chris Prentice, supported the various research trips that were required; and my friends, Lisa Marr, Simone Marshall, and Paul Tankard, made useful contributions. Robin Ramsey was a generous host in Vancouver, as was Minou Williams in the United Kingdom, but many others responded to my often esoteric inquiries. These include: Sue Sampson (Shire Hall), for details of Cambridge Castle; Peter Moore (Cambridge), for identifying his namesake's music shop; Ralph Crane (University of Tasmania) for taking me on a guided tour of Preston; and Annick Drösdal-Levillain (France) for assistance with Lowry's Norwegian. The staff of the UBC Special Collections, particularly Sarah Romkey, offered ongoing support; Renu Barrett, archivist at McMaster University, responded immediately to a cry for help; Einar Gustafsson, *historieforteller* of the Ålesund Museum, identified references to (and gave me a map of) the town in the 1930s; the staff of Oslo's *Nasjonalbiblioteket* facilitated my work on Nordahl Grieg; and the Library and Department of Foreign Languages at the University of Bergen offered both hospitality and assistance. I am particularly grateful to Erik Tonning for his help with the Norwegian elements of the book, for his encouragement of the project, and for his generous sponsorship of my time in Norway. I would also like to thank Erik, Matthew Feldman, and my editors at Continuum Press for their forbearance in allowing me to defer another commitment to finish this project, even though it took much longer than I had estimated.

My deepest debts, however, are to David Large (Universities of Sydney and Otago), for his unfailing interest and help, his close readings of my drafts, and his tenacity in tracing some of the obscurities that had eluded me; and to Colin Dilnot for identifying so many of Lowry's ships and locations, for taking me around Liverpool and the Wirral, and for his generosity, not simply as a host, but in sharing with me his vast cornucopia of information about the early Lowry. The first 75 percent of any set of annotations is relatively easy; the next 20 percent increasingly more difficult; and the last 5 percent almost impossible—but that last 25 percent is what matters most, and the greatest thrill of annotation is the revelation of the seemingly impossible. As Napoleon reputedly said, if it is impossible it will take a little longer: this has been, without doubt, the most challenging text that I have ever annotated, and without the unflagging support of these two *compañeros* my commentary would have taken much longer and would have been very much the poorer.

CHRIS ACKERLEY
University of Otago

Introduction

I.

In August 1952 Malcolm Lowry told his editor, Albert Erskine, that the manuscript of his unpublished novel *Dark as the Grave Wherein My Friend Is Laid* had been "deposited in the bank," adding, "it hadn't occurred to me till very recently that there *were* things called safety deposit boxes"; three months later he assured Erskine that two more works in progress, *La Mordida* and *The Ordeal of Sigbjørn Wilderness*, would be deposited the next day (*CL* 2:593, 608). In safeguarding these manuscripts Lowry demonstrated that he had finally learned a lesson that should have been impressed upon him two decades earlier when the typescript of his first novel, *Ultramarine* (1933), was stolen along with the briefcase in which an editor for Chatto & Windus had placed it. Although Lowry had not retained a carbon copy, the book was unexpectedly rescued by his friend Martin Case, who had held onto a late draft that its author had discarded (Day 158–60; Bowker 143–44). Even after this experience, however, Lowry would suffer another, far more traumatic, loss of a manuscript long before he finally began to rely on "safety deposit boxes."

On the morning of 7 June 1944 a fire broke out in the squatter's shack in British Columbia where Lowry and his second wife, Margerie, had lived for three years. They managed to rescue most of his papers, including manuscripts for *Under the Volcano*, but all that remained of another novel, *In Ballast to the White Sea*, were the few papers now stored in Box 12, Folders 14 and 15, of the University of British Columbia's Malcolm Lowry Archive: two small notebooks with preliminary notes for *In Ballast*, the first two pages of a 1936 typescript, a notebook with an earlier draft of Chapters I and II, and several small, circular pieces of charred paper from a handwritten draft and another typescript, both otherwise lost. Lowry never attempted to recreate the novel; instead, he mourned its loss and, in time, romanticized it as a (potentially) great book, its destruction one of the central tragedies of his life. He also referred to *In Ballast* and the fire in later writings, notably *Dark as the Grave*, whose drafts (also at the University of British Columbia) include a long discussion by the protagonist, Sigbjørn Wilderness, of his own lost novel, also called *In Ballast to the White Sea* (UBC 9:5, 341–59).[1]

In their discussions of Lowry's work, critics have relied mainly on these materials and two letters that Lowry sent in August 1951 to David Markson, who was then writing a master's thesis on *Under the Volcano* (CL 2:417–20, 423–30). In the first letter he told Markson that *In Ballast* was "once the sort of Paradiso of the trilogy of which the Volcano was the first, or 'Inferno' section" and claimed that it was "now incorporated hypothetically elsewhere in the whole bolus of 5 books—I think—to be called The Voyage that Never Ends" (CL 2:417). Despite Lowry's intriguing plans to include a new version of *In Ballast* in this projected sequence of books, there is no evidence that he spent any time on that act of reconstruction.

Yet during the years when Lowry told one and all that the only draft of his second novel had been lost there was someone who knew otherwise, much as Martin Case had when the manuscript of *Ultramarine* was stolen. That was Lowry's ex-wife Jan Gabrial, an American whom he had met in Granada, Spain (summer 1933), married in Paris (January 1934), and followed to New York (August 1934). Two years later, when they left for an extended stay in Mexico, Lowry and Jan entrusted a carbon copy of *In Ballast* to her mother, Emily van der Heim.[2] Although the trip was planned, in part, to save their marriage, by December 1937 the Lowrys' relationship had deteriorated so much that Jan moved to Los Angeles. Lowry followed in July 1938 and remained for almost a year before moving to Vancouver, soon to be joined by Margerie Bonner, whom he had met in Los Angeles; they married at the end of 1940, a month after he and Jan were divorced. Lowry and Jan never met or spoke after he left Los Angeles, and he rebuffed her attempts to remain on friendly terms. A few months before the divorce, when Jan wrote to say she might visit Vancouver and would like to see him, he responded curtly, implied (unfairly) that she had used his work as the basis for a story she had published, and refused to see her. Her reply (Gabrial 197–98) was, it appears, the end of their correspondence.

In her memoir *Inside the Volcano*, Jan says that she *almost* contacted Lowry in 1947, after he published *Under the Volcano*, but she was deterred by "the thought that he might view my letter . . . as self-serving, even opportunistic, and . . . by the memory of his final harsh, accusatory note" (Gabrial 198). In fact, she did write such a "letter": a message typed on a postcard with a picture of a Diego Rivera fresco on the other side. Jan congratulated "the big cat"—a pet name for Lowry—on the success of *Under the Volcano*, which she had read three times, and she called the novel "a shattering and miraculous and beautiful and very great book." She also expressed hope that both *In Ballast to the White Sea* and *The Last Address* (the early title for a novella that was posthumously published, in a badly patched together edition, under the title *Lunar Caustic*) would soon be published.[3] Having written this tribute to Lowry's work, however, Jan scribbled over it and set it aside, her dread of a negative response outweighing her desire to congratulate him.[4]

Had Jan sent her message of congratulations it is conceivable, although far from certain, that Lowry would have answered and would have told her about the loss of *In Ballast*. In that case, surely Jan would have remembered having left a typescript at her mother's house eleven years earlier and would have reminded him that the book was not irrevocably lost. Yet it is also quite possible that even as he wrote letters to David Markson about his "lost" novel Lowry himself remembered having given his former mother-in-law a full copy of *In Ballast*, as it then stood, eight years before the fire. Of course there is no way of knowing for certain, but I believe that Lowry did in fact remember, and that he preferred the legend of the tragically burnt novel[5] to the difficulties of revising an incomplete typescript without access to his later revisions (even if they were not extensive). Another, more intractable, difficulty was that since *In Ballast* was shaped by the politics of mid-1930s Europe it would have required considerable rewriting to accommodate the very different world situation of the mid-1940s. Lowry could also have had personal reasons for not returning to the project: he might have wanted to avoid angering his rather volatile second wife by making contact with his first wife or her mother, even over such an important matter, and he clearly wanted to break with his own past and with a novel that was closely associated with *Ultramarine*, which by then he had disowned.[6] Whatever the reason, if Lowry remembered the earlier draft of *In Ballast to the White Sea*, he seems to have told no one.[7]

II.

In its focus on the development of an artist figure, *In Ballast to the White Sea* is a modernist Künstlerroman in the tradition of Mann's *Tonio Kröger* (to which one of the characters alludes in Chapter V), Proust's *In Search of Lost Time*, Joyce's *A Portrait of the Artist as a Young Man*, and Lawrence's *Sons and Lovers*. However, it differs from these familiar examples in several ways, one being that *In Ballast* does not follow the life of its protagonist, Sigbjørn Hansen-Tarnmoor, over the course of many years but focuses on his response to a crisis, or series of crises, over a few months. In this way it resembles *Ultramarine*, for which it was conceived as a sequel and justification. Like Dana Hilliot in *Ultramarine*, Sigbjørn struggles with issues of authenticity and originality; moreover, Dana and Sigbjørn are younger versions of the typical Lowry protagonist. Whether he is named Sigbjørn Lawhill, Bill Plantagenet, Geoffrey Firmin, Martin Striven, Martin Trumbaugh, Sigbjørn Wilderness, Ethan Llewelyn, Sigurd Storelsen, Tom Goodheart, Kennish

Drumgold Cosnahan, or Roderick McGregor Fairhaven, the Lowryan protagonist is, inevitably, a portrait of the artist.

The early chapters of *In Ballast* focus on Sigbjørn (known within his family as Barney) and his brother Tor, two Cambridge undergraduates who were born in Norway but raised in England. Their mother died some years ago; their father, Captain Hansen-Tarnmoor ("Hansen" is usually dropped), is the head of a shipping company. The novel opens in early winter, with the brothers standing on Castle Hill in Cambridge, opposite a prison and allegedly on the spot where "the last hanging on the mound" had taken place. There are several ominous references to hanging and to other disasters, including one that has brought the brothers together, despite their "chemic dissimilarity" and unspecified "former differences": the sinking of a ship, the *Thorstein*, owned by their father's company. Sigbjørn has been a sailor and now wants to be a writer, beginning with a novel about his experiences; unfortunately, as he tells Tor, a Norwegian writer named Erikson "took the sea away from me." To confront his anxieties Sigbjørn would like to travel to Norway to meet Erikson and secure permission to adapt his novel as a play.

When the scene shifts to the streets of Cambridge, their conversation reveals several reasons for the tension between Tor and Sigbjørn, including intellectual differences—Tor regards life as meaningless, "standardless," a matter of "accident," while Sigbjørn believes in "a power for good watching over all things"—and rivalry over Nina, a young woman whom Sigbjørn loves. While the brothers are in a bar they learn that another Tarnmoor Line ship, the *Brynjaar*, has sunk and that human error seems to have been to blame. In Chapter III, at Tor's lodging house, they place a telephone call to their father to assure him of their support; then they go to Tor's room, to talk and drink Irish whiskey. The latest sinking seems to Tor symbolic of the universe, and as his mood turns darker he says that he has thought of committing suicide. Still, he also believes in the importance of social action, of escaping the prison of self through an identification with "the virile solidarity of the proletariat." Later, as Tor plays his violin, Sigbjørn falls asleep, waking up two hours later when Tor shakes him. It is almost time for Sigbjørn to leave, so as not to violate curfew, but first Tor shows him the room where he says he plans to turn on the gas and kill himself. Sigbjørn tries to convince himself that Tor must not be serious, but as he gets back to his own lodging house he feels that he is in a prison.

Given the ending of Chapter III, the form of Chapter IV, a series of letters from Sigbjørn to Erikson, is unexpected, and the movement away from narrative at this juncture means that Tor's suicide looms over the chapter as an unresolved narrative possibility. Yet, in his second letter to Erikson, Sigbjørn appropriates

Tor's phrase when he says that his "duty is with what is popularly called the virile solidarity of the proletariat." The phrase establishes a connection among Tor, Erikson, and (now) Sigbjørn as socialists. The fact that this letter breaks off with the words "My brother—" and two other letters end similarly is the clearest sign in this chapter that Tor did kill himself, and that Sigbjørn, guilt-stricken, has begun to adopt some of his values.

By the end of the novel Sigbjørn will seek out and find Erikson. In the meantime there are scenes in the Liverpool area in which Sigbjørn meets with his father or with Nina, followed by a train ride north from Liverpool to Preston, during which Sigbjørn happens to be seated across from Daland Haarfragre, the captain of a freighter on which he will be working. Later there are scenes in Preston, where a constable and a taxi driver try with mixed success to keep Sigbjørn out of trouble, and aboard the freighter, which was supposed to sail to Archangel (on the White Sea) but is redirected to Aalesund, Norway. Only seventeen chapters are numbered in the typescript, which continues with an unnumbered rough draft of Chapter XVIII, in which Sigbjørn finally arrives in Norway, and further notes.

Like *Ultramarine*, which he based on his experiences in 1927 as a crew member on a freighter, the SS *Pyrrhus*, prior to his first year at Cambridge, *In Ballast* grew out of Lowry's life: in this case, his experience as a Cambridge student whose attempt to write a novel based on his own life at sea is complicated by a growing sense of identification with another author. Around the time when he began writing *Ultramarine*, Lowry read two novels, each published in 1927, that immediately captured his imagination: *Blue Voyage*, by Conrad Aiken, and *The Ship Sails On*, a translation of *Skibet gaar videre* (1924) by the Norwegian writer Nordahl Grieg. Lowry would later tell Markson that *Blue Voyage* "was an enormous influence on me" (CL 2:412), and so it was; but the fact that in the same letter he could not bring himself to name either Grieg or *The Ship Sails On* is a sign that his anxiety over Grieg's influence went even deeper. Lowry borrowed narrative strategies, phrases, and the like from Aiken, but his emotional attachment to *The Ship Sails On* led him to imagine that his own novel, and perhaps even his life, had already been "written" in Grieg's book. In 1931, he attempted to come to terms with his identification with Grieg by sailing to Norway, where, through a set of improbable circumstances that were probably much like those described in *In Ballast*, he managed not only to meet Grieg but (he claimed) to secure permission to adapt *The Ship Sails On* for the stage—perhaps because Grieg, a successful playwright as well as a published poet and novelist, was more interested in working on new projects than in dramatizing his own novel; possibly also because Grieg wanted to humour Lowry. While he was still in Oslo, Lowry wrote a long letter to Grieg (CL 1:102–10), much of it devoted to Rupert Brooke, a subject of Grieg's current writing project. It appears that in a later note Lowry said he hoped to meet with Grieg again, but Grieg declined, citing the press of his creative work and saying, "as a fellow writer I know you will understand and forgive" (Bowker 130).

Lowry often exaggerated the extent to which *Ultramarine* was based on *The Ship Sails On*, even writing, in a 1939 letter to Grieg, "Much of U. is paraphrase, plagiarism, or pastiche, from you" (*CL* 1:192). Yet, despite his anxieties (or, perversely, because of them), Lowry borrowed from Grieg, as when he ended the fifth chapter of *Ultramarine* with the final line of Grieg's second chapter: "Outside was the roar of the sea and the darkness" (Grieg 26; *Ultramarine* 235 [1933 ed.]). He even smuggled part of the line into Chapter VII of *In Ballast*: Sigbjørn tells Nina, "Where I'm going to is the roar of the sea and the darkness, and the night."[8] Both Lowry's anxiety about borrowing from other writers and his determination to keep on borrowing are evident in a 1933 letter to Aiken about *Ultramarine*. After admitting that his novel could be classified as a "cento"—a patchwork of quotations from other writers—Lowry contends that "under the reign of [James Joyce's] Bloom & [T. S. Eliot's] Sweeney, a greater freedom seems to be permitted." In any case, according to Lowry, he could not help borrowing from Aiken: "Blue Voyage, apart from its being the best nonsecular statement of the plight of the creative artist with the courage to live in the modern world, has become part of my consciousness, & I cannot conceive of any other way in which Ultramarine could be written" (*CL* 1:116–17).

Still, after his trip to Norway, Lowry seems to have felt reassured that his fixation on Grieg and his identification with Grieg's protagonist Benjamin Hall need not deter him from continuing to work on *Ultramarine*: after all, Grieg had called him "a fellow writer." Besides, meeting Grieg gave him the basic plot for a second novel, *In Ballast to the White Sea*, in which a Cambridge undergraduate who wants to write a book finds that a Norwegian writer has already written such a book, and has done it better than he can. With its focus on a writer's dilemma and its fictionalization of Lowry's first novel as a book written by Sigbjørn Tarnmoor, *In Ballast* anticipates some of Lowry's post-*Volcano* fictions, including *Dark as the Grave*, *La Mordida*, and "Through the Panama," whose protagonist, Sigbjørn Wilderness, is Lowry's fictional counterpart and author of a version of *Under the Volcano* entitled *The Valley of the Shadow of Death*. In each of these later narratives the protagonist-writer echoes Lowry's sense, when he returned to Mexico in 1945–1946, that he was trapped within the world he had created in *Under the Volcano*, much as Sigbjørn Tarnmoor finds himself already "written" in Erikson's novel, *Skibets reise fra Kristiania* ("The Ship's Voyage from Kristiania," fictional counterpart to Grieg's *The Ship Sails On*). Formerly haunted by another author's novel, Lowry in his later works came to be haunted by his own novel, as descriptions like "[Sigbjørn] went down through the patio haunted by his characters" indicate (DATG 192).

The parallels between *In Ballast* and Lowry's post-*Volcano* (meta)fictions become especially interesting in passages such as this one from "Through the Panama," a story that consists of extracts from Sigbjørn Wilderness's journal:

> The further point is that the novel is about a character who becomes enmeshed in the plot of the novel he has written, as I did in Mexico. But now I am becoming enmeshed in the plot of a novel I have scarcely begun [*Dark as the Grave*]. Idea is not new, at least so far as enmeshment with characters is concerned. Goethe, Wilhelm von Scholz, 'The Race with a Shadow,' Pirandello, etc. But did these people ever have it happen to *them*? (*Hear Us* 30)

In his description of *In Ballast* for David Markson, Lowry also connected Goethe with von Scholz's play, noting that among the very few literary works that develop the theme of someone's "growing sense as of identity" with a fictional character is "a sinister German play running in England called The Race with a Shadow by one Wilhelm von Scholz, based on an idea by Goethe" (CL 2:418).[9] The point is also made explicitly in one of Sigbjørn's letters to Erikson in Chapter IV of *In Ballast*:

> I am well aware that Goethe said the relation of an author with his principal character may be a race with a shadow: I am familiar with von Scholz' play—it was playing in Cambridge not long ago—and I know the scenical idea of the doppelganger to be an old adage; and more mundanely one has heard of people writing to authors saying "I am your character Smith" or "I am your character Jones." I have also read, in a review, an account of a novel, which I have purposely for that reason refrained from reading, on a similar theme, by Louis Adamic. And there is a story by A. Huxley. But this is real, is happening, now, to me— (46–47)

These references to von Scholz point to Lowry's awareness that his themes have been anticipated by other writers, who in turn are dependent on still earlier writers, as when von Scholz "based [his play] on an idea by Goethe." Hence Sigbjørn's revelation that he has been influenced by Erikson's novel is followed immediately by a defence: the situation is not unique (although it is rare enough that Sigbjørn, and therefore Lowry, can claim some measure of originality after all!). Moreover, he says, this is not something happening in a book: instead, "this is real, is happening, now, to me—." Of course, in Lowry's case it *was* happening in a book, as well as in his life. Indeed, there was not much difference between the events of his books and of real life, as he set out to demonstrate in this novel and others.

Lowry alluded to von Scholz's *The Race with a Shadow* in an unpublished 1934 letter to Grieg: "So our destiny takes us—is it a race with a shadow?"[10] This letter is very strange; or would be, had it been written by anyone but Malcolm Lowry. After mentioning *Ultramarine*, which he claims (falsely) is being translated into French, he says that he has included in that novel "a kind of pastiche of one or two of your very earliest poems, which pass through the consciousness of my character," adding that if Grieg is unhappy with what Lowry intended as a "tribute," he will delete the passages from subsequent editions. He also defends the inclusion of passages from Grieg as unavoidable, since "I could not make my protagonist, my or Benjamin's doppelganger, think anything else. That was what he thought even if you wrote it." (Note the similarity to Lowry's claim, in the letter to Aiken cited earlier, that his absorption of *Blue Voyage* into *Ultramarine* was unavoidable.) Later, he says he has finished dramatizing *The Ship Sails On*, although he needs Grieg's help to make the play better; toward the end he refers, almost as an afterthought, to his marriage to Jan. Given his elaborate explanation and defence of his appropriation of "one or two" poems by Grieg, it is noteworthy that Lowry apparently did not send a copy of *Ultramarine* to the man whose book had been such a strong influence on it; moreover, like Sigbjørn, Lowry probably never sent the letter itself. Yet this letter is nonetheless significant, not only for what Lowry says in it but for what he omits: he confesses to plagiarism but provides no details, and mentions using lines from Grieg's poems but is vague about his more significant indebtedness to *The Ship Sails On*. The letter is typical of Lowry's tendency both to appropriate the language of other literary texts and to be so anxious about his borrowings that he has to defend himself against possible charges of plagiarism. Years later the same impulse would surface in a letter to Erskine about *Under the Volcano* in which Lowry said that he had considered "appending a list of notes to the book," to help readers to interpret it and also "to acknowledge . . . any borrowings, echoes, design-governing postures, and so on, as used to be the custom with poets, and might well be with novelists" (*CL* 1:595).

Michel Schneider's observations that "viewed from a certain angle, the history of literature is a history of repetitions, of the already written" and that "intertextuality not only affects but constitutes literary writing" seem especially relevant to modernist writers like Eliot, Pound, and Joyce who tend to incorporate other works within their own, in the form of parallels, allusions, or even direct quotations.[11] Lowry saw himself as part of the contemporary literary scene (he was of course living "under the reign of Bloom & Sweeney"), but his appropriations sometimes extended well beyond the modernist allusive technique that Eliot's friend Aiken had described in a review of *The Waste Land*, where he argued that Eliot and Pound attempted "to make a 'literature of literature'—a poetry not more actuated by life itself than by poetry" ("An Anatomy of Melancholy" 99). Aiken's characterization of *The Waste Land* and the *Cantos* as products of a "very complex and very literary awareness able to speak only, or best, in terms of the literary past, the terms which had moulded its tongue" would have applied with equal force to Lowry, for whom Aiken was also part of the "literary past" that shaped *Ultramarine*. According to Clarissa Lorenz, Aiken's second wife, as Lowry wrote and revised his first novel he showed Aiken numerous drafts, from which Aiken repeatedly excised imitations of passages from *Blue Voyage*. Even worse, when Lowry read a draft of Aiken's next novel, *Great Circle*, which included Aiken's dream of eating his father's skeleton, Lowry wanted to appropriate the dream as his own.[12] Of course, it is possible that Lowry played at testing the limits of influence with Aiken, appropriating material that he knew Aiken would recognize and delete from the manuscripts, but his very different relationship with Nordahl Grieg, whose name he would later conceal from David Markson, made it impossible for him to play the same game with the Norwegian writer. The result was not only that a passage like "Outside was the roar of the sea and the darkness" could make its way intact from Grieg's novel into *Ultramarine* but that Lowry would then write *In Ballast to the White Sea*, confronting and overcoming his sense of indebtedness to Grieg without acknowledging any debt to Aiken in the novel.

Elsewhere I have argued that Lowry's open acknowledgment of Aiken's influence might be read as an attempt to create his literary father—a father whom he believed he would eventually overcome (*Forests* 24). Grieg was too geographically distant from Lowry, and too close to him in age, to be a father figure, but Lowry certainly regarded Grieg as a kindred spirit. In any event, he was fully aware of how much he owed to the writings of both men. It is therefore ironic that the charge of plagiarism that Lowry always feared would come from Burton Rascoe, an author who had not influenced him and to whom he owed virtually nothing.

III.

Apart from the fire that destroyed his manuscript, the most traumatic event for Lowry during the years when he worked on *In Ballast to the White Sea* occurred in 1935, after his agent, Harold Matson, submitted the novel-in-progress to Doubleday, along with a copy of *Ultramarine* to demonstrate that Lowry was a published novelist. The materials were passed along to Rascoe, an editor at Doubleday, who looked into *Ultramarine* just long enough to decide that it was largely plagiarized from his story "What Is Love?" When the two met, Rascoe subjected Lowry to grossly exaggerated claims that an author less sensitive than Lowry to the charge of being derivative, one who had not already written a novel on the subject of his indebtedness to another writer, would have dismissed out of hand, perhaps with the threat of a lawsuit for slander. Instead, Lowry was "in a state of shock" (Bowker 193). In fact, he appears to have read "What Is Love?" and to have borrowed a few lines from it, all of them quotations from other works that amount to very little. Although both narratives use a stream-of-consciousness technique that neither Rascoe nor Lowry invented, their plots, locales, themes, and characters have almost nothing in common. Still, Rascoe threatened to expose Lowry as a plagiarist, and according to Rascoe, Lowry signed a confession to that effect. Rascoe's claim cannot be confirmed, and Jan Gabrial told Sherrill Grace she did not believe Lowry ever signed such a confession (*CL* 1:330). Nonetheless, there is no doubt that Lowry was deeply shaken by the accusation.[13]

Nearly two decades later, Rascoe, still claiming he had been victimized by Lowry's "plagiarism," wrote to a friend about the incident.[14] In the letter he mentioned in passing that when Lowry had gained some fame for a novel either entitled "Beneath the Volcano" or "Under the Volcano" (Rascoe used both titles), he had not read it, so he did not know whether that was the novel Lowry had submitted to Doubleday in 1935. Although by his own admission Rascoe had not read much of *In Ballast*, and could not remember its title, he recalled telling Lowry that the novel was clearly a version of Charles Morgan's *The Fountain*, with some borrowings from Céline and Malraux. Before Jan revealed that a manuscript of *In Ballast* had survived, there was no way of testing the veracity of Rascoe's claim that Lowry had copied Morgan, although a perusal of *The Fountain* would have shown that its style and themes were quite unlike anything in the Lowry canon. Now that the two novels can be compared, it is hard to imagine what connection Rascoe saw between them, unless it is that in each case the protagonist of the novel is himself writing a book or that both Lowry and Morgan use epigraphs to preface parts of their novels.[15] However, given that the volumes the protagonists are writing are quite different (Lewis Alison's archivally based study of "the development of spiritual concepts in England since the Renaissance" [Morgan 26] is a project unattended by the anxieties that plague Sigbjørn), and that Morgan and Lowry never use the same—or even, as far as I can tell, similar—epigraphs, these connections only underscore how fundamentally different the two novels are. It is possible that Lowry read *The Fountain*, but he did not plagiarize from it.

Rascoe's obsession with plagiarism seems to have equalled Lowry's, but his charges were always directed at other writers, never at himself: in *Titans of Literature*, for example, Rascoe accepted without question Norman Douglas's eccentric claim, in *Old Calabria*, that John Milton plagiarized almost all of *Paradise Lost* from Serafino della Salandra's *Adamo Canuto* (*Titans* 281). Lowry noted the charge against Milton in May 1940 when he wrote to Rascoe, apologizing once again for "the matter of the Latin Quotations, which, I assure you again, was not deliberate plagiarism on my part"; even so, he admitted that *Ultramarine* "was hopelessly derivative." At the end he added, "I reread the other day, and with delight and profit, 'Titans.' Milton absolved me a little" (*CL* 1:329–30). As Doyen (215) suggests, there was surely a connection between Lowry's decision to send Rascoe a conciliatory letter at this time and his concerns, as he prepared to submit the 1940 manuscript of *Under the Volcano* to his agent, that his writing might again come to Rascoe's attention. Doyen's suspicion seems to be confirmed by Lowry's letter of 27 July 1940 to Harold Matson in which he asks Matson to read the manuscript of the new novel, adding, "It is 'original:' if you fear for past Websterian, not to say Miltonian minor lack of ethics on my part . . . . It is as much mine as I know of" (*CL* 1:342). It is not clear how Lowry expected Matson to follow his allusion to Rascoe's claim that Milton was a plagiarist—a charge that, as Lowry put it, might absolve him a little—but the context is clear enough for readers who have access to both letters. The allusion to John Webster, however, takes us back to Nordahl Grieg.

In her remarkable essay "Respecting Plagiarism: Tradition, Guilt, and Malcolm Lowry's 'Pelagiarist Pen'" (1992), Sherrill Grace laid the foundation for subsequent studies of plagiarism and intertextuality in Lowry's work, including the "intense identification" with another writer that often led him to adopt the other writer's identity, "at least for his creative purposes" (466).[16] In this article Grace also used an analysis of Lowry's September 1931 letter to Grieg, which had only recently been discovered, not only to explore the Lowry–Grieg relationship but to bring three scholarly books into her study of Lowry's imagination. Two are theoretical texts written long after Lowry's death: Gérard Genette's *Palimpsestes: La littérature au second degré* (1982), which investigates forms of "transtextuality," and Michel Schneider's *Voleurs de mots: Essai sur le plagiat, la psychanalyse et la pensée* (1985), a psychoanalytic study with numerous insights into Lowry's obsession with plagiarism. The third book, however, is one Lowry had read and had discussed in the letter to Grieg: Rupert Brooke's *John Webster and the Elizabethan Drama* (1916). The letter to Grieg, written while Lowry was still in Oslo (*CL* 1:102–06), makes it clear that Grieg had told Lowry of his plans to go to Cambridge to carry out research for his book *De unge døde* (*Youth Died*, 1932), a study of poets who died young: Rupert Brooke, for example, and John Keats. Lowry mentioned both poets in his letter, but he devoted much more space to Brooke than to Keats, for his purpose in writing the letter was to make a strong impression on Grieg by demonstrating his knowledge of Brooke, and particularly of Brooke's study of John Webster. As he says in the letter, Lowry had no copy of *John Webster and the Elizabethan Drama* in Oslo. Thus, his ability to recall and even quote from Brooke's writing and from T. S. Eliot's "Whispers of Immortality" is indeed impressive, despite the fact (as Chris Ackerley has discovered—see annotations XVIII.47 and XVIII.49) that much of the letter derives directly from Houston Peterson's *The Melody of Chaos* (1931), which Lowry must have carried with him on his trip to Norway.[17] Still, it is clear that Lowry had read Brooke's study, and his fascination with *John Webster and the Elizabethan Drama* makes what Brooke has to say about allegations of plagiarism against Webster especially interesting for Lowry scholars. Toward the end of his Chapter V, Brooke draws on recent discoveries of Webster's sources to comment on Webster's reworking of phrases borrowed from other writers. Brooke says it is clear that Webster used notebooks to record passages from works he read, and later drew on those notebooks for his plays; this practice, he observes, does not mean that Webster was either a greater or a lesser artist than other writers, only that he had a poorer memory. Brooke's argument that complete originality is an unattainable, even an absurd, goal—"The poet and the dramatist work with words, ideas, and phrases. It is ridiculous, and shows a wild incomprehension of the principles of literature, to demand that each should use only his own; every man's brain is filled by thoughts and words of other people's" (Brooke 151)—is similar to Schneider's point that all literature is intertextual. Moreover, Brooke argued, great writers use other people's words imaginatively, and he cited examples of how "Webster reset other people's jewels and redoubled their lustre," even, in one case, improving a line he borrowed from John Donne (Brooke 152).

Although Grace had no opportunity to see the typescript of *In Ballast to the White Sea* when she wrote "Respecting Plagiarism," she recognized the potential importance of the 1931 letter to Grieg, with its commentary on Brooke's study of Webster, in relation to the "lost" novel:

> Given what we know about Lowry's own life and writing, it is possible to see in this letter to Grieg the earliest seeds of "In Ballast to the White Sea." Moreover, this letter outlines the "poetic theory" that informed that work and everything else that Lowry wrote. "In Ballast" represented Lowry's surrounding of Grieg's position as author . . . by . . . incorporating Grieg's text, Grieg's conversation, Lowry's letters to Grieg—and

> hence Lowry's construction of his relationship with Grieg—into his own text. (470)

Lowry's letter to Grieg is directly related to two crucial references to Brooke in the novel. The first occurs in one of Sigbjørn's letters to Erikson (Chapter IV):

> Uprooted and lost myself I had to find others who had suffered similarly in literature as well as in life which meant that I could not pass the stage of 'hysterical identification' which . . . is no more than a stage in, although an important experience of, the adolescence of a creative writer . . . . I discovered that my approach to literature had always been the same: I had been devoted more to the idea of Chatterton and Keats, the *idea* of their dying young, and to that being the most proper thing a young writer can do, than to their work; in fact I discovered a further illustration of this in myself when I suddenly found within myself the same attachment growing for Rupert Brooke, a passion, in fact, for his death, his fate whereas—although as a man and as a critic I found him worthy of respect—as a poet he is to my mind something of a cold potato, or could we say perhaps, a ghost laid by Old Leysians at Byron's pool? (48, ellipses added)

Here, Sigbjørn (Lowry) introduces the subject of poets who died young, including Brooke, but confesses to being more interested in the *idea* of the poet who dies young than in the poems themselves. In this way he anticipates the subject of the study that Erikson is just then undertaking, or planning to undertake. This is what most of us would regard as a coincidence: Sigbjørn has no way of knowing that Erikson plans to come to Cambridge, to his university, even as Sigbjørn hopes someday to meet with Erikson in Norway; he also has no way of knowing that Erikson shares his interest in Brooke. For Lowry, however, what appears to be "coincidence" is often a sign of an underlying affinity, as Ackerley has shown ("Coincidence and Design").

The second reference to Brooke in the novel occurs much later, when Sigbjørn finally meets Erikson and learns of his interest in Brooke's *John Webster and the Elizabethan Drama*. A note inserted toward the end of the typescript of *In Ballast* indicates that Lowry planned to reinforce the connection between his own experience and Sigbjørn's by having his character write the very letter that Grace would cite in her article: "Seated in the Røde Mølle 'under the geraniums,' Sigbjørn, drinking sherry and writing a long letter to Erikson about Rupert Brooke and the Elizabethans, is battling an alcoholic confusion as to whether a further meeting with the Norwegian writer actually took place."[18] The evidence of *In Ballast* confirms what Grace already knew:

> Brooke's remarks are such an uncannily accurate gloss on the methods, preoccupations, and psychology of Lowry that it is not hard to imagine how Lowry (plagued by his fear of plagiarism from his teens) must have felt while reading them, or why he would privilege Brooke the interpreter of Marston and Webster over Brooke the cult poet, and see in the former a vital link between himself and Grieg or between himself and the great Elizabethan tradition of English literature. ("Respecting Plagiarism" 472)

IV.

One final traumatic event in Lowry's life that was directly related to *In Ballast* occurred a few weeks after the fire destroyed his shack and his manuscript: six months after the fact, Lowry finally heard about Nordahl Grieg's death. Having escaped from Norway when his country was invaded by Germany, Grieg died when the RAF bomber in which he had been riding as an observer was shot down during a raid over Potsdam, Germany. Outside Norway, Grieg was not well known, and Lowry was living in a remote place, so it is hardly surprising that he learned of Grieg's death only much later, when he travelled to Ontario after the fire to stay with Gerald Noxon. Three years later, writing to John Davenport, Lowry followed a lamentation on the death of another friend, James Travers, with this description of earlier events: "And Nordahl [is also dead]—so is my book about him, died with our house June 7th 1944, in flames. We went East to discover Gerald Noxon doing a broadcast for Free Norway about [Grieg's] death six months before; he died on our third wedding anniversary, Dec 2 [1943]" (CL 2:47). For Lowry, the coincidences (Grieg's death on the Lowrys' anniversary and the destruction six months later of the manuscript that recorded Malcolm's identification with Grieg) were an ominous concatenation of events, what he often called the Law of Series. Even if (as I suspect) Lowry remembered the carbon typescript of *In Ballast*, Grieg's death would have given him yet another reason not to return to a novel that had been intended as a confrontation with, and exorcism of, his demons.

Yet, ultimately, Lowry planned for *In Ballast* to conclude happily, despite Jan's conviction that "the book would end with the cry which epitomized those nightmare visions Malc both fled and craved: '*My God! What shall I do without my misery?*'" (Gabrial 80).[19] That it was meant to end on a positive note, an affirmation of life rather than a downward spiral, is made clear by Lowry's references to *In Ballast* in his letters. At least as early as 1942 Lowry said he was writing a trilogy, structured on the *Divine Comedy*, entitled *The Voyage That Never Ends*, in which *Under the Volcano* was the *Inferno*; *The Last Address* or *Lunar Caustic* or *Swinging the Maelstrom* (three names for different versions of a novella set in a psychiatric ward in New York's Bellevue Hospital) the *Purgatorio*; and *In Ballast* the *Paradiso*.[20] The burning of Lowry's *Paradiso* led to his abandonment of the original idea for *The Voyage That Never Ends*; later, he used the same title for a much longer series framed by the two parts of a dream vision, *The Ordeal of Sigbjørn Wilderness*, a voyage into death and rebirth that in turn ended positively, with a simple scene of marital love.[21] In a letter to Markson, Lowry said that *In Ballast*, and thus the early version of *The Voyage* as a trilogy, would have had "a triumphant outcome" in which both A and X (Sigbjørn Tarnmoor and William Erikson) are "realigned on the side of life" (*CL* 2:420, 428). Moreover, according to Lowry, "with a few exceptions like the brother's death etc," *In Ballast* was based on events he had lived through (*CL* 2:428).

Since 1965, when the two letters to Markson about *In Ballast* were published (as one) in Lowry's *Selected Letters*, critics have relied on these descriptions of his lost novel. By contrast, readers of the present edition who compare Lowry's statements with the details in the narrative will find crucial differences: in the surviving text there is no "stormy love affair with an older woman" for which Sigbjørn risks being sent down from Cambridge, nor a "gigantic lawsuit" between his father and the Peruvian government, a "blind medium" who predicts the questions on Sigbjørn's Dante exam, or a pilgrimage by Sigbjørn to his mother's grave (*CL* 2:418, 419, 426, 427). Of course, this edition records only one stage in the composition of *In Ballast*, and it is possible that those details were all taken from other stages; it is also possible that they are related to the planned revision of *In Ballast* that Lowry claimed would have been part of the greatly expanded version of *The Voyage That Never Ends*, or even that he invented some details as he wrote to Markson. Other references in the letter, however, correspond to the text we have, and Lowry's explanations, although at times overly complicated and plagued by digressions, are immensely helpful.

One crucial scene of *In Ballast* that Lowry describes in terms that differ from its presentation in the novel involves the death of Tor, who is referred to in the letter only as A's (Sigbjørn's) brother. According to Lowry, A, unable to cope with his sense of identification with the Scandinavian writer, X, tells his brother about his dilemma. The result is that "he—the brother—derides X's book which enrages A to such an extent that inadvertently he causes his brother to turn all his venom on himself in a Dostoievskian scene that leads to the brother's death" (*CL* 2:426). In the surviving draft of the novel Tor does commit suicide, but the tension between the brothers has nothing to do with an argument about Erikson or his book. On the contrary, Tor tells Sigbjørn, "your experience [of identification with Erikson] is only an interesting recurrence of an eternal process. But you ought to get in touch with Erikson just the same" (Chapter I). The letter is also misleading in another way: Lowry's claim that the brother's suicide was one element of the plot that he had invented (CL 2:428), while basically true, is not the whole truth. For while none of Lowry's brothers committed suicide, Tor's death is based on the unhappy end of Paul Fitte, one of Lowry's Cambridge friends.

According to the *Cambridge Daily News* for Saturday, 16 November 1929, Fitte committed suicide on the previous day by sealing up his room and turning on the gas—exactly as Tor does in *In Ballast*.[22] Several of Lowry's unpublished or posthumously published writings, including *October Ferry to Gabriola*, *Dark as the Grave*, and *The Ordeal of Sigbjørn Wilderness*, record his enduring sense of guilt over Fitte, who is disguised as Peter Cordwainer in *October Ferry* and as Wensleydale elsewhere. In these versions, typically, the protagonist recalls having treated the Fitte character callously or at least having failed to take a suicide threat seriously. It is hard to say how much truth there is in this narrative, or for that matter in the earlier fictionalized version of Fitte's death: in Charlotte Haldane's 1932 novel *I Bring Not Peace*, where Lowry is only slightly disguised as James Dowd and Fitte as Dennis Carling. Dowd tries to help Carling deal with a blackmailer, but when Carling threatens suicide, Dowd tells him, "If you kill yourself . . . I shall never forgive you" (Haldane 286). Elsewhere (*Forests* 127) I have suggested that Lowry's involvement in Fitte's death, as he represented it in his fiction, might have been shaped as much by Haldane's novel as by Fitte's suicide itself. It is also quite possible that the scene in the third chapter of *In Ballast*, where Tor's threat of suicide is obviously serious but Sigbjørn manages to tell himself otherwise, owes as much to *I Bring Not Peace* as to Lowry's personal history with Fitte. If this is another example of Lowry's art imitating art, then Tor's statement that "They'll find me in the morning: lying, as you put it, all dead. It's a literary fashion" takes on another (probably unintended) meaning.

Tor's suicide is not, however, merely a fictional version of Fitte's (or Carling's): it is also a crucial element in the novel's archetypal pattern, the journey into death, or winter, followed ultimately by rebirth in spring (the narrative ends not long after Easter). Tor seems to have been introduced as a character in this novel so that he can serve as Sigbjørn's double, or his other self, much as Septimus Smith is Clarissa's double in Virginia Woolf's *Mrs. Dalloway*. In Lowry's novel, the death of one brother (or one part of Sigbjørn) allows the other to live. In this respect Tor's successful suicide bears comparison with a scene in *Dark as the Grave* in which Sigbjørn Wilderness cuts his wrist with a razor but is saved by his wife (DATG 187). The latter scene is based on Lowry's own attempt to take his life in January 1946, when the chances that *Under the Volcano* would be published appeared remote (Day 350, Bowker 355), but it parallels the *In Ballast* scene, and *Dark as the Grave*, which ends in a vision of the world as a fertile garden, has a pattern of psychological descent and ascent much like the earlier novel. The turning point of *In Ballast* occurs when Sigbjørn pulls himself together after Tor's suicide and finally makes the journey to Norway that his brother had recommended. In *Dark as the Grave*, a different Sigbjørn will pull himself together after his own suicide attempt and will continue his journey toward regeneration.

V.

Ultimately, all of these themes would have been developed, connected, clarified, interwoven in the ideal text of *In Ballast to the White Sea*: one written by Malcolm Lowry after several more years of revision, based either on a manuscript that somehow survived the 1944 fire or on the carbon typescript entrusted to Emily van der Heim. In all likelihood, the text would have been strikingly different from the one in this edition, if Lowry's revisions of *In Ballast* were as extensive as those that transformed the 1940 manuscript of *Under the Volcano* into the brilliant novel published in 1947.[23] In the absence of a text revised by Lowry, however, the best possible edition of *In Ballast* would have been based directly on the 1936 typescript that Jan Gabrial mentioned in her memoir when she wrote, "Some 265 pages of *In Ballast* still survive in carbon" (Gabrial 80). The 1936 typescript of *In Ballast* was presumably a nearly complete draft of the novel, at least through seventeen chapters, and somewhat more fully revised than the manuscript whose submission to Doubleday a year earlier had led to Rascoe's charges of plagiarism. Above all, it was Lowry's work, for better or worse, the last extant version of the novel that he had a chance to proofread and correct.

My expectation when I undertook this project was that the editing would be relatively straightforward: there would be none of the dilemmas posed by competing theories of copy text—for example, whether an author's final manuscript or the first edition of a novel or poem provides the best evidence of an author's final intentions, or even whether "final intentions" should be the primary basis for a scholarly text—nor would more recent debates about the concept of copy text itself play a crucial role in my approach to the edition. The existence of a single manuscript for *In Ballast* would render such questions moot. Yet as soon as I began looking at the New York Public Library's Jan Gabrial Papers I realized that the situation was considerably more complex, challenging, and intriguing than

I had expected and that, as far as I could tell, the editorial problems I faced were unlike those typically addressed in studies of textual editing. As a result, I have come more and more to appreciate Jerome McGann's contention that "the best scholarly editions establish their texts according to a catholic set of guidelines and priorities whose relative authority shifts and alters under changing circumstances" (McGann 94). Even more relevant, in my view, is A. E. Housman's striking description of the textual critic's role:

> [T]extual criticism is not a branch of mathematics, nor indeed an exact science at all. It deals with a matter not rigid and constant, like lines and numbers, but fluid and variable; namely the frailties and aberrations of the human mind, and of its insubordinate servants, the human fingers. . . . A textual critic engaged upon his business is not at all like Newton investigating the motions of the planets: he is much more like a dog hunting for fleas. If a dog hunted for fleas on mathematical principles, basing his researches on statistics of area and population, he would never catch a flea except by accident. They require to be treated as individuals; and every problem which presents itself to the textual critic must be regarded as possibly unique. (Housman 3:1058–59, my ellipsis)

A brief description of the primary materials in the Jan Gabrial Papers that form the basis for this edition will indicate why Housman's warning about the need to treat textual problems as individuals rings so true. To begin with, for the most part, the 265-page carbon typescript that Jan mentioned has disappeared. All we have left of the 1936 typescript are photocopies of Chapters I, II, IV, and XII and roughly half a page from Chapter XIV (NYPL 3:1, 3:6); what happened to the rest of the typescript is unclear.[24] There is of course no holograph manuscript for *In Ballast*, so the only complete manuscripts are two typescripts (rough and clean copies) edited in 1991 by Jan Gabrial. The survival of some textual evidence from the 1930s is, however, fortunate, since it enables us to compare Jan's edited version with her source, for part of the novel, and to see if she made any changes other than the correction of errors.

The answer is somewhat reassuring, at least for Lowry scholars who are familiar with the problems associated with such posthumous publications as the *Selected Poems*, *Selected Letters*, *Lunar Caustic*, *Dark as the Grave*, and *October Ferry*. However, when Jan retyped the earlier manuscript she often made changes in paragraphing, punctuation, and even phrasing.[25] In so doing, she would have been acting in a manner prescribed, in 1936, by Lowry himself: according to Gordon Bowker, just before the trip to Mexico Lowry wrote a will in which he made Jan his sole beneficiary and also specified that she should "try, in her own time, to make something out of the inchoate notes for the novel [*In Ballast*] I have left behind on the lines I have sometimes suggested in conversation with her" (Bowker 202). Although Jan's intentions were good, the result is that the text differs in many ways from the one Lowry appears to have intended. The changes are mostly small ones that have little effect on the narrative as a whole, but often they alter the tone or even the meaning of a passage.

An extreme example of Jan's revisions may be seen in a paragraph from one of Sigbjørn's letters to Erikson in Chapter IV. In the present edition, the passage appears as follows:

> Whatever it was therefore, and in the eclecticism of these alternatives its object must in some way be present by implication, I am left now, as I was three years ago, before ever I went to sea at all, as most of my generation, a sufferer from ἄσκησις, with an unconquerable aspiration towards a completion, a fulfillment of present existence. And I am left at the stage where it becomes necessary to set out again— (43)

This version of the passage is identical with the 1936 typescript except in minor matters: I have changed Lowry's *ἀσκησις* to *ἄσκησις*, adding an acute accent over the alpha, and substituted "left now" for the typescript reading in which "leftnow" is typed as one word (with a slash inserted by hand to indicate that the words should be separated); at the end of the quote and elsewhere in the novel I have made a distinction between hyphens and dashes that Lowry probably assumed a printer would make (he uses hyphens for both); and a double space before "as most of my generation" has been reduced to a single space.

Here is the same paragraph in Jan's 1991 typescript:

> Whatever it was, therefore, and in the eclecticism of these alternatives, its object must in some way be present by implication, I am now left as I was three years ago, before I ever went to sea at all, as most of my generation... with an unconquerable aspiration towards a completion, a fulfillment of present existence. And I am left at the stage where it becomes necessary to set out again- (NYPL 4:1, 75–76; ellipsis in typescript)

Jan added a comma after "Whatever it was," deleted one after "I am left now," and changed "left now" to "now left"; on the other hand, she did not alter Lowry's hyphen, or short dash. These are reasonable editorial decisions, albeit not ones I made. Yet the ellipsis in her typescript, which a reader might interpret as part of Sigbjørn's letter to Erikson, covers up a gap that we can recognize as such only because the 1936 typescript reading is still available. Apparently, Jan could not read the Greek word that Lowry inserted by hand, and since she had no idea what it meant she simply eliminated it, along with the rest of the phrase in which Sigbjørn identifies himself as "a sufferer from ἄσκησις." He means that he is an ascetic, a sufferer from *áskēsis* or religious self-discipline. The omission of this part of the passage eliminates not only the element of *áskēsis* from the image of himself that Sigbjørn hopes to create but also the intended religious context for his "unconquerable aspiration towards a completion, a fulfillment of present existence." Here, Jan's omission of part of the text distorts its meaning.

In the few chapters for which we have the 1936 typescript and both of Jan's 1991 typescripts, this is probably the most damaging change even though some others involve larger deletions of text. Had the 1936 text not been preserved for Chapter IV, it would have been impossible to tell that this passage had been altered: instead, the ellipsis might have been regarded as Lowry's attempt to represent the text itself as an edited (or an incomplete) document, or perhaps as Sigbjørn's acknowledgment that he has lost his train of thought. If there are similar problems in chapters for which we no longer have the 1936 typescript, most of the lost or altered text probably cannot be recovered. Still, at many places in the text it has proved possible to make emendations that restore the sense of Lowry's earlier typescript even when we do not have a 1936 typescript for comparison. Thus, in Chapter VIII, as Sigbjørn and his father play golf, the 1991 typescript tells us, "Dark clouds were blowing up from the sea, from the point of air: beyond, on the other side of the river in Flintshire, the Welsh mountains loomed leaden-grey" (NYPL 4:3, 233). Perhaps "the point of air" makes sense in another context, but in a scene in which someone stands on a golf course on the Wirral, looking across the Dee toward the Welsh mountains, it is clearly an error for Point of Ayr, the Welsh peninsula just north of Flintshire. Jan's unfamiliarity with places named in the novel led to other such errors in her typescript, many of which have been spotted through the annotations. In such cases, we can reasonably assume that Lowry would have corrected the names, or at least that he would have wanted an editor to do so.

The principles of emendation followed in this edition are described in the Textual Notes. Here, it will suffice to say that in general I have kept in mind G. Thomas Tanselle's warning that although even unpublished literary works normally should be edited as if they were intended for publication, "there are borderline cases: deciding, for instance, whether the manuscript of an unpublished novel is finished enough to serve as the basis for a critical edition or whether it is so rough and fragmentary that it must be regarded as a private paper"

("Texts" 17).[26] Given that the basis of this edition is, ultimately, a revision of a manuscript that Lowry submitted to Doubleday—albeit with disastrous results—it would seem to fall into the first category, but the typescript is also clearly that of a work in progress, so a scholarly edition of the novel should not regularize its features in ways that would make it seem far more "finished" than it actually is. For example, Lowry used more than one system to represent dialogue and quotations in this novel, an inconsistency that is evident in the remnants of the 1936 typescript. In the first two chapters dialogue is introduced by dashes (or by hyphens); there are no quotations in Chapter I, but in II there are a few quotations, all of them enclosed within single (British) quotation marks. There is no dialogue in Chapter IV, but, in the early part of the chapter, quotations, including single words treated as quotations, are placed within double (American) quotation marks. Later, however, the quotations (all brief, mostly single words) are placed within single quotation marks. The typescript of Chapter XII and the partial page from Chapter XIV use double quotation marks throughout, except that on one copy of a page from XII (the file has two copies of some pages from that chapter) Lowry added, by hand, a brief dialogue—using single quotation marks. Since there is no strong evidence that one system of punctuating dialogue should be used throughout the text, the inconsistency has been retained in the edition, with exceptions for obvious errors such as a quotation that begins with a double and concludes with a single quotation mark.

Likewise, the epigraphs to chapters of *In Ballast* have generally been allowed to stand as they are presented in the 1991 typescript except when an erroneous transcription obscures the epigraph's meaning or its relation to the main text.[27] This is most obviously the case with the epigraph for Chapter XV, a passage from Melville's *Moby-Dick* which in Jan's typescript reads, "Forehead to forehead I meet thee this time, Moby Dick!" In this edition the epigraph has been emended to the phrasing in the novel itself: "Forehead to forehead I meet thee, this third time, Moby Dick!" (Chapter CXXXV). Jan's reduction of "I meet thee, this third time" to "I meet thee this time" seems a small matter, and her reading would have been allowed to stand if it were likely that this was Lowry's preference. However, Lowry almost certainly used the Melville passage as an epigraph in that place in the novel to signal the theme of recurrence, which continues with the chapter's first two sentences, each of which begins with the words "Once more." Jan's omission of "third" was probably inadvertent, and in any case it obscures the relationship of epigraph to chapter.

On the other hand, the erroneous attribution of Chapter IV's epigraph to C. K. Ogden and I. A. Richards has been allowed to stand in the text itself while being corrected in a textual note. The reason for this decision is complex, and some background is necessary. Of the four chapters for which we have the 1936 typescript, this is the only one that has an epigraph; but instead of being part of the typescript itself, this one is written in Jan's hand on a separate page. We do not have a manuscript, notebook, or other document that authorizes the use of this epigraph, or any other, in the novel, but there is little doubt that Lowry chose the epigraphs: they are typically derived from works by authors to whom he was attracted, and they reflect the eclectic range of interests he brought to all of his fiction. In this case, the ultimate source of the epigraph is not a work by Ogden and Richards. Rather, the epigraph comes from the introduction by F. G. Crookshank to Charles Blondel's *The Troubled Conscience and the Insane Mind*, a volume with translations of two long papers, originally published in French, by Blondel, a professor of psychology at the University of Strasbourg. In his introduction Crookshank explains that "Blondel's persistent use of the French word *conscience*" in the context of "right and wrong in the sphere of intellect rather than . . . in the sphere of morality, or ethics" might pose problems for English readers. Even so, he notes that modern psychological theory is consistent in some respects with the English emphasis on morality, as in the position of "[Joseph] Butler, in his famous *First Sermon* [who] lays it down that we were made for society and to promote the happiness thereof just as we are intended to take care of our own life and health and private good" (Crookshank 14–15).[28] Soon after, Crookshank writes:

> So, after all, there may be fundamentally something more in common between the eighteenth-century Anglican bishop [Butler] and the twentieth-century psychologist at Strasbourg than an academician would—very properly—be disposed to allow. In fact, to use the terminology of Messrs. Ogden and Richards (in the *Meaning of Meaning*) two observers remote in time and space, each subservient to special social experiences and languages, while observing the same set of *referents*, have come to construct vastly differing *references* and yet, ultimately, to approximate very closely in matter of verbal *symbolization*. (15–16)

As to how a passage that refers to Ogden and Richards came to be attributed to them, my best guess, at this point, is that Lowry quoted it (from "two observers" to the end) in a notebook and added a note about its connection with Ogden and Richards—a note that he (or, more likely, Jan) later misinterpreted as indicating that they were the authors of the passage, not that it used the terminology of their book *The Meaning of Meaning*. In any case, the error will be identified, and the true author of the epigraph (which begins, "Two observers") named, in a textual note, but the epigraph will not be corrected in the text itself. Instead, the misattribution will be allowed to stand as a reminder that the current edition cannot be fully "corrected" because it is the product of earlier documents, including notes and drafts that might at times have been unreliable and that, for the most part, have been lost forever.[29]

In addition to the epigraphs there is other evidence that when Jan began retyping the manuscript she had access both to the 1936 typescript of *In Ballast* and to other papers whose exact nature can no longer be determined. The conversation toward the end of Chapter XIV provides us with another small piece of evidence: when Sigbjørn expresses surprise at how few people have been arrested for drunkenness at Easter, Constable Jump answers, "Celebrating the birth of a royal babe exhausted them at Christmas." The passage refers to the birth on 25 December 1936 of Princess Alexandra (later the Honourable Lady Ogilvy), a granddaughter of King George V. Lowry's reference is quite clear, but the passage could not have been included in the typescript that he left with his mother-in-law when he and Jan departed for Mexico several months before the birth of this particular royal babe. Most likely, the passage was written while the Lowrys were both in Mexico at the end of 1936 or in 1937, a time when the birth would have been in the news. Jan says that in September 1938, while she and Malcolm were both living (separately) in the Los Angeles area, Benjamin Parks, an attorney working for Lowry's father, had Lowry admitted to a sanatorium. After three weeks Lowry wrote to her, seeking pity and mentioning "the loss of *In Ballast* together with its notes (sent registered and insured from Mexico)" (Gabrial 189–90). She does not specify what later became of those notes, but if she had access to them, that might explain not only the epigraphs but the "royal babe" reference.

The folder with Jan's first printout of the final chapter also contains a typescript entitled "Notes for Last Three Chapters of In Ballast (from Malcolm Lowry)," the title indicating that the typescript is based on Lowry's own notes. Much of the final chapter, numbered XVIII in this edition, is based on that typescript, whose notes in turn are at least partly derived from documents that cannot have been part of the 1936 typescript or left with Jan's mother along with it. On pages 8–9 of the 1991 typescript Jan pointed to a major source for the notes that follow: "From Malcolm's notes on In Ballast as discussed with a Dr. Hippolyte in Haiti." This is both revealing and misleading. Dr. Hippolyte, a character in Lowry's *Dark as the Grave Wherein My Friend Is Laid*, is indeed Haitian, but the scene described here is set in Cuernavaca, Mexico.[30] *Dark as the Grave* is based on Lowry's *second* trip to Mexico (1945–1946), with his second wife, Margerie. In the novel, Sigbjørn Wilderness returns with his second wife, Primrose, to the scene of his unpublished novel *The Valley of the Shadow of Death* (*Under the Volcano*) and is haunted by reminders of his past. Not that he does much to try to put the past behind him: packed in his luggage are "fragments of manuscript, piles of it, even burned and unintelligent manuscript that Sigbjørn could never hope to put together again but which, equally, seemed too precious to be left behind, or to be trusted with anyone else." These fragments include "the burned remnants of the manuscripts of *In Ballast to the White Sea* . . . that had once contained his portrait of Erikson" (DATG 34).

Jan probably read the published text of *Dark as the Grave*, as edited by Douglas Day and Margerie Lowry, but she would not have found the scene she mentions in that version of the novel since the editors deleted it from their text. The scene does appear, however, in the typescript of the novel in the Malcolm Lowry Archive at the University of British Columbia Library (UBC 9:5, 345–52). Either Jan read Lowry's manuscripts for *Dark as the Grave* in Vancouver (unlikely but, I suppose, possible) or someone provided her with photocopies from the archive that she drew on for her notes on the ending of *In Ballast*. These manuscripts were not her only source—there are pages that I cannot trace to an archival document—but the incorporation of this material into the most nearly complete typescript we have for *In Ballast* raises the question whether or not to include in an edition of the novel passages that exist only as a result of Lowry's attempt, in his later fiction, to come to terms with the loss of *In Ballast* by passing that loss on to his protagonist and then letting the character find a way of coping with the guilt Lowry associated with his doomed novel. Lowry's life was so entangled with his works, and his works with one another, that editorial problems of this sort are probably inevitable. In any event, I have included the notes and drafts that Jan adapted from *Dark as the Grave* and from other sources that are not yet identified. These passages are part of the textual history of *In Ballast* even if they were composed with other ends in mind.[31]

My intention has been to produce a text as close as possible to the one Conrad Aiken read during a trip to Mexico in May and June 1937, a book he described in glowing terms:

> I'm reading Malcolm's really remarkable new novel, unpublished, very queer, very profound, very twisted, wonderfully rich—In Ballast to the White Sea. Gosh, the fellow's got genius—such a brilliant egocentric nonstop selfanalysis, and such a magnificent fountain, inexhaustible, of projected self-love I never did see. Wonderful. Too much of it, and directionless, but for sheer tactile richness and beauty of prose texture a joy to swim in. (*Selected Letters of Conrad Aiken* 218)

The (re)creation of this text has remained my goal, but of course it is an unrealizable one, since many chapters of the novel as it then stood are available only through Jan's 1991 typescripts, which simultaneously preserve and transform Lowry's text. Those typescripts are the only possible starting point for an edition of *In Ballast*, since there is no other text available for most of the chapters. However, the clear evidence that Jan made changes in the text and that she introduced versions of passages that Lowry wrote for a later novel into this one, as a substitute for parts of *In Ballast* that had been lost (or perhaps had never been written to begin with), means that in many cases the decision whether or not to emend the typescript has depended on my subjective sense of what seemed the more likely reading, one consistent with this work or Lowry's corpus as a whole.

The indeterminacy of Lowry's text, at least at some points, has been considerably reduced by the annotations, and by consultation with notebooks and draft materials for *In Ballast* at the University of British Columbia. This is not to say that readings that support interpretations developed in the annotations have been favoured, only that the annotations have necessarily been taken into consideration. Two examples may be cited from the opening chapter, the first being the epigraph, attributed to Rainer Maria Rilke: "Perhaps we always nocturnally retrace the stretch we have won wearily in the summer sun." Since the 1936 typescript has no epigraphs, I have followed the 1991 reading, which is either misquoted or altered from the first page of M. D. Herter Norton's 1932 translation of *Die Weise von Liebe und Tod des Cornets Christoph Rilke* as *The Tale of the Love and Death of Cornet Christopher Rilke*: "Perhaps we always nocturnally retrace the stretch we have won wearily in the foreign sun? It is possible. The sun is heavy, as deep in summer at home. But we took our leave in summer" (Rilke 11). Rilke's reference to a foreign sun might make more sense, thematically, than the typescript's reference to a summer sun, if we connect it to Sigbjørn's childhood in Norway, and the alteration of "foreign" to "summer" might be attributed to eyeskip, given that "summer" appears twice in the next few lines. Yet apart from the substitution of a period for the question mark, Lowry copied "Perhaps we always nocturnally retrace the stretch we have won wearily in the foreign sun" correctly into one of his notebooks for *In Ballast*, as Ackerley indicates in his annotation.[32] The fact that Lowry copied only this one sentence into the notebook means that if the notebook rather than the Rilke text itself was the immediate source for the epigraph, the substitution of "summer" for "foreign" cannot have been due to eyeskip. In this case, it appears likely that Lowry deliberately altered Rilke's line, and the alteration has therefore been allowed to stand.

An equally problematic passage in the 1991 typescript is this paragraph from Chapter I:

> Or, was it as if each had to face the world separately once again, with the icy courage childhood brings to the first walk alone? (Who can say who guards him? What dangers threaten that white head in his first tremulous setting forth?) (NYPL 4:1, 4)

In the present edition, the 1936 reading, in which the passage consisted of two short paragraphs, has been followed:

> Or it was as if each had to face separately again, the world, with the icy courage childhood brings to the first walk alone.
>
> Who can say who guards him? What dangers threaten that white head in his first tremulous setting out? (NYPL 3:1, 3)

Jan's revisions of the earlier reading are extensive: among other things, she changed the first sentence to a question, making it parallel with the other sentences; she also collapsed two related paragraphs into one, and then—perhaps to retain the distinction between the first sentence and the other two—she placed the last two sentences within parentheses. These and other changes are defensible if the aim is to improve the passage rather than to present it, to the extent that it is possible, just as Lowry wrote it, or intended to write it. Yet it is the final change in the passage, Jan's substitution of "setting forth" for Lowry's "setting out," that gave me pause, for Jan probably assumed (as I do) that Lowry intended an allusion to W. B. Yeats's "Among School Children," in which Yeats wondered whether a young mother who could imagine her baby son as an old man would still regard him as "A compensation for the pang of his birth, / Or the uncertainty of his setting forth." The allusion to Yeats is of course more obvious in the 1991 than in the 1936 typescript, but I have very reluctantly restored the 1936 reading on the grounds that there is no evidence that "setting out" was erroneous or that Lowry planned to change it to "setting forth." I still believe Lowry had Yeats in mind (Lowry's "white head" is the counterpart to the "sixty or more winters on its head" that Yeats imagines have turned the baby into an old man) and that Jan improved the passage, but all I can do is to attempt to restore the text, as much as possible, to readings that are traceable to Lowry himself. The irony, of course, is that Lowry incorporated so many writings of other authors into his text that distinguishing his writing from theirs is often quite difficult. The parallel processes of editing and annotating this text have pointed repeatedly to the element of indeterminacy in the novel, an element that renders absurd any claim for the "definitive" status of an edition of *In Ballast*.

Both the larger history of *In Ballast* and the indeterminacies I have described are related to the dilemma of the artist as described by Sigbjørn Wilderness in a scene in *Dark as the Grave* that reflects Lowry's anxieties after the fire destroyed his copy of *In Ballast to the White Sea*. Sigbjørn compares an author who is composing a literary work to "a man continually pushing his way through blinding smoke in an effort to rescue some precious objects from a burning building." The building, he says, represents "the work of art in question, long since perfect in the mind, and only rendered a vehicle of destruction by the effort to realize it, to transmute it upon paper"; moreover, the writer who returns to his creation after a night's sleep finds it has changed, like a house in which, during the night, "invisible workmen" replace a stringer with "one of inferior quality" (DATG 154–55). When Dr. Hippolyte suggests that his attempt "to get too much in" his book is the source of his problems and that "A little more selectivity might be in order," Sigbjørn asks, "suppose that you were in my position, haunted at every moment that a fire or some other disaster would step in and destroy what you have already so laboriously created before you have a chance to get it into some reasonably permanent form . . . would you not tend also to 'get too much in' . . . on the basis that it's better to get too much in than to get too little out[?]" (DATG 156). The relevance of this discussion to *In Ballast* is evident from the references to fire, but anyone who reads the novel will also recognize Lowry's aesthetic of excess, his habitual attempt to "get too much in" for fear of getting "too little out." This pattern is particularly evident in the many allusions, all of them at least potentially symbolic, within his narrative. When we also consider Lowry's anxieties about having his text changed by "invisible workmen" and the inevitable deterioration of an ideal work from the perfect form it assumes in the mind to the debased condition of a work committed to paper, along with those related to Nordahl Grieg, Paul Fitte, and Burton Rascoe, what seems most miraculous is that somehow, in whatever form, *In Ballast to the White Sea* has survived at all, and is now available for us to read and to compare with his other major projects of the late 1930s and early 1940s: *The Last Address / Swinging the Maelstrom* and the 1940 text of *Under the Volcano*.

NOTES

1. This discussion, and much more, was omitted from the published version of *Dark as the Grave*.
2. Jan's given name was Janine Vanderheim, according to the biographical note for the NYPL Jan Gabrial Papers, which is probably based on Gordon Bowker's biography (153); Sherrill Grace's note in her edition of Lowry's letters cites Jan's name at birth as Jennie Bermingham van der Heim (CL 1:121 n1). In her memoir Jan spells the family name "van der Heim" and says that she adopted the name "Jan Gabrial" as a stage name while acting in summer stock (Gabrial 11).

3. Vik Doyen's critical edition of Lowry's *Swinging the Maelstrom*, the significantly different later version of *The Last Address*, includes the earlier story as an appendix.
4. Jan Gabrial Papers, New York Public Library (NYPL 1:2).
5. It seems strangely prophetic of the 1944 fire that in a scene from *In Ballast* Sigbjørn hands his own manuscript to his girlfriend Nina, who was based loosely on Jan, and tells her, "And before I forget it, here's the manuscript of my novel. I didn't know whether to burn it or to give it to you." Nina answers, "Why thank you! Why that's like Hedda Gabler all over again, too." The possible burning of Sigbjørn's manuscript, which Nina compares to Hedda Gabler's burning of Eilert Løvborg's manuscript, foreshadows other burnings as well: most notably, in *Under the Volcano*, Laruelle's burning of the Consul's letter (end of Chapter 1) and Yvonne's hallucination of the Consul's burning book (end of Chapter 11).
6. In June 1951 Lowry wrote to Markson, "Ultramarine is very fortunately out of print (was never really printed as it was meant to be) and is an absolute flop and abortion and of no interest to you unless you want to hurt my feelings" (*CL* 2:401). Lowry's anxiety over *Ultramarine* was related to Burton Rascoe's charge of plagiarism.
7. Jan probably learned about the 1944 fire and the loss of *In Ballast* much later, from Lowry's *Selected Letters* (1965), *Dark as the Grave* (1968), or Douglas Day's biography of Lowry (1973). Even then she kept the secret to herself, although she later told Gordon Bowker, Lowry's second biographer, and Sherrill Grace, who edited Lowry's letters, asking them not to reveal the existence of the typescript. Only in 1997, when Jan allowed excerpts from her memoir to be read at the Malcolm Lowry conference (University of Toronto), could Grace reveal that a draft of *In Ballast* still existed (see Grace, "Three Letters Home" 25n7.). I suspect that one of Jan's motives for not disclosing the survival of an *In Ballast* manuscript for so long was to keep it from Margerie Lowry, who might have wanted to edit the novel for publication and, as Lowry's widow, might have had a legal right to do so.
8. The phrase also appears at the end of Lowry's story "On Board the *West Hardaway*," which he adapted from Chapters I and V of *Ultramarine* (P&S 35), and in the title of one of his poems and the first line of another (CP 99, 107).
9. In a draft of *Dark as the Grave* Lowry again connected his identification with Grieg (whom he renamed Guldbransen) with the theme of von Scholz's *Der Wettlauf mit dem Schatten* (UBC 9:5, 355–56). I am indebted to Frank Stringfellow, who found the passage in which Dr. Martins, having encountered a Stranger who believes his life is told in a novel Martins is writing, says, "Goethe hat mal notiert, ihm begegneten immer mehr seine Gestalten" ("Goethe once noted down that he was encountering his characters more and more"). What Lowry and Sigbjørn "know" about the statement attributed to Goethe seems to have been what was said in the English-language performance of *The Race with a Shadow* that each saw—Lowry in London, Sigbjørn in Cambridge.
10. Jan Gabrial Papers, New York Public Library (NYPL 2:11). Jan's suggested date of 1934 is confirmed by references to Lowry's marriage (January 1934) and to the publication a year earlier of *Ultramarine* (1933). Lowry gives his address as "Eure et Loire [sic] Near

Chartres," at the Hotel du Pont St. Prést, from which he also sent Sylvia Beach a letter that Grace dates to June 1934 (*CL* 1:152).

11. Schneider 16 ("vue sous un certain angle, l'histoire de la littérature est l'histoire des répétitions, du déjà écrit"), 311 ("L'intertextualité . . . non seulement affecte l'écriture littéraire, mais la constitue"). Schneider also describes every author as "in debt, not to the literary past but to his memory of it" ("Chaque auteur est en dette, non du passé de la littérature, mais de la mémoire qu'il en a"; Schneider 320). Christopher Ricks, who argues that it is easier to define plagiarism than to identify instances of it (150–51), nonetheless says that "if credited, allusion is a defence that must stanch the accusation of plagiarism" (160).
12. Lorenz 73, 87, 103, 125. On the Lowry–Aiken relationship see the biographies by Day and Bowker, passim; Sugars's edition of the Aiken–Lowry letters; Durrant; Grace, *Voyage* 123–27, 142–43; and McCarthy, *Forests* 20–24, 132–33. In a 1960 letter Aiken reported that he had just looked at the manuscripts for *Ultramarine* and had found "the description of the eating of the father's skeleton [in *Great Circle*], copied out in Malc's neat pencilling—an appropriate appropriation!" (*Selected Letters of Conrad Aiken* 307).
13. Studies of Rascoe's allegations began in 1973 with Vik Doyen's dissertation, "Fighting the Albatross of Self: A Genetic Study of the Literary Work of Malcolm Lowry" (46–47, 213–17). Doyen compared Rascoe's annotated copy of *Ultramarine*, in the Burton Rascoe Collection at the University of Pennsylvania, with the text of Rascoe's story and found that Lowry borrowed from "What Is Love?" a passage that plays on lines from Ralph Waldo Emerson's "Friendship" and Lewis Carroll's *Through the Looking-Glass* ("The rooty drop of manly blood the surging sea outweighs; the world uncertain comes and goes, the lover rooty stays. Beware the pretty face my son and shun the scrumptious chatter-box") and two Latin quotations: "*post coitum omnia animalia triste est. Omnia?*" (an abbreviation of the adage *post coitum omne animal triste est sive gallus et mulier*, "after sex all animals are sad except the rooster and the woman") and "*supinus pertundo tunicam*" (from Catullus's Poem 32, "nam pransus iaceo et satur supinus / pertundo tunicamque palliumque," a risqué passage translated by Swanson as "I'm lying, filled with what I ate, / watching my tunic stand up straight"). "What Is Love?" 718, 722; for Lowry's versions, see *Ultramarine* 158 and 169 (1933 edition), 118, 125 (1962 edition). On Rascoe, see also Bowker 192–94, Gabrial 79–80, and McCarthy, *Forests*, 28–29, 220–221.
14. UBC 3:13; photocopy of letter from the Burton Rascoe Collection. Rascoe's letter to "Edward" was accompanied by Lowry's letter to Rascoe (19 May 1940), on the recto and verso of which Rascoe typed a note, more than three times the length of Lowry's letter, characterizing what Lowry wrote as "a curious letter, showing at once a deliberate attempt to put into writing a falsehood and an evasion regarding a deliberate and conscious plagiarism" and claiming that Lowry took "whole paragraphs, word for word" from his story. (Lowry did no such thing.) For Lowry's letter, which I discuss in this introduction, and an extensive excerpt from Rascoe's note, see *CL* 1:329–31.
15. Since the surviving chapters of the 1936 typescript have no epigraphs except for one that Jan apparently added later, there were probably no epigraphs in the 1935 typescript that Rascoe saw.

16. On Lowry and plagiarism see also Grace, "Thoughts," "Play's," and *CL* 1:xxii–xxiv; McCarthy, *Forests*; Schneider, 93, 296–99, 301–302, 352; Sugars, "Recuperating Authority"; Vice, "Self-Consciousness" 162–70 and "Postmodern" 128–31. On Lowry's resentment at charges that he was a derivative writer and his work an "anthology," or what he called a "cento" (*CL* 1:116), see McCarthy, "Totality."
17. In a letter to Aiken three months earlier, Lowry said he had passed the first part of the English Tripos with "a fairly good essay on Truth & Poetry" in which he quoted Aiken as well as "Poe and the Melody of Chaos" (*CL* 1:95).
18. Cf. Lowry's 1931 letter to Grieg: "I was actually thinking out a letter to you when I met you in the Red Mill: and now can't be altogether sure about the meeting: it might have been imagination" (*CL* 1:102).
19. Jan made the same assertion in her "Introductory Notes to In Ballast to the White Sea," a six-page typescript collected in the Jan Gabrial Papers (NYPL 2:6).
20. See Lowry's May and August 1942 letters to his father and to Margerie's sister and mother, as well as his June 1945 and January and June 1946 letters to his British publisher, Jonathan Cape, and his American editor, Albert Erskine (*CL* 1:396, 407, 479, 503–504, 580).
21. For commentaries on *The Voyage That Never Ends* and *The Ordeal of Sigbjørn Wilderness*, see especially Grace, *Voyage* 6–11 and McCarthy, *Forests* 117–30. In the "Work in Progress" statement that Lowry sent to Harold Matson in 1951, Lowry indicates that the "untitled sea novel" he planned to include in the sequence would be "a complete rewriting" of *Ultramarine* (which he does not name but refers to as "a twelfth rate and derivative and altogether unmentionable early novel of mine") along with "what can be salved in memory" of *In Ballast to the White Sea* ("Work in Progress" 73).
22. "Suicide of Cambridge Freshman," photocopy, UBC 36:16. On Fitte's suicide see especially Bradbrook 113–16, 161–62; Doyen, "Fighting the Albatross" 15–16; Bowker 97–100, 190, 568; and Gabrial 76–77, 157.
23. The 1940 text of *Under the Volcano* was published in a limited edition by Paul Tiessen and Miguel Mota, who are now preparing a scholarly edition of the text with annotations by Chris Ackerley. Frederick Asals's *The Making of Malcolm Lowry's "Under the Volcano"* is essential reading for anyone interested in Lowry's revisions.
24. In 2009 Jan Gabrial's attorney, Stephen W. Kramer, verified that all of the papers related to *In Ballast* that were in Jan's possession when she died were donated to the New York Public Library.
25. It might be worth noting that Jan almost certainly typed the 1936 *In Ballast* as well, since Lowry's attempts at typing were usually restricted to rough drafts. On Lowry's resistance to the use of typewriters, see Wutz.
26. See also Tanselle's astute observation that "if we wish to experience the texts of works (or versions), and not simply the texts of documents, we must leave the certainty (or relative certainty) of the documentary texts for the uncertainty of our reconstructions" ("Editing" 259).
27. Comparisons of the epigraphs with their sources may be found in the Textual Notes.

28. Crookshank does not further identity Butler or his sermon, but his reference is clearly to "Sermon I: Upon Humane Nature" by Joseph Butler (1692–1752). Lowry also mined Crookshank's introduction for a passage in Chapter XVI dealing with cenesthesia, which Lowry changed to cinesthesia. (Thanks to David Large for tracing the epigraph to Blondel's book.)
29. The same principle has been followed with the epigraph to Chapter XVI, a passage from Marlowe's *Doctor Faustus* that Lowry attributed to Ben Jonson.
30. In *Dark as the Grave*, Lowry writes that "Dr. Hippolyte was a Haitian, had been the Haitian chargé d'affaires in Mexico at one time, but for some reason had not returned and still lived in Cuernavaca" (DATG 147). In *La Mordida* he is named Dr. Amann.
31. Jan's addition of material from *Dark as the Grave* into the typescript for *In Ballast* inadvertently points to the close connection between these two novels: the feeling that one is inside a novel is a theme in both works, and in each there are significant references to Melville's *Redburn*, Julian Green's *The Dark Journey*, and Arthur Schnitzler's *Flight into Darkness*, along with other novels. Sigbjørn Wilderness shares a name with Sigbjørn Tarnmoor, and as the Lowry surrogate in *Dark as the Grave* the later protagonist becomes the fictional author of *In Ballast*. The extensive discussion of the lost novel in the manuscripts for *Dark as the Grave* may be part of what Lowry meant when he told Markson that *In Ballast* was "incorporated hypothetically" in *The Voyage that Never Ends*.
32. UBC 12:14, Varsity Composition Book [p. 34].

WORKS CITED IN THE INTRODUCTION

Ackerley, Chris. "'Well, of course, if we knew all the things': Coincidence and Design in *Ulysses* and *Under the Volcano*." McCarthy and Tiessen, *Joyce/Lowry* 41–62.

Aiken, Conrad. "An Anatomy of Melancholy." *T. S. Eliot: The Contemporary Reviews*. Ed. Jewel Spears Brooker. Cambridge: Cambridge UP, 2004. 99–103.

——. *Selected Letters of Conrad Aiken*. Ed. Joseph Killorin. New Haven and London: Yale UP, 1978.

Asals, Frederick. *The Making of Malcolm Lowry's "Under the Volcano."* Athens and London: U of Georgia P, 1997.

Asals, Frederick, and Paul Tiessen, eds. *A Darkness That Murmured: Essays on Malcolm Lowry and the Twentieth Century*. Toronto: U of Toronto P, 2000.

Bowker, Gordon. *Pursued by Furies: A Life of Malcolm Lowry*. London: HarperCollins, 1993.

Bradbrook, M. C. *Malcolm Lowry: His Art and Early Life—A Study in Transformation*. Cambridge: Cambridge UP, 1974.

Brooke, Rupert. *John Webster and the Elizabethan Drama*. New York: Lane, 1916.

Butler, Joseph. "Sermon I: Upon Humane Nature." *Fifteen Sermons Preached at the Rolls Chapel*. London: James and John Knapton, 1726. 1–24.

Catullus. *Odi et Amo: The Complete Poetry of Catullus.* Trans. Roy Arthur Swanson. Indianapolis: Bobbs-Merrill, 1959.

——. *The Poems of Catullus: A Bilingual Edition.* Trans. Peter Green. Berkeley: U of California P, 2005.

Day, Douglas. *Malcolm Lowry: A Biography.* New York: Oxford UP, 1973.

Doyen, Victor. "Fighting the Albatross of Self: A Genetic Study of the Literary Work of Malcolm Lowry." Diss. Katholieke Universiteit te Leuven, 1973.

Durrant, Geoffrey. "Aiken and Lowry." *Canadian Literature* 64 (Spring 1975): 24–40.

Gabrial, Jan. *Inside the Volcano: My Life with Malcolm Lowry.* New York: St. Martin's P, 2000.

Grace, Sherrill. "The Play's the Thing: Reading 'Lowry' in the Dark Wood of Freud, Cocteau, and Barthes." Asals and Tiessen, *Darkness* 226–52. Rpt. in Grace, *Strange Comfort* 157–80.

——. "Respecting Plagiarism: Tradition, Guilt, and Malcolm Lowry's 'Pelagiarist Pen.'" *English Studies in Canada* 18 (December 1992): 461–81. Rpt. in Grace, *Strange Comfort* 103–22.

——. *Strange Comfort: Essays on the Work of Malcolm Lowry.* Vancouver: Talonbooks, 2009.

——. "Thoughts Towards the Archaeology of Editing: 'Caravan of Silence.'" *Malcolm Lowry Review* 29–30 (Fall 1991 & Spring 1992): 64–77.

——. "Three Letters Home." Asals and Tiessen, *Darkness* 14–28.

——. *The Voyage That Never Ends: Malcolm Lowry's Fiction.* Vancouver: U of British Columbia P, 1982.

——, ed. *Swinging the Maelstrom: New Perspectives on Malcolm Lowry.* Montreal and Kingston: McGill-Queen's UP, 1992.

Grieg, Nordahl. *The Ship Sails On.* Trans. A. G. Chater. New York: Knopf, 1927.

Haldane, Charlotte. *I Bring Not Peace.* London: Chatto & Windus, 1932.

Housman, A. E. "The Application of Thought to Textual Criticism." *The Classical Papers of A. E. Housman.* 3 vols. Ed. J. Diggle and F. R. D. Goodyear. Cambridge: Cambridge UP, 1972.

Lorenz, Clarissa M. *Lorelei Two: My Life with Conrad Aiken.* Athens: U of Georgia P, 1983.

Lowry, Malcolm. *Dark as the Grave Wherein My Friend Is Laid.* Ed. Douglas Day and Margerie Bonner Lowry. New York: New American Library, 1968. Cited as DATG.

——. *Hear Us O Lord from Heaven Thy Dwelling Place.* Philadelphia: Lippincott, 1961. Cited as *Hear Us.*

——. *The Letters of Conrad Aiken and Malcolm Lowry, 1929–1954.* Ed. Cynthia C. Sugars. Toronto: ECW Press, 1992. Cited as *Letters.*

——. *Malcolm Lowry's "La Mordida."* Ed. Patrick A. McCarthy. Athens and London: U of Georgia P, 1996.

——. *October Ferry to Gabriola*. Ed. Margerie Lowry. New York and Cleveland: World, 1970. Cited as OF.

——. *Psalms and Songs*. Ed. Margerie Lowry. New York: New American Library, 1975. Cited as P&S.

——. *Selected Letters*. Ed. Harvey Breit and Margerie Bonner Lowry. Philadelphia: J. B. Lippincott, 1965.

——. *Sursum Corda! The Collected Letters of Malcolm Lowry*. Ed. Sherrill Grace. 2 vols. Toronto: U of Toronto P, 1995, 1996. Cited as CL.

——. *Swinging the Maelstrom: A Critical Edition*. Ed. Vik Doyen with introduction by Vik Doyen and Miguel Mota; annotations by Chris Ackerley. Ottawa: U of Ottawa P, 2013.

——. *Ultramarine*. London: Jonathan Cape, 1933. Rev. ed. Philadelphia: Lippincott, 1962.

——. *Under the Volcano*. New York: Reynal & Hitchcock, 1947.

——. "Work in Progress: The Voyage That Never Ends." *Malcolm Lowry Review* 21–22 (Fall 1987 & Spring 1988): 72–99.

McCarthy, Patrick A. *Forests of Symbols: World, Text and Self in Malcolm Lowry's Fiction*. Athens and London: U of Georgia P, 1994.

——. "Totality and Fragmentation in Lowry and Joyce." Asals and Tiessen, *Darkness* 173–87.

McCarthy, Patrick A., and Paul Tiessen, eds. *Joyce/Lowry: Critical Perspectives*. Lexington: UP of Kentucky, 1997.

McGann, Jerome J. *A Critique of Modern Textual Criticism*. Charlottesville and London: UP of Virginia, 1992.

Morgan, Charles. *The Fountain*. London: Macmillan, 1932.

Peterson, Houston. *The Melody of Chaos*. New York: Longmans, Green, 1931.

Rascoe, Burton. *Titans of Literature: From Homer to the Present*. New York: Putnam's, 1928.

——. "What Is Love?" *The Second American Caravan: A Yearbook of American Literature*. Ed. Alfred Kreymborg, Lewis Mumford, and Paul Rosenfeld. New York: Macaulay, 1928. 716–25.

Ricks, Christopher. "Plagiarism." *Proceedings of the British Academy* 97 (1998): 149–68.

Schneider, Michel. *Voleurs de mots: Essai sur le plagiat, la psychanalyse et la pensée*. Paris: Gallimard, 1985.

Sugars, Cynthia. "Recuperating Authority: Plagiarism as Pastiche?" Asals and Tiessen, *Darkness* 39–46.

Tanselle, G. Thomas. "Texts of Documents and Texts of Works." *Textual Criticism and Scholarly Editing*. Charlottesville: UP of Virginia, 1990. 3–23.

——. "Editing without a Copy-Text." *Textual Editing and Criticism: An Introduction*. Ed. Erick Kelemen. New York and London: Norton, 2009. 253–80.

Vice, Sue. "Self-Consciousness in the Work of Malcolm Lowry: An Examination of Narrative Voice." Diss. Oxford University, 1988.

——. "The Volcano of a Postmodern Lowry." Grace, *Swinging* 123–35.

Wutz, Michael. "Archaic Mechanics, Anarchic Meaning: Malcolm Lowry and the Technology of Narrative." *Reading Matters: Narratives in the New Media Ecology.* Ed. Joseph Tabbi and Michael Wutz. Ithaca and London: Cornell UP, 1997. 53–75.

In Ballast to the White Sea

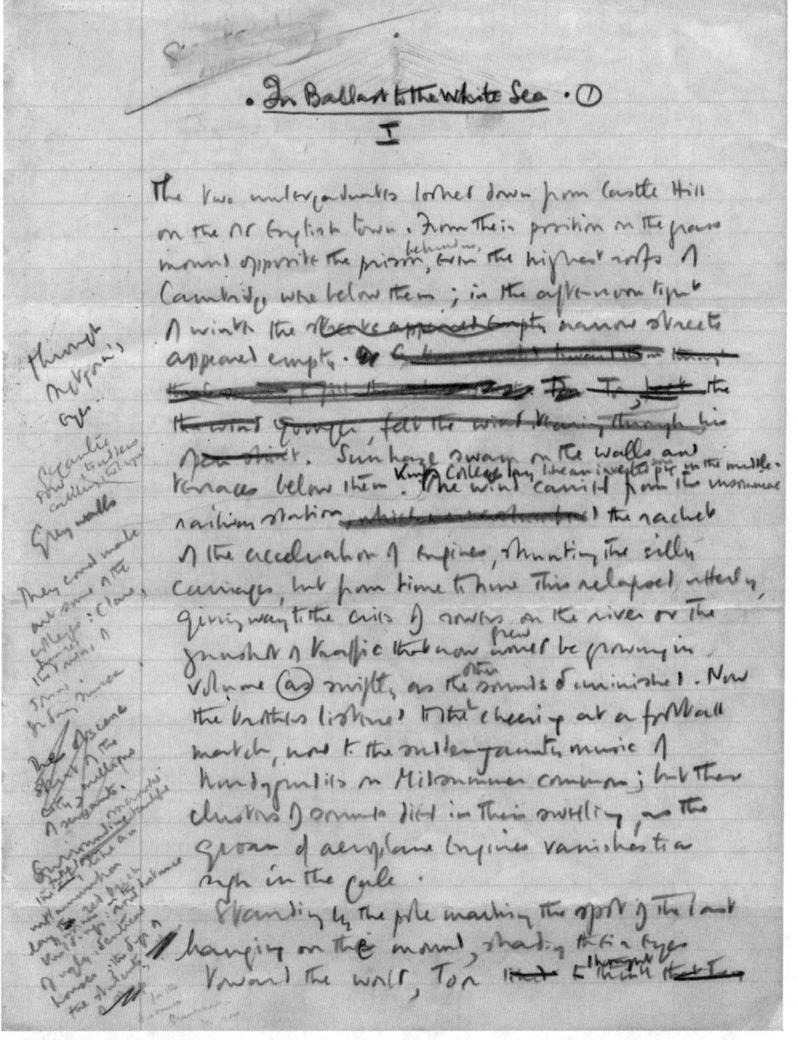
· In Ballast to the White Sea · 1

I

The two undergraduates looked down from Castle Hill on the old English town. From their position on the grass mound opposite the prison, behind, the highest roofs of Cambridge were below them; in the afternoon light of winter the narrow streets appeared empty. Sun haze swam on the walls and terraces below them. King's College lay like an inverted pig in the middle. The wind carried from the railway station the racket of the acceleration of engines, shunting the silly carriages, but from time to time this relapsed utterly, giving way to the cries of rowers on the river or the grumble of traffic that now would be growing in volume as swiftly as the other sounds diminished. Now the brothers listened to the cheering at a football match, now to the sullen gaunty music of roundabouts on Midsummer common; but these clusters of sounds died in their swelling, as the groan of aeroplane engines vanishes to a sigh in the gale.

Standing by the pole marking the spot of the last hanging on the mound, shading their eyes toward the west, Tor thought

SOURCE: RARE BOOKS AND SPECIAL COLLECTIONS, UNIVERSITY OF BRITISH COLUMBIA LIBRARY, AND ARE REPRODUCED BY PERMISSION OF PETER MATSON (OF STERLING LORD LITERISTIC) ON BEHALF OF THE ESTATE OF MALCOLM LOWRY.

In Ballast to the White Sea

I

Perhaps we always nocturnally retrace the stretch we have won wearily in the summer sun.

RILKE[1]

The two undergraduates looked down from Castle Hill[2] on the old English town. From their position on the grass mound opposite the prison[3] even the highest roofs of Cambridge[4] were below them; in the afternoon light[5] of winter the streets appeared spotless and empty, but sun-haze swam on sun-haze among the walls and towers and terraces far beneath. A brawling wind carried from the railway station,[6] which never slumbered, the racket of the acceleration of engines, shunting the drowsy carriages: but from time to time this would relapse utterly, giving way then to the cries of rowers on the river or the gunshot of traffic that now would be growing in volume as swiftly as the other sounds diminished. Now the brothers inclined their ears[7] to the cheering at a football match, now to the sudden jaunty music—loud, loud—of the hurdy-gurdies on Midsummer Common:[8] but again these clusters of sounds, each of them a hail and farewell from separate worlds of objectivity,[9] would die away almost in their swelling, as the groan of aeroplane engines quickly vanishes to a sigh in the gale.

Standing by the pole marking the spot of the last hanging on the Mound,[10] their fair hair blowing, their eyes bright with the sun and wind even when despair was behind them, they were like two castaways on a raft, shading their eyes towards the flat world against some vanishing hope, while all around them the surf broke, a spray not of sea but of dust and straw. But to Sigbjørn,[11] the younger, the wailing of the wind about the prison was like wind in the rigging of a ship, in the telegraph wires above them he heard once more the threnody[12] that the wireless aerial sheathes in the Bay of Bengal[13] and the banging of a loose shutter somewhere might have been the groaning of the strakes[14] of a boat labouring in a heavy swell; yet if he felt within him again that special anguish of the sea, for Sigbjørn had been a sailor, he could detect also within himself for the first time in some weeks today on Tor's[15] return from a brief stay in London the schism between them and narcissistically much of the ebb and flow of the other's very different feelings.

For between these two brothers there existed marked chemic[16] dissimilarity. In fact it was the first time since an accident[17] to them in childhood in Norway that they had been brought close together in spirit. Only six weeks had elapsed since one of their father's ships, the *Thorstein*,[18] had gone down off the coast of Montserrat[19] with enormous loss of life. Since that period, during the investigation and the resulting public obloquy, they had been in spite of former differences inseparable. They drew together in defence. An armistice was signed ceasing the spiritual hostilities[20] between them. They accepted now what they had formerly, and vainly, contested together or as against one another, the inner solitude of an environment which no familiarity with the other students, the English language, the flat countryside—after the mountain ranges and torrents of Norway their very hearts had to stoop to walk it—the life, and the chilled climate, could change from the permanently alien. This quality common to them both that separated them from the mass of students was not however implicit in their foreignness. It arose rather from an inability to contact life at first hand, even if only to connect[21] was their deepest desire: rather was it that each had become by virtue of the other's existence one place removed from life as though the body of one brother lay across the opening of the cave of self[22] in which the other lay captured, obstructing the light, yes, existence itself.

Each term, the train they travelled down on from Liverpool to Cambridge[23] gathered more and more students on the way. There were long waits on the platform. And their two bare white heads seen among the other golden brown English where they waited, might seem to an onlooker as freakish as a pair of white swallows among their dun fellows awaiting the signal for the summer migration. From Lincoln to Ely this term they had stood in the corridor, too shy to sit down: yet resting it seemed in their common grief. And all this term, neglecting their work they had stood together so: each walking every alternate day the two miles to the other's rooms: all the indignation of the past with each other melted away in this sorrowful, but warm fealty.[24] But now as the sea tugs at the very souls of the sister ships lying in harbour, or as the moon draws the disconsolate twin tides of the day to herself from the shore, so a dual magnetism seemed to be pulling these brothers out again towards the separate poles of their oceanic destiny.[25]

Or it was as if each had to face separately again, the world, with the icy courage childhood brings to the first walk alone.

Who can say who guards him? What dangers threaten that white head in his first tremulous setting out?[26]

—God knows, Tor was saying, I'm still frightened of something—you know what Dostoievsky[27] said—something I can't conceive, which doesn't exist, but which rises up before me as a horrible, distorted, irrefutable, fact.

—It may be the flood, who knows? Sigbjørn said, and laughed for the first time that term. Or Dante.[28] That Italian paper!

At this moment an object, evoked, Sigbjørn could not help thinking afterwards, by some evil malice, evil more by virtue of what it did not divulge than by what it did, and which he now saw to be a newspaper, had disentangled itself from a hedge below and was blowing towards them. Tor trapping it absently with his stick and foot peered down at the muddied columns. Sigbjørn stood by him looking over his shoulder.

Mount Ararat[29] *in eruption. Thousands panic.*

Now as if simultaneously released from the tension and shame of the last weeks both men started to shake with laughter, and as they did so into Sigbjørn's mind came a picture of two ships, their ropes cast off from the wharf, but their immediate passage through the dock gate suddenly obstructed.

—So there won't be anywhere to go at all now.

—But let's hope Dante is the only irrefutable fact.

—The old rascal is enough!

—But the *Inferno* is child's play to what readers of the English Tripos[30] must go through...

—Yes, Tor, where shall we go now in that ark of yours you always talk of building?

—The only thing I shall have in common with Noah now is I shall get drunk[31] perhaps. But to be serious, it's not that only, it's not only the fear of the exam—

Sigbjørn looked up at the stake planted on the site of the old gallows.[32] And for a moment he had the nightmare notion that this hill where they were standing was actually Mount Ararat itself. Why make any journey? But if that were true, if the papers could be believed, it was a dangerous spot. Indeed, already in eruption without their being aware of it! He exclaimed:

—Think of something else, of the last man hanged on this hill, think what he must have suffered. Twenty-two years ago! It's nearly that since we were born, Sigbjørn went on, but there are unhappier places even than this.

But Tor was absorbed in his own private joke about Mount Ararat.

—The station platform for instance, Sigbjørn said, is an unhappier place than this, a roar coming, and subsiding, as quickly as it had come, from that direction.

—Yes, the station platform, Tor replied at last. Where there are so many partings. Its heart cracked with grief, I used to think when a child, he added, and went on laughing, for were they not, after their penance, free to laugh once more? He peered down again at the trapped newspaper.

—And all wharves, Tor. That smoke which is so evanescent, so like pity, like love, like a dream of the sea.[33] Ah my God if only—But look here! The way must have looked just as easy and straight as it does now...don't you think so?

—What way? Tor was laughing. To whom? What do you mean?

—To him up there, of course. Sigbjørn was looking up at the stake and adding impatiently, to that last hanged man of course. Doesn't it seem so easy? As though you could walk to the North Pole[34] on a day like this. It seems so simple, so folded over in peace, and there's a kind of sea feeling to it too. Don't you see the meadows beyond; it's like a calm on the line,[35] blowing and furling...

—Mount Ararat, Tor shook, I'm sorry I can't get over it. It's the funniest thing I ever heard. And he laughed again, crouching down and bending over the fouled newspaper. Sigbjørn pointed out over the fens[36] towards the sea.

—My soul turns like a compass needle[37] towards the Pole.

—Other things lacking, it's polite to have a soul, Tor said relapsing as he did sometimes, into the broken English of his youth.

Sigbjørn still pointed, staring with sea-gazing eyes over the flat world, as flat as the grey sea which at noonday makes the sailor off watch dream of meadows at home. Now that his heart was still he could think again of the chain of watches, the abysmal concentric conversations[38] reflecting in a torrent of words his own distraction, the back-breaking work of coal-passing,[39] the ship staggering and wallowing in a green sea, the immediate experience of which had been intolerable with ecstasy; but the ecstasy was being withdrawn from him as quickly as around him the ebb of one tide of sounds was displaced by the flood of another: and as soon as he saw its exacting cause the mood disappeared altogether. How to break the circle of self,[40] even in the shadow of disaster, he knew that was the thought in the hearts of them both, how to break from this hill on which they were standing, the cursed coward circle from which neither had ever emerged.

Below them the lamplighter,[41] in hard daylight, like Diogenes, lit the lamps with his long pike against the coming dark—but who could say for certain it would curve towards them tonight? A sudden gust tore frantically at the hair of the grass: shadows drifted before the sun, and swept the mound where they were standing: a mournful shadow rested with them for a moment, enveloping them, as though they were its victims, then galloped off to westward.

—Darkness begins at midday,[42] was all Tor said, laughing.

—As the Chinese, is it the Chinese, say?

—You always bring in the sea, Tor said, temporarily controlled at last; I envy you your suffering. In spite of all you say to the contrary that was your university.[43] You had no need to come here.

Down below them a clock chimed,[44] four or five; *doom*, *doom*, the strokes came loud and each stroke was a curvature of sound, every odd one being inaudible: beyond the clock the thick spire of a church was falling against the swiftly voyaging clouds. The raised arm of Cain[45] that fell every day in some part of the world.

—But Erikson[46] took the sea away from me.

—What you say today is being shouted on the housetops[47] tomorrow anyway, you can never escape that. Even Erikson could not escape that. But you had something there in that experience, something intensely valuable to yourself, something that I needed more than you, and something you made no use of. And now it's too late for me to have it.

—You talk as though you're an old man. You're young yet.

—Did you ever read of an old man aged twenty-one who attained his majority in death?[48]

—Besides, it seems that I'm the one to kick. If you'd ever had the experience of writing a book, and then discovering it had been written by somebody else better, as I have, you might have some reason to feel fatal.

And just as the burden of the disaster of the *Thorstein* was being lifted from his shoulders, the old and bowing weight of this discovery replaced it. For here Sigbjørn's inability to connect had stood him in the worst stead. Eight months as a coal trimmer[49] on a freighter before he came to the University, searing though it must have been, socially revealing beyond all words as it might, it should, have been, Sigbjørn had returned home with his experience having apparently done no more for him than to convince him of what he already knew and of what everyone already knows, that life was as deep and as infinitely terrible and mysterious as the ocean. And when he returned, fire-scarred, thin, and hard and sleepless as he was at first, it was only to discover that his brother Tor while remaining at home had attained greater maturity. And soon under the stress of the utter incommunicability of his experience, and hence the ever increasing necessity to lie about it, the mask of his adventure fell away, leaving a face with even softer lines than before. It was not because he was a natural writer but because he was impelled to try even if the attempt were foredoomed to failure, to connect, to communicate, somehow, that had driven him to make a book of his experience. This was the way out. Otherwise nobody, perhaps not even himself, would ever know what he suffered—and indeed he must have suffered—or even have any related idea of what suffering he saw. For in reality he had found similar motives to those that restrained Tor from accompanying him, when opportunity offered, were now behind himself when he held away from giving himself over entirely to the workers. In a book this bridge might be spanned. But the unfeasibility of this way out of the wood had been only too cruelly shown to him. To discover that one's book has been written better by someone else is a sinister experience even to the untalented.

—I feel fatal without that, Tor said. I've never written a book, and I never shall. And I never want to. And your experience is only an interesting recurrence of an eternal process.[50] But you ought to get in touch with Erikson just the same.

—I thought of getting a Norwegian freighter this coming vac, and making *Skibets reise fra Kristiania*[51] into a play in my watch below. But can you tell me why when I think of Norway I always think of Russia[52] at the same time?

—Isn't it possible that for us, Russia is the future, and Norway the past?

—The future? To Dostoievsky's Christianity belongs the next thousand years?

—That's the worst kind of Spenglerian nonsense[53]. To Russia, perhaps. But to Dostoievsky's—

Again they looked out over the fens and the meadows, over the blackened corn sheaves, the sad harvest of that year, out beyond where the Cam wound through willows and poplars growing in the marshes.

—The past! Do you remember our underground railway, Tor, our *Holmenkollen*[54] at home in Norway? What do you suppose we were looking for in that old well shaft?

—The philosopher's stone perhaps. Or the quadrature of the circle.[55]

—The absolute.

—Anyway it always puzzled me how we escaped with our lives when it collapsed.

Norway! Cambridge, the fens, and beyond in the heart the world with its million ships and giant chimneys seemed to grow further and further away, the people, the trees and the waters, the hundred distractions of memory seemed to fade before the thought of this one single source of them both. They must go back! But at this instant the town of Archangel[56] rose before him in imagination, flat and sombre, with miles of piled timbers along the wharves.

—Would you come back to Norway, Tor?

—Why should I go back? Why do you go back or anywhere but to come home again?

Sigbjørn said nothing.

Now the rowers were coming back from Chesterton,[57] the river made its way through the town: flying out over the fens was a solitary, landless, gull:[58] and he felt the power of water moving through the spirit of all these things, of water everywhere seeking the ocean, as it is said the soul seeks Brahma.[59]

For a short time longer the sun spun before them like a thousand golden hoops afire: then its fierce light softened, it started to sink: the day drew in over the plain with its small waves of land, tiny dunes which were the sea's seal and small lakes, eyes of the sea,[60] and over the water which circulated invisibly there, threading all of this together with a grey thread, woods, villages, and land that was itself ploughed brownly as water churned by a steamer's propeller.

In the last light Sigbjørn said pointing:

—Look Tor, the way must have seemed easy and straight. Do you think that last hanged man saw the path stretched out before him, that although he knew his body would soon be swinging in the air...

—His soul went marching,[61] Tor began to laugh.

—Yes, his soul still crept on, huddled, bent over his endless walks like the Wandering Jew...[62]

—Perhaps like the man in the Tarot[63] pack he was hanged upside down. An old time penalty. He saw truth.

—Or perhaps, he saw himself.

—The singing slayer[64] remained mirthful to the end, said Tor, it's a fact. I read about him only yesterday in an American paper[65] in London. You know if I went anywhere I'd go to America!

—But what do you mean, singing slayer?

Tor passed his hand over his hair.

—Nattily attired, his black hair glowing, meticulous in his preparations for death, etcetera...

—Don't be a damned fool!

—As he sang, then prayed, he paid strict attention to details until he dropped through the trap; and as he stepped upon it—

—Come along, we ought to go, Sigbjørn said impatiently.

—And as he stepped upon it, Tor went on, and Tor executed a dance, he tested it with half a dozen light dancing steps...

Tor was dancing gloomily, a kind of death jig,[66] on the mound, slowly revolving, clods of dirt flying from his feet.

—Tap-dance of death, he remarked.

He stopped his dancing and with his stick freed the newspaper wrapped round the stake:[67] now it floated away. For a moment, like a lost soul, the poor paper hovered uncertainly in the air, then it drifted away down the cold coast of the houses.

Sigbjørn gathered his gown around him but still they both lingered waiting as the ship-boy on the masthead for the sun to sink.

—Since the *Thorstein* went down, Sigbjørn said, I've had terrible dreams. I dream of a figure being hanged in the snow, the executioner's fingers trembling, the death mask blowing away, it blows far away into the snow and the executioner stumbles after it.

—Like a man looking for his soul, said Tor, and put on his black gown.[68]

—And the other night I dreamt of the sisters of Le Mans;[69] one of them was hanged in an apple tree; her limbs were broken and the limbs of the apple tree were breaking.

—Then there was Pink the poet, Tor said. I'm dead as I ever will be, he said, to Dr. Styx[70] on being cut down.

—The murderer, who said, on Monday, on being led to the gallows: this week is beginning well.[71]

Now it was night. They laughed; what on earth gave rise to all this? Tor shuffled down the grass hill, laughing, digging his heels in the earth.[72]

Sigbjørn ran after him.

II

> Shut up talking, charming in the best suits to be had in town,
> Lecturing on navigation while the ship is going down.
>
> W.H. AUDEN[1]

The two brothers kept close in beside the prison railings.[2] The gravel path led to the main road from Huntingdon.[3] They started to walk down the hill towards the town and the world, leaving the prison behind.

—Do you remember the story of John Lee, the man they couldn't hang?[4] Tor asked.

But Sigbjørn could not attend to that, he was looking into the sunset. He had already forgotten their terrible conversation on the gallows' hill. For the time being even the *Thorstein* was forgotten. He loved life once again with the same strong love he had given the ocean. He even shivered, shaking the darkness from himself as a horse tries to shake off a whiff of chemicals[5] from a factory.

—We don't have enough sun. It would be good to build a house of glass![6]

—The sun would shrivel you to a husk.

—Isn't that all we are, husks driven before the storm.[7]

—I prefer the dark.

—God is the storm.

The men laughed at their mutual disparagement without gaiety or bitterness or indeed reality. They had reached the corner of Chesterton Lane[8] and Sidney Street where at the cross-roads the ways led north, south, east and west. Facing north, Sigbjørn said exultantly:

—Don't you feel sometimes the desire to rotate, to break away? Don't you ever feel the rondure[9] of the earth in yourself?

Tor was lighting a cigarette,[10] cupping the match against the wind.

—Barney,[11] I hate this unrelated energy, this glee, of yours, he said, and the cigarette alight, obeying the same instinct that made him the moment night fell, don it, an instinct that in a second-year man, betrayed an almost pathological fear of authority,[12] he struggled out of his gown,[13] Sigbjørn doing likewise.

They had walked on and were now passing Magdalene College:[14]

—but I envy you the sea—

And he touched the iron-spiked railings:

—Tactile suffering,[15] my boy! But if you're a fraud, he said, what made you go to sea in the first place? Perhaps I'm a fraud too but not such a gilded fake[16] as yourself. I may be a prig—and he struck a match for his brother, sheltering him from the wind—but perhaps, as has been suggested, as Telemachus[17] did in Menelaus, I meet an arch-prig in you.

—What *do* you believe, Tor? I often wonder...

—Show me the starving man,[18] Tor swung with his stick; quoting he traced a hieroglyph[19] with the ferrule[20] on the sidewalk. Show me the starving man I pay no attention to him. Show me the starving man on the point of dying, I grab up groceries and, he added quickly, I jump on him! Yes I jump on him! He seized Sigbjørn laughing:

—I cram bread down his mouth and stuff his eyes and his ears with potatoes. He forced his brother to the wall:

—I rip open his lips to hammer down more food, and bung in his teeth the better to stuff him. The explanation—it's the godlike in me!

He held him at arm's length against the wall, looking at him with a strange mingling of malice and dread.

—What do you mean by that? Take your hands off me. And don't keep quoting that Ripley-like philosopher[21] at me.

—I don't mean anything by that, Tor said, calmly releasing him. But like Charles Fort[22] who wrote it and who was no Ripley, I do mean something by the godawful meaninglessness of that. I mean, that's the law of supply and demand. That's the way it works. We're in the helpless state of a standardless existence.

They walked on in silence.

—I don't agree that it's standardless. There's a power for good[23] watching over all things. *Ens a se extra et supra omne genus, necessarium, unum, infinite, perfectum, simplex, immutabile, immensum, eternum, intelligens.*[24] Only yesterday you said...

—But I say now, all is accident.[25]

—As the infant Julian Green[26] remarked in the meat-market: *il y a beaucoup d'accidents ici*. That much may be admitted.

—The goal of the seeker of wisdom[27] is the juncture of two obliterations. One is of knowing nothing and the other is of knowing there is nothing to know. What do we learn in this damned place, only lies.

—Perhaps you learned what you just said. But don't you think sometimes everything in the world hints of secret knowledge,[28] buried somewhere? Yet there are no teachers for us, or we don't qualify...

—Nothing out of nowhere answers that.

—But only the other day you were saying...

—How Voltaire[29] would have hated you!

They walked on, nervously gesticulating[30] with their hands, among the dense traffic that hinted in vain, in spite of their awareness of it, of the magnificent thickness of things elsewhere, continually shrugging their gowns around them at the approach of imaginary proctors,[31] who could not possibly be on their rounds so early, their white heads luminously gliding,[32] lighting and relighting cigarettes that were neither enjoyed for themselves nor because they were forbidden. Since the dark ages millions of such men have threaded their way gesticulating through the narrow streets of Cambridge. Whither? Whence? For these souls, in spite of their reading, the serene brotherhood of philosophs might never have existed. For is not the common absolute[33] of the latter, the incommunicability of knowledge arrived at by intuition? An observer who had also the advantage of listening to their conversation might have said that the strangest thing about them was that like amateur scientists whose calculations have suddenly proved to them that they are moving along a fault in the earth's crust upon which any stress might cause the elastic limit[34] to be exceeded they were escaping from a danger which only seemed real to themselves. And to that observer their conversation would seem equally unreal and affected, the more so since as will shortly be seen part of its affectation always consisted in being aware of its unreality. But the strangest presumption of all is—supposing that earthquake should actually take place!

The two brothers came to a bridge crossing the 'backs.'[35] Here all was desolate, deserted, the punts drawn up into the boathouses and the sluggish stream, mournfully lit by gas-lamps, thick with fallen leaves. They leaned against the railings looking down silently on the dull, soundless, water, not so choked however that it did not in the infinitely tall depths below them shimmeringly reflect the hooded terrors that were themselves. Bitter nights at sea came back to Sigbjørn. And then, many nights he had stood with Nina,[36] leaning on a bridge, or on the rail of a deserted promenade.[37] The river had swept past them then and they had clutched each other with a sudden fear lest that rondure of the earth over whose face their destinies were being carried would separate them like two whirling atoms: now the movement of the river[38] was infinitely slow, yet it seemed to him a part in the mind of that other swift movement which in turn perhaps belonged to a single great movement outside either, to the sum of things flowing like a stream. Water, which wanders to the sea through wide fens, a bright certainty which feels its way cautiously, like a tendril parting out from a vine, through the parched and hostile country of philosophy: the soul, but what was that?

Something that flows through the air, swims in the water, moves imperceptibly[39] from mind to mind—

And themselves part of the stream being carried onwards to the sea!

Sigbjørn glanced sideways at his brother, who suddenly groaned aloud. He was about to say something, then hesitated. Tor really looked as though he'd seen a ghost. Perhaps he had. Perhaps he had seen the ghost of dead summers that lurked always in this place with its tenebrous memories of white and blue girls,[40] but this was a hovering misery nobody who knew Cambridge the year round could fail to see. He glanced at Tor again, wondering if it was the thought of the disaster that still made him look like a man who sees into hell[41] and doesn't know it. But this time Sigbjørn touched his shoulder. Straightening themselves, the brothers walked on. Their pace involuntarily quickened. And now Sigbjørn asked the question he had been avoiding.

—By the way, how's Nina? Did you look after her in London?

—Ah, Nina.

—Why do you say Ah Nina like that? Did you look after her in London?

They were passing Moore's Music Shop[42] window in which there was a small exhibition of manuscripts, spread out before a background of guitars and violins and glockenspiels. What is philosophy, the universe is a scroll of music, the window seemed to say to them as they passed.

—She's well!

They walked on past Bridge Street and the corner of Newmarket Road into Sidney Street.[43] Sigbjørn looked up, postponing all feeling. In a hundred lighted rooms men were working.

Up there a light snaps off and a young face turns on the darkness, on the thousand noises of the old town. What is there? Nothing. Only youth, birth, life, and death, ah, the women of Sidney Street! He will follow this way? No: there is no secret, no message under the stone for him, his desire is not that way. But suddenly he knows what he wants is in the room. It is in that stir behind the bookcase, rather than in the turned pages of the books themselves, in the closet, where is it? Imagination. No: there is some essence there, some hint of secret knowledge, some code implicit in the special blackness of the occasion. Something is there, he thinks as he turns away from the town and life and death, that will trouble him till the end of his days. And his mind drops away in its pursuits.

—She isn't in love with you, is she? he asked.

Tor was relighting his cigarette cupping his hands the flames illumining his face, and for a moment appeared not to hear. They walked on.

—In love, out of love, in and out of love, what does all this *mean*, he said then. Well if it comes to that I think we were all more or less in love with her. I remember that night at the party at Marmorstein's[44]—afterwards she was standing at the piano—and there was something in spite of that unity you used to talk about, so broken about her, as well as how shall I say, something absorbent—as if she would draw one into her own world...I longed to comfort her, but 'in love,' he laughed. All that mechanism of 'in love'!

—For God's sake, said Sigbjørn, Nina and I were trying to make a go of it, why must you interfere? Why must the world always break into something that's lovely like that?

—I didn't interfere.

—You have in some way interfered.

—I don't think private grief, private considerations, are of the smallest importance when there are so many—

—Nina used that phrase to me in a letter.

—None of us thought you were the person for her. She's so alive, so fresh, so sane, and you with 'my soul turns outward towards the pole,'[45] that fine soul which never turned anywhere but inwards, upon yourself.

—After all, it's not for you to interfere, even if you hate me. Good God, if you only knew the heartbreak, the foreboding, the lost hope which somehow or other was found again just in time, and hope...

—Creating, from its own wreck,[46] the thing it contemplates, Tor interrupted with finality.

—Hope that you couldn't share I was going to say: and the pilgrimage we made...

—Where?

—Where? Well...

Sigbjørn's echo hung in the air helplessly and then drifted away on the wind like a snowflake with no aim but with, philosophers maintain, infinite meaning.[47]

—Well, we were building something—

—Yes, yes, Tor said, you were. But there shouldn't have been all that struggle, struggle with false complications, towards an unreal goal.[48] There was in her I repeat too much ingrained sanity, like the sanity[49] in one of Shakespeare's comedies. Well, there's a good deal of theatricality in us, but of a fouler kind.

—What do you mean?

—In our lives and our actions. And hence in the influences that recur in our lives. Our hold on life is insensitive, and our view of spiritual problems anyway is so crudely external that we only appear to disagree, while we fail to evoke the inner truths of either. We study philosophy yet philosophy might not have existed for the arguments we indulge in. We're like players in an old and bad drama that has been on the road for years and years until the words we say no longer hold any meaning. We love and speak and gesture automatically and the drama is coming off, Barney. This joyless performance is definitely at an end.

—What do you mean?

—I mean that while in London I tried to free Nina even if I could not free myself. I tried to make her aware of the decay all around her. In short I gave her a manifesto of her whole life.

—Free her from what?

—But what are you worrying about Barney? Tor suddenly changed his tone. Of course everybody knew she was your possession...

—Possession. What do you mean? There was nothing of the kind in our relationship. There was only freedom.

—Freedom!

The brothers walked in gathering anger down Sidney Street. Suddenly the clock in the Round Church[50] struck 6. Opening time—[51]

In the old town six hundred doors opened and were fastened back.

They increased their pace, now they were walking so swiftly that it was impossible to talk at all. Avoiding the traffic congregated at the foot of Market Hill,[52] they crossed the pavement to Peti-Curi, where they mingled in the black crowd of townspeople and students moving like a slow glacier up towards the Market Square.

The Market Square itself into which they now emerged was a separate existence of coarse naked reality whose beings obeyed its own strong laws: only a few undergraduates were present here, lurking guiltily near the naphtha flares[53] and the gas jets steadily whirring, seeming almost to be straining nervously towards this objective world where so many hard bargains were struck.

The two men cut over to the left, into Bene't Street.

At the Bath Hotel[54] 'Family and Commercial,' opposite the Friar House and the Art School, to which it was indeed a pleasing alternative, the two men stopped. Here, with King's and St. Catharine's Colleges near and Queens' just beyond and Corpus and Pembroke[55] at hand, the shadow of the old University itself seemed to fall on them: it might have been an immense factory of knowledge where they were the humblest menial workers, shuddering in the yard in their flimsies at night, knowing little of its machinery or purpose.

They stepped over the brass sill, an action which was like entering a ship's cabin, into the dark interior[56] of the tavern.

They walked in slowly, as was the custom, looking for acquaintances, but with this departure from general practice, they were looking for acquaintances to shun. It was difficult enough for here in a cramped space, the record of life was playing wildly already, only twenty minutes after opening time. And as if torn from an electric fan the conversations were propelled from the various barrooms into which they peered: *and Jock said to this little bum run and he ran like a stoat and got away with it: threw a bottle of Worthington*[57] *at old Jigger and you should have seen this little bum run and get away with it: he ran like a bloody stoat and got away with it.*

They peered round into another bar. The Players![58]

It's all a race with a shadow, race with a shadow: prompt, damn you, prompt, after a long silence a voice came, from the wings, I've lost the bloody page: when they say yes, now, quick curtain, after that, quick: like this, whore! and then quick curtain, murderer!

At this moment Ginger[59] the barman came to the door.

—I was just going to say you could come to the dining-room if you wished, but these fellows are going out.

At this moment the bar-parlor was suddenly vacated. Tor was saying to Sigbjørn under his breath:

—How can even people who know us sympathize—sympathize, what a word! —about the *Thorstein*. I hate to see them try to. Well Ginger, he added when he had settled in a basket chair, we've decided that we're failures!

—Well, gentlemen, you've come to college late today, said the licensee over his shoulder and added, Failures, oh dear me, you mustn't give up hope, gentlemen! He nodded to Tor:

—I haven't seen you for some days, Mr. Tarnmoor.[60] Been away on a holiday?

Tor hugged his gown around him and raised two fingers. Sigbjørn nodded.

—Whiskey. Two large Irish, please.

The drinks were brought and Ginger retired to the shadow, calm and contemplative.

—You're trembling, Sigbjørn said.

—It must be Dante.

—Dante.

They lifted their glasses.

—*In la sua voluntade è nostra pace.*[61]

—Four things[62] I count worthy of sacrifice: Truth, freedom, justice, and peace, toasted Tor.

They drained their glasses, reordered. Now there was stillness in the tavern. But from outside came the sound of the tapping[63] of a stick: they raised their heads for a moment trying to shake off a sudden hint of impending disaster, mysteriously recognised by them both, in the clicking of that ferrule: then the tapping stopped, suggesting that the stick's owner had also stopped next door, at the Eagle.[64]

—No, Tor said, almost to himself, I really wouldn't mind getting away to sea. I almost feel that—*rondure*, as you call it. That little, self-conscious, rondure. What were you, Barney, a coal trimmer? What does that mean?

—I'd rather not talk about it, Sigbjørn said.

—Why not?

—Well, what does it mean? It means working like hell.[65] When the coal is near the stokehold floor[66] you can thank God for it and that you have some air to breathe, even if it's scorched. Sometimes you work alone, far below the waterline.

He stopped speaking, his face a petrified memory, for the unexpressed decision on both their parts to refrain from all mention of Nina only aggravated the immedicable[67] agony of the sea. But Tor persisted:

—Eyes like rings that have lost their gems![68] And a trimmer, by God, that does seem to fit into Dante well. Why, there's a pattern to the whole thing. The trimmers that were not good enough for heaven,[69] not bad enough for hell. Not one thing or the other. But anyway you look at it it's a terrifying idea. So that's what you long for is it, the fire of the unconscious, which is also the womb,[70] he said, ironically. For all things are composed of fire[71] and into fire they shall return.

—If fire didn't cause suffering the world would have been consumed by it.

—If fire did not cause pain!

There was silence between the two men in which the breakers of the mind crashed.

—In England as in Norway, Tor said, the sea is never very far away. Yet I've never gone. I've always longed for it and never had the nerve to go. Yes, in spite of anything I may have said. When you came back from your first voyage didn't people always say to you: Hello Barney, when are you going back to sea? With a kind of hopefulness, you will agree, that they might be asked to come along?

—I suppose they did, now I think of it.

—Of course they did! Hello, Barney. Hi, there! Drop in and have a drink, why don't you, between oceans? And then...Look: is there any chance you can take me on a voyage? And still more and more people, with whom I include myself, want to return to that element—even omitting the fire part of it!—more explorers who can't explore, poor creatures who just want to go to hell just the same.

—To the inferno!

—Exactly! A vast unhappy army of foolish virgins,[72] starved for beauty, for love, for life itself, voices crying in the darkness[73] for help, going down there; sailors who can't sail, stokers who can't stoke, communists who aren't revolutionary,[74] with private incomes, rushing down like swine[75] on the sea. I see it all, and what a picture it is.

—God help these.

—But of course he won't. Of course he won't, Tor repeated. For aren't they in the process of burning like the well known chaff in holy writ,[76] along with the other capitalist stinkers, with whom I include myself! You can't of course see them burning: they burn invisibly like, I imagine, a cargo that's on fire. But you can smell them probably, if you're lucky. In spite of ultimate negation, it's a fulfillment of ancient prophecy.

—It makes me think of suicides in Japan,[77] jumping down the volcano.

—Or skiers falling at the jump in Frognersaeteren.[78]

There was silence for some while and then Tor asked a question he had evidently been framing during it.

—Have you ever heard anyone speak of the unintelligent, the dumb man or woman, whether poor or rich, who doesn't and who never will understand the situation of which he has become the symbol? But who is never the less the result of all these words and phrases, the finished production of years of other people's toil and grief, of other people's distinctions, and contradistinctions, and lies, and evasions, the person they are all talking about...

He looked up as the lame newsvender tapped through the hallway into the far barroom.

—But never see, Sigbjørn interpolated.

—Because he is ashamed to be seen.

—And never hear—

—Because he is dumb. Yes, the man the wireless speaks of in the evening but who himself passes down the road on quite a different pilgrimage.[79] I drink to that man. Do you drink to him?

—To be sure. I drink.

—Very well then, drink, not to the unknown soldier, not to the unknown warrior,[80] but to the unknown human being!

Tor stood up

—Drink in the name of him who said I am and shall be. In the name of the Lord of Hosts, the Tetragrammaton: in the names of the globes, the wheels, the mysterious beasts and ministering angels. And the grand prince Michael.[81] To the unknown human being!

—To the unknown quantity.

The licensee was standing beside them with a grave face: gently, he unfolded the evening paper and handed it to Sigbjørn without a word.

Over the road the bell of Corpus began to toll: *doom: doom:*[82] a bell-buoy. 'Ware shoal! Shoal!

Tor was leaning over Sigbjørn's shoulder, and they read: *Forty Missing In Terrible Sea Disaster. Another Tarnmoor Line Tragedy. Deck Engineer Protests He Did Not Steer A Course. More strange navigation, amazing ignorance or an inexplicable horror wove the mystery of the Brynjaar,*[83] *the second Hansen-Tarnmoor liner to sink within six weeks. The disaster of the Thorstein six weeks ago...*

The bell stopped, leaving a concave silence.

The brothers said nothing, did not move, seeming to be transfixed with horror. Now the silence was filled by a noise: students, bells ringing on their hard bicycles, pedalling swiftly up Bene't Street to Freshman's Hall[84] in their various colleges. The silence of the dark town was filled with the tinkling music of their bells as a wood in spring is filled with singing. From Chesterton Lane, from Mill Road, from Bateman Street, from Peti-Curi[85] they came: now they had passed, as a wind[86] passes: for a moment or two there remained a hushing sound as when a swordfish goes through a shoal of bluefish:[87] then dead silence.

The final bell for hall started again.

A scene flashed before Sigbjørn. Leadenhall Street,[88] Lloyds. He saw himself there suddenly, reading the telegraph board; news of storms at sea, collisions, disablements, groundings, catastrophes. On the raised platform an official was tolling the bell of the lost treasure ship, *Lutine*.[89] Two tolls! What ship is it, what ship...

The Corpus Christi bell stopped.

—Hadn't we better go—

—No, said Tor. We obviously can't go to hall.

The licensee stood beside them in the gloom, his hands thrown out in an empty gesture: what can I do?

The tapping of a stick in the alleyway outside was the residue of the preceding chaos of sound.

—We must telephone father immediately.

—My God, Sigbjørn said.

The owner of the stick, a newsvender, a stooped bronzed man, peered round into the taproom:[90] he held a stick at arm's length, so that his sleeve was short on his wrist, showing tattoo marks:[91] a bathing girl, a flag, a crucifix, a barque in full sail: ex-sailor.

Round his waist he wore, like an apron, the announcement: *Another Tarnmoor Line Tragedy*.

—I just want a pint of bitter, panted the sailor.

The licensee went out. Sigbjørn turned to go, but Tor was standing absolutely motionless, looking straight in front of him. The sailor tapped over to the brothers, and shouldered his stick.

—You 'eard my old brassy ferrule, he said. He looked round furtively at the door, then back at them.

—Tell your fortune sir, he whispered.

Sigbjørn shook his head and motioned to Tor to come. But Tor, his face white as paper, was automatically holding out his hand. Sigbjørn felt a cold shiver down his spine as he watched. Suddenly this sailor said, with avidity:

—You're going for a long journey.[92]

III

If we really want to live, we'd better start at once to try;
If we don't, it doesn't matter, but we'd better start to die.

W.H. AUDEN[1]

At the rack downstairs in Tor's lodging in Trumpington Street[2] they paused to look for his mail.

—That's odd, decidedly odd: they've taken away your name, Sigbjørn said.

—So they have.

They stared foolishly at the name-board: Ames, Barrow, Carruthers,[3] and so on. All the rest were there as usual, but surprisingly enough the metal envelope enclosing the name T. H. Tarnmoor was vacant.[4]

—It must be a practical joke. Or drunks, more likely.

In the vestibule however there was a letter for him on the table and quickly as Tor snatched it Sigbjørn was able to recognise the handwriting: Nina's.

At a corner of the vestibule was the telephone. Tor took the receiver off.

—We'll try to get him again. He dialed the operator. I want a trunk call[5] through to Liverpool. Yes, Royal 4321. He replaced the receiver and took out his cigarette case.

—They're going to ring when they're through. There was the silent offer and refusal of a cigarette between them.

—Is that letter from Nina? Sigbjørn asked.

The telephone rang and Tor took off the receiver. He spoke sideways through his mouth to Sigbjørn.

—We're through. Is that Royal 4321?

Sigbjørn heard a distant voice say:

—Yes.

—May I speak to Captain Hansen-Tarnmoor[6] please. It's very important.

—Who's speaking? Captain Tarnmoor can't...

—His son.

The next moment Sigbjørn heard his father's voice faintly through the phone.

—Hello.

—Hello, Dad...He turned round to Sigbjørn. What shall I say?

—God knows. Don't worry him.

—This is Tor and Barney speaking. We want you to know we're with you to the end: whatever liability you've incurred, whether the accident was caused by a fault in construction of the ship or by failure in the human element, we know you alone, in yourself, are not to blame.

A pause, and then came, faintly:

—We don't associate such doom[7] with ourselves.

—What does he say? Sigbjørn asked.

Tor went on:

—Any plan you may have to make regarding us, involving us, even involving our withdrawal doesn't bother us: any sacrifice we ourselves may be called upon to make we shall make gladly.

A pause in which there was dead silence.

—Thank you, came faintly, at last.

—What does he say?

—He says we don't associate such doom with ourselves. That's all.

They started to climb the spiral[8] staircase. The sound of radios, each playing the same tune, crept beneath the doors as they mounted the stairs.

As they climbed, jealous anger mounted in Sigbjørn but it was as though this emotion were being experienced by somebody else for whom he was partially responsible but with whom he was not inwardly involved. Quite apart from this, from like thoughts of himself, he had the feeling another person,[9] unseen but enclosing them both, was climbing with them. The solitary mountaineer on Everest has felt, in making his final perilous ascent, that he was guarded, but this figure, he knew, did not guard them.

—When a bee dies,[10] Tor was saying above him, his hands lightly poised on the iron bannisters, does it cease to hum?

The grotesque absurdity of this jingled against Sigbjørn's consciousness, dropped away. He climbed on. Round and round, spiraling upwards, like the Tower of London,[11] he thought. He could not believe that only two men were mounting the stairs: the figure that suffered jealousy, the figure that had enclosed them, these hurried on. His nerves now peopled the ascent with a crowd of dense shapes of conscience, of fear, that stormed upwards with them.

— *Post mortem nihil est: Ipsaque mors nihil.*[12]

—Post mortem, anyway.

Tor opened the door, switched on a light. They passed down the corridor into Tor's study.

—Well, this is where the great mind speaks his thoughts.

—And there, too, is Golgotha.[13]

—Yes, Golgotha, Tor sighed. You'd think we were in the nineties.[14] The naughty nineties.

Sigbjørn walked over to the window. He looked out over the street to Corpus Christi which, with its one dim light burning in the porter's lodge, seemed to lean towards them against King's Parade[15] like the shadowy hulk of the *Oedipus Tyrannus*[16] lying alongside number six wharf in Singapore.

—Why did I say what I did? Tor ruminated. Of course he's to blame. The earthly author of my blood,[17] and of how many other people's God knows...

With his back to Tor, Sigbjørn asked:

—Why don't you open the letter?

—Why should I?

—Are you saving it, to read it alone?

Tor was walking over to the cupboard.

—Have a whiskey and soda? He brought out a bottle of John Jameson,[18] a syphon, two glasses.

—It's from Nina, isn't it?

Tor said nothing, pouring whiskey. Then, taking his glass and pushing one over to Sigbjørn who shook his head, Tor swallowed a long draught and sat down opposite the bookshelves.

—Whoever heard of D'Holbach[19] now, he asked rhetorically, eyeing his books. He rose, walked to a shelf, and with one finger, arched and refined, touched the D'Holbach...Yes, whoever heard of this forerunner of revolution?

—Tor, cut all this out. That letter's from Nina, isn't it? Stop acting. Give it to me.

—Well it's from Nina. So what? as the Americans say. So what? Stop acting yourself.

Tor pulled out the D'Holbach.

—Man is therefore in no wise bound, he read. And should he find himself unsupported he can desert a position which has become unpleasant and irksome. As to the citizen, he can hold to his country and his associates only by the mortgage on his well-being. If the lien is paid off he is free.

—It sounds antiquated. As well as being untrue. Am I supposed to take you up on that suggestion or is it for your benefit?

—My benefit.

—Yours? Weren't you thinking of father?

—No, Tor said, I was thinking of myself. Or rather, the measure of pain[20] can neither remain empty nor be more than filled. He was pacing about the room. But tell me, whom were you thinking about? Not of Nina, eh? Did you ever try to liberate her? Not of father. But of Barney. I! I! My! My! God, even when a thing like this happens it seems only to reflect the shipwreck of our own lives that we can hear breaking away on the sharp reefs of the world. Or collision.[21] The collision between...My mind is broken in the crash. The Lord is my hospital, he marries me pars partore parteth.[22] Do you remember Doctor Berg's[23] classic example of hobophrene?[24]

—Did you really try to liberate Nina?

—Listen, Barney, if you're to get anywhere, if I'm to get anywhere, this has got to stop! This whirligig[25] of self has got to slow up. If you're going to be any good as a man or as a writer it's got to finish.

—Why didn't we read science then, instead of English? Reports on the character of 600 tornadoes...That would have been the ticket! But what's the good of talking of the disaster? It's happened. It's over. The dead are frozen in the postures of the living.[26] It's over. No good talking any more. We've talked, talked, talked too much. If we could act that would be different!

—Listen Barney. Listen to this. Perhaps we can...

He resumed pacing about the room. His was a curious habit of opening a door for no valid reason, listening for a moment, then lingeringly shutting it again.

Sigbjørn's nerves were as frayed as his brother's and each time Tor did this it was like ripping the bandage off a wound. Now Tor went through the performance again, finally moving to the window where, on spotting a policeman under the lamp at the corner of Silver Street,[27] he hastily drew the blinds and resumed his pacing.

—Listen now: I heard someone suggesting that the design of the *Brynjarr* included a more efficient system of—watertight bulkheads?[28]

—Yes.

—Watertight bulkheads? then the vessel should have been able to return to port under its own power without appreciable loss and no loss of life other than those killed in the collision. The fact that she did sink, in a comparatively short time—whatever that was—...my mind is wandering...

Now almost every sentence spoken by Tor was accompanied by some fevered gesture, the opening and shutting of a cupboard door, the taking out and replacing of a book, now bending to straighten the carpet needlessly, and all these nervous movements were permeated by a kind of purpose, an irreducible logic round which his over-worked, emotionally exhausted, horror-stricken mind ceaselessly jostled.

—So, as I was saying, that shows the necessity for the formulation of an effective set of construction rules which will preclude a recurrence of this kind of thing! But it's important to remember the old man's other ships, the *Arcturion*[29] and the rest of them, still afloat, that under similar conditions might be expected to perform similarly. Now wouldn't that be something for you to investigate? something to take you away from yourself? And starting, moreover, like charity, at home!

—Why don't you get Nina to investigate it? Her sociological tendencies are more strongly marked.

—Barney, you're suffering, actually suffering, I'm convinced of it. But letting that pass, tell me if you don't agree. By the way, is it telemeter?[30]

—Is what telemeter?

—According to the paper the reason that the *Brynjarr* sank so soon after the collision was that the telemeter happened to be frozen—that the engineer happened to be at the...is it trick-wheel?

—Trick-wheel!

—At the trick-wheel! Exactly. Well, that the engineer was at the trick-wheel alone, that the change from the telemeter to the trick steering-wheel took place while the *Brynjarr* was at full speed and in comparatively close quarters sprang from the first cause, namely the faulty design of the ship. Agreed? Do you as a sailor agree?

—I wouldn't like to say.

—Very well. Now then...that the orders may have been misinterpreted at that particular moment may also be partially attributed to this cause. But that the orders should have been misinterpreted at all is the surprising[31] thing on a ship, isn't it? Doesn't it seem to you, as a sailor, surprising that the bridge should say port and that the engineer should go starboard?[32] At that moment?

—Yes, I suppose so. On second thoughts, yes. Incredible![33]

—Which suggests two things to me. One: how to formulate and promulgate a set of construction rules for thc world which will preclude the recurrence of this catastrophe, world-wide. Two: how man stationed in one dimension[34] can direct his life in accordance with a law belonging to another. These two problems, in one form or another are what must be solved, yet the negotiation of the first involves the negation of the second and a man could go mad trying to reconcile these irreconcilables.[35]

—Don't try to reconcile them then, Sigbjørn said. If you were consistent it would suggest no such problems. That's the sort of thing that haunts me, not you. Simply you would wish for safer ships to be constructed. Besides, haven't you said time and again that the rules are already promulgated?

—Yes, I have. I have. But remember this. You went down to the submerged tide-bank[36] of humanity, as one might say: you suffered with your fellows; you have all that suffering, that experience over me: I stayed at home and read. I am as they say an incurable petit bourgeois.[37] But what do you come back with from the sea? The last thing that might have been expected: a kind of vague mysticism that doesn't suit you at all. And it's that, in myself too (for like Voltaire dying,[38] I love God but loathe superstition, but unlike him I *am* superstitious, yet perhaps, perhaps...it's the northern love of truth)...it's that, then, that I've tried to deliver Nina from.

—But haven't you said that you...

—Yes, yes, I know. I'm implicated, too. I suffer anguish and dread. I feel sometimes the presence of God and try to fight him down. I feel sometimes I've wandered onto the wrong planet![39] If you knew how I suffered from the confusion. God doesn't explain another of our ships going down after the *Thorstein*, doesn't explain the *Thorstein*, for that matter; those currents that were 'unforeseen, unusual and incalculable.'[40] Nor does the thought of God mitigate the guilt of that shrieking sea.[41] Nor the guilt that is in us, Barney. But there's the rub: we forget Job.[42] That God is beyond this ephemeral accident. I don't really believe what I'm saying. I don't believe anything. I know despair is unfashionable these days. I feel myself giving in to it. All I ask is, didn't the first cause itself ever contemplate its lack of talent with agony?

—Well?

Tor had walked over to the window and stood with his hand on the curtain.

—What amazes me is that quite apart from this second disaster which seems more and more like a shocking nightmare than anything else, neither of us is real, is positive; we merge, one into the other; we're fake, fake things, fake patchwork, jumbles of old quotations and second hand experiences. You're something like me, something like father, something like Erikson. Even the *Brynjarr*!...

—At this moment it seems to me merely the reflection of a great wreck,[43] of a great collision somewhere else. Or perhaps it's merely the driving home of an argument, the stipulations of which were manifest in the breaking up of the *Thorstein*. Don't you think that if I died you could let all these contradictions and despairs, all the rest, pass into me as if I were a dying tree? But let me die, let me just fall away into the darkness and then you could advance, gliding away from all this like a ship, or no, not like a ship, not a ship...

—What on earth do you mean?

—I've been thinking of suicide, Barney.

—Well I've been thinking about murder, for that matter.

Tor laughed. And Sigbjørn, catching sight of his own face in the mirror, which at that moment resembled a circus clown in deepest distress, or again, Stan Laurel,[44] the comedian, laughed too. A grotesque phrase of Erikson's occurred to him then, and his reflection, like a character in an old film, mouthed the words soundlessly: 'Cain shall not slay Abel today.'[45] If there is no God then we may commit murder...[46]

—Well, why not? Sigbjørn heard himself say...

—Why not what?

—Kill yourself. Yes, why not? Go on and die and then they'll be sorry they treated you so mean. They'll see you lying there all dead and then they'll know how miserably you suffered.

Was it really himself speaking? Sigbjørn heard what he'd said as though he were listening to another; so oddly detached was he from his words. He took a long swallow of the Jameson.

—From the turmoil of the weary world,[47] Tor was saying slowly, I return at last to the mother that bore me and retreat into the haven of the womb.[48] So many of our friends are making that same journey,[49] for better or for worse. And after all, why not?

Tor lit another cigarette.

—Do you really believe that? Sigbjørn asked.

—Not really. And yet...No, I don't. Someone said everybody starts feeling like that when they wish they'd never been born. But all the same, if I killed myself, and you signed on a Norwegian ship as you're saying you will (just as I'm always saying I'll kill myself)...which got you back to Norway, or we both got on a Norwegian ship, signed on *down below*,[50] it'd be as if—

Terror suddenly struck its claws into Sigbjørn. Everything save fear was forgotten. He heard his mother saying again 'Don't let me catch you digging down there or you'll go down to the Underground Railway.'

Another spiral[51] had absurdly wound its way upward: now they were looking down into it.

Sigbjørn took a drink and his face, which had betrayed something like love for his brother, hardened once more into the vain mask of the world.

—I'm inclined to take your advice, Tor said. My God I'm sick of this place! What's the good of these godawful examinations anyway and why do we go to lectures when the available knowledge can be obtained from the books the lecturers themselves write? And anyway I've read all the books. All the books are read.[52]

—Well, we'll have to leave anyway.

—Even so, where would we go from here? All the books are read. Mount Ararat is in eruption! He paced the whole length of his shelves,[53] saying: Virgil, Dante, Homer, Orpheus, Logos, Mythos, Partisan Mists, Laboratory Statistics, what have you?

—What did you say you were? A trimmer? Neither good enough for heaven nor bad enough for hell! Isn't that what we were just reading in Dante?[54] 'Oh most unhappy souls of those trimmers who lived without disgrace and without praise...Commingled are they with that choir of angels who rebelled not, yet to God were faithless: all for self was their desire. Heaven refuses them lest they should stain its glory. And deep hell admits them not lest even the damned from them some glory gain. Their name on earth is as a breath on glass.'

Tor walked about ceaselessly, laying another halfsmoked cigarette down on one of the ashtrays from which already little jets of smoke were rising in all parts of the room, as from the deck of a steamer prepared for sea.

—What a terrible, lousy translation that is anyhow! All the books are read... He looked round his shelves.

—Do you know, from all these books,[55] Aristotle, Spinoza, Kant, Bergson, Croce, I can remember nothing at all. From everything I have, only two things haunt me now. Even if we accept Karl Marx![56] One from our, so to say, Søren Kierkegaard,[57] his statement to the general effect that although trained in strict obedience from childhood, he was equipped with the reckless faith that he could do everything but one thing: and that was to be free as a bird, if only for one day. And the other—you'll laugh at me—is Charles Fort's story of the Mad Fishmonger of Worcester.[58]

—The Mad Fishmonger of Worcester!

—Yes, the profound, imponderable, and altogether bogus story of the Mad Fishmonger of Worcester, the best fish story of all!

—I don't know it.

—Well, it appears that there were mysterious appearances of periwinkles and crabs in Worcester which is fifty miles from the sea, when the day before such a thing as a live periwinkle or a live crab in Worcester was unprocurable. Suddenly there appeared thousands and thousands of periwinkles and crabs but unaccompanied by shells or weeds. The occurrence conventionalized and out of it emerged the story of the Mad Fishmonger of Worcester. But nobody *saw* the fishmonger. The question is, if the fishmonger did the periwinkles did he do the crabs too, if he did it?

—And Fort's conclusion?

—His conclusion? Did you say conclusion? What else but that the Mad Fishmonger of Worcester is everywhere! Absolutely! What do we learn here but lies? What do we learn about ships that run aground[59] for no reason and ships that consummate their terrible union[60] in the dark?

—What indeed? But...

—Barney, all this makes me feel simply nasty. I think of us at this moment as just catamites[61]...is it catamites?...of the world's old age. Yes, just the little juices of his drooling, dribbling, quibbling senescence. To be sure, Barney, I'll make your flesh creep. The world is old and crazy and dirty and his member is withered between his legs. But you, won't you make something of that shocking old nightmare, make him run for us at least, make that verminous old man run for his life till he sweats out his lifeblood and his gallstones rattle and he drops in his tracks.

—And then what? as the Americans say! What could cause two disasters like that? Sigbjørn went on. What's the good of talking?

—They'll make a thousand explanations yet disasters will continue.

—Believed to be the work of reds.

—Yes, 'believed to be the work of reds'[62] the papers will say tomorrow. I'm beginning to be ashamed to live in this country...or is it that I'm ashamed to live in the world as it is, and as I am, now...

—I wonder if it isn't the future itself, as with the *Titanic*[63] and the disasters which preceded the Great War[64] sending out supernatural manifestations of some kind, of change, of revolution...

—Why then must innocent people perish?

—Nature was always lavish,[65] wasn't she? Even the Russians, at the very headquarters of the future,[66] can't avoid the future: a thousand apparently inexorable setbacks, in the face of which they manage to carry on. The sadistic patterns of nature would resist any human symbology, but if nature must, let her cut off her nose to spite her face: we shall build new ships; the world will be changed; like a revolving stage the world will be whirled round and in a minute a new scene will be playing.

—Strange that a thing like this should only increase one's desire to get away. But you're right...what's the good of talking?...In the face of it reason itself stands still. What do we know?[67]

—Chance, coincidence...No there must be some order in it, some meaning. I can't believe it's just blind malicious force.[68]

—Let us cultivate our garden,[69] Tor said. But perhaps Candide's answer is not so final these days. Where, for instance, is the garden? Unless it's a new society, a new world!

—Or where was it? Sigbjørn asked, his thoughts again abruptly centred on himself, it's this thinking you can do everything yourself. It's this quality of yours, this reliance on the will,[70] which is fatal.

—This is a bloody farce! I don't think I can do everything for myself, Tor said. I don't. But I struggle against the feeling that I can't. And I tried to uproot that feeling from Nina when I saw it planted there by you. And Nina is happier without it.

—But at the same time, Nina and I were happy until you came along. Yes! She was happy. But you promised a new kind of happiness. That's exactly what happened to Adam and Eve. The moment a person is vain enough to think he is entirely responsible for his own happiness, that he—so to speak—works the miracles, that happiness is taken away from him.

—If I came between you and Nina it was not for myself. It was for Nina and for you. I loved you both. Why, you join me to life, Barney, don't you see? But you can't—

Above the books the photograph of Nina smiled down on the brothers gallantly uncaring of all these words.

—Yes, Tor said, I wanted to liberate you both. I told her we had to change; that the days of sweet sadness, lost generation,[71] etcetera are over. Yes, and the days of 'I love only you,' as well. You've heard all this before, and it's uncomfortable... and it's right.

—And it's meretriciously false.

—For God's sake, look around you! Do you see the wood for the trees in this forest of ambivalence[72] where we live? Look out there in the sky, how the star Wormwood[73] is set and burns furiously for us both.

—If it's true you liberated Nina, Sigbjørn began, perhaps you wouldn't mind showing me that letter. Then I might be able to get some idea, possibly, just how far you did, as you say...

—You don't imagine that a few conversations could completely force her out of her former pattern, at least not against her will, but—

Tor handed Sigbjørn the letter but Sigbjørn found himself, surprisingly enough, shaking his head.

—I don't want to see it, he said and turning away poured himself a fresh drink, then, quite astonished at what he took to be his own hypocrisy, handed Tor back the letter.

—Listen, Barney, Tor said: It's no use substituting psychological explanations and evasions for social fact, economic fact. What do we build? What are we building? Who are these people cheating us? Why do we allow ourselves to be fooled from day to day, from hour to hour, like this? Why do we walk about in circles, listening to worthless lies while the ship is going down,[74] the world is going down? Are we too goddamned lazy to do anything about it? What did you do?

—Well, I went to sea...

—Why?

—To come back again, you always say.

—No. Not really. You went because you saw in school the same decay I now see around me, with this difference: I'm seeing it too late. It isn't a matter of politics alone, it's natural law. Our old selves have got to be reborn, have got to shed their stale environment, if not in conscious union with the 'virile solidarity'[75] of the proletariat—he paused—then everywhere, in everything truth strikes. And he concluded with a contrived shiver, as though truth had finally, and at that precise moment, been revealed to him.

—But for God's sake, man, Sigbjørn said, have you any idea of the 'virile solidarity' of the proletariat, as you call it? Have you ever had any experience of that solidarity, that virility, in any form whatsoever? Or do you just look upon it as a literary fashion?

—If a literary fashion, the world's waiting for that literary fashion just the same. When I think of Cambridge, he added in an enraged voice, I always think of that scene in Helgefjoss,[76] the boy jumping on the dead horse, enjoying the feel of its ribs.

—It's possible that we might strike an impartial observer in the same light, Sigbjørn said.

Tor was taking out a blue folder of tripos papers.[77]

—'Tragedy, as it was anciently composed,' he read aloud, 'hath ever been held the gravest, morallest, and most profitable of all other poems, therefore said by Aristotle to be of power, by raising Pity and Fear and Terror to purge the mind of these and suchlike passions. Discuss'.... What tripe it all is! It's not necessary to prattle of literary fashions. This is the tripe we have to recite blindfolded while the world runs away to her own destruction like an idiot child in the dark. Our world is waiting for revolution and that's all there is to it.

—But what kind of revolution? And was the world ever waiting for anything else? And whatever it was waiting for, is that any reason for you to be waiting too?

Sigbjørn stopped whatever he was going to say. He was standing at one end of Tor's bookcase opposite Marx' Das Kapital[78] and some books on the Soviet film: Pudovkin,[79] Eisenstein,[80] Fejos...[81]

—A social revolution?

He picked out 'Haveth Childers Everywhere.'[82]

—Or a revolution of the word?

Selecting with one hand Kafka's 'Amerika'[83] and with the other Kierkegaard's 'Essays,'[84] he asked:

—Or revolution of the soul?

He held up the 'Phantasia of the Unconscious.'[85]

—A revolution of sex?

Sitting down once more Sigbjørn said:

—The truth is, in none of these revolutions could we be counted on. Life has left us behind. We're like runners in a race who are so far behind—

—Perhaps they will win the next one.

—And meantime the goal has changed. When we started, the goal was God and in the certainty of our childhood perhaps it really was God but now the road is lost. It was so dreadfully vast—

—Yes, but isn't it worthwhile, Tor said, isn't the breaking down of barriers worth it? Isn't it worth the effort to make the transition? After all, you would have to break down barriers even if you became, as I always suspect you to be on the point of becoming, some sort of a mystic—not that I dare laugh at the *idea* of some sort of esotericism...in short, whatever act of faith you make you're not going to avoid torture.

Tor paced in silence before speaking again.

—It's an agonizing transition. Perhaps doubly hard for you who once cast your lot in with the workers. I sometimes think there are too many lives we can never forget. If we could only be purged of so much worthless knowledge and history. Over a past as clean as a snow-covered battlefield it might at least be possible to progress towards something like an attitude. But in this *teatre cruel*[86] in which we continue to rehearse it's practically impossible! Unless we know clearly what we have to sacrifice. Then, it's true, we might break away from it all utterly, start again.

He looked round despairingly at the books.[87]

Pythagoras, Xenophanes, Empedocles...

—One says the universe starts with fire; another, with air.[88] What can you do with these philosophers, anyway?

—Here's another says it starts with water...Actually, what *can* you do with them?

—Did anyone say it started, and will probably end, with blood?

Sigbjørn picked up the leather-thonged Empedocles.

—I know, Tor said. The only thing to do is to burn them. Or throw them overboard like Giraux[89] threw Oscar Wilde's works overboard. Scatter them to their own postulated first causes, to fire, to water, to the four winds?

—But you're right, Tor, Sigbjørn said. You can't avoid torture. Empedocles on Aetna: a moment of incandescent suffering:[90] we must all know that.

—Each soul must know its own Gethsemane.[91]

And as Tor laughed again, another old grief unfolded within Sigbjørn, a grief so bitter he had postponed ever truly recognizing it. Yet it had lain neglected in a corner of his consciousness for many years. Now it moved again, just as he had stirred in the womb, the pain of the memory of his mother's death stirred in him. More than this, perhaps, he began to feel at this moment, almost physically, the monitory presence of his mother in the room. *As a child from school who feels its own dead mother on the stair and sets her place at table and at chair.*[92]

That expressed the feeling, he thought. But although he understood this feeling, was aware of its presence, something held him back still...some fear, some fear of being possessed...from giving in to it.

But as if joined to Sigbjørn by some nexus of thought at this moment, Tor straightened their mother's photograph above them on the mantelpiece and said:

—I wonder really what she went through.

Their mother,[93] in the photograph, a young, fair-haired woman, typically Norwegian, with the sea-blue, sea-gazing eyes, looked down on them from the photograph above the books: but there was something unmalleable in that face, something forbidding, too, but at the same time not positive in those eyes even when one did not see the colour: as though whatever reality or conviction she held did not exist in its own right, but was simply a reaction to something else.

And the curious thing about it all to Sigbjørn, at this moment, was that his father's face seemed, in the photograph beside it, to express exactly the same quality: in this case the questing look in the eyes was refuted by a strong mouth: it was as though the eyes said 'Seek! find out!' while the mouth warned, 'If so, it is sufficient only to be that which you seek.'

It occurred to him, in fact that it might be said the eyes belonged to Hamlet, but the mouth to King Lear.[94] A chaos of a man,[95] indeed, who would try, in life, to play both parts at once.

At the same time, and this was the thought in the minds of both Sigbjørn and Tor, here were two people who had fought to the death for what they conceived to be their antithetical opinions.

Whereas so obviously in their faces was it betrayed that these opinions would merge into as many new approximations as they chose, they might just as well have decided to agree about life in the one essential they seemed to have overlooked, which was, after all, to live it happily.

But at the very moment this conclusion came to Sigbjørn he realized also how difficult it is to be happy, even if you do not know the reason for your misery, when the very system under which you live may render life untenable for thousands of others.

—Alma Mater, Tor was saying. It's strange how we come down to that symbol again, even in a university.

—Matriculation, for instance. By the way, what is a matrix?[96]

Tor pulled out a dictionary; Sigbjørn had risen again and was looking over his shoulder and the two of them having found the word, read its definition:

—Matrix: it is something holding...

—embedded within it...

—another object to which it gives shape or form...

—but also it is a die or mold as for the face of type.

—it is also a rock in which a gem is embedded.

—it is the uterus or womb; the substance beneath the cells of a tissue.

—the formative cells from which a structure grows

—as part of a cutis beneath a nail.

Tor replaced the book.

Sigbjørn took his seat again, poured a fresh drink; sat in silence. Matrix! The formative cells from which a structure grows! Was the structure even now growing? Certainly the small jealousies and sufferings were only as waves breaking upon the vast sea of misery that the *Brynjarr*'s loss created within him. But Tor was right: these billows lapped undeniably at a sort of sea-barrier between one life and another. He imagined the barrier broken down in a flood of water, the seas racing through, and now, his soul free again, he saw a three-master moving downstream, a tug gliding quickly with her, gulls like puffs of smoke in the steel distance. *Mon âme est un trois-mâts cherchant son Icarie!*[97] And now he saw another ship leaving the wharf, gulls circling her, the mate at the foc'sle head[98] with the bosun's watch: now heave away,[99] steady, all clear...

But now a ship was coming in, the little boats nose-dive at anchor in welcome, a seaman standing hears the cordage rattle, he waits for the bosun's call to muster, the twelve to four fireman's watch[100] is coming out on deck, the derricks are slowly raised for the port.

Far, far north[101] the shepherd who drives his flocks out in the morning meets his friend driving his flocks home for the night.

The needle respects all points of the compass alike.

—

—It's wrong she had to die, Tor said finally. She would have understood us now, have given us courage to strike out, to leap the Van Gogh prison wall.[102]

—I wonder.

—There was the same conflict between her and father as there was between—

—Or that you made...

—And that must exist always between man and woman,[103] Tor exclaimed—and between man and man, the conflict between pretensions to spiritual esotericism[104] and pretentions to physical emancipation. You don't imagine that had there been no pretensions between them, had it been *real*, they'd have destroyed each other like that: no, had there been reality on either side, or on both sides, they would have separated entirely or joined indissolubly, become one person.[105]

—Or let their pretensions, or reality, alone, said Sigbjørn. But I'm sufficiently haunted an individual myself to know how difficult that is. Thank God they don't expect us to have pretensions at sea,[106] however.

—Do you remember the day she died? Tor was saying. Just before we left Oslo.

Sigbjørn drew aside the curtain, and looking out of the window said:

—She said once that if it were not for passion[107] love would be eternal. You could say she was like the earth herself with its flowering in spring and heavy dreaming summer when there is all time to waste. And then, that winter, that shrunken, haggard face...I'll never forget her and her love for the sea, and rain, human things you remember when all the ideology is forgotten. Thank God she never lived to suffer these things, at any rate.

—She was human all right, Tor said. The day Uncle Bjorg[108] went bankrupt she went to his office and hanged herself, right there in his office, with the curtain cord. And father coming in by accident only just cut her down in time. Then they went out to drink. And father said once to me that it was one of the few occasions since their marriage that they ever talked as human beings.

—After that they both drank.

Tor took out his violin and played, walking over to the window. He was parodying a virtuoso. But in spite of this, the melody that he played, Sibelius' *Valse Triste*,[109] was curiously moving. Pictures[110] passed before Sigbjørn's mind, glaciers, fjords, forests that were symbols[111] in the heart; ranges that suggested the vast mountain change of humanity itself. His tear-ducts were quickening; he felt as if he might at any moment break down and weep, weep for those who were drowned, weep for his father, weep for Tor, weep for something he could never understand, weep because his life was only half real, weep because he liked this sort of music and not, as he felt he should, music that was stripped and winnowed.[112] Now he saw winter in Norway: a whole nation was on skis, all was white.... But *Drammensveien*[113] had somehow become confused with King's Parade. He slept.

The two children, Tor and Sigbjørn, stood under the shadow of the wall in the back garden of the deserted house. It was their birthday. Like conspirators they looked round to see nobody was watching. Then they started to dig. Work was laid aside, resumed again. Light slanted down between the branches of an apple tree. The light crawled over the children digging. Once more they looked round: all clear! Now they would dig down to the underground railway, the Holmenkollen.[114]

Suddenly, with a clatter, the vehicle shaft collapsed on them: all was dark. In the dark people were searching with lanterns. Sigbjørn glided under a low bridge: *Warning—Low Archway*. Now he was standing on a swamp. All around him were abandoned sunken roads and marshlands. A factory built itself before him. A big freighter slipped noiselessly along beyond the reeds where he stood watching. Nearby, the factory pulsed with sound; number three furnace[115] glowed. In the distance news of the electric Lysadis[116] flowed and flowed: *Tarnmoor Naufragung*.[117] Suddenly confusion, fire, machine-gun fire of rivets snapping off, all around people were screaming, a woman's bones crumbled, the trees' limbs were breaking, the world was crumbling.

Once more he was standing in the shaft and earth was falling on him; an avalanche of earth was falling over his dream. A fragment of verse learned in childhood whispered itself loudly in his ear: *little duck, good little duck, Hansel and Gretel here we stand, there is neither stile nor bridge to take us back to land.*[118]

—How now is Hamlet dead and Ophelia in a swoon?[119] Sleep is a friend to everyone they say.

The shadow of Tor rose up before him; he was shaking him.

—Often with a blade would I have delivered myself from its fortune but...

—Come on, man. Arise and shine[120] as you say.

Sigbjørn slowly came to his senses but once both eyes were open the sense of change or error came so potently he sat bolt upright.

—How long have I been asleep?

—About two hours.

—Have you drunk all the whiskey?

—No, here it is. Tor poured him out a glass and Sigbjørn, rising shakily, took a long drink.

—I had bad dreams. We were digging down to that damned underground railway again—

Tor said nothing. Then he went out of the room. What was in the air? For the next few moments the amount of external attention he was compelled to give while he put on his coat, combed his hair, re-established his awareness of the room, was sufficient to keep his thoughts relatively passive, although they were stirring the whole while, they were not themselves completely awake; but one by one, like eyes in his spirit, he felt them open, and each of them encompassed a disaster; now the whole battery of them seemed to be focussed in the full stare of truth. Good God! My God, the *Brynjarr*! This isn't true. Each incident, the hopeless task of mastering Dante[121] in time, Nina, and titanically, the disasters themselves, and now a hundred other smaller burdens of conscience, each one of them carrying its special vision towards its own inevitable molecular catastrophe,[122] weighted him down, were piled on him with the effect of physical blows, some heavy, some slight, from the cumulative effect of which he reeled. Did it feel like this when one waked to a real consciousness of real life? He fumbled round the room feeling not only the full freight of truth but also again, this queer peripheral change. What was it? Was it visible or chemic?[123] Where did it come from? This change, as though in a chess game his opponent had moved behind his back. But he was not quite sure what that move was. He looked around him. Yes, he was certain of it; just as the awakening wanderer is certain there have been small secret uncertain shiftings in the wood while he slept. Tor entered the room again.

—What's the time? Sigbjørn asked.

—Almost time you went, Tor said queerly. If you want to keep a twelve[124] you'll have to go. Now come and have a look at the bedroom.

Sigbjørn followed him along the corridor, drink in hand. Tor switched on the light.

—There, you see, I've blocked up the windows with newspapers.[125] So that no air can get in. Before I turn in, having finished off the whiskey, I turn on the gas: and there we are. They'll find me in the morning: lying, as you put it, all dead. It's a literary fashion.

—You fool, you're not serious, are you?

—Yes, Tor said, I'm serious.

Sigbjørn looked away. But was he such a fool?

—After all, Tor was saying, didn't you tell me to do it?

—Tell you to do it?

—And the little man[126] with one leg, 'you're going for a long journey.' It all fits in perfectly. It's all continuous and harmonious. Just as when the alarm clock rings in the morning and you're getting up, all fall in line. It's the only possible thing that can happen.

Sigbjørn said nothing this time. In the silence between them the men walked back to the study.

—It's twenty-five to twelve. If you want to have a bite of supper and keep a twelve in St. Eligius Street[127] you'll have to hurry. The landlady brought me something while you were asleep and I took it from her at the door. I thought it better for her not to see you. Tor walked over to the table by the fire.

—You'd better have some. You'll feel better.

Tor spoke jerkily but with extraordinary, calculated deliberation and between each sentence he closed a cupboard or put a book away.

—You're all knocked up,[128] Sigbjørn said, not believing all this.

Then the two brothers broke bread[129] silently together. Sigbjørn crumbled his food but when he had stuffed it in his mouth he could not swallow it. He opened and shut his jaws slowly and mechanically but the food did not taste. He caught sight of his face in the mirror and again another phrase of Erikson's occurred to him: it is worse to betray Judas than to betray Jesus.[130] Sigbjørn shivered.

—Tor, you don't mean to do it, do you? You're not serious?

—Yes, I'm serious, Tor said. I'm serious all right. It's a definite way out. The objectivity of the dead. It's party treason.[131]

—What do you mean? Sigbjørn's teeth were chattering. He took a sip of whiskey.

—What's all this tripe, objectivity of the dead? What the hell do you mean? You're crazy. Haven't we got any further than that surrealistic nonsense?[132]

—You can go a lot further. After, you can go further.

Sigbjørn took another drink and another. Suddenly it seemed clear that Tor was after all quite right. It was a way out; it was a desperate, definite way out; it was a tactile effort made towards something. It was for him—but was it for him? It was a stale death, some accident mentioned on a year-old newsreel in an obscure cinema. Nevertheless this was what he'd been talking about all evening. He could encourage Tor much as his own acquaintances had encouraged him to go to sea a few years ago: Go on, it'll be a great experience, but I haven't got the nerve to do it myself—

Besides at this moment he did not wish Tor well at all. Tor had beaten him out with Nina, had he? Very well, an eye for an eye, a tooth for a tooth. That was the strong, hard, law of life. But he could not believe in the issue, and as the threat of such an issue partook, anyway, of the latter's own inexplicable mystery, only increasing therefore its remoteness, the contest between them was reduced to the simplest terms of the simplest game.

He looked round him. Of course this was not serious, was not real, was just a play, a masque, a shadow of something else. We do not associate such...[133] No. Of course not. We didn't. Or was it because they always deceived themselves that they always found themselves confronted by an unreal fact? By the unreal fact of the *Thorstein* sinking, of the *Brynjarr* in collision? No, they were not sitting there coldly meditating Tor's suicide. His father's ship had not gone down. Nina awaited him with open arms: you were right about the necessity for...They were safe. For there were the family photographs and there the family philosophers. There Kwannon,[134] goddess of mercy, and here their good guardians, Kafka, Kierkegaard, Rilke, and there sitting opposite him—but why did he have to disguise himself as his brother Tor—watching his every move, was Erikson.[135]

Sigbjørn said suddenly, across the table:

—All right, go on and do it.[136]

Tor was watching him calmly.

—I suppose you congratulate yourself on killing me. But you're quite mistaken, do you hear me?

Sigbjørn was suddenly seized with a more violent fit of shivering: his teeth chattered, his hands clenched and clenched convulsively; a spasm of horripilation[137] ran through his hair. He took Tor by the arm.

—You pocket Judas! You goddamned posthumous play! You typographical error![138] Yes, go ahead! Good luck to you!

Tor sat calmly unmoved, looking at his brother. He said slowly:

—It would take a word the equivalent of a thousand years[139] to express what I feel.

—Give me that letter again, Sigbjørn demanded.

Without looking at him, Tor handed him a letter and stood up.

—Come with me,[140] Tor said suddenly.

For a moment, Sigbjørn hesitated. A feeling that Tor, for he had now convinced himself that it *was* Tor, was right, was going to break away to a life somehow colder, cleaner, better, swept through him. He hesitated only a second from accompanying him. But now it was Tor's turn to go to sea.

—Go alone, he said.

But hearing himself say this, he wondered: What made me say it?

—Now you'll have to go, Tor said without moving.

Sigbjørn was putting his scarf and coat on. He was in the corridor. He had his gown on. Suddenly he felt an impulse to embrace his brother. There were so many things left unsaid. Goodbye. Bon Voyage. Have you got your gaff-topsail boots?[141] But of course this was only a joke. Everything would be clear in the morning. Then he remembered the *Brynjarr*. Its memory barely touched him now, but it was enough, shade of a jolt though it was, to convince him that although events might have seemed generally fictitious lately, their reality in the morning remained unchanged. He turned to go back but the door had shut in his face. A clock on the stairway said 11:53. He ran down the stairs. On the first floor he heard the landlady coming up from the basement to let him out.

—Have to run for it, the landlady said, if you're to keep a twelve.

He ran into King's Parade. Once he looked round. High up in the house was an orange square, Tor's room. As he approached Peterhouse[142] he gathered his gown round him; passing Addenbrooke's Hospital[143] on the left he noticed the luminous clock on the dark facade: 11:59.

He slowed, his heart beating loudly: go back, it said, ticking crazily, and voices all round him said go back, go back, go back, go back. He stopped altogether. Addenbrooke's Hospital—a vague thought of an inquest there flickered through him a moment—post mortem, nihil.[144]

Go back.

The luminous clock started to strike the fourfold prelude to midnight: *Sing,song,hang,soon.*[145] He ran on again. No, he had to keep a twelve, that was all there was to it! In the morning all would be clear. *Soon, hang, sing, song*, the absurd slow bells beat in the wind after him as he ran on. He could even afford to imagine their echoes as whirring over the fens to the sea, to the soul's Atlantic—

His shadow ran before him along Trumpington Street. This was unreal, unreal, was in fact a race with a shadow. An exact description for here an advertisement loomed over him: Festival Theatre.[146] The Race With A Shadow.[147] By Wilhelm von Scholz. Nightly. 8:30. *He ran like a bloody stoat and got away with it.*

Ah, midnight must have started already without his hearing it. He stopped short again, his heart beating. Go back. He listened for the clock but the clock was not striking. It was, in fact, hesitating and it was hesitating before it said something. And this is what it said.

Womb—

Yes, it said 'womb': the clock was beckoning him back, the voices were murmuring to him, 'go back, go back, go back.' His mother stood over him: Go back. He heard the clock hesitating again and this time it seemed to hesitate far longer and the trees and the buildings seemed to be crowding nearer to hear what the clock was going to say next, and the clock said:

Tomb—

The clock said 'tomb' and he ran on again. The clock tore him away to frenzied action. If he failed to keep a twelve he could be sent down. If he returned he would be unable to get in. But then they'd have to leave anyway. Would they? The police? But they could scarcely be avoided anyhow. Here was a policeman now, but not looking at him queerly, because from all over the town undergraduates were running to get into their lodgings by twelve. In fact, somebody was running after him now, would catch him up if he wasn't careful. Both were running and gasping for breath. Tor would be gasping for breath too. He heard the sound of his own gasping. But this was a nightmare. He would wake up in sunlight after a night of horror. None of this was true. We do not associate such—

Doom,[148] the clock said finally.

At the top of the steps he leaned his head against the door and with what was practically all his remaining strength he pulled the bell. The bell sounded below, in the basement, subterranean, ting-ting. Beneath the sea, Ting-Ting: ting. Eight bells.[149] He gave the bell another pull and heard the landlord coming up.

—Good evening, Mr. Tarnmoor the landlord was saying at the door. Just twelve. Nobody saw you? What's that? Nobody but a policeman? No proctors? Very well, we'll mark you in at one minute to.

Over his books, his father and mother looked down at him. The room crowded with voices. Go back, go back, go, back.

Below them was a photograph of the *Oedipus Tyrannus*,[150] bearing down the Arabian coast with a load of frightened horses, burying and wallowing in her way: homeward? onward? He fell into a chair. Now in his brain he seemed to hear the creak of the encased steering,[151] the spinal cord of the ship, the vast sea noises of night, the water against iron plates, the scream of the gale in the jackstays,[152] and he saw again the sea rushing past him like a vast negative; or as a manuscript of music is unrolled, so was unrolling ceaselessly the dark parchment of the sea.

Go back.

He took out the letter Tor had given him but it was addressed to his father. It slipped out of his fingers. In the corridor he heard the landlord bolting the door. Unreasonably, he tried the windows, but they were barred and bolted. His limbs were crumbling: murderess of Le Mans![153]

He shook the windows; iron bars. He was in a lunatic asylum. He was imprisoned. That was it. They had been standing outside the prison, somebody had seen them, the police had taken him in. They had locked him up. That was all. But where was Tor? His head lolled to one side.

The Lord is my hospital I shall not want. He marries me, pars, parters, parteth, He leadeth me leadeth me leadeth...[154]

IV

Two observers, even if remote in time and space, each subservient to special social experiences and languages, while observing the same set of referents, have come to construct vastly different references, and yet ultimately to approximate very closely in matter of verbal symbolization.

OGDEN AND RICHARDS[1]

(a)

Trinity College,[2] D5,
Cambridge,
England

"Whence came you, Hawthorne? By what right do you drink from my flagon of life? And when I put it to my lips—lo, they are yours and not mine, I feel that the Godhead is broken up like the bread at the Supper, and that we are the pieces. Hence this infinite fraternity of feeling."[3]

To Hr William Erikson, c/o Christiania Bokhandel Forlag, Raadhusgt 199, Oslo, Norway[4]

Dear sir:

It is not gratuitously that I choose these words of the American writer Herman Melville[5] as an exordium to my letter. As you may not know, up North, in the deep ice, which burns as that great writer's spirit did to the human touch, when later he found his solitary spiritual steadfastness in Mount Monadnock,[6] it was written in a letter to Nathaniel Hawthorne, a colleague with whom he identified himself in some ways with less reason than I do with you. Nathaniel Hawthorne, although Consul at Rock Ferry[7] over the water from Liverpool, had not been to sea. But to be as concrete as possible:

My name is Sigbjørn Hansen-Tarnmoor.[8] I have written, without posting, several letters to you during the last few months and to the elucidation of my motives in thus approaching you I have devoted the best part of a year. I am of Norwegian descent. My mother, who is dead, was Norwegian and I myself was born in Christiansand[9] and spent my early childhood there and at Christiania which men now call Oslo, the town on the swamp![10]

When I was too young to remember we left the country and settled in Liverpool, my father being a shipowner there.

But Norway left me with a wound no summer has ever healed. Even as a boy whenever I saw a Norwegian flag I felt haunted. I would stand for hours on the wharf watching for Norwegian freighters. And when they came it was as though they had sailed into my heart.

Their names, the *Suley*[11] from Trondhjem,[12] the *Oxenstjerna*[13] from Bergen,[14] the town on the meadow at the foot of the hill, and more than any, the *Direction*[15] from Oslo, whose haunting name I chose for the ship in the book you will later hear of, to mention only a few, were more than a memory to me and when they left harbour again I felt as if I had lost old friends, and I became unaccountably desolate until they returned once more, which was often not for years. And always I dreamed I would sail for the country of my birth in one of them, but I never did.

At last, a few years ago, when I was seventeen, I did sail on a ship, as a coal trimmer on an English freighter. The voyage was to the Far East,[16] and the ship made her way slowly from port to port along the China coast, and, you will agree, as finally in the opposite direction to Norway as might well be—

Only the "voyage" remained true, in a sense the fulfillment of my dreams; the voyage within me, the voyage of my soul towards its heritage, while my body, tortured and torn away from it, suffered every torment of deprivation;[17] so that in spite of its nature I still feel this voyage was a return, or, should I say, a pilgrimage towards a goal, or towards a beginning—or towards an attitude!—that may never in this life be reached. Or was it to serve, wilfully, the bitterest apprenticeship to life I could find? To prepare myself for some vocation other than the sea? In search of secret knowledge? Or simply in search of life, of objective reality.[18]

Whatever it was therefore, and in the eclecticism of these alternatives its object must in some way be present by implication, I am left now, as I was three years ago, before ever I went to sea at all, as most of my generation, a sufferer from ἄσκησις,[19] with an unconquerable aspiration towards a completion, a fulfillment of present existence. And I am left at the stage where it becomes necessary to set out again—

(not finished)[20]

(b)

11 St. Eligius St,
Cambridge

To Hr William Erikson,

Dear sir, etc,

etc. I have contemplated writing you for a long time. Indeed this is only one of many attempts. How shall I begin?[21] First I should say perhaps that many and varied are the neuroses which have brought me to my present pass, that is to the position where I feel I must write to you, and many and various also are those which brought me to the pass or—excuse the phrase!—lack of a pass I arrived at a few years ago on the threshold of the first voyage I shall tell you of later. But they differ from, just as they resemble, each other, in one important particular. Three years ago I wanted to find myself, now I want to lose myself. Then I wanted to discover my place on earth, believing it to be that of a writer: now I know that I shall never find any true reality or permanence in my private universe, or multiverse.[22] Why? Because my duty is with what is popularly called the virile solidarity of the proletariat.[23] Yet although I know this I still seem to cherish within myself the privilege of being aware of, and of doing nothing about it. Religion, superstition, scepticism, experience, all are at the bottom of this. I repeat that, whereas before I was concerned with finding out what my vocation was, with private grief, with establishing myself in some particular mode, now I am equally concerned in forgetting all about myself, and devoting my gifts, such as they are, to the common movement for change. It is strange however that in this letter I seem nevertheless to be drawing a remarkable amount of attention to myself. My brother—

(not finished)

(c)

—

What shall we do without our misery?[24] Have you ever thought of a generation, asking, in one voice, crying for help, that question. I am now in a transition state, as it were between sea and sea, a state for which you are partly responsible, asking myself, and answering myself that question. But my brother—[25]

(not finished)

(d)

Trinity College,
Cambridge

To W. Erikson

Dear sir,

You don't know who I am? Yet a perusal of this letter must convince you that its writer is a very old friend indeed, whose message to [gap in TS] is a scroll of music[26] on which is written a revolutionary song. Revolution is the solution of existing problems. Without debacle revolution is impossible. I make a debacle of self.[27]

Yours, etc.

(not posted)

(e)

11 St. Eligius Street,
Cambridge

To Hr William Erikson, c/o Christiania Bokhandel Forlag, Oslo

Dear sir,

I have written you many letters, none of which have been posted, so it is perhaps only too natural that this should appear to begin in the middle. To be as concrete as possible. Of course I have the same difficulty in answering the question "Why did I go?" as you yourself have had for in *Skibets reise fra Kristiania* you write, introducing your protagonist:[28] "A young face paused on the quays, looking up at the ship, Benjamin Wallae,[29] the shipbroker's son, who wanted to find out what the sea was like before he took to the business." And perhaps that is just about as much as both of us care to admit. But we are open to be questioned.

It was not safety I wanted, for I deliberately sought the most dangerous job, not security, for I spent my pay recklessly in every kind of folly, not love I was starved for, not power for which I was frustrated. No! Or you could put it to me that having unconscious need of all those things I was still unconsciously seeking them. Or you can personify them all by my mother, and say that I was returning to the womb,[30] to the birth which is the death into new life, to the Alpha and Omega[31] of which the sea was the symbol, the beginning and the end: is eternity and annihilation, the A to Z, ah, Atlantic, gaudy-striped zebra of the Ultimate! You may say that Norway has nothing to do with it. You may say all these things and still be wrong, or far from the truth, if that truth exists.

But perhaps it was something like this unknown truth I was after, that we were both after: we were seeking knowledge, the secret built into the Sphinx,[32] the secret in snoring volcanoes,[33] and dismal islands shawled in snow, the secret in the one word equivalent to a thousand years;[34] but we chose to read it instead finally where it was most transient, in the frozen seas' storm, or in the heeling shadow[35] of the solitary albatross.

And soon in the light of what I experienced arterially at sea, I lost sight of that object, if object it can be called: it would be sufficient, I thought, more than sufficient, to tell man what the sea was like; that would be a fine thing to do, I was the only one who knew, the only sufferer in the world. I would write about it all, I would be the one writer who having lived his childhood dreams had yet preserved sufficient intensity and tractability of consciousness, had brought to that living sufficient urgency to find beauty in that region, to make the tale bearable in the telling; that was my plan before I discovered that it had all been written before, but more beautifully, more intensely, by yourself in *Skibets reise fra Kristiania*.[36]

I! I! I! What mockery it is that the truism "There is nothing new under the sun"[37] should take such a form. What a frontispiece also to the new book of life whose pages are only being cut today. Private grief, even when projected—how little validity it has! I am not sure that I feel its ultimate invalidity so strongly as when applying to those now, in this world, who do not live at all, whose grief is no grief, but only the meaningless anxiety of those eternally asleep, who awake would find themselves in a world where no conception of theirs of the meaning of pain would be comprehensible. Who can say if, someday, for a few, all this will somehow be changed.

But to return. Your book, then, not only made my own seem futile but robbed my voyage of its last vestige of meaning; in an important sense it cancelled that voyage; forced me out of the pattern of my destiny, so that the voyage has to be remade, the pattern pieced together once more.

At the time I was writing my book, my actual voyage had sometimes seemed something to which that book had become anterior, something which had not yet happened, and at other times that which was written seemed identified with what had happened. But who can say now what the truth is, or what forces our books may have aroused or released? Who can say whose ghosts are whose? And what would be such meaning in comparison with those whose lives have many voyages; what of them? You do not expect such voyages to have meanings any more than you expect your best friends to be geniuses: yet I feel this much to be so, that in those voyages, a soul may trace the beginning curve of its life, but it is precisely this curve which we do not see.

(not finished)

(f)

Mecca Cafe[38]
Liverpool

...

I am well aware that Goethe said the relation of an author with his principal character may be a race with a shadow:[39] I am familiar with von Scholz' play—it was playing in Cambridge not long ago—and I know the scenical idea of the doppelgänger[40] to be an old adage; and more mundanely one has heard of people writing to authors saying "I am your character Smith" or "I am your character Jones." I have also read, in a review, an account of a novel, which I have purposely for that reason refrained from reading, on a similar theme, by Louis

Adamic.[41] And there is a story by A. Huxley.[42] But this is real, is happening, now, to me—

(not inserted)

(g)

Kardomah Cafe[43]
Liverpool

...

But your book destroyed my identity altogether, so close was it to my own experience, both in fact and within my own book, that I begin to believe almost that I may be Benjamin Wallae, your character. But if that is so I ask myself, where and who is X, the projection of myself in my own novel which will never be finished. Where and who is he and who are you?

I have said that your book robbed my voyage of its last vestige of meaning. But as your evil art raised a being, a shadow here, who could answer to the name of Benjamin Wallae—

(Not inserted)

(h)

Kardomah Cafe
Liverpool

Dear sir, etc.

I have long been impelled to write to you. In fact I have written to you many times. But the more I write, paradoxically enough, the more complex my position becomes in relation to you and the more impossible it becomes to state my position clearly. For an accomplished spirit there is but one dialogue, says Barrès[44]—that between our two Egos, the momentary Ego we are and the ideal Ego towards which we strive. But let that pass. I cannot say truly that this identification (i.e. of that which was written with that which had happened, to *me*) was quite exact, for I did not transcribe directly from my own experience in that book. I would have described my 'actual' voyage as a 'spiritual' disaster which had broken my heart, which had in an important sense, killed me, preparing me for new 'physical' life, whereas what I had written was a 'physical' disaster preparing me for new 'spiritual' life. From your book I got the impression that Benjamin Wallae whom I assume a projection of *yourself*, was myself really, (as distinct from my projected self), moving among your characters in *Skibets reise fra Kristiania* with only the slightest differences as to documentation, mode, etc.—we except language—from my *novel unnamed*. But this is irrelevant—

(not finished)

(i)

Mecca Cafe
Liverpool

...

Let me be more explicit and tell you how this came about. When I returned from sea, after my first terrible voyage to China and Japan, I came up to Cambridge to study English Literature at the University. At College I discovered that Literature as a whole for which I had always assumed I possessed a passion, by this I mean the *stream* of Literature,[45] seemed to attract others with more objectivity than it did myself. Uprooted and lost myself I had to find others who had suffered similarly in literature as well as in life which meant that I could not pass the stage of 'hysterical identification'[46] which speaking now with maturer—although by no means mature!—judgment, is no more than a stage in, although an important experience of, the adolescence of a creative writer. After I came from sea, after an experience which has been called 'the breaking of the heart'[47] I discovered that my approach to literature had always been the same: I had been devoted more to the idea of Chatterton[48] and Keats,[49] the *idea* of their dying young, and to that being the most proper thing a young writer can do, than to their work; in fact I discovered a further illustration of this in myself when I suddenly found within myself the same attachment growing for Rupert Brooke,[50] a passion, in fact, for his death, his fate whereas—although as a man and as a critic I found him worthy of respect—as a poet he is to my mind something of a cold potato, or could we say perhaps, a ghost laid by Old Leysians[51] at Byron's pool?[52] So, I leave my guard open, I make an offering of my wounded precepts to you...Le suicide, est-il une solution?[53] We had descended as low as that; but when it came to the test, my brother—

(not finished)

(j)

Kardomah Cafe,
Liverpool

My supervisor,[54] a friendly critic of my work, excused me from lectures and attendance at hall to finish my novel of the sea. But when, in the Christmas vacation, I picked up in a Liverpool bookshop[55] a translation of your novel *Skibets reise fra Kristiania* remaindered from the publishers, and even in translation published seven years before, I...And this book made—

(not finished)

(k)

Mecca Cafe,
Liverpool

To W. Erikson

Dear sir, etc:

...etc. If to conclude, such a situation so engineered seems especially selected by some infernal fatality to further me to my end where by some evil magic I suppose the identity of my consciousness will disappear altogether I cannot help thinking nevertheless that my own special predicament is less remarkable than the general inferences to be drawn from it; but no sooner do I begin to make these inferences however than they cease to be true or rather they become relative to other far more complex speculations that in turn suggest others and so on, and so on, from impalpable to imponderable, progressing finally to, perhaps, say—'party treason'—[56]

(not finished)

(l)

(rough draft)

In my novel unnamed I did not draw from my physical experience but if I can so put it, if there is such a thing, upon my metaphysical. The character I chose, X, for the tragic hero, was a Norwegian (that is to say myself) and the novel treated of a painfully convulsive process of adjustment which communicated a real experience as lived from within towards the other members of the crew whom I personified by the Liverpool-Irish fireman W;[57] all names I had not decided on.

(But I had decided on the name of the ship: this was S.S. *Direction* called after a real ship[58] I had seen in Liverpool. But the ship I really sailed on was called the *Oedipus Tyrannus*.)

All the characters were affected by this process, the inner chaos of X expressing itself elementally, outwardly, resulting in *physical* disaster involving the entire crew.

Similarly, in your *Skibets reise fra Kristiania* the disastrous move of the sailor Aalesund[59] is only equivalent to that of your character Wallae, Benjamin Wallae, who might be my X, who might be myself, who might be you, in signing on the ship at all, of whatever name, and after that move or moves, as in my novel unnamed, destruction holds the joker.[60] Benjamin Wallae has had to identify himself with, to surround the position of, in fact, to be, Aalesund, the brute, the monster, before he is adjusted to the crew in the same way that my character X had to conquer Y to be, as it were, X plus Y, before a similar adjustment[61] to the crew and to life was possible for him. And the same with that shadow of those shadows[62] which is myself! But which is myself? From your feet falls the sandal[63] that is myself? What do we derive from all this? Simply, nada...Or that we have had similar experiences, and made strangely similar use of them. But whereas my book is preoccupied to the end with the precious destiny of X, you merge your characters completely in the mass, the future. If they die, it is for something they believe in. Your characters' pilgrimage is a process of adjustment towards the proletariat: my character is merely one more introspective pilgrimage[64] into that region of the soul where man also ceases to be his own factor. In my book the mass is only important for the personal adjustment it enables one man to make; in yours the personal adjustment is important and rightly important only because it sensibly strengthens the mass—

(not finished)

(m)

Bath Hotel[65]
Cambridge, 9:30 P.M.

—And new hands crawl up to take the leavings the old ones have left: this we take for granted: only Wallae and X remaining continually in focus, continually and visibly moving towards an end: the rest within a fixed, unified, symbol, are in flux. That we do happen to account for them speaks well for us as artists. All? No: there is Gustav[66] in *Skibets reise fra Kristiania*, and in my book a character (nameless) not accounted for. This represents the flaw, the injured nuance, which to my mind renders more perfect a pattern of destiny because we cannot see *all* and communication is impossible between the two dimensions,[67] between the divine conception on the one plane, and the sub-human execution on the other, and this flaw seems to me a recognition on the part of the artist that—

(not finished)

(n)

But what is the name of the ship[68] you really sailed on? Or is *Skibets reise fra Kristiania* entirely a work of imagination?

(not proceeded with)

(o)

Pseudo-Dostoievskian![69]

(p)

General Post Office,
Cambridge

private and confidential
To W. Erikson, Oslo

Dear sir:

Your book, *Skibets reise fra Kristiania* interested me extremely and as there is some field in England for Norwegian translations I am just sending you this card to ask you if any other of your works have been published in this country. If not although I do not myself remember much Norwegian I might be of some help. The process by which a sailor, a superman in courage and resource in his natural element becomes a weakling and a child when he takes shore leave has never been revealed with more agonizing truth than in your masterpiece.

Yours sincerely,

(not posted)

(q)

To J. Trygvesen[70] & Co., Ltd., 105 Charlotte Street, London

Dear sir:

Could you let me know the private address (as apart from that of his Norwegian publishers) of William Erikson, one of your authors, who wrote *A Ship's Voyage from Oslo* (1926) translated by S.H. Retach,[71] in my opinion a masterpiece.

Yours, etc.

Sigbjørn Tarnmoor

(r)

To Mr. S. Tarnmoor, Trinity College D5, Cambridge

Dear sir:

We regret we cannot let you have William Erikson's private address, but we shall gladly have forwarded to him any letters that you may wish to send care of this office.

Yours sincerely,

A.E. Smith (for J. Trygvesen)

(s)

William Erikson

c/o J. Trygvesen & Co. Ltd

105 Charlotte Street

London

Please Forward.

(no letter enclosed)

(t)

(from Sigbjørn Tarnmoor, Liverpool)

Benjamin Wallae, Esq.

Trinity College

Cambridge

(no letter enclosed)

(u)

Trinity College D5

To—

Whence came you Benjamin?[72] By what right do you drink from my flagon of life? And when I put it to my lips—lo, they are yours, and not mine. I feel that the Godhead is broken up like the bread at the supper, and that we are the pieces. Hence this infinite fraternity of feeling.

(not inserted)

(v)

What has thou man that thou canst call thine own?
What is there in thee man that can be known?
Dark fluxion all unfixable by thought,
A phantom dim of past and future wrought,
Vain sister of the worm—[73]

(w)

Trinity

Cain shall not—[74]
Abel shall not—
Judas shall not—
It is worse for Judas to betray Abel today.
Cain shall not slay Jesus today.

(not expanded)

(x)

Final conclusions. Here is the whole secret of our whole life, of the life of the world, if I could only read it: old creations erased by new real lives. A creation has physical significance and being, just as we have our being from god—for lack of a better word—who himself moves like a writer through his dark scroll.[75] And you Plotinus Plinlimmon![76]

(not inserted)

(y)

Dear William

(not proceeded with)

(z)

Dear Benjamin

(not written)[77]

V

When misfortune has singled out a man for its prey, it will follow him to the ends of the earth and he shall not escape it though he mount up to the clouds like a falcon or thrust himself deep down in the earth like the armadillo.

W.H. HUDSON[1]

The two men, father and son, drifted slowly up and down the Exchange Flagstones.[2]

In the incredible turmoil of Liverpool around them—of the shunting and shrieking of engines from the railway station;[3] from the electric railways as their trains ground over and under the houses; along the line of docks and the cry of trams; from the many-voiced Mersey[4] (misery?); in a hundred powerfully mutating smells; in a million nightmarish noises—there was something about Captain Hansen-Tarnmoor and his son Sigbjørn of the organic absoluteness[5] which defines the present.

Brokers, merchants, tartars,[6] lascars, workers and workless, cheaters and cheated hurried by them in one direction; there was on all sides, as this complex parliament of faces flowed past them from the sea (for it seemed that these creatures really had emerged from that element, and might be on their way blindly from that eternity to another), a flurried, inflamed, raging shiftiness and haste in the midst of which their own small endlessly retraced radius implied, as has been suggested, something fixed and true for all time.

And it was indeed as though father and son were aware of this absoluteness, as though it had passed, so silent were they, into their very beings, as though the past and the future, revelations too dreadful to contemplate, were under lock and key in the safe with the accounts and charters of the *Thorstein* and the *Brynjarr*[7] and Tor's college bills; equations which were to have been fairly balanced but which were now finished—with a blot.

It was from this and also from a sort of heartbroken consideration on the part of certain of his employees, more difficult to bear than the most general damning indignation, save on the parts of those actually bereaved, the former tending to lay the blame too heavily at the door of one man, when it was difficult enough in this case to lay it at the door of a system (even when that system was undoubtedly to blame), that they had escaped, first from an adjoining underwriter's room,[8] then from one of the firm's Norwegian lawyers, Mr. Tostrup, with his roll-top desks and ferocious Edvard Munch[9] engravings on the wall, and finally from the oddly inadequate private office of the Captain himself with its single, and at such a time tragically incongruous, water-colour of a sailing ship with furled sails,[10] as strangely calm as a sleeping gull on the sleeked waves before the tempest.

Escape? Hardly! For like murderers it was circumscribed by the consequences of the fact from which they were escaping. They were spread-eagled on this wheel.[11] They would have fled now as far as the Banks of Despair or Cape Desolation[12] had they not foreseen witnesses even at the ends of the earth. Therefore it was with a tacit admission that any further removal from the misery was fruitless when during the present investigations such pitiful constructive effort as was expedient had been already made, that they paced up and down the 'flags' as ceaselessly as they had in other days paced the foc'sle head from winch[13] to windlass and from windlass to lookout.

But today the breakers of the town smashed about their feet.

The Captain said nothing. As time passed, their beat shortened. They found themselves increasingly centred upon the statue of Lord Nelson[14] in the middle of the Square, walking like prisoners on a ship whose chains,[15] tautening without end on the ringbolt, enforce their weighted steps one more weary time to retreat. And every glance towards them contained a threat of punishment, every approach a possible diminishing of the little freedom still left to them.

—This is calamity without the salt of reason, the Captain said finally. If I'd only been there! If I could only have that time over again!

He looked down at his shoes which were perfectly polished. Indeed, he was more carefully dressed than Sigbjørn ever remembered having seen him, as if he had said to himself at every recent seduction of despair, Thou hast not got me down yet, oh World!

Indeed, were it not for an extraordinary nervousness, which, underlying his calm, took the form of his starting at every acceleration of traffic as a recruit starts at gunfire, and a look of absolute terror crossing his face whenever this particular sound—itself like the vast shaking of chains all over the city—was unusually protracted, Sigbjørn would have attributed to him a remarkable callousness, and even as it was, he was only now for the first time beginning to betray by something occasionally ruined and desperate in his talk the agony which he had endured and which he was continuing to endure.

—My purpose and my practice was throughout to accede to all arrangements consistent with dignity, he said now, with an extravagant concision. Outwardly I may be matter-of-fact, commonplace, mingling with colleagues. Inwardly...

The look of terror crossed his face again at the commingling of grinding gears and electric wailing when, almost simultaneously and on either side in Tithebarn Street and Dale Street,[16] the green lights flashed on against the noonday, letting the pent-up traffic pass.

—Abraham always stands by with a blunderbuss,[17] he added with a sort of sobbing laugh which, at the same time, constituted a patent warning to an acquaintance who had turned to regard him with hostility.

They continued their pacing, turning their backs; but Sigbjørn felt, on behalf of his father, the conspiracy on the part of these swiftly walking merchants and those others sneaking up on them; he felt slander from hypocritical sources, the presence of the devil; and his imagination filled the silence which fell between them with their voices: 'they're the Tarnmoors, you see that fellow, I'd like to get my hands on that fellow, trying to collect insurance on his ships, a disgrace to Liverpool, had two sons at Cambridge, drove one to suicide, that's the other, used to be a highly respected man'...

—It would have been just the same, father, Sigbjørn said. Nothing you could have said, nothing you could have done, would have altered anything.

They paused at the centre of the area exchange, leaning against the rail[18] surrounding the monument to the memory of Lord Nelson. And the regularity of this scene, every time Sigbjørn noticed it, served also to enhance that curious feeling of the present; the arcade, embracing three sides of the quadrangle two of which contained merchants' offices, and on the eastern wing the exchange and the underwriter's room, suggesting to him again that in the midst of much that was fluctuant and transitory—for this architectural solidity housed many bankruptcies—they were rehearsing something that might be indeed, as his father had curiously hinted, as manifest in all human relations as the intended sacrifice by Abraham of his son, Isaac.

His father now, with an oddly reactive predominance of interest in the statue as though it were in some way symbolic of what was happening, was reading the words inscribed at its base...

—Erected in 1813[19] from designs by Matthew Charles Wyatt Esq., being modelled and cast in bronze by R. Westmacott, Esq., the Captain read aloud.

—It's damned ugly I think.

—Let me see, the four figures round the pedestal presumably mean the four victories.

—Or the Angels Four[20] that there convened, said Sigbjørn.

—Well the figure of Nelson is the principal. And Victory is in the act of crowning the hero's sword[21] with another conquest.

—While Death—isn't that Death? —is seen stealing from beneath the folds of the fallen flag of the enemy touching the heart, yes, the heart no less, with his palm.

—Yes, I see. A chaste and classical palm, said the Captain. And meanwhile Britannia[22]—surely that's Britannia—mourns the fate of her son while there you see a dauntless seaman, the handsome sailor of fiction no doubt, starting forward with all the energy of life to strike a deadly blow. It's highly ironical, you will agree: 'England expects every man to do his duty.'[23]

—With the lowered flag he conceals his lost hand,[24] Sigbjørn said.

—Oh my God if only...With no warning, Captain Tarnmoor sank suddenly to the iron seat. Couldn't you have done something to help? Couldn't you have prevented it some way? Somehow?

He had turned so pale, so far had he bowed over, that it seemed he might actually collapse, much as the Spanish Captain Benito Cereno[25] had collapsed in the arms of his Negro servant. His next words came only faintly:

—I'm no Sir Arthur Henderson, or Currie, or Booth,[26] and what star do you steer your life by anyhow? Star Wormwood?[27]...His knees shook in an alarming fashion, and indeed his whole frame was trembling as Sigbjørn helped him to sit again in an upright posture. The Captain passed a hand across his head looking desperately at several unemployed cotton porters[28] who had wandered up to watch but who now turned away, emptiness in their eyes.

—God, rather than go through what I have again I would.... The Captain looked round slowly and shakily at the statue.

—Some have died of grief...[29]

Sigbjørn stood by him silently.

—The Battle of Copenhagen[30] was one of Nelson's, the Captain said, reviving somewhat. But don't you go back, back there up North, back to the fair-haired people,[31] like Tonio Kröger,[32] or they'll lock you up in the Public Library or the 'drunk for salties'[33] or whatever they did to him.

—I'm going back, said Sigbjørn. I don't want to be cruel, I'll do anything for you I can, but I'm going back.

—You're going back? What did you say? Yes, going back. But going back where? What do you mean?

—I'm going back to sea. And who knows, I shall be going back to the fair-haired people too.

He looked away as a long-drawn moan[34] came from the river as if in ironic comment upon this decision. When he turned to his father again he was surprised to see him lighting a cigar.

—There's something of the Micawber[35] in us all, the Captain said, emitting a flood of grey air. The trouble is, I've had no sleep. But I'll try and pull myself together, for a time anyway.

And almost immediately he threw the cigar away again. He rose, grasping Sigbjørn's arm, and they wandered over the flags towards Dale Street.

—I hate walking slowly across this Square, any time, he said. You see, the *Thorstein* was—

He hesitated, fumbling for words, and to Sigbjørn he appeared like a man in actual physical torment whose central agony had been pricked once more, who struggled painfully. His son had concluded that there were certain allocations of blame, of error, imputations to wrong causes and right rationalizations, evasions and perhaps an occasional facing of the truth that his father had rehearsed, but which were always referential to matters sometime before or sometime after the fact. It was as though in the centre lay a core of horror surrounded by a painful inflammation which itself could scarcely be touched. Meantime, however, he was still prepared to evaluate the strength of other affected parts of the system. But, the entire organism being affected, it was as impossible to avoid discovering distress almost anywhere as it was to avoid calling attention to it.

Now like something in a fantastic film cartoon[36] in which an automobile can spread wings at the cul-de-sac, he continued beyond the bad lands, at the other side.

—Yet I was prepared to take on a burden of guilt for that. I would have paid any penance for those lives. I wrangled with myself whether or not I should commit suicide and decided...We'll go here, to this Bodega,[37] and he pushed Sigbjørn through the swing door...decided a captain who thinks he has done his duty doesn't go down with the ship; as for the owner, he has responsibilities to discharge to those remaining. Granted that they remain. Or he may have sons—a son, yes a remaining son. The Captain ordered two sherries.

When they were brought the Captain did not drink but stared fixedly at the tawny liquid as though the thought of it could make him ill.

—I can't drink. I can't eat. But I like to be among people eating and drinking. He smiled. I feel strangely inclined to laugh at ridiculous trifles. And he wagged his head fussily at several acquaintances further down the bar who regarded him wide-eyed with a mixture of horror and astonishment.

—But there is no explanation for it, none at all. I can't fathom it. Now if your ship were going south and you wanted to turn east, what would you do, Barney?

—I'd starboard—no, port my helm.[38]

—She steers hard as hell tonight, said the Captain slowly. Then he turned on his son, the ambivalence of a cosmic doubt cleaving his mind with two separate traces, like the wake of two ships. Do you think I was responsible, Tor?...I mean Barney? Tell me, do you think I *was* responsible? The inquest said the helmsman was insane.

They huddled together like two conspirators.

—It's curious how you don't believe it, he went on. Feel that wood, it's just as hard. That tankard over there, it's just as cold. And there are our reflections; we know where we are,[39] but we don't associate such dooms with ourselves.

—Good God Almighty! he suddenly burst out. I can't be gloomy about this whole thing. I know your mother would have...Only there mustn't be any doubt. Don't leave anything doubtful. As if that were possible! The verdict at the inquest...

—Hush, he warned himself, lowering his voice...The verdict at the inquest, just like your explanations, was ambiguous. Tell me everything you know. I accept that Tor was dreadfully unhappy always. In some ways I could almost be glad for him he's rid of the burdens of life, if he isn't up against something worse. Only don't leave anything doubtful...as if there were anything else but doubt.... He pushed his untouched sherry towards Sigbjørn who shook his head...All this has put me in a hilariously morbid condition, not responsible for what I say. Break down! Yes, break down! Go under!

Sigbjørn, trembling, tried to control himself, pull himself together sufficiently to make some reply. He looked about him, holding the bulb of sherry, looked at the hostile faces around him, at the formidable casks, San Lucar, Pasto, Pale Dry; and the Port advertisement started an idiotic refrain[40] in his mind: *old port, light, delicate, Cockburn's very fine*[41]...but he could say nothing, looking round helplessly at the casks.

They got up to go, pushing their way out into the cold, tempered blue morning, blue...as blue as Nina's sea-voyaging eyes...

—I killed him!

For a moment, Captain Hansen-Tarnmoor recoiled against the window of the Bodega like a man struck by lightning. And Sigbjørn standing by him, waiting, it seemed eternally, for his collapse, saw in his mind's eye the elemental equivalent of this mental stroke, the lightning flash suddenly like a warning from a lighthouse[42] against a cloudless summer evening whose warning is also beckoning an invitation to the storm; the man who falls slowly[43] in the distance as the mowers move across the fields; handles that have burnt in the sun now turn like dark wings in the shade.

But as a fireman, worked after his debauch in port, manages to make his last half hour in the first watch out to sea, half-unconscious but propped up by some inner heroism as though the iron from his own blistering tools has entered his spirit, the Captain slowly, and with infinite, painful deliberation seemed to gather all his strength into one effort not to collapse. Then he said clearly, as if suffering had rendered him clairvoyant, or as if—for some other being into whose soul he had entered in another region where night had fallen—this same lightning flash had only illumined all that had hitherto tossed in darkness.

—What you say is not strictly true. I don't believe you.

They were standing looking down the street which inclined steeply towards the Mersey and Sigbjørn remembered how Tor and he had gazed down from the hanging hill[44] in Cambridge on a wintry world.

—Only in the sense that you brought his murderer into the world can you be held responsible, Sigbjørn said. And you can scarcely have expected to know you were going to do that.

—No, I don't believe you, his father said again.

They were walking now with slow bereaved steps down an obscure street near the docks: the huddled warehouses, the iron shutters, the roofs, the cables piled on the wharfs, seemed dumbly to want to speak to them: the truth is neither one thing nor the other, they seemed to say, you're all in the right, can't help yourselves, only the cause is in the wrong.

—I remember old captains here, sunburnt, going in and out, talking of Valparaiso.[45]

They looked up at the voyaging clouds, cargoed with memories of the past: a single cloud floated by far behind; White Ship[46] on a failed voyage.

The father now took the son's arm.

—You didn't, I know. I know the way of the world, my boy. I took my trick at the wheel. Did you ever take a trick wheel?[47]...I've paced the foc'sle head my boy.

—As though we were doing it now!

—Yes, I've talked with the men, I know the men as well as you. I've done my dhoby[48] with them, can make a handy-billy;[49] many captains were my friends. I was a captain myself, I crossed the Atlantic several times on—shall we say?—business...I seem to be wandering. Grief is a kind of delirium,[50] don't heed me. But the crazed live many years.[51] Barney do you know how shocked I was when I first saw you go to sea? Yet can you believe I was glad you had to go! How can we talk like this? But we don't associate such dooms with ourselves, Barney, do we? These things don't happen to most people. And those to whom they do happen, those to whom they do happen, aren't allowed—

—Aren't allowed what?

—Aren't allowed to participate in the mysteries,[52] should we say?

—What on earth do you mean?

—Something is being let loose...yes, something is being let loose. Do you know, it's as mysterious as the first cause of all things, and yet...did you ever read *Moby Dick*?[53]

—Many times, Sigbjørn said.

—Good! Well, possibly you'll have some idea then, some inkling, of the blind malicious force—and yet it seems *dual*—in the world, transcending...You know, and yet you're not superstitious, are you? By the way, Melville stood here,[54] wandered about here, in this very place. Liverpool. Yes, and it was here he must have spoken with Hawthorne. Melville really thought he'd found in Hawthorne a spiritual ally![55] Melville really thought Hawthorne had written all his own books better! Weren't you telling me you'd found some Norwegian who'd written your book better?

—William Erikson!

For the first time Sigbjørn extended his *hyrkontrakt*.[56]

—I hope to see him in Norway, he said. It's unfortunate that as far as I know my ship's going to Archangel.

—Your ship! what's the name of your ship?

—The *Unsgaard*.[57]

—*Aasgaard*![58] The old Norse myth tells us that Aasgaard itself would be consumed at last, and the very gods would be destroyed.

—The *Unsgaard*, I said.

The Captain took the green Norwegian discharge book received by Sigbjørn from the Norsk Konsulat[59] that morning in one hand, and placed on his spectacles with the other.

—Yes, I see. *D/S Unsgaard, Sigbjørn Tarnmoor, limper*, he read. *Skibets reise fra Prester til Archangel/Leningrad*.[60]

The Captain handed the book back calmly, as if he now accepted the voyage.

—Well! All the whaling is gone to the Norwegians now. I sold one of my ships to the Larvik[61] Fisheries, the *Sequancia*.[62] Well, that's where Moby Dick is now.

—That's where I'm going.

—Well, Oslo is the new Nantucket,[63] Larvik its 'Sconset.[64] That's where the hunt for Moby Dick starts, or does it start here where his great creator wandered? Alas, Liverpool itself was a dream in his mind once, said Captain Tarnmoor, but the *Baltimore Clipper*[65] disillusioned him. Riddough's Hotel,[66] where his father had stayed, and which he couldn't find—and where was it anyhow?—was it the next embitterment? The starving woman[67] in the cotton warehouse? But why go on?

—If he'd seen Liverpool today he'd have been more embittered perhaps?

—The second time[68] he came to Liverpool he left it for the Holy Land. Perhaps today, like you, he'd have gone to Russia.[69] Or perhaps he'd have stayed in Liverpool and anatomized its special heroism, its own disasters heroically encountered!

—The idea of Russia as a Holy Land is surely false!

—But apart from all this, what have you discovered? You weren't a writer at all?[70] Captain Tarnmoor digressed. Well, perhaps that's the most satisfying discovery of all, that you're not what you think you are, that your apparent colleagues are not your own at all, that...But why go on? After all, perhaps you're right, change this world, kill your old father, only above all don't write about yourself.

Sigbjørn winced.

—Did that hurt? his father went on. Don't listen. It only hurts me. I hope your books have all the success in the world. You have to find your place on earth, God knows.

Sigbjørn laughed, not from amusement, but one of those laughs de l'Isle Adam[71] was reputed to have indulged in when filled with an excess of bizarre, excited joviality which, repeated by nocturnal echoes, would make dogs howl or Adam turn in his grave. He looked up at the clouds, a fleet of clouds endlessly setting out.

—Tell me, his father said, you can tell me now. What happened in the morning. I know the rest.

—I went out early into the street, Sigbjørn said, as though reciting something long rehearsed in spirit. I didn't really believe he'd done it. The wind was blowing over the fens. And yet at the same time I knew somehow that he was dead. All night I had heard his heart beating in my ear.

—What do you mean?

—Like a watch ticking[72] in an empty room. And about six o'clock it seemed to stop. St. Mary's clock[73] was pointing to six. There was a fresh wind, cool and strong, like a wind coming round a headland. I felt curiously as though I had delayed sending an S.O.S. call.[74]

—Well? You can tell me.

—Suddenly a desire to do good, to assuage suffering, came over me...

—Yes. Go on...

—There isn't any more to say. Nobody can be good to a dead undergraduate lying on a camp bed.

—Who knows?

—But the future!...

Sigbjørn saw the ocean again, the grey combers slowly breaking, the Mother Carey's pigeons[75] scattering, the black French collier[76] sinking in the waves, and grey, grey, grey—

Oh, lovely ship, trembling in every mast:[77] I shall set out—

—Barney, listen. One of us must keep sane or we'll both crack up. I know all the facts of the case. I know what you didn't tell at the inquest[78] and what you did, by now. How you didn't dissuade him, and so on. But, laying all agony aside, we must stop talking in circles like madmen, Barney. We've got to be sane, however much carnage and sudden death is around us. First, I doubt whether there are many suicides like that, on a sudden impulse. Yes, without knowing it I can see how Tor had carried that death around with him for years. How he was surrounded by a strange fatality arising from it, just how his suicide, in fact, became his entire object in life. You say his name-plate had disappeared![79] Indeed, you mustn't blame yourself, for it was as if he had already ceased to exist. No, ultimately, it's still I that am to blame, for a thousand instances when I might have shown more understanding, more stir of fellowship,[80] it's as though at each opportunity I had denied him, betrayed him—

And hands, like frantic birds in a gale, flitting on the branches of the wheel, as the *Thorstein* drove on the rocks—

—What shall we do? Where can we go? Why do these things happen to us?

—How can we think of Tor? how can we even think of that when we've lost so many lives? each with their fears and hopes trembling in the darkness, now only voices crying somewhere, crying in the darkness for help; all night I hear them... imprisoned in the viewless winds![81] My God, there's no meaning to it!

Above them an aeroplane was manoeuvering slowly, incredibly slowly...circling against the high wind, and then its motor cut out, appearing to rest as a seagull does on its wing; then diving steeply once more, its engine picking up once again with a strong roaring; slow Immelmann turn.[82]

Warning: Low Archway

It is later than you think.[83]

They started to walk slowly along the road by the docks, but they were aimless, and did not seem to know where they were going now as they cut across the heavy-smelling bystreets and the open unloading warehouses, and stood looking down into gaping cellars as though they were staring into voids within themselves, and a dozen times they even started quite mundane topics of conversation. For the horror stood in relation to their scene as deliberate unreality on the stage may stand to a certain stylized play in which what matters is not reality according to life but according to the special reality of the theatre: both scene and illusion are satisfactory only when creating for the audience its own fantasy. And it was as though the Captain and Sigbjørn were spectators of this wreckage of their own lives in a play that seemed unending, in which the fantasy that took place was so recurrently unconvincing as to become uncared for either by conscience or sensibility.

They closed their eyes to it, feeling something of the boring pain that follows physical satiety. It was curious but they were victims of wandering attention at their own drama where it was even possible for long periods to forget it altogether until with a shock the ghastliness of the theatre's purposive illusion seemed again to be enclosed by their own lives, as in a play of which the audience is expected to make a part. And now as they walked they frequently forgot 'it' as one forgets the first cause of all things, the fall of man,[84] and all mysteries in a hundred trivial harassments which carry in themselves only implications of these things.

Without knowing it they were making a great circle[85] of the city which would bring them back once more to their starting point, the Exchange 'flags,' and also back, incidentally, to those questions which tormented them and which would never be answered. Their tragic sauntering traced within the city a huge question-mark. They paused at a traffic light in silence. When the green signal flashed on and the cars were released a flow of pent-up talk also would be freed between them, talk that covered old ground, anything to avoid what really gnawed at them. They climbed a gradient,[86] finding strange comfort merely in this, that for a time, however small, they were free to climb away from that element to which all gradients inevitably descend, to water, to the sea. Yet even as they climbed the father was saying for the tenth time:

—And so you want to go to sea again?

And for the tenth time, Sigbjørn was replying:

—Yes, I've got to get away, out, back into my own tracks, to the sources of my ancestry.

—That is, to your own mother, to Norway.

—Well...On a Norwegian ship. But she's bound to Archangel for timber. I don't know whether I'll touch Norway.

—Then what about Erikson?

—If I don't go to Norway I shan't meet him. But I shall be able to dramatise that book[87] in my watch below. And I shall see Russia, where the future is being hammered out...

Suddenly, rounding a corner near Gladstone Place[88] where the Sailor's Institute stood and out-of-work seamen and firemen hung about in little groups, their eyes turning to the lost ocean much as men off-watch at sea stare into the grey melancholy expanse of waters thinking of homes to which they may never return, they found themselves held up in a crowd.[89] A heavy smell of cloth, as warmly damp as the interior of a laundry, was penetrating their nostrils. Suddenly: shouts, the ringing of hooves, chaos.

They could not see, their arms were useless, their faces nuzzled coarse cloth. They were submerged in a dark forest of human beings. To pass through was as impossible as parting trunks of trees. But now a few, more resilient saplings gave way. For a second Sigbjørn suspected they had been recognised and some demonstration was being made against his father. But they soon realized it was a mass workers' meeting in process of being broken up by the police. For a few minutes they were carried on by the angry torrent which seemed to swell from north, south, east and west at once. Through all shrieked the whistle of an ambulance. Three policemen rode up before them, detoured them.

All was calm again now where they were in Post Office Road,[90] like boats hastily pulled up far onto the beach to safety while below the spent waves drew back again to their hungry followers whose predecessors, in their turn, raced round the headland out of sight. A little further up and naught could be seen of what had so quickly transpired. Scarcely a hint reached them now of that tumult driving on beyond their knowledge and—who knew?—to the future. But perhaps there had been no tumult. Perhaps it was just some chemical phenomenon reflecting their own distraction. Whatever it was had not shaken them free from their own appalling fixation upon the apparently trivial. Only it could be said, perhaps, that the foregoing chaos had abstracted in its headlong career some of the confusion in the Captain's mind.

—Then your purpose, or your lack of it, is dual,[91] the Captain said, as they walked along Post Office Road. You have to set out; you are on a Norwegian ship; and to that extent you are home already. And moreover, home without touching Norway at all which you are not sure you are going to reach anyway! Nor are you sure whether you want to meet Erikson! Or wait...for perhaps you do meet him, again without knowing it, for just as you are home already, in a sense, on that Norwegian ship, *Unsgaard*, you also meet Erikson, identified there as a member of the crew. In short, you meet yourself.[92] Only a new self. Or...But where's the *Aasgaard* bound to after Archangel?

—The *Unsgaard*? She's bound back again to Preston with timber.[93] But supposing I didn't mind where she took me! What would you say to that? For almost anything seems better these days than carrying your whole horizon in your pocket...[94]

They had crossed into the shopping centre[95] where mothers were fussing in and out of the huge department stores with their school-capped sons and there was a strong smell of coffee. Some bitterly distilling memory of childhood forced father and son to walk even more swiftly. Above them shadows of clouds raced across girders, swept tall buildings where soft fabrics gleamed from the upper windows. Trams[96] lumbered past to Calderstones, Old Swan, London Road, Islington, Mossley Hill, Aintree.

—You're lucky to have anything at all to carry about in your pocket, the Captain said, adding, as if he had to, Well, I give you my final word. You're twenty-one years of age and if you wish to go to hell, you must do so at your own expense. He quickly changed the trend of his remarks. But why, why, submit to the vulgarity of the voyage? If you sign on a Norwegian ship, well, doesn't that discount the inner necessity of your return to Norway? Why not, like Huysmans,[97] take the voyage for granted? After all, your spiritual gravitation towards Norway carries within it its own fulfillment. Moreover if, as it has been stated, revolution is the solution of present problems, then you had much better not escape but return home now with me, who to some extent needs your cooperation, feeling already the physical stimulation and the moral fatigue of a man coming back to his home after a dangerous journey.

—I'm not escaping. And after all, what good can I be to you?

—A brother, or a son for that matter, I agree 'is harder to be one than a strong city[98] and his intentions are like the bars of a castle...' I could have your room fitted up with advertisements of the P.S.N.C., the R.M.S.P.C.,[99] and so on. And advertisements for La Paz, and Buenos Aires and Batavia. Besides—and the Captain coughed and changed his line again—besides, haven't you done this sort of thing enough? China, Borneo, Japan—what more do you want? Didn't those places load you with finer mountains,[100] identify a finer scene?

Sigbjørn appeared to be talking to himself as he muttered, looking straight ahead of him as he almost ran along beside the Captain:

—I must go...I must! I've got to see Erikson...it's as though he stole my birthright.[101] And yet I don't feel envy, merely that I am his character. No, not that, I *am* Erikson...

The Captain was out of breath and panting as he replied:

—Well, similar coincidences, sometimes fallacious and imaginary, but sometimes quite real, happen in great inventions of man. Maeterlinck[102] points this out rather vulgarly in almost these words. They float in the air, so to speak! It's as though a few privileged individuals more sensitive or more perspicacious than the rest, simultaneously capture a warning from beyond the world and draw from the secret spiritual well which nature opens from time to time.

—That's not it at all.

At the steepest part of the gradient of Lord Street[103] which they were now climbing, the Captain panted:

—Well, gravitation itself is a put-up job[104]...so are higher mathematics. What do we know?

A memory of Tor flickered through Sigbjørn and was gone.

—Each soul knows its own Gethsemane. That's about all we can say.

They had curved round into Mount Pleasant, one of those streets which, with Great Homer Street[105] and others converging on the main channels leading down the Pier Head,[106] are like lesser tributaries of the Mersey itself. The signs of a cinema, built on an incline,[107] attracted their attention.

Century Theatre, the Home of Unusual Films. Pudovkin's The End of St. Petersburg.[108]

They entered unhesitatingly as if they had been making all along for this place of refuge. But once inside they were almost lost. Like blind men they felt their way to a seat. The main film was playing. Somewhere, people marching, Sigbjørn thought: a few, weary, crawl to the wayside. God help me...*The Kerensky Government is only the same thing in a different coat. No compromise!*[109]

Behind them—and on hearing them Sigbjørn turned quickly—a man was whispering to a girl, perhaps a student at the University.[110]

—You see how they don't complicate these workers any longer with souls? the student was whispering. They haven't time for neuroses, for talking about themselves, they have something else to do, they are ready to take over...

Near them another voice from the darkness said, admonitorily, 'Ssh, ssh!' and the conversation stopped.

The father and son sat in silence, leaning forward eagerly, seeming almost as if they willed to be transported from their own seats into this world, not indeed less tragic than their own, but where hope displaced sterility, and courage, despair; for although this film did not celebrate the accomplished fact—the success—however you preferred to look at it—of a workers' republic, nevertheless it was precisely the air of pleading in it for something which had not yet come to pass, and the quality of actually moving towards a fact, a solution, that transfixed them, even when its related object must have served only to remind them that, like two castaways, they could now hail any sail on the Barbary coast[111] of their lives with equally scant hope of succor. But here in this drama, whose shadows were at least more real to them than their own acquaintances, hope and not an out-distancing fulfillment was implicit, and they could take comfort from it.

Behind them the voices started again.

—God help us all[112] that worker's wife[113] said to the peasant, the girl behind them was noting. Yet they have destroyed God. There is no soul any longer there. Or is it true it was the priests who destroyed God and that the government only insisted they should do something useful?

—God help those that believe this and also believe in God, the boy said.

—Ssh! Ssh! the voice again warned from the darkness and there was silence.

The Winter Palace[114] was captured before their eyes. St Petersburg was declared Leningrad. The workers slowly filed into the palace, the strike leader's wife following after, carrying a pail of potatoes. On seeing her, and then the peasant from the country, the workers broke into slow smiles. Suddenly the screen grew bright, the lights went up. It was the end of the performance, which was not continuous. There would be no further performance until 8:30 and they got up to go. There was only a handful of people in the whole cinema, and in the last half-dozen rows where they had been sitting, only three persons altogether: the students, who seemed to be lovers, and who now sauntered away arm in arm, and the old man who had silenced them.

Sigbjørn never saw them again.

At the door, the manager was apologizing to them:

—I'm sorry we don't have continuous performance[115] any longer. No business...it seems these films are only for high-class audiences.

Father and son walked down Mount Pleasant in the direction of the Adelphi Hotel.[116] The Captain groaned aloud. If for a time they had managed to relieve the pain, it merely waited, like the conscience—in the dark of the nerves—for its next opportunity to pounce.

—Communism isn't just getting it back on the old man, the Captain said, for neglecting your precious sex education, and Sigbjørn nodded, if you will excuse that Delphic statement, the Captain added thoughtfully as they came in view of the façade of the hotel. A little further down they stopped at a hoarding of the picture they had just seen. And as they stared at the garish poster[117] of the poor peasant turning his face towards the city like a pilgrim, a slow, painful groping after something better there, Sigbjørn saw his own face reflected behind, another soul who sought to be reborn, who perhaps sought God in the very regions where he had been destroyed.

He took again from his inside pocket his *hyrkontrakt* and read over to himself: *Tarnmoor, limper, D/S Unsgaard, skibets reise fra Prester til Archangel/Leningrad.*

He said nothing but again he had the peculiar fancy that that ignorant peasant, God-haunted, staggering under the burdens of his old life, but turning his face towards the suffering, heroic masses, was himself. Father and son walked on side by side, individuals unaccounted for by life, rarely in the books.

—I suppose you think we don't struggle. Let me tell you, I've seen as much heroism here in its different way, in cotton, in shipping, as ever you'd see in...But what's the use of talking? Reactions always react too far...It seems absolutely fatal in this world to have a penetrating intelligence; I don't mean just to be clever, or brilliant...what am I saying?...but to know, to have an answer to everything. It's fatal, then, if you don't use your gifts, and fatal to everyone else around you...The whole thing is not to know.[118]

—I'm not sure what you mean but I don't *know*, Sigbjørn said, his mind on another tack. I'm as ignorant as that peasant, far more so, because I have only worthless knowledge, tag ends of quotations, other people's epigrams, copy-cat paragraphs, to support me. That peasant at any rate had some remnant even driven by starvation as he was, of the culture, of the soil, of that truth which is cored in growing things. I have no culture at all. I'm sure I never learnt anything but worthless lies at Cambridge. Meantime the wireless tells me what I am, what I should do, where I belong...while here I am—and he found himself repeating what Tor had said—'going down the street on quite a different pilgrimage…'[119] Hundreds are like that. And Benjamin Wallae was like that.

Above them as they walked down Lime Street,[120] the advertisements grinned down at them, each monstrous, grotesquely set face belonging to a flat apostle of rugged individualism. Take Phosphorine for the Nerves! Damaroids for the Brain! Carter's Little Liver Pills for the Liver![121] How confidingly they took you in, Sigbjørn thought. How like philosophers they were! And finally the self-same apostle with his rubric pictorial health invited them to drink such-and-such a whiskey in order presumably that their livers would be in a sufficiently receptive state for the soluble little pills, while thousands of unemployed decayed in the foul soil beneath. The vicious circle of capitalism!

At the same time, Sigbjørn wondered how men who tolerated such a civilisation could find time to do anything else but drink. Certainly that was one excuse for England's blindness.

As they moved from Lime Street down past the Washington Hotel[122] to the isthmus of Manchester Street,[123] a vision of Leningrad[124] was still super-imposed upon Liverpool in his mind's eye.

His father walked silently with him, lost in his own thoughts.

Sigbjørn scanned the faces of those moving down towards the Pier Head. Had death indeed undone so many?[125] Wasn't there one sign of life, one gleam, one spark of enthusiasm anywhere? Even as they walked he imagined wildly the nerves of these people shattered, their brains giving way, while even as this dissolution proceeded, the deceptive antidotes for these things, which they could not afford, mockingly fixed their gaze. These men walked down to the sea with the faltering steps of people who had been monstrously deceived. Who had deceived them? Whither that grey emptiness in the eyes of the unemployed? Whence those men pale as dried river beds, drifting down towards the Mersey, as it seemed, with the wind? It was horrible; he had never before seen its horror, its ghastliness, its tragedy. And even now he did not see it all, his vision springing rather from an intuition of this decay than from any immediacy of the experience. Perhaps he was quite wrong.

But now he saw something else:

Everybody, as far as the eye could reach down Dale Street, down which they were now walking, was limping. It was all like a procession of the cripples, the halt, and the lamed at Lourdes.[126] And suddenly he perceived that this was simply the halting gait of the old world monstrously reduplicated. The old world, clairvoyant in his last moments, who perhaps would be destroyed, miracles and all.

"Did you hear my brassy ferrule? You're going for a long journey."

And suddenly he felt that Tor was well out of it.

—Yes, Barney, the Captain was saying, the situation is tragic. Just simply, starkly tragic. Tragic because I can do nothing. I am in a position rather similar to that of a petty officer,[127] not a bosun,[128] say…a lamp-trimmer…petty judases we used to call them, who exploit the forecastle but who are themselves exploited by the bridge. You may see that, whatever my own convictions, I would be in a difficult situation with my political and economic alignments. If I work people as hard as I can and for as little as I can it is not because I make a fortune. On the contrary, I myself have been practically ruined. I've barely got enough to struggle on with now.

The word 'trimmer' reverberated in Sigbjørn's brain. What had happened? And again, what had happened? What did all this mean? Had his father deliberately…? But surely that was impossible!

—What happens to people like me is that bigger lines reduce my gross receipts by employing price-cutting tactics and so on. It's the old story—cutting each other's throats…Besides, the workers themselves, by striking, make lots of trouble for me. Not only the sailors, but the shore gang. Expenses are raised, and then there's an economy drive…

—Well, nobody could say I haven't worked desperately hard to keep you boys at Cambridge and one place and another. Even now, as I am—and I'm fighting as hell against it—I'm in an appalling state of breakdown…not in the least ameliorated by my being aware of its causes. Yet I am unable to take steps to be cured!

Sympathy flickered in Sigbjørn for a moment, like a light that is about to fuse. What were the implications of that? That they were in some way getting rid of their ships for the insurance and then crawling out of the entire situation by fixing the blame on a handful of ship's officers? That the delay in the S.O.S. call of the *Thorstein*, which cost a hundred and fifty persons their lives, was perhaps directly traceable to the policy of the ship's company to delay such calls in order to reduce salvage and rescue expenses for the stockholders?

But even that didn't explain it all. Sigbjørn speculated still further.

He had heard that every piece of evidence given by the survivors and members of the crew of the *Thorstein* had been ignored in the official report. Possibly this would also prove true of the *Brynjarr*. That made his father, then, a sort of tool, a tool in the hands of the system. And for the first time Sigbjørn understood the real meaning of the words 'middle-class.' But surely his father would not be a party willingly to such corruption! Not willingly, not wittingly. No. He had done it for him, for Tor; to keep them at Cambridge? That seemed impossible, too. Unless…?

In spite of what he had just said, was it possible, Sigbjørn wondered as they walked on in silence, that his father had taken refuge in complex and ruinous speculations, not from financial reasons alone, but at first as a strong compensation for something else that had failed? That his life was an example of *alopecuria*,[129] the habit of the fox that has lost his tail.

What then, precisely, Sigbjørn asked himself, had been this first failure? What sinister loss had he first sustained? What shame had he known? Perhaps the answer was buried with his mother in Norway. He would never know.

But as he tried to think of this, strangely enough the entire life of a simple man, not his father, swiftly unfolded before him. He saw this man, perhaps a writer, growing in proportion as he became ashamed of his simplicity, envious of the apparently enormous conclusions of his contemporaries, and finally taking refuge in their abstractions to hide a naive heart that had cried out too painfully before, but with honesty, that honesty which has caused him shame, to a God outside at any sign of suffering or injustice. And then Sigbjørn saw these frontiers[130] becoming too treacherous for him, saw his crossing of them ending, as most half-hearted attempts to explore beyond the boundaries of human knowledge do end, in madness and despair.

Now they were approaching a traffic light, the cars were thickly crowded, soon they would have to stop. His father still walked in silence. Sigbjørn's thoughts were racing through his brain. He could, of course, sympathize with the exploitation, but for the evil that informed it, if explicable evil it was, there could be no possible sympathy. If his father had entered it all in a spirit of envy, in a spirit of compensation, or merely as a sort of game, it had all come now, disastrously, to an end.

Perhaps much would be in the dark even when it seemed all was explained; the spider might be dissected but the web still remain an inexplicable mystery.

—Who knows, his father was now saying as they waited at the red light[131] across the road, I may be aware of the implications of the class struggle, of the intrinsic dirtiness of the very newspapers I read. But perhaps I am too wearied by battling crushing organizations—and I assure you they are crushing to me—not to be amused by those very newspapers. Perhaps, perhaps, who knows? Is it any wonder if I find myself rationalizing my actions? God knows I could scarcely oppose your feeling for the masses. On the contrary, Scandinavia has always been suggestible to all ideas of emancipation. Hasn't Norway always followed with especial vigilance the great shocks, even the least oscillations, that stir, or only skim the surface, of the larger countries? Don't forget the great Herman Bang[132] who gave up the ghost in a Pullman car in Utah.

The ghost of Herman Bang sat bolt upright in a railway carriage in Salt Lake City and said, in Sigbjørn's voice,

—There is no solution, gentlemen and generations without hope of the present day, only in the inexorable conclusion of capitalist decay and the victory of the working class...

—It's pretty to think so,[133] the Captain said. But if I ever implied that some form or other of esotericism was an escape from reality rather than an escape towards it I only underestimated myself. And that's one thing you don't want to laugh at!

—I didn't imply it! I didn't laugh. But what do you mean?

—No, then Tor did. He—

The green lights were flashed on. They passed trams halted in Dale Street from Islington, Everton, Scotland Road[134] going down the Pier Head to the sea. Sigbjørn did not hear the rest of his father's reply in the roar of traffic going in the other direction.

—And besides, it was a dummy company, the Captain was saying, even more mysteriously, as they turned into Exchange Street West.[135]

—If the system is partly to blame, he went on, fate took a hand against it. But it's the last straw you should talk to me about Russia, the Captain digressed once more, as though it were the Absolute! For I assure you in advance that it's nothing of the kind. Besides I'll be surprised—even if you do get there—if they'll let you go beyond the wharf.

The day was ending. There was a wild vermillion sky in the west as they walked down the street back towards the flags; but above them, white afternoon clouds as evening garnered them in, still hurried by, ceaselessly.

—You'll just have to sit in the foc'sle while the ship lies alongside, playing fan-tan[136] like any old Chinaman on a Blue Piper.[137] What you say is all rot, if you'll excuse me. You should stay here. Of course if the cry in Cambridge wasn't, as it must be by now, fashion being what it is, Down with Psychology,[138] I might make a few remarks to you, and perhaps I shall do, too, on a soundly psychological basis. After all, psychology is a much-neglected study.

The men stopped stock-still in the road. It was not that they wished to protract this scene between them but perhaps the fear of facing the world again alone, which they would have to do when they had returned to their starting point, the flags, that halted them.

—However perhaps you can unravel your own conflicts as well as I after I've informed you that since you've returned from Cambridge you've ascribed your motives for wanting to go to sea again to more than a dozen different causes. Surely you don't want to go because of all of them!

—Is it as important why I go as that I am going?

—Yes it is. That's the whole point...if what you intend to do is not to be simply childish. You can't stand off from me with that purity, that remote untouchableness of adolescence! Not this time! For you can't want to go to Russia[139] if your motive is to see Erikson, who is probably in Norway. And if you want to go to

Norway, the source of our ancestry, as you put it, you would scarcely choose to sign on a ship that went to Russia.

Sigbjørn thought, and when the answer came it was as though Tor spoke it.

—Erikson in some way connects me with the future.

—But, I repeat, why go at all? Take—

An aeroplane was flying over, rigidly, iron against blue steel. The men started slowly to walk again, looking straight up in the air at the machine.

—Who flies the Atlantic?[140] There are so many preparations, hesitations, interferences from the press, and annoyances of one sort and another by the time the pilot comes actually to do it, that he feels he has flown it a thousand times already. Why go? Were you younger, it would be excusable. Now, and especially now, it's a regression. Don't go....

Suddenly he saw that he was pleading, and hesitated for a moment, then went on:

—Oh, well, what's the good? A few years ago young men like you used to be aesthetes, now they're communists.

—What's the good of...

Warning! Low Archway

It is later than you think.

Above them the aeroplane circled. For the first time Sigbjørn noticed it was advertising something: *Dewar's Whisky*.[141] This was its mene tekel[142] for them on the wall of the sky as they craned their necks upward. Now only the first word was left. As they watched the D and E of this were dispersed. And from this evanescence in the sky, only the one word: *War*.

Now the aeroplane circled again away from them, tracing slow patterns of despair.

—Oh well, if you love your own misery[143] so much! The Captain took out his watch, looked at it, and compared it with the clock on the Exchange.

—That clock's fast, he said.

They stood still, facing one another; for once more the raving of the city had enclosed them in the small square, the Exchange flags. Only now an endless dense procession was hurrying in the opposite direction, down to the sea, to the black voices of the underground.

—And you talk of the death of private grief.[144]

Under the anaesthetic[145] of the afternoon new wounds had been opened. Now they were fully conscious but still did not look at each other for pain. The Captain replaced his watch.

—Well, it's time we put an end to this more or less unsuitable conversation.

Behind him loomed the coal-blackened statue[146] of Lord Nelson, bleakly profound in its perfect meaninglessness, evil with its cyclopean eye[147] turned towards that signal which a million wakeful ones[148] shall countervail.

The aeroplane dropped, dived down the sky northwards; a regatta of white clouds scurried after, before the wind.

—I've an appointment with one of our lawyers at the Mecca Cafe.

—Very well then, sir! You to Mecca, me to Archangel.[149]

VI

> So it is in intermediateness, where only to "be" positive is to generate corresponding and, perhaps, equal negativeness. In our acceptance, it is, in quasi-existence, premonitory, or prenatal, or preawakening consciousness of a real existence.
>
> CHARLES FORT[1]

The day declined in the poor streets where Nina and Sigbjørn stood arguing.

...Everything seemed over between them. All at once she broke away from him. Sigbjørn stared after her. He made one step to follow her, then let his arm fall with a hopeless gesture. Rain fell in his eyes, sharp drops. Misery. For their last evening together they had chosen a little restaurant where they had once been happy[2] and moreover which had then done good business. Now it was on its last legs. Their waiter had lolled in a chair, half asleep; a gramophone playing cracked records had continually run down. Altogether the situation had been a sinister, cruelly laughable, abstraction of their own relationship. The tragic aspect of it which might indeed have lent dignity to their scene had seemed, on the contrary, continually to be verging on the ludicrous, as indeed many tragic situations do, as if they called for some such comment on life as: I can't help laughing at its funerals. They had left the cafe without finishing dinner. The memory of Tor had squeezed its painful problem between all that had been really fine and true between them. And this, the memory rather of his existence than of his death, had been a forbidding censorship even to that haughty frivolity above mentioned which can alone mitigate the boredom of intolerable suffering. Why then was it that they had agreed to meet tomorrow before she went on board the *Arcturion*?[3]

So suffering, like a wounded tiger, can drag itself wearily on through the undergrowth of human lives.

Sigbjørn had not moved. He was still standing in the place where Nina had left him gazing idiotically after her. It was not yet late. They had met early and the undergrounds[4] were still swallowing the people up. Nina, no more than a disappearing white light, a light which it must be admitted had been fast disappearing for some months past, was soon extinguished in the crowd. Gone. It was as if some powerful substance had drawn her and was now quietly drawing everyone else in Liverpool beneath the earth; a force from which they could not escape tugged at them, as, clinging to their umbrellas, to their papers, to their hats, they were dragged down into the Central and James Street subways of the Mersey Railway. It seemed to him as he stood above the great city, poised on a huge wet street like a wing, like Mr. Cavafy[5] at an angle to the universe, that the inhabitants were aslant, were flying, winged with struggling umbrellas; souls swept by a tidal wave down a gully, souls driven like husks,[6] like leaves before the storm.

The clock in Water Street[7] said 6:30.

Water Street, he thought, water flowing through all things, threading all things with a colourless thread; rain for parched lives...Somewhere, people marching. The newsboys cried around him 'Last Yacko and Exprey'[8] and the cries of the city broke like surf about them.

TARNMOOR LINE DISASTER.

The last business men continued to be transported through the city as if by a current to where the black vortex of the Underground, the disappearing point,[9] yawned for them. They were dragged along there; then they were gone in a moment. Now the city was empty. The clangour of the trams resounded as if within some vast empty shell. But soon bells struck, and another tidal wave of people burst down the street, thronging the pavements and the piazzas and filling the city with sound as they fought against the icy wind bearing down to the river. The booming of traffic and the moans of the electric[10] rose together with the thousand other cries of the city and sea only to be lost continually, like the song of life itself, in the wind. For a moment all would be still; only for the whole city, the next moment, to undulate with noise as from the trembling of an enormous flexitone.[11] Sigbjørn mingled with the rough current of working life swirling down towards the Pier Head and he was carried along uncared by it for some time and then left like a log that is swept with the stream and caught up in the rubbish by the river bank. For some time he stood, pressed up against the outside of the Honduras Building.[12] Why did he behave in this curious fashion? Was he a creature from some other planet? Strayed by mistake to this earth? Some sort of Casper Hauser![13] Like the poor blank newspaper that had fluttered down from Castle Hill; that day with Tor he drifted along. Down the streets he drifted, down Water Street, down towards the Liver Building.[14] At Goree Piazzas[15] with a kind of automatic perversity he bought an *Echo* and glanced at it in the light of a street lamp. In Spain there was a revolution.[16] In Italy—rumour of war.[17] Everywhere, dark rumour of war, revolution, disaster, change. He turned over the page. Everywhere, debacle. Somewhere, people marching. Some march to death, others to new life...

TARNMOOR LINE DISASTER. BRUUS' EVIDENCE.

Another paragraph caught his eye and he read it with strange avidity, with the greedy relief he felt when he realized there was other, interesting news in the world.

"Yokohama. From a special correspondent. For a long time Kegon Cataract,[18] an almost vertical waterfall 260 feet high was the shrine of the unhappy and self-doomed. Into that vortex hundreds cast themselves and their bodies disappeared forever. When the authorities decided the cataract had claimed enough victims, they closed all accesses with barbed wire. Shortly afterwards, candidates for suicide discovered the little volcanic island of Oshima[19] off the coast. In greater and greater numbers people flocked to the island to be cremated in incandescent lava..."

He looked up, seeing in his mind's eye the bodies falling into the volcano,[20] and then, all over the world, bodies falling in battle, and bursting in fire. In his mind bodies fell all over the world like ski-jumpers[21] at Frognersaeteren. He turned another page. There the news glared, and the words swarmed round him fearfully.

"Captain Nils Bruus,[22] Master of the Tarnmoor liner *Thorstein* and one of its fifty survivors when it was wrecked on the Antigua Bell rocks,[23] defended his seamanship yesterday afternoon before the inspectors at the Custom House.[24] The inspectors announced they would withhold a decision until they had further studied the evidence. Captain Bruus appeared, facing a charge of criminal negligence in navigation, which was brought by the inspectors after a hearing several weeks ago at which he explained his handling of the ship the night of the disaster. He summoned the one surviving officer of the *Brynjarr* and two other sea captains acquainted with the Leeward Islands[25] to support his claim that he had acted as he should."

That he had acted as he should! Sigbjørn retraced his steps.

Warning, Low Archway.

It is later than you think.

Leslie Howard[26] *in Outward Bound.*[27]

He had stopped outside a cinema hoarding which depicted this time no Russian peasant, but a ship of the dead setting out into the imponderable, to navigate the nexus between this world and the next, crowded for the grave; outward bound.

"To support his claim that he had acted as he should." These words tormented Sigbjørn; what would Captain Nils Bruus have to account for on the Judgment Day? But possibly he was only a scapegoat. Now four sailors speaking Norwegian were swinging down the street past him. These and the creatures[28] for whom they searched now took possession of the great city. Here they came, more sailors, and with the struggling gait peculiar to them. Would he too soon be playing the game as seriously as the others?

They sought life, after bitter watches at sea. What did Sigbjørn himself seek?

On an errand of life man sped frequently the swiftest way to death. Who could say who could escape?

He followed them a little way as if he too had been drawn by a magnetic current; or as if his very being had been caught in their swell so that he was attracted to them only to be left yawing and rocking behind in a cavity of the spirit as blank as the walls of the womb. The walls of the womb which would expand once more to bear out his soul streaming on the objective cataract of life.

He stood bent over the threshold of an old life, between two worlds, the one a dismantled old world with decay at its very centre which was already collapsing, its props of memory, precept and conclusions, all the old idealopogy collapsing like a sinking freighter's samson posts[29] and derricks before the Atlantic flood of new life and energy rolling over it in the mind, and the other only as yet a lengthening shadow of a world, apprehended now only by his true substance, the shadow of himself, the self that was to come. Death, to the old evaluations, despairs, hopelessnesses, sophistications, and to the old sacrifices too, death to the old life built on these staggering foundations! Death to a life where men were visible only in public lavatories and railway trains! He would set out, through water to fire; through fire to earth; through earth to air that he could breathe. Suddenly he remembered Tor's saying "If I die you could let all your confusions pass into me as if I were a tree"; and he knew that this in fact had happened. Or a self had died a little every day since Tor's death. Soon it would pass out of existence altogether and all that would remain was an intuition, a part of that divine and not secular law that determines a man's place on earth!

Seeking quiet from his thoughts he pushed his way into a tavern, the *Legs of Man*.[30] Ordering a beer he went to a corner and sat down. Mechanically he took in the notices around the bar: Bass in Bottles;[31] Caergwrle Ales;[32] Do not offer checks in payment, a refusal often gives offence; Special Lunch, Beef and Potatoes 1/6; Our Special Cheesy Hammy Eggy[33] 1/9; Sausage and Mash 1/3; Futurist Theatre,[34] Leslie Howard in Outward Bound. But even here was no sanctuary. His eyes wandered to the window. Through it he could see the tall panes of his father's office, and the flag, a red cross on a white ground[35] with H.T. in contiguous sections flying defiantly on the roof.

HANSEN-TARNMOOR LINES
OSLO, LIVERPOOL, NEW YORK
CRUISES TO THE WEST INDIES

Also offices in London, Glasgow, Bremen, Antwerp, Havana, Cienfuegos, Guantanamo,[36] Montreal, Naples, Marseilles, was what he read. And below this on the blackened wall someone had chalked, recently (for no attempt had been made to erase it), "We wish you a pleasant voyage to hell,[37] if not now, next year." His hand shook violently on the glass he had just been brought. His thoughts stormed within him. Although the conversation in the tavern at this hour was subdued the room was full of noises which usually he would not notice but which now jangled on his nerves. The trickling of beer from the pull, the eternal creaking of the swing-door, even the shuffling movements of the landlord's feet were like a torture to him and from outside the ringing of iron-shod boots on the pavement and the bitter song of iron itself as the overhead rattled along the line of docks were to him like cries from the damned, from the heart of the Malebolge:[38] a verse of idiot creaking came to him: "The world is the Isle of Man,[39] locate it in Castletown, on a far shore, always on a far shore conceive..." He tried to shut out all thought of himself from the world, all thought of Nina, of Erikson, of his father, to free his being on existence itself; the strain of this effort suggested to him the curious idea that he was actually taking part a second time at his own parturition; but it was transient agony as yet, and he knew as the sound of the world came back that it was not yet time for his release. The sounds of the world were transformed into the creaking of a ship at night, the wooden creaking of the bunks, the iron creaking of the steering gear, was this again the persistent sound of decay at the centre of the world? The old world creaking woodenly like a deserted house empty of music and light and tapestry, the myriad noises of the gnawed timbers were molecular, atomic, the feeling of the sound of the world within himself cracking like the west wind in trees, distant sound of the axes,[40] turned his soul into rotten wood that ticked, into the tavern of life, life itself was already flowing ceaselessly, bringing the smell of voyages and far, turbulent towns into life's room, interpenetrating it, washing round it as he had seen a big sea wash round the petty officer's messroom so that afterwards the door opened from the other side: he tried to distinguish life's faces, the speciality of special faces, the different particular tragic sense of each life, tried to imagine what made life possible for each, and then, with horror, he realized the truth: he could not distinguish one face from another; this was what he had been brought to; all the faces were the same!

And now all the faces were his own. And sounds now, and sounds only, utterly, peopled his world! Was this the beginning of madness or the darkness that precedes a new birth? From darkness to darkness. From eternity to eternity. This was collapse, breakdown, debacle. He had exploited himself to exhaustion, had reached the final frontier on every level of his being. He could either go into a lunatic asylum, could give in to this, could console himself for the rest of his life with the exquisite and terrible polar indulgences of madness, or he could let one part of himself, or one self, sink down utterly into this darkness, and abstracting from it all its disordered, kinetic power into the service of human courage, whose source was ever timidly explicable, but whose quality is absolute, he could go forward. Get out! Back to the sea. Or to fire!

He paid for his drink and left the tavern, his head singing. Yes: it was almost as though, in fact, he were leaving his old body! But a typhoon raged in the watery abyss[41] between the two. The noises, transforming themselves into voices, were following him, whispering like the wind from all sides, inviting, repelling, approving him. Break, they said, break, break, break[42] the coward circle. While the ship is going down. While the world is going down. Break the coward circle. Release yourself on life, flowing down on you from all sides like lava. Break.

Warning! Low archway.

Terror struck up like heat strikes at noonday from the iron and wood superstructure of the overhead that overarched and enclosed him. He turned away, once more seeking sanctuary, as the tavern, *The Baltimore Clipper*[43] rose up before him. Here, with the ghosts of Melville and Redburn to keep him company perhaps he would find respite. And suddenly, as at sea the foc'sle door shuts out the tempest the noises and voices were shut out behind him. At the bar a sailor and one of the shore gang were talking and Sigbjørn found himself listening to them calmly. Here were the voices of the inheritors of the future in which the sea itself stormed, as far removed from delirium as it was from those eunuchs at Cambridge giggling limericks[44] with their stinking breaths, or from elegized talks in smoky rooms. He ordered himself a beer and sat down in the corner.

—Remember the old *Peleus*,[45] you know, Jesus, she nearly rolled all the sticks out of her. She only had an icebox you know, no fridge.

—The old *Achilles*,[46] you know.

—We put back three times[47] to Amsterdam. Under the Dutch flag!

—Ah, but she's laid up now.

—City boats laid up at Preston.

—Ah, if we'd only—

—She's laid up now.

—I'd give my right hand to be sailing again!

—Fair breaks your heart to see these ships laid up.

—But sure, we'll get a ship!

They stopped talking, their faces a petrified memory.

And they would sail again, Sigbjørn thought. Yes, and those unemployed ships would sail again too! would sail of themselves through the world trumpeting their wrongs aloud. His eye caught the Blue Peter[48] flag pinned behind the bar. Strange, to find himself once more at the starting point. Blue Peter!

He knew there were only three people in the bar-room yet it seemed that the room was dense again as it had been climbing Tor's staircase with haunting shapes of conscience,[49] of fear. Yes, the starting point, a voice muttered at his shoulder; yes, go forward old fool, forward melancholy masochist, forward into the past, seek still further within the bloody thesaurus of suffering. Forward, another said, you're right to suspect it—for what machinery is it that drives men back and back? Futurity broods on the ocean,[50] a third added, life has no time to waste. Yes, but what is it that calls them, a fourth asked, that hints to them from the dark of voyaging once more even when it's impossible? Is it the voice of memory? asked the fifth, stronger than all necessity, crying to be relieved? Is it forgotten hope that it is possible to change the past, interposed a sixth, that torments their very souls? The future can change the past,[51] a seventh said...

Sigbjørn looked up again forcing himself to face reality. The sailors were talking. Sigbjørn tried to listen, tried to fight down the voices whirring up at him from the abyss and tried to fight down also the utter exhaustion that claimed him. But he did not bargain for what he heard. So close indeed was it to the dictates of his own conscience that at first he was not properly aware of it. The picture they daubed[52] was too close to his own eyes. And even though he must have been aware that everywhere in Liverpool such conversations were taking place, out of sheer self-defence his mind wandered away from them, and he looked round the room.

—That boat and that gear was bloody frozen. So were the blocks,[53] eh.

—Surely. Everything was sacrificed to a drive for profits.

...No, the tavern had scarcely changed since Melville's day. Though he had never bothered to notice it before. There was still, just as Melville had written,[54] 'the narrow little room with red curtain looking out on a smoky yard,' just as he had written 'the dull lamp swinging overhead placed in a wooden ship suspended from the ceiling'! The same walls 'covered with a paper representing an endless procession of vessels of all nations circumnavigating the apartment. And by way of a pictorial mainsail to one of these ships a map hung against it.' All as he had written. And from the street even the same confused uproar of 'ballad singers, bawling women, babies and drunken sailors.' But most extraordinary of all, the same decay at the centre of it all, the same monstrous deception in the ravening heart of the misery. His mind ran on like this for some time and it was not until the two words 'breakdown,' now so charged with affected meaning, started out of the conversation that he turned his attention once more to what the sailors were saying. Astonished, as before, that there were only two people in the room when he seemed to be surrounded by a host he composed himself to listen.

—Breakdown was due to this bloody fact, Horsey,[55] that the mixture of glycerine[56] and water in the steering machine froze, either because there was too little of the stuff, or because the glycerine was of, you know, an inferior quality like.

—I said right out, you know, the *Thorstein* is a bloody death ship.[57]

—Yes, let me tell you. I was in it with the shore gang, shore bosun,[58] eh. And let me tell you another thing. I seen the boats with all their gear frozen stiff. Yes, all the blocks and all. Jesus, they had plenty of time to get off if the lifeboat gear had worked properly...

—There shouldn't have been a single life lost on that ship!

—And all the davits caked up with ice. An economy crew, eh. It don't provide for no emergencies.

—If the hand steering apparatus had been hooked up!

—Criminal economy!

Sigbjørn buried his face in his hands. It was as though fate had been waiting to drive this wedge of truth through his haunted mind. Yes, it was true, whatever supernatural ambiguities *Moby Dick* might have circumscribed in his flight from modern thought or through his own brain, nothing had altered the powerful fact of the white whale's actual existence. Fact! White whale! White Sea![59] The wedge—or was it a harpoon?—of agonizing truth was driven further in and he trembled with the pain of it. These tragedies could all have been avoided. They could be avoided in future. But that safer ships should be built was not enough. The only way out was a new society in which such economy drives were impossible. No, the blind, malicious force in the world, he said to himself, although as he sat there he seemed to be speaking to many others, cannot always, perhaps, be eluded—least of all when we pursue it—but the greediness and evil in the present state of affairs in the world leads only into a playing into the hands of that force. For, his heart hammered, deep in the original unity of that society, lies the old harpoon[60] of its inevitable, festering annihilation. Capitalist society carried her own rusted presages of disaster within her as the whale did the lances whose wounds weakened it at the final attack. How would he serve that attack? isolated, without a place on earth, perhaps not wanted[61] by either side? He would sail again anyhow, no shirking that. Broken as he was, he would go. Was it an empty gesture? Not only an empty but selfish gesture as to pursue his course of action somebody more needy must go without a job? Money? He had fifty pounds in the world of his own. And he was never going to ask for any more. Perhaps he could actually be called needy himself. He looked through the sooty window. Lime and soot...if order and disorder could be so distinguished no wisdom would be needed.

Outside, rain was falling, darkly patterning the sidewalks under the street lamps as it blew in from the sea. Ceaselessly, ceaselessly, the overhead cars rattled. Trams whined past. A Liverpool newsboy walked by slowly, and silently, hoarse from shouting. But the hoarding he carried now said:

TARNMOOR DISASTER SENSATION. STOP PRESS. BRUUS' SUICIDE[62] ON LEAVING DOCK!

He disappeared.

What fresh horror was this? Sigbjørn wearily only half believed it. He brushed it away as a sick man in a hospital brushes away a figure that passes. What is this dark colossus that strikes at my eyelids? Now it is gone. Bruus' suicide. Tor's suicide...A ship's suicide on leaving dock. If he had read that the world itself had committed suicide he would not now have been surprised. For it seemed that this world was anyhow breaking up[63] all round him. This new fact neither assisted nor hindered her in her headlong decline. It even glided off his consciousness. Liverpool *Echo*? Then this was an echo of an echo. An echo also of the undergraduate's suicide of shame[64] that had prefaced the deadly and negative catalogue of events in the newspapers surrounding Tor's death, whose horror only it now evoked. And it was now the guilt and ghastliness of those days that struck up against the street, from the lights against the evening, and from the tavern voices, and crushed him, bore down upon his shoulder with a weight of conscience even more terrible than any thought of death itself, a horror darker than the night whose shadow had already been cast. To him Bruus might have been a dream whose name he had once dreamt: Tor's was the face that every heartbeat hammered into a pulp. Sigbjørn murmured something that was very like a prayer: which way would you go,[65] Melville, if you were alive? Then, although still like a blind man, he understood something around him, the barman drying glasses, the two seamen, the lights in the yard and the street, and the melancholy sea-rain falling. He fell asleep. The voices of the two sailors spoke through his dream but transferred into those of himself and one other in a scene poised in a different time. He was standing in the dark high among desolate sandhills. Below him the sea drew its breath hoarsely. He leaned away from the sea towards the world and heard himself saying:

—Oh Mother Earth[66] who art no more my mother and into whose bosom this frame shall never be received. Oh Mankind whose...

(—Hello there, where are you? where? a voice said.)

—brotherhood I had cast off and trampled the great heart beneath my feet. Oh stars of heaven that shone on me as of old as if to light me onward and upward: farewell, and all and forever come deadly element of fire!...henceforth my familiar phase...embrace me as I do thee...

The furnace doors of the *Unsgaard* opened before him. A spiral of flame shot out. The fire fluttered like a flag, the wavering flag[67] that covered the trimmers in the *Inferno*! The fire leapt out in the form of his mother to embrace him, to clasp him in the maw of the flames. Eight bells. On deck the trimmer off watch lowered the corpse of his mother, wrapped in the Norwegian flag,[68] into the sea. But through the wavering flames were still outlined the sandhills.

—Why if it isn't my old character, Erik Brandt![69] Old Benjamin Brandt! What are you doing here among these melancholy sandhills?[70]

—Why, Nathaniel! Is it you? Only going out at night as usual?

—Why, Herman!

—Right. The truth is, old fellow, my tripos—sorry, hypos![71]—has the upper hand of me again, once more I bring up the rear of every funeral I meet...The truth is I had pretty well made up my mind to be annihilated. I—

—At it again, Melville. Isn't your own the form in which destiny has embodied itself, yourself the chief agent of the coming evil you have foreshadowed. Does fate impede its decree?

—Right, Nathaniel. If I hadn't fooled you this time, Plotinus Plinlimmon![72] if I hadn't fooled you by surviving myself. Fooled you, Erikson! By my death and my burial being locked up in my chest. And with it—what do you think? The unpardonable sin.[73] The sin of an intellect that triumphed over the sense of brotherhood with man. The unpardonable sin! I go forward to my comrades. My old body is but the lees of my better being.[74] Take my old self who will. Take it I say, it is not me.

He turned round, facing the ocean!

...Healed of my hurt[75] I bless the inhuman sea,
Yes bless the angels four that there convene.
For healed am I ever by their pitiless breath
Distilled in wholesome dew named rosemarine.[76]

VII

A web of snow slowly weaved itself into the air above Sigbjørn as he paced the Pier Head tram circuit[1] waiting for Nina, and above the river flowing endlessly out to sea, above the white city,[2] into a pattern—he wondered—of the fourth dimension.[3] Snow, grey-white water, and snow again as far as the eye could reach. A gull circling from the westward swayed momentarily, poised as if trapped in the web of snow, and then freeing herself vanished rapidly into the darkness from which she had emerged, with harsh raucous cries, trailing a skein of feathery mist. Snow, dark nimbus of cloud, cirrus[4] of snow falling on Woodside,[5] on Goree Piazzas, on the Brocklebank dock, swirling down on outgoing ships: why make the voyage to the White Sea?

For here in Liverpool he was already there in Archangel as he imagined it: in a vast white calm where sky was confused with sea and from which new order, or new chaos, would emerge for him where new order already was. It was as though the ghost of the White Sea had come to him in the fearful form of the elementary spirits sailors see in the mists of Okee Chobee.[6]

Debacle of self,[7] his mind nervously lingered with the phrase he had once used: was he capable of it? Did not in every move that old self-consciousness intrude, that old pain of self, self, self return, thrusting into every immolation its greedy problems?

If he had made any immolations!

Debacle of self; he stamped with the cold, watching the circuit of trams and then the slow shunting procession setting out for Calderstones—gallstones!—Mount Pleasant and Old Swan.[8] He stamped again swinging his arms in the 'cabman's lift'[9] as he watched the steam of horses' breath rising to mingle with the fluttering snow. Turning up his coat collar and shivering as he walked to the railings of the Pier Head which, like a ship's, were looped with heaving lines and lifebelts.

Standing with both his hands on the railings he looked out to the sea until he grew rigid with gazing.[10]

Saturday morning...

This was the day the ships went out in the full tide; together they steamed slowly to the end of the river as Nina's ship would steam—where their wakes would spread out like the broad hand of a god across the sea, within whose fingers the special destiny of each ship was traced, to China, to America, to Costa Rica.

As the discursive sirens called through the wild weather a certain freighter fixed his attention: she was slipping swiftly down the Mersey with the tide, the

Norwegian flag[11]—a red cross on a white ground—flying high from her stern. On her side was written in tall white letters: *Direction—Oslo*.

It was thc ship after which he had called the freighter in his book (the mss. of which he held under his arm). Almost she was an imaginary ship even though she was bound by short stages: one was the berth to which she was now warping downstream to Glasgow for orders.

Even so, that ship, the S.S. *Direction*, carried his longings and his disappointments with her, and like the gulls which circled her in the snow—ambassadors to the ship—they flew before her to Port Said,[12] skimmed the Bitter Lakes to the Gulf of Bab-el-Mandeb, drifted through the Indian Ocean to Penang.[13]

Three years ago, he thought, on just such a day as this,[14] in just such wild weather! and in imagination the vast, tilted parallelogram[15] of the *Oedipus Tyrannus* rose up before him again, and the ruled diagonal of the bow that produced was the foremast.

Now it seemed to him that on his last day in Liverpool before sailing once more he lost those three years since he had sailed in her; that he was once more on the threshold of that first voyage. It was as though almost today, and having conjured with the idea so long he felt no fear at it, he was to take farewell not only of Nina but of himself.

Perhaps truly the past could be changed...

Farewell, *Direction*, but your creator Sigbjørn also carries such a cross—

He strained his eyes into the murk after her and as if in answer to the questioning in his heart, the multiform clarion voices of the world responded: sirens of freighters everywhere savagely and appalling commenting from that white darkness as if the chords of a cathedral organ should be struck tangentially by a village idiot! He turned away from the sea, and through the furling mist and snow, the cathedral,[16] high up over Liverpool like a warehouse, appeared momentarily in front of his eyes; there she was, alone, a castle she seemed now swimming alone into darkness over cliffs of mist; a feudal castle for priests; unfinished, the crane on top. We were the young apprentices, the young workmen, wavering scaffolding. Ah, Nina, what have we abandoned?

Above him now the clock[17] on the Liver Building was visible, its jewelled finger, which Nina and he had watched so often, moving on towards eleven. How often had poor creatures waited here for the hoped hour, the news of the *Titanic*,[18] of the *Vestris*,[19] of the *Lusitania*,[20] and now of the *Thorstein* and of the *Brynjarr*? for news of those claimed by the icy dregs of the unvintageable?[21] for news which even when it came was fragmentary, piecemeal, and untruthful?

God, how could he be dreaming now, as blind to that aspect of reality already experienced as he had been blind then to the horror awaiting him...the dreams of three years before? How could he want to be crucified[22] again...? Knowing the mystery of the volcano why should he desire its terror once more? And perhaps the sum of all this mystery was only a woman after all. Sphinx, tell me your secret! Sphinx, Jocasta!...*Oedipus Tyrannus.*[23]

The clock struck eleven and for some minutes afterwards every woman approaching seemed to be Nina coming over the snow to greet him. Hello, hello. A score of times he thought he saw her and a score of times he ran to meet her, his heart beating. Wrong again! In his mind he saw her many times as she had come to him before, over the snow with the snow plows ranged round like armoured cars, coming late into the Café Cantante,[24] running to greet him in summer; blue girls. And how the blue girls do and how the white ones are![25] Nervously he examined the L.N.E.R.[26] timetables, and recalled uneasily their conversation of the night before. What if she should have decided after all not to keep their appointment here! That terrible last night in the restaurant—

But suddenly there she was, long-legged and smiling, scarlet umbrella tilted toadstool-wise to the snow slanting in a sudden tumultuous gust like arrows of rain, striding towards him as though nothing had happened. They said nothing as they walked swiftly down the pedestrian's runnel of the automobile slipway down to the wharf. Beside them the cars came slowly and shakily down over the quivering iron gangway to the floating pier,[27] their windscreen wipers twirling their antennae; below them a crowd was gathering, now it was well-nigh sweeping them off their feet. Here cars in bottom gear moved also very slowly and jerkily towards the Woodside and Rock Ferry and Egremont boats.[28] They could see passenger ferries edging away from the tide, sidling across the Mersey like crabs. Over in Birkenhead the snow drifted past gantries[29] standing up back against the sky. A fourmaster was being towed down the river, *Herzogin Cecile*,[30] from Wallaroo. Behind them, with chains webbed on balloon tires, the snow whirling around them, cars still struggled to the wharf. The *Herzogin Cecile* disappeared. 'Rounding the horn, white feathers in the snow—the gulf claims,'[31] the verse ran through Sigbjørn's head as they waited despairingly for the crowd to move on.

Near them, almost against their faces, notices and advertisements were plastered, L.N.E.R. Timetables; Futurist Theatre;[32] Leslie Howard in Outward Bound; Crazy Week at the Empire, twice nightly; 6:30, 8:30. What had these idiot messages to do with this outward-going, this parting with its heart-break, and its memories of unfulfillment, of past things? But both Nina and Sigbjørn laughed, inclining their heads to them.

Then they were carried on with the crowd.

The *Arcturion*[33] lay toppling hugely at the wharf. At any moment it seemed that she would crash down upon it. Canvas-clad gangways slanted up into the ship and stewards with gladstone bags[34] rushed through them in an endless race; near at hand a moving staircase was winding flat luggage slowly in its spool: *perpetuum mobile:*[35] but the board where the ship's name should have been was empty.[36] In its place was nothing.

...A sudden terror seized him, but the thought that had come was inadmissible. This couldn't be true, it was a nightmare dreamt in prison while he awaited execution for Tor's murder. He touched Nina's coat, feeling the texture of the cloth; but this visible touch of reality brought no comfort. So they had taken away Tor's name—

He forced his mind out of the pattern of this sinister coincidence: that way madness lay.[37] Instead, he watched, as they were halted again, the unemployed around the feet of the gangway: those whose very purpose in life had been transferred into a farewell: whose farewells each day might be frozen somewhere, he could imagine, in patterns of ice, mind-undreamt: those whom hope forsook daily, making the tide.

Nina and Sigbjørn were standing, coat collars turned up under the scarlet umbrella, looking up at the ship, waiting for the crowd.

—Do you feel a sort of paternal pride in it, Nina asked.

Sigbjørn said nothing, laughing shortly.

—Of course I chose it on purpose! I want to see what's really afoot...I've got to make certain inquiries; get certain things straight in my own mind! *and* I've got to make a report...Apart from everything else, America's the only place for me to go to. The rest of the earth is as dead to me as the mountains of the moon.

The crowd was moving on.

—Come on aboard, now.

But a further confusion delayed them just as they were stepping on the gangway. Another crowd had been waiting at the far side, perhaps for some celebrity, and now this crowd closed in. They struggled to see what was going on, whom the crowd waited for. Now they saw. A pair of Siamese twins[38] were being carefully escorted along the wharf. Together they glided up the gangway, followed by their escort, who had momentarily stood, or rather reeled, aside, who perhaps was their manager, a man with a face like an over-ripe apple that soon would fall to the mould, now advancing unsteadily after the twins, as though already adapted to what he perhaps considered a suitable shipboard gait. The crowd stared up after them curiously but with no visible emotion. Pity that dare not approach, Sigbjørn thought, terror that will not retreat.[39] But the crowd at length fell apart and Nina and Sigbjørn followed up the gangway.

They strolled into the alleyway of C deck, where an oval of bannisters formed the well at the bottom of which was the tourist dining-room. At a distance, invisible, the ship's band toiled at *Faust*.[40] Nina went down the alleyway to see the purser while Sigbjørn waited.

In the salon some young men were eating prematurely as if by some special right. Perhaps they had not left the ship at all. Beside him in a lacquered and bedizened[41] alcove passengers were sending their last telegrams. They huddled together, leaning against each other's shoulders, their tortured mouths moving silently, forming the difficult letters.

He looked down in the salon again. It was strange, but he could never rid himself of the notion that a passenger liner was a fake thing when compared with a freighter and with no stronger base for prejudice than this he would have found himself hating the *Arcturion*. The hypocrisy of it, he found himself muttering, the wicked deceit of it! That gelatine, those hams dressed up like French poodles and the ship itself, like a gigantic frilled corpse, no less, its dying agonies composed to a superficial grin. What shares were here, decked out in pleasantry and persiflage,[42] what cornucopias[43] filled with dividends! Nothing less than the best for our patrons! What 'art' was here too, for those who live graciously and die painfully! And as he watched the life around him a hatred of his father smouldered within him, but a hatred—he was forced to admit to himself—based at these moments on a quite superficial estimate of the unpleasantness of the life around him. His hatred responded to the meanness in the stewards' faces rather than to the causes of that meanness, just as it did to the officers with indigestion, the wireless operator even now fomenting disturbances in the pantry;[44] and the greasers,[45] wipers, thieves, eternally drifting through the ship from deck to deck, from bulkhead to bulkhead, to the soft, cruel unctuousness common to every one of these domestic servants on this vast treadmill in hell. *No trust*,[46] read the notice outside the barber's shop. That was it. No trust! Exploitation...He tried for a few minutes to surround its economic position. But of course his impressions would be essentially spurious! That was a foregone conclusion. He wouldn't be able to understand it. How indeed could he be expected to understand a matter so complex when he failed to notice such things as he supposed must be quite obvious to others as somewhere a really human face, illumined with a friendly smile; passion in cabins; danger on deck and ambition on the bridge; allotments left behind, misery of departure in individual human beings, not to mention the responsibility or heroic toil of these beings; in short failed to see the faith which no philosophic or economic speculation can affirm for certain is not cored in struggle, even towards necessarily mutable ends.[47] And if he failed to identify this was it likely he could sense the thousand economic implications arising from it?...But perhaps what he did see, he told himself, and not so superficially as he might suspect for the precise reason that he was standing within it, was the soul not only of the ship, but of his own class, and this—however much of an abysmal mystery—was a spectacle without joy. Yes—did he see so superficially? He did not of course understand what he saw but he was ready to admit at this moment that his willingness to call his true feelings superficial might spring from the same cause as the undoubted superficiality of his knowledge: namely, the unwillingness to be confronted with the truth. Truth, that certainly was a word, the meaning of which must not be allowed to deviate.

—Hello, Nina, he said.

—Well!...

—I've been standing here and hating with a great hatred, Sigbjørn went on.

—You may hate all you like but if anything happens to this ship they'll attribute it to red sabotage.

—'Believed to be work of reds.' I once actually swallowed that sort of thing.

His words trailed off fatefully for how easy it was to assume that nothing could ever happen to a ship, even a Tarnmoor liner—

—Have a cigarette?

—Thanks.

They smoked, leaning against the bannisters, talking easily.

—Well, here you are with your views going to Russia, Nina said at length, and here I am with mine, going to America. It's all a little confused.

They laughed again.

—Views? What are views? Have I any views? Sigbjørn exclaimed. Last night everything was perfectly clear to me. And it was made clear, paradoxically enough, by a sort of mystical vision.[48] My course of action, the inevitable process of adjustment, its inevitable result and so forth, everything. But today I'm in the same muddle once more.

—I've lost ground with myself in the same way in the past, Nina said sympathetically. But she showed no more curiosity than this.

—It's bad when you can't tell a mountain from a valley, or—he ran his finger along a stanchion—rust from the iron facing—

—And endurance from decay.

—Exactly.

They both laughed again as if in gentle badinage, for the first time in many months in a purely friendly fashion, as if indeed each were already released from the bondage in which the other's presence held him.

—Well, supposing you do go to Russia...what'll your next movement be?

He noticed that a certain scorn had now crept into her tone, a scorn that Sigbjørn sympathized with. Indeed, what was his next move, if he ever reached Russia? He simply didn't know, and would evade the fact that his journey, which seemed again to him how only towards such a tenebrous solution as Novalis'[49] 'really better land' covered an unrelated object.

—I'm not sure I am going to Russia. But I do feel this—that I am under sealed orders,[50] that I shall soon know what I *have* to do, where I have to go. And that when I do know, when I do see my star, I'll follow it till I die.

In the silence that followed Sigbjørn examined this statement which now, as it were, hung in the air before him. He undoubtedly meant every word of it. But if true, it was not very convincing.

—Well, Nina said finally, I can't help thinking, if you'll excuse me, that the flag should always be flown at half mast whenever a really good artist becomes 'metaphysical.'

—Thanks for the 'really good artist.' Sigbjørn smiled in a too-friendly fashion.

—When you really consider that the human status is an adaptive organism,[51] Nina was going on...

But Sigbjørn clenched his hands angrily in pain. It was this sort of thing that always infuriated him about Nina. This insulting of the soul, before which he became as a child, helpless because he could not defend something that seemed to die in him every time it was attacked.

—An organism, Nina was saying, caught in an unbroken equilibrium[52] of forces, from the electrons sowing new stars in the void to the electrons vibrating in the bonc lamps of our brains, you can't achieve that mystical 'peace'—there is no peace...

He did not hear the rest of this, but then:

—from which it is but a step to the basis of all organized religion which you will agree is...

—Yes, but my God I hate you, Sigbjørn interrupted. And yes, there may be peace, too. And what right have you to assume that an abstract concept of God has the remotest connection with the Church? Although I grant you these considerations might be shelved!

He was the more insulted since only yesterday he had decided that he was in complete agreement with her.

—It's all part of the same thing, Nina said now. Let's go downstairs. She moved away towards the staircase.

—Not at all, Sigbjørn shouted angrily, following her just the same. How on earth can a brilliant creature like yourself, moreover with your knowledge, more or less tractable, make such a mistake? And most of you women are like that! Hang it, it isn't all part of the same thing at all. He pursued her down the stairs.

—Either this sort of thing—he was speaking hurriedly as he almost had to run to keep up with her—this sheer lumping together of all religious thought with the organized capitalist hokum, or you suitably distort the teaching of

Jesus Christ to suit your own ideals of erotic immolation[53]...he shouted as he descended—from which I might add—he had now reached another deck, following her—the hokum springs. That's all a horrid distortion of something that was never intended for you in the first place. And *you've* distorted it. You've done it. Right through the ages you've done it. And now you have the condescension to assume that you are discarding, along with the evil organizations which you undeniably recognise, but not as your own responsibility, something, that has never belonged to you. You...

But his words were lost in the chaos on the next deck, in a confusion of stewards, porters, pursers, among whom they had a sudden glimpse of the twins, standing aloof, askance by their luggage; 'The New Chang and Chen,[54] Schenectady, Hotel Nazareth,[55] Galilee'; and old ladies weaving more and more slowly and feebly in the gloom, like lizards, the process of petrifaction that the voyage would complete already set in motion within them, and old men, at once more hearty, more deliberate or more circumspect, according to nature, in matters demanding their authority, than was their wont on shore. 'A fat man with a steak and bottle, Revives my faith in God almighty.' Now he followed down the third staircase. 'But women who read Aristotle, Shake my faith in Aphrodite.'[56] Down, down, about and about, what goes on beneath the consciousness of a ship, murderous extremities down where God is, where it is hot and dark—

Held up in the crowd for a minute he realized that he had quite lost sight of Nina.

Still, Nina was safe. She was not like Spender's Aristotle woman either, he thought. In fact it was impossible to say what she was like, or rather, what form she would take, this woman of the future. Certainly she was magnificent, and as certainly she would die for what she believed in! And perhaps her very being, so compounded of gallantry and ruthless materialism and beauty, the sheer physical beauty of revolution, identified a far finer energy than he might be expected to expend in the 'going about and about'[57] the mountain of truth. Perhaps this energy of hers would coalesce with a more active entity, with a finer elemental,[58] in the very inner world it denied—

But he caught sight of her far below waiting for him. And perhaps without knowing it—his thoughts ran on as he descended, now released by the crowd—she was really helping him to build the Ark[59] against the inevitable flood while he merely speculated in the outer darkness as to what shape the Ark would take. Perhaps of all people of the future, while he still wavered—and perhaps Tor had been right—he belonged to the most meretricious order. And when the flood came there he would be left to be swallowed up in the darkness, of no more consequence than a Mother Carey's chicken[60] on the face of the waters. Or, like the skunk,[61] he would only be able to sign on at the last moment under company regulations, to avoid being thrown overboard.

But this was not to deny, he thought as he ran down the last steps to F deck, the existence of those that—

But here he was.

In the cabin Nina's suitcases had already been piled in a corner; the porthole was clasped shut against the snow; the light was burning in its wired globular shell. The clean ship-folded blankets, the shining brasswork, suggested a deceptive order. It was indeed a niche in the stormy world's cliff whose security was not to be relied upon.

Nina tried the bunk with the palms of her hands and at last sat down upon it, inviting Sigbjørn to sit beside her. As she took off her hat Sigbjørn found himself flushing, not with desire—nerves were too played to death for that; even though she was desirable—but with guilt. Yes, guilt. Here was something between them that he had wrecked for himself with his own mind and that he had not the equipment to salvage.

Nina had stood up and was patting her hair.

—You don't look happy, she said brightly, speaking into the mirror.

—How can I be? I'm so divided against myself.[62] Divided...All breaking up perhaps.

—Well, she sighed, it's really simple. There's the bad on the one hand; and the good in a united front against the evil.

Now she was combing her hair in the mirror, smiling; and he wondered at the furies that could lurk behind that innocent brow.

—It sounds simple. A matter of black and white.

—It is simple. But not really so simple as that. And nothing like so simple as sitting on the fence like you do.

She was steel, this woman—a machine, he thought. Inexorable in time of war, a bomber, bringing death to the killers.

—That's bad, Sigbjørn said, taking a cigarette. But do I? After all I couldn't help my upbringing. It nearly crippled me. They are crippling disadvantages, say what you will, that an English public school equips you with. And habits, too, principally that delightful one you mention of sitting on the fence. They forge all real values for you so that when you go out into the elemental world[63] and your checks are simply dishonoured, you're left with nothing. Of course I'm aware that many continue to be prosperous and survive without ever passing the counterfeiting stage, or being questioned about it, or even questioning themselves. But these stay in the dungeon, they accept it as it is. They do not wish to escape because they do not know they are in prison—

Nina was silent and went on combing her hair. The sounds of the wharf and the winches on deck were muffled in here. What had he said: prison? Great gates slammed in his brain.[64] Was this then where he really was? The shadow-play of something that must have happened in another existence flickered in his mind. He lay in a prison, looking up at the ceiling, hour after hour, condemned to death for his brother's murder. If he could only escape! A tremendous effort and the bars, the walls, the outer gates, the pickets, melted away. He lay under the sky in summer. But here, now that he had escaped in imagination, the real horror of his conscience waited to fasten on him. It hung over him. It was a wind-hover,[65] a hawk, now it dropped like a weight; he closed his eyes in terror to this reality and before it could capture the shivering mouse of himself he was away again, projected astonishingly somewhat in the manner of Jack London's *Star Rover*,[66] far away, into the cabin of an Atlantic liner where he said farewell to a girl named Nina.

—But it's too literary with you, this girl was saying, you can come out of that wood of perplexity where you winter and face facts. Do you hear me? Facts. And with courage. Just as you had to face Tor's death as a fact, now you have to face the death of a class—your own class.

She laid down her comb by the mirror and settled herself on the bunk beside him.

But is it, Sigbjørn wondered, a fact? Was Tor's death a fact? Wasn't his influence everywhere, like the sea rolling on through the mind? But if sunlight would only pour over the wintry darkness of his memory!

And as for the death of a class—

—The important difference between Tor and yourself, Nina said, is this: he didn't look outside himself for help. The world to him was a crazy game of chance. And he didn't pretend to see any order in it. And he didn't try to force a significance upon things that are not significant at all. And he saw only one way out, one way in which man could, to a certain extent, elude that natural malevolence and maliciousness and force, even canalize[67] that force for his own benefit, a way of living in which man would at least suffer as a human being and no longer as an animal: and that was through revolution and that revolution's goal, a classless society—

But was Tor's death a fact? Did not something of him live on afterwards, unseen? look on and help? (Something also of him demand help?) Something that existed in essences he might never suspect, such as in those noises in the London streets that at night sounded like voices endlessly shrieking with pain or crying for help, help which no one gives or knows how to give.

And as for the death of a class—

—Tor was right. To an extent I'm right too, he said.

—Oh no. No.

—No? Before Cambridge, if not for a long time, at least for the most important time in my whole life, I led the life of a worker. And the day after tomorrow, as swiftly as the day after tomorrow, I am a worker again. It must seem to you at any rate that I bring to my life the proper need for new orientation.

—No, no, Nina said. All this would be very fine if the tragic sense of life were all that mattered...I don't accept that. No personal, or intellectual cross that you or your kind may bear—

—Of my kind! That *is* a little...But don't go on, I know what you're going to say!

—In a word, I hate all you metaphysicals.

Sigbjørn did not take the bait this time. He laughed and offered her a cigarette.

—That's a queer phrase. It reminds me of the barmaid in Cambridge who said to me: 'I do love to meet you *celebrates*—'

—I hate myself for the smart-alecky conversation, Nina laughed, as well as for the *au grand sérieux*[68] manner. There's always one of the two and it's as bad as anything.

—I hate myself for it too. How long before the ship sails?

—About an hour.

—What's your route?

—Oh it isn't the usual one; we go round the land at first. I think we put in a day at Belfast.

—And after that?

—Glasgow. That's really our starting point.

—Then we might pass each other.

—Ships that pass[69]...Would you like the window opened? she asked suddenly.

—Porthole.

—Porthole. In the army we call it porthole.

He leaned across Nina's bunk to open the heavy-rimmed disk; a gust of sharp air came into the cabin with fresh sounds from the sea and city borne upon it. Snowflakes on this—at the moment—leeward side drifted past; one flake settled on the pillow; already it was beginning to disappear. They both looked out of the port on the Mersey. The gantries in Birkenhead no longer stood up with an air of stark black permanence; they would be invisible for a time and then swiftly, almost as though they were sliding into place, they would mysteriously reappear, still gaunt against the snow but illusively nearer. The tugs and ferry-boats crept across the river at half-speed. Engine-room telegraphs on ships that could not be seen jangled with an eerie sound, almost sullenly, as if from beneath the ocean. Sirens mourned from the grey darkness. The river drifting past seemed more like a glacier moving stealthily on its fatal way. And it seemed to Sigbjørn that this scene where sea was confused with sky was like life itself—all-powerful, all-corroding—but disclosing only fragments of its real nature, a ship, a prison, a mast, a cathedral, a gantry, unrelated objects between which the nexuses were difficult or impossible. Well, life was here, and death, too: absolute death life gave lavishly to many lovers, as did the sea who imaged them both. *And here's the horror of the cracked church bell*[70]... In a sudden terror he closed the port again on this desolation.

—I can't stand it...It's somehow haunted. Or it's like the flood, the end of the world, dissolution.

—It's not that *you* can't stand, but your vision of it, Nina said. Not *that* as it is.

—But how do I know that you see it as it is?

—I? Why I?—

—Anymore than I know that your materialism doesn't arrest the motion of thought, and is therefore false. Not only false, but reactionary. Not only reactionary but ultimately suicidal. So—not I, reactionary, but you, you!

—Oh no, Nina said. But it is only after the triumph of the workers, as has often been pointed out, that we can be concerned with social issues that are not pressing. The new world order will not be static. It will contain contradictions of its own. People will still argue about their responses to a scene such as this one, and a thousand other things beside. But this is scarcely a pressing issue at the moment.

—My God, then, Nina—well, it's as I thought—can you mean that absolute materialism is only a weapon at the moment and that after a classless society has been established—in the course of time problems of this kind will become of importance...

—Problems, more specifically of what sort?

—Did I fail to mention that? Well, problems the nature of which we've given the merest hint; do you mean that in the course of time these can become of importance again, to a few? The only point being that they should be shelved now, *postponed*...

—Well, all of this is old stuff, but no organized—

—No, nothing of the kind, Sigbjørn interrupted, and was silent, thinking. These last words he had spoken seemed again to him a kind of revelation. Postponed? That was it. The elucidation of the enigmas and contradictions of the universe would be postponed until after no contradictions of class remained. But gradually this 'postponement' began to seem as much an evasion of real issues as it had seemed a moment or two before to be a revelatory solution. Further, was it not a personal feeling simply? Did he not want these matters postponed for the very personal reason that his intellect was wholly inadequate to deal with them at the moment! Their postponement would give him time to find a teacher. But, teacher? What did he mean, teacher? What false premonition in the unconscious, logic in the metaphysical was this?

—The trouble is...he began.

But what was the trouble? There was no trouble. On the contrary, everything was only too clear. In fact at this moment he could foresee that premonition in the very act of being created in what men call the unconscious itself: it was in the act of foreseeing it that he was himself blinded by the rays, which like a revolving drummond light[71] that vortex discharges at the approach of all but the boldest spies, and in which both intuition and reason are in danger. Only in the darkness that followed Sigbjørn found himself the richer for a conviction: that the travail of a rebirth in consciousness which was demanded must not be confused with the actual childishness, the literal infantility of thought and feeling with which he was now enveloped and into which so often lately he had found himself escaping. 'Become as a little child again.'[72] It was true that one must. But the direction in which he now ran for succor—and moreover he ran obliquely—was not the true way.

Although he now knew this:

—The trouble is this ignorance again. I don't *know* anything. Nothing. You are probably aware of it. Don't think it's not affected by poverty, exploitation of workers or natives. I am. I was a worker long enough to feel it and to hate the suffering that is caused by a class system. It's that I haven't anything of value to say about it. To twist an intolerable remark around: *La bêtise est mon fort.*[73] It's my strong point, my armour. Take that away and there's nothing left, just as there was nothing left for Tchekov's old lady[74] when they took away her religion.

—That's all lying, evasion, Nina said. And as for—

—Of course I shall contradict myself[75] in a minute. But one thing you must admit: if I have anything of value to say, before I can *do* anything of value certain personal adjustments must be made. Even a lunatic would see that.

—That's still all part of the same thing, Nina said steadily. First you hint that you are so magnificent you're quite beyond human judgment, then that you are so stupid you can't understand anything at all, finally the complaint is that you are ill and that you must be cured first before you *begin* to understand.

—But I am ill. I *must* be cured first.

—You mean that you don't function in a merchant society? What artist of your type does? Surely all this is only a method of calling attention to yourself. First you say on failing in that society: '*noli me tangere*,[76] I'm in search of the Holy Grail.'[77] When the Holy Grail is proved illusory your argument is: 'it's only my stupidity that I can't find it.' From which it is but a step to: 'how much less then can I understand the economics of Ricardo!'[78]—it being admitted by yourself meanwhile that the Holy Grail was for you the easier object. After which you may well say: 'I am ill, and therefore before I can grasp anything, I *must* be cured.'

—But before I can understand anything I *must* be cured.

—Oh, what craziness are you up to now? Nina sighed and there was something like love in her voice...But almost immediately, as if saying a firm 'no' to the seduction of such a feeling, she added: And it's then you start to look outside yourself, to God, to a personal God, to a guardian angel:[79] or conversely, you turn inwards towards some form of esotericism. Never a faith in life, in action.

—But the guardian angel exists, Sigbjørn exclaimed, even though that itself is a contradiction of, perhaps, the Holy Grail. And yes, that exists too. But it surely isn't craziness simply to look outside yourself, Nina, he went on. Isn't it reasonable to suppose that man's existence is the justification of the angel that guards him?

—Have some Chianti,[80] Nina said.

She was opening her suitcase. Now they were far apart as they had never been; heart and lungs apart; as far as ships moored contiguously in the Bay of Yokohama[81] drift away at their berth in the change of tide.

Nina was taking out a straw-covered bottle of Orvieto and a corkscrew. While she produced some paper cups Sigbjørn opened the bottle.

—I thought of this, she was saying. It's silly to part quite hating each other. We'll drink to your living phantasy of the unconscious.[82]

Sigbjørn poured some wine into his cup, filled hers, then his own. The perfect gentleman, he thought with hatred. But what am I? And the strange remark overheard, of the lamp-trimmer on the *Oedipus Tyrannus* occurred to him: 'I hate that bloody no-class Tarnmoor.'[83] What angel was that?

—All right. He raised his glass, laughingly. Have it your own way, let's drink. Man does not yield himself to the angels[84], nor unto death—utterly—save only through the weakness of his feeble will...Selah[85], I give it up.

They drank to each other. Nina got up to stretch her legs. She looked in the mirror, patted her hair, powdered her face and then stood quite still gazing deep into her own eyes. Deep brown eyes like the earth. But how was this reconcilable with her strange machine-like quality? Perhaps she had the same sort of correspondence with the earth that a tractor had! And behind her, watching, his own eyes, blue, wise but without humanity: pitying but cold and abstract like the sea... Well, perhaps they were both machines! but of a different type. Even memories were mechanical. Was that a memory of Tor moving in her face? Never mind, they could resume relations on a different plane; on the abstract plane of machines, now they knew that they were subservient to different laws, different gearing, and reacted differently to atmosphere, even though perhaps ultimately they were being driven by different routes towards the same goal.

—I wish you no harm, this machine called Nina laughed. On the contrary.

—Here's how, the machine Sigbjørn said, drinking. I know it's a gallant story.[86] You give me the air for *my* sake because you wish to see me become strong and self-reliant. And we shall always remain friends. Just like brothers, in fact. Oh well, here's to our darkness and our brightness, may they part with a gesture of extreme—

—*À votre santé.*

They laughed. The Chianti was warming them. Well, this was life at present, a glass of Chianti. So it would go on. They were right to laugh. It was even funny.

—Besides, he said, you talk of your precious singleness of motive in going to the States as against the dubious multiplicity of my own in going to Russia, but I could think of at least a dozen reasons for your going and two dozen objections to it also, if I were clever enough—

—Well, tell me *one.*

—Strange, I can't think of one offhand.

Perhaps it did not suit him after all quite to destroy his own amour propre.

—Anyway, he said, I could think up some *confusions* in your own thoughts. Here are you, a communist, seeking 'outside' yourself for your destiny, and not content with draining private misery into a common well—God knows what I *was* going to say—

—The truth; we have real wrongs to right, real enemies to fight, real grievances to redress. We don't tilt at windmills.[87]

—But my way is not to fight, but drift; to be blown like a whirring wind, like a grindstone, and yet it is to fight. To fight with contradictions, not against them—the electron that is at the same time a bullet and a wave.[88]

—Not at all, he thought. I don't mean this, I'm lying. But then why do all conversations with Nina descend to such intoxicating nonsense? Break with the past! Oh, break, break, break, on thy cold grey stones, oh sea!

—But Sigbjørn, can you really be so weak as to look outside yourself to a God for help?

—Did I say I did? Well, if I do, it's not because my psyche has disintegrated. And moreover it's because we deny this that we're thrown out of our Eden. You make the mistake of thinking everything can be done by yourself. And there's the whole secret of the fall of man! That's why we've broken up, are leaving each other, and finally that's why Tor died.

—Why did he die?

—He didn't realize that he would be helped.

—By whom?

—No, that's not right either....Anyway, even if he hadn't died, you would have destroyed him...No, I take that back too.

Nina was silent a moment, then said slowly and bitterly:

—Aren't *you* getting confused?

—Yes, I'm sorry...I'm also sorry I denied the help. And why did I deny the help? For the simple reason that when the help is denied it is withdrawn.

—For instance you used to say that the truth lay inside you, the kingdom of heaven lay inside you,[89] Nina was saying. How can it be inside, and outside as well? It seems to me you don't know what you do mean.

—Something that swims in the air, moves in the sea, and burrows under the earth.[90]

—But it can't be both inside and outside at the same time.

—Not unless substance is as much open as shut!

—What! in Spinoza's sense![91] Substance? Are you crazy! Well, not any more than you can be inside and outside a movement at the same time.

—Or any more than you can be aboard one of my father's ships and yet inside the movement.

—All this proves nothing.

Snow[92] drifted soundlessly past the porthole, snow falling on tugs in the Mersey, snow forlornly burying land and sea, burying the past and the future, snow that falls on the people of Liverpool falls also on Alfred Gordon Pym[93] in captivity under barbarian hordes where his life drains away on a desperate coast at Land's End, at Dead End. Gulls also drifted past the porthole, with outstretched sadistic beaks, dead sailors, they said—more likely dead philosophers—winged hostility; the *quack quack* of positivism,[94] the sea-gull symbol in human consciousness. Snowflakes clung to the outside of the glass. The evil he had done to Tor, at first no more than a flake, and then like the slowly-moving glacier outside; a glacier powerfully carrying everything in its path, consequence and cause alike. This thought having the effect of stifling him, perversely enough he pulled up the metal bolt once more and swung up the brass-rimmed disk of glass, disclosing within its circular frame the white Mersey, the *real* white sea, he thought for a moment, rather than the world of imagination dimly shaped through the pane, as though his objective had been suddenly moved into place before him when the porthole was flung open to the icy air. But a moment's contemplation and again this sea became what it was, an abstraction: as indeed are most appearances, on the leeward side of life.

He drew in long breaths, looking out over—what? The end of the world? Cataclysm? Not a single class but the whole outer circle of the world, awaits its coup-de-grâce. The stupid doggerel[95] scrawled itself on his brain. By which time,

Nina had implied, all that would be left of him—would be his own irreducible logic. Well, what did that matter? But almost immediately something told him that it might matter considerably. It had sometimes occurred to him by intuition that nature might be lavish in her attempts to produce something or somebody self-evolving; did not, in some men's lives, a choice arise, without their knowing it, between following cool spirals,[96] one that wound upwards to real life, and the one whose course was downward, to the stony ground of real death? From the dark cavern of his life he had emerged before this staircase that coiled down infinitely below him, but also towered upwards like a fantastic spring infinitely into the equal darkness. Which direction should he choose?

Or should he choose neither and retreat to his niche, the cavern, carefully askance from all action, a sort of conscious fungus on life. Perhaps to Nina such choices did not consciously present themselves, and therefore no congruency in argument could ever be reached with her. These considerations had that effect upon him of that produced by a play he could not follow or a book he read half asleep. A dull creating impulse of one's own followed with wandering response the outlines of reality for a time; then struck out tangentially on its independent course; invariably sleep was the cul-de-sac on this road. Outside, the snow mists cleared, gathered again; a freighter was moving down the river. One moment she was in full view, the next she had vanished as absolutely as if she had sunk. It was the same way with life. Yesterday, when Nina was away, everything had seemed clear. Now, relatively at the same moment, on the verge of her departure, as they stood looking out of the porthole at the bitter weather, everything was as muddled as before; sea with sky; reflection with reality; cause with effect. Perhaps their parting alone, itself affective of so many old antagonisms, separations, agreements, economic squabbling and the like, was sufficient to load him down like a coffin-ship[97] with its ill-distributed burden whose ponderous trimming made his very being cleave and sag within him. Quite apart from any other cargo...

—Maybe I'm just unconsciously supporting my father, he said, in the face of the enemy. Perhaps that's why I can't go the whole way.

—You have to commit murder, no less, Nina said.

—Murder, he began...

But his mind could not travel on these lines. To increase his confusion, the memory of words his father had once used to him: 'our philosophy is based on no faith,'[98] now returned to mock him and to mow at him. What did that mean? Perhaps the best thing to do was intellectually and spiritually to heave-to for the moment and let the mutable gale blow itself out over the treacherous mountains of the past. Besides he now had the idea that it was philosophy rather than anything else, and not its fruits either so much as its debris that had him loaded down below the plimsoll—[99]

In ballast to the White Sea indeed! Throw the cargo overboard—including the captain's wife.[100] Still, a ship in ballast was none too easy in a heavy sea, and should she run into really dirty weather—

—There's a vacuum in the centre of every well-conducted tornado, he said. I don't really know what I'm talking about.

Nina poured out another glass of Chianti for him.

—I repeat, if you're expecting, or advocating, some other sort of revolution, a psychical revolution or some such, before a social revolution, why you might as well expect to revive a corpse[101] with a shot of this.

—Or talk about revolution in the Midland Adelphi Bar...[102]

—Or for that matter on the S.S. *Arcturion*, queen of the Tarnmoor fleet, built under contract with the Government, and outward bound for hell—[103]

She poured herself a glass. They drank to each other.

—Or in any kind of penthouse bolsheviki.

—You're right.

—If there's to be a revolution of the soul, or of the word—or of the worm— she went on, for the worm will presumably turn, or whatever you're hinting at, prejudice apart, very well—a private and personal thing, all right—but then it would not be organized capitalistically for the simple reason that—

—Only a few are chosen,[104] Sigbjørn said. I know. I'm sure you're right. Unfortunately the next moment I shall find myself dissenting. Of course that's no good; to go over to you is an act of full belief. It's a complete thing, and I'd have to give myself to it as completely as I'd have to give myself over to the other.

—What other?

—Something I don't know about. Something like death, but also something like new life.

—Can't you be more concrete? Do you mean you're going to join the Elks?[105]

—Well, he laughed, I'm in a kind of no-man's-land at the moment—is that being concrete?

—Not very.

—Well, anyway, here I am. To twist another aphorism,[106] myself the subject, no teachers to be found far and wide! Only spirits like yourself, and at one time Tor, and in a different way my father, all on the verge of tremendous abysses, or creations, but who never-the-less have *affirmed* life! Standing fast means shaking off the grasp of hands, you know that. They drag you every way and you can't grasp them all.

—But didn't you say 'to fight with contradictions'?

—Did I? Probably I did. But it's not what I mean at all. Unless I meant by it that you can't prevent these contradictions entering your very psyche. Well, shall I say you can't change as easily as jumping into a tub of warm water. I probably belong to your side, am gravitating to your side, that is if your side really *means* revolution. Well, of course it does, of course, of course. Anyhow I could be beguiled by its sheer beauty if by nothing else.

—Not a question of beguiling, Nina said shortly. And then she emphasized this angrily:

—Beguiling has nothing at all to do with it. But fighting with contradictions, as a matter of fact that is curiously more what I mean, for dialectic—

But her own previous annoyance had started in Sigbjørn a train of objections which were already beyond this stopping point of their possible agreement. No beguiling he was thinking, not listening, but there's something devilishly obstructing about your mind. What precisely it obstructs is, when carried to its logical end, the motion of the mind itself beyond materialistic standards. But then my mind obstructs also, and what precisely it obstructs is, when carried to its logical end, the motion of human justice. He said:

—I suspect you of being spiritually unjust.

But he thought: 'physical,' 'spiritual,' what do these words mean? What uncritical judgments are these?

—I suspect you of being spiritually dishonest, Nina was forced to retort, all opportunity of agreement now lost.

—Why did you say that?

—I never said I suspected you of being, say, an opportunist, he explained. I expected you to reply and indeed was inviting you to reply: 'I suspect *you* of being humanly unjust.' Why don't you fight with the weapons I offer you?

—Very well, I say it. You are—however you expressed *what* you are.

—I suggest that there should be a reconciliation of these disharmonies then: two minuses after all make a plus.

—Well, the reconciliation might come unconsciously if you *lived* rather than talked about this religion, unknown, of yours.

—Just as it would come with you? If you lived what you believe in?

—I am going to live it.

—Don't you talk rather too much about yourself? asked Nina.

—Too damned much.

But I am going to live it, he thought. I am going to change. First there is the psychologic pattern to retrace. But then again how can I say for sure when I feel only partly free? When I seem partly controlled, partly under orders from something or somebody outside myself, whose demand for right is absolute—the little old one[107] in the unconscious? No: then—'I must confess I never experienced this oceanic feeling myself,' Freud said.[108] Here again, an incomplete synthesis.

—I am going to live it, he said.

—I wonder.

He thought: 'whose demand for right was absolute?' and for whatever is unquestionably right it is obvious, although I distrust the word, that sacrifices must be made, even of that which within its own enclosed scene (and irrespective of its corrupt causes of which it is helpless), is all right.

—Perhaps I shall join you after all, he said.

—Words, words, words...[109]

—I know.

—Let's go out on deck. It couldn't be colder than this. We let too much air in here.

—Or we didn't let in enough!

Not by a damn sight, Sigbjørn muttered as he bolted the porthole.

Boat Drill at 3 p.m. this afternoon.

Passengers are requested to put on their lifebelts when the signal is given and stand to the positions assigned to them which they will find in their cabins.

Boddy Finch life jacket.[110]

Arcturion: Liverpool.

They were standing on a lower hurricane deck on the lee side looking over towards New Brighton;[111] there was a hush in the tempest between them and for the time being they were alone, no passengers or sailors disturbing them. From far above them the galley boy was dumping garbage down the ash-chute. The garbage shot past them with a swish into the sea. So many half beliefs, spurious beliefs, beliefs that one couldn't be wrong, to be got rid of. Another load of garbage slid past. Get rid of all confusions. Dump them overboard. Sculls there;[112] dump over this little lot, will you boy? They were only two human beings that had loved and had been betrayed by their own refracted vision of the tree of knowledge, and were now parting. What transcended the agonizing truth of this?

—Nina, Sigbjørn exclaimed. Don't go on this damned ship, let's go away together somewhere. I won't go on the *Unsgaard* either. We'll go away somewhere and start again. It'll be a—

—Rebirth.

—Yes, it will be. Yes, the only truth is in us, is in our love, is in our—

—Well, where would we go to?

—I don't know but don't go on this ship anyway. You don't know what sort of tub you're in.

—Oh yes I do. And I shall know a good deal more by the time we dock in New York. Well, I'm waiting for an answer. Where would we go?

Mount Ararat in eruption! Where indeed? An absurd adolescent fancy, he saw them cruising low over the vermillion waves, like two seagulls flying: *io, io*,[113] where the cockle fishers dabble with their fists in the salt silt: two seabirds flying together endlessly and so happy in one another. *Io, io*. Or was it quack quack? Don't go on this ship? But where? Ararat in eruption! A single snowflake curved in under the projecting deckhead and lighted on his palm. Where? At the moment of parting, of exquisite pain, one drop of God's blood[114] falls like a benediction. Or is it a tear, the salt taste of eternity? Now it had evaporated.

—Before it's too late, Nina, voyage with me, not to America, not to Archangel, not to Lyonesse,[115] but into the province of that pain.

But they merely walked away towards the stern: along an alleyway, through a little smoking-room in which magazines and leaflets of the company were arranged—Sigbjørn taking one of the latter absently—and up a companion ladder to D deck in the poop, at length coming to stand at the stern itself under the protection of the deck-head of the decking bridge: this was the entire extent of their escape, the limit of their common voyage.

A little aft of them and above them on its ice-covered staff, the flag furled and fluttered; the flag that covered the trimmers in the *Inferno*, wavering and fluctuating, with a noise like the very fire that tortured them. The flag, the cross—[116]

—We may pass each other, Nina was saying, if you sail from Preston.

—I pointed that out to you before but you weren't interested.

She looked over his shoulder at the leaflet[117] he was examining.

—But this should interest you. Listen to this: 'Being equipped with a most polite and efficient steward service one is made to feel altogether at home on a Tarnmoor liner. It is this feature that has earned for the ships of this line an unequaled reputation for quality and variety. The ships of this company are all built under contracts with the Government and are required to undergo a rigid examination by naval officers before being placed in the service. Exceptionally seaworthy vessels. Well lighted and ventilated staterooms.'

A bugle sounded distantly and both started to walk forward moved by the same impulse—to say their last farewell.

—It's all settled, it's final then, Nina said.

He had folded the leaflet. Now he handed her his *hyrkontrakt* again: *Sigbjørn Tarnmoor, limper, 21: skibets reise fra Prester til Leningrad/Archangel.*

—Yes. All final.

—I do wish you good luck, Nina said. I suppose you feel as I do, that you're going out to a new land, some new found land[118] where—

—As though you were going to discover America for the first time.

—Like Erikson.

—Leif Erikson.

—Or Christopher Columbus in the *Nina*. Wasn't it the...Don't you remember you used to say...Well, I do hope you have a good voyage.

—Well, I suppose I've got to get off now.

An officer in gold braid, blue prussian collar turned up and his face hidden in it like a chestnut in a burr, muttered in passing them, almost as if to himself:

—No hurry, children, plenty of time. Only the first bugle. Three quarters of an hour yet before this wash-basin sails.

He vanished.

—'Passengers who go with the Tarnmoor Line for the first time do not fail to remark the unusual interest taken in the comfort and enjoyment of the voyage by the officers of the ship.

—'Also we avoid unknown sailings and this feature will at once impress regular travellers as well as the occasional tourist for nothing is so exasperating on arriving at a connecting point as to find that the steamer expected to leave within a short period might not start for two or three days causing considerable inconvenience and expense.'

They laughed. Sigbjørn took her hand. For a few moments it was as though they were reprieved; no conflict had been born within them, there was no revolt or misery: they were spared; there was no hurry to leave paradise.[119] This instant was their marriage. This was what their relationship should have been: never again would they be parted.

Then the moment was over.

—God, I'm sorry that you're going, Sigbjørn burst out finally, squeezing her hand. Do you remember the Norwegian poem:[120] 'Sea and time sundered us, and nights of the west are gloomy'—how does it go? He burst out laughing.

—Sea and time, it doesn't sound very good now.

Still holding her hand he drew her closer to the rail: See that old piece of driftwood down there? See it?

They craned over the side watching the moving debris of the port: old papers, orange boxes, blocks of melting ice, refuse all coated with grimy snow.

—Yes, there it is. I see.

And the two of them looked at the old piece of driftwood. The ice had melted round the ship. The waves raced along at the speed of an express train but this piece of driftwood as the waves swept under it seemed to be making no advance at all, merely rising and falling with a fatigued movement, to and fro.

—Do you see how a human soul[121] can be like that? Sigbjørn asked.

Nina was silent for a moment, then she said:

—I see how it is in the form only, and not the substance of the waves that travels over the surface.

—That's it precisely. But can you see, Nina, how a human soul can be like that poor log, absolutely alone? Chaos breaks over his head but moves him only slightly, now nearer, now farther from his goal, that goal toward which he is inexorably traveling. But can you see how alone he can be, for perhaps centuries, how absolutely alone in the universe like a bit of wreck in mid-Atlantic?

—I wouldn't think of it. And besides it isn't alone, it has the companionship of other jetsam. I would think of the rolling Atlantic itself. But Barney, you know you don't have to think of yourself like that, you're not lonely, you don't—

—I admit I imagined it out at sea. And then that soul dying like some lonely sailor that dies there, as if a wave should break for the last time and be no more heard and seen. Real death. That's frightful. Do you think Tor died, really, like that? That his soul really died? That he passed right out of existence, that he is dead, as dead as this moment is dead? Or do you think you can be reborn? Even in this life? Do you think so?

—He had the courage to do it; I'm sure he got what he wanted. Nina spoke dreamily with an impartiality she was obviously very far from feeling. I'm sure he got what he wanted, she repeated and added, almost with acerbity, but I couldn't as a rule have any sympathy with what he did (do, though).

—Tell me, did Tor so much convert you? Or had you arrived at these conclusions independently?

—I think I attached him to life, to men. That's what he told me. Deep down he may have resented the fact that I, and not himself, stood between *you* and life.

—*You* stood between?

—To him, yes. But he did try to liberate me, to make me free. Free within myself, and that's what you never wanted to do. And Tor really did love humanity, he loved it as something of which he never could become a part. And that's one reason why he—

—No, that isn't why...

—What did he want? Tell me, what did he want? What...

—Don't...

A door banged behind them in the engineer's mess-room and a torrent of conversation poured out of it as if it had been pent up there...'port boiler was leaking so bad they plugged the tubes in the bottom row...' 'port feed-pump[122] was out of order,' 'starboard feed-pump was bucking,' 'well, what the hell, both those damned boilers leaked badly,' 'injector out of order,' 'bucking the bucking feed-pump,' 'lost lubricating-oil—thirty degrees list,' 'port-hole glasses cracked,' 'because the feed-pump was bucking...'

An engineer in yellow dungarees banged the door; the conversation was shut out.

—But I don't see that log as a symbol of the soul, Nina said, as you call it. I see it as something small that has broken away, perhaps from a dam, where it was rotting, but which will still find its way in the chaotic dark of the sea, towards its goal. Just like you said, in fact: only different.

—It will still rot; or it will get water-logged and sink. Besides, having broken away from the mass, hasn't it lost its purpose? It could, of course, mean anything.

—It could mean anything of course.

—*That bucking feed-pump was bucking.*

...*Boat Drill at 5 P.M. this afternoon. Passengers are requested to put on their lifebelts when the signal is given, and stand to the position assigned to them which they will find in their cabins*

Boddy Finch life jacket

For the benefit of our patrons...the Arcturion is equipped with nine water-tight bulkheads with electrically equipped water-tight doors, nine steel deck-houses, nine automatic electric fire-detecting systems, nine two-and-a-half gallon portable fire extinguishers, nine fire hydrants and nine lifeboats seating nine each...Safety first...nothing less than the best for our...

Gentlemen.

They were walking swiftly aft, past lifeboats, whose gear, they say, was frozen and useless, pushing through windily-creaking brass-silled white cabin doors, which stewards, loaded with baggage opened with their knees, wandered on through the soulless and expensive ship, surrounded on all sides by ventilating systems, elevator shafts, the mezzanine balcony—for the ship had been built for the tropical trades—and extravagant hangings and furniture; in short, by everywhere the worst kind of capitalist decor. In places by hatches that they must pass where cargo was not being worked, the deck was like a wedding cake, but most of the tarpaulin had been rolled away and wedges knocked out in preparation for the luggage and merchandise which were being swung inboard in slings and then dropped soundlessly down into the hatches; winches were rattling furiously; and in the hatches the stevedores would work in a kind of fever, and then stop suddenly, releasing the rope net, turning up their faces to the black sky, to the shore bosun leaning over the brink of the well, to the snow, as they waited for the signal to receive the next load. At these moments Nina and Sigbjørn would dash for security on the other side.

—Well it might represent bourgeois civilisation, Nina was saying.

—What might represent it?

—Why, that piece of lumber.

—Oh, that!

—Yes, timber that everyone thought meant security; wood, calculating and expedient...A ship. But it is rotten. The mass sweeps over it, vast, chaotic, powerful, a passionate Atlantic. It sinks.

—That's rather disproportionate, isn't it?

—Not in terms of good and evil.

—But chaotic? That way madness lies, or at least leads to 'the aphorisming eclectic,'[123] Sigbjørn said.

—Word splitting. What are we trying to avoid anyhow?

—Is it parting?

Now they stood on the starboard side near the bow, the windward side where the wind itself cut through them to the bone. Here everything seemed more concrete, more real, than on the leeward side; it was as if the world here had abandoned its elemental, abstract pose, and was trying to offer a quite different appearance. On the other hand, even the concrete, the tactile, the obvious were subject to the same disabilities of presentation; all could not be shown at once; nor even a single part for a long enough time to arouse an adequate response. At one moment the melancholy docks, shawled in snow,[124] stretched before them; at the next, again as if a screen had hidden them, and another scene had been moved across into place, the Overhead Railway[125] appeared: and in a similar manner, the warehouses, the offices floating into sight, appeared in turn, tier on tier, prison-like dwelling on prison-building, ugly, ugly, singly disclosed, and above all—blank embodiment of the day's evil[126]—the cathedral.

—Well there it is, up there...

—We were the young apprentices, the young workmen—wavering scaffolding—

—We were building something too, and now we've left it. Unfinished, with the crane on top. Perhaps in time it will disassemble altogether.

—Just like New Brighton tower[127] over there—

—Which you can't see today—

—Has been dismantled.

—Exactly, or rather...Let's save a little, it's cold, cold.

...Boat drill at 3 P.M. Passengers are requested to put on their...

Boddy Finch life jacket.

Arcturion; Liverpool.

—What I said at first! What is there in us that drives us apart? that's always been at work, in both of us, breaking us up?

—That's what I said at first to you, Nina said. But you wouldn't listen. Our separate needs were many and various; we should accept them and at the same time be glad we had each other. Differences were not themselves culpable. But you could not accept that, you had to try and absorb me!

—But that is precisely...what I ought to have done. A man and a woman should be one. Tor—

—No, that's where death sets in. Anyway, you weren't right, you weren't the right kind of pioneer. Not the right prospector. And moreover you were prospecting in forbidden territory. I wouldn't follow you.

—But Tor—

—I wouldn't follow you.

—But you would...

—Don't talk of it.

—But Nina, Nina, for God's sake, we were building something. We were. We were! Nothing is so sad as a building left unfinished, abandoned by its soul, by all love, just left hopelessly to rot.

Snow drove across the apparition of the cathedral which they had turned to look at once more as they again retraced their steps to the stern.

Beware of the propellers! Tourist passengers not allowed on this deck!

—On the contrary, nothing can be so triumphant as to leave it. But there has to be more than mere parting...there has to be death. It's not that I'm naturally cruel.

—You are!

—No. A certain amount of force is necessary, that's all. But to be quite ruthlessly frank with you, we built with bricks of straw.[128] And you know it! And you know it! It's really the end. Better to cut everything off with a knife, much better. I know this is treason to youth, to admit that we're defeated.

For a moment the pronoun 'we' seemed to comfort him. Then his heart turned cold.

—But we're not defeated. How can we be defeated when I've agreed with you all along really?

—But you've wavered,[129] you can never be counted on ... No! Better to finish. Tor's death decided that for me. End! Finish!

—Did Tor mean so much to you then? My God, there's the bugle!

From down below the bugle sounded, followed by the thunderous roar of the dinner gong for first lunch. Pain! Private grief! The gong crashed again. Pang! Break! Break! Pang! Farther down the alleyway a sailor, astride of the bulwarks, in a shining oilskin speckled with snow, loosed a Turk's Head[130] with a marlinspike.[131] He worked with feverish haste. An easy birth for the poor ship. Cut the knot. Get it off with a knife. Cut all the knots. The bugle sounded again with monitory finality.

Last Post! Reveille![132]

Nina laughed:

— Someday I'm going to murder the bugler.

—Someday they're going to find him dead, Sigbjørn said. Someday they're going to find that bugler with his bugle broken over his head. So, Heloise,[133] this is the beginning of the end.

—No, the end.

Last Post! Reveille!

They were moving away; but the same officer rose up before them again, muttering in his stride as he vanished into the bosun's locker:

—No hurry...Half an hour yet...Plenty of time before this tin can sails!

Reprieved again! But this time the feeling was not so satisfactory. Not unlike being the victim of an unsuccessful attempt at hanging.[134] They stood in silence, their faces averted from one another, warders of themselves. He looked down the length of the ship. In two days he would be on board the *Unsgaard*, a vessel not half the size. Yet, on both, the watches would turn-to on deck or down in the stokehold at the same time. The current of life in the forecastle was in the same stream. Yet with what essential differences! On board the *Unsgaard* he imagined Captain, officers and crew to be one with the labouring vessel herself. But what was the *Arcturion*? An old-fashioned hotel, an expensive restaurant whose business was waning; a telegraph office, a public lavatory, a gamblers' den, a burlesque show in which Siamese twins were top of the bill, but also a kind of phantom, a rough integration of infinitely small activities, an entity as elusive and as casual as the *Zeitgeist*;[135] a composite world from which, indeed, many essentials were omitted, going to pieces before their eyes! Or capsizing. And in his mind's eye he saw the over-loaded *Vestris* leaving Hoboken[136] with a heavy list, and slowly, slowly overturning in the grey seas, like the topheavy system of which she was the symbol; like the overburdened world that carried within her the seeds of her own destruction.

What, indeed, was this ship? Like the Tao,[137] a square with no angles, a great sound which cannot be heard, a great image with no form.

This second postponement had the effect of making them impatient of their own inability to part: in spite of differences it seemed that they were as inevitable to each other as the New Chang and Chen whose separation might cause death to both, or, more terrible, one death.

—Well, here am I—it's ironic—signed on as a coal passer going God knows where, and here are you, in at least comparative—

—The difference is this. You're not making an act of full belief. And I am. Everything you've said to me is only proof of your wavering. And it's neck or nothing.

—But I'm going. You should talk of neck or nothing. If it comes to that, are you making an act of full belief?

—Absolutely. None of the old ideology is any good any longer. It is such an act. Yours—although it may seem on the surface like an identification with the proletariat—is still simply an escape from yourself.[138] It's more of a tense, personal, religious matter with you than anything else.

—Religious? The sea? I don't follow.

—What I wish to convey to you is not that in your own way you are not brave; on the contrary, your courage is as blind as the forces you invoke; but that what you're doing is not rational, not criticized by thought, and is therefore, in short, sentimental.

—Sentimental!

—For Pete's sake can't you see that all this business about going home, to Russia, or Norway, or Spitzbergen,[139] or wherever it is, is just one more attempt on your part to crawl back into Grandma's beaded bag?[140]

Sigbjørn laughed loudly.

—Bitter words, Nina. But what about your returning to America?

But Nina overlooked this:

—You must see that yours is not a class-conscious gesture at all, she said, but simply an act of primitive revolt. Barbaric...Moreover it's the giving of yourself over to the dark forces of the unconscious, so celebrated by your Mr. Lawrence,[141] from which it's but a step, also made in the dark, not to Communism but to Fascism. It's like going to war—there's that same quality of blindness about it. As a matter of fact I think a great many in the same position as yourself feel that they must take some such violent step in the dark as a compensation for what their brothers and fathers went through in the war.

—Bitter words, Nina. But seven years makes a difference. Lawrence would have gone over to your side if he'd lived. He always suspected psychic disintegration in 'spiritual' people. He'd have seen the danger to the world in his 'blood consciousness' creed; I think he'd have gone 'red' in your sense. But apart from all this you said yourself that the first step must be made in the dark, out of a willingness to walk blind that comes in the creation of a new and unseen thing.

—Right. But the blind man must know he's crossing a bridge. His blindness is related to an object.

—What's your object, then?

—Well, there's definitely work to be done in America.[142] That country is also in danger of Fascism, and if she's to be saved it must be done in the next two years. Besides, I've been offered a definite job.

—So have I. But that's personal. What about the object; the related, the disinterested object?

—Well, writers are a strong force in America, there's more respect for them than here. Far greater, I should say, than here, where no writers save a few exiled Americans can breathe. And they can only breathe because with them disillusion has extended to a cosmic despair. Their breathing's no longer full-lunged. And there are a great many like that in America. Their despair is rooted chiefly in the fact that they're not wanted, that they're not necessary, that their art is only a playing with coloured blocks. Remove that feeling, and given the talent, they become our allies.

Sigbjørn smiled.

—It sounds simple. Why not let charity begin at home?

—I'm trying to make you see. But you're much more difficult. You're a kind of a false radical. In a sense you're just part of an unpredictable university fashion.[143]

—It won't be the fashion long if this is the way it gets treated, Sigbjørn said. But what if I were genuine? Or another sort of revolutionary?

—Well, we'll see. The only other sort of revolutionary to my mind is the revolutionary petty bourgeois; the wolf's mask of a Goering,[144] revolutionary of war.

—You're more ruthless than Hedda Gabler![145]

—Far more!

—But what about myself—betrayed by my own stupidity—who never meant to do anything more ruthless than to discount the attraction of a new idea?

—Other things lacking, I repeat: stupidity is polite.

Sigbjørn recoiled. 'Stupidity is polite!' Other things lacking, it's polite to have a soul, hadn't Tor said? This odd, characteristic misuse of the word aroused an uneasy suspicion. He repressed it, however. It was strange enough in all conscience to reflect upon the nature of personalities flowing into one another, the essences of a first caught or rejected by a second, the spiritual front a third put on to society mingling and interweaving with the very being of a fourth, no one quite separate, nothing entirely one's own, without further complicating it by special jealousy; for what he had apprehended as self indeed carried the refrain of water, being a mere interpenetration with others, imitation of Christ,[146] of this teacher or that, water in water, that flowed through all things. Nothing entirely one's own indeed! Erikson?...But perhaps the feelings simply arose from an economic basis in the psyche itself.

—It's true I've been frequently betrayed by it, he said, but in my own way I'm struggling after the principle of good. Won't you help me?

—You'll have to fight yourself, Barney. You have your own particular legacies which I can't touch. At least not more than I'm already touching them. As for walking blind, it is true you have to, to a certain extent. But that's different from *pretending* you are blind, or from any other infantilism, much as, say, your friend Hawthorne going out only at night...

Hawthorne, white Hawthorne,[147] where are you going? where are you going, my bonny,[148] my love? They had paused between two ventilators in a kind of niche on the hurricane deck.[149] They were facing again the Cheshire, the Rock Ferry side of the Mersey where Hawthorne had been Consul and which at the moment was as clear as though seen through binoculars, with the dangerous clarity that presages storm. The Woodside and Egremont ferries edged swiftly across the river. In the distance the old Eastham ferry[150] was slowly paddling downstream. A big German freighter had just dropped anchor in the middle of the river. Sea birds screamed out to her.

Nina was silent as they stared out at the ship.

—That's our common enemy, their eyes seemed to say, focussing on the soulless swastika.[151]

(Hawthorne crawled blindly down Old Ropery,[152] tin cup clenched in an outstretched, trembling fist. Tap-tap. Veteran of four wars. A penny for my eyes;[153] tappy-tappy; my brassy ferrule. 'Is that you Melville? You're going for a long journey, Melville.' 'Yes, the Holy Land.' 'A Zionist?[154] or is your mind still made up to be annihilated?' 'Annihilated?' 'Annihilated.')

—You wouldn't fight with them?

—Fight with them?

For a moment the sound of the winches above them was the clattering of machine-guns. The snow-mists, the terrible vaporous metallurgies[155] of aerochemistry, the sea that raced past a thick river of blood. Goering's bloated face rose up before him and he smashed it to jelly.

—I'd rather die than fight with them.

—You would?

—I swear to you I'll fight everything they stand for.

—Well be careful you don't give them aid unconsciously.

—Unconsciously?

—Yes, isn't your lovely Norway the apex of Nordic culture,[156] of all your heathen religion? And haven't they the raw materials, the ores and woods useful to—she nodded out towards the Nazi ship. And aren't you busy with your 'program of salvation,' and your 'Nordic League of Nations.'

—I was never busy with them, Sigbjørn laughed. I haven't been to Norway since I was an infant. It had always seemed to me a place in the world that was free and good.

—So would almost any country seem in a childhood spent in a wealthy family.

Sigbjørn said nothing. That's not true, either, he thought. The trees striding down to the harbour from Frognersaeteren, fir trees and hawthorne trees, white hawthorne covered in snow! 'Look, they haven't had a headache[157] as long as I have,' Melville said. In the distance the sandhills where he had walked with Hawthorne could be dimly seen from the deck of the *Arcturion*, a daub of undulating waves in Chinese white,[158] white sea, seen through a network of snow. But surely the destroyer would spare Norway.

—Be careful you don't give them aid unconsciously, Nina repeated.

Gusts of wind blew up icy spray in their faces, but they leaned further over the iron side of the ship from which water poured endlessly. Further along the side, steward's heads peeped out of heavy brass-rimmed portholes; below them on an iron platform another steward in a dark waistcoat appeared suddenly and nervously dumped some garbage overboard, remaining for some time transfixed by his actions. Then he threw away the cigarette he had been smoking and vanished.

—You're right, Nina. I know you're right. It's true what you say. I suppose I'm still not much more than a child who wants to be an engine-driver. I wouldn't have the impudence to call myself a communist, not yet. But those enemies of yours are my enemies.

—A dog running after its own tail would have described me better a year or two ago, Nina smiled.

—It's been hard to find my place on earth. It's hard for millions of others like me.

—Yes.

—But at any rate I'm not sticking on the lee side,[159] Nina. For a time we both had found a safe niche in the world. But we renounced it. Both of us. I'm not afraid of this, it had to be done. But you can't despise me... Where I'm going to is the roar of the sea and the darkness,[160] and the night. Isn't it? Isn't it?

—You are afraid, though. You're trembling, Nina said gently.

—Aren't you afraid though? aren't you? aren't we all rounding...every life has its Cape Horn...[161]

The snow streamed and tumbled. Snow forlornly burying land and sea, burying the past and the future, snow falling into the sea, melting into water, spindrift[162] of ideals, dreams—fleeting, indeterminable—drifting out to a littered Atlantic of civilisation...

—Yes, Nina, and every life has its Tierra del Fuego, dangerous island of fire...

—Are you rounding Cape Horn?

Last Post! Reveille!

Before them the waves raced on. The ghost of Tor seemed to speak through the silence between them. 'All is as a wave that breaks *perpetuum mobile*. Revolution.

Absolutely. You'd be surprised if I told you there was no afterlife as it seems to you. Oh, life here's as easy as falling off a log or at least stopping off one of the old man's ships rotting at a mile a minute. Astonished, aren't you? At such a mundane message from the astral world?'[163]

Again Sigbjørn had the curious notion that this was all a nightmare—he was in prison, condemned to death—of extraordinary detail and documentation, but never-the-less a dream; a dream in which one set out, weighed down with the ballast of the past, to the White Sea! But what was that? Did he go in pursuit of that whiteness which strikes more of a panic to the soul than redness[164] which affrights in blood? Or was it of that very redness, the redness of the star of revolution,[165] beautiful over the White Sea? Where was he going? Moving towards Novalis' really better world, or to Cummings'[166] vicariously infantile land of slogan? Whose star did he follow, was it his own or Myers'[167] cold north star of his self-mistrust?

—I'm afraid I'm not very gay, he said.

Nina was silent.

—That's curious, too, he added, for like Heine[168] I'm usually most amusing when...

—When what? Let's move. It's freezing cold, Nina said impatiently.

—When my heart is breaking, Sigbjørn said to himself. I suppose I was going to say.

...Arcturion: Liverpool, Post Drill at 3 P.M. this afternoon. Passengers are requested to put on their lifebelts when the signal is given and stand to the positions assigned to them which they will find in their cabins...Boddy Finch Lifejacket.

—And before I forget it, here's the manuscript of my novel. I didn't know whether to burn it or to give it to you. There you are.

—Why thank you! Why that's like Hedda Gabler[169] all over again, too. But no, seriously, Barney, thank you.

Gymnasium.

Swimming Pool

No admission except on business.

Arcturion: Liverpool

Again they were feverishly pacing the length of the ship, in and out of doors, into the stewards' department, the third class, the steerage,[170] Nina carrying the manuscript under her arm and occasionally feigning interest: now they were going down below again, asbestos covered pipes and boilers everywhere; the stokehold ladder descended into a sea of heat, into his future, he thought; further along, the barber snipping, *no trust*; charity[171] begins at home and is kind...

From eternity to eternity—[172]

They leaned against iron bulwarks far down in the *Arcturion*. The sound of water pouring here was louder, the sounds of the vessel itself more urgent. It was as if in moving closer to the time they must part they had also moved closer to the heart of the dense complexity of the ship itself. From here, the cold waste of waters, so much nearer to their eyes, lost much of the lovely identity it had seemed by comparison, in spite of all, to hold from the upper decks; so much more desolate was it indeed that the sight of the cabins around them, already lit against the noonday, alone prevented Sigbjørn from breaking down; as in Nina's cabin, there was a glow around them, a warmth here, a hint of sanctuary. But below them still drifted sacking, half-melted panes of ice, flotsam of every kind. Nina leaned over as if to see something better; then she gave a cry.

—There, I thought so. It's that piece of timber of ours. It's still there!

Sigbjørn was standing on the steam-piping beside her and leaned over.

—Well, so it is.

—Yes. But do you see *what* it is?

Sigbjørn peered closer.

—No, I don't.

—Look again!

Sigbjørn stood on tiptoe beside Nina on the steam-piping, craning over.

—No, I don't see.

—Well, it's a wooden leg.

He burst out laughing, looking down.

—Well, my God, so it is! Who would have thought of that?

He looked again. Ridiculous. A wooden leg, there was no doubt about it. He was asleep, of course, this was a nightmare. He was asleep in prison: still, what a sinister coincidence! none-the-less sinister for being quite meaningless. Absurd! Goodbye, old masthead.[173] Keep a good eye on the whale while I'm gone. We'll talk tomorrow when the white whale lies down there, tied by head and tail.

—It's Captain Ahab's wooden leg, actually!

—Who was Captain Ahab? oh, I remember—well, but why Captain Ahab?

—Don't you see? He's given up the struggle. His soul's ship has sailed out on its last voyage. And only his wooden leg left, like Job,[174] to tell the tale. The whole business is already over. Coendet.[175] Fini. Ridiculous even to think of beginning again!

—What *are* you talking about? And what's all this stuff about *Goby* Dick[176] anyhow? And wasn't Melville a weak, contentious old man, who shouted because he was afraid of life, because he was just a che-ild at heart?

—Even so, if he lived today, he would be strong. And still some ships sail from their ports and ever afterwards are missing, Sigbjørn said.

—The *Arcturion* is, of course, queen of the fleet, Nina said.

In the distance they heard the ship's band strike up once more the Soldiers' Chorus from *Faust*.[177] A literature of war. It must be nearly time to leave. They leaned in silence, looking over towards Bidston Hill[178] where they had once made love, but which was now invisible. He recalled the strange duplicity of a favourite remark of hers: 'Isn't it fun just *lying* together?' There was silence for a moment and there seemed no reason why the ship didn't sail. Below them, a porthole was thrust open and a drunken voice said:

—The devil[179] knows so many people that the devil dances...And the voice added, with finality:

—In Sicily![180] And wears rubber pants and legs!

A peal of drunken laughter, like thunder, followed this; everybody in the vicinity was laughing uproariously.

—What did he say, Nina? Dances in Sicily?

—Oh he's just a drunk.

But the voice went on, still more drunkenly:

—Haven't a conscience, I'm an atheist, said the devil. Dead men tell no tales. Come here, steward. Do you think you could push a trunk through there?

—Sure, the steward could be heard replying, in a low but jocular tone. Sure, Davy Jones[181] would take care of it.

—But I haven't got a trunk big enough for the two of them.

The bugle blew sharply again. Last Post! Sigbjørn lit a cigarette. They started to walk again. Are we the mirror of universal law, he said to himself, laughing. Or is all our effort incommensurable with divine law?

Tourist passengers may not pass this barrier.

Down, down, further down, that which takes beneath the consciousness, murderous extremity of burying alive. They were in a low, cavernous, uncarpeted corridor upon which a few cabins abutted; a heavy smell of soup greeted them; and one of the portholes opening on the corridors framed in it the horse's grin of the man they had just heard speaking from above.

—Hello, hello, I give an interview to very few people said the devil, taking his hat off. I come from Barbary Coast,[182] said the devil, when it was *bare*. When it was *bare*, the man now shouted at them, for Nina and Sigbjørn had arrived opposite his cabin. *Bare*, he baa-ed.

A steward in black serge whispered:

—It's the manager of the Siamese twins on the shilankobozzle—[183]

—On the what, said Nina and Sigbjørn.

—On the shilankobozzle. One wants to go back to the States and the other to Bangkok.

—It's a pretty problem.

—Isn't it? Show-business or back to home and mother? Well, that's what comes of being joined together by *Merther* Nature.[184] Yes *sir*!

He moved away. Sigbjørn and Nina retraced their steps to the end of the corridor, paced back again. But the manager of the New Chang and Chen seemed to be waiting for them.

—The Barbary Coast is still bare, he stated, and turning away poured himself some whiskey. Got any Scotch?

A bottle fell with a thud. Laughter came from inside the cabin. They walked back to the door; paced up and down, quickly, against time. Outside a galley a clock ticked nervously on. A bugle sounded distantly, nostalgically.

Reveille!

The manager stumbled out of the cabin and followed them, taking Nina's arm.

—Got any Scotch? We don't say any more names, said the devil, he exclaimed. Or we might speak out of our turn...

He whinnied, his face like a horse's skull; clasping brass-bound bannisters, he followed them down a sour corridor, red-plushed—at sea a hill to climb—watchchains jangling on him like fetters.

—I've never been upstairs and downstairs as well as I had been. Can you eat gold? said the devil, the man asked. The exchange is silver, what are you going to do? said the devil. Eat, said the sympathetic gent, he added.

He rolled off towards the dining-room, but a waiter, with a firm forefinger, gently propelled him into the alleyway. He struggled against it, struggling to rejoin Nina and Sigbjørn.

—I name no names. Shame upon them, he babbled. I put my foot upon the tablet...The Ivory Coast,[185] when it was *bare*.

—Come on now, the Steward remonstrated with him. Come on, sir, come on...

—It surely must be Caesar Imperator himself, Sigbjørn whispered to Nina.

Last Post!

He shouted meaninglessly over his shoulder as he see-sawed along the corridor between two stewards; their hold loosening, he collapsed against the bulkhead.

—Yes, Imperator Capitalismus,[186] said Nina.

—It's too much for him anyhow, he's liquidated.

Reveille!

From the quartermaster's room another burst of conversation came like shrapnel shot. 'By crimes,[187] she's a coffin ship.' *Brynjaar*! 'It steers harder than the...' 'Last trip it was so ploody tough steering on the whateffer'...'Glycerine when the ploody wheel sticks.' 'And carrying a ploody cargo of barium peroxide on this ploody ship.' 'Sure, sweatrags and wool,' 'Carbolic acid and napthaline,' 'Acid and napthaline and fusel oil.'[188]

The gong crashed, releasing a torpedo of sound through the tube of the corridors and alleyways.

It was as though he had suddenly come across this maniac that called himself Sigbjørn raving on the top deck.

—Tor was right, he was shouting.

—I suppose you think he did it on account of *you*, Nina was saying passionately. I suppose you think it's very grand to go away and forget what *you've* done to him.

—Well, he didn't kill himself for you. He didn't give two hoots in hell for you, Nina.

—What do you know about him?

—I was his brother; and his best friend.

—What do you mean? He knew me much better than he knew anybody, much better than he knew you!

—That's all cruel nonsense! shouted Sigbjørn.

—I knew him better than you knew him.

—What do you mean? Do you mean you were his mistress?

—Yes! I was!

For a moment Sigbjørn was silenced; then he said quickly, but with venom:

—I see. I shared the same womb in more senses than one!

For a second or two they stared at each other with hatred, then Nina turned and ran down the alleyway.

Sigbjørn stood where he was for a moment, then he started to run after her just as he had done the night before. But he had lost sight of her.

—Oh, I'm sorry, sorry Nina, he muttered. For God's sake come back, I didn't mean...

But the bugle sounded the ultimate, the inescapable, notes.

Eurydice! Eurydice![189]

The siren roared, diapasoned:[190] *doom*. Pang, the Burmese dinner gong jangled, pang-pang-pang. Break! Break! 'All visitors get off the ship!' 'Are you a passenger? no, then off the ship!' 'Everybody off the ship.' 'Off the ship!' 'Ship.'

Come back, where are you? Where are you?

He thought he saw her and tried to make his way along through the push and press of the corridor but, ridiculously enough, he had to stand aside for the Siamese twins to pass. The ghost of schism,[191] of division, living dialectic of evil, passionless personification also of the incalculable, the absurd, the illogical, the synthetic, the superhuman, the sanctified—they drifted past him aft, luminously gliding against the grey darkness. Tardy reporters darting at either elbow. Twin faces expressionless, one turned towards Schenectady and the other towards Siam. At a distance, their resurrected manager, his blue overcoat powdered with snow, spun and reeled after them. The shark glides white through the phosphorus White Sea.[192]

—Hello, old fellow, the manager grabbed him, but Sigbjørn shook him off. He passed on.

Too late now, even too late to make a joke about forgetting her quadrant, her sea-sick pills, her gaff-topsail boots. Or even to make that one about the fustian[193]...he had been waiting for his opportunity to say it all morning, waiting for Nina's favourite remark: 'that's just your fustian,' as the band struggled with Gounod:[194] 'Never mind, it's just my fustian Faustian.'

Break!

There was a lull, then the deep, deafening, rhythmic sound of the engines vibrated through the vessel.

—All passengers off the ship, please. Are you a passenger? no? then off the ship, please.

He went to the gangway but the manager of the New Chang and Chen had followed him round.

—Hullo there...been looking for you all over. You hungry? said the devil, the manager said. Starving said the poor boy. Where do you live? said the devil. On a nice burg[195] said—

Sigbjørn shook him off and picked his way down the gangway.

—Well, if you must go, the manager shouted after him, goodbye, bon voyage.

No sooner was he down than the gangway swung in with a high clatter; above, the manager swayed at the gangway head in the arms of the second steward.

The *Arcturion* was moving slowly away from the wharf. Moored to the side, forward of her, so far below her that he had not noticed from the deck, was the *Direction*, and as the *Arcturion* drew level with her, she started to strain on her ropes. Crack, crack; suddenly, like snapped elastic, the rope flew up into the crowd. As if drawn by some magnetic force, the *Direction* slipped sideways towards the *Arcturion*. A collision seemed certain.

—Let go, for God's sake, didn't you hear me?

—Let go! let go! let go!

On the wharf, Sigbjørn started forward. Streamers were being thrown half-heartedly, almost ironically, through the snow. Draped in streamers, the manager of the New Chang and Chen waved to Sigbjørn. Nina was nowhere to be seen. Collision mats[196] were hurriedly lowered on both the *Arcturion* and the *Direction*.

But on the wharf men had ceased to wave; they ran about in confusion.

The *Arcturion* no longer had way on her, but the suction she was causing stopped and a tug came alongside the *Direction* and nosed her to the berth.

Now the *Arcturion* proceeded dead-slow: white birds, sea-voyaging, gleamed after her: there was a foreboding in their cry as if they already hovered over a shipwreck. Now she seemed to be gone—

The clock on the Liver Building started to strike twelve. Sigbjørn stood on the wharf, where there was still confusion. Arms that would have waved were dropped to the side in desperation. There was a hopeless commingling of emotion, for at the shadow of distress all had started involuntarily forward to help their loved ones. Now all were left with a stoop in their souls.

Farewell, farewell country of counterfeit architecture[197]....Farewell!

Suddenly, in a frenzy, Sigbjørn started to run after the ship.

Doom.[198] The last stroke of twelve from the Liver Building merged in the melancholy wailing of the wind that seemed now to be blowing up the essences of those lovers parted forever by the terrible ocean, of all who were parted, who eternally embraced and turned to one another again on this eternal wharf. The smoke drifted away down the gusts mingling with the turmoil of the snowflakes, wavering as love itself wavers between love and hatred for the ocean, that gives him his livelihood, that gives him his death.

The snowflakes fluttered like a thousand torn-up manuscripts thrown from the windows of the past. The *Arcturion* had gone.

Sigbjørn stopped, exhausted, a vacancy in his heart where the ship had been, a vacancy that deepened swiftly to an infinite void, an abyss of ignorance in which the cradle-song and threnody of the sea,[199] the sense of division and dissolution around him: everything he knew or had known were engulfed; even that pervading feeling of the immedicable horror of opposites[200] disappeared; no love, no more sense of loss, no hate could live in that blackness.

Then he saw that the ship's disappearance had been an illusion; the mists had lifted for a moment and she was there again, trembling in every mast,[201] all her lights burning, and quite close to the wharf, so close indeed that at first he thought he could read her name; he walked a step or two forward, 'A,' 'N': he could read the first and last letters; and then as if by some cinematic device, the screen of his vision had suddenly broadened, adding to it another dimension: he saw the name—or it seemed to be the name—quite close at hand: not *Arcturion* but *Adam Cadmon.*[202]

Adam Cadmon? Absurd, surely there was some mistake, and now as the *Arcturion* drew away once more so that he could no longer see any name, he knew it only to have been a trick played by the misty day. But the name persisted in his mind. Why Adam Cadmon?

Then he remembered. It was the ancient name for man he had learnt at school and which now returned as a memory strong enough momentarily to distort his vision.

Well, let the ship be man then, he thought dully, a liner in which there were many transients, each directed to his own destination...a separate unit in the complement, yet to himself the centre of the steamer...her heart; but this composite liner of which they were a part did not know her own goal even if fools called it New York or Belfast.

The *Arcturion* plunged into the terrible whiteness like the grey sleeping mass of the psyche in the midst of which its factions slowly and mechanically prowled, each inevitably lighting up around itself its small special porthole, enclosing also for each its molecular disaster, or fulfillment, or change; it was those terrible eyes, of which two had been most dear to him, that now burst through the murk, growing dimmer and dimmer until they disappeared.

And long after the ship had severed herself from the wharf's grey womb,[203] Sigbjørn stood there, seeking her, watching from that shore where the soul breaks in anguish with the sea.[204]

VIII

> The illogical surd, the incalculable element, the residual difference between the momentous transition and the inadequate cause.
>
> E.T. BROWN[1]

From the sandy road as they passed the iron bridge[2] with its rusted builder's plate "Cheshire Lines, 1840" they could see the low mist scurrying over the finger-high grass between the deserted fairways of the first and ninth holes.[3] Captain Hansen-Tarnmoor held out his hand, upturned to the moisture.

—A sea day...

—We could make a go of it. What do you think?

From the horrible to the commonplace is but a step,[4] Sigbjørn thought. They opened the door into the club-house;[5] the club-room was empty. It smelt sweet and clean, the hearth was blazing, richly welcoming them. The Captain now stood with his back to it, stretching the wet palms of his hands behind him to the fire.

—I haven't been here for ages, he said.

Sigbjørn was looking around him at the trophies, the enlarged photographs of members putting, at the piled back numbers of *The Golfer*.[6]

—I expect they've got your handicap up, he said, and walked over to the board. They certainly have: to fifteen. They forget that day you won the monthly medal.[7]

—Yes, they forget soon.

—Ten years is a long time, Sigbjørn said. They've put mine up to twenty.

—Ten years, is it as long as that?

—Ten? It must be sixteen since you played with me: it's about ten since I last played. It was the first year we came from Norway, when I was seven. You used to give me three strokes[8] a hole...Hullo, Macleoran.[9]

The professional and caretaker was standing at the doorway of the bar which he was on the point of opening. A smile of recognition seemed to flicker for a moment on his face, disappeared, flickered again, went: then his suspicion became wholly enlightened.

—I'm very pleased to see you again, he said with nervous pleasure. He shook hands with both of them but his expression soon changed to one of inarticulate suffering, as if between them all moved some horror, as indeed was the case, one too fearful to express. Then the mask of the world settled on all three of them.

—It's the way it is, you haven't paid us a visit for a long time, he said finally.

—Have things much changed?

—They're making us eighteen holes,[10] he said. Otherwise, not much. It's the way it is, there's a tee in the wood now and you drive back across the pond over the third green; and the fifth[11] is a dog-legged hole, like the first at the Royal Liverpool,[12] instead of being a straight run.

—That's bad, Sigbjørn said.

—No. It's the way it is, a great improvement, Macleoran said, lifting his eyebrows. And when we're the eighteen hole course...

—You'll rival Hoylake, eh? said the Captain. Well! It's extraordinary to think of all these changes going on under our noses, and ourselves involved, and not noticing them.

—You better get us a drink,[13] Macleoran, Sigbjørn said. And one for yourself...Very well, three Irish. Extraordinary, he added to himself, is this possible? Are we such callous people—and surely we are not—that we can still talk like this?...

—I suppose you've read about it all, the Captain said.

Macleoran, his back to them in the bar, nodded but said nothing.

—It's lucky it's a weekday. There never used to be anybody here on winter afternoons: we took a chance on it. The Captain cleared his throat. My boy's going away tomorrow.

Macleoran nodded again as he brought the drinks towards them, but it seemed to Sigbjørn that when he drank, he did so with reluctance. To say the least of it, he immediately qualified this surmise as he himself drank.

—Your clubs will need cleaning, sir? was all he asked.

—No, you better leave them. Bring me a few golfballs[14] though. Better give us half a dozen Dunlop 30, or have you any good repaints?

—We don't have Dunlop 30 anymore, or balls like that.

—I suppose the Chemico Bob has died out too, Sigbjørn said.

—And the Zodiac Zone?

—That's gone, too.

—All right, I'll go and see for myself, the Captain said.

He went out with Macleoran into the room beyond.

Sigbjørn peered through the window at the desolate course. A hell of a day!... Soon all this would seem meaningless to him and he would see this encounter with Macleoran, this forthcoming game if it were played—which absurdly put him in mind of Drake in Plymouth[15] at bowls before the Armada—through a mist,[16] yes, a mist as dense in the mind as that through which he now saw, actually, the ninth green with its drooping flag and pools of casual water; only with the difference, the remarkable difference, that he would be standing, not in a mere club-house, but on an iron well-deck,[17] or in a coal-bunker rather than in a sand-bunker. Why did they choose to play at all? he asked himself. Neither callousness nor a selfish neglect of problems around them, left carelessly unsolved, he flattered himself, seemed properly to account for their presence at the club-house: perhaps it had arisen from the complex desire of the father to be as near as possible to the son he might never see again, however much that son had added to his other liabilities!

With some difficulty Sigbjørn located his locker, which opened stiffly: on top of it were two balls rotted away with the damp down to the elastic core, giving them the appearance of onions, from which layer after layer had been stripped, revealing at length the innermost bulb.[18] Zodiac Zones. Examining his clubs[19] he saw that with the exception of a strong-shafted niblick, and although rusted, they were otherwise the same as when he had laid them aside ten years before. He withdrew and grounded a mashie-iron on the locker-room floor. Uncle Bjorg's cast-offs serving him when he had outgrown his first clubs. Strange to think how large they had seemed, one reason for his loss of interest, and that only now when they were warped and rusted had he grown up to them. He tried them one after one. Clock, spoon, Braid-Mills putter, jigger. All these clubs out of date now; clock, who had ever heard of a clock? Still they could be played with. It was good to hold them again. He replaced them in the bag and at the same time noticed that his father's clubs had fared not much better. But doubtless they also could still be used...He looked round at the iron-barred lockers; ten years, he thought, prison! But the sound of his father's footsteps dispelled a growing illusion, or was it a growing sense of reality?

—It's the same for both of us, the Captain said, entering with the repaints. Let's make up our minds. Shall we make a go of it—or not?

—I say, yes.

—Come on, then.

As they went out they saw Macleoran standing behind the bar, absolutely motionless; his ear was applied to the door and he seemed by his posture to be wishing to give the impression that he listened for something, although the room beyond was perfectly empty; and as his father swung, re-teed,[20] and finally drove a somewhat sliced, topped[21] shot that echoed dully from the bridge, a tentative reason for this occurred to Sigbjørn: Macleoran could not bring himself to watch the two old members set off without giving some sign which he did not want to have mistaken for a sign of sympathy; although this was not because he felt no sympathy or because he was not a sympathetic man; it was simply that the Captain and his son, by virtue of the disasters which had happened and continued happening to them, had grown akin to monsters whose very touch was chaos; and this was why Maclorean, their old friend, was standing with his back half turned and with his ear at the door of an untenanted room, as Voltaire might have imagined Pangloss[22] listening for the eternal harmony.

The mist was clearing as they walked up the first fairway, but the sky was overcast and windy. Dark clouds were blowing up from the sea, from the Point of Ayr:[23] beyond, on the other side of the river in Flintshire, the Welsh mountains loomed leaden-grey: but the Mostyn[24] furnaces were lashing vermillion against the angry sky, as though something, or the shadow of something, were there, gesticulating in the furnace light. From the Irish Channel,[25] sirens called.

The tide was going out, leaving the sands[26] strangely printed, the channel sunk in the centre flowed fully, and fishing boats were slanting outward, always outward, from Neston[27] and Parkgate. With a whip of rain coming as Sigbjørn played his second shot, he could almost feel it hurling into the eyes of fishermen at their tillers.

The snow had been largely swept from the course but still lay between fairways or piled thickly in bunkers, in brilliant oases of white.

The men did not meet until they reached the green; the hole, which had been badly played by both, being halved, Sigbjørn picked out from the water-filled cup; the smell of the shining repaints with their meshed diamond tracery distilled a memory of Norway.[28]

They walked slowly to the second tee,[29] turning once again to look at the mountains and the ocean and moving clouds. There was a salt tang in the air: in spite of all, a cleanness that made it good to be alive.

—Do you remember the old days, with Tor?

—On Saturday afternoons three-ball matches,[30] dodging balls all the time? It's strange to think of playing without him.

—Three. There's always three, it seems.

—He's happy now, at any rate.

—Do you think he is?

—But where has he gone?

Where, indeed, had he gone? The wind shirred[31] over the course, through the reeds, chased over the pools, the ponds and grasses and natural hazards[32] and patches of snow; it was like a care that passed, frowning the face of the waters.[33] Trailing a solitary snow-backed carriage, an old engine, with her fireman standing wide-legged on the tender, meandered along a single line[34] edging the course, towards Thurstaston.[35] And to Sigbjørn Tor's presence really seemed to be, in these minutes, in the smoke blowing flustered and chaotic; a suggestion of him lurking as well in the winds borne from the sea; in these sands and humming grasses; in the echo of wheels ringing against the iron, and the evanescence of the steam.

—After fifteen years I still socket,[36] said the Captain who had driven with a mid-iron.[37]

This time their drives were lying together on the fairway; the Captain sliced his second into the wood and a minute later the two of them were hacking among the tough grasses and hunks of snow. High above them the dripping plumes of the trees, whose trunks groaned, tossed and circled. Sheep[38] stumbled away from the men, flashing and scattering snow as they approached, to a further shelter near a pond, where they huddled together, nuzzling one another for comfort. The men looked for the balls.

—I know you were thinking of Tor, the Captain said. But how dare I think even of my own men when hundreds of innocent men and women have been drowned? The thought rises up to jeer and mow at me in everything I do. You know—and he hacked at a groundsel—that any rational philosophy or at any rate a philosophy that you have been taught to consider rational, would certainly exclude the idea of punishment. And yet that's just what seems to be happening to me. The cause is beyond us all.

He hacked.

—People say that I am a murderer, but that's not what I believe I am. I'm a tool. Of course, whenever there's disaster, a man must be the scapegoat. They say there weren't enough boats, that the passengers were not given boat-drill, that the officers were insufficiently trained...They say jobs were given to men on the cheap, without their having proper discharges.[39] Well, if it's so, I didn't know it. The privity[40] of the master is not always the privity of the owner, even when it is so deemed. He exploded a shell of snow with his niblick.

Sigbjørn said nothing. But after a while he began:

—The fault is the system.

But Captain Tarnmoor interposed:

—We'll give this up. It's your hole.

They walked to the next tee[41] and drove off.

—Now what were you going to say?

Sigbjørn was following the trajectory of his ball with his eye: a good shot, taking it all in all.[42]

He picked up his bag and also his father's, carrying one over each shoulder as the men drifted past the bunker guarding the pretty.[43] It was as though he already made excuse by this action for what he was about to say.

—I was going to add that the same or similar thing happened in that Norwegian novel I was telling you about: *Skibets reise fra Kristiania*.[44] The ship on which the principal character is working goes to the rescue of a ship afire, one of a line to which disasters are happening. The rescuing ship sends double watches down below and all personal grievances and griefs are lost in the solidarity of the firemen, and the seamen who 'mutually assist'[45] them, as they raise as much steam as possible; the troubles and fears of the principal character disappear in the common purpose of the unit.

—That sounds like the plots of almost any book. But nothing like that happened to you anyway, did it?

—Listen, the point is, this character, this Benjamin's troubles might have been my own. I might have been that man. I saw him dream and work and suffer. The feeling was as intense as if I were watching a moving picture of myself; I was completely identified with him; I *was*—him.

—What was the name of the ship?

—The *Henrik Ibsen*.[46]

—Never heard of it. Well?

—Well then. All this of course tallied with the foolish, narcissistic projection of myself I had given in *my* book. Only this was much better done, even that part of it. The difference in the two books was that whereas mine was entirely preoccupied with

—You better play your shot.

Sigbjørn played and watched the ball disappear over a bunker. His father played an iron, then turned to him. Sigbjørn shouldered their bags again.

—Preoccupied with the personal destiny of the hero and ended with some attitude or gesture meant to emphasize his individual importance; in this other book the importance of Benjamin disappeared with his gesture of merging himself with the powerful solidarity of the workers, fighting for something they believed in, yet going to the rescue of the burning ship—

He thrust his thumb in the strap of the golf-bag at his shoulder.

—Representing undoubtedly, the Captain said, the capitalist system.

—They only went to the rescue of *life*.

—Well, said the Captain, I see it all clearly. To make it complete you have to have the burning the work of reds, red sabotage!

—That's absurd. Besides, it wasn't.

—And as for the capitalist system, even though there may be some grounds for thinking it unsatisfactory, it seems to me that you yourself have benefitted very clearly from it. Why not substitute the world?

—Because there's nothing wrong with the world, Sigbjørn said. Or is there? All I've been trying to say to you anyway is what I said to Nina: I'd die for communism but I haven't the impudence to call myself a communist. Another thing, I don't suppose they'd have me.

—When you have such queer experiences I can quite understand your dying for anything. You can't reconcile them with the Godhead, said the Captain. Under such a circumstance, it is, to say the least of it, opportune to find something to die for.

—Well, here we are, surrounded by a strange fatality, and among other things being driven into another war[47]...Can't you see that the system is rotten right through?

The Captain played his third.

—What system?

—The capitalist system.

—I can see that I am driving into the wood, the Captain said, watching his ball disappear over a shelter. Ah no, saved.

—It's not a matter for jokes.

Again they were shoulder to shoulder, the Captain carrying his own bag once more.

—It's desperate; call it opportune, but it still remains desperate; here you are, you've lost a son, you're losing your ships, your—our—whole life is disintegrating all around us into mania, the very elements[48] with hostile slidings and collidings of matter are fighting against us; the whole business is like a psychotic nightmare! and not content with this, I repeat that we're being driven into another war.

—Who is? The Captain stopped.

—You are...And I am, without knowing it.

—Oh, the Captain said slowly. I'm driving you into another war now, am I?

—Well, maybe if you lose another...thing, you'll be satisfied. Good God, making a decision to get away from it all is at least as easy as stepping off one of your ships...Sorry.

—That's all rot anyhow, if you'll excuse me, the Captain said. We're not just a firm of Girdlestone.[49] That's all nonsense. These things are just manifestations of the senseless force[50] in the world, blind, malicious, destructive, operating with the senseless fixative persistence of an infant or a lunatic.

Infant or a lunatic! Or the mad fishmonger of Worcester...Those periwinkles[51] were just a racket!

The Captain without addressing[52] played a perfect approach shot that landed on a patch of dry grass ninety yards away and ran up to within a few feet of the pin; the white repaint resting there glittered like a tiny ball of snow on the emerald green, twinkling.

—Another thing, my boy, he said, pleased. One is apt to draw these conclusions simply from the public responsibility, or rather the responsibility as it appears to the public. Disasters like these create liabilities which are practically unendurable but it is not possible to base moral conclusions upon these liabilities; of course people do, lazily assuming the final in the oblique and it is this that makes almost everything we know as human justice so ultimately unsatisfactory. If it comes to that, the British law is the most onerous of all maritime laws limiting liability, but then we are of course not entirely concerned with the British law.[53]

Sigbjørn's chip-shot rose far into the black sky, was suspended there for a moment, a white whirling world, a ping-pong ball in interstellar space, and then fell between the Captain's and the flag; it rested where it fell in its own self-made matrix.[54]

—Stymie,[55] said the Captain. Or not quite. I think I can negotiate it with a putter.

But his putt ran past the hole, and by a fault in the ground was even deterred wide of it as Sigbjørn expectantly raised the pin.

—I walk unseen,[56] the Captain said bitterly, on the dark, unshaven green.

Later they walked on down the hard fairway of the fourth[57] in silence; Sigbjørn was two up; there was ice in the footprints and a drift of white in the gulley.

—But as Candide said, let us cultivate our garden...[58]

—Is that answer so final, Sigbjørn said, taking a divot,[59] and did Candide say anything about replacing the turf?

At the next hole, the fifth,[60] the new hole Macleoran had cautioned, Sigbjørn drove with a strong slice, carrying the pond, but his father, who had expected to go out of bounds on the other side, strongly pulled his drive so that the ball dropped over the railings into the deep wet grass of the embankment where it disappeared. Having found his, Sigbjørn left his bag alongside it and taking an old niblick walked across the course to help his father; climbing over the rail, he dropped into the tall grass. They hacked down among the roots of the groundsel and the big unflowered marguerites[61]...down here where God is, where it is hot and dark. Below them, a goods train passed; fifty-six trucks of asphaltic slag[62]—Sigbjørn counted them—for Llay Main;[63] and the climbing of the trucks made a sad song in the air, a melancholy incantation: *Llay Main, Llay Main, Llay Main.* It was a name that suggested unutterable lostness, loneliness, desolation—or loose gear clanging somewhere on a freighter at night as an exhausted man lay in his bunk. Where was Llay Main? The train had disappeared northwards. A black bird—a Brueghel bird,[64] his father said, lifting his head at that moment—flew swiftly after it, over the humming wastes, north.

—Where is Preston?[65] Sigbjørn asked.

—I'm surprised you don't know if you're taking a ship from there. It's on the confluence of the road to the North between Manchester and Liverpool.

Surprised you don't know, his father repeated, producing his pipe, but I suppose you signed on at the Norsk Konsulat[66] in Liverpool.

—The road to the North!

—We'll give it up, his father said.

They climbed over the fence. Again they were walking side by side, through wet, frosted knee-high grass. The Captain smoked his pipe.

—I may be ruined, imprisoned. God knows what will happen. If you want to prove that I'm doomed, don't trouble to. I know that, boy. Duns, lawyers, the underwriters, the police—have you ever feared the police?—of course, I know you have...around me all day. We're probably being watched at this moment.[67] Well, they bring it home to me, old chap. Even when I write, it's as though a devil perched on my pen. But my own fate is immaterial,[68] we can leave that out, damnation holds no terrors for me. But the future, insofar as it concerns yourself, is of more importance...Here's your ball. I should play a full mashie[69] right up into the wind. You might as well play, even if I'm a non-combatant.

Sigbjørn was addressing the ball.

—Keep a stiff left arm. Take some turf. Aim at those men over there, banking the turf[70] for the new nine holes. The wind'll take it round...

But after a topped, low, indeterminate shot, the ball only fell in the mud on the edge of the wood. A niblick shifted it about a foot; now it was deeply buried in the mud and melting ice; another divot of mud and grass, and the ball was even more firmly embedded. The Captain was quietly laughing. Then the ball disappeared altogether, and giving up yet another repaint as lost they went to the sixth tee.[71]

But unfortunately, the Captain, who had upturned his bag and was shaking it vigorously, was saying:

—We haven't any more.

But at last a first, then a second ball did fall out.

—Gutties,[72] the Captain exclaimed. Oh, the imperishable gutty.

—What are gutties? asked Sigbjørn. They look like Silver Kings.[73]

—Gutta-percha balls. Twenty years old, the Captain said triumphantly. Harry Vardon[74] used to win the Open Championship at Hoylake with them...He teed one.

—You try.

Sigbjørn drove one of the balls about a hundred yards along the ground.

—It's like wood, he said.

The Captain's drive followed, a hard sharp crack against the imperishable gutta-percha, producing a similar effect.

—Another daisy cutter,[75] the Captain said. We serve the obsolete.[76]

But beyond the pot-bunker[77] guarding the green, their approaches soared up high against the wind, and rabbits scuttled away from them among the hummocks.

—Tor freed a rabbit[78] from a snare here, Sigbjørn said. We used to go round with niblicks letting them out.

—Somebody must be dormie,[79] the Captain said. Is it you, Barney?

At the seventh tee[80] the Captain offered:

—You must drive to the left, else the wind will carry you into the wood.

Sigbjørn drove to the left, to the west, towards the Irish Sea, but a powerful gust coming seemed to gather up the ball, which had been driven the wrong side of the wind, and hurl it from sight over the cliff;[81] the Captain played with the same result. At the edge of the cliff they looked down at the estuary. A big wind was blowing it up; although the tide was low, the wind stooped and whipped at the sea so that it raged in the shallows; far out in the Irish Channel a freighter was rolling, and its smoke drifted over the cold moorland of the county. They gazed down on the shore where close against the cliff was huddled the crumbling ruin of a Roman turret.[82]

—Childe Roland to the dark tower came.[83]

Jesus, and it was so dark, too, and wasn't the damned thing built of ivory, Sigbjørn thought maliciously.

Or Roland Childe.[84] Do you remember the lines? 'The moving pageants of the waning day; Heavy with dreams, desires, prognostications, Brooding with solemn and Titanic crests, They surge, whose mantles' wise imaginations Trail where Earth's mute and languorous body rests.'

—I used to lie here in summer, Sigbjørn said, listening to the wind, looking out to sea, years and years and years ago.

—You thought too much. Do you know, I brought you and Tor here when you were kids the first year after we left Norway. I brought you here to see the *Lusitania*[85] go out, on her last outward voyage. We looked at her through a telescope.

Sigbjørn squinted one eye through a circle of his thumb and forefinger:

—I can imagine it now.

And in Sigbjørn's imagination, the plunging freighter[86] was suddenly close to his eyes, the vague outline of well-deck and hatch rising to the bridge was photographically distinct; a group of seamen talking on the foredeck as instantly plain as if they were only fifty feet away also appeared; the quartermaster[87] stolidly gripping the wheel who turned aside to strike eight bells, then gripped it again, for it was four o'clock; and a trimmer who at that moment clattered down to number one hatch, bucket on his elbow, going off watch to the firemen's forecastle; and the log-wheel[88] at the stern which endlessly spun...Yes, it was as if he were already aboard the *Unsgaard* from whose deck he now imagined himself seeing not Wales but Norway: here he was, already in his new life, peering at Norway or Russia, counting the waves.

—Wasn't it the *Lusitania*'s last voyage out of Liverpool? he asked.

—It was. I just said so.

—I didn't hear you...And now they've salvaged her.[89]

Exhumed, under swinging hurricane lamps, they disinterred Tor's body; pressing the lids back they found only holes; no minute lens[90] on which was photographed the victim's murderer. The twelve bones[91] rolled back in the grave. But keep the wolf far from thence or with his nails he'll dig them up again.[92]

—Is it true what they say, that they've salvaged her?

For an instant the men looked at each other in silence, then they both laughed, wildly and hysterically, grasping one another for support. They looked out over the darkening world, almost, it seemed to Sigbjørn, they looked through the world into the chaos of wind and rain and murk flowing ceaselessly out of the southwest: the clouds rolling up were an Armada,[93] he thought again, a vanquished Armada of cloud blown over from the great mountain chain of Wales on the other side of the Dee, Pen-y-Pass, Penmaenmawr, Snowdon, Cader-Idris;[94] and now from its base in the heart Norway rose once more, black, all-enveloping, infinite, and it seemed to Sigbjørn as the day ended that they stood on the brink of the midnight of the world, a world that would never again leave a message under the stone for the pilgrim, and it was as if the chaos which man had brought to man by his greed and deceit and betrayal of his own birthright was mirrored in the swiftly drifting, tattered wreckage above them.

—See Hilbre Island[95] over there, the Captain said, pointing out towards the Irish Sea. That's where Lycidas was drowned.

—Once more ye laurels and once more...

—Rich happiness that such a son is drowned.[96]

There was a sudden hush in the wind as though the world had caught its breath: and for a moment this lull, as in a tropical dawn, when the day workers troop from the fo'castle for the bosun's orders, held spellbound the two men; the change of the tide—

Then they started to climb down the cliff. At the start, sand whipped up in their faces. Further down, below where the sand martins[97] nested in summer, there was thick clay and the shelter of the crag. They climbed slowly down. Now there were only a dozen feet to go; that could be done in a moment.

The Captain stumbled down first, his shoes laden with dirt, onto the shore.

Sigbjørn ran after him.

A seething coursed like electricity along the shore's rim. Further down, the palpitant sand rustled as the two men trudged forward among shells and driftwood where no found ball shone for them like a nugget.

Over in Flint against the Welsh mountains the Mostyn furnaces[98] lashed red against the blackness.

Near them moved the dark face of the ocean, tragic and haggard.

IX

> To one who has lived long, there is not one spot of ground, overgrown with grass and weeds that is not equally sad. For this sadness is in us, in a memory of other days which follows us into all places. But for the child there is no past: he is born into the world light-hearted like a bird; for him, gladness is everywhere.
>
> W.H. HUDSON[1]

—The great thing in life, said the Captain, is not to do what we have just, in miniature, absurdly done.

—What's that?

—Give up, turn back, abandon...

—That sounds sententious; and I seem to have heard these sentiments before.[2]

—Where?

—Oh, from the Boy's Brigade.[3] Or from my own conscience. Or somewhere... Perhaps it was the Salvation Army.[4]

—Well, it's truer than even they may think. As a matter of fact, it's the whole point, and what I must again and again emphasize as your father before you go... now that your departure is inevitable.

—I don't altogether get it. Supposing you were on the wrong road, for instance if you were starting a war, surely it would be a good thing to turn back.

—That's just a perverted form of the same truth. And its perversion, for that matter, is in the commonest usage in life, in business, in the church, and elsewhere...But let that pass. In some form or another it always holds good. But how many people are going the right way is quite a different kettle of fish.

—Well, who can say what that is?

—Never mind. I said *if* you were going the right way, go on. For if you turn back you *loose*[5] something terrible, something which no one may arrest...By the by, what's the first image that strikes you?

—The first image? Of what? Oh, I see...Of what's unloosed. Well...Let me see...A derrick crazily adrift[6] in a hurricane when it's impossible to check the topping-lift,[7] perhaps somebody's up there jammed against the crosstrees trying, but it's futile; and nobody seems able to prevent the derrick's furious battering against the hatches...how's that?

—Exactly. You loose on a world into which at any moment the sea will come flooding the now-unleashed undirected strength and impulse of your first breaking away.

—I don't altogether...

—Do you think it sounds romantic? You want an enemy that you can see. Not something you just call destiny?

—Call what destiny?

—What I say means more than it appears to mean.

—I wish you'd be more concrete.

For some time the men walked on in silence.

—I can't explain. Once I tried to, and to the wrong people, and it turned out a fraud, and I'm afraid it might turn out a fraud again. Only I do seem to see hope for you. And like a man who is captured and can free himself only by answering his captor's riddle, so am I, even without your knowing it, held captive by you.

—But I asked you no riddle.

—One has to be solved just the same.

Sigbjørn lit his pipe and the ash blew over his shoulder. Around them the wind howled with a dark melancholy wailing. On the rim of the cliff he could see the silhouettes of the turf-cutters[8] going home, marching together: men marching against the sky, moving in the chaotic dark of a new creation.

—Yes, Barney, it's just like the riddle of the sphinx,[9] in the end you'd kill your father and marry your mother, the sea...Ah well. But there are some antagonists, unlike the sea against the earth, which are invisible.

—And it's that you say I think is romantic? I'm puzzled.

—I didn't say it was. I asked you.

—If I could believe it was romantic, impossible, I'd go to sea or something, throw in my lot with the workers of the world, with the future—tomorrow.

—But you are going to sea tomorrow his father said gently and took his arm. That's precisely what you are going to do.

Sigbjørn laughed.

—Yes. I'd forgotten.

—We were forgetting a lot. But why should that knowledge encourage or hinder you?

Sigbjørn made no answer, not knowing what he meant.

They walked on, kicking the pebbles, and again the hideous reality of the situation thrust itself between them; in affection, he now took his father's arm, trying to close it out, but soon sorrow, as inevitably as the following shadow of the night, had fallen on them; now, as they walked, its darkness of anguish moved slowly with them; when they spoke it was as though they did so through a pall. They were like two patients in a hospital, neither knowing which of them would survive but having for each other the extraordinary consideration[10] that only the sick can have for another in torment when the infirmity of jocularity of the one is at once a dismissal of his own pain, and a recognition of the other's greater need. But a rising wind making it increasingly difficult to hear or to be heard, they became at length silent. To avoid the dark skeleton[11] of a wreck, they moved closer to the incoming tide; further out, in the shallows, they could see, stooped in the last vermillion glare, the cockle fishers.[12] Once more they were walking in the teeth of the wind.

—Newton played on the seashore, the Captain said suddenly, now and then finding a smoother pebble—he kicked one—or a prettier shell than ordinary.[13]

Sigbjørn, catching this remark on a gust, said:

—Or sometimes treasure.

—Sometimes treasure, but the ocean of truth lay undiscovered before him. Well, may God keep us from single vision and Newton's sleep!

Sigbjørn made some reply but the wind whipped his words away. The tide was closing in swiftly on them so that now there remained, as the cliff's jagged circumference[14] jutted out to touch the arched plenitude of the beach, only a narrow tangent on which to walk; beyond, the sea, bottomless abyss of metaphysics, dark ocean[15] without shores or lighthouse and strewn with many a philosophic wreck!

—Kant, he was beginning, in Kant's...

—What did you say about Cambridge? his father shouted.

—Cambridge?

—Didn't you say Cambridge? I can't hear...

—I didn't, Sigbjørn shouted. I was going to say...but never mind. Yet since you suggest it I'll say that at Cambridge we were like we are now. Like men walking in a gale, and not being able to hear fully, or to understand ourselves, completely, either what we said or what we were being told about ourselves.

—What? The father cupped his hands: What did you say?

—I said I couldn't make use of Cambridge, neither of us could. Besides, we hadn't the teachers, Sigbjørn shouted. And nobody seemed to have the time! It was an opportunity—I suppose it was an opportunity—but one thrown away. Not absolutely our fault! Or we were like men knowing nothing, walking along a street and hearing as we walked along, from the wireless, disconnected scraps of knowledge...

—What? Walking along a heath did you say, a desolate heath?[16]

—Or like men walking along the shore, as we are now, along the fringe of knowledge. Occasionally, from the absolute, scraps of the spume of reality flung in our faces. Our discoveries, fireman's boots, old messkits thrown overboard by stewards...

The tide flung restlessly onto the beach, sucking its breath over stones and shells that carried in their drums, muted, the recorded Atlantic. Father and son were now driven closer and closer to the cliff wall. Now the gunshot of the sea boomed and spattered against this. They were silent again as they climbed slowly up the cliff path at the west of the last green; they felt their way over the rough; the Captain stumbled, with an exclamation, over the pin flattened by the wind; now they crossed once more the mound of the first tee, unlatched the meshed wire gate opening on the putting green,[17] and crunched over the gravel path towards the club-house. In the members' room a single electric globe was burning. A policeman[18] vanished suddenly round the angle of Macleoran's shed. But Macleoran was nowhere to be seen. The clubhouse door was locked and the wind moaned around it, blowing up a surf of rubble and straw. Here, shut out from the tempest, they might, as they had half intended, have been cabined for the night, taking the first train in the morning from the nearby station[19] for Birkenhead[20] where Sigbjørn's seabag had been stored. But the sight of the policeman suggested to them both the advisability of the alternative of returning home.

—We spent too much time looking for balls, Sigbjørn said.

But his father was saying:

—Who is the more conceited? The man who thinks he has an answer to everything or the man who refuses to believe such an answer may exist?

—Perhaps neither of them could be called philosophers.

'*Members only. Trespassers will be prosecuted with the utmost rigour of the law.*' The gate swung to behind them.

Once more they had passed under the old iron bridge[21]—1840—and once beyond the tarred declivity leading down from the tiny station they were soon in Fleet Lane,[22] trudging deeply in the sand. They turned up Kings' Drive, rounding the hairpin bend Tor had called Cape Horn, where both had agreed so often, laughingly: 'There's a Cape Horn in every life.' At the crest of the drive a sweep of the road led between parchment-coloured birches and sweet-smelling heather towards Grange, but a mile before it should have joined the main road to Chester and the North it stopped abruptly and thenceforward a path was the safest course for some way beside the ruin of the abandoned road,[23] then almost losing itself in moorland shrubbery; and it was along the abandoned cutting that the two men now made their way.

Blocks of red sandstone[24] rose in the path. Once Sigbjørn stumbled against a notice along which the Captain focussed a torch: again: '*Trespassers will be prosecuted with the utmost rigour of the law.*' The trees stirred blackly beside them on either side and the wind moaned as if in the struts of a bomber; wasn't it here somewhere, on one of these trees, Nina and he had carved their names?

The Captain's light revealed from time to time overturned trucks, heavy flanged wheels, long detached, blackened and rusted; piles of jagged stone once assembled for the building and now overgrown with moss. Rusted iron lines leading nowhere, uprooted sleepers, a donkey-engine[25] lying on its side. A rabbit paused, considered, vanished. In the far distance the lights of Liverpool[26] could be seen; and small red and green lamps floating down the Irish Channel—ships voyaging out—ships returning. A lighthouse flashed. Cars purred up Thurstaston Hill, brilliant wings swept the fields. Under the powerful gaze of electricity a gate grew high and vanished, and in every one of these distant lights, and nearer in the warmth of the lights of homes, there seemed a possible sanctuary from the hopelessness of the way they had chosen. The Captain shouted again:

—What do you think of this, Barney? Here's purpose abandoned. Do you look at it that way? An absolute abandonment. Do you see it like that?

Now they were walking on the path.

—I see that the true road[27] has not been trodden on for so long it is difficult to find. The way is so dreadfully vast!

—But those who really turn back are doomed, are lost. More lost even than the foolish virgins, those who set out unprepared. Are you prepared?

Sigbjørn could not hear and said nothing. And here was the tree, what sort of tree he didn't know—he didn't know any of the names of trees, to him just further proof of his ignorance—and here their initials—S.T., N.L.[28]—carved in the bark, but somehow these initials, momentarily under the torch, seemed to have grown larger than he last remembered their being: could it be true that they had increased from year to year with the growth of the tree, as some said was possible? He paused only a moment and walked on. He had taken his father's clubs again, and with a bag slung crosswise over each shoulder he appeared oddly bowed down as by some Christian's burden.[29] But a hope now moved with him—could not men's thoughts then develop into new forms of relations[30] with man's growing mind, the growing mind of the new world, the growing world?

Now they were walking down the steep rock path, ravaged by hail and fire, through the burnt gorse bushes that led to home. Down below the lights of the house shone warmly through trees that roared like a waterfall,[31] a tumult whose savagery was uncaring of the muted song of a small stream nearby, and noting this as he walked Sigbjørn remembered how slender real waterfalls in Norway could appear from the railing corridor far below, no more in fact than tiny frescoes on the rocks, and then the surflike clamour of the wind in the trees above them, loud-tongued as the passage of an express itself, a gathering impetus, a Niagara of sound, reverberated in the night with what to him might have been the cry of the sea, of the torrents falling forever from cliff shoulder to creek down Skjaeggedalsfoss.[32]

In the light from a lamp among the whirling shadows two lovers were saying farewell.

And this, in turn, was the shadow of his own real home-coming. To return home after long grief and pain only when another, more bitter, journey was about to begin!

—Are you prepared, I said, the Captain repeated more loudly.

—Prepared? Well, Sigbjørn answered, waking from his reveries, I'm prepared to the extent of four pairs of dungarees, a dozen chain-breaker singlets[33]—he emphasized each item by kicking stones as he descended the path—three pairs of fireman's slippers and a fireman's cap; much soap for washing, a camera, and iodine, and a plate, cup, spoon, knife and fork, packed in a seabag and waiting at Birkenhead Park.[34] Do you mean that?

The Captain did not reply for a while. Then he said, shortly:

—Prepared for a long journey.[35]

X

> He rushes after facts like a novice on skates, a novice, moreover, who is practising in a place where it is forbidden to skate.
>
> FRANZ KAFKA[1]

—A trial by fire,[2] did you say? But perhaps you'd better keep fire out of it. You never know what you may set alight by your idle words.

—A trial by fear.

—A trial by fear is better. Do you begin to be afraid already?

—It would be foolish of me to deny it.

—The day of the 'Hairy Ape'[3] being over, are you sure you can pick on a coal burner? There aren't many left.

—You know that I've signed on a coal burner[4] as a coal passer, a *limper*.[5]

—Of course, *Skibets reise fra Prester*...Well, draw up your chair to the fire. See how the world is a forest of symbols.

—It makes a noise like a flag.[6]

—*L'homme y passe à travers des forêts de symboles*[7] *qui l'observent avec des regards familiers.*

—I drink to you, father. Farewell to the symbolic, to the wings of folly.[8]

—Farewell to the infantile.[9]

—The Parnassien.[10]

—'During ages without number the shifting seas and slow-moving mountains have pressed down the sun's vintage[11] on the coal-beds of the earth.' Well, Barney, all I can say is you'd better make the most of this. Tomorrow, comfort will be something imagined and dreamed of. It will be: Come on there! You've got to turn out on deck and heave ashes![12]

—You're horribly right.

—That will be reality. No more talking abstractions.

—No more...

...Say something. This silence is maddening.

—Does it remind you of anything? Put that piece of coal back on the fire.

—Yes, the dead stillness down below in port...Or, listen to that—*ssspang*[13]—the coal shifts in the bunkers.

—I was thinking of Tor and you falling down that shaft. It was a narrower squeak than even you can have thought. They told you not to dig on the beds because if you did you would go down to the underground railway.[14] That was enough for you both. You had to dig down to it. The opening was to be on your birthday...It was all something nobody could ever forget.

—Did it cause much trouble to get us out?

—Well, to the extent of a mechanical shovel operated by the aid of flashlights! And we had to fasten cables to our bungalow and make them fast to trees on the other side of the crater—yes, it could be called a crater—to hold the house in place. Strangely enough, it's your birthday again the day after tomorrow.

—At least that's when the outward event is celebrated.

—Machine diggers had to dig a shaft parallel to the well, and then cut across to the spot where you were entombed. It was Caesarian! It was positively inconceivable that two children could be so ingenious. And all because you wanted to be an engineer like Uncle Bjorg.[15]

—The strangest thing of all is that the incident has absolutely no significance.

—None whatsoever.

—There was really no need to bring it up then, father. Or do you begin to see some—

—No, as a matter of fact I was thinking of something else. I read somewhere that the dreams of workers underground are much more closely allied with the world of living reality[16] than with a subconscious adventure. Dreams of falling, slimy walls slipping past, the roaring of steel conductors, howling and shrieking from the void, coal shifting in the bunker. It was just a thought that passed, very like a dream itself through my mind, perhaps, because I suddenly realized that you have to make such a synthesis in your own destiny between the real world and the unreal.

—I wonder if it can be done.

—It's difficult to talk.

—Why?

—Why? Because a mirror stands between us, Barney. At least that's the simplest explanation. Life is a hall of mirrors, someone said.

—A sort of Versailles, in fact.[17]

—In fact, yes. That's probably why Nero[18] wished to destroy the world: because it looked like himself.

—That's good.

—It isn't really. There are really many things I want to say to you before you go, but they're not organized in my mind. They're all on different tacks, or rather they're like the little gusts and eddies themselves, not to say possibly unpredictable little squalls—but all of them nevertheless carrying on the craft of my argument towards a safe anchorage. Or say that like dialectic itself, the movement is rather from temporal towards co-extensive consistency.[19]

—You mean that while you talk to me we have to imagine we're on the artificial lake[20] at West Kirby.

—That's about it.

—Well, go on—

—All right then, Barney, we're away on our first tack![21] And flying the red burgee![22]

—Wait a bit, what about getting the boat out of the boathouse and rigging the mainsail[23] and getting it down to the jetty. And finding someone to trip the lug!

—This is becoming really contentious. But I assume that in your life this has already been done.

—I'm not so sure, father. But at any rate let's assume it.

—Done. Well, I wish to suggest these things to you...first, that what may appear to be supernatural may in reality be subnormal,[24] by which I mean that a man driven half-frantic by inexplicable coincidences may feel that they *mean* something and be right. But what they do mean really is that his passionate attribution of meaning to these coincidences has aroused a similar enthusiasm in the subnormal world for producing them. Second, that it will not perhaps decrease my own naïveté in your eyes if I say that what abstractions you have enmeshed yourself in hide away from yourself your own. Third, that our own lack of intelligence is no measure of intelligence itself. Fourth, that it has been pointed out that to ignore metaphysical problems[25] is not to abolish them...to all of which I might add that they might be postponed and that in the order of facts they may well be very far down the list.

—I thought of that myself.

—It's worth thinking of again, Barney. Shall I go on?

—Do! As a matter of fact all conclusions seem final within me, even when I know them to be mutable.

—Yes, everything changing but at the same time, for once, all of them are going somewhere.[26]

—Yes.

—All right, then, Barney; you agree. I'll go on. Help yourself to a drink. And now we're getting on another tack. This interval is the going about.

—Will you have a drink, too?

—Thank you...Thanks. Now: As D'Israeli remarks,[27] nothing is so capable of disordering the intellect as an intense application to any one of these things: the quadrature of the circle; the multiplication of the cube; perpetual motion; the philosophical stone. In youth we may exercise our imagination on these curious topics merely to convince us of their impossibility: but it takes a great defect of judgment to be occupied with them at an advanced age. It is proper, however, says Fontenelle,[28] to apply oneself to these inquiries because we make as we proceed many valuable discoveries of which we were ignorant...At the same time a point of view may be reached where such a standpoint as this appears purely condescending. Quite apart from which the pursuit of the material equivalents of these things, the achievement of the apparently impossible, might be considered simply as the revolutionary principle, the will towards the future.[29]

—I heard Tor say often: the vacancy of the imbecile is the ideal of the scholar.[30]

—Doesn't that only appear to be so because of an habitually false conceit of the ideal itself that dwells in us even as we search for the image without? But to return to the matter of the mirrors: in all essentials you must understand how little we disagree. Besides, it's all a question of substitution, of terminology. There's no very clear differentiation between what many of us think—don't you see that?

—You mean we're all after the same thing...

—There is such a thing as an absolute demand for right. But witness the astounding similarity in the origin of religions themselves, however one may account economically for their eventual inadequacy or deterioration. But to return to the mirrors. I've already said that Nero couldn't stand it and told you why he wanted to destroy the world.

— Nero is a good example, a very, very good example at just this moment.

—And wasn't it D'Israeli again who mentions in his *Curiosities*, the case of Le Brun,[31] a Jesuit Latin poet, whose themes were religious? Anyway he got the idea of substituting a religious Virgil and Ovid merely by adapting his works to their titles. His Christian Virgil consists, like the pagan Virgil, of Eclogues, Georgics, and of an epic of twelve books with the sole difference that devotional subjects were substituted for fabulous ones. His epic is the Ignaciad or the pilgrimage of St. Ignatius. The Christian Ovid is in the same taste, everything wears a new face. The Epistles are pious ones: the Fasti, the six days of the creation: the Elegies, the lamentations of Jeremiah: a poem on the love of God is substituted for the Art of Love...and so on. By the way, what about yourself in that regard?

—Isn't it a bit late to tell me the facts of life?

—It's preposterous, I know. But were you ever really happy?

—Isn't it a bit late in the day to ask? But please go on; you were talking about the substitution of the crucifixion for the scene between Dido and Aeneas[32] in the cave, or something. Or was it the resurrection? The stone was just being rolled away, I believe. And have you entirely forgotten Ulysses?

—All of which reminds me of Kafka's dictum[33] that in elevating the body to the cross the saints are at one with their enemies. However, was it with Nina?

—Was what with Nina? Oh, I see what you mean. I suppose so, yes.

—Was Tor in love with Nina?

—I never thought of it, until...

—Could that have caused his death?

—Certainly not.

—Are you so sure?

—Yes, I'm so sure. In the first place her whole being seemed to be keyed beyond that kind of love.

—She sounds tiresome. But that explains nothing. The surest way of winning a person's love is to persecute him, and then to deny him—

—That's not right either. But Tor was not so damnably in love with her. There was no object of happiness between them, at least not happiness in the ordinary sense. Besides, does one want that sort of happiness anyhow? For instance, when I was happy with her, when I finally achieved a unity, a completion with her, then, then...

—Then what?

—Well, all at once I would become violently unhappy!

—Unhappy? Why?

—It sounds absurd, doesn't it? Well, I don't know how to explain it, frankly. But it was just as I say. At such moments I suffered terribly—and I really mean suffered—from a sensation of parting, of unbelievable heartbreak!

—Well, can it be explained? Surely not even the true genius of a man like Freud could explain that feeling you mention, that being wrapped about with fear, disquietude, death, at such a time: especially since no one knows the origin of sexuality, and by analysis only the centre of gravity of the suffering is shifted anyway! Substitution![34] For the reason, a feeling: for the feeling, an idea. For the mental expression, a mental expression. Well, it's all a much neglected study and a very expensive pastime. But what really broke you up?

—We were always quarreling. Besides, she was a communist who actually belonged to the party. I had the temerity to claim to have a soul. It was this temerity she disliked and insulted.

—A soul! How pretentious you sound. It's no wonder she left you. But what do you really mean by a soul? Be more concrete.

—I don't know. How can you be concrete about a soul?

—Well how can you have an allegiance to something you can't be concrete about?

—Very easily...Well, to put it roughly then, it was a clash on a very obvious religious ground.

—Supposing she is right? Suppose that hers is the only, although it is certainly not the inevitable, solution? Are you going to hang off because of your precious soul? And even if she does slight such pretentions, isn't it reasonable to suppose that she does so because that happens to be at the moment the technic of the transition?[35] Eventually, if the whole man is to be involved, as to my mind he must, the wisdom of religious thought and the miraculous powers of men must also enter the revolutionary movement. For no facts can hurt it! That's the point. All that is left outside—the corruption, the rationalizing, the running away from life, the degenerate miscarried faith and its praelectors.[36]

—The trouble is that she didn't really disagree with that viewpoint, a viewpoint I must in course of time have adopted from you without knowing it.

—A confusion certainly does arise from the fact that while we may pretend to antithetical opinions there may be very little evidence of these in our lives. That even as we speak, we are borrowing, not only from each other's pockets so to speak, but from each other's voices as well, however controversial these may be. But still all of it is being carried somewhere.

—Yes.

—And: did I say an expensive pastime? What I should have said is that it is being increasingly realized that the pastime in question must challenge the inquiry of the entire background of our personal and social habituations.[37] Which means that without the open knowledge of our financial position, our relationship is false. But to return: Do you see anything so fantastic as a truth—and by truth I mean something that is not deviating towards, or in the process of becoming,[38] something else—emerge from all this?

—Nothing of us but doth strange...[39]

—It is man that changes. The rebirth of man is the truth. And surely it is as painfully convulsive a drama as that which more generally we know as birth; and just as in the latter, nature working with secret plastic vision, stealthily but not, perhaps, inevitably, assists the development of the embryo into the child, so with the concentrated underground forces that determine the travail of rebirth[40] in man's consciousness. And this just as the other, depending for a successful outcome upon our will and usage, and not merely upon the mechanical march of events, makes ourselves important. You've spoken to me in letters in the past of the 'debacle of self,' of 'the death of private grief,'[41] but this renunciation is quite absurd. The debacle is not, as a matter of fact, of your own self, but rather of myself: of that self which knows but does not act on its knowledge.[42] The health of the whole and the health of the part being one, my death, the death of a bad habit, or the plucking out of an offensive corrupting organ,[43] is as important as your life: much more, it makes your life possible. Something that is quite dead can no longer corrupt the whole.

—I more or less follow you, these ideas having circulated, but more sluggishly, in my own mind...

—Just as a child, at a certain age, must become adult or go down into degeneration,[44] so man stands at this hour.

—I'm suggestible to good advice. I am ignorant, credulous, able to believe anything; such strange patterns destiny makes with our lives. Go on!

—Well, the truth at the moment is that we have to go about now, have to get on a different tack again.

—Where have we been up to now?

—We've been sailing close-hauled[45] without much trouble. Now you'll have to do some boom-dodging, and perhaps later even some bailing. Are you ready?

—I'm all set.

—All right, round we go...

—Round it is.

—All right. We're away. This time we may even get a little off our course. The question is—Erikson. He spreads above us like—what? The sky? You below are the sea, the mimic reflector,[46] credulous as the moon...And does the sea think she's blue from some quality of her own? And Erikson? Call him what you will... call him the Absolute...but how much has he created himself?

—If he were, that question would scarcely arise.

—I told you you would have to do some bailing. Anyway, the boat leaks. But still, in the present situation it's perhaps interesting to speculate on the part played by contemporary influences, etcetera...On what share in an artist's growth they have—these scions,[47] so to speak—snatched living from different trees. More interesting, even, what remains of the art when these secretions, these wandering seeds blown by the wind, so to say, are swept away? With what sap and with what light has he grown his crop?

—I don't think it's of the slightest importance.

—Let me say my say. The only things that stand like Athanasius[48] against the world are the opinions we hold at the moment. A cloud[49] no bigger than a human hand appears on the economic or on any other horizon and we are lost once more to a new faith. Scandinavians have the habit most of all. Philosophies, religious forms of art, of thought, explode within us with an irresistible violence. We dash into intellectual adventures with the enthusiasm with which explorers start for the Pole. But the extremes are never reached, the philosophies are not absorbed, but are rather scanned by a feverish tired mind already greedy for richer and more indigestible food.

—Well, what's the point?

—The point is, these debauches are all roads by which we endeavour to reach the unknown. But the unhappiness, the loss of identity, the guilt that seethes in you, the disasters like hidden mines exploding about us—and consequently the very need to reach the unknown itself—are all engendered by the purposelessness[50] of the vile society you live in, by the inadequacy, the utter tentativeness,[51] of the known.

—And it's this that has to change.

—No; not that *has* to change. That you have to change.

—But I have to change myself first.

—Not first. You are the change. What you have to get into your head is not that you are *not* the problem, but that you are the problem.

—You mean I've got to get it back in my head.

—Yes. For in England there is loyalty to many groups. But in a classless society there is only one loyalty: to the group, and that is, to yourself.

—Or to yourself, but that is the group.

—Exactly.

—But that's just the same as saying that every hair of my head is numbered.[52]

—You don't have to go further than the seventh century for Dorotheus' statement[53] that if we love God then to the extent that we approach him through love of him we unite in love with our neighbours; and the closer our union with them, the closer our union with God also. A statement liable to dangerous misinterpretation, for by neighbour Dorotheus didn't mean the swindling ship's chandler[54] who lives next door.

—Well, even so...

—Even so the fact that to 'neighbour' an esoteric definition should not blind you to the truth of that as demonstrated in Russia. One can supposedly love one's neighbour as one's self[55] there because perhaps there is no good reason not to! And if there is a swindling ship's chandler next door he is speedily removed! Or so one gathers. They do live a religion there, despite vexatious incidents, that's the whole point.

—I understand that. But I am not in Russia. I may never go to Russia and even if I did I should probably be thrown out on my ear. And besides, I don't belong to a party.

—Without knowing it, you do. For there still remains the choice between life and death, in which you would choose life.

—That doesn't follow.

—You have to remember that no matter from what alternative abyss, I am still the dynamic urging you on. To put it more briefly, I am telling you the truth as only a dead man can...

—...Yes, and mind you: Priam was not the only father of Oedipus.[56] What of those who led him when he was blind? It seems to me that life is often simply a process of the *exchange* of fathers, influence, and the like, in the hope that one will be led eventually to a position that with love and labour may be rendered irrefragable. That is, the eternal recurrence of the father surrogate.[57]

—In a society with much contradictions of class no position is irrefragable, even taking into account that men were not born equal, that is to say with equal powers.

—Quite so; but the pilgrimage continues, even when there is no absolute; one still hopes to find the person, even if out of the pages of a book, who will dare to leap the walls[58] of the prison, who can point to a richer, warmer life,[59] who knows the secrets of the sea[60]...Lacking such a person, by the way, it is quite conceivable one eventually takes his place oneself.

—All these are half-truths, still...Logical, perhaps, but untrue pseudo-logic. Even if approached from the exterior, I don't know...And where are all the teachers who would tell us anyway who could tell me? And what do you *mean* by—

—Never mind that. We're going around on another tack now.

—All right. Pass me the decanter.

—I'll have one myself if you don't mind! Well now! There are several things I have to say...I'll say them in the order they occur to me. First, it seems to me that the imaginative flight[61] into the past may be psychologically a real flight, a running away from life, and so on. Just simply cowardice, in short, a disgrace. Or it may be something quite different.

—What, for instance?

—It might be, or it seems to me that it might be, a flight not from present day evils but towards a state of mind from which their existence may be more properly surveyed and possibilities for their solution studied. Towards, in fact, although it may sound laughable, a controlling of reality—in fine, of the very object to which those who scoff at such matters have related themselves.

—Is this a rationalization?

—Not at all. The frontiers of physics, chemistry, mathematics, have been prolonged. It has been said that death can be indefinitely postponed[62]...Somewhere or other the frontiers of the real and unreal vanish. What of the magical powers of man? The magic of the prelogical? There are more important things, one says, than these, which anyway smack of the infantile, of quackery, of the coteries, of black magic. Very well, they do—but what of their reality? Their material use? And what if you found yourself in your own voyage, a voyage which is the antithesis of the actual, of the material, but which at the same time is, in part, a voyage of primitive return, caught up by a recurrence of a pre-logical condition where miracles are as common as daisies?

—It sounds unlikely to me. But what of it?

—All right, we'll leave that; I don't wish to develop the idea. I merely wish, so to speak, to sow a few seeds of thought in you which will bear fruit in their own time...Now here's something: I think I notice in you the same tendencies that Ruge and Echtermeyer[63] objected to in the German romantic school,[64] a sort of medieval consciousness, a tendency towards mystical and ecclesiastical terminology which makes me think that you might, under certain circumstances, turn Catholic: for there is in you a strong tendency towards Catholicism in its mystic form.

—Towards Catholicism?

—Yes, you always showed it in your letters. By your love for words like 'spiritual,' 'soul,' etcetera...

—Soul etcetera? What do you mean by soul etcetera?

—And also by a general evidence of more humble and utilitarian vocables.[65] Which makes me think once more of the German romantics. Your conviction, or what appears to be a conviction, that the end of the world is near, and that in the arts it has already taken place; a belief, or what appears to be a belief, in spirit as the only reality, a feeling you often betray that all is vanity,[66] that there is nothing new under the sun, for example; there is Erikson, the futility that pervades you because of him, 'everything has been done before,' and so forth...all that is part of the same thing.

—So what? As the Americans say...

—Nothing, save that to do so—that is to join the Catholic Church—for you, I feel, would be a mistake.

—But whose lot creeps into the church to keep its metaphysics[67] warm?

—That's simply cruel. And here again, if one is not careful, one will succeed in being only condescending. Let's leave it simply at that: it seems to me it would be a mistake.

—Santayana[68] said that he believed in the Virgin Mary as one would believe in a wife one knew but did not like to think was unfaithful.

—We leave all that...

—All these different structures unfinished, with the crane on top.[69]

—Exactly. Which brings me to my point that forbidding censorships are up to mischief within you.

—Censorships?

—Yes: that will erase everything that excludes the possibility of a salvation that you can comprehend. One—dare I say the only?—possibility, and a seemingly paradoxical one, is in communism. Another possibility of refuge is in some form of esotericism, unclear to you, with which perhaps you have long and rightly suspected I was involved. And from which you have indirectly drawn a great many moral dispositions. These possibilities you admit?

—Yes.

—But what perhaps you have not had the honesty to admit to yourself is the extent and power of your own hatred. Intellectually your heart may cry for the brotherhood of man[70] but under certain circumstances you have betrayed this: in your own brother you have perhaps killed it. It will rise again. But the wherefore of all this is no longer of much importance, its logical fiction having extended to deeper tragedies.

—I don't get this at all.

—Never mind. It's damnably difficult to make any sense when the validity of everything you say is cancelled by the central contradiction in your own life.

—Damnably, I should say.

—But in the furnace of this life into which allies and enemies, survivor and dying, rebel and reactionary, have been pitchforked, a steel fort is being forged. It is emerging, I should say...

—Or like the red-hot thought that threads its way through the bursting brain of a man in the electric chair...

—We're going to swing right round[71] now. Right round, leaving all that.

—All right, I'm set. I'm ready to tip the lug.

—All right, then. Right! We're going round. But this is a little more uncomfortable; an intellectual transition, should we say, from fire to ice...[72]

—Ice?

—Yes. Put it another way, it's a difference in the rate of vibrations, if I may so express it, rather than in the substance. Watch ice change into water for example, or hence into steam, vapor and gas, and it still doesn't change it...

—Substance which all the while is H_2O! That much I am sure of!

—Exactly. It's still two atoms of hydrogen and one atom of oxygen, not changing its substance at all and only increasing the rapidity of its atomic and electronic vibrations...So the question before the house is: what happened when Europe entered the Ice Age?

—The Ice Age? I don't know. Or at least...Well, I remember Jensen's book,[73] the wild animals[74] rushing madly through the darkness from the oncoming glaciers...

—Yes, that's right, uncaring of old enmities they rushed hip by haunch, from the glaciers.

—And the people had already fled.

—Yes. And a single youth set his face to the numbing rain of the north to conquer the new enemy. Well, this is what I was getting at, the Northern peoples were descended from him and the girl he found. And we are so descended. The memory[75] of the land in which the childhood of a race was spent lives in our dreams as a lost Eden or the Blessed Isles. This yearning made us Vikings[76] and explorers. This was shown in the migration of peoples that broke the strength of the Roman Empire and in the great discoveries which initiated the modern era. (And so on and so forth.)

—I'm not going back to Norway on a flowery excuse like that.

—Can you say you don't yearn for such a land?

—Certainly not. And even if I did and I reached it I could not recognise it or my own forests or they me.

—Well, I only wanted to ask you—

—At least I don't think so. As a matter of fact I feel rather shaken by the suggestion...But no, it's altogether too dramatic and perfect.

—Still, it's strange that the cry you seem to hear is back, back, back to coal, back to the womb. Well, even if it were true it would perhaps be better to go than to stay here where time has become a stagnant horror like the stillness in the heart[77] of a man who has committed murder.

—Better to go. Yes, better to go anywhere. But damn it all, do you believe yourself all this back to the womb business?

—Listen to the fire...

—It's a friendly thing.

—Friendly! Well, I'll tell you, it's strange how it sometimes works out. It's all so plausible.

—What's plausible?

—It's interesting to wonder, for instance, if there's any basis for believing, as some psychiatrists maintain, that the ego instincts are death instincts[78] and the sexual instincts—life instincts.

—And then what? What's that got to do with the fire?

—It's not the fire so much as the coal, and not the coal so much as the elemental quality of fire, and the ancient inanimate quality of coal. For supposing what I said a moment ago to be true, just which cluster of instincts would draw you back to Norway? And which, out to Russia?

—Probably not either would draw me in the way you describe.

—Probably not. But at the same time, it's very interesting for a moment to suppose that they do. For instance, if for Norway I substitute—

—Substitute? But then I suppose I've thought of all this myself. Only it sounds so queer coming from you.

—Yes, substitute. Supposing, I repeat, Norway to be death, your mother's death (and so forth) and of course your own and Tor's birth, and death to be a manifestation of the same force—supposing, I say, Norway to personify death, or rather the rocky inanimate whose reinstatement your ego-instincts desire—then would it be altogether fabulous to suggest that those instincts which draw you out to Russia, which make you sympathetic to Communism, are life instincts, in fine—sexual instincts?

—I don't think I associate death with the inanimate anyway. On the contrary, I've always been out of step with this life when I have believed it to be simply a preparation for the next one. Besides, I have never really studied mental hygiene[79] and therefore lack suggestibility to that kind of symbology, to the catchwords... Wait a minute, I dare say even that's not quite true.

—Not quite true, eh?

—I would say that at any rate those instincts which draw me to Russia do at least encompass the idea of *life* and that therefore that much of what you say is true. Not so very long ago I scarcely took this intermediary into account.

—Insofar as those instincts partly belong to an extension of your identification with Erikson, they are sexual.[80]

—What does it matter? They belong to *life* I say.

—I'm glad to see you don't like to be pinned down by qualifications or by terminology that will soon be out of date anyhow. But more concisely I take it that you hold in common with Roback and Macdougall[81] and others the opinion—to my thinking, the very sound opinion—that the innate structure of the human mind comprises much more than instincts alone anyway, and that there are many facts, into which we won't go, but which would, under other circumstances, compel us to go further in the recognition of innate mental structure.

—Yes, more or less...Speech is given to man to disguise his thoughts.[82] What you said was logical but not necessarily true.

—You mean that the arguments of a charlatan, as White[83] has pointed out, are made for those who do not know and who are seduced by a fine logic to think that when conclusion follows premise with such certainty there must be truth.

—As you—or White or whoever—suggest: just because a conclusion is contained in the premise and follows logically therefrom, is no reason why the conclusion is necessarily true.

—Exactly. Now we may proceed.

—A little slower if you please.

—All right, slower. Anyhow this time we're not going about, merely a little closer to the wind, that's all. You have to look out that we don't gybe,[84] though... in fact we're going just as close to the wind as we can. You're born. We can't go much closer than that.

—All right, I'm born. Have a drink, by the way.

—Thanks. You, too. Now...You're born and it's not so simple. But at first things are ideal. All your needs are simplified. This is very, very old stuff, but it must be said. In your world you're an imperial highness, a viceroy...

—It's absurd to say it was my ideal. It's true I have still a deep love of Norway but things were not ideal. As matter of fact I have almost no memories of childhood and those I have are unpleasant. No, that's not true either. Love of Norway, though, of one's home, is a different matter...

—I repeat that whether you remember it or not things are ideal for a time. Then, all that you *do* remember probably: sudden chaos, upheaval, wrenching apart. You find yourself having to face a very cold world indeed—not much of a substitute for the old—and face it alone. Or worse than alone, you face it with a brother of whom you're becoming extremely jealous. (All this has nothing to do with your accident.)

—I remember quarreling with Tor. But was I jealous?

—Anyway, and this is the point, if you could express your deepest desire at that time it would be to turn back: to turn back to the old world, of despotism, a world in which even if you had a rival[85] you were scarcely conscious of it...But that is not your only desire. On the contrary. You do wish to be active. It's a funny thing, but you do! In an important sense you've outgrown your space and your forces are pushing for more activity, like a crocus in spring pushing through the lawn outside...That's logical, isn't it?

—I understand that. But where does it get us? All this pseudo-logic...I don't know. It suddenly occurs to me for no very good reason that you might as well say, deriving from the lines of these arguments, that imperialism is simply an enthronement by the masses of the infantile,[86] the powerless, which is nevertheless invested, just as the child often is, with all the *insignia* of omnipotence,[87] and that this enthronement fulfills a deeply-felt want even in those who are exploited by it: who continue, therefore, vicariously to enjoy...And so on, and so on. Which might be quite logical but also might not be true. And it wouldn't get us anywhere.

—All right then, if you're not satisfied, we'll go even further back. Back to yourself at the very moment of birth. When even then you are of two minds. One is desirous of the womb where you were adjusted—as indeed never since—to your environment;[88] the other wishes once more for action, to kick and stretch, to break away; a conflict which is solved temporarily and very nicely by your mother's answering your every need. All the same this dichotomy is never resolved.

—What do you *mean* by environment?

—If you ask me what do I mean by it now, as opposed to then, which is obvious, you're at the root of the matter. What indeed do I mean by it? Adjustment to present-day bourgeois society is in itself like becoming adjusted to the padded cell. It's a lunatic asylum. A society on the verge of war, the great castration[89] when, mark you, suicides practically cease;[90] if there'd been a war on, Tor might be still alive. Well, what are you going to do about it?

—What are you going to do about it?

—I'm going to pass out of your life, possibly out of life altogether, probably out of existence. I can't stop myself now.

—It's almost as though two worlds were speaking.

—Thus the old world addresses the new. Where is another chaos, where? But the question is, what are you going to do about it?

—Will you tell me?

—I'll do my best. But first let's look at what I've said already. In effect, it is this. The revolutionary principle is the will towards the future.[91] And there must be no back, back, for its own sake. No psychological probing down, or pressing of the reason below the feeling must alter that will to go forward. No passion for the unconscious at the expense of the conscious, nor for the affective at the expense of the intellectual, must hold you back.

—You didn't say that at all. On the contrary you said that if I went back, back as you put it, I should possibly apprise the pre-logical—whatever that may be—on the way, and that that and the power which co-exists with it on the frontier where the real and unreal meet are indeed nothing but the miraculous potentialities of man which are his birthright and which must enter the revolutionary movement if the whole of man is to be reborn and not just to become an abortion.

—It's true that I said that as well. But if you were to receive correct instructions they would have to be in no known language. The next best thing I can do is to warn you not to let the lesser cheat you of the greater while remembering at the same time that the lesser is also part of the greater.

—And which is the greater?

—At the moment, the more immediate. And now, for the last time, we've got to go round once more. Tostrup-Hanson[92] tells me you were down at the Arcturion yesterday.

—I was indeed.

—Then you may have noticed the Siamese twins.

—Yes.

—Well, it's a preposterous illustration, perhaps, but nevertheless a good one. And when I'm through with it I'm through with your instincts once and for all, and you can just take or leave everything I've said..

—Well, I'm waiting.

—With not even a ray of an hypothesis having penetrated into the obscurity of the origin of sexuality,[93] the argument advanced by Freud and others was that a certain myth possibly derives an instinct for the reinstatement of an earlier situation.

—This is all apropos of the ego instincts again, etcetera—the desire for the inanimate, for death.

—More or less. Of course you know that part of Plato's *Symposium*[94] where—

—Yes. I know what you're going to say. It was Aristophanes. He said that there were originally three sexes, not, as today, two. He said that besides the male and female, there existed a third sex which had an equal share in the two first when Zeus divided them up.

—That's quite right. And this same thought is also in the Upanishads, to be precise, in the Brihad-Aranyaka Upanishad.[95]

—It is also suggested, father, by St. Paul.[96] In the idea of sanctity.

—Not to say by Bernard Shaw.[97] I'm surprised at your knowledge. Well then, here we are. We're on the last lap now, round the last lifebuoy, heading for home. What are you going to do about it? Forget...that's what you're going to do about it.

—Forget?

—Yes. The thing is—forget for the time being. Or rather, to renounce, temporarily, forget, in that sense, all these truths and doctrines and speculations which cannot be entirely put aside, together with the other facts which are not yet wanted: just as you have to forget the lies, the evasions, the empty gestures, the abstract symbols, the other facts long pooled in the memory: the discussions in Parliament; the judgments from the benches; the superstitions, even when they prove grounded, and so forth! Let them have no place in your new life, think in different categories; so much belongs to your past, your Caliban past.[98] What is true will be found sifted from the rest when more immediate contradictions have been removed from the whole.

—But you said, and then you were talking about instincts, and besides we—

—Yes. Well, my last word on that subject is that I agree with Roback[99] that an instinct of expression is no more than a particularization of an act involving one's own self, and that principles we are discussing really represent universalization, involving naturally the individual who is acting, but directed towards humanity in general, of which this or that person appears as a case. And we could visualize by a synecdoche, yourself as that person.

—I don't know what that word means, and this forgetting seems to contradict—

—Only seems to! For all wisdom will be needed sooner or later on the side of the oppressed. If you can somehow forget the wisdom for the time being, without slighting it, until the hour is ripe for its application, and *then* remember: that is what I mean.

—All that seems a bit phony, as the Americans say. To forget, and yet not to forget. To remember and yet not to remember.

—All the same it is what perhaps goes on behind the phenomenon of birth itself, as Thomas Mann has pointed out—that is, an ethical renunciation[100] of infinity, of all weaving in spaceless and timeless night.

—I do begin to see that. A renunciation of infinity, as the form shapes itself with gathered desire from a world of possibilities. I can see something wonderful in that.

—You see it?

—A renunciation of infinity...You've turned the tables on me in a strange way.

—Yes. Your rebellion against authority is a failure. Nobody's going to stop you where you're going. Everybody's going to help you where you're going. I'm doomed, at an end. The voices[101] you hear helping you speak from the very brink of the grave. What greater affirmation of life can there be than that?

—What—

—...Listen to the roar of the sea and the wind.[102] The storm's already in the house, trying the doors.

But at this point both worlds were becalmed.

XI

> To his astonishment the whole house was lighted up. Then gradually came the reflection that even the most extraordinary visitation of fate does not express itself at once in a decisive alteration of the outer forms of living.
>
> ARTHUR SCHNITZLER[1]

All he heard was coal, coal, an avalanche of coal[2] falling over his dream. All at once, rising on his elbow, he woke with a start, his heart beating loudly. Where was he? What had he done? What nightmare waited only the relieved disproving of daylight? That dream of coal falling...

...Where was he? Somewhere a storm roared, a storm of trees or sea—no, that was in his mind. But that siren calling, that was surely real? All hands on deck, something wrong...He grabbed under his bed for his sea-boots. Nothing there, he was not at sea yet, that was plain. Suddenly he sat bolt upright on the edge of his bed, shivering with terror. That dream he had had, what haunting shapes of horror or anguish even now were poised bears, scarcely yet in retreat?

He swung himself into bed again and pulled the blankets up to his chin. There was something wrong with the room, he felt, it was different; it was getting to be dawn of course, though, and perhaps that partially accounted for it. But the room certainly was not as it had been[3] the night before when he staggered up from the armchair in the dining-room almost asleep to fall unconscious in his bed. Even now he could recall the sea-whispering around the house and the shadows of the green waves of nameless trees pouring over the frosted glass in the bathroom like the Atlantic over the scuttle.[4] That talk with his father, how much did he recall of it now? Words, words. A renunciation of infinity?[5] Well, time would show what would come of this renunciation. Or perhaps he had only been talking to himself. At once he almost cried aloud as he sat up in bed once more.

He was going to sea today, these were his last few moments of comfort—his last few hours possibly on earth—

He lay back in bed, feeling the warmth of the blankets with sudden gratitude. The last morning, they're going to hang me at dawn...What was the good of delaying, better make an end of it instantly, and he swung himself out of bed again to try the icy rape of daybreak. He dressed with an almost feverish haste, as if he feared to give in to the temptation to return to bed and sleep past the time at which he was to take his train for Preston. As he tied his tie he saw that what seemed changed about the room was in reality a change outside; he had opened the window and instantly shut it again on the yellow, drifting light of fog. As he washed he heard the lights being turned on and the remote clatter of jugs from upstairs, the maids stirring. And he remembered them as they had been the night before at dinner, circulating with averted faces, as if they, too, shared in the general guilt. For a moment another time shone with extraordinary clearness on his soul. The quiet stir of a freighter's foc'sle before the watch turns to at dawn, in the east a wild glint of yellow, already a banging of pans in the galley, the watch standing in the foc'sle entrance with cups of coffee in their fists and peering out into the murk: and all around them the high grey seas, grey, grey, a mountainous wilderness—

He went downstairs into the hall and looked at the barometer. 29.00. And outside a thick fog, as though all the smoke of Liverpool and Birkenhead, not to say of Chester and the furnaces of Mostyn, were hanging concentrated over the Wirral Peninsula. A gloomy prospect.

He opened the door into the dining-room. He could smell the fog in there. Through the window he could barely see beyond the tennis-court,[6] grimly silent, when only last night the wind had set up a jingling of the rings on the outer nets like a ghost of sleigh-bells.[7] That story in Erckmann-Chatrian[8] of the man who murdered the Polish Jew by burning him in the lime-kiln!...And Ethan Brand.[9] 'From that time onwards Ethan Brand was a fiend.'

He rested his hands on the back of a chair, then absently picked up last night's newspaper lying on the seat. Fog expected...It had already been expected then. He shook the paper straight. Plenty of warnings[10] of everything if he only had the wits to understand them. 'Strange collision in channel. Cutters rushed from the Zuyder Zee...'[11] But fancies from the caverns of nightmare wove patterns over the print. He rubbed his eyes, hang it all, he was still half asleep...He laid the paper down and let himself fall into the chair.

The consummation of the love of two ships. In the fog they softly collide, interpenetrate; the sea, their soft marriage bed, is also their deathbed...Collision. The dithering crack[12] of two ships that smash into each other in the fog, collision of old and new. 'Mr Otto Hurwitz,[13] furrier, 37, up from his cabin, his sea-gown scarfed about him, noticed nothing unusual. Perhaps he was not even questioned...'

He stood up and simultaneously realized that he was so apprehensive of the consequences of the step he was taking, so afraid of the reality he was embracing, that his mind instantly erected a partition between himself and any immediate semblance of it. With a start he now noticed that his father was asleep on the sofa. He shook him and woke him up.

—I came down here again to read the paper. I dozed off when you were down here, but couldn't get to sleep again, the Captain said. Why there's a real Baker Street fog.[14]

—A real pea-souper. The trains will be delayed. How shall I get to Park?

—It's elementary, my dear Watson, we'll take the car.

—Elementary is right.

Sigbjørn sat down and watched his father as he threw the blankets off himself and stretched. As Sigbjørn watched him he could almost feel the cold presage of disaster clutching at him and then loosing him as he imagined his thinking automatically: such things cannot happen to us, do not happen to me: and then the knowledge that calamity was real and cogent, growing with the light, his apprehension of it ebbing away with its acceptance, leaving him strangely assured, even brisk, in manner.

—You better go and warm up the car[15] if you want to catch your train from Exchange.

—If there is one...I'm going out in a minute. I'm just looking at this room for the last time.

—I understand that, his father said, pulling on a sweater.

—I wonder if you do.

For here, at any rate, some happy ordered thoughts clung, remote from nightmare. Years ago he had been happy in this room, eating, smoking, talking. For a long time Tor and he had sat facing each other over the table, playing checkers; and he remembered the absolute peace and the peace that also seemed to be flowing from the hearts of those present—yes, even from the very objects in the room, even from Brueghel's 'Fall of Icarus with Statue,'[16] even from the books, and the peace that flowed like moonlight from the beauty of old silver, on his first night home from the sea. Good people; but were there any longer good people in the world? That sort of goodness seemed to have died. The lighthouse that lighted the storm invited it once more.

—But better to fall with Icarus[17] than thrive with Smith, he remarked to himself.

The Captain stared out of the window. From the darkness, chords of sirens blended. Still lingering, Sigbjørn's glance wandered over the room, a big room, lofty and dark...a darkness which the Brueghel engraving alone rendered luminous...and filled with furniture: several large tables; bureaux; cupboards in which were kept books and papers of some sort. The wide sofa that had served Captain Tarnmoor as a bed was covered with a rug he himself had bought from a hawker in Belawandello,[18] Sumatra. Apart from the Brueghel reprint, the pictures on the walls were dark and grimy; it was difficult to make out what they represented and he had never troubled to find out. Two or three books covered with folded newspapers were lying on a table, one of them with a bookmark; he picked it up and glanced at it.

'Eventually if the whole man is to be involved, as to my mind he must, the wisdom of religious thought and the miraculous powers of man, now slighted by the technic of transition, must also enter the revolutionary movement. For no facts can hurt it!'[19]

The Captain regarded Sigbjørn with embarrassed relief as he saw him lay the book down and his eyes stray to the shelves. Strange that he hadn't noticed it before, how these books of his father presented almost an organic, continuous view of history itself. Through them he now saw the idea of revolution running like water, like a widening river to the sea, through the Patrists, the Gothic builders, the sixteenth and seventeenth century founders of modern science; through Spinoza and Hegel to the turbulent estuary of Marx; books whose purpose was strangely at variance with the Captain's own dissident life but which must indeed have often purged him of the gloomy conclusion of average and of the underwriters.

With these thoughts Sigbjørn left the room without a word and in a minute he was out of the house.

In the garden,[20] the fog was so thick that he twice stumbled against frames and flower-pots in his path. Under the trees the daffodil and hyacinth shoots lay quiescent in the winter and he made his way carefully so as not to hurt these tiny nerves and muscles of the nativity of spring. Cows lowing at a distance from the mangers in Mapleson's farm[21] merged queerly with the tenor warnings[22] of grim toilers in the Irish Channel. To his surprise the car engine started without much flooding of the carburettor and in five minutes he had managed to drive round, with due circumspection, from the garages to the front door. He covered the radiator with a rug and entered the house. Breakfast was ready and father and son ate quickly and in silence. Another five minutes and they were ready to start.

—Goodbye.

—Goodbye.

—Goodbye Sigrid, goodbye Eva, goodbye Cookie.

—What, you're not going to sea again?

—No sooner you're home than you're off again!

A man in muddied leather gaiters stood by the car, twisting his cap inside and out, in his face moving the same inarticulate sympathy that he had noticed in Macleoran's. The gardener.

—Goodbye, sir, he said quietly. I was dreadfully sorry, I don't know what to say—that Master Tor—it's all too much for us all, like...—

The gardener[23] opened the door of the car for him.

—Thank you. Goodbye and God bless you. I may be going to Norway!

—To Norway.

Sigbjørn blew the horn sharply.

—Well, ha, the helmsman, said the Captain, struggling with his great coat. What's it to be, dead reckoning?[24] Or on the planet Vulcan?[25]

—By the great circle...[26]

In bottom gear the car moved slowly up the drive: the bare bushes rustled by, a long branch like a sudden tentacle sent out by the house itself as a last resort to hold them back, clutched at the windscreen, dropped behind with a futile gesture; on every hand the dark boles of the trees, imperfectly materializing through the fog, were like symbols of a growing strength, of a growing reality: the telegraph poles[27] which marched through the garden hummed interminably, a hushed agony of sound, the moaning of Tor's violin.

The gardener had followed them up the drive and shut the gate behind them. They waved, and the house, lighted against the fog, looked back, itself a ship, her bearings lost, a few scattered eyes[28] straining through the gloom. Then it disappeared.

—Well, we're going forward to meet the pall...[29]

Sigbjørn changed up to top.

—Change down again, you'd better, the Captain said.

Sigbjørn obeyed and the engine hummed in a higher register, feeling her way along slowly. Then he changed down into third, proceeding at little more than a walking pace. Patches of white lay in the fields and from a distance might have been either snow or fog. Further down in the valley the latter lay as thickly as poison gas. Ghosts and wisps, detached from detumescent bladders of fog, drifted past them. Several other cars had come up behind and there was the steady sound of purring cylinders. An engine would be put in neutral, then steps would be heard above the sound, steps in retreat, always in retreat, ringing out on the pavements. Sigbjørn double-declutched[30] into bottom. They were approaching a cross-roads.[31] A pillar of lights sprang up before them.

—Starboard lights. Go through.

—No. Red. Stop! Danger!

Sigbjørn threw out both brake and clutch, and moved the lever to and fro between the gear gates in its neutral position, then revved up the engine once or twice and waited. Alert for changing lights, he removed his gloves, blew in his hands, peered around. The light flashed green. Go. And they moved on.

—I don't see how you drive so well for such an absent-minded person. It seems to me, Barney, that most of your troubles are over if you can drive a car.

—Very often, permanently, Sigbjørn said.

For a time the road seemed to lift right out of the fog and to take advantage of the clear interlude they increased speed. Soon they had turned the dangerous Frankby[32] corner into the Greasby road, passed the village green and the village cross, and roared into the straight. At the corner, by the Coach and Horses, he slowed down.

—To a horse, a house jumps out of the way, the Captain said, looking out. I think the road's clear.

—Strange how there seems to be almost no fog here.

They pushed on, taking advantage of the dangerous temporary clarity and it now seemed that almost everyone else on the road was of the same mind. Cars lurched both past and towards them, so swiftly sometimes it seemed that they were participating in an immensely speeded-up news film: each car that approached suggested inevitably a frightful collision that by some legerdemain was always avoided.

—It's an awful thought. One Christmas Day I felt the same as that horse...

A huge grey limousine hurtled past them like a shell.

—What was that? A Rolls or what?

—The owl of Minerva[33] takes its flight in the evening.

—A red light!

Warning. As Sigbjørn took off his gloves again to blow into his hands he saw that they had pulled in beside the limousine. Saluting an acquaintance in the car he noticed that a hasty conference was instantly called by its occupants and he knew that their lips were moving in the same conspiracy of sympathy or of condemnation: he could almost feel the substance of their words moving about him:

'A terrible, terrible thing. That's Captain...'

(And the name that would have coincided with the change of the light to Caution not mentioned for fear it would be overheard or apprehended.)

'And that's his son, they're awfully nice people really, they say! But their ships...But his brother...a terrible thing, such a terrible, terrible thing.' Go...

The fog had parted for them like the waters of the Red Sea[34] and the snow in fields and on roofs was now distinct as snow. Still the way was clear as they continued past the Bromborough[35] omnibus stop, over the Upton[36] railway station bridge, and down the incline beyond, faster here, to get a run for Bidston Hill[37] where trees, hedges, and houses rushed up to them as from a screen, to be instantly transferred into new, ever-changing scenes; and soon they had reached the summit where it was so clear they could see the Observatory through the trees. Sigbjørn gasped as he suddenly felt the breath of the sea on his face and for an instant he took his eyes off the road.

—Look out, Barney. Port your helm[38] quick.

Sigbjørn spun the wheel instinctively to the left and then, disaster almost upon them, to the right as the Bromborough-West Kirby omnibus, toppling with its load, lurched heavily towards the hedge.

—To a man a bus jumps out of the way.[39]

He changed down, accelerated, double-declutched, changed down again, accelerated, changed up and was in the straight. Noctorum[40] on the right and Bidston Common[41] on his left. With huge and tattered sails the old windmill loomed before them like a derelict being driven before the storm on the dark sea of the moor where snow patches on the heather were like white crests of waves.

—What on earth did you say port for, father, when you meant right?

—I forgot that now when you give the signal, starboard, wheel, rudder, ship, all move to the right, and...

But suddenly he was silent.[42]

At the Oxton[43] cross-roads they were again held up by a red light, and Sigbjørn, taking his hands off the wheel, was relieved that his own trembling would only seem to be a movement in sympathy with the vibration of the engine. Here also they were as clear of the fog, which seemed to be drifting northwards away from them, as if they had been flying above the clouds: only a thick low blanket lay on the river far below. And it was quite possible to see from this point, high over Birkenhead, with its monotonous roofs far below them, over the Mersey to Liverpool where the Liver Building—the clock-face was bleached by distance—rose waggishly through the fog.

Sigbjørn shivered with the cold and with terror as he contemplated all this: terror of the coming voyage, of the new faces, of the work, and of the death the outward configuration of which had only just been avoided.

Down the river rose the four masts of a White Star[44] liner as she steered slowly towards Seacombe and Egremont,[45] moving through the whiteness, dwarfing any flagpole or tower on the foreshore. Nearer at hand the crosstrees of the *Herzogin Cecile*[46] were fixed above a bleak warehouse, boys perched on them, the maintop and the rigging like urchins chestnutting, or sloths hanging from trees. To the west of the float the docks led inland past Poulton and Liscard to lesser tributaries where, shrouded in fog as for the grave, old ships lay up the reaches.[47] Beyond them, the mist piled up in snowbanks of white across the waterfront of Liverpool; the sun, fighting to bleed through, gave Sigbjørn the sudden impression that the pain of the travail of the world was momentarily centred here, at this point, long after its muscles and organs were complete.

—A Turner sunset[48] at nine o'clock in the morning, the Captain remarked. Very odd.

All around, engines were still purring steadily and with the same gesture of recognition, made perhaps with a little more conscious politeness to the people in the limousine, came an old reflection: how little they all knew about each other! What did he know of them? Or they of him? Certainly they could scarcely tell at this moment, when he acknowledged them, that he was experiencing the horror of a man who sees into a new world but who is still attracted by the life behind, a man who knows that the old world will never be the same, will always be too narrow for him, but whose courage and awakening consciousness are as yet insufficient to encompass the new.

—Thalassa, Thalassa,[49] he remarked suddenly for no valid reason, and blew the horn twice.[50]

The green light flashed, Go.

—Go!

Looking towards Liverpool as he drove on he experienced the sensation once more of seeing straight North, straight on towards the Pole, a vast white calm where sea was confused with sky: and he remembered with a shock that beyond lay Preston from which he would set out; it seemed to him as though ever since that day on Castle Hill in Cambridge with Tor, his own real being (however circumambient), his corporate self had been moving towards this in an undeviating line, as the Captain of a Line[51] follows the ruled plan of his Admiral.

—Mind you, his father was saying, anything I feel about the world is not based on *faith* but there is this much that is the same: that there is in life just that same incommensurability between divine and human law. It says starboard: we go to port, and onto the rocks. Or into a collision. Its demands are not ambiguous from its own point of view, but from ours. Oh well, I'm not sure Jacobsen[52] wasn't right after all.

—I'm damned sure he was, Sigbjørn said pallidly, not listening, but keeping his mind on the road. I'm sure he was damned right.

They coasted down the hill turning to the right to cross the Tranmere-Woodside tramline[53] and throttling down as he steered cautiously through the Park gate: in the Park they followed, as if engulfed in a whirlpool, an ever-narrowing series of concentric circles, finally disgorging them by the Birkenhead Park[54] football ground, the grandstand of which appeared bare and stark through the trees.

—I dropped a goal[55] there once, Sigbjørn said, slowing for a Rock Ferry tram.[56] A moment later they were in Duke Street by Birkenhead Park Station[57] and he was reversing into his position in line in the garage.

Underground...

He unchecked his sea-bag which he hoisted over his shoulder; they hurried down to the platform. They were sitting on straw seats, the sea-bag beside them, absently watching their own reflections opposite them lurking behind framed advertisements for theatres and cinemas: *Futurist Cinema, Leslie Howard in Outward Bound, continuous performance, 2–11*[58]...In a moment the train had plunged from the ghostly light into the abyss: soon they were at Hamilton Square.[59] Then they were away again. The train was swaying and shaking and it felt as though the whole world beneath them was tottering to its disaster.

Futurist Theatre, Leslie Howard in Outward Bound: Crazy Week at the Empire: 6:30, 8:30: Popular Prices...Fragments of conversation dislodged themselves from the solid wall of noise set up by the swaying train.

—Do you remember Gaillard?[60]

—And the old Hippodrome?[61] And the Argyle?[62]

—Brown's Bioscope.[63]

—...Liverpool Irish![64]

This time they felt themselves plunging deeply down into the earth, deeply under the water,[65] and Sigbjørn felt momentarily as though he were being actually retraced through this dark cavern to his beginnings. Matrix.[66] The two men sat in silence while the train hurled on like a projectile through the oval tunnel beneath the river. It was strange to think of the weight it had carried, of the million ships and cargoes and destinies that in their time had moved slowly outwards over it, or homewards to rest, whether in the bright departure of day or secretly on the bosom of the Mersey at night.

At James Street Station,[67] the men left the train. Ascending gravely by the lift to the upper air Sigbjørn felt again around him the conspiracy of sympathy, and the strange mixture of indignation, curiosity, and ghastly glee that characterizes human beings in the presence of those to whom great disasters are happening. But they fixed their eyes steadily on the framed advertisements that seemed to Sigbjørn to make, solipsistically enough, idiotic comment on the situation, and did not move their heads or seem to recognise anyone. Soon they were swept out onto the street. Water Street...but from Water to fire!

Outside, where the fog was thick again, it was as though they had drawn the community with them. Given the opportunity, it would follow them to their destinations, would stand round the office door and touch its wood, as sacred as the real cross. The last taxi had been taken and only an old horse-cab drawn up at the rear of the stand, its muffled driver half asleep in the cold, offered means of escape. They climbed in.

—To Exchange.[68]

The cab clattered up Water Street, the horses' breath mingling with the fog.

—We serve the obsolete.[69] We rush from all havens astern.[70]

—But the ship backs from the wharf before she swings round for the open sea.

The Captain polished his pince-nez on his sleeve. Then he looked at his watch.

—Five minutes!

The cab driver's tall hat towered up into the fog. By an adroit move, they had avoided a traffic jam: buses, vans, cars, trams that could do no more than jerk spasmodically forward a few feet at a time, were left behind and as they entered the gloom of Exchange the roars of the city, the clangour of changing gears, warnings and directions, the subdued subterranean pulse of a hundred running engines, like the vibrant thrumming[71] of a ship's turbines, interrupted once by a clash of glass, ebbed away into the deafening detonations within the immense black dome of the station. *Exchange*. The Captain paid the cab driver and they hurried towards the barrier.

—Better run, we've only got a few minutes!

—All right, sir, don't bother with a platform ticket,[72] you've only got a minute.

Sigbjørn hoisted his sea-bag over the turnstile. He held out his ticket: Preston, 3rd class. They swung through. Now they hurried down the platform. Above them a clock-face snapped at the minutes. By the train, standing with its open doors ready for them, a man and a woman were in each other's arms.

—Isn't that like mother?

—Yes, it is. But never mind. You must get in. Hurry! His father smiled at him. For the last time, psychology!

Sigbjørn climbed into the train and stowed his sea-bag in the corridor. A door slammed. On the other side of the platform, another train was drawing in, its long belly sliding, its long angles of driving-rod driving.

He came to the window to say goodbye to his father, but the man, now separated from the woman, was opening the carriage door. The man and he stood together in the corridor; the woman and his father on the platform. Sigbjørn tried to open the window but it was jammed. He tugged again at the thick, perforated thong. The strap would not give, the window was shut between them.

He could see his father now as he pulled at the window. The man standing by helped him but it was useless. Now the train was moving out and explosions were echoing from the black glass roof. A barrier of iron and timber and glass had arisen between him and his father.

Exchange...

Their mouths moved on either side of the barrier forming inaudible phrases[73] of parting, of love. Now his father was running with the train, he was saying something Sigbjørn could not hear. The sheds were moving, the stationary train opposite seemed also to be moving...'*Exchange*'...Sigbjørn turned away. What had his father been trying to say? Who could tell? He would never know, only those detonations which seemed to be blasting from the platform, blasting the special past[74] and he recalled the words, 'cracked with grief.'

From the fog emerged, but oddly enough not with remorse but with a fatal delight, a final acceptance—yes, even a dreadful triumph, only these two certainties in the heart:

—Murderer.

—Fratricide.[75]

XII

> The tragedy of our spiritual quest: we don't know what we are searching for...[1]

"What could happen?"[2] asked the man seated in the third class compartment opposite him.

Sigbjørn looked at him in bewilderment. The stranger was tall and bearded with a florid, earth coloured complexion in which his eyes shone oddly like two blue flowers. A seam-like scar ran down one side of his face from temple to chin. With hands laced and knotted like boots he was searching for a cigarette. He found one; now he was short of a match...

"How do you mean, what could happen?" Sigbjørn struck a match for him.

"Thank you...Well anyway, that's what the gentleman outside was trying to say," the other said, drawing on his cigarette. "If anything happened you were to follow certain courses of action not specified. Cigarette?"

Sigbjørn shook his head, opening and shutting his hand on a new pipe.

"I'm really a pipe smoker, too," said the other. "I prefer the old donkeyboiler[3] anytime."

"By the way did you mean my father just now?"

"Your father was it? Very well, it was your father; but the question to ask yourself, the question I always ask myself is: what could happen?"

"Yes, indeed, what," Sigbjørn repeated automatically.

There was silence and the shuffle shuffle of the train. Then another train passing, although slowly, in the opposite direction, startled him. Zzzzt! It was gone quickly, after all.

But it was returning home while he was committed so irrevocably in the opposite direction.

Yet in an important sense it might be said that he too was returning home. He felt a sudden stab, like a stab of love. He crossed his legs, pressing his knees tightly against one another to stop himself trembling. He was now getting into quite a panic, it was like going back to school, he thought. Nothing is as all-poisoning as this fear which sinks into the pit of the stomach and spreads icily through the entire system.

But it was astonishing to feel how alike this was to the actual, wasting, sickness for the sea itself and with this realization a perverse longing for the ocean gripped him; but this was not, he felt, glancing sideways out of the dull window, for any sea which should await him so much as for one that belonged to the shrouded country receding from him even if his immediate vision of that country were limited to the iron works near at hand, slag heaps, gas retorts, cylinders, tall black shafts growing through the fog— "The Bootle Cold Storage[4] and Ice Company." Rattle-shuffle.

Somewhere in the corridor a door banged. The train swayed...Something seemed to come to an end, he thought, abruptly, like a shut door: that also seemed to finish it: but there was nothing on the other side, no reality, no exchange, so much in life was just a fade out, on two figures walking alone in the sunset, or one was alone again oneself and the sirens called through the fog.[5]

Yet somehow here he was beyond that sunset, beyond that door, beyond—almost literally—that fog and life still managed to go on when everything ought to have been finished.

Rattle-rattle-shuffle-rattle-rattle. The train leaned far over for a corner, and it was beautiful the way she did so, graciously arching her iron jointed body; the telegraph poles took a short cut over a yard, but soon the wires stealthily undulated after them again; rattle shuffle, rattle shuffle. And *wheeeee*, said the train. *Wheeeeeeee!* Short and long whistles like a freighter entering port. *Wheee! Wheeeeee!* But entering what port? Archangel or Leningrad or—

"Do you do rock climbing?" the man opposite interrupted his thoughts.

"What?"

"Climbing with a rope."

He inclined his head over his shoulder towards a photograph among a block of others on the compartment wall advertising hotels of the railway, and such landmarks as Carnarvon Castle[6] and Llanberis Pass[7], of a square stone unlovely building standing at the foot of towering mountains: Sigbjørn peered closer and read: Gorphwysfa Hotel, Pen-y-Pass.

"At that hotel there," the man went on, "I've been doing some climbing with a rope. I stayed at that hotel there, however you pronounce it...Anyway, to cut a long story short, I did rock climbing there. A very fine sport. Oh yes."

Rattle rattle rattle. The train seemed to be a special entity whose noises filled the gaps in the conversation; their heads nodded between phrases with the motion of the train and even certain words themselves seemed to be a logical emphasis by it here and there.

"They certainly bleed you in Wales. Don't you have a saying: Taffy[8] was a Welshman, Taffy was a thief?...By the way do you like a glass of whiskey in the morning?"

"Thank you very much." Sigbjørn drank deeply from a proffered flask.

"My name is Daland Haarfragre."[9]

"Mine Tarnmoor."

They rattled on through Aintree,[10] but he could distinguish no sign of the imminent Grand National; if preparations were being made for [it] they must have been going on underground. There was dead silence for a time until they were well outside the town when the man broke the quiet with what was almost a shout.

"I was interested because of what your father said—that something might happen. Now all I ask is, what? That climbing is as dangerous a thing as you might attempt anyway, otherwise, isn't that so? Then something might have happened to me only this time it didn't!"

"No," Sigbjørn said,

"Do you climb the Devil's Kitchen?"[11] the man asked. "I climbed it once in nails for my own pleasure and once in rubbers for the glory of God."

Sigbjørn's thoughts spread and wandered away with the rails on either side of the train. A man stood with pick upraised at their passage. At street corners, along the tracks, at the entrances of unopened public houses, loitered the unemployed, gazing with empty eyes into the lifting fog, eyes like stones[12] that had lost their gems. A few provincial cinemas were already lighted.

"I climbed the Parson's Nose,"[13] his companion was saying.

"How long did it take you?"

"Oh, I went up in three-quarters of an hour. I found the rocks very easy."

"There's a saying that you can come down in two minutes and find the rocks very hard."

Haarfragre laughed prolongedly. "For a Welshman I must say you're a damned good man," he added with unction. "But all racial discrimination is bad. If you really are a Welshman I'm prepared to admit you're as good as me."

"Thank you," Sigbjørn said. "I hope I have Welsh blood."

"Look at Poland[14]...At the whole matter of national minorities...The Ukrainians! But of course the problem of Wales[15] is not primarily a national one. It is only the problem of workers everywhere."

"Life is damned queer."

"Queer! I'll say it's queer, but that knowledge won't get you very far...Queer, sure it's queer: my crew are queer, going on strike about some old scrap-iron, rightly enough, and the police are queer too, but we've got to act—that's all there is to it—for tomorrow you may be denied the right to act."

"How do you mean?"

"I mean that we must ally ourselves with our own class, the working class now or with the open forces of reaction."

"Yes."

Sigbjørn turned away, afraid. Wasn't he acting now? Allying himself with his own class...Or was it something else again? Not an alliance so much as an excursion to the working class, a sort of Prince of Wales[16] trip to the stokehold. Dreary houses with mediaeval plumbing and henruns in the back yard glided past; an environment, sordid, grassless and pitiful, unfolded itself and clutched at his conscience. He was a member of the human race living in an equal darkness, but of the soul, that luxury commodity. Ah Peer Gynt, that onion without a core![17]

You could as soon stop the running mind of the Northern man as you could the Midnight Sun[18] circling the saucer of the horizon. Nothing is solved by it, yet everything is obvious—

They had now stopped at Maghull,[19] and the droning of an aeroplane[20] engine filled the silence. Sigbjørn, who for some obscure reason could never resist aeroplanes, rushed to the corridor to look, but saw nothing.

When he returned to the compartment he saw that Haarfragre was buried in a newspaper. It was the Norse paper, *Aftenposten*.[21] Leaning forward Sigbjørn could read, but not translate, its now almost unfamiliar language.

Trelast damper paa grunn i Maaløystrømmen. Skibet kom av, men da for skibet begynte paa reise fra Omega til Prester og som man ser full lastet med trelast fra russiske sagbrukene...[22]

"What's a trelast damper?" asked Sigbjørn.

"A timber ship, son."

"Is that so? I'm just signing on—or rather I've just been signed on one—as a fireman."

"Is that so?" Haarfragre smiled at him queerly. "Really?"

"Yes."

"That's very interesting." Haarfragre hummed as he went on reading.

The train pounded on; far to the east were the factories of Wigan;[23] they huddled in clusters, their chimneys in the clearing, but still leaden, distant, seeming like the smokestacks of Mississippi river boats[24] flaming in a mad race. They fell behind, their smoke hung heavily. Towns collapsed before a bombardment of noise, but these were mild agricultural towns and indeed the country through which they were passing was essentially pastoral, and was about as much a part of Lancashire as Sigbjørn was himself, which is to say, a good deal more a part of it than was apparent. To the west, over those plains, the sea was invisible and Sigbjørn was conscious of a sharp sense of disappointment, almost, of betrayal. They rushed through Ormskirk.[25] Stations, villages, thickets, telegraph wires, snapped off, sank deeply in the train's swell; she mounted a cutting like a ship rising to a slow, grey, comber. Sigbjørn looked at the back of the paper again.

Skibet som med la propplasten gaar til sjøs...Slik saa dampskibet "Viets" ut, da det i fjord gaar og kom inn til Kristiansand efter sin fryktelige reise fra Arkangelsk. Som meddelte i morgennummeret igor ble styrmannen, da stormen raste som verst, slaat over bord. Paa billedet...[26]

"A lot of storms you seem to be having," he said, understanding perhaps three words.

"Yes," said Haarfragre without raising his eyes, "This is the season of fires and disasters."

...Piddlededum, piddledee, sang the train. Melville's Caergwrle Ales.[27] Piddlededeeeeee! Author of Pegdog and Piddlededee;[28] the man who lived among the cannibals. The wheels cried out against the iron. In a wet field before him on the left a game of football[29] was being played; a three-quarter broke away; sold a dummy; sold two dummies; now there was none to stop him save the fullback, it was really amazing that so much activity could take place in a few seconds. Sigbjørn craned round—would he make it? No. Two roars, one of disappointment, the other of exultation, from the crowd, met and mingled with the racket of the train as the fullback tackled the three-quarter low and brought him slithering down in the mud and slush of snow. Sigbjørn had to imagine the rest, the forwards gathering round, the referee hesitating to blow his whistle. Or, in all that welter of sound, with which was mingled again the roar of a plane, did he distinguish its infinitesimal pipe? Get up, get up, get up, the party is in danger. Gone...

But instantly they were upon another game in which a try had just been scored; the stand-off half poised the ball for the kick, and a moment later the try had been converted into a goal.

The thought pursued, the problem balked but now finally solved; the solution signed. And behind the goal the linesmen's flags flew up in triumph!

For some time Haarfragre had laid aside his reading and he had been watching Sigbjørn with a smile. Then Sigbjørn saw that he was holding an envelope with a foreign but familiar stamp towards him. He leaned forward and read:

Captain Daland Haarfragre,
c/o Smith and Hermannsonn,[30]
D/S Unsgaard,
Prester,
Lancs. England.

Haarfragre was smiling but said nothing, still holding the letter in front of Sigbjørn's eyes as though it were a rag with which he had just flicked a speck of dust from the bridge house. Then he pocketed the letter.

"You're the man I heard all about at the Konsulat," he said.

They both started to laugh.

"I'm sorry I didn't catch a chance to speak to your father on the platform. But we have had many talks as a matter of fact, in those little Mecca cafes[31] you have there. I knew him before you ever got your job. Of course he helped you get it."

"Nonsense. My father was terribly shocked when I told him I was going to sea again."

Haarfragre shrugged his shoulders. "Exactly. Well, it was not your father who helped you get the job, I was not quite accurate, it was a gentleman named Jump[32] who interested himself in you, God knows why. Your father's help came later."

"Good God!" Sigbjørn experienced a complicated emotion in which was mingled thanks for his father's generosity, whatever form it had taken, and remorse that the world would never let him grow up into a man.

"Yes," Haarfragre laughed, nodding. "Your father put in a good word for you, so to speak. He guarantees your good behavior, promises you will not desert the ship, but, what is really sensible, gives you a note[33] to draw on the ship's chandlers in Oslo anytime you like. That's more important than you think for the simple reason we don't know where we're going or when we'll lay up."

Sigbjørn was thinking of Jump, but he suggested imponderables that did not bear thinking of at all. So he suppressed them instantly.

"You mean even the captain doesn't know where we're going," he said.

Haarfragre took a long breath. "What sort of a ship do you think we are? Do you think our freight's paid with time bills?"[34]

"I know you're in ballast."

"Well, there's no need for a lien on our cargoes. No charterers pay her freight in advance. Still, there's this much certain, the *Unsgaard* sails as soon as she's finished unloading. Tomorrow I should say."

Sigbjørn fell silent, looking out at a little pine wood—wood for timber, wood for fire—gliding past the window. One trembling hand rubbed on top of the other. Haarfragre was also looking out. On the last tree a stray advertisement was stuck. *Douglas Fairbanks Jr.*[35] *in Outward Bound...Futurist Theatre...*

"And what sort of captain do you think I am?" laughed Haarfragre. "You must think I'm rather queer, leaving my ship to go climbing, eh?"

"Nothing will ever be queer again to me now."

"Come, come, what if I was like Captain Christoforidas?"[36]

"Christopher—"

"Christoforidas. He was the man who left his ship in Quarantine. The ship was examined and—what do you mean?—fumitigated,[37] but then the skipper left it. Yes, he just left it and took all the papers and half the crew with him. And they couldn't move the ship! No they had to leave it there, riding her anchor, and getting in the way of other boats endangering small boats carrying customs and public health officials and so on."

"Maybe when he sobered up and discovered that had happened he decided not to come back."

"That would have been bad."

"That would be."

The fir woods of Croston[38] were still sliding past the train. Now he was really committed, there was no getting out of the transaction now. Was it by a stroke of fortune, that the future had fallen into his grasp?

He remembered his last voyage and thought suddenly that the landscape beyond the trees that they were now passing was extraordinarily like the Kwantung Peninsula.[39] He remembered the crews of junks standing wide-legged and looking up at the ship. Cape Esan, Tsugaru Strait, Hakodate in a hurricane of snow, the Sea of Japan, Korea...Dairen![40]

For a moment his mind sought refuge among these memories, and they seemed good. It had been the height of summer when the *Oedipus Tyrannus*[41] had made Dairen. It was strange that what was a comfortless experience should have an almost nostalgic attraction for him in retrospect. Plagues of flies, naked boys running for coins on the wharf, natives starving under the bloated bellies of the Socony[42] Oil tanks, the crust of bread that fell into the oil on the wharf and the man that ate it, the brazen heat, the quilted sky, what components of a happy memory were there here? Well, there had been a hint of Russia,[43] of enormous things up country—Manchukuo[44] now.

"Did you ever go to Dairen?" Sigbjørn asked. Perhaps the past was more comfortable than the present anyhow.

"Dalny? I'll say I did. What makes you ask?"

"Nothing."

"Well, anyway we won't go to a dirty spindle head[45] like that no more," Haarfragre said. "You shall have a beautiful voyage on our rotten ship. And in Leningrad you shall see—perhaps, perhaps—the wide Neva, its waters so blue where it turns abruptly! And so beautiful where she forks among the beautiful, pretty, islands, looking for the Gulf of Finland and the ocean."

"There are white nights there, just as in Norway?"

"Oh yes, white nights in summer. Leningrad[46] is built on a swamp[47] too you know."

Sigbjørn looked away again. When he looked back the other's countenance was black as a thundercloud.

"Damn it, it's not as simple as that, young fellow." His eyes glared at him under thick brows. "So you want to be a fireman, do you?"

"Why not?"

"Why not? No reason. But suppose I told you we had no need of a fireman on our vessel? What would you say to that?"

Sigbjørn said nothing. Rattle shuffle rattle shuffle.

"Suppose I should say this: I'm the captain of the *Unsgaard* and consider that we have no need of you or of any more firemen at all. What then?"

"I understood you were short of men."

Captain Haarfragre laughed. "I understood a hell of a lot of things when I was your age...Let me see your *hyrkontrakt*."

Sigbjørn handed it to him and he examined it for a while in silence. "Of course 'limper' means that you are a coal passer," the Captain said at length, "you don't look on that as a job, do you?"

"A hell fire job, some say."

"But it's not the job for you, is it? You weren't cut out for heaving coal, were you? Why, it's a slave job!"

"If not for the heaving coal, then for what else?"

The train rattled and shuffled on.

"Supposing I were to tell you the ship was an oil-burner."[48]

"An oil-burner!"

The train was passing over a bad stretch of rail and the two men were jogging in their seats like horseback riders in their saddles.

"Or if it was one of those funny ships you stoked all by yourself" it would be unfortunate, too, Haarfragre added as if to himself. Then another drollery seemed to strike him. "Supposing," he said, handing the discharge back, "my ship turned out to be an old windbag."

"A windbag?"

"Yes, sir, a windbag, bound for Cape Desolation or the Horn,[49] you'd be out of luck, wouldn't you? Or if she turned out to be some kind of an old orange boat,[50] or balloon boat or some old haystack like one of them there famous bloody laundry boats going round picking up washing, you'd be quite out of luck, wouldn't you? But if my old can burns coal you'll be all right unless I say I don't want a coal passer, isn't that rightee?"[51]

"Rightee," said Sigbjørn with a wan smile.

Haarfragre started to hum to himself. They were approaching Farington,[52] and the fields they were passing now had been flooded and had not yet thawed. A procession of men were skating along the fields parallel with the train but Sigbjørn had the idea it was only one man they saw, skating eternally with the train.

There was a gleam of flame in the smoke that billowed over their heads from the engine. Fear possessed him and he imagined this man as death.

Death was a dark skater[53] hurtling over the mound; crouched down he streaked towards you; he circled you with his hands outstretched; then he was away again over the flooded fields; he was gone, gone forever, the danger was past.

But it is then that more quietly, more swiftly, than ever before he slides up behind you and you are lost—

"Supposing," said Haarfragre, "I were to tell you that my vessel was not going to Russia at all, or indeed to any place that you or anybody else had ever heard of, supposing I told you that we were not going in ballast to the White Sea or any other sea, but to some place quite different, but not altogether unfamiliar perhaps, what would you say then?"

Sigbjørn rubbed his eyes: was he asleep? But the shuffle rattle of the train was louder, more urgent. That was real. And what was that shadow galloping over the fields, that tiny, cross-like shadow? Could it be an aeroplane? If it were so he couldn't hear it, its shadow moved noiselessly towards its aim.

"Or supposing," Haarfragre continued, "she turned out to be some old hulk, and I crammed all sail on her and sailed her nearly to the Horn and then back again when I decided she was overloaded, and made the owners reload her.[54] What would you say to that?"

Sigbjørn laughed, but said nothing. When you half shut your eyes there seemed to be many people in the compartment, he thought, it was as though Haarfragre's nonsensical remarks had created a kind of density in the atmosphere.

"Or if I told you she rolled so much we had to take her into harbour; that she was out there rolling in the Irish ocean and we took her into the Ribble[55] and she just went on rolling and rolling from side to side and she rolled all the sticks[56] out of her and all the spars and the coal, and even when we got her alongside we couldn't stop her, and maybe she's rolling yet. What would you say?"

"I'd say that was a goddam funny ship."

"Yes, sir, and there is such a ship, too; such a ship, and going to Archangel. She rolls so that she makes a big hole in the wharf and then the Marine Superintendent and the Harbour Master and the shore bosun[57] tell her to put to sea again, and then what happens? Why, she strains, and opens in her upper works, her coppers and grates[58] fall down...We lose the upper irons[59] of our rudder, we have to live on tiny small biscuits and salt water...We make a machine for steering the ship. In the end we have to *tie* the ship together, frap it,[60] like St. Paul. In short, the ship is a complete wreck, and when finally we get her home she does not require much trouble to break up."

"Or supposing it turned out to be the Flying Dutchman,"[61] Sigbjørn suggested. "That would make one feel like going back home."

"I often think the world is like that ship that rolls people off it," said Haarfragre, producing his pipe.

"Yes, it's difficult to hang on."

They had stopped by a signal box; Preston 9. The silence that followed was again filled by the roar of a plane. Passengers went out into the corridor and peered out at the isobars[62] of smoke rising over the city they were approaching. They stretched themselves out of the windows but they were not tall enough to see the machine.

"Seriously, why are you going?" Haarfragre asked, passing him the flask once again. "In precisely what manner do you intend to make use of us?"

"I don't know. I'm confused in my mind," Sigbjørn replied, then, asking the other as if tangentially, "By the way, have you ever heard of a Norwegian author, William Erikson?"

"An author?"

"Yes, the author of a book about the sea—I wonder if you've read it—*Skibets reise fra Kristiania.*"

"I've heard of it, yes," Haarfragre said reflectively. "Well, I've read it if you like. But that book is all nonsense. When all the mens is ashore all the time and getting diseases. The sea is not like that. A man takes one voyage as a deckboy and then writes a book like that telling us what the sea is like. You don't seriously imagine that the greatest enemy of the sailors are drink and womens, do you?"

"You didn't get to the end, did you?" Sigbjørn said with a smile.

"I read far enough."

"Not at all."

Sigbjørn's anger was quenched by the fear that poured through him as finally, irrevocably, the train started once more. He sent out a prayer to the little patches of snow in the station yards, a last supplication to the past, to miracle, to Christmas, he felt rather than Easter. But there was no stopping the train and there was no stopping whatever might come after. By a level crossing a man had reined in his horse to watch them go. The horse champed at the bit; breath was white on the air.

"When the world possesses reason race-horses[63] are reserved for hauling dung. When without, war horses are bred on the common..." Haarfragre said musingly and started to hum again. "I once heard a story about an English captain...Shall I tell it you."

"Surely. Go on."

"Well, he was rolling all round the world on some old tub and he always made very good and profitable voyages for his owners. But he was very fond of horse back riding and bills for this never failed to appear in his accounts. Shall I go on? Well, the company told him not to let them see any more bills for the nags. Well, sure enough the next voyage home there were no bills for the horses, and the company congratulated him, but the captain said, 'Although you can't see the horse, he's there just the same.'"

They laughed. The train was drawing into Preston.[64]

"Now, have a last glass of whiskey in the afternoon, eh." He offered the flask.

"Good luck."

"Good luck."

"Now," said Haarfragre, drawing on his coat, "I've got to say goodbye before we get there." He held out his hand. "We had a very pleasant conversation. But remember, when we are at sea, I am the Old Man.[65] No chinnings, no whiskey, no talk. Nothing very jocular." He wagged an ingratiating finger. "You have a saying, not too many jokes with the officers! Well, goodbye, I hope you find it not too bloody hot down below. And, by the way, there's no need to come on board till as late as you like tonight. You better have something to eat at the station and get well filled up. You'll need it, with our scallywag of a cook."

The men shook hands. Haarfragre dropped down onto the platform. The *Aftenposten* was left on the seat. Sigbjørn pulled his sea-bag from the luggage rack.

Suddenly the captain's head appeared through the corridor window. He was laughing as he said:

"We won't be able to see you but you'll be there just the same."

XIII

> Being great it, the Tao, passes on; passing on, it becomes remote; having become remote, it returns...[1]

A lone airman,[2] that wintry Easter, was flying over the Irish Sea. Now that the fog had cleared completely he was following the line of the old telegraph stations[3] to Liverpool: Holyhead, Cefn Du, Point Lynas, Puffin Island, Great Ormes Head. Making a spurt, he covered the seventeen miles between Llysfaen over Veryd to Voel Nant in seven minutes.

Like a needle his machine threaded cloud and cloud. Its song was heard over the estuary of the Dee and far inland over the Peninsula.

Marvelous weather, thought the pilot, smiling. Especially since the day had broken in thick fog and flying had at first seemed hopeless. Previous days had been shrouded in wet, driving snow with occasional clear intervals, like yesterday afternoon.[4] In the evening, the expected rain had turned to snow, melting as it fell. Ice and snow drifted down the rivers.

Now the fog had dispersed, the sun was shining brilliantly and the world seemed to hang between winter and spring, a gulf through which a northeast March wind, blowing all the way down from Norway, rushed howling to both.

Sea birds scattered at his approach, mewing with terror: *Meev, Meev, quark, cli, klio, io,*[5] dropping very low to cruise rapidly away with a steady beat of their white wings, a handsbreadth from the water.

Suddenly all that could be heard on board was the crying of the wind in the struts. The plane, with its engine cut out, was diving over Hilbre Island.[6] The retreat of white birds became more disorderly, more panic-stricken. Did the pilot dive then, remembering Lycidas, the drowned scholar? This is, one thinks, where it happened...or was it in Anglesey?[7]

But no thought of Milton crossed the pilot's mind: he dived purely and simply out of love of life. He was heading across the estuary of the Dee. Below him a tug with a string of barges made its way up river; from the cockpit they looked like large animated shoes. Reaching the shore of South Wirral he decided to follow the coast and changed his course accordingly.

He reeled along the cliffs. Below him, the snowy fields were now streaked generously with green; on this westerly, wind-bitten seaboard many golf courses were plotted.

His eyes glancing away from his route, spotted a red brick house[8] standing apart from its village, which belonged to a Captain Tarnmoor, ship-owner, but it was not the house that fascinated the pilot so much as the road which led away from it. This wound in great curves over the back of the Wirral, rolling between white-brimmed fields splashed with emerald to one cross-roads, up a steepish slope, between acres of moorland to another, where, dropping down through marshes, lower-lying fields, and villages of rain-dark stone, it mounted a final hill at the other side of the county, thickly wooded and crowned by an observatory and an ancient windmill. This was Bidston and the last station[9] of the ancient Telegraph. Beyond lay Lancashire and the North.

The road had been taken by Captain Tarnmoor and his son, Sigbjørn, not two hours before. They had driven along it in a dense fog. The pilot avoided it.

Below him now the world seemed to move very slowly and spasmodically: it would give a jerk forward, appear to stop, then advance, gliding; he dived and the world spun madly as in delirium. He did not speculate as to whether the crazily-spinning battery of our existence might not itself be part of a great delirium; he was not interested; opening the throttle, he looped: a Crosville 'bus[10] crawled slowly above him, on the sky, upside down.

As he roared directly over the Royal Liverpool[11] Golf Club, a man standing on the green at the 'Telegraph' shook a putter at him. It glittered in the sun like a little brooch. From time to time someone waved at him gaily from Hoylake Promenade[12] but he was already far beyond, racing over the Meols shore where only the remains of an old forest looked up at him gloomily with a face of black, antediluvian stubble.

A little later he spat to leeward in the hope of hitting what was left of the Star Chamber in Leasowe Castle.[13] Rock Point Fort[14] now lay below the airman on the left and again he prepared to dive, this time not only without shutting off the engine but with such accelerated deliberation that a spectator might have wondered if his intention were not to actually open fire. The pilot, himself, considered it interesting enough to speculate on what would have happened had he done so, given the machine-gun, of course, and he even accompanied his rapid, angry, and—in the strictest sense of the word—quixotic, descent with a phut-phut-phut-phut, uttered through clenched teeth, as though there were something about the Fort he hated violently and wished removed.

There was not much to be feared, he reflected, from the six thirty-two pounders mounted on cast-iron traversing platforms, or from the sixteen thirty-pounders, two in the casements of the tower. These were not nimble enough for aircraft. Nor would they have time to heat shot in the furnaces under the walls as they did in the years when Karl Marx and Queen Victoria were born. Perhaps the real danger would be of his own making. A direct hit on the magazine in the centre of the tower would cause instant explosion of the whole, a hurricane of dowels and trenails,[15] an eruption of cement and volcanic puzzilani, harder than stone and for this reason brought over from Mount Aetna more than a hundred years before.

But he knew these old defenses of the Industrial Revolution—just as the ancient telegraph whose line he had been following—to be obsolete, and therefore as harmless as the game he himself was playing. There was, however, and it must be repeated, a menacing sound to this game. And as he came out of his dive, circling the marble lighthouse[16] with his machine side-slipping and yawing in a snow-edged wind that might also have sprung from the sides of Mount Aetna, then zooming up and up and up until he hung like a windhover[17] above the estuary of the Mersey, it was not impossible to conceive of him as an emissary of the future, perhaps even—as Ricardo[18] appeared to the House of Commons—as a terrestrial visitor; anyhow, many who saw him heard something more than the temporal future rattling and knocking on the doors of their minds.

The Estuary spread westward to the horizon. Standing out there was a group of apparently motionless trawlers and steamers. Nearer in, two liners that had missed the top of the tide[19] were waiting to dock on the ebb.

The Estuary flowed eastwards into the Mersey which flowed inland to Runcorn[20] and beyond; the Manchester Ship Canal branched off it. Waterways were spread there like the veins of a hand. A violent wind now buffeted him and his machine seemed to buckle against it. He banked to eastward.

Below him, like a huge fish, a dredger glided, and he dropped lower to read her name.

'*Leviathan.*'[21]

But no thought of the White Whale entered the pilot's mind; he made no overtures to the supernatural at all; as a matter of fact he only wondered for a moment what had happened to the other Leviathan which never made any money for its owner and whether or not it was still tied up in Hoboken, New Jersey—and then forgot both altogether.

He headed down the Mersey. Far to his right, beyond the brow of the hill and winding away into the distance, was the road he had remarked from South Wirral and on which Sigbjørn Tarnmoor and his father had journeyed by car that morning, by way of Birkenhead, to James Street and Exchange.

On both sides of the river lay graving-docks[22] and ship-repairing yards. Between them, ferries sidled. A Greek timber ship[23] with a list to starboard made its slow way along the New Brighton side. A Geordie collier[24] passed over the place where only the day before the *Arcturion*[25] of the Tarnmoor Line had so nearly fouled the *Direction*,[26] outward bound. On the Birkenhead side the sailing ship, *Herzogin Cecile* from Wallaroo raised her spires nearer heaven than any church in sight.

From the air, the three rings[27] at the tramway stop below the Liver Building looked like targets. Phut,phut,phut,phut, muttered the pilot, but flying on, tried to imagine, in a more human mood, the life below him. Down there perhaps a new sea-apprentice in new stiff clothes and shiny cap took a ride on a Pier Head tram gazing down from his special altitude on all that trafficking in curious merchandise. His shoulders were thin with inexperience as he looked on the shrieking lorries labeled with the names of undreamed of harbours where he would go. And it was really strange if he should think of those places when at hand was the most romantic of all.

While an old, drunken woman in Milk Street[28] sang (throwing, with a magnificent gesture, two corners of her black shawl over her left shoulder) 'My Old Man's a Fireman On an Elder Dempster Boat,'[29] two hundred unemployed sailors with blue books[30] stormed a certain superintendent: "Here, I've got enough discharges to sink the *Mauretania*,"[31] and several wheat-broker's apprentices were called in line to receive their bonus—"Mallalieu,[32] my boy, we'll bear the brunt of the wheat market on our broad shoulders!"—while another apprentice in a marine insurance office received an inscribed picture of the heads of the firm as reward for many years faithful (and unpaid) service in the interest of the laws of average.[33]

At the Cotton Exchange[34] the loud-tongued tolling for another bankruptcy shattered the silence of many minds as ruthlessly as the tonger-tong of the bell of the treasure ship *Lutine* at Lloyd's spelt the doom of some iron freighter not long since pregnant with the issue of the ocean, and low as a submarine awash as she laboured in her agony.

While the pale corpses of cotton porters rotted in the stifling economic weather near Tithebarn Street, four hundred ex-soldiers rattled dominoes and dice in smoke-filled cafes. And, finally, while a red-faced broker, broken, drank an early, guilty, bemusing draught Bass at the scarcely opened Oyster Bar, his brain a circus ring of rampant bulls[35] and non-performing bears (what activity before a bank holiday could match the ceaseless scrambling in his own conscience?) many whose lives were not a directionless nightmare at all but who had achieved their goals, walked, shoulders erect, and happily serene in the light of ancient faith; or without ancient faith but nonetheless serene, to offices, barbershops, golf, or wives and children.

For some there was only hope or disappointment; nothing between. To others life seemed good: a toughness ran through their veins like self-extending tree roots; and there actually existed on the part of many a sublime, unselfish acceptance of the smash-and-grab,[36] of the root-hog-or-die philosophy,[37] while elsewhere rolled a seething phosphorescent gleaming of revolt.

Or so the pilot speculated. But from the air you cannot see decay.

Captain Tarnmoor, or Hansen-Tarnmoor, to give him his correct name, who had left Exchange Station about half an hour after seeing his son Sigbjørn off to Preston from number three platform, had loitered in the station buffet almost too overcome to move, but who was now as delighted as he could allow himself to be delighted by anything, by the way the fog had lifted and the sun come out, wondered, turning into the Mecca Cafe,[38] if the machine above were the same he had noticed two days before skywriting whiskey advertisements. The thought disturbed him as he stood looking up, stroking his beard.

The pilot passed over an aerodrome. The tall, oddly evocative letters of its name stared up whitely from the flying field: Speke.[39]

The densest population in the world, and an area so dynamic its influence was felt in every part of it, now spread itself before his eyes. From the air it seemed like part of a country of the future, which had spread horizontally rather than vertically, but of a stupendous greatness, and where there was a continual outgoing and incoming of all that was necessary to people in an island state; and on water, earth, and in the air a continual, raving flux, beginning at one end of the world and ending at the other.

He put the nose of the plane down and held it there, watching over the side as though he were going to land. But now there were no outlines of a field below where his wheels, first gently, then heavily, would touch the ground; but perhaps he wanted only to try and understand, instantly, without even the distraction of the sound of his engine, that inchoate yet strangely ordered mystery of gigantic traffic.

Soon his engine caught again, with a roar.

The Industrial Revolution! Lancashire, thought the pilot, was certainly the county where that age had driven down its roots. Glass, factories and cotton mills, weaving sheds,[40] puddling furnaces,[41] docks and dynamos, railways running on three levels...and intertwining them, a green, windblown countryside, thundering with horses' hooves, jagged with colour, groaning with crowds at the racetrack and at rugby matches, and the whole cabled and flexed with steel rivers and canals! It was marvelous but where was it all going to lead? For a moment, but only for a moment, he wondered what lay behind all this spinning, roving,[42] carding, what secret could be hidden in these towns that seemed from a great height to be laid bare as the abdomen in an operation, so that it might seem to require only a small effort of the imagination to see right through these gasworks, for instance, into rooms full of retorts beneath, he imagined, like a fireman's dream of eternally shut furnaces in a clean stokehold, what secret lay beyond and below its obvious relations of exchange and property? But below him now were shunting trucks, evanescent as drops of sliding mercury...

The future would be simple as a waterfall, he thought, opening the throttle...

A little later he was flying over the ship canal where an oil tanker seemed to be crawling mildly through fields of potatoes.

From Manchester, towns opened out of northeast and northwest, towns in whose very names clanged and shattered the music of the Industrial Revolution: Bolton, Blackburn, Accrington...[43]

He flew north.

Cutting the county in two was the River Ribble, running southwest from the Pennines[44] to Preston. The Norwegians called the latter Prester. The southern half was also cut in two, but from north to south, by a high road[45] running from Warrington to Preston. East of that was industrial Lancashire. West of it was an agricultural belt, given over to the growing of potatoes, the pasturing of cattle, the intensive production of eggs.

Along this pastoral strip, far below the pilot, Sigbjørn Tarnmoor proceeded in a third-class railway carriage to Preston to join, as a coal passer, the Norwegian timber vessel, *Unsgaard*. Opposite him, without his yet knowing it, sat the captain of the ship. Once, when the train stopped, Sigbjørn heard the aeroplane. He rushed to the window to look, but he saw nothing.

As he was traveling along, Sigbjørn felt a queer empathy with this part of the country, although he couldn't fully explain this feeling to himself, or make any comparison clear in his mind; this pastoral belt wasn't Lancashire and neither was he, that was the first point!

Yet in some way he was as mysteriously interwoven with capitalist Lancashire as the past is mysteriously and wonderfully interwoven in all our lives. At the same time he had this feeling of not belonging and although smoke and fire hung heavily on all horizons, this country west of Wigan and St.Helens responded to him; when he looked further west and couldn't even see the ocean, which, like Poseidon,[46] he considered belonging to him anyway, his sensation of being set apart was completed; in spite of it he was still able to reflect that like those other byproducts of coke and tar and sulphate of ammonia,[47] once dumped in the river but now beginning to recover millions of pounds, he might still prove to be of value, even if this were unrecognised, or at the moment, unrealisable.

The truth is, he would have felt just as isolated anywhere else for although he had lived in various parts of Lancashire and Cheshire since coming over from Norway as a child, he knew his way around surprisingly little and had small enough correspondence with life. For instance, he hadn't known Preston was a seaport at all though he had been to sea before.

Towns were just names and products in school-books: St.Helens, glass; Wigan, coal and iron; or what a town was reputed to be, but was not, remarkable for such as Birkenhead, where the first steam tram was run.[48] And the names of certain Lancashire towns fascinated him just as names to the exclusion of their possible significance: Culcheth, Flixton, Upholland, Newton-in-Makerfield, Oswaldtwistle...But he had never visited these towns.[49]

Now he occupied himself by trying to decipher the Norwegian in Captain Haarfragre's *Aftenposten*, occasionally turning to watch a football game through the carriage window, for in the Easter season in Lancashire games were often played in the mornings.

Meanwhile the lone airman, having flown over the Manchester ship canal in a great circle, was now returning over Maghull in the direction of the sea; once more he changed his course. For a time he loitered in the air. Then, as though he had come previously to a decision, he started to fly swiftly over Coppull towards Leyland in the direction of Preston.

From the air he could see the rivers, Lancashire's original divulgence of power, coming down in spate after the thaw as no more than garden brooks; and over the countryside, the pastureland and moors, marching pylons carrying high-tension wires. Roads, too, drove down the country and the one he followed, that had once carried munitions, dropped down from Shap Fell[50] to Preston to strike south through Derby to London behind him.

He passed over densely populated towns where mills were idle, and one town that seemed empty, like a city of the dead that seemed already to be paralysed, cut off from substance and hope, awaiting only its own devastation, for its smokeless chimneys were like mute howitzers[51] it would one day train on itself; but everywhere there were churches raising their brittle, metal masts to God, and a little further on there would be the same confusion of moving merchandise as before, the same multitudinous activity denying disaster; and there was one town dark with smoke but lit against its own darkness, and the pilot imagined the mine shafts[52] running underneath the central streets, dark caverns where the power was dug that kept the arc-lamps blazing above.

In the train below, Sigbjørn thought suddenly of Cambridge, his university. Hadn't men of mechanical genius flocked to Lancashire just as the scholars had flocked to the universities in the Middle Ages? But now the descendants of these men had different ambitions for their sons. They desired for them the Universities again. And so the circle was complete, he thought, men eternally passing from one class to another.[53]

Yes, but now the more enlightened wished not to climb further up, but if possible to go lower down.

He wondered how he could express these thoughts to Haarfragre, with whom he had struck up a conversation. But this unreality and, yes, the horror of what he was doing overwhelmed him and he tried instead to imagine that the train was going in the opposite direction.

The pilot, too, was thinking, looking down: all that seems to remain permanently here is the habit of trying out new ideas. By that magnet, commercial as well as mechanical ability had been drawn. How will Lancashire fare in the future and what ideas will be tried?

Preston docks,[54] which he was now approaching, seen from the air at certain points, seemed to be shaped like the head and shoulders of a man drawn in angles: a neck of water supporting the wide but faceless head of the dock, and its jaw distinctly ruled so that it jutted sharply to the north; below the neck, this man's shoulders of gleaming metals raised up on both sides to arms and wrists and hands that were, on the left, angles of a road, and on the right, of a canal:[55] it was indeed as if at this central point of Lancashire, within the womb, as it were, of this Alma Mater[56] of industrial civilisation, by some electrification of chosen reality, these docks and metals were struggling to take on a human form that was already capable of at least the appearance of a gesture, for it seemed to be stretching upwards with already created, cracking, muscles of pyramids of coal.

But the rest of the crescent body was not formed at all; its legs trailed off in wasteland, poverty grass,[57] scrap-iron.

A second downward look two miles further on and this illusion had disappeared, gone in the space of a minute; and instead of any image being afforded, everything started to look alike. Roads ruled parallel to the dock, reflecting the sunlight, were indistinguishable from the dock, and the dock from the canal. The factory chimneys were like funnels and the pyramids of coal like the endless and soulless gables of factory buildings. All the people looked alike and everything seemed to be an interminable, interpenetrating plagiarism of everything else.

And all of it was swept by the tiny, black, cross-like shadow of his own machine.

Only the river was clear as a solution to be followed; it wound out, a magnificent blue, like the Susquehanna[58] in Pennsylvania, as though it were being drawn like steel from the furnaces of the town. He followed it with his eyes all the way to Freckleton and St. Annes-on-the-Sea.[59]

He had been circling Preston curiously for about a quarter of an hour when the little train bearing Sigbjørn Tarnmoor and Captain Haarfragre of the *Unsgaard* approached.

It streaked ahead on the last stretch from Farington like a little terrier...the smoke was the bone in its mouth.

The pilot flew on. He saw a timber ship down there unloading. On her side was painted her name in enormous letters: *Unsgaard*. From a thousand feet he could read it. He flew north always north.[60] He left the factories behind.

Instead, there were waterfalls and caves below him, and where the country was steeper, mysterious rivers, underground...

XIV.1

Christophorus then carried him over, but now for the first time found a burden which almost exceeded his powers. This little child was a marvellous child, it grew heavier and heavier, and the river swelled beneath him, the darkness closed before him and became doubly dark, it was as though the elements would swallow him. The child weighed him down, never had anything been so heavy. Such is the weight of Life's germ, Life's beginning and the time to come of which we have no knowledge. And yet it seemed that the burden itself sustained him, else he would never have come across without straining himself. When at last he reached the opposite bank it was as though he had carried the whole world on his shoulders.

JOHANNES V. JENSEN[1]

The revolutionary hour at which we live is but the present phase of the process, centuries old and destined to outlive almost the memory of economic conflict, whereby man (not a privileged, exploiting class, but man as a whole) will merge into a conscious culture: even as a child at a certain physiologic stage must become adult or go down into degeneracy, so man stands at this hour. The key of the long phase is economic, therefore the importance of the class struggle and the imperative of entering it on the side of the workers.

WALDO FRANK[2]

In all Lancashire there was not a happier man than the little taxi driver, Christopher Burgess.[3] Even the diurnal attempts[4] of winter to take possession of the city did not disturb him—the worse the weather the better the business if it came to that—though none liked a bright sun in a clear sky more than he.

When his taxi was idle and perhaps a shift of winds from the north to the southwest had sent the temperature rising quickly once more towards a spring off-guard and unable to hold it, he lit his pipe and pulled out a bit of dirty paper to write some rhymes.

When both spring and winter called a truce to let a curtain of fog come slowly down over their turn he laughed and wrote another verse.

The dark buildings of Preston seemed to drop a curse as one passed but there was something even in their soullessness that responded kindly to the traveller when Mr. Burgess' taxi drove him by.

He was a small, round, dark, tough man of about forty with heavy moustaches who smoked incessantly and, when on the job in winter, always wore several waistcoats and a brown muffler. A heavy arc of watch-chain spanned the uppermost waistcoat. He had been a soldier, sailor, riveter, mechanic, hawker of poems. He loved and was loved by his wife and child and if he had any other strong feelings about life, they swam like fierce fish far below the serene surface of his mind.

But this morning his wife and child were to go away for a short holiday and he woke early with the odd feeling he would like to make a speech or break a window in the course of the day.

As a matter of fact it was going to be a sort of holiday to him also since by an arrangement between the mushroom, or owner, drivers, of whom he was one, the journeymen and the flatraters[5]—that is, between those drivers hired by their cab-owners (who took half) and those who virtually rented their cabs from the owners and took all—his fares had been limited to a percentage which he would exceed over Easter if he taxied anything like the normal number of fares. So he planned to lay off today, perhaps taking just one or two if the fancy struck him. He drew back the curtain by his bed and saw fog: the weather had decided it for him.

At half past eight he was peering out of his kitchen door at his garden. It seemed literally filled with scurrying wisps of fog.

Stooping, he fondled the ears of his cat, Dandy Dinmott[6] with one hand while with the other he stroked his moustaches. Snow, beginning to melt, was still encrusted on the black soil; the view was melancholy, even more so for Dandy Dinmott, had she known five dead cats were buried under the grape arbour he was admiring, for he still admired it even without being able to see much of it through the murk. He soon turned away, shutting the door to give himself over fully to the magnificent smells of breakfast cooking.

'Did you give William his breakfast allright,' he asked his wife, who nodded, shaking the frying pan vigorously over the blue-yellow gas flame.

'He likes his chow, that one,' he said. 'I wrote what you might call a little piece about him this morning.' He produced a piece of paper from his waistcoat pocket. 'Now, listen, Agnes,[7] it's called "A boy should eat more than his father." Would you like to hear it?'

'Now then, come and have your breakfast,' said Mrs. Burgess as she set bacon and eggs before him. 'You and your poetry. Mr. Jump[8] will be having you locked up one of these days.'

'I'll read it to you just the same' said Mr. Burgess, with an agreeable smile. '"Father of mine, awaken, I pray thee, to the truth: Two helps of egg and bacon are requisite to youth; and since thy little nipper needs much more food than thee, Deny thyself that kipper and hand it on to me."[9] What do you think of it? Good, eh?'

'Now then, eat your breakfast,' said Agnes Burgess. 'I've got to catch the train in twenty minutes.'

'Well, I'll bet you he asked for two helpings.'

'You get along with your own breakfast, now.'

As Mr. Burgess finished, the rest of the little piece ordered itself in his mind: 'The meal no longer dull is, Dad, chuck across the toast. For at last my empty stomach says I should rule the roast. Hunger must have its calm allayed, Beyond my wildest dream, Go slow there with the marmalade, Let me scrape out...' And so it went on.

He was pleased with his effort and still pleased when, twenty minutes later, he was warming up his Beardmore taxi[10] preparatory to taking Mrs. Burgess and their twelve-year-old son, who were to spend Easter with her mother in Windermere, to Preston North Station.[11]

'That's a mackerel sky,[12] ain't it?' he remarked to his son, William, looking up, as they drove along infinitely slowly, at a little rift in the greyness.

'Wish it was a herring one,' was the reply and Christopher turned round to Mrs. Burgess. 'He says he wishes it were a herring one, Mother.'

And they all laughed until they reached the Preston North.

But when the excursion train to the Lakes had parted them, or rather had been blasted away from him with detonations and fog signals, he felt so lost that he would gladly have remained on the station rank which he was not at liberty to do. So he became, willy nilly, for a time, a cruising cab.[13] Nobody would have thought that the driver of any cab would have cruised in the fog just for fun, but for a lack of a better word, that was what Christopher was doing. Meantime the fog was clearing.

When he stopped to pick up a random fare, one of three he'd decided he would take during the day, he was absurdly glad for the man's company, for by now his feeling of loss without Mrs. Burgess had approached despair. He dropped the fare in Lune Street and cruised slowly down into Fishergate.[14]

On one hand was an immense, vacant lot, surrounded on three sides by ruined open walls of warehouses and filled with scrap-iron of all kinds. The fourth side was a timber wharf where the Norwegian freighter *Unsgaard* which had arrived in Preston six weeks ago, was now unloading the last of her cargo. Skirting this as far as the wicket gate[15] in the fence by the police lodge was a road.

Mr. Burgess stopped his engine and watched the *Unsgaard* with a kind of longing, while around him the fog lifted more and more. What did that mean, *Unsgaard*?[16] Guardian or something—or what? The eternally swinging derricks recalled his sole voyage to sea, way back before the war on an old Adriatic boat.[17] He wished momentarily he had stuck to the sea that had such a curious way of washing out all unpleasant memories connected with it so that sailors spat on it and longed to return to it at the same time.

The milky grey sky was beginning to break up; in several more places it was becoming blue. Christopher swung around in his seat with one arm encircling the wheel and suddenly stared into the scrap-heap between himself and the *Unsgaard* as if into a vacancy within his own life.

The lot, which was more like a glimpse into the very soul of the obsolete, was filled with such remnants of the industrial revolution as hoop iron, circular and long bellows, ancient anvils, patent cartwheel hoops,[18] springs for conveyances, rain waterfall pipes, gutters and heads as well as sham stoves, antique toilet seats, copper kettles, cruet stands,[19] fish knives, locks, hinges and nails, wringing machines[20] and patent waterfall washing machines, not to speak of brewers' hydrometers, saccharometers and thermometers,[21] the properties of publicans and distillers of seventy-six years ago.[22] Christopher grew tired of looking at it.

He raised his head and saw the tall figure of P. C. Jump approaching along the wharves. Christopher now forgot all about the scrap-heap. Instead, he thought of Jump whom he watched with both misgivings and curiosity.

With misgivings because relations between the police and taximen were never happy, even at their best: when you were trying to get your license they troubled you; then, when you'd got that, they never let you rest, not for one moment...but kept pinching you on one pretext or another...and of course there were always those arch-enemies of cab drivers, the mobile police.[23]

If he watched Jump with curiosity it was because the Constable was the sort of man about whom legends grew though he could not have said precisely why this should be so since legends often do not appear to spring from their heroes' exploits but on the contrary to delight in making mysterious what is not truly mysterious at all.

Such a one was Jump. According to one story Christopher had heard, the Constable was a demoted Superintendent who had been transferred from the Tottenham Court Road district in London for calling the Chief-of-Police a short-armed bastard.[24] And there were other stories; that he had come from the Police Department at Cambridge after some brush-up there. Still others claimed Jump was a detective operating incognito.

For what had made him come to Preston if he were not actually a detective since it was here that northwest England's equivalent to Scotland Yard[25] was located? True, though it was plain to see that he now worked with the Docks Police,[26] that he should have been so transferred from a County or Metropolitan Police Force was inconceivable—well, at any rate, unlikely—since had he been transferred from London, for instance, his further service would not be pensionable.[27]

Christopher debated: an intriguing problem? Or was it only curiosity which made it seem like one?

He watched as P. C. Jump continued strolling along the wharf and keeping a sharp lookout for everything. With an air that appeared perhaps a shade too professional, he tested one mooring rope after another, even seemingly intent on loosening one of the *Unsgaard*'s wire runners (almost as if he feared the strangulation of the bollard over which the bight was cast). Finally he tugged on another hawser,[28] leaning back like the leader in a tug-of-war; when at last he stepped back to brush the cuffs of his pants he had the air of a man actually disappointed at failing to take the ship along with him on his morning rounds.

He was a man of strikingly handsome appearance. His measured tramp rang out on the hard road and the nostrils of his long nose twitched at the iridescence of the sea smells and snuffed in long breaths of air poisoned with sulphur dioxide.[29] He twirled his baton on his thumb.

"Hullo there, Constable," Christopher called. "Happy Easter."

"Oh yes, happy Easter," replied Jump. "What are you doing here?"

"Looking at this junk," said Christopher. "This is what caused all the trouble, ain't it?"

Police Constable Jump blinked. "What? More trouble?"

"No, this was the scrapiron they had brought down and were going to load in that ratcatcher over there, that Skowegian.[30] If it hadn't been for them fellers going on strike and...but you know all this."

Jump sniffed. "Ha, hah," he said mirthlessly, swaying backwards and forwards on his heels like a stage policeman. "Come and have one at the Trelast."[31]

"What? Out of hours?"

"Ha, ha." This was a chuckle. "I'll fix that."

Without further ado Jump climbed into Christopher's taxi. The hell through which they were soon passing and which was paved with the good intentions[32] of having a bitter at the Trelast Arms was also a wilderness of torn-down warehouses and objects that can have served nothing but the obsolete.[33] Half-erased advertisements for long-bankrupt firms, and forgotten remedies for maladies no one heard of any longer plastered the walls. 'Bowker's celebrated Tic-pills,[34] an infallible remedy for Tic-Doloreux or Faceache. These pills have obtained an international reputation both in England and abroad as a cure for that dreadful malady, Tic Doloreux, and for all neuralgic affections of the head and face. The most popular remedy extant,' the Constable was reading, and thought: "It should have been *extinct*," when suddenly Christopher Burgess, who had been so surprised by the Policeman's invitation that he hadn't said another word, reversed into the yard of the Trelast. "What about the skipper of that packet?" he asked turning off the petrol.

"Daland Haarfragre? He was with the strikers. He backed them up," replied Jump as he got out of the car. "He's a damned mysterious person."

"Mysterious person," echoed Christopher, following the Constable to a back door where they knocked and waited. "What about yourself?"

The Constable rapped again on the door and laughed, "Me? I? There's nothing mysterious about me." A face appeared behind the transom[35] above the door and a moment later they were admitted into a dark passage. "Go straight in," a voice said behind them.

"*...decked at the foot of Johnson Avenue.*[36] *In Jersey City this was. Of course I followed the sea in them days. Well, we were all dark*[37] *and most of the crowd was asleep when this damn bolshevik come aboard, yis*......Good morning there..."

An immense, heavy man named Webb,[38] an unemployed sailor, who was wearing a thick cap that might have been made of roofing felt and which he fingered nervously as he spoke, was telling some story to the landlord. Jump nodded as he entered, and called for two pints; 'old and mild'[39] were decided upon. The landlord's wife who had let them in, retired to an inner room where she could be seen sewing. A clock over the bar said it was thirty minutes before legal opening time.[40]

"Yes, Captain Daland is a queer one; he took a holiday from his ship and went climbing in the Welsh mountains."

"Climbing in the..."

"*...tried to chase him off but he just wouldn't go, that's all there was to it. Then they sent in what they call a riot call, you know, but not till he'd beaten up three of us...*"

"Daland got in today; he's around here somewhere."

"*...then the cops arrived, sssh, no offense intended—the cops, the policemen, lor lumme bloody days! Two squad cars, an emergency truck, two cars, and cops on feet. Well this bloody fellow he takes one look at the cops then gets hold of a hammer and darts down into the hold...*"

"Well, how do you know?

"How do I know? Because I've got them watched."

"Then you *are*... But why *them*? I thought were just talking of Daland."

"There's another man with Daland, to be precise, a trimmer..."

Christopher opened his mouth and then thought better of it.

"...a trimmer to replace the one who was shot here."[41]

"But I don't see why they had to get a trimmer from—where's Daland coming from?"

"Liverpool."

"From Liverpool, when there are plenty out of work here..."[42]

"Well, that's just—coincidence..."

"*....Sergeant McGlone and the others, leaping like a bloody chamois with McGlone close behind. Well down into the bloody hold they go now and across the cargo of scrap-iron...*"

"Scrap-iron, did you say, Webb?" Jump interrupted himself, speaking right across the room.

"Sure, any objections, sergeant?"[43]

"None at all."

"*...well, anyway here were all these cops swarming after him and jumping on members of the crew and all thinking it was this fellow when all the while he was asleep behind a coal bunker.*"

"But why do you have to watch the trimmer, too?"

"Now listen," said Jump, leaning over close towards Christopher and speaking in his ear, "the thing to remember is that they are being watched. In England you can't get mixed up in anything shady without being watched forever afterwards. That's why some of them go and live in America."

"*Did I say asleep? Well, he wasn't, see, not exactly asleep...Someone tossed three tear gas bombs, then rushed in to pinch him but this chap got up and whacked this cop on the head with the hammer and got away. In the end he got behind a boiler, where he belonged anyway, and the cops, forty of them they say there were, got him. He said he thought his own ship, some Greek freighter, the Ariadne Pandelis[44] or something of that, had sailed without him and he'd decided to sail on ours and catch it in mid-ocean. I tell you, that Norwegian chap got all that was coming to him, too.*"

"Which Norwegian chap?" Jump called over.

"You ought to know, you're the new policeman down there, aren't you? I mean the young fellow who got shot; mark my words, he asked for it. These damn' Bolshies deserve all they get. That Mussolini's[45] a civilising influence. Now I'll tell you, big Red Russia's no more than just a great balloon."

"I was a seabird once," said Mr. Burgess musingly, as if to himself. Then he said quietly to Jump, "But why does the new trimmer have to be watched too?"

"In England, everyone is watched."

"Do you mean you've got me down in black and white?"

"Sure. We know everything about you. It's because of that I spoke to you as I did. I know, for instance, that you are trustworthy."

"In England, trustworthy people don't trust the police. But I don't see...Here am I; I've always obeyed the law, I've led a pretty good life as lives go. I'm not ashamed of anything I've done."

"Well, you've been mixed up with the police yourself."

"Oh, you mean the mobile police," Christopher said wrathfully. "I don't call them the police. That's different."

"Nevertheless you see how it is. A man isn't free in England, even if he prides himself on not being a slave.[46] Take for instance this man, this trimmer, coming in on the train with Haarfragre."

"Yes, what about him? You didn't answer my question about him."

"Well, he's just a young fellow, a college student; we really haven't got anything on him though he was mixed up with a very peculiar business at Cambridge."

"Cambridge?"

"He was an undergraduate."

"You mean he's running away to sea, like?"

"Yes and no. He thinks he can start again, find a new reality, you might almost say. But there's something that keeps pursuing him, something he can't outrun..."[47]

"I don't follow you at all," said Christopher. "What's the poor lad done?"

"Well, there are certain circumstances, a letter maybe, a conversation overheard by the landlady, but there's no proof...we've nothing concrete on him. So it's not so much what he may have done already as what he may be going to do next."

"I never heard of such a thing. What's the chap's name?"

"Sigbjørn Tarnmoor."

"Tarn...Is he any relation to the Tarnmoor of the Tarnmoor Line?"

"Yes, he's the son. His father's in a peck of trouble too, but it's the son's our problem at the moment. We've expected at any time to be able to make a case against him, if only for drunken driving, but we've never caught him on the mat."[48]

"Come to think of it," Mr. Burgess said thoughtfully, "I read a bit about that Cambridge case a while back in the papers."

"But we haven't got him on the mat all the same," Jump was repeating. "And not only that, I'm finally beginning to wish him well."

"Wish him well?"

"I know you won't believe me when I tell you this but I do want him to break clean at last. I'd actually like to have him get away."

"You expect me to believe...? You want me to...? You're fooling me...What are you after?"

"What I'm trying to say is that he'll never get away by running but he'd have a better chance if he went to earth somewhere, and somewhere out of England where he could learn to accept life."

"I don't understand at all. And where do I come in?"

"If you go up to the station in half an hour you'll find him drinking at the bar, half seas over,[49] perhaps, but harmless as a child. You ask him where he wants to go, but wherever that is, just take him to the ship. You can take him free. I'll pay for him myself."

Police Constable Jump withdrew five silver coins from his pocket and held them out, shining on his palm.

"Look here," said Mr. Burgess, "I'm damned if I'm going to do any informing or giving anyone away."

"You're not expected to. And you don't have to understand. All you do is just take him to the ship."

"But why?"

"Because that's the first step. He's one of those fellows who can't make up his mind, but once he gets his dunnage[50] on board ship, even if he then leaves, we'll get him back to her."

Christopher scratched his head. "Then why don't you meet him?"

"I don't want to frighten him any more than he's already frightened."

"Well," Christopher said, "I admit you do give a fellow the creeps. How shall I recognise him?"

"You won't be able to miss him. He's got bright yellow hair, is a little bit taller than you, a little bit shorter than I, comes up to about here...He's more or less unshaven, wears an old blue serge suit with a black polo sweater—you know, comes up to the neck—and has a sea-bag with him. He's probably half drunk but he holds such a lot you may not be able to notice it unless his back teeth are actually under water. Now then, let's have a drink on it and don't tell anybody else: they may not understand."

"I wouldn't be a bit surprised," said Christopher, and for whatever reason he shook the Constable's hand.

"Above all, I don't want him to turn back. You remember what happened to Vanderdecken,[51] who turned back from the Horn, after swearing he'd round it."

"I wouldn't know about him."

"Never heard of the Flying Dutchman, eh? Never mind, have a game of darts." He rose, stretching his limbs. "How about it, Mr. Webb?"

He moved to the blackboard by the darts target and sponged it clean. "Mr. Burgess?...The duties thrust upon the police these days," he said, giving the board an extra swipe, "make police work of the most vital importance to the community.... Rightly carried out..."[52]

He stepped aside. "...it ensures that degree of orderly life for the state."

"Oh crap," said Mr. Webb, tossing a winged barb into the double fifteen.[53]

"...It is an honourable career for a man of ability and character," Jump continued, taking the darts from Mr. Webb and swaying forward balanced on his left foot, his right raised gracefully from the ground like a ballet dancer's, "but it contains a call for service and..."

He threw the first dart wide of the board: "...should be approached from a high sense of..."

"How about a call for service here? Mine's a Guinness."[54]

"Mine's an old."

"A mild and bitters please."

"It is an arduous life," continued Jump, taking another three darts. "Frequent visits, for instance, must be made to Public Houses..."

"We agree there!"

"...to see that they are properly conducted and that the licensing laws[55] are not infringed....Well, I give up." He handed his darts to Webb and, beckoning Christopher over to a corner, pulled out his notebook. Licking his thumb repeatedly, he flicked over its pages. Christopher looked over his shoulder.

"You see? No secrets."

There were indeed no secrets, or so it seemed to Christopher, for at first the book was filled with old dates of petty sessions, details of licensing returns, lapsed licenses and those requiring confirmation, tramps census,[56] and so forth—but then his duties seemed to change: from the book one would have gathered that his time was now entirely taken up by wharf duties: he scrutinized ships, tugs; tested the security of mooring ropes; watched for overloaded barges; in the event of fire he had to be prepared to summon floating engines[57] and maintain order while the firemen worked. He had to keep watch[58] at the wicket gate for suspicious characters. On the other hand, strangely enough, it seemed now quite unnecessary for him to visit Public Houses.

Once the phrase 'Unsolved Crimes' started out of the page and Christopher felt a sharp unease as he realized that everything in that notebook would indicate that Jump had indeed, as speculated, been transferred here from a County or Metropolitan force, and that an exception[59] had been made for him.

He stared at the Constable. "What are you then?"

"As you see, I'm a bonafide policeman—who must now, by the way, be getting along." He rose, tucked away the notebook, and called "Good afternoon, all," to the room at large.

To Christopher he added, sotto voce, "Check with me later in the lodge by the dock gates," and smiling, added, "You can't refuse; it's an order."

As he left, the clockwork cuckoo over the bar, a bar filled with bottles of John Jameson, Old Hollander[60] and 'port type wines, as if by *force majeure*,[61] was impelled ten times swiftly from its recess. Everyone in the bar tapped their heads knowingly, looking after the Constable.

"The only thing is," said Mr. Webb, scoring a double, and thus opening a game in which no one seemed willing to participate, "he's high up. I've heard there isn't anyone so high up."

"That fellow's so high up he's in the clouds—proper barmy, he is."

The far moan of an aeroplane engine reached the dull room, changing key as the pilot dived.

"Hullo," said Mr. Webb. "It must have cleared up."

"It's the loveliest day now," called the landlord's wife from the inner room.

They pulled the curtains aside and looked up at the aeroplane. The landlord unbolted the doors and customers from the real world came in. Everything surely moved back to the plane of the normal, the legal, the hard, the bitter, the actual, the quotidian.

What had taken place before might have happened in another world, and indeed otherwise it could scarcely have happened at all anywhere else.

XIV.2

Sigbjørn, short-sighted but subject to correction, stood in the Preston Station Restaurant,[62] one foot on the rail, leaning against the bar. In a corner of the glum room stood his new sea-bag which had fallen forward over his suitcase in a protective manner. He ordered another whiskey and felt himself actually shuddering with fear. This quickened to desire and when he had received his whiskey he started to talk with the barmaid in low, excited whispers. How easy, though, it would be to stay here, to fool his destiny, not to go on the ship at all, to escape completely from himself...Perhaps the very choice between life and death had been presented to him. He had wanted to return to the past, to be reborn if you like, but he hadn't counted on the future being so near. And with this realization and another whiskey he decided to choose life.[63] Even if he only paid a visit to life, something might be changed by it.

'Is it you I'm leaving behind?'

'What did you say, ducky?'

'Nothing. I was just thinking how attractive you were.'

After all, there was nothing else left that he really loved save, perhaps, comfort. He stared for a moment at some empty sandwichless bulbs of glass[64] and an appalling spasm of fright ran through him to be succeeded instantly by that electric wave of lust. Extraordinary!

Through the window behind the bar he could see over the roofs of Preston, which for the most part seemed nothing like a seaport at all, but a grey, heartless place with iron avenues that might have been a hundred miles from the clean smell of sea salt. He thought of having another whiskey but instead decided to buy a small bottle. It would remain to be seen if he could quench his fear with it, but standing at the door looking out as he waited for the barmaid to wrap up the bottle, he knew that it was as useless as trying to quench a wind with water. His fear swept every other consideration but that of itself before it, conquering even desire.

'Is it you I am leaving behind?' he thought, shaking the barmaid's hand, but said, 'If I ever get back we'll go to the Bear's Paw[65] together.'

'Or the Three White Mice...Goodbye and good luck. And bon voyage.'

'Goodbye.'

'And bon voyage'....For about a minute, until he had engaged a taxi—Mr. Burgess' Beardmore—these words held him fast as ropes from the sweep of his fear. But once inside and speeding towards the wharf, he was gathered up again in its headlong tumult, a tumult in which the elements seemed to be about to join, for the taxi itself staggered and sweated, almost seeming to buckle against a sudden lash of wind and rain. Soon there was nothing but fear about him, in the explosion of streetcars, in the disastrous rip of tires on the frozen asphalt, and even in the sight of the crowds released from the office buildings. They too seemed to be in some kind of a mysterious panic, which perhaps accurately describes them, for most of them were doing their holiday shopping. Only one thing Sigbjørn was sure of, that it was the last time in his life he'd be able to afford a taxi.

On the other side of the glass, smoking a pipe contentedly, for he was amused at the young man and his sea-bag, sat Mr. Burgess, jingles running through his head in time with the purring of his Beardmore.

'To your castle good fellow pray drive me
Then damn it come in and dine (He sounded the horn twice.)
On barons of beef[66] and fat capons,
On filetted peacock and old wine...'

He turned round with a smile as if to ask: how do you like that? but Sigbjørn sat peering forward into the mist, pale with fright and whiskey.

Suddenly there came the sharp tang of the sea in his nostrils and on his face the caress of damp sea smoke. There lay the *Unsgaard*. What did that mean?[67] Guardian of our life, perhaps? Perhaps there was nothing much to be frightened of after all. She lay there so meekly, a pitiful object herself, with a big list to starboard. Standing within a wicket gate, in a fence that towered above them, a constable challenged them in a friendly fashion. They passed through into a bleak vacant field with torn-down goal-posts and cans and lidless bins and the wind whining in vacant boilers and blowing up patches of snow.

A pile of sweet-smelling timber, partially snow-covered, stood beside the ship where they were now going. Further to the left, poverty grass grew among the wandering tracks, and there was the gleam of snow on the metals at the edge of the huge reservoir of the dock. UNSGAARD AALESUND.[68]

All the cargo was being hoisted onto the wharf; no barges, as at a saw-mill, were alongside.

Carrying his bag, Sigbjørn picked his way among the litter of the well-deck and climbed the ladder to the waste. 'Where's the firemen's foc'sle?'

'I don't know, but aft, aft...'

A man pointed his hand twice in the direction of the stern. 'All the crew are ashore.'

'Where's she bound for?'

'I don't know but I heard a rumour it might be Newfoundland.'[69]

Fyrbøter...[70]

He crawled down a ladder and ducked his head into the foc'sle which he saw immediately was quite empty. Not a soul. He dumped his sea-bag in a corner of the mess-room and looked round the bunks, which were in separate cubicles abutting on the alleyway and the sailors' foc'sle on the other side.

It was a strange arrangement but not unpleasing. Each man had a certain amount of privacy from his fellows. There were clean-looking showers. And each had seemed, also, to be trying to outdo the other in the matter of colourful curtains to the bunks. The whole foc'sle was spotlessly clean and gave him somehow the impression of a school common-room rather than what it was. He left his sea-bag and case where they were and went back up on deck.

Nobody...Now even the stevedores were departing. But Mr. Burgess still stood on the wharf with a gentle but scandalized expression on his face.

Sigbjørn climbed slowly down the gangplank and approached him, smiling.

'Do you mean to tell me that you're one of the crew of that ratcatcher?' Christopher demanded. 'What are you? You're English, aren't you? A mate?' He started to roll a cigarette.

'A trimmer.'

'A drag?[71] Don't kid me! Let's look at your hands.'

Sigbjørn extended them.

'You're no trimmer!'

'Not yet. I shall be soon.'

'When's she sailing?'

'Tomorrow, I think.'

'You think?'

'Well, the crew's all knocked off. There's not a soul on board.'

'What are you going to do now?'

'I don't know. What about a drink?'

Sigbjørn handed the taxi driver the bottle. Christopher shook his head. 'I don't drink when I'm working. Well, perhaps just a little one. Happy Easter!'

As he handed the bottle back he asked, 'What makes you go to sea, anyway? You're not a sailor, are you?'

Sigbjørn ignored this. 'Let's get out of the sleet.'

'Can I give you a lift anywhere, buckshee?'[72]

'If you're going up to town, many thanks...'

As they were driving Sigbjørn leaned forward. 'As a matter of fact, it's not a ratcatcher at all but a pretty good ship.'

'What do you mean, pretty good?'

'Well, as far as I can see at the moment they make good provision for their men.'

'Are you the man they sent on board in place of the man who got shot?'

'I don't know anything about that,' Sigbjørn said. And he began to tell Christopher about Haarfragre and the events of the day.

'You must be the man,' Christopher said, decisively. "Look here, meet me in thirty minutes at the Trelast...anybody'll tell you where that is.'

At six o'clock Sigbjørn entered the Trelast. The bar parlour was perfectly empty but a newly-made fire burned brightly in one corner. He ordered a beer and strolled over to it, staring into it as though it held a secret for him. The landlord brought his beer to him, and he drank deeply. Then, sitting on his heels, he warmed his hands. The fire meant comfort, refuge and the past, but it also meant the future, the trial in which his weaknesses would be put to the test; it meant pain; it might mean death...

'There's someone waiting for you in the Public bar,' the landlord called.

Sigbjørn started. How stupid of him! Somehow it seemed characteristic of his whole life that he should have chosen the Private.[73]

To get to the Public he had to go out in the street and the sudden cut of wind was like reality itself.

In the Public bar he found Christopher playing darts by himself. They greeted each other and took turns at the board.

'Well I wonder what sort of food you'll get at sea,' said Christopher. 'I'll bet you don't get decarbonized plaice and carburettor sauce[74] there, do you?' He impaled the double fifteen with two barbs.

'I wouldn't know.' Sigbjørn laughed.

Christopher withdrew the three winged darts from the pitted cork target. The bar was filling and many of Christopher's friends greeted him but Christopher went on talking to Sigbjørn.

'Or gasket of beef or piston of pork with Texaco sauce and two bottles of distilled water with a dram of carbolic[75] acid thrown in. You won't get any of that. It'll be like a, you know, new life...None of the old stuff.' His tone managed to be savage and bantering at the same time.

They stood aside from the board for two others to play.

...forty thousand bloody seamen out of work ...

I ain't telling you the word of a bloody lie,[76] *there's twenty thousand officers without jobs in this country...*

They'll get the maximum of profit with the minimum of bloody labour....

Scrap nine million tons, boy, that'll give them profits all right...

increased competition for employment will increase unemployment....

a cook with his overtime earns more than a second officer...

I got back from a voyage down the China coast and couldn't even get a holiday...

Take a look at all these bloody ships laid up in Preston...

These conversations, presaging as they did what he was to hear on board the *Unsgaard* for perhaps many months, filled him with dismay; in the first place he was so out of touch with the world and man that he scarcely understood it although its interest was peripheral to his own—how much less, then, would he be able to understand the language of Norwegian workers on board the *Unsgaard*, even when their language had once been his own? And how much less would they care to call him one of them?

The fact that his future shipmates were at the moment nowhere to be found increased his feeling of isolation. The rumour had only to be bruited about that he was going aboard for the whole crew to scatter like rats. Where to? Were they underground, fomenting in basements? 'Building from the black base upwards,' as he had once read of communists in a poem.[77] He had again a sudden urge to escape while there was still time, to burrow underground himself from his dread of the future, whereupon into his mind's eye came a vision of a solid line of small and continuous works, hidden and ready to receive their defenders at a moment's notice.

He saw low steel and concrete forts, linked by smaller turret-like pillboxes, and underneath a labyrinth of tunnels with barracks, ammunition magazines and power houses. From embrasures[78] of shell-holes, light artillery and machine-guns could be fired. Sallyports provided exits for quick raiding detachments. And generally speaking, there would be no escape.

Sigbjørn felt suddenly very dizzy. Turrets, tunnels, magazines, powerhouses reeled in his mind.

To make matters worse, the landlord started to lead him to the door. "You've had enough; get home now."

But Christopher Burgess came to the rescue: "You can take a kip on my sofa if you like until you feel well enough to go on the ship."

The next thing Sigbjørn knew, he was standing in a room that contained a watering can, five umbrellas, a silver-topped cane, four Christmas robins, a stuffed squirrel, a lovebird and five stopped clocks in glass cases. There were also a good many cups and shells with 'present from Ryde'[79] printed on them, and in spite of the Beardmore, for it was Christopher Burgess' house in which he found himself, a New Year's calendar from Daimler's.[80]

"Let me show you the house, if you're feeling a little better," said a voice behind him, and Sigbjørn followed Christopher Burgess into the kitchen where he lit the gas.

With a despair absolutely foreign to him, Christopher announced, "The world's going to the dogs. Mark my words, nobody has a chance these days. Come, I'll show you my garden."[81]

"I must have slept for hours," Sigbjørn said. "I hope I wasn't much of a nuisance."

"You weren't. But look here, I suppose I ought to tell you this: the police are looking for you."

Sigbjørn seemed not to understand, or, if he did understand, seemed curiously unimpressed.

"They haven't been looking as long as I have," was all he said, and the subject was not referred to again between them.

Although he had waked in a gaslit room and the kitchen gas had been lit in his presence, Sigbjørn only now realized that it was dark and when, with a "Let me show you my garden," Christopher opened the door on what had now become a tempest, a howling chaos, an infinite misery, Sigbjørn's astonishment turned to fear as he suddenly tripped, nearly falling on his face.

"Never mind Dandy Dinmott," Christopher said. "That's only a favourite big cat."

Mr. Burgess pointed out into blank darkness. "Over there's my grape tree. Three hundred grapes on that. And five dead cats underneath it. Oh, dead cats are fine for fruit!" He stopped to stroke Dandy Dinmott, but at this moment the gas blew out. Mr. Burgess managed, with some difficulty, to close the door which muted the sounds of the storm. "I have an old affectionate poodle, too."

Soon the gas jet steadily whirred again in the little kitchen. In his basket snored the old affectionate poodle.

Christopher pointed to a photograph on the wall: "There are my three brothers, all of them dead now." He spoke as though for the first time aware of this as anything but a whim of destiny.

"That one there, that first one, he got killed by a tram...he got a bleeding muscle. And this second one here, he got a nail in the toe. And this young fellow, he got all set up in a pub, and died two days later. Nobody's got a chance these days. And there's my poor sister, she got carried away in the 'flu epidemic of '18."[82]

They went back to the front room where Sigbjørn asked the time, but Christopher didn't know. They glanced round at the stopped clocks.

"I'll tell you what," said Christopher, "I'll rustle you up some bread and cheese. You must be hungry. I'm so hungry I don't know where to sleep."

"I'll see first if I can get another bottle before closing time," said Sigbjørn, to whom hunger had become identified with thirst. "I'll bring it back for you."

"Not for me," Christopher shouted after him. "And not for you either. You'll be a dead man on your first watch and nobody'll love you. I was a seabird once and I know."

But Sigbjørn had gone out.

Left alone, Mr. Burgess, who had had only a few in the course of the day but more than normally, and who felt temporarily torn out of his pattern, disestablished from the awareness of his own periphery, both by the fact of Mrs. Burgess' absence and of Sigbjørn's recent presence, and those nightmarish conversations in the Trelast that he could not believe he had had at all, was seized with a desire to smash things.[83]

He longed to sweep the stopped clocks from their pedestals and the Christmas robins from their perches; and he imagined the delicious crash of glass smashing to smithereens. But for a sudden pang of love for his wife, who he vaguely imagined had some attachment to these things, he would have demolished the room.

Staying his hand, he too went out into the street, yet outside he was seized with the urge again. Passing Mr. Webb's shop,[84] which sold creepy books and 'useful books for practical men,' and which was shut and dark, he gleefully smashed its window.

An electric eye[85] fixed above the chemist's shop and left working by mistake, winked at him, a disturbing orange against the indigo of night. He recalled a dream he had had persistently many years ago about the time he had failed an eye test. In his dream, an eye had appeared, and then an eyeglass before the eye, but a young doctor had told him his dreams had nothing to do with his eyes at all: that the eye was what he really felt deep inside himself which had to be corrected by the glass of what he himself knew; that a man must study his nature and his possibilities and heed the guidance of his intuition; tack like a sailor with the winds and tides. The eye could see through a concealing fog; scan the invisible; and, like an unmanned machine-gun, was automatically primed to bring down whatever lay within its range.

Whereupon, ashamed of his futile gesture, Mr. Burgess ran as fast as he could to the docks' police lodge and there gave himself up.

Meantime, Sigbjørn had lost his way back to Mr. Burgess. As a matter of fact, he was lost in the field of scrap-iron; the wind whistled in the copper kettles, sluiced the rust down the rain waterfall pipes, frolicked and gamboled about the patent cart-wheel hoops, blew in the bellows and shouted up the toilet seats.[86] Suddenly he stumbled and fell flat on his face.

The instant he fell, the dream started; he dreamed he fell like this and that scoops and shovels were at work, their necks swinging and bowing as they loaded the scrap-iron on a vessel bound for Brindisi.[87]

He had no legs, but he crawled on his stumps back and forth at a tremendous rate, trying desperately to evade the merciless mechanism till at last a shape stooped in the darkness for him, too, and slung him into a coal bunker on the vessel. Now it was all right to go to sleep again. He lay down in the bunker and awoke.

It was only a dream. It was perfectly all right to go on sleeping in the coal bunker. On the other hand, now he was awake and could make good his escape. It was only a dream and he must wake up if he didn't want to freeze to death in the snow.

His dream ended as he slowly rubbed his hand across his head to feel if there were any blood. There was none. It had begun half a second earlier when his head struck the iron but it had seemed to last for hours. He groped for the rum bottle and found it intact. Now for Mr. Burgess, or, failing Mr. Burgess, the *Unsgaard*.

But a figure who had identified an almost mobile smell of liquor rose before him. "Where are you going? What's that you've got there? Had a few, eh?"

"It's a bottle of rum. Would you like some?"

"A rhetorical question," Constable Jump said briskly. "Come along now—no, this way."

As he pushed Sigbjørn before him into the little station house he gave an enormous wink, and remarked to no one in particular: "Here's another one under arrest."

Christopher was sitting down, and when he saw Sigbjørn, started to shake with laughter.

"He's been smashing windows," said Jump. "Sit over there," he instructed Sigbjørn, pointing.

In spite of that day's uncharacteristic exchange of conversation, Jump was highly normal, but would have been quick to acknowledge that the warnings and orders he had given Christopher possessed something of that remote, staring quality which, as Empson declares,[88] belongs to the beauty of the ideas of the insane. Yet long after he had retired from active detection he had willingly allowed himself to drift from place to place in the country, filling needful niches as they arose; it was, therefore, natural, that having come North he should gravitate to Preston, which was, as it were, the Scotland Yard of the northwest of England; sheer caprice, however, had mandated his stint as Dock Policeman; which had only been suggested to him as a joke.

Accident alone[89] accounted for his arrival in Cambridge, shortly before the death of Tor Tarnmoor. The circumstances struck him as sufficiently mysterious to capture his attention and he had interested himself in Sigbjørn and in his activities, perhaps, as he had hinted to Christopher, more as potential wrongdoer than as criminal.

Hence he had watched Sigbjørn's development since the tragedy with the meticulous interest of a master gardener in a rampant and unfamiliar shrub. In Liverpool he had studied Sigbjørn's indecisiveness, his wavering and incorrigible duality, his countless trivial hesitancies (as though his wretched and inescapable soul-searching were a mandate) and come to feel a comprehension of that haunted mind which devolved ultimately into the barely formulated belief that this somehow imposed an obligation he must meet. For Sigbjørn, it was clear to him, was foundering.

It was because of this that, once aware of Sigbjørn's clumsy attempts at obtaining a *hyrkontrakt*, Jump had interceded with both Haarfragre, in Preston, and the Norwegian Consulate in Liverpool, even before Captain Tarnmoor had done likewise. There may have been an unacknowledged impetus for such intervention, for the sorrow of Jump's life was childlessness.

At the Docks' office, Sigbjørn was circling about, for one drink from his newly acquired bottle had left him unsteadier than before he went to sleep. His slurred voice, when he spoke, sounded perplexed.

"Aren't there any more drunks than this on Easter Eve?"

"Not this year." Jump eyed him thoughtfully. "Celebrating the birth of a royal babe exhausted them at Christmas."[90]

"Bitter words from the Force," said Sigbjørn, examining his head, which seemed unhurt, in a mirror. "But I mean the despairing ones." He dropped into a chair.

"Oh, they're all locked up long ago."

"And the fighting ones?"

Jump pointed to Christopher. "That one," he said. "He's been fighting shop windows. He's lucky he's got someone who can clear the mess he's made."

"It won't do any good smashing shop windows," said Sigbjørn.

"Nor getting cock-eyed either," Jump told him, with a glance at Christopher which meant 'Here he is anyway, if not quite in the way we expected.'

"Now then, tell us what your line is."

"I'm an economic student,"[91] mumbled Sigbjørn, his voice sinking to a whisper. "Collapse of..."

It was obvious he was of the verge of passing out.

"Maybe he wants a drink of rum," suggested Christopher, but Sigbjørn's head fell forward on his hands.

Jump looked at Christopher. "He's out."

And indeed Sigbjørn had already given way beneath the table.

"Well, you've got him on the mat now," said Mr. Burgess. "Now, when I look at it, my point of view, it'll kill him working on that ship."

"He could stay here," said Jump, lighting a cigarette.

"Yet you seem precious anxious for him to sail."

"I am."

"It would be a kindness to leave him. Let him stay here. He ought to be in a home."

"Damn it now, I've half a mind to turn the young bastard over to the City Police."

A wind from the sea rattled the windows of the little Police Lodge. Sirens called[92] from the river, close at hand. In the distance the chemist's eye winked at Christopher. The gunnerless machine-gun...the aeroplane finder...*follow your intuition...*

"Now when I look at it in my point of view and personal light..." But what was his point of view?

He remembered his one voyage, the ship making little headway against raging northerly gales: malevolent squalls washing the ship from stem to stern. The ship was dragged under water but she shook it off and lay trembling in every mast.[93]

But that grey, poor light could illumine the rebirth of man on the side of life,[94] with only a curtain of wind and rain for privacy.

Later, Jump followed them with his torch along the wharf as, this time on his shoulder,[95] Christopher carried Sigbjørn again to the ship, *Unsgaard.*

XV

Forehead to forehead I meet thee, this third time, Moby Dick!

HERMAN MELVILLE[1]

Once more[2] a young face paused on the quays looking up at the ship. Once more Sigbjørn wondered: Is this your place on earth?

The iron ship lay wearily against the wharf; a pile of wood was stacked beside her, where he stood hidden.

Suddenly he pressed his lips against the sweet wood as if to draw from it some of its generous strength. Wood, wood, all goodness, all rightness were in that sweet texture!

That morning when he had waked his eyelids had been heavy to lift. There was nobody in the forecastle. In a panic, he had gone out on deck; the few hands there took him for an agent or a tally clerk.[3] He had gone forward to report himself but the chief engineer's door was closed and the captain was nowhere to be seen. Only a few hands were visible, working forward under the mate.

He hesitated to go down below but he looked down from the fiddley[4] into the engine-room; lever weight and fulcrum[5] slept there, but all was poised: co-ordination was expectant in every nut and bolt.

Perhaps he could slip away without being observed...

Even when on the wharf, he had no intention of leaving the *Unsgaard*. He had felt only that there his own purpose would become stronger to him; standing away from it he would see it, like the ship, as clearly, as bare, as moulded as iron. He would no longer be enclosed by it as it is said man is enclosed by his soul.[6]

Yet now every nerve within him did really bid: Escape! Escape utterly from the ship and from any dream of that purpose.

He tunneled through a fragrant wilderness of pine until he came to a clearing from which he could see the *Unsgaard* again, perhaps for the last time! The huge bows of the ship rose up before him and seemed to stare at him through its eyes of hawse-holes[7] like an elephant. He laughed aloud at this absurd fancy but his laughter sounded idiotic, like gibbering.

Behind him, metals ran into the desolation of the scrap-heap and were lost in half-frozen pools and basins of rain among which old propellers and anchors rusted away; a little poverty grass that grew there was the only sign of life. Before him loomed the ship!

He burrowed back to his former position, leant his elbows on a ledge of pine, and watched the *Unsgaard*, sniffing in the good smell of resin. Ah, wood! the wood of good trees, wood for building, for the warmth and goodness of fire, but also for the fire that makes of wood itself only chaff.

Bells pealed out wildly from the city. Of course! It was Easter day.[8] He touched the wood with his fingers. There was innocence about wood too, like that of little children, as yet almost devoid of life but later to be vivified and perfected; and then the one to crucify, the other to be crucified, and Sigbjørn wondered if the young trees swaying in the forests of the White Sea already talked of what life held in store for them.

As he watched, suddenly, without any apparent preamble, the *Unsgaard* backed away from the wharf. Now she was swinging out deliberately into the middle of the stream. A plume of smoke shot from her siren; the siren roared. The sound eddied back and forth among the sheds, a sharply echoing racket in all that iron loneliness!

He ran forward with a shout. Too late! The ship would not wait for him. Like life, she had no time to waste. Anyone might profess to prefer certainty but none wished it in his heart. Ah, well...

He started to walk slowly in the direction of Preston, and hung his head as he passed through the wicker gate. What could he say to Constable Jump? But this time nobody stopped him.

The desolate streets flowed back into town and Sigbjørn was aware of the contour of every house; a piece of glass on the roadway; a tall workman's pike left by a wall; the creaking gable outside a Public House; and his senses recoiled from all these sharp impressions because every one of them meant suffering. Thoughts of Nina arose to further trouble him; he imagined the ocean between them flowing into his heart, its Atlantic billows foaming there ceaselessly as if to engulf the fires of his pain.

The sound of an organ playing an Easter hymn and the sight of crowds pouring from a church waked him temporarily from this obliteration of self-consciousness, but these men in black walking slowly together as if in mourning under a grey sky like wet sacking was unspeakably depressing.

He recalled a day like it when everything had been changed to brightness by a letter from Nina; then, humble words penetrating his whole being had become rays of sunlight. Today, when there would be no such letter, it struck him that it might none-the-less be comforting to again go to a Post Office.[9]

He entered through a door on which was pasted the notice: *On Easter Day, open from 12–2 p.m. only.*

Here for a moment he was safe from the onslaught of his thoughts. Should he send a telegram to his father? Perhaps he had been a coward in the first place ever to think of leaving when so much was unravelling behind. But now was he to return again?

He had been standing transfixed in the middle of the floor; now he walked to the desk and started to write a telegram, but it was not to his father: it was not to anyone at all.

The words he wrote were words of love, affection, *darling, love, darling* but darling whom? And to whom? He didn't know.

Here in the Post Office life roared about him, everyone was on an errand of life, however belatedly. He took up a telephone book, turned its pages, but not to look up any name he knew, when suddenly, from its leaves, the mocking image of Candide arose.[10] *Let us cultivate our garden...*

He shut the book with a bang, startling a young lady in tweeds with quantities of fair hair who was standing at the next desk. For a moment their glances met.

"Is it you that I'm leaving behind?" Sigbjørn asked her mysteriously, and pushed through the swinging doors into the street.

On an errand of life! A memory, grey in the mind, cloying, flickered through him as he passed down Fishergate. Rebirth; the travail of a rebirth in consciousness; at some time or another, long long ago, he had experienced this indecision, had seen his ship sail away in just that manner. Rebirth! Yes, what Tor said had been right, he was being reborn in some mysterious way: that must be what was happening.

Even now, he was struggling in the womb; on all sides there was anxiety, flurry, in response to this, the uterus of consciousness that held him dilated in slow pain.

As if this incident were in meaningless empathy with such a feeling, at the corner of Main Street an obviously pregnant woman passed him.[11]

"Will you help me up these steps?"

Sigbjørn, taking her arm, gently helped.

"Ah, the pain is so bad, and I am alone; I have no one to help me. I am alone!"

Someone opened the door and she passed inside. The door slammed in his face. He knocked softly on the door. Perhaps he could be of some assistance. He knocked louder: still no answer.

One never knew. It might be desperately serious. He knocked again, almost crazily, this time, and after a moment the door opened, a face peered out, and an angry voice snapped: "Go away now, get out, we're proper fed up with you, we're not giving away any more this Easter!"

Sigbjørn walked on, distracted by this bewildering incident which might almost have had, by its very meaninglessness, some significance.

Rebirth! All was pain! The pavestones would heave themselves up, the streets contract and dilate before his eyes, the factory chimneys stretch themselves until they cracked their very roots...

Even now the city groaned as for one still crucified; soon the whole world would be convulsing itself again in order to create something self-evolving!

He started, as though he had been tapped on the shoulder. The ship!...He stopped for a moment, then walked on. Well, let it go. But how had he ever got on the ship in the first place? Yes, how? There had been that taxi man reciting poems, and then the policeman, the police station, Police Constable Jump...Like a specter in a nightmare the last night squeezed its flabby face against him but divulged nothing.

Why had he ever wanted to go on a ship? Why was he Sigbjørn? Or was he nothing? A spirit still driven to and fro by the conflicting impulses which had finally destroyed him on earth?

He stepped from the road to the pavement. A fire engine hauled past, clanging terror, followed by a screaming ambulance. He turned into a small inn at the corner.

The peace and safety of the place entered into him as he sat down; what dangers he had avoided by not taking the ship! He ordered a beer and looked round. And yet, in the sanctuary of the inn itself, one might easily imagine oneself to be in a forecastle; the low benches, the dim lamp, the scarred cedarwood table at which two old men were murmuring like able seamen in the middle watch,[12] gave that impression; but Sigbjørn felt again that something around him, in the very substance and the pattern of the scene and the time, was trying to communicate with him.

The first old man looked at him and raised his glass. "Happy Easter," he said. "Will you drink with us?"

At this moment Sigbjørn's drink arrived and he held up his glass politely. "Happy Easter! But I've already got a drink."

"*Nel mezzo del cammin di nuestra vita*,"[13] toasted the second old man. "Good health to you. Sure now," he added, raising his mug, "Preston was Dante's original."

"Do you know Dante, too?" Sigbjørn asked thoughtfully. "He was an obscene old man."

"He was a great poet," said the first.

"We've taught at Preston for twenty-five years," added the second.

The first old man laughed. "*In la sua voluntade è nostra pace.*"[14]

At this, Sigbjørn laughed too.

"It's a great town," chuckled the first, "a great old town. Being a college student yourself of course, you'd know that coal was discovered here by Richard Coeur de Lion[15] in 1200..."

"As long ago as that?" asked Sigbjørn, tasting his beer.

"Of course it was Alexander[16] who first discovered its usefulness."

"Although Theophrastus[17] wrote of the stones he found in Liguria and Elis. Did you know that?"

"No." Sigbjørn smiled and said nothing. He thought not of the ship but of the thickness of things, of the depth of Preston, where each tree with its mandrake[18] root struck far down into the earth, into the ancient mass of igneous rock, where each chimney[19] could be imagined as magnetic to a star,[20] and the soul, too...but what was that?...thrusting downwards and upwards, in-dwelling, self-extending, ubiquitous. The marriage of heaven and hell![21]

He shook hands with the old schoolmasters. "Well, Happy Easter! You must excuse me; I must be off to the crusades too now," he laughed, and pushed out into the street.

...Why the crusades?...?[22]

In mediae nostra vitae...Well, no Virgil[23] would lead him through the *Inferno* today. No Christophers were on duty either, if it came to that.

Nor was today, like yesterday, a day of making peace with authority, the authority of Police Constable Jump.

Then he remembered his father's words: 'Nobody's going to stop you where you're going. Everybody's going to help you where you're going.' But where would they help him to this time now that hope had sailed with the tide? And not only hope, but all his luggage as well? *In mediae nostrae vitae!*

He was standing on the top of a hill,[24] looking down on the town; far, far away in the gathering evening were the wharfs and the ships, and again he thought of standing on Castle Hill with Tor: perhaps in reality the sea and its ways had been nearer to him then than now.

Some instinct presently bade him return, if only to the wharf the *Unsgaard* had left, to the womb from which she had been severed. That emptiness was a wound within him.

Not so much as a murderer returns to the scene of his crime and a lover to the house where the beloved has once lived, or as he revisits the embankment to see the bright rails[25] that carried her away from him, Sigbjørn returned to the docks.

A 'docks' tram was swaying down the street and he boarded it at a run. There was something about this swift decision that amused him. He had thought life could no longer be snatched in passing. There was a Norwegian proverb that said life lurched by so swiftly that if a man tried to jump aboard he only split his skull against the pavement.[26]

The tram was empty and his thoughts shrivelled up inside him. The conductor stood by the ticket machine outside; his eyes bore that kind of vacancy Sigbjørn associated with those old seamen who had gazed so long at the rolling wastes of the ocean that its infinitude seemed ultimately inscribed upon their sight, and he recalled the words of a fellow-seaman[27] on board the *Oedipus Tyrannus*: "When I get home I'll get a job as first mate on a tram."

"On a tramp?" he'd asked.

"No, on a tram!"

They had laughed, standing in the middle watch by the red-throated ventilator. Could that seaman, Frank, now be this conductor?

He peered at the man quickly, as quickly turned away, and the next moment saw the conductor do likewise—his glance neutral, once more indefinite.

If you want a good boot go to France, to W. France, 117 Fishergate, Preston; Mr. Bowker's Tic Pills; Spectacles and eye preservers of the best quality, carefully adapted to vision by Messrs Cartwright, Opticians, 122 Fishergate, Preston.[28]

If it *was* Frank what should he say? Perhaps the conductor was thinking the same thing...

The tram stopped and a girl climbed in. She was the same girl with the luxuriance of fair hair he had addressed so strangely in the Post Office. A queer courage possessed him and very deliberately he rose from his seat and went over to her.

"I'm sorry if I frightened you in the Post Office this morning," he said.

She looked at him, recognizing him, but without any fear at all. "I didn't understand what you said."

Sigbjørn regarded her, then laughed. Edging nearer to her, he took her gloved hand in his.

"You're awfully pretty. Look here, I haven't much time, do you mind if I kiss you?" But he said it in such a way that no one could have been offended; it was indeed as though all the tenderness and simple love that he considered his life had missed had gone into the request.

She laughed. "Don't be silly. Besides, you smell of drink."

"It's Easter Day," said Sigbjørn. "That makes all the difference."

He looked round to make sure he was not observed by the conductor, then took her in his arms and kissed her, again and again, as if indeed he were pressing his lips against the very source of life itself.

The girl did not protest but at the next stop she left the tram without a word. Sigbjørn watched her as she hurried down the street. Whether the conductor was his same friend or not he hadn't seen him kiss her. Or had he? The girl waved, and he half rose from his seat to wave back.

Now a new problem presented itself. Should he follow the girl or go down to the docks?

As he approached the docks he felt that the ship had not gone but that on the other hand, had she sailed—now that life was a thousand times more lonely without the fair-haired girl—it would be more than he could bear to return to the place where the *Unsgaard* had been.

For obscurely related reasons, he did not want to make quite sure that the conductor was his shipmate-friend; though as the tram approached ever nearer to the waterfront his desolation became so great that the certainty he was not would have inflicted upon him a sense of almost final bereavement.

Finally he dropped from the tram and walked a little way after the girl, in the opposite direction to the docks.

A policeman[29] was moving slowly towards him, and for fear it might be Jump, whom he was ashamed to meet because he hadn't taken the ship, or another policeman, informed of his assaulting a girl in a tram, or indeed any policeman at all who shadowed him for the murder of his own brother, he turned away; but his feet were leaden and his heart beat painfully with fear.

He tried to turn his thoughts away from himself to the schoolmasters, and forced himself to believe for a minute or two that the eternal pattern of three[30] was one of the secrets of existence which no one bothered to investigate; that, although those men would never remember him, would never even speak of him perhaps, nevertheless, the fitful pattern they had traced in those few minutes was eternal. Now he wondered about the conductor: could that really have been Frank? And where was Christopher Burgess today?[31]

The tram, with Main Street on its forehead was now returning and Christopher looked towards the wharves.

Once more there was no one to stop him at the wicket gate, and there beyond it, as he had already suspected, was the *Unsgaard*, perhaps a quarter of a mile from her original position, and having done no more than warp away from the wharves to the coaltips, where she lay meekly as before but this time under a dark skeleton of iron.[32]

Well, today he had to ferry himself over the stream.

He walked quickly over to her and clambered on board. Above him, coal poured clattering down a belt; dust drifted everywhere, and he remembered his dream.[33]

A man rose up beside him and he was instantly and shockingly reminded of Tor.

"I've been told to look out for you," he said. "I'm Silverhjelm.[34] It's lucky you came: we're sailing before our time."[35]

"Before your time? I thought you were sailing this morning."

"We had our holiday yesterday. Work today. The others the same." He looked up at the iron structure above them.

The avalanche of coal slackened, followed by an extraordinary, complete stillness on board the *Unsgaard*, broken only by what Sigbjørn surmised was the sound of men steadily chipping on the other side of the dock: *tuco, tuco, tuco,*

tuco,[36] it went, until he realized it was only the beating of his own heart, and when Silverhjelm spoke, he was once again reminded powerfully of Tor.

"You're in my watch for the time being—the twelve to four."

Tuco, tuco, tuco, tuco. His heart's hammering began afresh, like sharp blows struck through hands and feet.

"Plenty of time," he said. "Here, have a cigarette." And Silverhjelm replied "Yes. Tusen Tak."[37]

In silence, they strolled slowly forward.

The *Unsgaard* was at last ready for sea: was he as prepared for what might now befall him, whether of good or evil?

Forward, the carpenter was at the windlass; wire runners and hawsers were taken in; for some minutes there was confusion. Then the bight of the last hawser was thrown into the water by an unwilling shore gang and the *Unsgaard* backed away. Once more she blasted on her siren and it echoed backwards and forwards in the strange city just as it had done in the morning.

Silverhjelm and Sigbjørn leaned on the rail, smoking.

Now they were steaming ahead towards the Ribble.[38] Looking back, he noticed suddenly that Police Constable Jump was leaning among the timber; beside him was Christopher Burgess in his taxi. They appeared to be searching for him and as the *Unsgaard* gave vent to several short blasts Christopher honked back in ironic sympathy. There on the wharf Jump did a little, grotesque dance, ending by shaking his own hand aloft as a victorious boxer accepts the plaudits of the crowd.

Sigbjørn and Silverhjelm waved back, the former with a sense of genuine loss; they had become his friends. As he watched, they diminished to the size of puppets.

It was strange to be drawn out quietly from the stage like this while two friendly comedians danced on the threshold of one's old life. Or perhaps....? Had the P. C. only wanted to arrest him for assaulting a girl on a tram? At this thought Sigbjørn pressed his lips against an iron stanchion. It left a bitter taste.

The sky, which had been cobalt, now deepened to a deadly white. The gun[39] sounded for stop work, for there were those who seemed to work even on such holidays as Easter. It was a volley fired over a dead life while factory chimneys, at the angle of the dock, circled away like a cluster of howitzers. Lights came on in what now became a far, fantastic city.

"Where are we going?" Sigbjørn asked.

"We haven't got our charter yet," was Silverhjelm's reply. "It might be Archangel or Leningrad. Or even back to Aalesund."

From the receding city winked the electric eye[40] of Messrs Cartwright, Opticians, 122 Fishergate, adapted to perfect vision, and Sigbjørn imagined the chemist there busy with his tubes and rays, perhaps seeking for some further metallurgy[41] of death...or did he seek the elixir of life? Just as in the laboratory they sought perpetuum mobile and in the library, the philosopher's stone.[42]

It was after all good to be sailing out again into the Arctic Circle where the vessel would be filled with the ripeness and strength of wood, to be with her where she advanced, slowly gliding down river, towards her initial goal: the sea; gliding[43] silently as it is said the soul glides through existence, bearing with her an entire world of shadows.

And it was for this he must thank Christopher and the Constable, whoever had been the more instrumental in putting him on board; now he himself must ratify that decision in, as it were, cold blood, for he knew that had the ship not been his starting point that morning he would never have returned to her...that fact a tiny rider on the scales of his emaciated self-esteem.

The evening was unusually warm for the time of year and Sigbjørn and Silverhjelm lingered at the railing. Along the line the City boats[44] were moored, their wire runners and hawsers interlaced, a map of the world scrawled in rust on their iron bodies.

Good-bye, *City of Warsaw*! *City of Hong Kong*! Good-bye, *City of Paris*!

In their shrouded stillness Sigbjørn said farewell to a million glittering cities, and their shadows seemed to be sailing along with them as memory lapped their sides.

Ashore, an apron of lights flashed on over the cinema fronts. Lights shone in Public Houses where drinking out of hours was going on; a procession moved through a street, banners aloft; outside another cinema, a man lingered as though haunting. He will take refuge there and see, on a cartoon, a caricature of his most private passions. Silent as Charon's boat,[45] the *Unsgaard* glided between the marshes bordering the River Ribble, marshes as mysterious in their way as the deserts of Egypt and Arabia,[46] north and south of the Suez Canal; but instead of the Arab's watchfire, where glowworms flickered in summer, there now gleamed the faint spark of a cigarette. Poor lovers, with no rooms to go to and no money for the cinema, wandered there, and pausing, strained their eyes towards the lights and shadows of the ship.

"How small she is..."

Now the river was opening out into the Irish Sea, as the Suez opens to the Bitter Lakes. Orders flashed from the bridge where Haarfragre paced ceaselessly: *Halvt: Fullt: Sakte.*[47]

By the light of cluster lamps[48] on the foredeck, the crew worked. A dimming twilight cast its faint radiance on snow, still on the meadows, and crawled along the marshes.

Under the direction of the boatswain the crew gathered the timber discards and threw them overboard. From the pulpit,[49] a first voyager was heaving the lead.

(But deeper, deeper lie the well-springs of the past...)

Haarfragre called out *Igjen!*

Beyond, seas mountainous as the Alps awaited them. These they had to cross, like immigrants of old,[50] to discover for themselves what lay beyond.

XVI

Come deadly element of fire, embrace me as I do thee!

NATHANIEL HAWTHORNE[1]

Why this is hell, nor am I out of it!

BEN JONSON[2]

Between meridians of westerly longitude, between parallels of northerly latitude, lay the line, the track of the *Unsgaard*. In the chartroom were pencil, protractor,[3] a piece of rubber, a thermometer, a speedometer. The freighter could make nine knots.[4]

Haarfragre paced the bridge, the ship following the course he had plotted. Once he spoke to the quartermaster:[5]

"Starboard your helm[6] a little...a little more...Steady...Now then, what's the course?"

"Course N-79-W."[7]

"Good. Keep her like that."

In the wireless shack on the upper deck, Sparks[8] sat with the receivers over his ears, listening to the thousand electric voices of the world telling of wind and weather and derelicts in the same breath with Easter greetings and rumours of revolution and war.

Soon, Haarfragre turned in. Now only a watch-keeper[9] and a quartermaster remained on the bridge. The ship was silent above decks as a dead planet.

Sparks also prepared to turn in as a hand from the seamen's forecastle, called a wireless watcher,[10] inhibited his stride over the brass step as he came to relieve him.

As he went he peered in at the engine-room entrance to check the carpenter's tank soundings[11] on the blackboard. From the fiddley he could look right down into the stokehold.

The coal was near the stokehold floor[12]—this much he noticed—so that the trimmer on watch could afford to take more swigs of oatmeal and water[13] than usual.

A fireman slammed the furnace door with his shovel, dropped the shovel on the deck, wiped his forehead on a sweatrag. The trimmer stood under the ventilator. Another fireman was leaning on his slice,[14] while yet another was relieving himself in a bucket.

Sparks turned in.

Behind him, in the humid atmosphere, was the clamour of tossing metal.

The solitary tramp[15] was now shipping bitterly cold seas. She pitched slowly and heavily in the long swell. It was a world of semi-darkness, the sunset lost behind ragged clouds.

From down below came ringing of a shovel.

In the fireman's forecastle a dim light was burning. By its limited glow men sat stitching. Outside, the wind started to blow with a dark melancholy wailing.

A piece of stuff was ripped up, then there was silence broken only by the tremendous roar of the screws.[16] Silverhjelm was already snoring in his bunk. He alone spoke a passable English which was why Haarfragre had bade him keep an eye out for Sigbjørn on the gangway. *Expectamus te.*[17]

The others had much to talk about; much indeed must have happened, for good or evil, in their months away from Norway; there was, for instance, the man who had been shot, whose place Sigbjørn was now filling; and there was melancholy at the thought of loved ones left behind in the dark city, but whatever they said, although in what had been his birth-language, Sigbjørn could no longer understand.

With his head in his hands, he sat thinking. For once, the heart slept. Conversation occupied the table; a story bobbed like a cork in a sea of interruptions. For Sigbjørn, there was nothing to contribute: only now and again he nodded Ja or Nei. The lamp swung impartially. A kitten slept in the arms of one of the firemen.

Once, someone patted him on the back and produced some broken English. "Sigbjørn okay." Then conversation was resumed and the sea itself stormed in their words. Sigbjørn stared at the notice which hung over the messroom table as though he hoped thereby to relearn his native speech.

Signalisering og reglene maa nøye efterkommes.
Kvinner, barn, passasjerer, og hjaelpeløse personer
skal sendes i land för skibets besetning.
Kristiania 1901.[18]

He turned away, and following another trimmer's example, spread some sugar on a hunk of bread and munched it hungrily.

Though he wanted to concentrate on the events which had led to his arrival on board, this memory too seemed communicated in bits and pieces and a foreign tongue. He took another bite.

What had happened since Tor's death? He couldn't remember this clearly either. There seemed a void where his memory had been.

But quite suddenly it ceased to be a void, and filled with whirling fragments; like snowflakes they drifted ceaselessly to some hostile area of his brain where, for a hundredth of a second, each fragment became a fact, then melted and was gone.

Simultaneously these fragments echoed the particles, the tiny components of the incomprehensible vocables that swept over him as he sat munching bread and sugar in the firemen's foc'sle of a Norwegian timber ship bound, it was said, in ballast to the White Sea.

Or wasn't she bound for the White Sea? And if not, where would she take him? Would he also, like Columbus,[19] overtake imaginary realities to emerge with truer ones?

Or would reality, like the White Whale or the Magnetic Mountain[20] destroy the ship once in range of its devastating powers, so that the *Unsgaard*'s ironwork would explode; rivets would scatter like machine-gun bullets; timbers and hatches and bulkheads burst asunder; and the ship part and sink, with only the raised arm of a Daggoo[21] hammering the red flag to the disappearing masthead to show what faith had moved her voyaging?

He recalled one night three years before when, as a sailor on the *Oedipus Tyrannus* in Dairen, when as they lay alongside, he had taken his 'donkey's breakfast'[22] out on the hatch to sleep and had lain there for a long time staring at the mainmast and the stars when suddenly he became aware that some Chinese firemen were chattering at his elbow. Not knowing a word of their language, but listening intently, lulled by the rhythm of their speech, he had fallen asleep.

In sleep, their conversation penetrated, became comprehensible: an older fireman was advising a young trimmer how to wash his clothes. "Don't dry your dungarees below: they get stiff from the boilers. And wring out a singlet every time you come up. And get soap from the second steward, English soap; give him some samshaw[23] for it..."

He recalled waking several times in the space of a few hours but the Chinese, continuing to talk, took no notice of him. And what they said was again incomprehensible. He slept, and once more all was clear.

Now, under the torrent of talk, he felt himself drowning. In his exhaustion, aching in every limb, he nodded several times, leaning forward on his hands. Each time he waked it was with a start, his mind and ears filled with the meaningless hubbub and the roaring of the propellers and wind.

No one took any notice of him as he sat in a corner of the forecastle, although at one time he knew he had been talking to himself. Probably he had not uttered a sound. At the next moment the voices of the crew, like the repressed cinesthesia[24] of the madman that persistently invades the sphere of normal consciousness, had seemed to start out of the dark to touch him.

They appeared to be trying to express what he himself felt, where his experiences were beyond the resources of linguistic reserve, so that, as the cinesthesia took on a disorderly verbal expression, he became conscious of the antagonisms between his experience and these verbal symbolisms, and suffered the sense of integration and alienation which emotionally characterize the insane mind.

But when he fell asleep for a third time, he knew he was about to re-encounter that facility he had momentarily acquired in Dairen among the Chinese firemen: a linguistic déjà vu; that again his dreams would open doors to comprehension, even clarity:

..."nobody knows why that is..."

"In the old days, my God, there were wooden ships soaked with grease; they put to sea with as many fires aboard as the old whalers needed in boiling down their oil..."

"Why do they go? Nobody knows."

"There's too much danger of fire."

"Of fire—"

"Now you can haul a dead whale bodily aboard, have a fleet of seven catchers, get 2500 barrels of oil a day..."

"Factory ships[25] working their way through the ice, getting heavily battered... too much danger."

"Oh, jolly is the gale[26], And a joker is the whale, A'flourishing his tail, Such a sporty, funny, gamy, jesty, hoky-poky, lad, is the ocean eh!"

"Fire...factory ships working their way through the ice...getting heavily battered...too much danger..."

Sigbjørn knew he was asleep, but he braced himself as he would in consciousness, so as to hear every word. He knew too that although Silverhjelm was likewise asleep, he was frequently addressed and this was curious.

In his dream he waked, a sailor shaking him. "Coffee time."[27]

"What makes you take a Norwegian ship," asked one fireman.

"I was born in Norway. I'm going back to the country where I was born."

"But we won't touch Norway," said another. "We're going straight to Archangel."

"But maybe we'll go to Leningrad," said the first.

"But what makes you want to go to Norway?" a third persisted.

He took a wild shot.

"Have you ever heard of William Erikson, of a book called *Skibets reise fra Kristiania?*"

There was a stir at this.

"Yes, Gustav[28] sailed with him. He's a Bergener," said one of the older men.

"Everyone in Norway knows his book...but it's a lot of rot," another said.

"And it caused a fury in Norway." The first man again.

"He was a deckboy on a Wilhelmsen[29] liner."

"No. He was a limper. I will say that."

"He'd have been much better playing at Christ Jesus in the temple,"[30] said the first.

"It's a scandal, a kid like that, having one trip and then thinking he could tell the whole world what it's like."

"Let me tell you," said the first, excitedly, "as good people come out of the Norwegian mercantile as from any other walk of life."

"That young fellow tells the whole world that we do nothing but drink and go with women. What I call that is a lot of damn nonsense."

"But after all, what else do we do?" laughed the donkeymand,[31] "when we get into port *but* drink and go with women?"

"We go on strike for instance," said one.

"That's all in the day's work, but we have to have women as well, that's plain..."

"Yes, Bjorne's right. After all, what else do we do?"

There was laughter. "Yes, what do we do?"

"All the same, Jesus loves us and will save us in the end," insisted a new voice, and Sigbjørn knew that this conversation was a mockery of that which had occurred.

"I'd like to kill that Erikson," muttered the first fireman, "but now we've got to turn to."

"Down the little hell[32] and get rid of the beer," suggested the donkeymand who, for his part, had no intention of sweating very much.

"Time to turn to," a voice said in Sigbjørn's ear, and now he really did wake up.

They shuffled out on deck into an icy blast, for though the evening had begun mildly, it had grown bitterly cold. Far above them, Haarfragre was pacing again, with a gait rendered unsteady by the tossing sea, an ocean deeply sinking, laboriously rising, circling and dropping, so that the very bridge itself seemed convulsively to trace and retrace the outlines of the Cross.[33]

Sigbjørn imagined Ahab's dread question again re-echoing: "Hast seen the White Whale."[34]

But now a thousand fathom sea of heat, of density a thousand times that within the Pyramid of Cheops,[35] closed over them.

Down below in the bunker, working alone in the dark wandering room, far below the waterline of the ship so that it seemed that all the weight of humanity itself, with its unreal burdens and worthless history, were pressing on him, Sigbjørn thought again of Erikson.

In a bunker similar to this he must have worked.

But what could have driven Erikson to sea? Was his failure, perhaps even as Sigbjørn's own, now made clear to him or was his purpose still obscure, the secret for which he'd searched yet undisclosed?

And what was all the talk of purpose after all? What did we know of intent and of object? The secret lay buried: clay stopped the mouths of knowledge as it did of corpses. The Kingdom of Heaven[36] might exist but could man recognise it? Perhaps it was only the Island of Cipango,[37] which Marco Polo pictured as abounding in gold, whose dream would hold them as an article of faith.

Never falter, they'd told him. Go on, and always on. And as he thrust his shovel deep into a resisting pile of coal he realized that in thus working with his comrades and such simple tools, even though the language barrier continued to obstruct, even were he not to be accepted by them, there still existed something he had never found before but which had glowed before his reeling vision as clearly as the landing-lights that will direct the pilot.

He might not fully understand it yet. Meaning? Purpose? The words fell tinnily. But as with the Chinese firemen in his dreams, their clarity would come.

He descended to the stokehold from the bunker and drank a long swig of oatmeal and water from the can that hung below the ventilator. The work wasn't so bad after all, he thought, although the nearness of coal was always honey to a trimmer.

Already the skin was starting to peel from his hands,[38] though. He even laughed to Silverhjelm, who at that moment flung a slice away from him, with a strangely eclipsed face.

From a distance six bells were striking. One hour more. He could manage that.

An engineer came down the ladder, hesitated, then started to say something with avidity.

There was a pause in the work, everybody speaking at once. Then the engineer disappeared.

Work was resumed with redoubled activity. Before eight bells, another watch came below.

"Hurry up," shouted Silverhjelm. "We must get all steam..."

"Hurry, I said, work like goddam."

"What is it?"

"Hurry. A ship in distress. Don't talk. Hurry!"

"What ship is it?"

"Don't talk. Hurry!"

Sigbjørn shoveled like mad until he could take another spell. Erikson had been through all this. Hadn't something similar[39] happened in *Skibets reise fra*

Kristiania? A ship in distress! Down here Erikson had dreamed; his dream had been to tell what the sea was like. Could it be said of him he had succeeded, when even the actors in his dream renounced it?

The blasting heat smote with a breath that, it might be supposed, would have scorched and shriveled him but like Hawthorne's Ethan Brand he now bent over the terrible body of the fire like a fiend on the verge of plunging into his gulf of intensest torment. Like a fiend[40] he worked without thought, for all hands were now taking turns at the furnaces, until the nine firemen of the three boilers gave them respite again.

But this time when he took a spell under the ventilator he nearly collapsed. He fought against the drowsy nausea which overcame him, holding up his arms. And this time he had the sensation of being cheated by himself.

Although he managed to throw himself back into the work it was now clearly ineffectual. The crew seemed not to notice his presence at all; he could not rid himself of this feeling as he stretched, striving to stretch himself out of a deadly cramp; so Ethan Brand had stood and raised his arms on high.

At last he stumbled out on deck and lay face downward on a hatch. Not long ago he had had the pretentiousness to assume that, like a cause working back from the future, his belief in the brotherhood of man would comfort him in his perpetual tilting with despair. How was it possible that now, having willed himself to be its partisan, he could no longer comprehend its language? Four hours earlier had he taken refuge in its dream; was reality now to prove less logical?

Surely, his pounding temples told him, he had not committed the unpardonable sin: that of an intellect which holds itself triumphantly above this new-found brotherhood? Had he then, toiling before his prison-house of fire, cast off such claims of brotherhood? And was he, even now, trampling such beliefs, even such faith, into a paste of ashes?[41]

Silverhjelm appeared beside him and he rose. The former pointed northward. "An English ship on fire! The *Arcturion* out of Liverpool!"

"The *Arcturion*!!"

Sigbjørn, trembling, struggled for comprehension.

His father!

Nina!

Shouts and cries filled the night as the two young men stumbled up on deck. There was a shattering explosion and broken powdered glass was flung into the faces of those nearest.

On the far side of the deck firemen off watch had gathered; Sigbjørn and Silverhjelm joined them. In mid-distance, the *Arcturion* and a pier were blazing; scorched air heavily impregnated with their smoke.

Near at hand another ship lay off to provide aid and in sudden terror Sigbjørn wondered whether it might be the *Direction*. Choking, he could neither hear nor speak but for once he was ready to act without equivocation,[42] but only, he thought bitterly, when plainly there was little he could do.

For it was not only the *Arcturion* but seemingly the old world whose skeleton, like the ribs of a wicker basket, was burning to the water's edge. Smoke-laden flames, in murderous competition, streaked ever higher in an obscene parody of the Mostyn furnaces[43] which had once seemed to Sigbjørn to threaten the body of the night.

Some of the sailors, tiring, began to shuffle towards the forecastle, but Sigbjørn and Silverhjelm remained, transfixed and motionless.

Two young faces turning together to look on death.

XVII

Captain Haarfragre, wearing an old mackintosh, in bare feet, and with what felt like an extremely bad hangover, looked out of reddened eyes over the sleeked leaden surface of the water.

It was six o'clock in the morning, the ship's lights were still burning, and the day workers were only just turning to. The *Unsgaard* carried no boatswain,[1] and near him on the bridge an able seaman was getting his orders for the day from the first mate. The captain went over to them.

"Set that new man we took out of the stokehold to work in the forepeak,"[2] he said. "He can clear the timber from the deck and hatches forrard and the planks that are worth saving he can pile in there, too, eh?"

"Very good, sir," said the first mate, and turning to the A. B.[3] added, "You heard what he said, Bjorne, set that man working forrard and the rest of you get soogie[4] and wash paint on the boat deck."

"Very good," said Bjorne and turned to go, but Haarfragre caught him at the head of the companion ladder[5] and asked him, but not within hearing of the mate, who had sauntered to the other side of the bridge, "By the way, what about the man we took aboard in Prester, how does he get on with the men?"

Bjorne shook his head. "I don't care to say nothing about him."

Haarfragre smiled. "I don't want you to give anything away of course—you can trust me—it's just that I want to know how he's making out with all of you."

"Well," replied Bjorne, "it's difficult for me to say, like, for he signed on as a trimmer and lives in the fireman's quarters, and now that he's working on deck we don't see much more of him, but ever since the fire he's seemed to me to be in bad shape."

"How do you mean, in bad shape?"

"Well, for one thing, he doesn't seem to know why he's on board and if it comes to that we're not much wiser. I think that fire turned his head a little."

"He had a girlfriend on board that ship," said Haarfragre, "if that makes anything clearer to you. That may account for a lot."

"What! Did she die in the fire?" Bjorne asked sympathetically.

"No, she didn't. I got a wireless about five minutes ago. I haven't told him yet...she was picked up by an American freighter and she's well on her way to New York by now. So that makes things a bit better. But what I was going to say was...don't be too hard on him if he doesn't mix well, so long as he does what's he's told, of course. I really have a feeling of responsibility for him—don't say anything about this in the forecastle, but...Well..." Haarfragre tailed off.

"I think I understand," said Bjorne, and there seeming no more to be said on the subject, he disappeared down the bridge ladder.

Haarfragre sighed and entered the chart room where he dropped into a swivel chair. The events of the last days, during which he had hardly slept at all, seemed nightmarish even within his own extremely full memory. He had been through fire and earthquake, flood, and almost every kind of disaster, from which there had always proved to be some unexpected refuge, the unforeseen sanctuary where it was possible to lurk as men can beneath the tumult of Niagara[6]...or just as a ship is securely hidden by the headland from the maniacal typhoon...but nothing he had ever seen or experienced had seemed to him as dreadful, as sickeningly final and inescapable, as the burning of the *Arcturion*.

Yet survivors there had apparently been, even though the duty of the *Unsgaard* had consisted eventually in simply transferring a cargo of death.

Not all had been burnt or drowned or had been found frozen in the postures of the living,[7] for by some polar conceit of nature the temperature had dropped some twenty degrees during the time they had taken to reach the scene of the disaster, and Nina had been among those saved.

The quartermaster at the wheel struck four bells,[8] and was almost immediately relieved. Haarfragre muttered some greeting to the new man at the helm, for the wheel was immediately forward of the porthole at his elbow, but the relieving quartermaster just shifted his feet, nodded politely enough, and said nothing at all. Indeed, he could not. Ever since the disaster there had been a peculiar silence on board the vessel, silence on deck, silence below, silence both on and off watch.

Sometimes, like a fading coal,[9] it would hiss and flare up into a bright flame of argument and conviction or devastating criticism, only to subside into the burnt out wreckage of memory. Or, like the little fires that spurt up on the charred moorland after a great burning, but weaken and die since there is no longer even death to feed on, these arguments were starved of their real fuel, the harsh, dry bracken of hate. It was too early to hate, when they could never be sure they were not hating the dead.

So the quartermaster said nothing, contenting himself with keeping the course. And the others, too, heard now from the chartroom only as a tramping on deck; the clang of a shovel down below; and held their peace; a grimace, a shrug of the shoulders, gritted teeth, two outstretched, upflung hands shaking the forearms with silent fury, expressed, however, a common determination. No one was resigned.

Haarfragre was watching for Sigbjørn to go forward, but after a while, suspecting that he had been detained, he bent over his charts.

From these it would have been possible for even a landsman to deduce that the coastal waters of Norway are quite unlike those of other European countries. Norway itself appeared, obviously enough, as an irregular mass of rock furrowed and cleft by an indefinite number of gullies and valleys, its coastline winding in and out of bays and fjords cutting deeply into the mainland, a variability intensified by the numerous islands, holms[10] and rocks lying strewn at various distances from the mainland.

Along the predominant part of this coast, the chart showed what looked like tall, pointed mountaintops, and Haarfragre's finger, itself like a companion pinnacle,[11] was now pointing to one, but rising from the bottom of the sea nearly up to the surface of the water. And these hidden rocks and shallows, with dividing furrows and channels, were responsible for a still greater variability in the formation of the sea floor, which was the earth.

Haarfragre's finger now slowly moved along this sea floor, thousands of feet along which his own ship made her way, without the assistance of Sigbjørn, at a dozen knots, and the strange thought quickly came to him, and passed more quickly, that it had its correspondence[12] perhaps in the most dangerous and slippery heights and imponderable depths of the human consciousness.

For instead of sloping evenly from the shore to an outer ridge of banks—a formation common elsewhere but in Norway limited to just a few stretches—the sea floor descended in gigantic terraces with steep, mountainous precipices.

So the normal processes of man's thought may sometimes drop in encroaching steep down-slopes, steepened and rendered horribly luminous by nightmare, into the deeper, unconscious layers of the mind.

It had always seemed remarkable to Haarfragre that it should be so difficult to find any considerable area with a quite even floor; for even the shallow parts further off had an uneven surface with mountain-like tops projecting upward!

The Captain now examined the map of the east, south and part of the west coasts where the coastal bank descended from the shore in a very steep slope towards the *Norskerennen*,[13] the Norwegian channel, which ran from the Norwegian Sea[14] west of Aalesund, continuing as a wide, deep sea channel along the coast nearly to the Oslo fjord;[15] after which he seemed to be satisfied and swung round in his chair. Then he put on his boots.

Good God, he knew it all, or thought he knew it all—every channel, every natural division, every shallow level, he thought, threading the thick, tough laces through the damp hide—and what steep slopes there were west of Aalesund, going down to those vast depths and expanding into submarine plateaus between Norway and Spitzbergen.[16] And yet he often wondered, as he was wondering now, rising and returning to the bridge, from which he clearly saw Sigbjørn duck into the cavernous depths of the forepeak, how it was possible to guide a ship safely at all through such complexity. Just seeing they were all charted was a wonder in itself.

Even more of a marvel was it that these mountains and declivities under the sea should remain reasonably faithful to the reality, the scattered logic, of their aberration, that they did not wander when such powerful currents swept the floor.

Standing beside the quartermaster, Captain Haarfragre gazed north for a full minute, as though to encompass the voyage far beyond the coast of Finnmark[17] and the North Cape[18] of the White Sea, that the *Unsgaard* might still make, then he slowly descended the bridge companion to the foredeck and made his way to the forepeak.

Nor was it necessary for Sigbjørn to understand the nature of the framework enclosing him for him to be affected already by its correspondences, crosscurrents, and harmonies.

The forepart of the ship was deserted but Haarfragre would probably have seated himself regardless, and without embarrassment, on the step of the forepeak.

Sigbjørn must have seen him but said nothing, just paused for a moment in his work of shifting timber to glance up at the quartermaster, braced at the wheel on the bridge, who at that moment struck five bells.[19] Since they carried no lookout, no answering echo came.

The silence persisting, broodingly, the Captain rolled a cigarette and composed himself to inspect more closely the strange, wild figure which was Sigbjørn, Sigbjørn in singlet, soaking dungarees, and Blucher boots.[20]

"Your girl's O.K.," Haarfragre said at length. "I didn't rush to tell you, for some reason."

Sigbjørn seemed hardly to have heard him. "Yes, Bjorne told me. But I'd felt it all along."

"Bjorne told you, did he? I didn't tell him to tell you, but perhaps it's as well he did. Well, that's some good news at any rate."

Sigbjørn still said nothing and appeared so distraught that Haarfragre had to ask, "Aren't you glad?"

"Don't mistake me," Sigbjørn replied. "But why do you make a special point of telling me of Nina's rescue when so many others...hundreds, perhaps..." His voice trailed off, conveying only hopelessness. It was clear to the Captain he was still in shock.

Perhaps the loss of the Tarnmoor Line *Arcturion*, following so shortly on the earlier tragedy of the *Thorstein*, and the realization of what this must mean to his father, even his father's life...the Captain thought sympathetically.

"Yes, well..." he began, but yes, well, what? He made an abortive gesture, partially extending a hand and as swiftly withdrawing it, and stood up. "When we touch Norway, if you'd rather..." he began again, but he didn't finish this sentence either and Sigbjørn did not appear to notice as he left.

To Silverhjelm, when he next saw him, he remarked, "Better to keep an eye out for the Tarnmoor lad; he's taking all this quite hard."

The glance they exchanged was one of understanding.

XVIII

> Man has much in common with a house filled with inhabitants, the most disparate. Or better, he is like a great ocean liner on which are many transient passengers, each going to his own place for his own purposes, each uniting in himself elements the most diverse. And each separate unit in the population of the steamer orientates himself, unconsciously and involuntarily regards himself as the very centre of the steamer.[1]

#####

> (The three closing chapters, as indicated in Lowry's outlines, of which Aalesund would have been chapter 18.)

#####

Somewhere north of Scotland, the *Unsgaard* receives word that her charter to Archangel has been cancelled, and that she is to proceed to Aalesund,[2] her port of registry, at that time a fishing village with many little islands dotting its fjord. Lowry describes Aalesund itself as an island off the west coast of Norway, and the province of the ancient nobles of Møre.[3]

They enter Aalesund, which at first appears a romantic paradise: white buildings beyond the fjord; girls in rowboats, playing guitars; but its character seems to change as the ship warps further along into the desolate fjord, still part of yet distant from the town. At night the ship is so far from town that Sigbjørn is the only one who wants to go ashore, although Silverhjelm accompanies him as a kind of foreganger,[4] and in him Sigbjørn feels, as before, the influence of Tor.

What seems to him "strange, almost dreamlike," is that Aalesund is also the name of a principal character[5] in *Skibets reise* though Lowry acknowledges the possibility that the seaman could have been native to the village and hence so tagged.

Since they elected to "make fast to a treestump"[6] on one of the many little islands out in the fjord, it was assumed, wrongly, that the town, "a mile or so away," lacked a wharf for deepsea ships.

Next day Sigbjørn wakes late to find himself alone on board save for the mate and the donkeyman, the rest having gone ashore to learn the status of their charter.[7] Sigbjørn, following them, puts up at a dockside hotel called the Møre.[8] Then, having only English pounds, he seeks to change them at a kaffistove,[9] and it is there he makes the acquaintance of Carsten Walderhaug,[10] a teacher who is to aid him in his search for Erikson, one of whose books, Sigbjørn noted, he was in the act of reading. It deals with Erikson's experiences in China[11] in 1927, at the very period Sigbjørn was likewise there.

Sigbjørn learns that Erikson, too, has visited Aalesund and recited his poetry at the gymnasium.[12] Walderhaug describes the Norwegian author as "right from the heart" and indicates he has become so popular that he is forced to live, from time to time, under an assumed name.

He tells Sigbjørn of a newspaper clipping[13] in the form of a poem to and about the author, and promises to bring it next day, should they meet again at the kaffistove. Partisan and disciple that he has become, Sigbjørn eagerly agrees.

When he next encounters Haarfragre, this time at the ship's chandlers, the Captain informs him that their latest orders are to proceed to Archangel after all, but now that a large portion of the crew has been paid off the chances of replacing them in this fishing village, currently half strike-bound,[14] are at best dim. As atonement for the brevity of Sigbjørn's voyage, he offers to introduce him to the skipper of a collier who has voiced need for a coal passer and for firemen, and a next day's meeting is arranged.

Though it now turns out to be possible to go alongside in Aalesund after all, the *Unsgaard* remains tied up to its distant tree stump. The promised collier, on the Aalesund side at the coal tips,[15] is invisible behind a vast black cloud of smoke.

Next day, in company with a Norwegian who has lived in America and speaks English, met by chance at the Hotel Møre, Sigbjørn keeps his appointment with the collier skipper, whose vessel is a filthy decrepit tramp, caked with rust, covered stem to stern with coal dust and lacking even a gangway. She is registered in Bergen and her name is *Nina*.[16] The skipper firmly announces 'all bets are off,' that he is obliged by law to engage only Norwegians. With which pronouncement he disappears up a rope ladder.

Understandably relieved, Sigbjørn now meets with Haarfragre who informs him that the latest in the stream of orders directs them to tie up for the present: the charter for Archangel has once again been cancelled. Should Sigbjørn elect to wait it out and remain in Aalesund, Haarfragre will be reachable at either the ship's chandlers or on board.

The teacher, meanwhile, true to his promise, has brought the clipping, a poem addressing Erikson as the Hope of Norway and managing to incorporate most of the titles of his numerous works. The poem is signed: Nina.

Walderhaug, as addicted to jazz as is Sigbjørn, is in addition a violinist who furthers his income by playing from time to time at the cafes and nightclubs. He dreams of forming a small 'Jazzband' to be called Rumba.

More to the point, he has brought Sigbjørn news of Erikson. Through a friend he has learned that the writer now lives on Bygdø Allé[17] in Oslo when he is in town. His friend does not know the number but this is at least a start and to Sigbjørn Erikson begins to appear approachable. From Haarfragre, too, he has been given an Oslo address: that of the shipping company[18] which operates the *Unsgaard*.

Sigbjørn remains in a state of wretched indecision. His voyage has ended much too soon to fulfill the need to learn more of the lives of Norwegian sailors in order to successfully dramatise *Skibets reise fra Kristiania*. On the other hand, there is now a stronger possibility of meeting Erikson.

It seems to him that while his own decision is in suspense, the division in his mind has been reflected in the constant, contradictory messages to the *Unsgaard*; can it be that his indecision places the destiny of the ship within his grasp? that he is, as it were, the agent of one whose orders are sealed[19] but for whom he is the messenger?

His frame of mind is hardly enlivened by a series of near mishaps: a heavy pane of glass, collapsing from a window, nearly crushes him; a car, out of control, demolishes a light standard against which he had moments before been leaning; now, sitting in the sun at a cafe and eating smørbrød[20] with an unaccustomed glass of milk, he feels a nearly overwhelming compulsion to run, to hide.

Taking refuge in a nearby book store, he examines, without understanding, several of Erikson's books and wonders whether, in these, his future is written in a language he cannot understand.

A storm flies after the train in which Sigbjørn travels to Oslo. He stares from the window at the desolate iron land of his birth. Darkness is falling as they pound over the frozen wastes. Now a crag overhangs the train; now a foaming torrent seems about to engulf them; in the wet night he gazes out at his birthplace, Helgafjord.[21]

He pillows his face on his arm, and while sleeping deeply he dreams that his own mother stands above him, bending over him like a dark crag, as huge as the darkness itself.

His companion has taken a violin[22] from the rack and is playing softly. A melancholy yearning mingles with the racket of noise which is tossed back to them from the ravines and glaciers, but through his sleep this tiny thread of melody persists, a song as lost as some poor memory, which, like a muted string, is hushed and small.

In night and in the darkness of sleep he travels through the country for whose sake he has dreamed his life away. And again he dreams, of coal crashing down over him.[23]

The land lies buried in snow, snow half way up the stalks in the woods, the earth everywhere hidden, a single white snowfield as far as the land extends, white, shores along the Cattegat, white over in Skoane, on both sides of the sound, Kullen,[24] like a headland of snow running out to sea, the isles now isles of snow, and between all the buried coastline, the sea, open and black, sparkling with frost. The sounds too are closed with ice a fathom thick and the snow smooths out all countries into one.

'Only he in whom the past is stored is freighted for the future.'[25]

When he wakes, he is in Oslo.

Once in Oslo I bought myself a new mackintosh, a bottle of whiskey from the Bimmonpolet,[26] and told a taxi driver to drive me down the Bygdø Allé, my plan being to get off halfway and trust to luck. Very few people in Norway speak English and it was sometime before I understood from the taxi driver, first, that he had never heard of Erikson, and secondly that the Bygdø Allé,[27] while beginning as an avenue, continued as a road that went some 20 or 30 miles to the town of Bygdø. On hearing this I stopped the taxi and in English asked the first person I saw if he knew William Erikson or where he lived. To my astonishment he replied that he lived quite near and he knew him slightly. I accordingly offered him a lift home, which he accepted, and on arrival there...he lived in a lane just off the Bygdø Allé...he told me if I would wait outside while he did some telephoning he would conduct me to the apartment building where Erikson lived and was of the opinion there would be no difficulty in meeting him if I would just leave the matter to him, provided always that Erikson was in Oslo at present.

He was such a very long time returning that I dismissed the taxi feeling more and more isolated, even abandoned, and finally that perhaps I was the victim of some obscure hoax. I could not very well follow him into his house, the entrance to which was through a door in a high wall, out of which he came at a great rate just as I had given up hope of his coming at all.

He explained that he was a ship's broker and had had to put in a long distance call on behalf of one of his ships, and I discovered with some surprise that the ship in question was the *Unsgaard*. My chance acquaintance was none other than the deus ex machina[28] whose contradictory messages had had such a bearing upon the ship, her captain and myself. It turned out he did not think much of either Erikson or his work although granting the writer could say things that 'jump at you,' such as 'Cain shall not slay Abel today' and 'It is worse to betray Judas than to betray Jesus.'[29]

The apartment where Erikson lived, #68, was ultra-modern, and after refusing a drink in the restaurant which occupied the bottom floor, he escorted me up in the lift, showed me Erikson's door, and departed quickly.

I hesitated, knocked on the door in trepidation, the door opened, and there was Erikson, 'straight from the heart' and with 'his hair parted in the middle,' just as the little teacher in Aalesund had said. Perhaps he was, as the ship's broker had described him, a sloppy chap too, but I was struck by his extreme kindness.

Suffice it that, had I done nothing in my life but make that miserable trip, with all its coincidences and bafflements, and knock on that door in Oslo, my life would still have some meaning. So shattering an impression did the whole incident make on me that I not only remember every word he said but everything I did in detail: for instance, I walked all the way back down the Bygdø Allé, it was a stormy night with the trees thrashing, and stopped in a little bookstore near Biblioteket[30] where I bought a copy in the Tauchnitz edition[31] of a book called *The Dark Journey*.[32] I had two drinks on Erikson, who had to go out to dinner that night, and I hadn't even removed my mackintosh. We became friends, but as my father had prophesied, he didn't like having his work interfered with...He had become a dramatist himself; a play of his[33] was due to be produced at the National Theatre that winter and he was working hard. He was also preparing to take a trip to Cambridge because he was writing a book on the Elizabethan dramatists.[34] Although a dramatist himself he showed, to my surprise, no particular interest in helping with the dramatisation[35] of *Ship Sails On*, which he had finished seven years before.

However he was impressed with my knowledge of it, even going to far as to say 'You know more about that book than I shall ever know,' and generously gave me carte-blanche to dramatise it. To tell the truth I believe he was more impressed with the dramatic possibilities of our relationship than anything else, for he once said, "We should write a play about this thing—you *should* have written the book but unfortunately, I have—the play turns on that—and in the end, *you* kill *me*."[36]

Notes from Malcolm's outline for In Ballast:

The next evening Sigbjørn sets out towards the Bygdø Allé; he walks slowly and uncertainly, pausing to look in shopwindows and bookshops, seeking anywhere an excuse to loiter, to postpone the finality of his action, seeking even for some possible objective which will take him quite in the opposite direction. For instance, there is the National Gallery[37] he had not thought to visit during the day, nor has he been to the harbour; in the Kristian IV's gate,[38] there is an exhibition of Munch's pictures;[39] they are giving Kataev's play[40] at Nationaltheatret, there is a circus opposite the Holmenkollen and Sigbjørn wastes ten minutes on the way surveying the advertisements for Circus Revy,[41] Circus Globus Springboart and Tumpling Act. It would be good fun there and there was a possibility of adventure, etc., etc.

But as he passes Biblioteket he takes a taxi to whose driver he says, Til *Bygdø Allé*. The taxi goes at a great pace and he realizes that very soon they will be out of Oslo altogether, in fact in Bygdø itself, as the name of the avenue suggests.

Sigbjørn curses himself for not having made inquiries, for not having had the courage to enter the Kristiania Bokhandel,[42] Erikson's publishers, that morning, and making more specific inquiries about him. But he is abandoned to the situation, and now feeling that nothing he can do will alter the fixed curve[43] of what is going to happen, he prepares to obey the first impulse which comes to him.

He therefore hails a man at random and asks him if he knows where Erikson lives and it so happens that this man, whose name is Christensen, while not knowing, nevertheless has an intimate friend who he feels would know. Surprisingly enough, Christensen knows English, and Sigbjørn offers him a lift home. On the way, Sigbjørn asks him about Erikson.

"It's good of you to trust me," said Sigbjørn, "but it happens to be essential that I see him. I am an English writer and I'm making a play out of *Skibets reise fra Kristiania*. I don't know whether you know the ....(end of fragment...)

...stairs. In the corridor he sees a door with the card[44] of William Erikson pinned to it. He passes the door several times and then, taking courage, is about to knock when the door opens and it seems to Sigbjørn that again intention and object have overlapped.

"Can I speak to William Erikson?"

"I am William Erikson."

Sigbjørn has expected to meet his double but on the contrary Erikson is his exact opposite. Whereas Sigbjørn is fair-haired, Erikson is dark. Sigbjørn is tough looking, broad-shouldered and of medium height: Erikson is tall and slender, fragile, even tragic looking; everything perhaps that Sigbjørn as a child had wanted to become. But the room and Erikson's books are, in a sinister fashion,[45] like his own. An extraordinary, laconic conversation begins between the two in English, while Erikson, who is quite young, gives the other a whiskey. Sigbjørn does not manage to explain himself satisfactorily and the conversation peters out, in a conversation—again—about literature, during which Erikson says that as a matter of fact he is leaving in a week or two for Cambridge to write a book about Rupert Brooke.[46]

"But first I shall go to London and I shall take a little bed in Bloomsbury and sleep there like a little dead childrens."

"I always think Brooke had something nobody else had," said Erikson.

"You'll find his stock very low in Cambridge," said Sigbjørn abruptly, and then sat silently, alarmed. Good God, what travesty was this? And why had he ever made the journey at all? —

Sigbjørn feels himself for a moment to be again fooled by his own romanticism. Rupert Brooke—good God! But in the course of conversation it appears that *John Webster and the Elizabethan Drama* is the book which had given him the idea.[47]

Sigbjørn then tells him of his notion of making *Skibets reise* into a play and Erikson encourages him. As a matter of fact he has himself since become a playwright, and a play of his is to be produced at Nationaltheatret in the autumn... (end of fragment...)

Seated in the Røde Mølle[48] 'under the geraniums,' Sigbjørn, drinking sherry and writing a long letter[49] to Erikson about Rupert Brooke and the Elizabethans, is battling an alcoholic confusion as to whether a further meeting with the Norwegian writer actually took place. Yet he recalls distinctly their visit to the Viking ship,[50] one of that sculpted fleet which ravaged Europe, stormed east into Russia, ranged South to the Black Sea, and traded with the golden lands of the Far East; unconquerable for the 200 years the Viking Age endured.

And he remembers, too, how they had stared with awe approaching veneration at the lissome grace of the great ship and that when they spoke their voices dropped to whispers.

Erikson, Sigbjørn and Birgit[51] are lunching in the Tostrupkjaelderen cafe,[52] high above Oslo. There has been the first fall of snow which seems to Sigbjørn to cover the past, leaving all clean and purged. They look down on the harbour where the freighters lie at anchor and it is as though the world, too, lies at anchor below them.

Erikson says "That's where *Skibets reise fra Kristiania* began."[53]

Once again Sigbjørn felt the scorched air about him and heard the fire roaring like wind in sails. White heat! Pain, he thought, looking down on the harbour. Think of the Arctic, the haunted mind with its black ravines, Cape Horn;[54] this was all life was. When it is conquered, when you think it can no longer bring you to your knees, and the spirit is full of the rich ports welcoming, when you are most happy, what you construe as chance will punish your conceit for presuming that you achieved that peace yourself and without help.

For what other reason were Adam and Eve[55] thrown out of the garden?

As they look down at the sunlit harbour, one of the freighters is weighing anchor and they watch her pass out beyond the bay, beyond the fjord, beyond their dreams and knowledge.[56]

Sigbjørn, who believes in communism,[57] also believes that the soul is going out on its journey in life to seek God, but Erikson believes in nothing[58] save that man is utterly base. He has had every belief and discarded all of them.

"The great thing is to see the truth of all religions, and the categories permanent in each one...All these things are good; even war would be good but it no longer serves its purpose. Once, I think, that was to purge the world, to turn away the chaff. War used to be truth for some. Now it is up to us to stop it, and we'll have to stop bothering about ourselves until we have done our best to put the world right...Yet wars again will start, and all from the same cause, religion. If people would only see that they were all true, all the same."

This is the pole where the ideal and the real meet,[59] Sigbjørn thinks, and it is a moment of perfect ambivalence and pain. But suddenly he feels that Tor has somehow helped him to this situation and he is unaware that the same principle of destruction from which he has been escaping has again overtaken him, when he recalls Erikson's words:

"Cain shall not slay Abel today. Cain shall not slay Abel today."

But Erikson was continuing: "As the poet says, the day of privacy[60] is over and you must engage yourself in the struggle common to us all. After all, your voyage has not been quite useless."

"I discovered many things. I discovered that man can be reborn."

"But you also have discovered that only a few in life are important[61] and that you may not be one of them. Just as you were a character in that book, so has your long voyage brought home little more to you than that you are a pawn in the game which must be won to make the world livable for those who come after us: if that pawn suffers, who shall hear of it?"

"I once thought that God would."

"Why did you come here?" Birgit asks.

Gazing at her, Sigbjørn grasps that this woman holds in her glance the Norway he has longed for and has loved. Fata Morgana[62] encompassing his life from childhood, his mother, his brother, his dreams—his search for Erikson. And at that moment he falls suddenly and fatefully in love with her.

Erikson indicates that should Sigbjørn produce a workable play of *Skibets reise*, it might be produced at Nationaltheatret[63] and gives Sigbjørn a copy of his latest play.[64] Although Sigbjørn cannot understand it, he feels his future written there, even as in *Skibets reise* he discovered his own past.

"But why did you come here?" Birgit asks again.

"To seek my truth," says Sigbjørn. "And although I did not find it, like the hanged man[65] in the Tarot, I was hanged upside down just the same."

Looking at Birgit he is certain that he will know her more deeply, more fully, than anyone he has ever known before. He also knows that loving her may bring suffering and treachery, that it could be a nightmare, but that it is inescapable.

"And now you are as an infant[66] and must start again," Erikson was saying. "Or you leave like Tchekov's old lady, without anything."[67]

"First you take away my religion and now you take away my despair."

Birgit leans towards him, half earnestly, half laughing. "You must have to make a depth-charge of your grief."[68]

"But dear God!" Sigbjørn cries. "How shall I live without my misery?"[69]

[THE END]

See them rotting in football fields, have seen
ball at the Central. They are [illegible] horrendous
really, worse than [illegible] cartoons [illegible].

Gigantic pimply so-called students. Why do they
go on living? what are they being educated for, the
great ball fields, I wonder. They just sound like
pigs — it's impossible to find any meaning in all
their activities. Life bores me to death here, Tor.
I don't like any part of it.' 'Well I [illegible]

Tor smiled, screwing up his eyes
like his brother. 'And what about Peggy,' he asked. 'Does
she love you to death? How would she like your
going to sea?'

'Peggy's hell bent to go to America anyway,'
said his brother, kicking up the earth, 'She's got
a brother [illegible] a cop in the States. Besides
I think she wants to marry me, but you know.'

'Well,' asked Tor, 'why don't you marry her
after all. And go to America with her. Mother
used to say that that was the best place for Norwegians
to go.' 'And take me with you.'

'Jesus, do I want to commit suicide so young.'

There was a silence —

'Sigbjørn —' Tor broke it. 'You don't
mind my asking — but is it good, well, being
with Peggy — what's it like, you know, [illegible]
her.'

'Well' said Sigbjørn, 'If you've ever
[illegible] a girl you know.'

'Oh, I have' said Tor, 'Lots of them.
At least — all the same, I can't quite see you

SOURCE: RARE BOOKS AND SPECIAL COLLECTIONS, UNIVERSITY OF BRITISH COLUMBIA LIBRARY, AND ARE REPRODUCED BY PERMISSION OF PETER MATSON (OF STERLING LORD LITERISTIC) ON BEHALF OF THE ESTATE OF MALCOLM LOWRY.

Annotations

> Two books are being writ, of which the world shall see only one, and that the bungled one. The larger book, and the infinitely better, is for Pierre's own private shelf. That it is, whose unfathomable cravings drink his blood.
>
> —Lowry, of Melville's *Pierre* [UBC 9:5, 382]

Malcolm Lowry's *In Ballast to the White Sea* is indeed two books: that which has survived in typescript form, and that which it might have been, had it been rewritten and subjected to the same rigorous processes that *Under the Volcano* underwent in its transformation from the crude 1940 *Volcano* to the later masterpiece. Much of the novel lies latent within the surviving typescripts; these annotations, through their identification of Lowry's reading and borrowing, seek to see that "larger book" and the patterns of thought that underlie its surface action, or, indeed, its lack of action.

Annotation, by its very nature, is an inexact science, each note less an affirmation than a hypothesis destined to be replaced by another of greater explanatory power or elegance. The principle behind each entry is that expressed in E. D. Hirsch's *Validity in Interpretation* (1967), as deployed in my *Under the Volcano* website, and as summed up in his opening statement that "each interpretive problem requires its own distinct context of relevant knowledge." The present intention is to provide that context, to facilitate interpretation.

Lowry's relevant writings and sources appear in a bibliography, which differentiates between specific texts used (cited by page) and standard authors for whom any edition suffices (cited by chapter or part rather than by page). This principle extends even to writers like Melville and Freud, who are quoted frequently. Lowry's personal library has been consulted where possible. References to Shakespeare are by title of play; biblical quotations respect the King James Authorised Version. Lowry's works are cited in abbreviated form (UTV, DATG, OF, 'Sumptuous Armour'); and other studies by author's name (Bowker) or short title, as seems appropriate. Typically, a first citation is spelled out then a briefer format preferred. For the sake of clarity and economy the following non-standard practices have been adopted:

- single quotation marks for titles of poems, essays, and short stories; but also for citations; double quotation marks for passages and items quoted.
- square brackets for editorial intrusions, including references.
- occasional interpolation of words or phrases in a smaller italic font indicates Lowry's later (and often tentative) changes to his manuscript text.
- bolded cross-references, of the form [**#XIII.25**], to other annotations; an instruction such as "See **#XVII.7**" implies greater urgency.
- cross-references to the 'Textual Notes' to avoid duplication of material.
- inclusive punctuation only when such details are quoted; punctuation is placed outside the quotation marks if it is not specifically part of the quotation.
- commas as determined by logic and rhetorical emphasis, rather than prescription.
- Roman capitals [CXXV] for chapters and sections; but Arabic numerals for page numbers.
- 'on' to suggest later additions to manuscript or typescript; but 'in' to refer to details that are part of the original draft.

TITLE

In Ballast to the White Sea: a ship "in ballast" carries no cargo, but is weighted by scrap-iron (like that on Preston wharf [**#XIV.18–21**]). Grieg's *Mignon* leaves Norway thus [*Ship Sails On* 34]. Applied to the writer, it implies unwanted, useless, waste; one theme (belied by the work, surely, a return with good timber) has Sigbjørn finding he is not a writer [**#XVIII.61**]. His ostensible destination is the **White Sea**, an inset of the Arctic Ocean in northwest Russia, bounded by the Kola Peninsula and Archangel [**#I.56**; **#V.149**]; the *Unsgaard* [**#V.57**] is diverted to Ålesund, reflecting a tension between his Russian and Nordic goals [**#VII.156**]. *Whiteness* prevails [**#VII.2**; **#VII.164**]: Melville's "whiteness of the whale" invokes "thought of annihilation" [**#V.54**], like Poe's whiteout ending in *Arthur Gordon Pym* [**#VII.93**] or the sepulchral city of Tlaxcala [*UTV* 302]. 'Peter Gaunt and the Canals' envisions "a dry world / Washed white" [*CP* #15], where Soviet canals link Leningrad to Archangel, the Baltic to the White Sea. *Antigone*'s paean to death (an epigraph to *UTV*) invokes "the white sea"; Lowry's film script accentuates the "power that crosses the White Sea" [*Tender* 162], which, he told David Markson, represents death [*CL* 2:426].

CHAPTER I

I.1 [Epigraph] Rilke: Rainer Maria Rilke (1875–1926), Austro-Bohemian poet whom Lowry admired for inscribing the ineffable in a tumultuous age of disbelief and for his mystical attraction to Russia. Early drafts lack this epigraph, from the outset of *Die Weise von Liebe und Tod des Cornets Christoph Rilke* (1906), the threnody of a cavalry officer, translated by M. D. Herter Norton as *The Tale of the Love and Death of Cornet Christopher Rilke* (1932). Norton's "foreign sun", copied correctly into the 'Varsity' CB, became "summer sun".

I.2 Castle Hill: a natural hill in Cambridge, with a Norman castle (1068), of which but a few stones and Castle Mound [**#I.10**] remain. Like Kafka's Castle [**#VII.106**], it commands the town; like that in *Christopher Rilke*, it rises above the hovels [**#I.34**]. All drafts begin thus, but an early note specifies November. The 'Pegaso' NB proposes revisions: Paris (Café Chagrin); the quarrel with Nina "objectified"; "remembrance of mother in Norway"; "Looking north"; "'Mother significance' of drink"; "Erikson"; and "In Café Chagrin section he meets the Norwegian in the john". Three new chapters might have echoed Claude Houghton's *Julian Grant Loses his Way* [**#II.41**; **#XVIII.69**]; Julian, unaware he is dead, awakens in a café (compare Robinson's *Amaranth* [**#I.70**]). Sigbjørn would dream of 'Metal' ('June the 30th, 1934'), as his tensions with Tor increased.

I.3 prison: the Castle stronghold, a gaol within its precincts until 1803, and a gallows in the moat. The gatehouse of the new County Gaol (1807), facing the Mound, had a flat roof for public executions; its stones helped build Shire Hall and the new colleges.

I.4 Cambridge: once *Grentebrige* or *Cantebrigge*, a crossing of the Granta (as in its upper reaches), or Cam (the fallacy that *Cambridge* means "bridge over the Cam" is ineradicable). Castle Hill had Anglo-Saxon settlements, then a Norman castle [**#I.2**]; in a first draft, as the brothers descend, "The Middle Ages closed over them." Cambridge challenges Oxford for precedence; Peterhouse, its first college [**#III.142**], dates from 1284. Hugh recalls its founder, Siegebert of East Anglia, the old monk's "strange dream" [UTV 176]. Like Hugh, Lowry entered St. Catharine's [**#II.55**]; like Geoffrey, the Tarnmoors attend Trinity [**#IV.2**].

I.5 afternoon light: the 'Varsity' CB cites "Hjalmar Bergman", a Swedish author (1883–1931) whose grotesque humour offsets his pessimism: "In the afternoon light the streets appeared spotless & empty, sun haze swam on sun haze. Only from the never slumbering railway station could be heard the furious snorting of the engines as they pushed the drowsy carriages along the rails." In *God's Orchid*

(1924), on the day of the matriculation exam (6 June 1913), a ruthless innkeeper uses bribery to advance his beloved child, who, he learns, is that of his bitter rival. Lowry invests Bergman's *morning light* [9] with "sun haze".

I.6 railway station: when the railway came (1845), a long single platform eventuated outside Cambridge, the University opposing closer access (to dissuade young gentlemen from the London fleshpots). Quauhnahuac inherits hill and station, and distant sounds of *fiesta* [UTV 4–6]. Lowry elsewhere links the "train theme" to "Freudian death dreams" [CL 1:521].

I.7 inclined their ears: Psalm 102:2: "Hear my prayer, / O Lord, incline thy ear"; in earlier drafts the brothers "listened". Over the football match [**#I.72**] they hear: **hurdy-gurdies**, barrel-organs, with pipes, bellows, and rotating pins, on which buskers crank out programmed music; **hail and farewell** (a Latin tag, *Ave atque vale*); and a ubiquitous **aeroplane** [**#XIII.2**].

I.8 Midsummer Common: backing onto the Cam near Jesus College.

I.9 worlds of objectivity: mystically, the Otherness of Others [**#IV.18**].

I.10 Mound: the last remaining *motte* (raised earthwork) of the Keep, and highest point of Castle Hill [**#I.2**]; site of the "last hanging" [**#I.32**], and thus intimating 'grave'.

I.11 Sigbjørn: earlier, "Harald". Other Sigbjørns feature in 'Strange Comfort' ("an American writer in Rome"), 'Gin and Goldenrod', *La Mordida* ("pobres Canadianos"), DATG, and 'The Ordeal of Sigbjørn Wilderness'.

I.12 threnody: a death-song. Aiken's telegraph wires sing "multitudinously in the wind, a threnody" [*Blue Voyage* 308]; compare UTV [115], or 'In Le Havre': "LISTEN, *the far threnody of sirens in the haze; remembered telegraph wires, multitudinously distant*" [462, 466]. Jan de Hartog's "whining of the gale in the telegraph-wires and the banging of a loose shutter" [*Captain Jan* 198] is uncanny, as his ocean tugboats appeared in 1952.

I.13 Bay of Bengal: between India and Thailand. Lowry claimed [DATG 25; 'Panama' 29; 'Forest Path' 260; *Mordida* 188] that his maternal grandfather, Captain John Boden (1839–1884), a Norwegian [**#III.6**], died heroically when his command, *The Scottish Isles*, her crew dying of cholera, was destroyed there at his request by a British gunboat. More prosaically: Boden, her English first mate, was lost at sea [Bowker 3–4].

I.14 strakes: strips of planking or plating, running lengthwise along the side or bottom of the hull to constrain other planks or plates.

I.15 Tor: Sivert, in Grieg's *The Ship Sails On* [15], has a brother Tor.

I.16 chemic: *alchemical*; the archaism recurs [**#II.5**; **#III.123**] before Tor dies.

I.17 accident: the collapsed tunnel [**#I.54**; **#III.50**; **#XI.2**; **#XVIII.23**].

I.18 Thorstein: ON "Thor's stone" [**#VIII.35**]. Thorsteinn Eriksson, youngest son of Erik the Red [**#VII.118**], recovered from Vinland his brother Thorvald's body.

I.19 Montserrat: one of the Leeward Islands [**#VI.25**]; en route to Cape Cod (1929), Lowry climbed a mountain there [U 190; 'Panama' 72].

I.20 spiritual hostilities: the first draft offers physical enmity, puerile talk of "banging" girls under hedges and bridges, and crass rivalry over "Peggy" [**#II.37**].

I.21 only to connect: echoing Forster's mantra in *Howards End* (1910): "Only connect . . . "

I.22 cave of self: as in Plato's cave [*Republic* VII], occluded from authentic existence ("obstructing the light"). Compare Sigbjørn's "dark cavern" [**#XI.66**].

I.23 Liverpool to Cambridge: from Liverpool Central, changing at Nottingham for **Lincoln to Ely**, thence Cambridge. In 'Sumptuous Armour', Dick travels from Lime Street to Euston, taxis to Liverpool Street, for a Cambridge train. This (now from King's Cross) is quicker, as cross-country routes entail lengthy changes.

I.24 fealty: fidelity; as in the final exhortation of Melville's 'The Enthusiast': "never fall / From fealty to light" [**#XI.29**; Mumford 330, 343].

I.25 oceanic destiny: Freud's "oceanic" feeling [**#VII.108**]; here, two brothers as "sister ships" (of one line), feeling different pulls of the same tide.

I.26 setting out: Jan's 'setting forth' [1991 typescript] accentuates an allusion: what youthful mother, Yeats asks in the fifth stanza of 'Among School Children', would think her son with "sixty or more winters on its head" a compensation for "the uncertainty of his setting forth?"

I.27 Dostoievsky: Fyodor Dostoevsky (1821–1881), Russian master of the troubled soul. Lowry claimed his protagonist has "a Dostoievskian brother" [**#IV.69**; CL 2:418]. From William Fielding, *The Caveman within Us* (1922): "a frightful fear of something which I cannot define, of something which I cannot conceive, which does not exist, but which rises before me as a horrible, distorted, inexorable and irrefutable fact" [166]. Fielding echoes Joseph Grasset, *The Semi-Insane and the Semi-Responsible* (1907), who called *Crime and Punishment* "insanity with conscience" [Grasset 15]: Raskolnikov, maintaining that exceptional individuals might murder, cannot reconcile this internally. This precise sense of *crime* and *punishment* permeates Lowry's novel.

I.28 Dante: Dante Alighieri (1265–1321), whose *Divine Comedy* defines the "Italian paper" of the Tripos, Part II [**#I.30**].

I.29 *Ararat*: Turk. *agri dagh*, "mountain of pain"; a dormant volcano in eastern Turkey (with no eruptions in recorded history). Noah's ark [**#VII.59**] grounded there after the Flood [Genesis 8:4]; but an active volcano offers no sanctuary. 'Fyrbøterer' [CP #94] associates Ararat and the Ark with the sea; the headline returns in *October Ferry* [234].

I.30 Tripos: Cambridge Honours; after the three-legged stool on which candidates defended their theses. Part I is broad (Lowry described the eight papers to Aiken [CL 1:87]); Part II (which the brothers are taking) more specialized, with a language paper [**#I.28**], Tragedy [**#III.77**], and Practical Criticism [**#VIII.84**]. Lowry salvaged a Third.

I.31 drunk: Noah celebrated the new dispensation by planting a vineyard, getting drunk, then cursing his son Ham for seeing his nakedness [Genesis 9].

I.32 old gallows: until 1864, on the gatehouse roof [**#I.3**]; thereafter, in a wooden shed within the prison walls. The *Capital Punishment (Amendment) Act (1868)* ended public executions; the last man hanged publicly was John Green, a Whittlesey maltster, executed (1 Jan. 1864) for strangling Elizabeth Brown, whom he dumped in a malthouse furnace [**#XI.8**]. The last Cambridge hanging (4 Nov. 1913) was Frederick Seekings, Brampton, "of limited intellect and a demon in drink", for murdering Martha Jane Beeby, found in a ditch with her throat cut. Nothing on the Mound [**#I.10**] records this. "Twenty-two years" approximates Lowry's birth (28 July 1909); but by placing that hanging in "1911" the 'Pegaso' NB implies a present of November 1933 [**#I.2**; **#III.125**].

I.33 dream of the sea: the unconscious as creative matrix, as Lowry told Jan [*Inside* 6]. Compare the "vision of the sea" in 'The Roar of the Sea' [CP #97; **#VII.160**] and 'The Western Ocean' [CP #117]. Revised, this scene would enter a dream [**#XVIII.69**].

I.34 North Pole: Castle Hill, reputedly, is the highest point between Cambridge and the Pole. In the 'Varsity' CB Lowry notes, as if from *Christopher Rilke* (it is not in Rilke's text): "and at the pole, not a cairn but a castle" [**#I.2**].

I.35 calm on the line: at the equator, before a storm. In Melville's 'The Piazza', an August noon broods on the meadows "as a calm upon the Line, but the vastness and lonesomeness are so oceanic" [4]. The *Samaritan* awaits her U-boat, "A dead calm on the line" [UTV 32].

I.36 fens: once-extensive East Anglian marshes, now drained as rich arable land.

I.37 turns like a compass needle: William James likens consciousness to a magnetic field, where "our centre of energy turns like a compass-needle" [*Varieties* 187]. Earlier, 'Harald' said: "the pole gets me. My soul is turned towards it like a compass" [**#IV.64**]. Compare Day Lewis, *The Magnetic Mountain* (1933), Poem #3: "Compass and clock must fail"; or Poem #4: "When you're up the pole and you can't find your soul" [**#XVI.20**].

I.38 concentric conversations: words encircle Dana, whose school-boy fear of geometry includes the "silver compasses" of the Liver Building clock [U 17].

I.39 coal-passing: the *trimmer* [**#I.49**] passes the coal; the *fireman* feeds the furnace.

I.40 circle of self: in 'Poem Influenced by John Davenport and Cervantes' [CP #159], "The tavern is the centre of my circle". Compare the opening of Maria Cummins, *Haunted Hearts* (1864): "Every circle has its centre"; hers being Stein's, a convivial Old Dutch tavern.

I.41 lamplighter: igniting gas streetlamps by a long wickèd pole, and snuffing them at dawn. Compare Maria Cummins, *The Lamplighter* (1854). Cambridge, a "dark city", lacked adequate street-lighting until the 1950s. **Diogenes** the Cynic (c.412–323 BCE) lit a lamp and walked the streets in daylight, seeking an honest man.

I.42 Darkness begins at midday: Yeats prefaces 'The Cat and the Moon': "now that the abstract intellect has split the mind into categories, the body into cubes, we may be about to turn back towards the unconscious, the whole, the miraculous; according to a Chinese sage darkness begins at midday" [*Wheels and Butterflies* (1934), 140]. From the *I Ching*, or, Book of Changes [III:lv: "When the sun stands at midday it begins to set; when the moon is full, it begins to wane . . . How much truer is this of men, or of spirits and gods!"

I.43 university: any value his writing had, Melville concedes, must be ascribed to whaling, "for a whale-ship was my Yale College and my Harvard" [*Moby-Dick* XXIV].

I.44 the clock chimed: that above the West Door of St. Mary the Great [**#V.73**], King's Parade; here striking five but in earlier drafts six ("The pubs are open"); portending **doom**.

I.45 Cain: first-born of Adam and Eve; murderer of his brother Abel; fugitive and vagabond [Genesis 4]. His evasion provokes Sigbjørn: "Am I my brother's keeper?" The theme echoes Grieg [**#III.45**; **#IV.74**; **XVIII.29**].

I.46 Erikson: otherwise Nordahl Grieg (1902–1943), whose *Skibet gaar videre* (1924) was translated by A. G. Chater as *The Ship Sails On* (1927) [**#I.51**]. The usual Norwegian form is *Eriksen*. Lowry in Cuernavaca read about an American named William Erikson, shot and thrown down a *barranca*; Jan describes the effect this had [*Inside* 122]. In *DATG*, Erikson, like Grieg, dies in an air raid over Berlin (2 Dec. 1943).

I.47 on the housetops: Matthew 10:27: "What I tell you in darkness, that speak ye in light: and what ye hear in the ear, that preach ye upon the housetops."

I.48 attained his majority in death: reached legal independence. Melville's *Encantadas* ['Sketch Tenth'] records: "Here, in 1813, fell in daybreak duel, a Lieutenant of the U.S. frigate Essex, aged twenty-one: attaining his majority in death."

I.49 trimmer: one who "trims" coal heaps, passes coal to the firemen [**#I.39**], hauls ashes, dumps them overboard, and chips boiler scale. Trimmers did the dirtiest jobs, got the lowest pay, and bunked and messed separately. For Lowry, a Dantean image of the lost soul [**#II.69**]. Grieg uses the word [*Skibet* 96; **#I.51**].

I.50 eternal process: Nietzsche's eternal return, the universe recurring infinitely. The notion spread from India to Egypt, thence the Pythagoreans and Stoics. As antiquity declined and Christianity grew it faded, until Nietzsche revived it to affirm life after the death of God.

I.51 *Skibets reise fra Kristiania*: Nor. 'The Ship's Voyage from Kristiania', echoing Sigbjørn's *hyrkonrakt* [**#V.56**]. For the play based on Grieg's novel, see **#V.87**. *Kristiania* was a former name of Oslo [**#IV.4**]. The *Mignon* is "A Moloch that crushes the lives of men between its iron jaws" [*Ship Sails On* 2]. Benjamin's nadir is Cape Town, where he gets VD. Holding the mangy ship's dog, he scales the after-rail to jump, then, returning, accepts the worst the ship can do.

I.52 Russia: in the 1930s, before Stalin's atrocities were known, many Cambridge left-wingers supported Russia. In Charlotte Haldane's *I Bring Not Peace*, Michal comments, "If you are not enthusiastic about any one thing in present-day Russia, or if it is obviously just bad, they say, 'That's not Communism, that's transition'" [272]. Yet the "next thousand years" intimates the Third Reich [**#VII.156**]. Arriving at Ålesund, instead of Archangel, deflects the compass of Sigbjørn's Socialist soul (attracted by Grieg) towards a Nordic pole; his father later suggests why this might be [**#X.78**].

I.53 Spenglerian nonsense: Oswald Spengler's *Decline of the West* (1918–1922) describes civilizations evolving cyclically from youth to death, with Europe in its throes. Geoffrey Firmin's "a sort of determinism about the fate of nations" [UTV 309] echoes his namesake of 'July the 30th, 1934' [P&S 43].

I.54 Holmenkollen: an elevated district of western Oslo, with a spectacular ski-jump. *Holmenkollen* railway, Oslo's first, was extended (1916) west to *Frognerseteren* [**#II.78**], then linked (1928) to *Nationaltheatret*. It was not an underground, but that link was Oslo's first and (in 1931) only subway (others were being built); hence Lowry's misapprehension here and in his 1933 letter to Jan [CL 1:131; **#III.114**; **#X.14**; **#XI.2**; **#XVIII.48**].

I.55 philosopher's stone: the *lapis philosophorum*, turning base metals to gold. An elixir of immortality, the Stone signifies alchemical transmutation, its attainment spiritual perfection, and its discovery the Great Work. One of D'Israeli's 'Six Follies of Science' [**#X.27**]; another is the **quadrature of the circle**: forming a square identical in area to a given circle, in finite steps by compass and straight-edge; this was refuted in 1882 when *pi* was recognized as transcendental.

I.56 Archangel: the major port of the White Sea, on the Dvina River, kept virtually ice-free by the Gulf Stream; an export centre (timber, furs) to the West. The 'Pegaso' NB underlines 'Watchfulness'; hence a Rilke-like 'Archangel' [**#V.149**].

I.57 Chesterton: now a northeastern suburb of Cambridge [**#II.8**].

I.58 solitary, landless, gull: in the 'Varsity' CB, Lowry revised his Spitzbergen notes: "at all this [*lavish*] beauty Tor looked disapprovingly, preferring [*to it all the simplicity of*] the solitary, landless gull". The "landless gull" migrates from *Moby-Dick* [XIV]; but compare **#IV.35**.

I.59 Brahma: the Vedic Ur-universe is water, with isolated drops intimating the separation of *Atman*, the individual soul, from *Brahman*, the world-soul.

I.60 eyes of the sea: from Rimbaud's 'Drunken Boat'; more usually, mountain tarns immeasurably deep (not East Anglian fens). In the first draft, the ship ploughing these waves (Aristotle's exemplary metaphor) takes Sigbjørn to Archangel.

I.61 His soul went marching: 'John Brown's Body' lies "a-moldering in the grave", but his soul goes "marching on".

I.62 Wandering Jew: Ahaseurus, "Striker of Christ", who for impiety (taunting the cross-bearing Christ) wanders the earth till Judgment Day. He appears in *Maelstrom* [45], and repeatedly in *October Ferry* (chapter XX is 'The Wandering Jew').

I.63 Tarot: early drafts depict the last hanged man, his pathway North stretched before him. Ouspensky's *Symbolism of the Tarot* (1913) describes Card XII: "a man in terrible suffering, hung from one leg, head downward . . . a man who saw Truth . . . . In his own soul appears the gallows on which he hangs" [62]. Invoked later [**#XVIII.65**], and in *Maelstrom* [47].

I.64 singing slayer: Louis Kenneth Neu, hanged (1 Feb. 1935) in New Orleans for murdering Lawrence Shead (bludgeoned with an electric iron), a wealthy New Yorker, and Sheffield Clarke, a Nashville businessman. A last plea for commutation (syphilitic insanity) was denied. Neu wanted to be a singer, despite a history of mental illness. He sang during his incarceration, and composed a threnody: "I'm fit as a fiddle and ready to hang," he chortled, dancing as the noose was slipped about his neck. His last words were, "Don't muss my hair." His appearance in the first draft dates its composition as 1935.

I.65 American paper: Tor's "London" source is probably the *New York Times* (2 Feb. 1935): "Nattily attired, his black hair almost glowing, the 'singing slayer' remained mirthful until the end. Meticulous in his preparations for death as he sang, then prayed, he paid strict attention to the details until he dropped through the trap. As he stepped upon the steel trap door, he tested it with half a dozen light dancing steps."

I.66 death jig: a *rigadoon*, a Provençal dance, or *battement de tambour* marching culprits to punishment. Zola's *L'Assommoir* (1877) depicts Coupeau's death, dancing deliriously until he collapses after four days, his feet continuing a spastic rhythm. For Lowry, *Drunkard's Rigadoon* denoted Charles Jackson's *The Lost Weekend* (1944).

I.67 wrapped round the stake: in *Ultramarine* [73], and 'Goya the Obscure' [278], a page from the *Liverpool Express* blows along the road: "It clings finally to a lamppost, like some ugly, cringing wraith."

I.68 black gown: of an executioner; in a first draft, Sigbjørn tells Tor: "you were the boy hanged in the snow". Undergraduates in town had to wear gowns after dark [**#II.13**].

I.69 sisters of Le Mans: Christine and Lea Papin, reticent French maids, who murdered the wife and daughter of M. René Lancelin, a retired solicitor (2 Feb. 1933). Christine's capital sentence was commuted to life; Lea received ten years [**#III.153**]. The case was argued as symbolizing the class struggle; it provoked Genet's *The Maids* (1947).

I.70 Pink the poet . . . Dr. Styx: dream figures in E. A. Robinson's long poem, *Amaranth* (1934). **Pink** is one who, lacking talent, wastes his life in art. When

Amaranth gives this verdict, he accepts it lightly: "Excuse me," he says, "while I go and hang myself" [21]. **Dr. Styx**, of the Tavern of the Vanquished, accepts mediocrity yet lives contentedly in the wrong world. After Pink hangs himself from a rafter, his eyes open and lips move; when asked is he alive or dead, he replies: "I am as dead as I shall ever be, / . . . and that's as near as a physician / Requires to know" [33]. Styx asks again [99], but Pink is not cut down. The interlude is fatidic: Tor goes but Sigbjørn remains, in the "wrong world". Compare Julian Grant [**#I.2**].

I.71 beginning well: from Freud's *Wit and Its Relation to the Unconscious* (1922), exemplifying *Galgenhumor* [OF 49], "gallows humour".

I.72 digging his heels in the earth: as in a draft of 'Sumptuous Armour' [UBC 11:12, 28], revised for 'The Voyage that Never Ends'. Events would be retrospective ("All this takes place in memory at sea"), with the hockey match framed by "the hanging hill". Cambridge events observed from Castle Hill [**#I.2**] might include this game.

CHAPTER II

II.1 [Epigraph] Auden: W. H. Auden (1907–1973), British poet later resident in the United States, who rejected Modernism for socialism. The epigraph, not in the first typescript, is from *Poems* (1930), numbered XXII in the second edition (1933), but thereafter excluded [**#III.1**]. The poem begins: "Get there if you can and see the land you once were proud to own". It describes a blighted industrial landscape, expresses the urgent need for action, harangues the bourgeois dead, and vilifies those who escape authentic life [**#III.75**].

II.2 prison railings: all evidence of the prison (except the steps) has long gone [**#I.10**].

II.3 Huntingdon: a market town (birthplace of Oliver Cromwell) northeast of Cambridge. Castle Street here becomes the Huntingdon Road.

II.4 man they couldn't hang: John 'Babbacombe' Lee of Devon, sentenced to hang (23 Feb. 1885) for the brutal murder (15 Nov. 1884) of Emma Keyse, his employer. After the trapdoor thrice failed his sentence was commuted. He was released in 1907.

II.5 whiff of chemicals: the 'Varsity' CB records Billy Budd sensing evil, "as though he had suddenly inhaled a vile whiff from some chemical factory" [*Billy Budd* XVI; **#I.16**].

II.6 house of glass: an inset to the 'Varsity' CB reads: "Life. Life. I would like to build a house of glass to let the sun in"; echoing the final lines of Maeterlinck's 'The Hot House': "My God, my God, when shall we feel the rain / And the snow, and the wind, in this close house of glass?" Compare the broken greenhouse [UTV 279].

II.7 before the storm: Job 21:8: "as stubble before the wind, and as chaff that the storm carrieth away."

II.8 Chesterton Lane: once a turnpike to Chesterton [**#I.57**]. Magdalene becomes Bridge Street, thereafter Sidney Street, southeast of Castle Hill; 'cross-roads', haunted, imply suicides [OF 212]. Intersecting byways (Castle, Northampton, Magdalene, Chesterton) run not to the cardinal points but diagonally; Sigbjørn, facing north, confronts his destiny.

II.9 rondure: in an early draft, 'Harald' calls Cambridge a "dead loss", rejecting history for "categories of the present which are permanent . . . in the rondure of change, I see implicit certain universal principles." In Whitman's 'Passage to India', *rondure* expresses the transcendental hope of regaining the pre-lapsarian Paradise, a unity lost in Eden. Hart Crane's *The Bridge* (1930) invokes "this turning rondure" (Sigbjørn wants to "rotate").

II.10 lighting a cigarette: compare the opening lines of 'Men with Coats Thrashing' [CP #158]:

> Our lives we do not weep
> Are like wild cigarettes
> That on a stormy day
> Men light against the wind
> With cupped and practised hand . . .

II.11 Barney: Melville's pet name for his son, Malcolm, who committed suicide (1867), aged eighteen [**#IV.5**].

II.12 pathological fear of authority: Lowry's terrors, attributed to his characters [**#III.27**].

II.13 gown: a black, shortened BA gown. Undergraduates caught by a *Proctor* [**#II.31**] in town after *hall* [**#II.84**] without a gown or *square* (mortarboard) could be fined.

II.14 Magdalene: a smaller Cambridge college (that of I. A. Richards), founded 1428 as a Benedictine hostel; known for its "traditional" ways.

II.15 tactile suffering: a pathological sense, often hallucinatory, of physical texture (sensory impressions reduced to touch); sometimes associated with alcohol withdrawal.

II.16 gilded fake: hypocrites wearing gilded cloaks that dazzle, but are leaden and heavy within [*Inferno* XXIII].

II.17 Telemachus: ending the Introduction to the 1932 translation of Homer's *Odyssey* by T. E. Shaw (Lawrence of Arabia): "the priggish son who yet met his master-prig in Menelaus" [vii]; cited in *Time* [28 Nov. 1932: 51].

II.18 show me the starving man: until "It's the godlike in me!", verbatim from Charles Fort's *Lo!* [759; **#II.22**].

II.19 hieroglyph: compare Hart Crane, 'At Melville's Tomb':

> And wrecks passed without sound of bells,
> The calyx of death's bounty giving back
> A scattered chapter, livid hieroglyph,
> The portent wound in corridors of shells.

The "livid hieroglyph", Crane told a bewildered Harriet Monroe, editor of *Poetry*, is the vortex created when a ship sinks, wreckage arising as the water encloses it. Crane created one, jumping from the *Orizaba* (27 Apr. 1932) into the Gulf of Mexico. Unwitting irony: Crane's father, Clarence, invented the candy, Lifesavers (1912).

II.20 ferrule: L. *viriola*, "bracelet": an [iron] ring to prevent a cane splitting; thus, the cane.

II.21 Ripley-like philosopher: Robert Ripley (1890–1949); his "Believe It or Not" column was widely syndicated. Fort was, Tor says, "no Ripley" (sensationalist), but rather explored the cosmic laws behind curious phenomena.

II.22 Charles Fort: American eccentric (1874–1932), who made "the explicable seem more dramatic" [CL 1:315]. His *Book of the Damned* (1919), *New Lands* (1923), *Lo!* (1931), and *Wild Talents* (1932) record curiosities: frogs and fish falling from the skies, disappearances, spontaneous combustion . . . . Compare the Consul's "lost wild talents" [UTV 199], the latent gift, harnessed by adepts, of affecting phenomena by psychic powers; manifest, Lowry feared, in his self-destructive induction of fire: 'The Element Follows You Around, Sir' [OF XVIII]. *Lo!* proclaims, "we are in a state of **standardless existence** . . . the appeal to authority is as much of a wobble as any other of our insecurities" [558].

II.23 power for good: the 'Varsity' CB records from Federico Olivero's 1931 study of Rilke's poetry and mysticism: "All things are watched over, by a spirit of goodness ready for flight, Every stone & flower, & every child in the night" [17; citing Rilke's *Stundenbuch* (1905)].

II.24 *Ens a se extra . . . intelligens*: "Being above all kinds, necessary, One, infinite, perfect, simple, immutable, immense, eternal, intelligent"; a Scholastic definition of the deity, quoted from William James's *Pragmatism* in Will Durant's *Story of Philosophy* (1926) [559]. Such "intellectual finality" (says James) means nothing unless interpreted pragmatically; Sigbjørn must reconcile that scepticism with a "power for good".

II.25 all is accident: Donne examples the atheist who sees in sudden death or punishment of a sinner not God's miracle, but believes that "all is Nature, or all is Accident, and would have been so, though there were no God" [*Sermons* #49; **#XIV.89**].

II.26 Julian Green: or, his publisher's preference, *Julien* Green (1900–1998), born in France of American parents, a devout Catholic homosexual who wrote mostly in French. In Oslo Sigbjørn acquires, as Lowry did, his *Dark Journey* (1929) [**#XVIII.32**]. Arnold Bennett's *Journal* (1933) records Eleanora Green's little brother at the central meat-markets, Paris (*Les Halles*), as saying, "Maman, il doit y avoir pas mal d'accidents ici" [236].

II.27 goal of the seeker of wisdom: the "dance of the seeker and his goal" [UTV 286] derives, Lowry said, from "some gruesome Maeterlinckian drama, for in these movements a certain identity of the searcher with his goal was expressed" [UBC WT 1:5, 5]. The actual source is Fort's *Lo!* [**#II.22**]: "The seeker of wisdom departs more and more from the state of the idiot, only to find that he is returning. Belief after belief fades from his mind: so his goal is the juncture of two obliterations. One is of knowing nothing, and the other is of knowing that there is nothing to know" [762].

II.28 secret knowledge: as the Consul comments of his great work on Secret Knowledge, "one can always say when it never comes out that the title explains this deficiency" [UTV 39]. Madame Blavatsky's *magnum opus* was *The Secret Doctrine* (1888). Tor's "nothing out of nowhere" (*ex nihilo nihil*, "nothing out of nothing") affirms that "all is accident" [**#II.25**].

II.29 Voltaire: François-Marie Arouet (1694–1778), scourge of superstition and religion [**#III.38**; **#VIII.22**; **#VIII.58**; **#XV.10**], would have "hated" hints of secret knowledge.

II.30 gesticulating: Laruelle sees two ragged Indians wandering through the dusk, like Sorbonne professors [UTV 12]; in the 1940 *Volcano* [255], they are from Clare College.

II.31 proctors: L. *procurator*; university officials who administered finances, officiated ceremonies and examinations, and enforced discipline, with authority to impose fines for minor offences. With their "bulldogs" they patrolled streets and pubs after dusk [**#II.13**].

II.32 luminously gliding: as Melville's white shark [**#III.43**; **#VII.192**; **#XV.43**].

II.33 common absolute: an act of mind whereby various things are conceived indifferently, disregarding their individual differences [accidents], as subordinated to a common absolute [universal] concept. Lowry mocks the "common" notion that sensual knowledge (intuition) cannot be communicated (unique experience lacks a common absolute).

II.34 elastic limit: the *yield point* of a substance, up to which it returns to its original shape when stress is removed, but beyond which deformation is non-reversible; a term often applied to faults and stresses in the earth's crust. Such matters might be discussed (from 1928) in *Scientific American*'s popular "**amateur scientist**" column.

II.35 'backs': college grounds abutting the Cam (John's, Trinity, Trinity Hall, Clarc, King's, Queens'). Magdalene bridges have existed for 1,200 years; this dates from 1823. **Hooded terrors** are, more usually, cobras.

II.36 Nina: surname untold [**#IX.28**; **#XVIII.16**]. Earlier 'Peggy', her attributes (good teeth and legs, freckles) were overdone. Charlotte Haldane is one model: Lowry told Markson that his hero, troubled by a stormy affair with an older woman, risks being sent down [CL 2:418].

II.37 deserted promenade: Egremont, where Dana strolled with Janet [U 140].

II.38 movement of the river: Jan's 1991 typescript (unlike the 1936 one) invokes Robert Frost, whose 'West-running Brook' (1928) melds Lucretius and Bergson into the "stream of everything" flowing in endless cycles: "The universal cataract of death / That spends to nothingness". *La Mordida* [333] cites this poem. By changing 'country' to 'crater', Jan accentuated volcanoes [**#I.29**; **#VI.19**]. See the Textual Notes.

II.39 moves imperceptibly: John Cowper Powys, *The Meaning of Culture* (1930):

> Culture does not show itself among men as something ponderous, majestic, pompous, imposing. It does not 'show' itself at all! Like the *Tao*, so subtly

> described by the philosopher Kwang Tze three hundred years before Christ, it flows through the air, swims in the water, burrows in the earth, moves imperceptibly from mind to mind, and 'by doing nothing does everything.' [290]

In Ballast, Lowry said, celebrated the notion that "the ideas float in the air" [DATG TS, UBC 9:1, 119; 9:6, 394]; this derives from James [*Varieties* 27; **#V.102**].

II.40 white and blue girls: from the Perse School for Girls, Cambridge; in *Maelstrom* [48], a vision of innocence. Compare Rilke [**#VII.25**]. Baby Goya's pyjamas are "blue with a white stripe" ['Goya' 275], like Dana's [U 69], or Lowry's [Bowker 156].

II.41 sees into hell: Julian Grant, after a life of emotional suicide, awakens in hell [**#I.2**].

II.42 Moore's Music Shop: the 'Pianoforte & Music Warehouse' of Wm. James Moore, then at 22 Magdalene Street.

II.43 Bridge Street . . . Newmarket Road . . . Sidney Street: Magdalene Street continues as Bridge, then Sidney Street [**#II.8**], into the old town. Jesus Lane runs east off Sidney Street to the Newmarket Road. The **women of Sidney Street** embody *Les demoiselles d'Avignon* (1907), Picasso's five nude prostitutes, mocked for their angular shapes.

II.44 Marmorstein's: Lowry's contemporary, the 'Emile Cohen' of Charlotte Haldane's *I Bring Not Peace* [199–205]. Emile Marmorstein enjoyed ribald libations, but lacked typical Cambridge left-wing sympathies and lamented the passing of Empires, both the Austro-Hungarian of his Jewish ancestry and the Ottoman that became his life, as BBC advisor on Islam. Lowry told Marmorstein he had ceased dining in Hall as he kept seeing Paul Fitte [Bowker 99]. Tony Kilgallin records other recollections [18–27].

II.45 'my soul turns outward towards the pole': compare W. Wybergh, *Prayer as Science* (1919): "a cyclic procession of the Divine Life outwards towards the pole of matter, inwards towards the pole of spirit" [9].

II.46 from its own wreck: Demogorgon, concluding Shelley's *Prometheus Unbound*:

> To love, and bear; to hope till Hope creates
> From its own wreck the thing it contemplates;
> Neither to change, nor falter, nor repent;
> This, like thy glory, Titan, is to be
> Good, great and joyous, beautiful and free;
> This is alone Life, Joy, Empire, and Victory.

II.47 no aim but . . . infinite meaning: an aesthetic paradox: each snowflake has a unique structure, but that lacks purpose (Kant's "ohne Zweck"); subjective responses of pleasure are so various as to permit no common absolute [**#II.33**], but only empirical approximations and hence infinite degrees of beauty.

II.48 unreal goal: faith in Russia; like Columbus, Nina seeks America [**#VII.118**].

II.49 ingrained sanity: unidentified with respect to Shakespeare, whose comedies were generally regarded as inferior works.

II.50 Round Church: St. Sepulchre, at Bridge Street and Round Church Road; a 12th-century Romanesque structure attached to the Hospital (later, College) of St. Johns. One of four English round churches, it models Jerusalem's Holy Sepulchre.

II.51 Opening time: the Defence of the Realm Act (Aug. 1914) restricted opening hours from noon to 2:30 p.m. and 6:30 to 9:30 p.m., with minor dispensations [**#I.44**; **#XIV.40**]; this lasted till 2005. The first draft added a "medieval" touch to **six hundred doors**: "as though six hundred hunchbacks of Notre Dame had suddenly come to life."

II.52 Market Hill: west of Sidney Street; **Market Square** hosted an open-air market; **Peti-Curi**, or 'Petty Cury' (*Parva Cokeria*, the "little cury" where cooks lived), runs off Sidney Street towards Market Hill; it leads into Guildhall Street, and towards **Bene't Street**, named after St. Benedict's Church (1000–1050 CE).

II.53 naptha flares: flammable liquid mixtures (paraffin, white spirits) of hydrocarbons, distilled from petroleum or coal tar, used for street cooking [UTV 24].

II.54 Bath Hotel: 3 Bene't Street, whence Sigbjørn writes to Erikson [**#IV.65**]; advertised as "Family and Commercial". The **Friar House**, 12 Bene't Street, is a timber-framed 17th-century house; in the first draft the two drink here, resenting Cambridge's medievalism. The ***Arts School***, 14 Bene't Street, rose from a 14th-century Augustinian friary.

II.55 King's . . . Catharine's . . . Queens' . . . Corpus . . . Pembroke: Cambridge colleges of the "Old University" (ancient foundations, not later colleges):

> **King's**: on King's Parade [**#III.15**], right of the brothers, who are at its corner with Bene't Street. Founded in 1441 by Henry VI, and renown for its chapel, 'The King's College of Our Lady and Saint Nicholas in Cambridge' originally took Etonians.
>
> **Catharine's**: Lowry's college, left on Trumpington Street. Founded in 1475 by Dr. Robert Wodelarke, and named for St. Katherine of Alexandria who

was broken on a wheel (the college emblem) [**#V.11**]. Lowry often wrote 'Catherine' the Oxford way.

Queens': on Silver Street: 'The Queen's College of St. Margaret and St. Bernard' is invariably *Queens'*: Margaret of Anjou (wife of Henry VI) founded it (1448); and Elizabeth Woodville (wife of Edward IV) renewed the foundation (1465).

Corpus: *Corpus Christi*, opposite St Catharine's; founded 1352 by the Guilds of Corpus Christi and Blessed Virgin (the only Town foundation); a smaller college, renown for the treasures of its Parker Library.

Pembroke: on Trumpington Street; the third oldest Cambridge college, founded 1347 by Marie de St. Pol, Countess of Pembroke.

II.56 dark interior: stepping over the brass sill is to enter the limbo of *Outward Bound* [**#VI.27**], which, as Firmin says in 'June the 30th, 1934', had a bar: "Oh yes, it had a *bar!*" [P&S 41]. Compare *dark cavern* [**#XI.66**].

II.57 Worthington: brewed at Burton-on-Trent; bought by Bass in 1927. A **Jigger**, on Merseyside, is a back-entry from an alley, with connotations accordingly.

II.58 The Players!: from the nearby Festival Theatre, rehearsing von Scholz's *Race with a Shadow* [**#III.146 & 147**]. In earlier drafts, Webster's *Duchess of Malfi* had sounded brotherly betrayal by the Echo scene: "like death that we have" ("*. . . death that we have*") . . . "to fly your fate" ("*. . . oh fly your fate*"). Two echoes persist: "WHORE!" and "MURDERER!"; von Scholz ends thus: "Dirne! . . . Mörder!" [**#XI.75**].

II.59 Ginger: pantry-boy on the *Oedipus Tyrannus* [U 53]. The 'Pegaso' NB reconsiders: "II as before: but Ginger section dramatised."

II.60 Tarnmoor: Melville published *The Encantadas* (1854) as Salvator R. Tarnmoor, the name never explained. Mumford suggests "isolated mountainous lakes" and the baroque art of Salvator Rosa [239]. The cock that crows over the dead Lithuanian [UTV 353] came "from the Tarnmoor farm" [Asals 424].

II.61 *In la sua voluntade è nostra pace*: It. "In His will is our peace"; Dante, *Paradiso* [III.85; **#XV.14**], with several misspellings [see the Textual Notes]; regarded by some (Gladstone, Arnold, Eliot) as the loveliest line in literature.

II.62 Four things: Jorgenson likens Arnulf Överland, socialist poet, to Grieg "in the intensity of his earnestness", and records this toast [*Norwegian Literature* 520]. The 'Varsity' CB adds "*Hundred Violins*", a volume of Överland's poetry (1912).

II.63 tapping: like Old Pew, blind beggar of *Treasure Island*. Lowry noted that *stekel* means "stick", and Stekel described sleep as "re-experiencing the past, forgetting one's present, and pre-feeling one's future" [UBC 9:3, 181]. Wilhelm Stekel (1868–1940), in *The Will to Sleep* (1922), disputed Freud's interpretation of dreams as reversion to the inter-uterine state.

II.64 Eagle: 'The Eagle and Child', a coach-house (c.1600) in Bene't Street, beside the Bath Hotel; here, Crick and Watson announced the structure of DNA (1953).

II.65 working like hell: firemen as Dante's lost souls [**#II.69; #V.125**]. "I have to work as hell" was Grieg's evasion [Dahlie, 'Grieg Connection' 34].

II.66 stokehold floor: if the coal is near the furnace and the fire well-fed, trimmers and firemen might briefly lean on their shovels.

II.67 immedicable: in the UTV short story version, Popocatepetl, like Moby-Dick, presages "some disaster, unique and immedicable" [P&S 188]. The "immedicable horror of opposites" [**#VII.200**] returns in 'Jokes Aloft' [*CP* #119], *Last Address* [155], and *La Mordida* [171], from Shelley's *Prometheus Unbound* [II.2.4]:

> Evil, the immedicable plague, which, while
> Man looks on his creation like a God
> And sees that it is glorious, drives him on,
> The wreck of his own will, the scorn of earth,
> The outcast, the abandoned, the alone?

II.68 lost their gems: Dante's "Parean l'occhiaie anella sanza gemme" [**#XII.12**]: the empty eye sockets of the once-gluttonous [*Purgatorio* XXIII.30].

II.69 not good enough for heaven: in *Inferno* III, Dante encounters the wretched chasing a banner. These lived without infamy or praise (neutral angels of the War in Heaven, the lukewarm on earth); they have no hope of death, nor shall report of them live. He is told to look, but pass by [**#V.125**]. Carlyle writing on Mirabeau (1837) first called them 'trimmers', for having edged their spiritual obligations; others followed his example [**#I.49; #III.54**].

II.70 womb: the Freudian (or Lawrentian) conceit that integrates the unconscious with the womb, the return to the one embracing the other [**#III.96; #X.78; #XI.66**].

II.71 composed of fire: Heraclitus of Ephesus (c.500 BCE) contended that all things are composed of fire and unto fire shall return; the universe is One, begotten from fire and returning to it in endless cycles; and from this strife of opposites harmony evolves. This attracted many mystics (Swedenborg, Blake). Water, like Heraclitan fire, is another **element.**

II.72 foolish virgins: Matthew 25:1–13: ten virgins attend a wedding, carrying lamps to await the bridegroom. Five bring extra oil; five have none. The bridegroom is late; the foolish ask the wise for oil, but are denied; while they buy some the bridegroom arrives. The parable has apocalyptic overtones, of preparation for the day of reckoning.

II.73 crying in the darkness: in Tennyson's *In Memoriam* [LIV], the hope that good will somehow come from ill, as an infant crying in the night, "with no language but a cry".

II.74 communists who aren't revolutionary: Aiken reprimanded Lowry (1939): "the influence of the Complex Boys, these adolescent audens spenders with all their pretty little dexterities, their negative safety, their indoor marxmanship, has not been too good for you" [*Letters* 239]. Jan's "Communists who can't commune" [1991 TS] is more dexterous.

II.75 swine: Mark 5:11–13: Christ met the man of unclean spirit, whose name was Legion; He sent the devils into a herd of swine, which ran violently into the sea, and drowned.

II.76 chaff in holy writ: Luke 3:17: God will "thoroughly purge his floor, and will gather the wheat into his garner; but the chaff he will burn with fire unquenchable." The soul may **burn invisibly**, like a fire in a sealed hull (lacking oxygen), when denied its spiritual destiny.

II.77 suicides in Japan: Sigbjørn reads about these in the *Echo* [**#VI.19**].

II.78 Frognersaeteren: the *saeter* (high pasture) of Frogner, west of Oslo with a remarkable view of the city [**#XVIII.52**]; terminus of the Holmenkollen line [**#I.54**]. Lowry described it to Aiken as "a swell place", and to Jan as "just the best thing in the world" [CL 1:110, 130]. Dana recalls an inexplicable lost boomerang [U 16]. The ski-jump is not at Frognerseteren, but at Hollmenkollen, 190 meters (and five stations) below.

II.79 different pilgrimage: Sigbjørn will recall Tor's words [**#V.119**].

II.80 unknown warrior: in Westminster Abbey, the tomb of an unidentified British soldier killed in WWI in France.

II.81 I am and shall be . . . grand prince, Michael: esoterica: in Masonic ritual, the Lost Name of God, JAH-BUL-ON, that cannot be uttered: "I **am and shall be** Lord in Heaven on High, the Powerful the Father of all." Out-blustering Exodus 3:14, God to Moses: "I AM THAT I AM". The **Tetragrammaton** (Gk. τετραγράμματον), or "four letters", is the sacred name of God, given in Hebrew as 'Jehovah' or 'Yahweh' to conceal the True Name, the utterance of which is death. For the **globes . . . wheels**, see Ezekiel 1:16: the chariot of God, with four wheels, each "as it were a wheel in the middle of a wheel" (*globes*), symbolizing God's freedom to move as He wishes. Ezekiel's Chariot (Tarot Card #7) signifies successful projection. For the Consul, who has abused his mystical powers by drinking, it connotes the DTs [UTV 174]. Hugh explains: "At sea we called 'em the wheels" (one's head spins round). The **grand prince**, **Michael** is St. Michael the Archangel, who smote the rebel Lucifer in the Battle of the Angels, and in coming days of darkness shall arise to protect the children of God. These details derive from Edgar Saltus [*Anatomy of Negation*]: the rabbinical education of Spinoza, his refusal to assume that profession, and his excommunication:

> The great ban, the Schammatha, was publicly pronounced upon him. For half-an-hour, to the blare of trumpets, he was cursed in the name which contains forty-two letters; in the name of Him who said, *I am that I am and who shall be*; in the name of the Lord of Hosts, the Tetragrammaton; in the name of the Globes, the Wheels, Mysterious Beasts and Ministering Angels; in the name of the great Prince Michael; in the name of Metateron, whose name is like that of his master; in the name of Achthariel Jah. The Seraphim and Ofanim were called upon to give mouth to the malediction. Jehovah was supplicated never to forgive his sin, to let all the curses in the Book of the Law fall upon him and blot him from under the heavens. Then, as the music swooned in a shudder of brass, the candles were reversed, and through the darkness the whole congregation chanted in unison, Amen! [112–13]

II.82 bell of Corpus . . . doom: malediction, as befitting *Corpus Christi* [**#II.55**]. This is no compassionate "*dolente . . . dolore*" [UTV– 373]; rather, it summons the forces of Fate. Hence, the **bell-buoy**: a floating bell, anchored, warning of wrecks or shoals. The mundane sense of "strange navigation" [**#III.31**, **#V.38**, **#XI.38**] intimates an interpenetration of the spiritual and material, "inexplicable horror" and the everyday.

II.83 *Brynjaar*: ON *brynja*, "armour", and *arr*, "warrior"; hence *breastplated*.

II.84 Freshman's Hall: the evening meal for first-year students, 'freshman' limited to such archaic usage as this. Practice varies: at 'Formal Hall' students and fellows dine in regalia and grace is read; at 'Informal Hall' ('First Hall'), an earlier sitting, gowns are optional [**#II.13**].

II.85 Chesterton Lane . . . Mill Road . . . Bateman Street . . . Peti-Curi:

Chesterton Lane: near Magdalene College [**#II.8**].

Mill Road: from Parker's Piece, past the station, to Brook's Road, where a windmill once turned at Covent Garden corner.

Bateman Street: off Trumpington Street [**#III.2**], near The Leys. Lowry lodged at 2 Bateman Street [Bowker 96].

Peti-Curi: or *Petty Cury* [see **#II.52**].

II.86 a wind: Psalm 103:16, of life's brevity: "For the wind passes over it, and it is gone".

II.87 bluefish: a western Atlantic gamefish. Aggressive and voracious, they attack smaller fish in a "bluefish blitz" and are in turn the prey of larger predators, such as swordfish, which scythe through a shoal, thrashing their "swords" to kill or stun [*Blue Voyage* 307].

II.88 Leadenhall Street: Lloyds of London began (1688) in Edward Lloyd's coffee house, and since incorporation (1871) as a Society of "Names" has been the leading UK insurance firm. Their office at 12 Leadenhall Street opened in 1928.

II.89 Lutine: Fr. *lutine*, a female "imp" or "sprite"; a French frigate taken by the British (1779), then lost off Holland with a cargo of gold, mostly unsalvaged. The *Lutine Bell* was recovered (1858) from the wreckage. Hung in Lloyds's Underwriting Room, it was struck when the fate of an overdue ship was known: twice, if safe; once, if lost (a practice now ceremonial). Lowry has erred; his intention is surely doom.

II.90 taproom: where beer is pulled; equally, blind Fate "tapping" [**#II.63**].

II.91 tattoo marks: Andy Bredahl likewise sports "a Norwegian flag, a barque in full sail, a heart" [U 15].

II.92 long journey: to death, as Proverbs 7:19: "For the goodman is not at home, he is gone a long journey"; anticipating Jensen's *The Long Journey* [see **#X.73**].

CHAPTER III

III.1 [Epigraph] Auden: ending 'Get there if you can', the source of the previous epigraph [**#II.1**]. See the Textual Notes.

III.2 Trumpington Street: extending King's Parade [**#III.15**], towards The Leys. Lowry roomed at 70 Trumpington Street (1929), until evicted for drunkenness [Bowker 96]; Paul Fitte died there [**#III.125**]. Tor's digs, opposite Corpus near Cat's, imply that setting.

III.3 Ames, Barrow, Carruthers: 'William **Ames**' was the Consul's early name [**#I.46**]. Isaac **Barrow** was Trinity's inaugural Lucasian Professor of Mathematics. Old '**Carruthers**' was Praelector when Geoffrey was there [UTV 175; **#X.36**]; C. J. Carruthers (BA Trinity, 1928) was Lowry's contemporary. In the 'Pegaso' NB, 'Escruch is an Old Man' depicts Mr. Carruthers, a remittance man living in 'Q' [Quauhnahuac], who leads an "abstract" life [UTV 224].

III.4 vacant: the Captain later says: "as if he had already ceased to exist". The *Arcturion*'s slot is empty [**#VII.36**], but Erikson's is not [**#XVIII.44**].

III.5 trunk call: long-distance, requiring an operator. Liverpool had several exchanges ('Bank', 'Central', 'Royal'), each with limited subscribers. Like 'ABC' [**#III.3**], 'Royal 4321' is obviously patterned ("counting down"); it was not Arthur Lowry's number.

III.6 Hansen-Tarnmoor: the Old Man's name has a Norwegian inflection, like that of Lowry's maternal grandfather [**#I.13**]; 'Tarnmoor' has the requisite Melville ring [**#II.60**].

III.7 associate such doom: 'How Plash-Goo Came to the Land of None's Desire', in Edward Lord Dunsany's *Last Book of Wonder* (1916), tells how the giant, Plash-Goo, went to the mountain and there fought the dwarf, who by cunning forced him over the precipice that dropped to the land of None's Desire, the giant as he fell not truly believing this was so, "for we do not associate such dooms with ourselves" [172]. In 'China', distant guns thunder "Doom! Doom! Doom!" [P&S 49; **#III.133**; **#III.148**; **#V.39**].

III.8 spiral: suggesting Dante's *Inferno* and Grieg's *Skibet* [**#III.51**; **#VII.96**].

III.9 another person: Ernest Shackleton described in *South* (1919), crossing the icy mountains of South Georgia with two companions, his sense of being accompanied by another, a figure of Providence. This became Eliot's third "who walks always beside you" in *The Waste Land*. Compare the apparition of Providence in Dostoevsky's *The Brothers Karamazov* [XI.vii], where Ivan becomes aware of his complicity in Fyodor's murder. Reinold Messener made the first solo ascent of Everest (1980); Lowry intends the fated attempt by George Mallory and Andrew Irvine (1924). Mallory attended school in West Kirby and studied at Magdalene.

III.10 When a bee dies: varying the diverb, that when the bee ceases to hum the world will cease to turn. Compare John Clare's 'Noon': "Bees are faint and cease to hum." Dead bees release pheromones that alert others to dump the corpses outside the hive.

III.11 Tower of London: the northeast turret of the White Tower, where a spiral staircase winds to an observatory [**#III.8**].

III.12 *Post mortem nihil est: Ipsaque mors nihil:* in Seneca's *Troades* [II.397], Achilles's ghost demands Polyxena's sacrifice as recompense for honours denied on death. From Edgar Saltus, *Anatomy of Negation*, where Seneca's "After death is nothing; death itself is naught" [135–36] foreshadows d'Holbach on suicide [see **#III.19**].

III.13 Golgotha: Aramaic, "place of the skull"; where Christ was crucified.

III.14 nineties: the decadent 1890s, when the "tragic generation" died young.

III.15 King's Parade: locus of several Cambridge colleges [**#III.2**; UTV 79].

III.16 *Oedipus Tyrannus:* Dana's ship in *Ultramarine*, the 1933 *Nawab* rechristened to bless later works. In Sophocles's *Oedipus the King*, the son of Laius and Jocasta solves the riddle of the Sphinx [**#IV.32**], but is destined to slay his father, marry his mother, then blind himself on discovering his crimes.

III.17 earthly author of my blood: Henry Bolingbroke, son of John a Gaunt, about to fight Thomas Mowbray, Duke of Norfolk, farewells those present [*Richard II* I.iii.364]. Lowry echoes his 1931 letter to Grieg [*CL* 1:106].

III.18 Jameson: since 1780, the Irish whiskey of choice. In Charlotte Haldane's *I Bring Not Peace*, James Dowd prefers Irish: "Spell it with an 'e.' Looks so much better" [90].

III.19 D'Holbach: Paul Henry Thiry, Baron d'Holbach (1723–1789), atheist, encyclopaedist, and author of *Le Système de la nature* (1770). Denying the deity, he saw the universe as the play of accident [**#II.25**]; he was, as Tor says, a forerunner of revolution. Edgar Saltus [**#III.12**] praises him as one of the few courageous enough to advocate suicide. Engagements between Man and Nature are neither voluntary nor reciprocal:

> Man is therefore in nowise bound; and should he find himself unsupported, he can desert a position which has become unpleasant and irksome. As to the citizen, he can hold to his country and associates only by the mortgage on his well-being. If the lien is paid off, he is free. "Would a man be blamed," he asks, "a man who, finding himself useless and without resources in his native place, should withdraw into solitude? Well, then, with what right can a man be blamed who kills himself from despair? And what is death but an isolation?" [142]

III.20 measure of pain: Tor quotes Schopenhauer, *The World as Will and Idea* [IV.407], on Assertion and Denial of the Will, where suffering is "a measure which could neither remain empty, nor be more than filled", however its form might change.

III.21 collision: in *Maelstrom*, of Gary's broken mind; here, the *Brynjaar* [**#III.33**].

III.22 The Lord is my Hospital, he marries me pars partore parteth: Psalm 23: "The Lord is my shepherd; I shall not want. / He maketh me to lie down in green pastures, he leadeth me beside the still waters." In Karl Menninger's *The Human Mind* (1930), a brain-damaged patient says: "The Lord is my Hospital I shall not want. He marries me green pastors partners. He leadeth me leadeth me leadeth" [228]. Ben Lucien Burman, an irritated flea, used this to attack "the cult of unintelligibility" (1952), insisting that Modernism was indistinguishable from insanity. Sigbjørn revisits this [**#III.154**].

III.23 Doctor Berg: the protagonist of Alban Berg's brutal opera *Wozzeck* (1925), based on Georg Büchner's play, suffers from paranoid schizophrenia. A letter (15 March 1933) from "Harry" [Waters] recommends "of all modern works" *Wozzeck* as likely to appeal to Lowry [Huntington, AIK 2583].

III.24 hobophrene: a vagriant of *hebephrene*, a schizoid with adolescent delusions. 'Where do you come from?' ends, in Aiken's voice, "on Hebephrene's steep" [CP #47]; compare 'ηβηφρενε' in Lowry's 1931 letter to Grieg [CL 1:104], that "spiritual ambivalence" from which Sigbjørn suffers.

III.25 whirligig: something whirling bizarrely; as the "improvised whirligig" of the fair [UTV 211]. Lowry's "whirligig of taste", echoing "Jerry" Kellett, shows Grieg the "cultural cataclysm" of literary fashion [CL 1:106; **#V.129**; **#X.49**].

III.26 postures of the living: as the deck-crew of the *Unsgaard* [see **#XVII.7**].

III.27 Silver Street: off Trumpington Street towards the Queen's Road; location of Queens' and Darwin colleges. Tor's reaction [**#II.12**] signals intent; the 'Pegaso' NB records: "Fear of the police".

III.28 bulkheads: partitions dividing the ship into watertight compartments, to stop cargo moving and contain flooding if the hull is breached. After the 1912 *Titanic* disaster, when water from holed holds poured into others, designers used double hulls and raised bulkheads (an "effective set of construction rules" to preclude "a recurrence of this sort of thing"); yet in 1916, striking a mine in the Aegean, the *Britannic* sank quickly, with thirty lives lost. These White Star disasters underwrite those of the Tarnmoor Line [**#III.33**; **#VII.18**].

III.29 ***Arcturion:*** the doomed whaler of Melville's *Mardi* [**#XIII.25**].

III.30 **telemeter:** a device for recording or measuring far events and transmitting data (by radio) to a distant receiver. A **trick-wheel** is a steering wheel in the engine room or emergency location; the helmsman operates it on signal failure from the bridge, receiving orders by telephone [**#III.33**].

III.31 **surprising:** yet human error and ambiguity have determined the accident. Historically, orders were given in terms of the tiller, which, turned to port, moved the ship to starboard. Recent steering mechanisms were geared to turn the wheel as the ship; but "starboard your helm" [**#V.38**] still required the helmsman to turn the wheel to port. Dick Diver lists among causes of maritime disaster "the order to starboard taken as port" [*Tender* 172].

III.32 **port . . . starboard:** facing forward, *port* ('larboard') is on the left, with a red light; *starboard* on the right, with a green light. *Port* derives from the practice of mooring on that side, to prevent crushing the steering-boards (*starboard*) affixed to the right. If collision is imminent, ships must defer to the red light.

III.33 **Incredible!:** after WWI, some nations gave helm orders as the ship should turn; others retained the older system. A 1928 London conference proposed consistent use of 'left' and 'right', outmoding 'port' and 'starboard'; and a 1929 National Convention for Safety at Sea urged that steering orders be given directly, *to starboard* meaning that wheel, rudder, and bow should all turn that way. On 24 January 1935, the *Mohawk* crossed the path of the Norwegian freighter *Talisman* off New Jersey; her forty-five fatalities included the captain and most officers. The *Mohawk* deployed the new steering orders, but her back-up was older; when the main system jammed, "10 degrees starboard helm" effected a turn to port. Seeing the danger, the steersman turned the emergency system to starboard, hence the ship further to port. After an inquiry, the United States adopted the new rules. This incident, involving a Norwegian ship, shaped the *Brynjaar* disaster, as the 'Varsity' CB confirms, Lowry noting the heroism of Ingalls, the wireless lad, who kept signalling from his hut on deck directly above the fires.

III.34 **one dimension:** in Dunne's *Experiment with Time* (1927), displacement of time in a serial universe "explains" this issue, why orders from bridge to engineer (from telemeter to trick-wheel) seem different to all concerned. The "faulty design" reflects the universe, where time, in a conceit Lowry relished, is an illusion to stop things happening simultaneously.

III.35 irreconcilables: the "eternal horror of opposites" [UTV 130; **#II.67**] reflects *occult strife* (light and dark, life and death); *equilibrium* as their reconciliation; *eternal horror* when this fails [**#VII.200**].

III.36 submerged tide-bank: compare Macbeth's "here, upon this bank and shoal of time" [I.vii.6], as he thinks to "jump" the life to come [**#XIV.8**].

III.37 petit bourgeois: the lower middle classes, despised by Marxists; perfidious shopkeepers who do not increase capital but exploit the labour of others.

III.38 Voltaire dying: Voltaire's last words (28 Feb. 1778): "I die adoring God, loving my friends, not hating my enemies, and detesting superstition" [**#II.29**].

III.39 wrong planet: compare the "wrong world" of *Amaranth* [**#I.70**]; "another planet" [**#VI.13**]; and Laruelle's alienation since Geoffrey's death [UTV 9].

III.40 'unforeseen . . . incalculable': Nietzsche's 'Dawn: Thoughts on the Prejudices of Morality' (1881) asserts that "in all the original conditions of mankind, 'evil' signifies the same as 'individual,' 'free,' 'capricious,' 'unusual,' 'unforeseen,' 'incalculable'" [I:9].

III.41 shrieking sea: perhaps, Rider Haggard's *She* (IV, 'The Squall'), when a dhow founders off Zanzibar. The four survivors include the uncomplaining servant, **Job**.

III.42 Job: tested by Satan, Job bewails not God's injustice but the day he was born [**#VII.174**]. The crux, which Tor raises, is why he was so tested; Job replies, he is unworthy even to query this. Tor asks, is God beyond the ephemeral, untouched by the "accidents" [**#II.25**] of this insubstantial world; or does He, as Aristotle's **first cause** (a not-unmoved mover), despairingly contemplate the chaos of His failed creation?

III.43 great wreck: what Cardinal Newman calls in Chapter V of *Apologia Pro Vita Sua* (1865) a "terrible aboriginal calamity". Tor subsumes "contradictions and despairs" like "a dying tree"; intimations of Christ's sacrifice are unavoidable [**#III.129**]. Such atonement might facilitate Sigbjørn's "advance", but Tor struggles with the metaphor: "not a ship" (denying rebirth), but "gliding" (obscurely summoning Melville's white shark [**#II.32**; **#VII.192**]).

III.44 Stan Laurel: Arthur Stanley Jefferson (1890–1965); Oliver Hardy's thinner foil.

III.45 'Cain shall not slay Abel today': Benjamin, bitter, sees Sivert's smile and relents: "Cain could not slay Abel today" [*Ship Sails On* 146; **#I.45**; **#IV.74**;

#XVIII.29]. 'A Poem of God's Mercy' [*CP* #93] begins thus, but ends: "For at dawn is the reckoning and the last night is long."

III.46 If there is no God . . . : in *The Brothers Karamazov*, Ivan rejects God's world as built on a foundation of suffering, where "all is permitted". Mumford concludes: "if there is no God . . . then we can commit murder" [185].

III.47 turmoil of the weary world: see *Carmina Mariana* (1894), songs to the Virgin. Hymn XV, written by Novalis [**#VII.49**] and translated by Henry Curwen as 'Sorrow and Song', ends: "since then, the roar and turmoil of the weary world is stilled / And with harmonies of heaven hath my daily life been thrilled."

III.48 haven of the womb: Freud's *Das Unheimliche* [the uncanny] (1919) propounds the impossible dream of return to the womb (of which death is an expression) as the ultimate homesickness (Ger. *Heim*, "home"). See **#X.78**.

III.49 same journey: joining the International Brigades (1936) to fight (or die) in Spain, like Lowry's Cambridge contemporaries, John Cornford and John Sommerville.

III.50 *down below*: as in the shanty, "Fire in the galley, fire down below"; the inferno (hell for suicides, the stokehold) a common destiny. The **Underground Railway**, that childish warning so lightly recalled [**#I.54**], reveals Freudian terrors of the womb and the *Inferno*.

III.51 Another spiral: attributed to 'Erikson' [**#XVIII.43**]; Grieg's Benjamin looks into hell [*Ship Sails On* 167]. The phrase repeats in *DATG* [46]; in a 1940 letter to Whit Burnett [*CL* 1:337]; and in Lowry's film script, as Fate slowly ensnares Dick Diver: "another spiral had wound its way upward" [*Tender* 90].

III.52 All the books are read: Mallarmé's 'Brise marine' [Sea-wind]: "la chair est triste, hélas! Et j'ai lu tous les livres", read by Lowry as: "The flesh is sad, alas! and all the books are read" [Symons 189]; farewell the *ennui* of study for shipwreck and sailors' song. Lowry's scrawl survives: "All the books, all the bloody books are read—but do I want to hear the bloody sailors sing. No, hell no" [NYPL 2:36]. Ararat is another shipwreck [**#I.29**].

III.53 his shelves: an eclectic collection:

Virgil: Publius Vergilius Maro (70–19 BCE), poet of the *Eclogues*, *Georgics*, and *Aeneid*; Dante's guide through Hell and Purgatory.

Dante: Dante Alighieri (1265–1321), divine comedian [**#I.28; #III.54; #XV.13**].

Homer: *fl.* 850 BCE, author of the *Iliad* and *Odyssey*; father of Western literature.

Orpheus: whose music charmed wild beasts; who descended into Hades to regain Euridyce [**#VII.189**]; and whose bloody death inspired Orphic cults.

Logos: the Greek rationalist tradition, rather than the Christian Word incarnate.

Mythos: cultural narratives; notably, the opposition of *logos* and *mythos* (science and mysticism) in Jung.

Partisan Mists: in American politics, after a crisis, differences may be set aside to clear the "partisan mists"; alternatively, a foggy vista of the *Partisan Review*.

Laboratory Statistics: unspecified.

III.54 Dante: in *Inferno* III, Virgil castigates those undone by death as worthy neither of salvation nor damnation, so destined to swirl aimlessly for all eternity [**#I.49**; **#II.69**]. The "terrible, lousy translation" is by Jefferson Butler Fletcher (1931), cited almost verbatim ('caitiff' omitted; 'name' replacing 'fame'; one hiatus ignored) from Burton Rascoe's *Titans of Literature* (1932) [130]. Given Rascoe's fury (1935) over Lowry's "borrowings" from his 'What is Love?' (*In Ballast* he dismissed as equally derivative), this further appropriation assumes titanic ironies.

III.55 all these books:

Aristotle: (384–322 BCE), student of Plato and tutor of Alexander; the first great systematizer of Western thought.

Spinoza: Baruch (Benedict) de Spinoza (1632–1677), lens-grinder and philosopher, whose *Ethica* scrutinize Cartesianism [**#II.81**; **#VII.91**].

Kant: Immanuel Kant (1724–1804), German philosopher whose critiques of rationalism and epistemology reconstituted the Western tradition [**#IX.15**].

Bergson: Henri Bergson (1859–1941), French philosopher of duration and exponent of the Life Force. His *Creative Evolution* (1907) with its image of the cinematographic mind influenced Lowry [**#XVI.24**].

Croce: Benedetto Croce (1866–1952), Italian philosopher who defined abstract philosophy as the manifestation of history.

III.56 Karl Marx: (1818–1863), German political theorist whose *Communist Manifesto* (1848) and *Das Kapital* (1867) [**#III.78**] shaped international socialism.

III.57 Kierkegaard: Søren Kierkegaard (1813–1855), Danish philosophical theologian who affirmed Christian existentialism. Tor cites his 'Personal Confession', as translated in the *European Quarterly* (1934), where Kierkegaard describes the religious authority in which he was trained, and the melancholy he suffered. The 'Varsity' CB records his wish to escape the code of absolute obedience and be "free as a bird if only for one day" [120]. Kierkegaard likens himself to a fish watched by another power, but not yet drawn in; hence . . .

III.58 The Mad Fishmonger of Worcester: from Charles Fort, *Lo!*:

> Upon May 28th, 1881, near the city of Worcester, England, a fishmonger, with a procession of carts, loaded with several kinds of crabs and periwinkles, and with a dozen energetic assistants, appeared at a time when nobody on a busy road was looking. The fishmonger and his assistants grabbed sacks of periwinkles, and ran in a frenzy, slinging the things into fields on both sides of the road. They raced to gardens, and some assistants, standing on the shoulders of other assistants, had sacks lifted to them, and dumped sacks over the high walls. Meanwhile other assistants, in a dozen carts, were furiously shoveling out periwinkles, about a mile along the road. Also, meanwhile, several boys were busily mixing in crabs. They were not advertising anything. Above all there was secrecy. The cost must have been hundreds of dollars. They appeared without having been seen on the way, and they melted away equally mysteriously. There were houses all around, but nobody saw them. [549–50]

Fort rejects the notion of a mad fishmonger scattering periwinkles as nobody saw him, and since those retelling the tale "forget the crabs and tell of the periwinkles" [**#VIII.51**]. He affirms synchronicity: "the Mad Fishmonger of Worcester is everywhere." His next chapter concludes: "in phenomenal existence there is nothing that is independent of everything else".

III.59 ships that run aground: the inexplicable accidents afflicting the Tarnmoor line manifest (Tor reasons) a Fortean universe where such happenings are endemic.

III.60 consummate their terrible union: Dostoevsky's first novel, *Poor Folk* (1846), ends in sleazy rapture: "The new and terrible union was consummated." Lowry echoes Hardy's 'The Convergence of the Twain', the "consummation" of the *Titanic* and her iceberg.

III.61 catamites: nasty Senescence, drooling at the prospect of firm young flesh. Jo, Dickens's Fat Boy of *Pickwick Papers*, says: "I wants to make your flesh creep" [VIII].

III.62 'work of reds': a recurrent phrase (if in doubt, blame the Bolshies). In October 1931, a bloody demonstration provoked Home Secretary Sir John Gilmour to claim, "This is the work of Reds", as the National Unemployed

Workers' Movement (which organized the strike) "has a material connection with Moscow."

III.63 Titanic: the White Star liner [**#VII.18**] that hit an iceberg on her maiden voyage. The 'Varsity' CB records: "A black year—other marine catastrophes will follow the Titanic wreck. Cataclysms threaten on all sides". In the *New York Times* (24 April 1912), "Mme de Thebes" foretold dire events: "The year 1912 is a black year. Other marine catastrophes will follow the Titanic wreck. Cataclysms threaten on all sides. The sea especially is marked out as a source of danger. The dangerous epoch will last until March 21, 1913."

III.64 Great War: maritime disasters (Fort would agree) portended the storm: the *Florence* off Cape Race (1912); the *Southern Cross* off Newfoundland (31 March 1914), 173 deaths; and the *Empress of Ireland*, struck by a Norwegian collier in the St. Lawrence (29 May 1914), 1,012 deaths. This is the whirligig of time [**#III.25**]. For other warnings, see **#XI.10**.

III.65 lavish: Tennyson's *In Memoriam* protests nature's profligacy, so careless of the single life, so careful of the type.

III.66 headquarters of the future: a socialist truism [**#II.74**] that Sigbjørn now questions (Tor notes, he wants to get away).

III.67 What do we know?: Lowry told Markson (1951): "Another spiral has wound its way upward. Reason stands still. What do we know?" [*CL* 2.428]. This reflects Benjamin's guilt after betraying Anton [*Ship Sails On* 80; **#III.130**].

III.68 blind malicious force: manifest, beneath all, in the White Whale.

III.69 cultivate our garden: echoing the ending of Voltaire's *Candide*: "Cela est bien dit, répondit Candide, mais il faut cultiver notre jardin" [That is well put, Candide replied, but we must cultivate our garden], where Candide rejects Leibniz's optimism, and pre-established harmony. Sigbjørn will repeat Tor's words [**#VIII.58**; **#XV.10**].

III.70 reliance on the will: Sigbjørn implies that Tor has infected Nina with Nietzsche's "fatal" doctrine of the Will to Power. Their contention is an *agon*, or struggle for supremacy, from which Tor resigns.

III.71 lost generation: Gertrude Stein, of American artists in Paris after WWI; the epigraph to Hemingway's *The Sun Also Rises* [**#V.133**].

III.72 forest of ambivalence: compare Baudelaire's 'Correspondances' [**#X.7**].

III.73 Wormwood: Revelation 8:11, the star that fell upon the third part of the rivers and fountains of waters, "and many men died of the waters, because they were made bitter". Compare 'Only God Knows How III' and 'The Ship is Turning Homeward' [CP #74, #92].

III.74 going down: echoing Auden [**#II.1**].

III.75 'virile solidarity': from Granville Hicks, *Proletarian Literature in the United States* (1935), Auden's conviction that the self must die out of its old environment and be reborn in conscious union with "the virile solidarity of the proletariat" [Hicks 335; Asals 149].

III.76 Helgefjoss: "sacred waterfall". Not located, but in an early draft Tor asks 'Harald': "Do you remember Helgefjoss?", associating it with "The day mother died". En train to Oslo, Sigbjørn observes a foaming torrent: "in the wet night he gazes out at his birthplace, Helgafjord" [**#XVIII.21**]. That, too, is evasive, but this may be the *foss* in question. Charles Fort's only novel, *The Outcast Manufacturers* (1909), begins: "A dead horse lying in the southside gutter; boys jumping on it, enjoying the elasticity of its ribs."

III.77 tripos papers: past exams, as 'tripe'. Part II required a paper on Tragedy; hence Milton's Preface to *Samson Agonistes*:

> Tragedy, as it was anciently composed, hath been ever held the gravest, moralest, and most profitable of all other poems: therefore said by Aristotle to be of power by raising pity and fear, or terror, to purge the mind of those and such-like passions, that is to temper and reduce them to just measure with a kind of delight, stirred up by reading or seeing those passions well imitated.

III.78 *Das Kapital*: the analysis of capitalism by Karl Marx [**#III.56**], edited by Friedrich Engels (1867–1894). Contending that labour exploitation is the driving force of capitalism, Marx critiques Western society by the dialectic of political economy thus premised.

III.79 Pudovkin: Vsevolod Pudovkin (1893–1953), Russian director and screenwriter. A student of physical sciences, Pudovkin was three years a German POW before escaping to Moscow, where, working on cinematic propaganda, he was inspired by Griffith's *Intolerance* (1916). Best known for the trilogy, *Mother* (1926), *The End of St. Petersburg* (1927) [**#V.108**], and *Storm over Asia* (1928).

III.80 Eisenstein: Sergei Eisenstein (1898–1948), Russian director of *The Battleship Potemkin* (1925); *October* (1927); *Alexander Nevsky* (1938); *Ivan the Terrible* (1944, 1945, 1946); noted for innovations of camera angle and montage. *¡Que viva México!*, filmed and partly released in the 1930s, informs UTV (Laruelle resembles Eisenstein).

III.81 Fejos: Paul Fejos (1897–1963), Hungarian-born director of four American films: *The Last Performance* (1927); *The Last Moment* (1928); *Lonesome* (1928); and *Broadway* (1929).

III.82 'Haveth Childers Everywhere': part of Joyce's 'Work in Progress', published by the Fountain Press (Paris, 1930) and Faber (London, 1931); the finale (1939) of *Finnegans Wake* III.3 (532–54). The "**revolution of the word**", a surrealist manifesto, appeared in *transition* 16/17, the experimental journal, edited from 1927 by Eugene Jolas, who published bits of Joyce's forthcoming work. Its declaration of a new artistic age, abolishing barriers between content and form, was signed by many writers (not Joyce), but soon became a curiosity.

III.83 Kafka's 'Amerika': *Der Verschollene* [the man who disappeared]: Kafka's first novel, unfinished and posthumous (1927), tells of Karl Rossman, a young European who goes to New York to avoid the scandal of his seduction by a housemaid [**#X.1**].

III.84 Kierkegaard's 'Essays': Kierkegaard's *Philosophical Fragments* (1844) first appeared in English in 1936 [**#III.57**].

III.85 'Phantasia of the Unconscious': *Fantasia of the Unconscious*, Lawrence's study of Freudian psychoanalysis (1921); integrated (1923) with *Psychoanalysis and the Unconscious* (1922). The six essays challenge the "incest motive" of Freudian orthodoxy, substituting Lawrence's feelings and insights [**#VII.82**]. Here, 'transition' signals the necessity of 'rebirth' [**#X.35; #XIV.94**].

III.86 *teatre cruel*: a tortured form of Antonin Artaud's 'Le Théâtre de la cruauté (manifeste)' (Paris, 1932), seeking to restore to theatre a more passionate conception of life, one that saw the human condition as cruel and broke barriers between audience and stage.

III.87 books: editions unspecified:

> **Pythagoras:** Greek philosopher and mathematician of Samos (c.570–495 BCE), celebrated for *that* theorem, whose contributions to mathematics, music and philosophy deeply influenced Plato and Western thought.
>
> **Xenophanes:** Greek philosopher (c.570–475 BCE), whose elegiac poetry satirized the pantheon of anthropomorphic gods; an originator of scientific investigation.
>
> **Empedocles:** philosopher of Agrigentum, Sicily (c.480–430 BCE), who resolved the universal conflict of Love and Strife by jumping into Etna [**#III.90**].

III.88 fire . . . air . . . water: among the pre-Socratics, *Heraklites* considered fire the primary creative element; as *Diogenes of Apollonia* did air; and *Thales* water.

III.89 Giraux: Stanley Rogers, in *The Atlantic* (1930; a title shared with Grieg [**#XVIII.33**]), says that Gerbault [*sic*] threw overboard some works by Wilde, whose "lack of sincerity jarred upon a temperament rendered simple by contact with the sea" [68]. Alain Gerbault (1893–1941), "Hermit of the Seas", aviator and tennis champion, left France in 1923 on a six-year voyage in his thirty-footer, *Firecrest*; Rogers cites *The Fight of the 'Firecrest'* (1926) [20].

III.90 incandescent suffering: in 'Empedocles on Etna' (1852), Arnold's sage, tired of life, plunges into the crater. Aiken asks, "Why do we all want to be crucified, to fling ourselves into the very heart of the flame? Empedocles on Aetna. A moment of incandescent suffering. To suffer intensely is to live intensely, to be intensely conscious" [*Blue Voyage* 17; **#VI.19**].

III.91 Gethsemane: the garden outside Jerusalem, where Christ spent the night in prayer before the Crucifixion and was betrayed by Judas. Sigbjørn recalls these words [**#V.104**].

III.92 *As a child from school . . .*: the psychological autobiography of William Ellery Leonard, *The Locomotive-God* (1927), invokes the felt presence of one who has died: "And sets her place at table and her chair" [290]. Sigbjørn cites *The American Caravan* 1 (1927) [200].

III.93 mother: "remembrance of mother in Norway" would be enhanced in revision [**#I.2**].

III.94 Hamlet . . . Lear: like the Droeshout Shakespeare, composite frontispiece of the First Folio (1623). The 1940 Consul resembles "King Lear in full face, Hamlet in profile" [69].

III.95 chaos of a man: Lawrence, 'The Primrose Path', in *England, My England* (1924): the mother loves her two children "like a cool governess" and the father has "an emotional man's fear of sentiment". Their relation is difficult: "For after her cool fashion she did love him. With a chaos of a man such as he, she had no chance of being anything but cold and hard, poor thing. For she did love him."

III.96 matrix: L. *womb*, associating the Mother with 'Alma Mater' (Cambridge) and 'matriculation' (entry to her) [**#II.70**; **#XI.66**]. The dictionary is Webster's *Second*.

III.97 *Mon âme est un trois-mâts cherchant son Icarie*: Baudelaire, 'Le Voyage': "My soul is a three-master seeking its Icaria"; with 'notre' changed to *mon*, as in *La Mordida* [xxiii, 365]. *Icaria* is an island near Samos; Icarus fell nearby. In *Ultramarine* [186], "troismâts" follows the sentiment: "books, I shall throw them overboard" [**#III.52**; **#III.89**]. The "cross-trees" of a three-master, ending chapter III of *Ulysses*, offer Stephen Dedalus the prospect of Calvary and a long journey [**#IX.7**; **#IX.35**].

III.98 foc'sle head: the upper deck before the foremast, where the wheel is located [**#V.46**]. The *bosun* does not usually take a watch, but commands the deck crew.

III.99 heave away: an order to haul in mooring cables around the capstan; '**steady**' holds the vessel on the current course; '**all clear**' confirms that matters are in hand; **cordage** denotes ropes and cords, especially those of the rigging.

III.100 fireman's watch: the afternoon watch begins at noon; like the seamen, firemen are divided into two watches. The bosun's call to "muster" prepares for arrival.

III.101 Far, far north: the Index to Bulfinch's *Mythology* defines *Laestrygonians* as "A race of cannibal giants visited by Ulysses in their northern country . . . having days so short that the shepherd driving his flock to pasture in the morning will meet the shepherd coming home at night." At the magnetic North Pole "**all points of the compass**" are one.

III.102 prison wall: *The Prison Courtyard* (1890), painted when Vincent Van Gogh was "imprisoned" in the Saint-Paul-de-Mausole asylum, Saint Remy [**#X.58**; *CL* 1:125].

III.103 man and woman: Nietzsche's eternal sexual conflict, where woman tries to control man's will; Tor extends the analogy to man and man, in Nietzsche's doctrine of the Will to Power [**#III.70**]. The strife over Nina might have developed this motif in revision [**#I.2**].

III.104 spiritual esotericism: Madame Blavatsky argued that throughout mystic literature "we detect the same idea of spiritual Esotericism, that the personal God exists within, nowhere outside, the worshipper" [*Teachings* 119].

III.105 one person: Jensen's Man of will finds a Woman to share his vision and on her fathers the Nordic race [*Long Journey*, **#X.73**]. In marriage, the twain shall be of one flesh [**#X.96**]; in Plato's *Symposium*, each separated "one" yearns for its other [**#X.94**]. In the 'Varsity' CB, Lowry's "Proudman by Murray Constantine" invokes Katharine Burdekin's novel, *Proud Man* (1934, under this pseudonym), where "human" beings of the distant future [**#X.97**], unlike the "subhumans" of her time, are ungendered.

III.106 Thank God . . . at sea: echoing Herman Bang's *Ida Brandt*, from the 'Varsity' CB: "Ah, said the Admiral. Well, thank God they don't expect us to be scandalized at sea" [305].

III.107 passion: for the Norwegian-Danish writer, Amalie Skram (1846–1905), "life was a perpetual curse which through the commandment to multiply in the earth had gained the force of natural law". Her unhappy marriage reflects that of the Tarnmoors [**#III.95**]; her pessimism affects Tor. Lowry recorded in the 'Varsity' CB: "human beings are but puppets driven forward by the urge of their own bodies, slavishly obedient to the natural law of propagation. 'If passion did not exist, love would be eternal. What difference would it make if mankind ceased to propagate its kind? It seems to me that many have lived enough already'" [Jorgenson 349]. Jorgenson links Amalie Skram's naturalism with Grieg's *The Ship Sails On*, concluding that since heredity perpetuates the curse of passion, "the logical deed for all mankind is suicide" [352]. Tor has inherited the family impulse.

III.108 Uncle Bjørg: curious, as 'Bjørg' is the feminine of 'Bjørk'.

III.109 Sibelius' *Valse Triste*: an orchestral piece by Jean Sibelius (1865–1957), from the incidental music to *Kulema* [Death], a drama by Arvid Jämefelt (1903). The waltz depicts a son at his sick mother's bedside; when (like Sigbjørn) he falls asleep, she in weird gaiety is visited by Death. The music featured in the 1934 film, *Death Takes a Holiday*. Compare Grieg's poem, 'Oktoberaften paa Karl Johan' [October evening in Karl Johan's Street], "hvor nervene spiles til døde og synder som violiner / i trods og smertelig jubel, fordi vi endnu er til!"; as translated into *Ultramarine*, where "nerves are played to death and sing like violins in defiance and painful exultation, because we still exist" [86].

III.110 Pictures: in the 'Varsity' CB, a paragraph headed 'Sixteen violins':

> Pictures are moving before my eyes. I see a ship lying at the wharf, the ships gone. Now somebody is signalling to me out of a window. It must be important—he's frantic. Now I hear violins, thousands of them, the whole world is turning into a piece of music. All the same I'm still conscious that I'm here, am speaking to you . . . Hello, did I go to sleep. My conscience must be weighing me down.

The verso cites Amalie Skram [**#III.107**], of whose art it was the power and the limitation that she reproduced what she had seen and heard.

III.111 forests . . . symbols: anticipating Baudelaire's 'Correspondances' [**#X.5**].

III.112 stripped and winnowed: as grain from the stalk, the chaff blown away.

III.113 ***Drammensveien:*** an Oslo street, running forty miles west towards Drammen. Lowry wrote to Grieg from *Hotell Parkheimen* (Drammensveien 2) [**#XVIII.49**]. Dana stands in *Drammersveien* [sic] with Janet [U 54]; the 1933 text [71] is correct.

III.114 Holmenkollen: Sigbjørn's childhood catastrophe explained [**#I.54**]. The sign, ***Warning—Low Archway***, is another such memory, deriving from the bridge near the golf course [**#VIII.2**].

III.115 number three furnace: foundries are thus named (like ships' holds, or concubines).

III.116 Lysadis: correctly, *Lysavis*, "illuminated sign", as *Aftenpostens Lysavis*, for Oslo's main newspaper [**#XII.21**]. Recalled by Dana Hilliot and Dick Diver [U 54; *Tender* 148]; not in *Drammensveien* as Dana implies, but set upon the *Østbanestasjon* to report the 1930 election. An imagined electronic news-ticker offers persistent flashes of the Tarnmoor disaster; the "strange type" invokes *Lycidas* [**#VIII.95**] and other drownings.

III.117 ***Naufragung:*** Gerfregian for *naufrage*, "shipwreck"; in French maritime law, loss or destruction of a vessel by waves or storm. The carnage anticipates the end of UTV [**#VI.20**].

III.118 ***little duck . . . :*** in the Grimm brothers' tale, 'Hansel and Gretel', the children, fleeing the gingerbread house, try to leave the forest. They reach water, but as there is neither bridge nor boat Gretel entreats a white duck, in precisely the words cited.

III.119 How now . . . Ophelia in a swoon: a potpourri of *Hamlet* petals: Ophelia does not swoon, but when Gertrude drinks poison during the final duel Claudius says: "She swoons to see them bleed" [V.2.308]. When Hamlet kills Polonius he says: "How now? A rat? Dead for a ducat, dead" [III.iv.23]. "Often with a blade . . . " (unidentified) implies his quietus with a bare bodkin [III.i.83–84] and desire to sleep: "To die, to sleep; / To sleep, perchance to dream" [III.i.71–72]. Sigbjørn's "bad dreams" continues the motif: Hamlet might count himself a king of infinite space, "were it not that I have bad dreams" [II.ii.258–60].

III.120 Arise and shine: Isaiah 60:1: "Arise, shine; for thy light is come, and the glory of the Lord is risen upon thee"; to rouse the laggard: "Arise and shine / For the [Tarnmoor] Line."

III.121 mastering Dante: Lowry told Markson that "he" gets through the Dante exam by consulting a blind medium who foresees the questions [CL 2:426].

III.122 molecular catastrophe: that in phenomenal existence nothing is independent; tiny atomic movements trigger concatenations; hence "molecular disaster" [*Blue Voyage* 288; **#VII.202**]. Lowry cited (to Aiken) Robinson's 'Man Against the Sky': "blind atomic pilgrimage" [*CL* 1:83 (1931)]; in 'Ordeal', he offered "Atomic Rhythm" [UBC 22:20, 1].

III.123 chemic: like Billy Budd sniffing evil [**#I.16**; **#II.5**]. Or coal gas.

III.124 keep a twelve: Sigbjørn must return before the door is locked at midnight.

III.125 blocked up the windows: like Paul Fitte, with or without Lowry's aid, on the night of 14/15 November 1929. Bradbrook reports: the headline, "CAMBRIDGE TRAGEDY. STUDENT FOUND DEAD IN GAS-FILLED ROOM"; the inquest; chief witness, "Clement Milton Lowry", unwittingly commenting, "it was the last thing in the world he would do." Fitte was being blackmailed, with homosexual overtones to disgrace his wealthy family. The incident, with its moral complicity, features in 'Panama', 'Ordeal', and *October Ferry*, where Jacqueline's mother makes *sure*: "They found her hanging in a gas-filled flat" [32]. Lowry often treated it as hanging [**#XII.11**]. Charlotte Haldane describes that evening in *I Bring Not Peace* (1932), which is dedicated to Lowry, with James Dowd based on him and Dennis Carling on Paul Fitte:

> Then there was gas poisoning, quite the prettiest of all, coal-gas poisoning was. You turned on the tap and there was that sweetish sickly smell which like the stuff at the dentist's gave you muzziness and the grandest dreams in no time, better than alcohol it was. James had read that the carbon monoxide combined with your blood, knocking out the oxygen or preventing it from getting in, and it kept you a lovely pink colour, quite the pleasantest thing for those who had to find you and clear you up. [176]

III.126 little man: the vendor who promised Tor a long journey [**#II.92**].

III.127 St. Eligius Street: off Bateman Street [**#II.85**]. Saint Eligius, patron of goldsmiths and blacksmiths, shoed a recalcitrant horse by removing its leg then restoring it.

III.128 knocked up: Lowry's 'Byzantium' [*CP* #183] is subtitled: "(or getting a bit knocked oop now)"; less sexual innuendo than total fatigue.

III.129 broke bread: as Christ at the Last Supper: "in the same night that he was betrayed, took Bread; and, when he had given thanks, he brake it . . . " (Communion Service).

III.130 betray Judas: Benjamin (a seaman) recalls how he rejected Anton (a fireman), "despised and infinitely lonely" [*Ship Sails On* 79]. Realizing he has obscurely murdered Anton by withholding kindness, he concludes, "He had a grudge against Anton, but what excuse was that? It is worse to betray Judas than to betray Jesus" [**#XVIII.29**].

III.131 party treason: putting one's self ahead of the Cause [**#IV.56**]. Sigbjørn will recall "the objectivity of the dead" [**#IV.18**].

III.132 surrealistic nonsense: suicide as an aesthetic act [**#IV.53**], or a literary fashion.

III.133 we do not associate: "such dooms with ourselves" [**#III.7**; **#III.148**; **#V.39**].

III.134 Kwannon: *Kuan Yin*, in Chinese Buddhism the *bodhisattva* or spirit of compassion. Demarest reflects: "I will pray to Kwannon" [*Blue Voyage* 164]; and: "Kwannon, Goddess of Mercy, serene and beneficent idol, Cathayan peace! Smile down upon me" [207].

III.135 Erikson: Sigbjørn Wilderness recalls: "Erikson was N. but at one time Erikson was also the evil principle" [DATG TS, UBC 9:22, 668; **#IV.40**].

III.136 go on: as Lowry said (or imagined saying) to Paul Fitte [**#III.125**]. Ethan recalls: "All right, Mr. Peter Bloody Cordwainer . . . . Go ahead and do it" [OF 68].

III.137 horripilation: L. *horripilare*, "to bristle with hairs"; poetically, bristling with horror [UTV 126], as "when your hair walks backward on cold feet" [*Blue Voyage* 264].

III.138 typographical error: as Kent's abuse of Oswald [*King Lear* II.ii]: "Thou whoreson zed! thou unnecessary letter!"; with the "posthumous play" of being written. Laruelle recalls when an individual life "was not a mere misprint in a communiqué" [UTV 5].

III.139 thousand years: compare Aiken's philosophers [**#IV.34**].

III.140 —Come with me: Peter Cordwainer says: "Ethan, you come too" [OF 69].

III.141 gaff-topsail boots: Redburn, all at sea, laments his melancholy wardrobe, ill-adapted to his new life; notably, his beautiful high-heeled boots that trip him in the rigging. These the sailors call (in Chapter XV) his "gaff-topsail-boots". The ***gaff-topsail*** is a triangular sail, extended along the *gaff*, an upper spar to which a mainsail is attached.

III.142 Peterhouse: Trumpington Street; the oldest and smallest of the traditional colleges, founded in 1284 by Hugo de Balsham, Bishop of Ely.

III.143 Addenbrookes: a teaching hospital (1766) on Trumpington Street; relocated (1976) to the city south. Ethan recalls running furiously, the clock striking twelve: "I was staggering and running and gasping and I recall passing the hospital, where they held the inquest the next day. I had to be in my digs by twelve, you know, and I just made it" [OF 215; **#V.72**].

III.144 post mortem, nihil: "after death, nothing" [**#III.12**].

III.145 *Sing,song,hang,soon:* as 'Sing Sing' (New York's maximum security prison; compare the "singing slayer" [**#I.64**]). The tone is familiar: "Ding dong, ding dong; dong ding, ding dong"; then twelve slow "dongs". For the effect, see the Textual Notes.

III.146 Festival Theatre: Newmarket Road; a rare Regency venue outside London. Opening as the Barnwell (1814), it struggled financially and became a mission hall (1878). In 1926, Terence Gray, a millionaire racehorse owner, revived it as an expressionist theatre, with a revolving stage and cyclorama. It led the avant-garde, with both contemporary and classic productions, but by 1935 had faded, closing in 1939.

III.147 Race With A Shadow: Wilhelm von Scholz (1874–1969) was a German playwright and loyal Nazi intrigued by Goethe, mysticism, and fate [Grace, CL 2: 422]. His major success was *Der Wettlauf mit dem Schatten* (1920), or *Race with a Shadow* (1923), about the rivalry between a writer and his characters. The Royal Court staged it successfully in 1921, the first post-war German piece in England; it did not play at the Festival Theatre. Lowry mentions it in 'Panama' [27], and told Markson it was "a sinister German play running in London" [CL 2:418; **#II.58**; **#IV.39**].

III.148 *Womb- . . . Tomb- . . . Doom:* the "Dongs" [**#III.145**] compounded with Freudian inevitability and the "terrible fatality" of *Moby-Dick*, as in Lawrence's *Classic American Literature* (1923): "Doom! Doom! Doom!" [XI]. Yet we do not associate "such dooms with ourselves" [**#III.7**; **#III.133**; **#V.39**].

III.149 Eight bells: four double strokes, ending the watch.

III.150 *Oedipus Tyrannus:* on which Sigbjørn sailed [**#III.16**]. A handwritten insert to the 'Varsity' CB adds: "as an overladen Indiaman bearing down the Hindustan coast with a deck load of frightened horses, buries, rolls & wallows on her way." In *Moby-Dick*, an old bull whale thus heaves its aged bulk [LXXXI; **#VI.60**].

III.151 encased steering: cords and cables (like nerves in the spinal column), translating steering decisions into motion. The 'Varsity' insert notes: "The encased steering, the spinal cord of the ship unwound [*like a spool which*] [*or like music*] [*or a manuscript* ****] continually unrolling the huge [*dark*] parchment of the sea." A pod of whales leaves a great wake, "as though continually unrolling a great wide parchment upon the sea" [*Moby-Dick* LXXXI].

III.152 jackstays: battens stretching along the yards, to which sails are attached to steady the mast against strain of the gaff (the spar rising aft from a mast to support the sail-head).

III.153 murderess of Le Mans: adding the asylum to the earlier image [**#I.69**].

III.154 The Lord is my hospital . . . : Menninger's patient [**#III.22**], the setting now explicit madness.

CHAPTER IV

IV.1 [Epigraph] Ogden and Richards: F. G. Crookshank, in his introduction [16] to Charles Blondel, *The Troubled Conscience and the Insane Mind* (1928) [**#XVI.24**], discusses Ogden and Richards, whose *The Meaning of Meaning* (1923) criticized Saussure's dyadic model (the relation of *signifiant* to *signifié*) for "neglecting entirely the things for which signs stand" [8], in favour of a triadic model (their semiotic triangle) including reference. The "same set of *referents*" is Sigbjørn's experience shared with Erikson, which despite "differing *references*" explains the approximate "verbal *symbolization*" [plagiarism?]. See the Textual Notes.

IV.2 Trinity College: the largest Cambridge college, founded by Henry VIII (1546). Renowned for its Great Court (with emblematic fountain) and the Wren Library; the *Alma Mater* of Donne, Marvell, Newton, Byron, and Russell, and (for Lowry) John Cornford, Aleister Crowley, and Geoffrey Firmin. 'D5' is the desirable Room off Staircase D from Nevile's Court. Lowry, back from Oslo, took "number two on D staircase" at St. Catharine's, despite feeling that the College was "still haunted by Fitte" [Bowker 131].

IV.3 "Whence came you, Hawthorne?": Melville told Hawthorne of his "pantheistic" feelings and "Ineffable socialities", saying he would "sit down and dine" with him and "all the gods in old Rome's Pantheon". His fervent cry comes from Mumford [200], who cites a letter (17 Nov. 1851) from Rose Hawthorne Lathrop's *Memories of Hawthorne*. Melville's tragedy, said Mumford [264], was that Hawthorne could not respond to this call.

IV.4 Christiania Bokhandel Forlag: Oslo was 'Christiania' (1624–1877), then 'Kristiania' until 1925, when it reverted to 'Oslo'. Nor. *bokhandel* is "bookshop"; *Forlag*, "publisher". *Raadhusgt* is 'Rådhusgata', from the *Rådhus*, or Town Hall ('gt' is *gate*, 'street'; earlier orthography preferred 'aa' to 'å'). '199' is impossible (perhaps a mistyping of '19'), as the highest number is less than 40. 'Gyldendalske Bokhandel, Kristiania' was the Oslo branch of the Danish publishers of *Skibet gaar videre*) [**#I.51**] until 1925, when Grieg's brother Harald helped *Gyldendal Norsk Forlag* attain a national identity, their office at Rådhusgata 23. 'Hr' is 'Herr', a formal courtesy.

IV.5 Herman Melville: (1819–1891); Lowry's shipmate on the voyage that never ends; and father of Malcolm, who committed suicide [**#II.11**]. *In Ballast* draws widely from Melville, with *Moby-Dick* (1851) ubiquitous [**#V.53**], and *Redburn* (1849) and the fraught friendship with Hawthorne [**#IV.3**; **#V.54**; **#VI.71**] nearby. An **exordium** is the 'proem' (introduction) to an oration; Lowry flourished the word to Aiken [*CL* 1:61 (1929)].

IV.6 Mount Monadnock: Melville's home (1850) was 'Arrowhead', in Pittsfield, where he first met Hawthorne, a neighbour, and found respite from the sea. Mount *Greylock* (a nearby *monadnock*, or peak of hard residual rock) inspired Moby-Dick's great "Monadnock hump" [CXXV]. Lowry compounds the error (later corrected) of Mumford's first edition [200].

IV.7 Rock Ferry: in Birkenhead, then a major ferry terminus. Hawthorne as Consul (1853–1856) lived in Rock Park, with his office "over the water" in Liverpool; the house was later (1970s) demolished for a bypass. Martin Trumbaugh last saw his sick mother "at Rock Ferry Station, Birkenhead (where Nathaniel Hawthorne was Consul)" ['Panama' 69].

IV.8 Hansen-Tarnmoor: Sigbjørn emphasizes the Norwegian link [**#III.6**].

IV.9 Christiansand: a port in south Norway, named (1641) for King Christian IV. If (as seems likely) Lowry returned from Norway [Sept. 17?] on the *Calypso*, the Ellerman's Wilson Line *Passengerdamperen* (Oslo to Hull, Thursdays), he would have called at Kristiansand. Sigbjørn later says he was born at 'Helgefjord' [**#XVIII.21**].

IV.10 on the swamp: Harald III founded Oslo in 1048, its name supposedly implying "mouth of the Lo" [**#IV.14**]. Sigbjørn's "which men now call Oslo" has the heroic timbre; but although Christiania "stands low" with much "on a level with the swampy grounds" around it [Latham I:43], "on the swamp" more readily suggests St. Petersburg [**#XII.47**].

IV.11 Suley: the *M/S Soløy*, of the Erling H. Samuelsen line (Oslo), built in Malmö (1929); torpedoed in the Atlantic (24 June 1941). In 'Hotel Room in Chartres', the narrator journeys "from Exchange to Prester to join the *Suley*" [P&S 22–23].

IV.12 Trondhjem: *Trondheim*, the Viking capital; Norway's third city, three hundred miles north of Oslo. One recruit on the *Mignon* is "a Trondhjem lad" [*Ship Sails On* 216].

IV.13 *Oxenstjerna*: "Ox-forehead", a Swedish senatorial family, the ship named for its most illustrious member, Count Axel Gustafsson (1583–1654), chancellor and vice-regent, who led Sweden through the 17th-century religious wars. Dana and Janet saw in Oslo the "Norwegian tramp steamer" *Oxenstjerna* (Tromsö) [U 27]; in Birkenhead they see her again [66]; she reappears [203] as a final affirmation of their love.

IV.14 Bergen: Norway's second city; ON *Bergvin*, a meadow between the mountains. Sigbjørn's "meadow at the foot of a hill" is more truly an etymology of *Oslo* [**#IV.10**].

IV.15 *Direction*: suggested, Sigbjørn says, by "a real ship I had seen in Liverpool" [**#IV.58**]; probably the SS *Director*, built in Glasgow (1926) for the Charente SS Company, Liverpool. Like most of Lowry's vessels she was fated: torpedoed by a U-boat (15 July 1944).

IV.16 Far East: Grieg was in China [**#XVIII.11**] as Lowry sailed by on the *Pyrrhus* (1927).

IV.17 torment of deprivation: as Marlowe's Mephistopheles, his soul separated from God [iv.80]: "Why, this is hell, nor am I out of it" [**#XVI.2**]. He is "tormented with ten thousand hells / In being deprived of everlasting bliss."

IV.18 objective reality: Tor sought "objective reality" in death [**#I.8**; **#III.131**].

IV.19 ἄσκησις: religious self-discipline, *asceticism* [see the Textual Notes].

IV.20 (not finished): Demarest's letters to Cynthia tail off, unfinished, unsent [*Blue Voyage* VII]. Aiken recalled Hambo's poetic ship's log, that "mythopoetic logarithm, of a letter, that mythopoem (in imitation of D.'s own) to his all-too-imaginary Nita" [*Ushant* 30].

IV.21 How shall I begin?: and (like Prufrock) how should he presume? Sigbjørn is writing from his rooms in St. Eligius Street [**#III.127**].

IV.22 multiverse: Durant [*Philosophy* 560] quotes William James [**#II.24**] as saying that the cosmos is not a closed harmonious system, but shows itself "not as a uni- but a multiverse". James coined this usage (*Will to Believe* 1895), for how one's private universe might differ from that of others. He was attracted by "the endless varieties of religious experience and belief"; described them with "an artist's sympathy"; saw "some truth in every one"; and accepted the reality of "another—a spiritual—world" [Durant 562]. Lowry did likewise.

IV.23 virile solidarity of the proletariat: Hicksville [**#III.75**].

IV.24 without our misery?: Lowry's projected ending [**#XVIII.69**].

IV.25 my brother: compare 'June the 30th, 1934', the huge ox eyeing a tiny pot of Bovril: "Alas, my poor brother!" [P&S 45].

IV.26 scroll of music: destiny, as yet unrolled [**#III.151**; **#IV.75**].

IV.27 debacle of self: Sigbjørn uses this phrase (and 'private grief', in the next letter) to his father [**#VII.7**; **#X.41**]; 'debacle' suggests the Communards of the 1870s (and Zola's *La Débâcle*), whose failures heralded the 1917 Russian revolution.

IV.28 your protagonist: Benjamin Hall "appears on the quay in the darkness" [*Ship Sails On* 2; **#XV.2**]. Lowry summarizes, rather than quotes; Benjamin, a shipbroker's son, is learning about the sea before taking to the business [17].

IV.29 Wallae: as *Wallasey* (Germanic *Wahla*, "stranger", with Celtic *ey*, "island"). Grieg's protagonist is Benjamin Hall; their fictional doppelgängers are Erikson and Benjamin Wallae. Sigbjørn Tarnmoor identifies with Erikson (as Lowry with Grieg); Erikson's protagonist thus equates to Benjamin Wallae, who owes his surname to Lowry's Nikolai Wallae ("I am the one they call Nikolai, but my real name is Wallae" [U 17]), who in turn takes his Christian name from Grieg: "Sivert, though he was christened Nikolai" [*Ship Sails On* 6].

IV.30 returning to the womb: in *The Last Address*, Lawhill, having considered himself a ship (after the celebrated four-master of that era), adopts a foetal position [180].

IV.31 Alpha and Omega: Revelation 1:8: "I am the Alpha and Omega, the first and the last"; hence A to Z, Atlantic to zebra. In the 1940 *Volcano*, the Pacific is "striped like a zebra" [63]. The "**gaudy-striped zebra**" flee in A. W. Roler's 'The Modern Wild-Animal Trapper and his Captives', in the children's magazine, *St. Nicholas* (1909) [162].

IV.32 Sphinx: the monster guarding Thebes, demanding that passersby solve a riddle, and devouring those who failed. When Oedipus succeeded, the Sphinx, mortified, destroyed herself, as in Cocteau's *La Machine infernale*, which Lowry saw in Paris (1934) [UTV 221]. The "riddle of the sphinx" [**#VII.23**; **#IX.9**] implies Secret Knowledge; in Ouspensky's *New Model of the Universe* [362–65], her icy stare annihilates any transient sense of self.

IV.33 snoring volcanoes: 'In Cape Cod with Conrad Aiken' concludes: "I tell you this young man / So that your outlook may perhaps be broadened. / I who have seen snoring volcanoes / And dismal islands shawled in snow" [*CP* #13]. Hirosige's *Snow on the Kiso Mountains* (1857) was a cherished print at Aiken's Cape Cod home. Lowry revisited "snoring volcanoes" [U 30] and "shawled islets" in 'Outside was the roar of the sea' [*CP* #105].

IV.34 thousand years: one philosopher of 'In Cape Cod' (and in Aiken's 'Landscape West of Eden') has discovered a language so complex "it would take a thousand years to synthesise a single word". The other replies that in his language one word is "the equivalent of sixteen thousand years" [*CP* #13; **#III.139**]. Aiken recounts the dream to his children, John and Jane [*Letters* 153 (1929)], and in *Ushant* [167].

IV.35 heeling shadow: as in 'Outside was the roar of the sea' [*CP* #105]; compare the "solitary albatross heels over in the gale" [U 201], where Lowry envisages "den ensomme albatross" of Grieg's 'Rund Kap det Gode Haab'.

IV.36 *Skibets reise fra Kristiania*: expressing Sigbjørn/Lowry's belief that Erikson/Grieg had "stolen" his novel.

IV.37 ". . . under the sun": Ecclesiastes 1:9: "that which is done is that which shall be done; and there is no new thing under the sun."

IV.38 Mecca Cafe: of several in Liverpool (none survives), that in Water Street, under the India Buildings recently built for Alfred Holt's Blue Funnel Line.

IV.39 Goethe said . . . race with a shadow: a sentiment (an author's rivalry with his characters) that generated, Lowry says, von Scholz's *Race with a Shadow*. A Stranger appears to Dr. Martins, as Mephistopheles to Faust, a doppelgänger who believes his life is being told in Martins's current work. The rivalry derives from an author's unlived being, manifest in his creation. After the *Fremder* departs [I.iii], Martins explains to his wife Berta his sense of being in a race with this shadowy figure, saying: "Goethe hat mal notiert: ihm begegneten immer mehr seine Gestalten" [45], that Goethe has observed that one meets one's characters more and more. Lowry is recalling the stage-play (in English) [**#II.58**; **#III.147**].

IV.40 doppelgänger: intimating another order of reality; Erikson's "evil art" [**#III.135**] that created Benjamin Wallae as "another" Sigbjørn is more than "accident".

IV.41 Louis Adamic: Slovenian author (1899–1951) who emigrated to America at fourteen and became a writer. In the DATG typescript, Lowry calls him "a gifted Croatian" [UBC 9:5, 356]. Grace identifies his "rather minor, if good, but scarcely helpful book" [CL 2:418] as *Grandsons* (1935), a self-reflective novel by the "shadow" of the narrator [422].

IV.42 Huxley: Aldous Huxley (1894–1963), English novelist who discovered America in 1937. Lowry alerted Markson to his "feeble short story", which Grace identifies as 'Farcical History of Richard Greenow', from *Limbo* (1920), about a split personality writing different works under his male and female personae [CL 2:422].

IV.43 Kardomah Cafe: this popular chain, with many outlets, first poured its tea at the 1887 Liverpool Exhibition. The name, brewed by the Liverpool China and India Tea Company to suggest *Arabia exotica*, complements 'Mecca' [**#IV.38**]. No Liverpool Kardomah survives; this may be that once located at Whitechapel and Stanley Street.

IV.44 Barrès: Maurice Barrès (1862–1923), aesthete, Catholic, and egoist, best-known for the "metaphysical fiction", *Sous l'oeil des barbares* (1888). In *Le jardin de Bérénice* (1891), the heroine awakens to beauty in a garden of impressionistic delights, as Sigbjørn notes: "For an accomplished spirit there is but one dialogue—that between our two Egos, the momentary Ego we are, and the ideal Ego toward which we strive." Bérénice, alas, marries the wrong man, and dies like a flower in a cellar. Lowry plucked his fine flourishes from James Huneker's *Egoists: A Book of Supermen* (1921) [223].

IV.45 *stream* of Literature: Washington Irving noted in 'The Mutability of Literature' (1819) that paper and press have made everyone writers: "The stream of literature has swollen into a torrent—augmented into a river—expanded into a sea" [182].

IV.46 'hysterical identification': in Chapter IV, 'The Distortion of Dreams', of *The Interpretation of Dreams* (1898), Freud introduced this term to explain how one ego, perceiving significant analogies with another, constructs a distorted (hence hysterical) identification until that process is complete. Lowry admitted an "hysterical identification" with Aiken, Melville, and Grieg [Bowker 86, 98], using the phrase in *The Last Address* [144].

IV.47 'breaking of the heart': a term Freud popularized in 'The Unconscious' (1915), his example being the death of Lear.

IV.48 Chatterton: Thomas Chatterton (1752–1770), poet and forger; the "marvellous boy", whose suicide left his promise tragically unfulfilled. Lowry invokes him in 'But I shall live when you are dead and damned' [CP #52]; and (with Brooke) in 'Those who die young will look forever young' [CP #305]. Grieg's *De unge døde* [**#XVIII.46**] ignored Chatterton.

IV.49 Keats: John Keats (1795–1821), a Romantic poet who died young, of the TB that (as a medical student) he knew was inexorable. In 'Strange Comfort' Sigbjørn Wilderness visits his house in Rome. Lowry told Grieg (1931) that Keats "saw in the death of Chatterton the consummation of his own poetic theory so that he was ready for and even delighted by the prospect of his own death" [*CL* 1:105]. He offered Markson instances of authors absorbing another: "On the tragic plane you have Keat's [sic] identification with Chatterton, leading, Aiken once suggested, to a kind of *conscious* death on Keats [sic] part" [*CL* 2:429].

IV.50 Rupert Brooke: (1887–1915), the "young Apollo" who died young, unromantically, when an infected mosquito bite ended his glorious Trojan war. He epitomized the best of his generation; the futility of his death is a later accent. His poetry shows promise unfulfilled; Lowry told Grieg (1931) it had "germs of a metaphysical inquisitiveness which he had not time to develop" [*CL* 1:103], noting of *John Webster and the Elizabethan Drama* (1916) the "Dark Self that Wants to Die" and Marston's sinister influence [**#XVIII.47**]. Brooke inspired Grieg's *De unge døde* [**#XVIII.46**]. Lowry self-evaluated his Norwegian odyssey: "No Rupert Brooke, and no great lover he / Remembered little of simplicity" [*CP* #35].

IV.51 Old Leysians: Old Boys of The Leys, the "strict Wesleyan school" [UTV 18] that the Lowry brothers attended, might censure the pun on 'laid'.

IV.52 Byron's Pool: in the Cam, at Grantchester, where Byron had bathed. Lowry told Carol Brown it was "the world's worst place for bathing. Reedy and foul" [*CL* 1:44]. Rupert frolicked there naked with Virginia Woolf, to the aesthetic approbation of both.

IV.53 Le suicide, est-il une solution?: asked by André Breton in *La Révolution surréaliste* (Jan. 1925). To prove the desperation of the rational world, the journal reprinted impassively suicide reports, using this as a catchphrase [**#III.132**].

IV.54 My supervisor: Lowry's supervisor, T. R. Henn, was sceptical, but *Ultramarine* was accepted as an "original composition" should he be borderline. In the first draft, "Old Lupus" has let Sigbjørn submit the book instead of the thesis. The "friendly critic" was Hugh Sykes Davies, who deputized when Henn rejected his unruly charge.

IV.55 Liverpool bookshop: perhaps, Howell's bookshop (46 Castle Street), known for its unusual holdings. Lowry found *The Ship Sails On* in 1929; the *DATG* typescript notes it was *ex libris* and cost two shillings [UBC 9:1, 352]. Translated by A. G. Chater [**#IV.71**; **#X.73**]; not to be confused, as Douglas Day was [117], with Rev. A. J. Chaytor, Provençal scholar and "moral tutor" to whom Lowry was vainly assigned [Bowker 94].

IV.56 'party treason': betrayal of Socialist convictions (affirmed by Grieg) by accentuating individual aspirations over the Party's greater good. By viewing his predicament as "special", Sigbjørn, using one of Tor's last phrases [**#III.131**], betrays his professed ideals.

IV.57 Liverpool-Irish fireman W: Erikson's 'Wallae' [**#IV.29**]. Lowry defined his hero to Markson as 'A' and "a Scandinavian novelist" as 'X' [CL 2:418], noting that the more A reads X's book the more he identifies with its principal character, 'Y' [for the "old algebra", see **#IV.61**]. Here, as relations between 'A', 'X', and 'Y' entwine, no 'W' resolves them, let alone a Liverpool-Irish fireman.

IV.58 real ship: vertiginous reality: one ship (the *Direction*), seen by the fictional Sigbjørn in Liverpool [**#VII.11**], that identity uncertain [**#IV.16**]; another (the *Oedipus Tyrannus*), on which Dana Hilliot sailed [**#III.16**], as Hugh in UTV; whereas (1) in *Ultramarine* (1933) she was the *Nawab*; and (2) in Lowry's life the *Pyrrhus* . . . . If fiction postulates an authentic reality, then fictive characters are equally real, as Sigbjørn affirms when he becomes (imaginatively) Grieg's invention [**#IV.29**].

IV.59 Aalesund: a seaman on the *Mignon* [**#XVIII.5**], whose fate anticipates Benjamin's. Handsome but brutal, he brings onboard the young sister of Anton, a fireman, and tells all who intervene to "go to hell". When Aalesund gets "ill" (syphilis) [44], he packs his bag and flees; Benjamin, later, chooses hell by staying on board.

IV.60 joker: capable of trumping any other card, so controlling the game; it derives from the Fool of the Tarot, the Jungian Trickster of ancient mythology.

IV.61 similar adjustment: the old algebra [**#IV.57**]: 'X' (Sigbjørn) must consume 'Y' (Erikson) to become 'X plus Y', a composite Benjamin/Nikolai Wallae figure [**#IV.29**], to prove himself (as Lowry failed to do, though Dana, Hugh, Benjamin, Redburn and Lord Jim vicariously succeed), and/or experience rebirth.

IV.62 shadows: of an author's rivalry with his characters [**#III.147; #IV.39**].

IV.63 sandal: Deuteronomy 25:5–10: when one brother dies the other should take his wife as his own; should he not wish to do so the wife shall pull his sandal off his foot and spit in his face: "So it shall be done to the man who does not build up his brother's house. / And its name shall be called in Israel, the house of him that had his sandal pulled off."

IV.64 introspective pilgrimage: Stephen Dedalus, in *Ulysses*, says Ireland is not important because he belongs to it, but because it belongs to him: *argal*, socialism is not important to Sigbjørn because he belongs to it (as Erikson does), but because it belongs to him. This is party treason [**#IV.56**]. His pilgrim 'X' (or 'X plus Y' [**#IV.57**]), unlike Erikson's Wallae, will turn the compass of his soul [**#I.37**] from Russia to the North.

IV.65 Bath Hotel: 3 Bene't Street [**#II.54**].

IV.66 Gustav: Grieg's fireman, who rejects burnt porridge [*Ship Sails On* 51]; witnesses the death of Anton [81ff.]; blames himself [98]; evades his watch when Benjamin joins the stokehold [100]; sits with a prayer book when others go ashore in Cape Town [148]; and proclaims his salvation [168] when many, including Benjamin, are damned.

IV.67 two dimensions: the Consul's "correspondence between the subnormal world itself and the abnormally suspicious delirious one within" [*UTV* 355] entails the recognition that "phantoms" surrounding him correspond "to some faction of his being" [362; **#VII.202**]. Sigbjørn's "not finished" [*consummatum non est*] reflects this imperfect interpenetration between the spiritual and material realms, and the writer's struggle to reconcile them [**#X.24**].

IV.68 name of the ship: Grieg sailed on the *Henrik Ibsen* [**#VIII.46**].

IV.69 Pseudo Dostoeivskian: Lowry told Markson (1951) that the "Dostoievskian brother" [**#I.27**] derides X's book, so enraging A that "inadvertently he causes his brother to turn all his venom on himself in a Dostoievskian scene that leads to the brother's death" [*CL* 2:418].

IV.70 Trygvesen: Olaf Tryggvason, King from 995, reunited the realm of Harald Haarfagre [**#XII.9**], formed a national government, converted the Vikings to Christianity and founded Trondhjem. Charlotte Street lay in the bohemian heart of London's Fitzrovia; 105 is random (the Spectrum Gallery, once home to Albert Ludovici, painter). **A. E. Smith** is unknown.

IV.71 Retach: anagram of 'Chater' [**#IV.55**].

IV.72 Whence came you Benjamin?: hysterical identification [**#IV.3**; **#IV.46**; **#VI.65**].

IV.73 What hast thou man: from Coleridge's deathbed poem, 'Self-Knowledge', which Aiken had used as epigraph to *Blue Voyage*, as he later would for *Ushant*:

> What hast thou, Man, that thou dar'st call thine own?
> What is there in thee, Man, that can be known?

Dark fluxion, all unfixable by thought,
A phantom dim of past and future wrought,
Vain sister of the worm,—life, death, soul, clod,
Ignore thyself, and strive to know thy God!

IV.74 Cain shall not: commit fratricide [**#I.45**; **#III.45**; **#XVIII.29**]; **Judas shall not**: betray Jesus [**#III.130**]. Today.

IV.75 dark scroll: God's parchment unwinding [**#III.151**]. In the 1933 *Ultramarine*, life opens "like a blurred scroll read in a dark dream" [18; in Lowry's copy, struck through]; in 'Work in Progress' (1951) death is inscribed on "the accepted manuscript of one's life" [74].

IV.76 Plotinus Plinlimmon: in Melville's *Pierre; or, The Ambiguities* (1852), the flamboyant author of a pamphlet found by Pierre Glendinning, a would-be writer, "metaphysically and insufferably" entitled 'Chronometricals & Horologicals' [Bk. XIV]. Such time-keeping distinguishes between Christ's "chronometrical morality", which cannot be acted on locally, and "horological maxims" that are false to higher truth; absolute opposed to relative virtue. *Pierre* is considered either a satire of Transcendentalism (*Plotinus* a 3rd-century neo-Platonist; *Plinlimmon* ["Five rivers"] a Welsh mountain), or the *reductio* of Melville's mysteries [**#VI.72**], fires of Optimism leaving the ashes of despair.

IV.77: (not written): Aiken's final intrusion [*Blue Voyage* 345] on Demarest's increasingly vain attempts to say just what he means [**#IV.3**].

CHAPTER V

V.1 [Epigraph] W. H. Hudson: (1841–1922), a British naturalist who lived in Patagonia. 'El Ombú', in *Tales of the Pampas* (1902), describes a house, now ruined; and Don Santos Ugarte, its misfortunate owner. Lowry mildly misquotes [see **#V.12**; and the Textual Notes]. In *Far Away and Long Ago* (1918), an armadillo (an Infernal Machine) pulls Hudson into the earth [IV; UTV 113].

V.2 Exchange Flagstones: a large square in Liverpool's commercial district, behind the Town Hall. An Exchange Building opened in 1808, but business was often conducted "on the Flags" (flagstones) until a purpose-built Cotton Exchange, where Arthur Lowry had his office, opened in Old Hall Street (1906).

V.3 railway station: originally Tithebarn Street Station (1850), terminus of the Ormskirk and Preston railway that Sigbjørn will take; renamed Liverpool Exchange (1888), with links to Manchester Victoria, Glasgow Central, and the north. Damaged in WWII, it closed in 1977. The "incredible turmoil" arises from the Underground below [**#VI.4**], the Overhead at the foot of Water Street [**#VI.7**], and railway viaducts north of the Flags.

V.4 many-voiced Mersey: the deep "Moans round with many voices" in Tennyson's 'Ulysses'; 'misery' is naval slang for *Mersey*. The "terrible city" offered two enduring visions: the "lunatic city" inside which Lowry felt trapped; and the pathway to the sea, "the risk-laden escape route from lunacy into uncertainty" [Bowker 2; **V.34**].

V.5 organic absoluteness: as cited in the 'Varsity' CB: Edwin Muir in 'The Contemporary Novel' (1934) argued that Joyce's *Ulysses*, by breaking into another kind of present, "complex and multi-facetted", destroys "the traditional organic absoluteness of the present" [74]; whereas Kafka's *Castle* [**#X.1**] offers an "absolute protest" against the philosophy of flux.

V.6 tartars: swarthy persons of vaguely Asiatic origin languishing in Liverpool; ***lascars***: Indian sailors and militiamen, serving on British ships under special 'Lascar' agreements that gave owners control (cheap labour) over their conditions.

V.7 *Thorstein . . . Brynjarr*: ill-fated ships of the Tarnmoor Line [**#I.18**; **#II.83**].

V.8 underwriter's room: an attractive room in the Exchange Buildings, as Lloyd's of London, to accommodate "gentlemen concerned in the business of the insurance of ships", and "supplied with shipping intelligence, newspapers, &c" [*Picture of Liverpool* 104]. **Tostrup** was in Oslo a respected name [**#XVIII.52**].

V.9 Edvard Munch: expressionist painter (1863–1944), who fought a disapproving father and repressive environment to become Norway's best-known artist [**#XVIII.39**]. Munch held his first exhibition (1892) in the Tostrup building, *Karl Johans gate*.

V.10 furled sails: rolled up and bound to the spar, anticipating a storm.

V.11 spread-eagled: "breaking on the wheel" (St. Catharine), a horrendous mode of execution with excruciating variants: the victim lashed to a wagon wheel, limbs broken as it turned, the mangled remains (yet alive) braided through the spokes and raised for birds to eat.

V.12 Banks of Despair: shallow shoals, Bunyanesque emphasis given by, um, *capitalization*. **Cape Desolation**, at the entrance to the Magellan Channel [**#XII.49**], was named by Captain Cook because total bleakness followed. Lowry's "ends of the earth" amplifies Hudson [**#V.1**].

V.13 winch: a mechanism to wind a rope. A ***windlass*** (horizontal winch) sits on the foredeck, its ratchet geared to control the anchor (a vertical winch is a *capstan*).

V.14 Lord Nelson: the Nelson Monument, bronze statuary on a basement of Westmoreland marble, at the centre of the Flags [**#V.2**]: honouring Horatio, first Viscount Nelson (1758–1805), victorious in death at Trafalgar (21 Oct. 1805). The tableau, or *Apotheosis Group*, depicts a defiant Nelson, one foot on a cannon and the other on a "rolling foe" [*Redburn* XXXI]; a flag conceals his lost right arm. Victory crowns her hero as Death emerges from a fallen flag [**#V.24**]; Britannia, kneeling, mourns her lost son; and a lance-wielding seaman advances, to avenge his death [**#V.22**]. The plinth proclaims, above four prisoners enchained: 'England expects every man to do his duty' [**#V.23**]. This "obscure statue in an obscure square" was, Lowry told Gerald Noxon, "a favorite place of assignation" [CL 1:429 (1943)].

V.15 chains: the prisoners depicted on the Monument remind Redburn of "African slaves in the market-place" [*Redburn* XXXI], and Liverpool's history of slavery. A **ringbolt** is a bolt with a captive ring at one end and threaded at the other; attaching each prisoner to the mouths of laurelled lions beneath the plinth. These abject figures, often associated with slavery (William Roscoe, the major donor, was an abolitionist), represent captives from Nelson's triumphs.

V.16 Tithebarn Street and Dale Street: continuing Chapel and Water Streets north-east, beyond Exchange. Hugh pawned guitars "in Tithebarn Street" [UTV 155].

V.17 Abraham . . . blunderbuss: Abraham, obedient to God, prepared to sacrifice Isaac, his son [Genesis 2]. D'Israeli's *Curiosities of Literature* [**#X.27**] recalls a "laughable" Dutch picture, Abraham with a blunderbuss (a muzzle-loader), and an angel "urining in the pan".

V.18 rail: the Monument was briefly railed off, enclosure dates uncertain. The Flags form a **quadrangle**, bounded on three sides by offices, and, to the south, by the back façade of the old Town Hall. The Cotton Exchange was in the eastern wing [**#V.2**].

V.19 Erected in 1813: the monument has no inscription. The Captain "reads" Thomas Kaye's *Picture of Liverpool* (1834): "In the centre of the area . . . was erected in the year 1813, a splendid bronze monument to the memory of the immortal Lord Nelson. It was modelled and cast by Richard Westmacott, Esq., RA, from designs, by Mathew Charles Wyatt, Esq. The whole expense, mounting to £9000, was raised by public subscription" [65–66]. The crowns designate Nelson's "glorious achievements": St. Vincent (1797); the Nile (1798); Copenhagen (1801) [**#V.30**; **#V.147**]; and Trafalgar (1805). The "four figures" represent French prisoners, emblematic of "the subdued and humbled condition of those enemies who had aimed to bring England into subjection" [66–67].

V.20 Angels Four: in Melville's poem, 'Healed of My Hurt' [**#VI.75**].

V.21 crowning the hero's sword: Victory rewards the "gallant hero" by "presenting to him a fourth naval crown, received on the point of his sword" [*Picture* 66]. The *Victory* was Nelson's final command. A skeletal figure of Death, reaching from the fallen flag to clutch with bony hand at Nelson's heart, fascinates Redburn: "A very striking design, and true to the imagination; I could never look at Death without a shudder" [XXXI].

V.22 Britannia: an emblematic woman armed with shield and spear and wearing a Greek helmet, as on British coinage. Kneeling behind Nelson, she is "overwhelmed with the sense of her loss" [*Picture* 66]. By the 1930s the "dauntless seaman" had lost his lance and rust had stained his brawny arm. The "handsome sailor of fiction" is Billy Budd.

V.23 'England expects every man to do his duty': Nelson's command, from *HMS Victory*, as battle began. The signal read 'will do', but *to* persists in popular parlance, as on the plinth.

V.24 lost hand: as Victory proffers the fourth Crown [**#V.21**], "the maimed limb is concealed by the enemy's flag" [Kaye, *Stranger in Liverpool* 231].

V.25 Benito Cereno: Melville's novella, in *The Piazza Tales* (1856), about a slave rebellion (1799) on a Spanish merchantman, its crew forced to act naturally when an American vessel offers assistance. As the captain, Benito Cereno, tells his story he faints and is sustained by the Negro who seems his attentive servant, but is Babo, ruthless leader of the insurrection. Delano, the American captain, belatedly redresses the situation.

V.26 Henderson . . . Currie . . . Booth: Sir Arthur **Henderson** (1863–1935), Labour politician and Leader of the Opposition. As Foreign Secretary under Ramsay MacDonald he worked with the USSR and League of Nations, winning the Nobel Peace Prize (1934). Lacking a knighthood, he was diplomatically called Sir Arthur. George **Currie**, of the *Wanderer*, a Liverpool barque built in 1891 and dismasted off Tuscar Rock (Wexford) that October, was killed by a falling yard. Masefield's *Wanderer of Liverpool* (1930) calls him "a perfect sea-captain . . . at his best in a gale" [28]. William **Booth** founded the Salvation Army [**#IX.4**].

V.27 Wormwood: the bitter star of Revelation 8:1 [**#III.73**].

V.28 cotton porters: responsible for moving cotton bales from the docks, after "lumpers" had unstowed them, to the Exchange; then stacking, weighing, marking, and reloading them to send (by truck, train, or barge) to the mills. During the Depression they struggled to find work.

V.29 died of grief: a nation's sorrow enters the Captain's allusion [**#V.51**].

V.30 Copenhagen: Nelson led the attack (2 April 1801), famously disobeying Admiral Sir Hyde Parker's order to withdraw. He had lost his right eye in Corsica (1793); receiving Parker's signal on his flagship, the *Elephant*, he told his Flag Captain, Foley, that he had only one eye; then, holding the telescope to his blind eye, said he really could not see the signal [**#V.147**]. With Copenhagen threatened with bombardment a settlement was quickly signed.

V.31 fair-haired people: intimating *The Long Journey* [**#II.92; #X.73**]. Chesterton in the *Illustrated London News* [14 May 1910; rpt. in Chesterton 526] mocked the Aryan supremacy that Jensen affirms:

> that Europe was divided into dark-haired people and fair-haired people, and that all the good had come from the fair-haired people and all the bad from the dark-haired people. Also all the fair-haired people lived in the north of Europe and loved light, liberty, justice, and civilisation; while, on the other hand, all the dark-haired people lived in the south of Europe, and were very fond of darkness, misery, oppression, superstition, and failure.

V.32 Tonio Kröger: protagonist of Thomas Mann's *Tonio Kröger* (1903), his name reflecting the conflict between his Mediterranean and Nordic origins. A respected but disillusioned writer in southern Germany travels to his ancestral Denmark, escaping from aesthetics, to find his parents' house now a **Public Library**. Mistaken for an escaped criminal, he is questioned by the police, but allowed to continue his voyage. The story ends with him confessing to a fellow artist how love for humanity has surmounted alienation.

V.33 'drunk for salties': a 'salt-box', or brig for drunken sailors.

V.34 long-drawn moan: compare "one long continuous moan"; the words (in the 'Varsity' CB) of a witness at the *Titanic* inquiry, of those not saved [**#V.4**]. In the DATG typescript, Lowry added, "tears for the dead who shall not come homeward to any shore or any life. (In relation to this also the ships that sank in In Ballast to the White Sea . . . Adriane N. Pandelis, etc)" [UBC 9:22, 691].

V.35 Micawber: hopelessly optimistic, as Wilkins Micawber in *David Copperfield* (1850), always confident that "something will turn up".

V.36 film cartoon: Exchange Street West [**#V.135**], fancied as a cartoon cul-de-sac, then a narrow gulch in the "bad lands" of a cheap Western.

V.37 Bodega: a tavern visited by Des Esseintes, on his "long journey" in Huysmans' *À rebours* [**#V.41**; **#V.97**]. A curiosity: *La Bodega* (1905), by Vicente Blasco Ibánez, has a hero named Fermín.

V.38 starboard,—no, port my helm: by the old rules [**#III.31**], Sigbjørn's first impulse is correct, as "Port your helm" commands the helmsman to turn the wheel to starboard; under the new code his revision applies. Hence the *Brynjaar* disaster. Sigbjørn later "instinctively" turns the wrong way to avoid a collision, almost causing one [**#XI.38**].

V.39 we know where we are: as Melville's Bartleby, imprisoned: "I know where I am." The Captain echoes his earlier "**dooms**" [**#III.7**; **#III.148**].

V.40 idiotic refrain: compare the "verse of idiot creaking" later in the chapter with "A verse of idiotic clang reeled dully in his brain" [U 172]; from "Der slingrer et vers i min hjerne / av sløv, idiotisk klang", in Grieg's early poem, 'Stormnatt' [Night of Storm].

V.41 San Lucar . . . *Cockburn's*: Des Esseintes visits the Bodega [**#V.37**; **#V.97**]:

> He looked about him. Here, the great casks stood in a row, their labels announcing a whole series of ports, strong, fruity wines, mahogany or amaranth coloured, distinguished by laudatory titles, such as "Old Port," "Light Delicate," "Cockburn's Very Fine," "Magnificent Old Regina"; there, rounding their formidable bellies, crowded side by side enormous hogsheads containing the martial wine of Spain, the sherries and their congeners, topaz coloured whether light or dark,—San Lucar, Pasto, Pale Dry, Oloroso, Amontillado, sweet or dry. [*Against the Grain* XI]

V.42 lighthouse: Lowry's first (unpublished) anthology, *The Lighthouse Invites the Storm*, intimating Henryk Sienkiewicz, *The Lighthouse-Keeper* (1882). Compare the Farolito: "The Lighthouse, the lighthouse that invites the storm, and lights it!" [UTV 200]. The image is of self-destruction, the light inviting the ship to ground herself on the rocks it illuminates.

V.43 falls slowly: in Auden's 'Musée des beaux artes' (1938), Icarus dies in humdrum circumstances. The poem was too late for *In Ballast*, but Lowry shares Auden's inspiration, Pieter Brueghel's *Landscape with the Fall of Icarus* (1560) [**#XI.16**]. 'The lighthouse invites the storm' [CP #87] features "Icarus' circus plunge".

V.44 hanging hill: Castle Hill, Cambridge [**#I.32**].

V.45 Valparaiso: "Valley of Paradise", Chile, a refuge from Cape Horn: "the earth was a ship, lashed by the Horn's tail, doomed never to make her Valparaiso" [UTV 287]. The rhythm is that of 'Prufrock': women "come and go / Talking of Michaelangelo."

V.46 White Ship: sunk in the Channel off the French coast (25 Nov. 1120), after striking a rock, with only one survivor. Those drowned included William Adelin, only legitimate son of Henry I. No ship, they said, brought so much misery to England; Stephen de Blois usurped the throne, and the Anarchy followed.

V.47 trick wheel: the pun reminds the Captain, relentlessly, of the *Brynjaar* [**#III.33**]. The ***foc'sle head*** is the foredeck, where the regular wheel is mounted.

V.48 dhoby: a *dhobi* collects and washes dirty linen [**#XII.50**]. In 'West Hardaway' [P&S 30], Dana does his "dhoby". The Captain means he has worked as a hardy seaman, but echoes Nelson's dying words: "Thank God, I have done my washing."

V.49 handy-billy: a winch assembled from a double and single block (pulley).

V.50 delirium: in Hudson's 'El Ombú' [43; **#V.1**], Nicandro, an old gaucho, tells of Donata, who waters each day the spot where her husband Valerio died: "A great grief is like a delirium, and sometimes gives us strange thoughts, and makes us act like demented persons."

V.51 the crazed live many years: in 'El Ombú' [67], Monica is distraught when she learns of the death of Bruno, Donata's son: "Some have died of pure grief—did it not kill Donata in the end?—but the crazed may live many years. We sometimes think it would be better if they were dead; but not in all cases—not, señor, in this" [**#V.29**].

V.52 mysteries: secret rites and rituals (Orphic, Bacchic, Eleusinian, Cabbalistic), known to adepts and intimates, leading to enlightenment. Ouspensky's *New Model of the Universe* (1931), which Lowry recommended to Margerie's mother as a "rewarding book" [CL 1:314], calls them the journey of the soul [*New Model* 26]. For "let loose", see **#IX.5**.

V.53 *Moby Dick*: wherein call-me-Ishmael recounts the search for Moby-Dick, a white sperm whale on whom Ahab seeks revenge for his leg, lost in a previous encounter. The vendetta ends when Ahab harpoons the whale, which rams the *Pequod*, destroying its crew. 'The Whiteness of the Whale' [XLII] identifies the "malicious agencies" of Nature; the Captain's '*dual*' expresses the interpenetration of two realms: "in the world, transcending" [**#V.91**].

V.54 Melville stood here: in November 1856, travelling to the Holy Land to seek spiritual assurance, Melville reached Liverpool, where Hawthorne was Consul [**#IV.7**]. They spent time together, congenially, but Hawthorne recorded in his *English Notebooks* that Melville suffered from "too constant literary preoccupation" and a "morbid state of mind": he "began to reason of Providence and futurity, and of everything that lies beyond human ken, and informed me that he had 'pretty much made up his mind to be annihilated'" [**#VII.2**]. This was said on Southport sands [**#VI.70**], north of Liverpool, Hawthorne having left Rock Ferry.

V.55 spiritual ally: Melville regretted that his longing to discuss "ontological heroics" with Hawthorne (in a letter of 29 June 1851) aroused no comparable ardour; compare the Lowry/Grieg and Sigbjørn/Erikson meetings. Melville did not believe Hawthorne "had written his own books better", but his review of *Mosses from an Old Manse* (1850) had earlier admitted, "this Hawthorne has dropped germinous seeds into my soul".

V.56 *hyrkontrakt*: Nor. *hyre kontrakt*, the formal agreement outlining the conditions of Sigbjørn's hire (Lowry's word, oddly, is Swedish). See the Textual Notes [**#X.5**].

V.57 *Unsgaard*: recorded in the 'Varsity' CB, first in a list of sailors (Qvam, the Bull, Silverhjelm, Nicholas Skull), then as a ship (Nina, Fidèle). Unsgaard, central Denmark, is home to Bang's Ida Brandt and Rilke's Malte Laurids Brigge [**#V.132; #IX.30**].

V.58 Aasgaard: Åsgård, citadel of the Aesir, ruled by Odin and Freya, as recorded in the *Gylfaginning* [Tricking of Gylfi] of Snorri Sturluson (1179–1241), who predicts *Ragnarök*, the twilight of the gods. Mumford supplies the Melville link: "the old Norse myths told that Asgard itself would be conquered at last, and the very gods would be destroyed: the white whale is the symbol of that very force of destruction" [184–85].

V.59 Norsk Konsulat: 29 South Castle Street (no longer extant), Liverpool, Johan Vogt, Vice-Consul; where Sigbjørn obtained "the green Norwegian discharge book" [**#XIII.30**]. Hugh signed on with the Marine Superintendent in Garston [UTV 157]; Lowry at the Company office (India Buildings, Water Street), three days before sailing [Bowker 65]. Lowry outlined to Markson [CL 2:427] a scene where 'A' returns to Liverpool to sign on at the Consulate, there being none in Preston, and meets his brother. In *October Ferry* [236ff], Ethan's younger brother,

Gwyn, a trimmer on a vessel in ballast from Preston to Archangel, was lost at sea off Aalesund [**#XVIII.15**]. The two drank at Exchange before Gwyn leaves; at Preston he could not sign on, so returned to the *Konsulat*, and again met Ethan. This attempt to integrate *In Ballast* within the unending *Voyage* entails (Lowry admits) a third brother.

V.60 *D.S. Unsgaard* . . . *Archangel/Leningrad*: "the Steamship *Unsgaard*, Sigbjørn Tarnmoor, fireman . . . the ship's voyage from Preston to Archangel/Leningrad" [**#I.51**; **#V.56**; **#X.5**]; 'D/S' (*Dampskibet*) is "the steam-ship".

V.61 Larvik: southwest Norway, once a whaling port. Lowry's *Fagervik* ("fair bay") was built there (1922), for Nilson, Nyquist & Co., Oslo. Bombed and sunk in Narvik (May 1940), she was salvaged and continued service until 1969.

V.62 *Sequancia*: unregistered.

V.63 Nantucket: an island south of Cape Cod, heart of the whaling industry; the *Pequod* leaves from there. To Starbuck, her first mate, "two thirds of this terraceous globe are the Nantucketer's. For the sea is his, he owns it . . . he alone resides and riots on the sea" [*Moby-Dick* XIV]. By 1850, even as Melville was writing, US whaling had declined: "there are no whaling ships in New Bedford now: the Norwegians maintain the trade" [Mumford 26].

V.64 'Sconset: *Siasconset*, as this Nantucket town is rarely called, means "near the great whale bone". Larvik, like 'Sconset, is an attractive settlement no longer important.

V.65 *Baltimore Clipper*: Redburn sups at the *Sign of the Baltimore Clipper*, flanked by "the British Unicorn and American Eagle" [*Redburn* XXVIII]. Liverpool had no such pub [**#VI.54**]; but an *American Eagle* nested in Paradise Street (the hotel long gone, the Eagle remains). Baltimore Clippers were agile two-masters; the word defines ships of exceptional speed and beauty.

V.66 Riddough's Hotel: in his "prosy old guidebook" (the 1808 *Picture of Liverpool* [**#V.19**]), Redburn reads his father's hand: "Walter Redburn / Riddough's Royal Hotel / Liverpool, March 20th, 1808". He cannot find the hotel, at the foot of Lord Street: previously *Bates Hotel* (1805 edition), it became 'Riddiough's [sic] Royal Hotel' [1808 edition, 174], before the area was turned into shops.

V.67 starving woman: Redburn sees in Launcelott's Hey, an alley lined with prison-like cotton warehouses, what once had been a woman, clutching a dead babe to her shrunken bosom. Assistance is vain, and she and two other children are soon dead [XXVII].

V.68 second time: Melville first visited Liverpool as a boy on the St. *Lawrence* (1839); he returned in 1856 [**#V.66**]. Back from Jerusalem, he revisited Hawthorne (4 May 1857), who did not record this visit.

V.69 Russia: like many intellectuals, before Stalin's excesses were known. H. G. Wells (1920) insisted that decay was not the product of Bolshevism but the cause. Shaw met Stalin (1931), and dismissed stories of famine as slanderous: "I saw no underfed people there, and the children were remarkably plump" [Preface, *On the Rocks*].

V.70 weren't a writer: Erikson remarks, "in the end, *you* kill *me*" [**#XVIII.36; #XVIII.61**].

V.71 de l'isle Adam: Jean Marie Mathias Philippe Auguste, Comte de Villiers de l'Isle-Adam (1838–1888), Symbolist aesthete, whose "cruel jeering, a gloomy jesting" resembled Swift's "black rage against humanity" [*Against the Grain* XIV].

V.72 watch ticking: Ethan, having run to his room [**#III.143**], wakes at dawn, with a heart beating in his ear, growing fainter. Aware that if he roused his landlord and the police, Peter would be indicted or imprisoned, certainly sent down, and hence "would commit suicide anyway", he returned to sleep, waking with a hangover and a farewell letter in his pocket [OF 215]. 'Thirty-five Mescals in Cuautla' [CP #25] insists: "This ticking is most terrible of all . . . You hear it everywhere, for it is doom; / The tick of real death, not the tick of time." In Aiken's *Great Circle*, this is the death-watch beetle [**#V.130; #VI.40**]. Poe's 'The Tell-Tale Heart' tells of one who affirms his sanity after murdering an old man, but whose guilt creates the delusion that the heart still beats, with a low, dull sound, like a watch enveloped in cotton.

V.73 St. Mary's clock: see **#I.44**.

V.74 delayed sending an S.O.S. call: like the *Vestris* [**#VII.19**].

V.75 Mother Carey's pigeons: Mother Carey's chickens [**#VII.60**], *Oceanites oceanicus*, storm-petrels reputed to brood upon the ocean. 'Mother Carey' derives from *Mater cara*, an epithet of Mary for the Portuguese sailors who first saw them.

V.76 black French collier: a "Shadow" of the White Ship [**#V.46**].

V.77 trembling in every mast: like Vigil Forget [CP #78], sailing to oblivion [**#VII.201**].

V.78 inquest: Ethan says: "of course I didn't tell the truth at the inquest, partly for Father's sake, partly to defend myself" [OF 215; **#III.125**].

V.79 name-plate had disappeared: noted earlier [**#III.4**], and later [**#VII.36**].

V.80 stir of fellowship: James Thomson, *City of Dreadful Night* (1874), 'Proem' [stanza 5]; anticipated in *Ultramarine* [186]:

> Yes, here and there some weary wanderer
> In that same city of tremendous night,
> Will understand the speech and feel a stir
> Of fellowship in all-disastrous fight;
> "I suffer mute and lonely, yet another
> Uplifts his voice to let me know a brother
> Travels the same wild paths though out of sight."

V.81 viewless winds: Claudio's terror: "To be imprisoned in the viewless winds, / And blown with restless violence round about / The pendent world" [*Measure for Measure* III.i.124–26].

V.82 Immelmann turn: an aerial manoeuvre attributed to Max Immelmann (1890–1916), WWI German ace; an ascending half-loop and a half roll, changing course 180 degrees. The plane, from the opening page, intimates that power for good watching over all [**#II.23**].

V.83 *later than you think*: an evangelical warning, from Robert Service: "Yet I glower at pen and ink: / Oh, inspire me, Muse, I pray, / *It is later than you think*." For the "Low Archway", see **#VIII.2**. The two are walking towards Canning Dock.

V.84 fall of man: the sin of disobedience in Eden, the Captain says, let something loose, "mysterious as the first cause of all things" [**#IX.5**; **#XVIII.55**]. Milton asks, "say first what cause / Moved our grand parents in that happy state, / . . . to fall off from their Creator" [*Paradise Lost* I.28–31]. Liverpool's Paradise Street lurks nearby [**#V.88**].

V.85 great circle: the intersection of a sphere and a plane passing through its centre (as of the earth); an arc connecting two points on this figure. Aiken dissuaded Lowry from plagiarizing his 1932 novel of that name [**#XI.26**].

V.86 gradient: from the docks, up Canning Place to Paradise Street. The "strange comfort" anticipates that 'Afforded by the Profession'.

V.87 dramatise that book: Lowry told Grieg (1939) he had adapted *The Ship Sails On* [CL 1:192], but nothing survives beyond two rough pages in an early 1929 draft of *Ultramarine* [Huntington, AIK 3381]. The DATG typescript notes the ambition "to dramatise his masterly novel about Norwegian merchant seamen, somewhat in the manner of O'Neill" [UBC 9:5, 343]. 'The Ordeal of Sigbjørn Wilderness' recalls "that manuscript of the play he wrote with Gulbransen", adding unhelpfully, "if he ever wrote it" [UBC 22:19, 117].

V.88 Gladstone Place: *Canning Place*, two Prime Ministers transposed in jest (Gladstone rehabilitated prostitutes). This rare violation of topology [**#V.103**] offers a marriage of heaven and hell, with Salvationist halls nearby but red lights equally so. The **Sailor's Institute** is either the Liverpool Sailors' Home, in Canning Place at Paradise Street (demolished 1973): an 1840s philanthropic venture with "cabins" rather than rooms, offering sailors respite from the sea, grog-shops and "nightingales"; or, in nearby Hanover Street, with similar aims, the Gordon Smith Institute, the Liverpool Seamen's Friends Society and Bethel Union (1820).

V.89 crowd: Redburn in St. George's Square hears a Chartist addressing an orderly throng, which the police disperse. The 1930s saw the Trade Union movement grow, and entrenched authority resisting that; depression, unemployment, and declining trade often erupted as street protest. On 13 September 1932 (Lowry was in Liverpool), 10,000 unemployed assembled, the police making arrests and indiscriminate baton charges.

V.90 Post Office Road: the crowd has carried them past Old Post Office Place [*sic*], between Church Street and School Lane, towards the shopping centre [**#V.95**].

V.91 dual: echoing the Captain [**#V.53**].

V.92 meet yourself: Peer Gynt, after long wandering, returns to his mother, but meets at the crossroads his Other. In the Farolito, a fair young man embodies what once the Consul was [UTV 360]. Stephen quotes Maeterlinck thus [*Ulysses* IX; **#V.102**].

V.93 Preston with timber: in 'Hotel Room in Chartres', near St. Prest [P&S 23], the narrator recalls *Prester* and timber from Archangel [**#XIII.23**].

V.94 horizon: in *Ultramarine*: "those who carried the whole horizon of their lives in their pocket" [36]; or 'China': "you carry your horizon in your pocket wherever you are" [P&S 54]. Lowry's source is Grieg's poem, 'Rund Kap det gode Haab', in which the weary soul goes about his daily work "og bærer med sig i lommen hele sitt lives horisont" [and carries in his pocket the entire horizon of his life].

V.95 shopping centre: in Church Street, near Liverpool Central and Lime Street stations, Joe Passilique and Dana Hilliot see mothers in warm-smelling furs "fussing with their school-capped sons into the Bon Marché" ['Goya' 277; U 73].

V.96 trams: to various suburbs: **Calderstones**, Allerton, named for its Neolithic stone relics [**#VII.8**]; **Old Swan**, an inner-city suburb, after an old pub at the A57 junction; **London Road**, from the inner city to the University of Liverpool;

Islington, a district of Vauxhall; **Mossley Hill**, south, near Allerton; **Aintree**, north, home of the Grand National [**#XII.10**].

V.97 Huysmans: Joris-Karl Huysmans (1848–1907), author of *À rebours* (1884), translated anonymously as *Against the Grain* (1903). Des Esseintes, indulging his love of Dickens, decides to see London. Awaiting his train he visits a bookstore (to buy a guide), then a tavern full of Dickensian characters, to dine on English dishes. Holland, he recalls, disappointed compared with his picture, built of Dutch paintings; *ergo*, there is no point going to London. He and Chapter XI conclude: "What was the good of moving, when a man can travel so gloriously sitting in a chair? Was he not in London, whose odours and atmosphere, whose denizens and viands and table furniture were all about him? What could he expect, if he really went there, save fresh disappointments, the same as in Holland?" He returns home, feeling "the physical exhaustion and moral fatigue of a man restored to the domestic hearth after long and perilous journeyings." His "long journey" [**#II.92**; **#V.37**; **#X.73**] mocks Sigbjørn's.

V.98 'a strong city': Proverbs 18:19: "A brother offended is harder to be won than a strong city: and their contentions are like the **bars of a castle**."

V.99 P.S.N.C. . . . R.M.S.P.C.: the **Pacific Steam Navigation Company**, their Liverpool office in the Pacific Building, James Street, offering passages to South America; and the **Royal Mail Steam Packet Company**, a British agency founded by James Macqueen in 1839, for South America, the West Indies, and Caribbean. Operating from St. Thomas in the Danish Virgin Islands, it brought that colony brief prosperity. The world's largest shipping company when it acquired the White Star Line (1927) [**#XI.44**], it ran onto financial rocks: its affairs were investigated, the Chairman (Lord Kylsant) imprisoned for misrepresentation, and the company restructured. **La Paz**, the capital of Bolivia, is land-locked, but PSNC had a ship so-named. **Buenos Aires** was an RMSPC destination on trips to Brazil and Argentina. **Batavia**, or Jakarta, capital of the Dutch East Indies, was far from these routes, but the Blue Funnel Line ran to Freemantle via Singapore, Batavia, and Darwin.

V.100 finer mountains: from Edward Thomas, *A Literary Pilgrim in England* (1917). Keats planned a northern tour (1819): "to gain experience, rub off prejudice, enlarge his vision, load himself with finer mountains, strengthen his poetry" [40; U 186]. The chapter concludes with Keats, coughing blood, about to catch the steamer "carrying him to his Roman grave" [43].

V.101 stole my birthright: as Esau did Jacob (Genesis 25:30–34), gaining his brother's inheritance for a mess of pottage.

V.102 Maeterlinck: Maurice Maeterlinck (1862–1949), Belgian writer and Nobel laureate (1911). Lowry admired *Pelléas et Mélisande* (1892), and Debussy's opera thereof (1902); two brothers vying for one girl strikes various triangles. *The Unknown Guest* (1913), exploring precognition, argues in Chapter III that there are perceptions not of a pure future as a present not yet known; the "unknown guest" is that impulse within that permits some, acuter than others, "to capture a warning" from beyond the limited present that most experience. These ideas "float in the air" [**#II.39**].

V.103 Lord Street . . . Mount Pleasant: swept into Paradise Street, the two follow School Lane and Old Post Office Place [**#V.90**] into Church Street, then Ranelagh Street to Ranelagh Place and the Adelphi Hotel [**#V.116**], briefly into Brownlow Hill, and Mount Pleasant, an elevated road leading southeast (away from the Flags). The "steepest part of the gradient of Lord Street" is misleading: Ranelagh Street branches off Church Street (a continuation of Lord Street); but Lowry intimates Calvary: 'Paradise', 'Church', 'Lord', and 'Gethsemane'.

V.104 put-up job: God's workings, like those of higher mathematics, are mysterious, though the **gradient** reifies their empirical consequence. The Captain's "**What do we know?**" echoes Grieg [*Ship Sails On* 80], and Tor [**#III.67**]. **Gethsemane** and a flicker of betrayal provoke Sigbjørn to cast himself as Judas: again, ideas "float in the air" [**#II.39**; **#III.91**; **#V.102**].

V.105 Great Homer Street: north of Mount Pleasant, in the Vauxhall area [**#V.134**], where Andy Bredahl (*Ultramarine*) lives. Joe Passilique evades a syphilitic policeman gliding down this street ['Goya' 271]; Dana imagines himself there, stricken with disease [U 73].

V.106 Pier Head: St. George's Pier, terminus for Liverpool trams [**#VII.1**; **#XIII.27**], Mersey and Isle of Man ferries [**#VI.39**]. Water Street channels the conceit of tributaries [**#VI.7**].

V.107 incline: like that of Quauhnahuac [UTV 6]. The **Century Theatre**, "Home of Unusual Films", once a Wesleyan chapel, was a Mount Pleasant cinema featuring such rarities as Fejos's *Last Moment* [**#III.81**] and Pudovkin's expressionist works [**#III.79**].

V.108 *End of St. Petersburg*: a silent film (1927, eighty minutes), directed by Vsevolod Pudovkin (1893–1953), Russian master of montage; one of a trilogy filmed for the tenth anniversary of the October Revolution. Pudovkin charts the fall of the city. His hero, a politically awakened peasant (played by Ivan Chuleyov), comes for work but is drawn into events; he accidently betrays a friend, a labour leader. Sent to the capitalist war, he returns, steeled for revolution. The staged scenes are vividly realistic. Lowry told Gerald Noxon the film had made him weep, by its "sheer beauty" [CL 1:324 (1941)].

V.109 Kerensky: the Provisional Government of Alexander Kerensky (1881–1970), leader of the February revolution (1917), deposed Nicholas II. Kerensky became Minister of Justice, then Prime Minister; but his liberal policies and handling of the war met disapproval. Opposed by Lenin, he lost support in Petrograd, as the city was renamed. After the October Revolution, power passed to the Soviets; and Kerensky, after futile attempts to regain control, took exile. These words do not match the real subtitles. **No compromise!** was a Bolshevik slogan, before the revolution to reject Kerensky's wish to negotiate, and after, when the Conciliationists tried to exclude Lenin and Trotsky from coalition. The film ends with the revolutionaries triumphant [**#V.114**], though Bolshevik control and proletariat ideology was not yet assured.

V.110 University: Liverpool (1881), a leading "red brick" academy.

V.111 Barbary coast: northwest Africa, synonymous with pirates and slavery; also, a 1935 film, directed by Howard Hawks, set in San Francisco's "Barbary Coast". Bob Hope and Bing Crosby's *Road to Morocco* (1942) parodies the formula; like Webster's *Dictionary*, Redburn's guidebook [**#V.66**] is morocco-bound.

V.112 God help us all: not in the subtitles; but iconic crosses on the graves of dead soldiers reject a faith that offers no bread.

V.113 worker's wife: Vera Baranovskaia provides the human interest in Pudovkin's film [**#V.108**], as she loses her Bolshevist husband then regains him. She guides the peasant from political naiveté to Marxist consciousness, and when he is wounded at the **Winter Palace** tends his injuries. The film celebrates her resilience: though starving, she shares (from a tin pail) her few **potatoes** with the revolutionaries.

V.114 Winter Palace: on the Neva; once the royal residence, now the Hermitage. Kerensky's headquarters [**#V.109**], it was stormed in the October Revolution, a defining moment in the Soviet state. A signal from the fortress of Peter and Paul tells the revolutionaries to attack, and the film ends with "Long live the city of Lenin". St. Petersburg (from 1914, Petrograd) became **Leningrad** only after Lenin's death (1924); when Soviet Russia collapsed (1991), it reverted to St. Petersburg.

V.115 continuous performance: cinemas typically reran programs (newsreels, cartoons, main features), patrons coming and going at will. A charred fragment of the revised typescript suggests Mickey [Mouse] as one "short" [UBC 12:14].

V.116 Adelphi Hotel: Liverpool's largest hotel, in Ranelagh Place at Renshaw and Lime, opened 1826 and rebuilt 1912. In 20,000 *Leagues under the Sea*, the salon of the *Nautilus* is like the Adelphi. A **Delphic statement** is an ambiguous utterance, typical of the Delphic Oracle; the Captain, swayed by 'Adelphi' [brothers], implies Oedipal complexities.

V.117 garish poster: the original Russian poster for the *End of St. Petersburg* (designed by Israel Bograd) offered a striking pose, black against red, of the Bronze Horseman; this one depicts the hero against an urban backdrop, soldiers in readiness and icons crumbling.

V.118 not to know: that is, the agony of consciousness; rather than, as Sigbjørn understands, not to acquire knowledge. Compare the "two obliterations" [**#II.27**].

V.119 'different pilgrimage': as Tor's man who "passes down the road" [**#II.79**].

V.120 Lime Street: earlier Limekiln Lane, after the kilns there. The area from Mount Pleasant to Lime Street Station was known for its "Maggy Mays", or lamp-lit ladies, its cinemas and theatres. It attracted gatherings like *Redburn*'s Chartist protest [**#V.89**].

V.121 Phosphorine: 'Fisher's Phosphorine', an arsenic and strychnine-based tonic, popular in WWI to combat "nerve strain"; it came in long thin bottles and tasted so vile that it had to work. Its active ingredients were alcohol, quinine, phosphoric and sulphuric acids. **Damaroids** were sold in boxes of thirty-six; a "Safe and Sure Cure of General Weakness, Physical Decay, and Loss of Nerve Power . . . introduced for nervous and all exhausting diseases"; in effect, sugar-coated coca. **Carter's Little Liver Pills** relieved constipation, bisacodyl stimulating enteric nerves to induce colonic movements. See 'Sumptuous Armour' [P&S 45].

V.122 Washington Hotel: Lime Street; once Liverpool's finest, but long inoperative.

V.123 Manchester Street: a small diagonal connecting Old Haymarket and Whitechapel with Dale Street; created (c.1830) for easier access (avoiding an incline) of stage-coaches to the London Road. The "cut" through the "isthmus" (Lowry's metaphor) was later blocked.

V.124 vision of Leningrad: Pudovkin's *End of St. Petersburg* [**#V.108**]. The vista from Lime Street to St. George's Hall, with Georgian buildings flanking the way and an equestrian statue, curiously resembles Saint Petersburg, from Neva Prospect to the Hermitage.

V.125 undone so many: in *The Waste Land* (ll. 62–63), crowds crossing London Bridge suggest the futile in Dante's *Inferno* [III.55–57], chasing a whirling banner and tossed by a great wind: "*si lunga tratta / Di gente, ch'io non avrei mai creduto, / Che morte tanta n'avesse disfatta*" [So long a train of people, that I should never have believed that Death had undone so many]. These are the 'trimmers' [**#II.69**]. In *Israel Potter* (1854) [XXIV], Melville's "gulf-stream of humanity" pours "like an endless shoal of herring" over London Bridge, into that City of Dis [**#V.145**].

V.126 Lourdes: in the Hautes-Pyrénées, where miracles relieve the afflicted, by the grace of Our Lady's apparition to Bernadette Soubirous (1858) and the healing waters in her Grotto.

V.127 petty officer: neither seaman nor officer. Fr. *petit*, "insignificant", or "small-minded"; "petty judases", betraying masters to the men and vice-versa; "Mr. Facing Bloody Both Ways" [CP #116], who enters (*sans* 'bloody') 'The Days like Smitten Cymbals of Brass' [CP #196], despised by all. Compare *The Ship Sails On* [55], and 'China' [P&S 50].

V.128 bosun: the *boatswain*, or petty officer supervising deck work and watches. The **lamp-trimmer** is the P/O who tends the oil-lamps (starboard, port, masthead), reporting every half-hour at night navigational lights as correctly burning.

V.129 *alopecuria*: making a virtue of deficiency. In *The Whirligig of Taste* (1929), "Jerry" Kellett, former master of The Leys who tutored Lowry for his Cambridge entrance [**#III.25**], examines literary taste from primitive societies to the Victorians, denying permanent critical principles [**#X.49**]. He identifies a psychological quirk for which, "as there is no single English word, I may invent a Greek one—*alopecuria*, the habit of the fox that has lost his tail" [25]: imitators, unable to match their originals, have like the tailless fox "vaunted defect as merit" [26]. The wit arises from *alopecurus*, Foxtail Grass.

V.130 frontiers: the death-watch beetle precedes Andrew Cather in *Great Circle* "on his march to the frontiers of consciousness" [**#V.72**]; the Consul insists that the "final frontier of consciousness" is within [UTV 135]. Aiken's 'Literature in Massachusetts' calls Melville "the writer who carried fatherest and deepest that perilous frontier of mystic consciousness."

V.131 red light: "class struggle" as deference to that beacon.

V.132 Herman Bang: (1857–1912), Danish author who described the "quiet existence" of trivial lives in loveless relationships (the 'Varsity' CB cites *Ida Brandt*

[**#V.57**]). Bang's later years were embittered by homophobic persecution and poor health. During a lecture tour of the United States he took ill on a train, dying of apoplexy in Ogden, Utah; his death was rumoured to be suicide, by poison. Lowry depicts him to Grieg (1939) as dying of grief, "sitting bolt upright in a Pullman car, in Utah: without a country" [CL 1:192; U 72]; this is *De uden Faedreland* (1906), or *Denied a Country* (1927). Bang's *Haabløse Slaegter* [**generations without hope**] (1880), about a relationship with an older woman, was banned for obscenity.

V.133 pretty: Hemingway's *The Sun Also Rises* [**#III.71**] ends: "Isn't it pretty to think so?"

V.134 Islington ... Everton ... Scotland Road: working-class areas in Vauxhall, northwest of the city centre. Scotland Road, once a turnpike to Preston, is a major artery, near Great Homer Street [**#V.105**]. Trams radiate from Pier Head, ascending Dale Street.

V.135 Exchange Street West: a passage past the Town Hall into the Exchange Flags.

V.136 fan-tan: a pile of beans is tabled on a board marked one to four; players bet on a number; then chips are removed in fours, until four or fewer remain. Winners share the stake.

V.137 Blue Piper: the Blue Funnel Line, Alfred Holt, Liverpool (1865), with its white and blue smokestacks ("pipes") operated regular services ("the China Company") to the Far East.

V.138 Psychology: until recently, a branch of philosophy. I. A. Richards invested English Letters with scientific principles drawn from psychology and linguistics [**#IV.1**; **#VIII.84**].

V.139 Russia: by signing for Archangel Sigbjørn will reach Oslo, his destiny written. In the DATG typescript, Lowry imagines discussing this with his father, admitting that Archangel was no way to meet 'Gulbrandsen' [Erikson/Grieg], but he would be among Norwegians and might visit a Norwegian port [UBC 9:5, 344]. His father, disapproving, "like many of the Manx had a certain power of divination", and predicted that he would see Gulbransen, who would be a good host but would not like "having his work interfered with" [345].

V.140 flies the Atlantic?: Captain John Alcock and Lieutenant Arthur Brown made the first transatlantic flight, from St. John's, Newfoundland, to Clifden, Ireland (14/15 June 1919). Charles Lindbergh, in *The Spirit of St. Louis*, made the first solo flight, New York to Paris (20/21 May 1927). These events generated huge public interest.

V.141 *Dewar's Whisky*: a Scotch, blended by John Dewar (1846) and (as here) advertised aggressively. Their 'White label' (1899), blending forty single malts, survives.

V.142 mene tekel: at Belshazzar's feast [Daniel 5:25–28]: "And this is the writing that was written: MENE, MENE, TEKEL, UPHARSIN. / This is the interpretation of the thing. MENE: God hath numbered thy kingdom, and finished it; / TEKEL: Thou art weighed in the balances, and art found wanting". Compare UTV [145], the Consul's writing on the wall.

V.143 love your own misery: see **#XVIII.69**.

V.144 death of private grief: an iterated obscurity [**#IV.27**; **#VII.7**; **#X.41**].

V.145 anaesthetic: Prufrock's evening is spread out against the sky, "Like a patient etherised upon a table." The "endless dense procession" swells the Waste Landers flowing over London Bridge with those undone by death in Dante, the Underground their emblem [**#V.125**]. Masefield's "down to the sea" adds another tonal touch.

V.146 coal-blackened statue: the Nelson Monument [**#V.14**]; until cleansed for the Trafalgar bicentenary (2005), it was as black as the slaves many thought it depicted [**#V.15**].

V.147 cyclopean eye: the Magnetic Telegraph Company (1856) wired the Observatory clock at Waterloo Dock to Henley's Electro-magnetic clock in the Exchange. The "signal" is the Observatory time-ball falling at precisely one o'clock, letting mariners and lubbers check their instruments. Given its accuracy, the clock cannot be fast [**#XI.37**]. The "cyclopean eye" (that of Homer's Polyphemus) is equally Lord Nelson, his blind eye turned to the "signal" at Copenhagen [**#V.30**]. The *Unión Militar* headquarters glower at the Consul thus [UTV 339].

V.148 wakeful ones: Watchers [Daniel 4:17], angels alert to divine bequests [**#II.23**]; rather than Hawthorne's "wakeful one" of 'The Haunted Mind' (1837), telling the midnight strokes.

V.149 Mecca . . . Archangel: the Captain heads to the Mecca Cafe in the India Buildings [**#IV.38**]; despite the socialist ironies, Sigbjørn cannot resist the pun [**#I.56**].

CHAPTER VI

VI.1 [Epigraph] Charles Fort: celebrant of the peculiar [**#II.22**]. From *The Book of the Damned* [161], of the pure and perfect: "We can have illusion of this state—but only by disregarding its infinite denials. It's a drop of milk afloat in acid that's eating it. The positive swamped by the negative. So it is in intermediateness . . . a real existence."

VI.2 happy: in Oaxaca, Geoffrey and Yvonne "had once been happy" [UTV 349].

VI.3 *Arcturion*: Melville's doomed vessel [**#XIII.25**].

VI.4 undergrounds: infernos, with crowds undone by death [**#V.125; #V.145**]:

Central: opened (1892) as the Liverpool Central Low Level Underground, linked to the main-line station; terminal of the Mersey Railway from Birkenhead.

James Street: first Liverpool stop after the Mersey Tunnel.

Mersey Railway: advertised as the "Quickest Route to Liverpool". The second oldest Underground (1886), it ran from Green Lane via Birkenhead Central and the Mersey Tunnel to James Street, connecting with the Wirral railway, with extensions to Rock Ferry (1891) and Central (1892).

VI.5 Mr. Cavafy: Constantine Cavafy (1863–1933) moved as a child to Liverpool where his father ran a business; he returned to Alexandria in 1885. Forster images him in 'The Poetry of C. P. Cavafy' (1923): "a Greek gentleman in a straw hat, standing absolutely motionless at a slight angle to the universe" [91], an eccentricity offering oblique insights into human foibles.

VI.6 driven like husks: echoing the exchange with Tor [**#II.7**].

VI.7 Water Street: from the Flags [**#V.2**] to the docks. The clock may be that on the Liver Building [**#VI.14**], at the foot of Water Street [**#VII.17**].

VI.8 'Last Yacko and Exprey': last editions of evening newspapers, the liberal *Liverpool Echo* (1879); and conservative *Evening Express* (1870; folding 1958). In 'Goya the Obscure', boys cry "Yacko!" and "Last Echo and Exprey"; their papers say: "Liverpool Liner aground" [278]. Dana reads: "Norwegian liner aground in Mersey" [U 73].

VI.9 disappearing point: compare '*Punctum Indifferens Skibet Gaar Videre*' [At the point of no return the ship sails on], later part IV of *Ultramarine*. Nautical imagery (current, shell, bells) enhances the conceit of *Water* Street, swirling towards Pier Head; "vortex" invokes both volcano [**#VI.19**] and maelstrom [**#II.19**].

VI.10 electric: the Overhead Railway, Liverpool's first electrically operated line, running (1893 to 1956) six miles along the docks from Seaforth Sands to Dingle.

VI.11 flexitone: a high-pitched percussion instrument, with a flexible metal flap and steel surface against which a fixed wooden ball, controlled by the player, produces sounds.

VI.12 Honduras Building: presumably, the *India Buildings* [**#IV.38**].

VI.13 Casper Hauser: a boy who appeared (26 May 1828) in Nuremburg, claiming to have lived in a darkened cell. Cared for by a schoolmaster, he learned essentials and revealed a talent for drawing. Many sought to establish his origins, or prove he was an imposter. On 14 December 1833 he came home, wounded in the breast, and died three days later. Melville mentions him in *Billy Budd*, *Pierre*, and *The Confidence Man*. Charles Fort intuits teleportation: he might have been "a citizen of another planet, transferred by some miracle to our own" [*Lo!* 711; **#III.39**].

VI.14 Liver Building: the Royal Liver Building, Pier Head [**#V.106**], built by the Royal Liver Assurance group (1911). Long the highest Liverpool building, it is crowned by two fabled Liver birds; one (male) looking inland to ensure the pubs are open; the other (female) seawards for handsome sailors. One of the "three graces" (with the Cunard and Port of Liverpool Buildings), it is the city's best-known landmark. The Consul recalls his Q-ship landing, the "Liver Building seen once more through the misty rain" [UTV 131].

VI.15 Goree Piazzas: two massive warehouses near Pier Head with arcades ('piazzas'), built (1773) to handle colonial goods flowing into Liverpool; named for an island and slave depot off Dakar, Senegal. Iron rings set in the walls reputedly secured slaves, though few arrived. The last "blackbirder" sailed in 1807, but the trade long sustained Liverpool's wealth. Dana recalls "the Goree Piazzas, where they used to chain the slaves" [U 67]. 'Imprisoned in a Liverpool of self' invokes "gutted arcades of the past" [CP #233].

VI.16 Spain: the Civil War began July 1936, with the Fascist takeover of the Balearic and Canary Islands, before a mainland landing by Foreign Legionnaires encouraged Andalusian garrisons to revolt. Previous years had seen increasing restlessness, inconclusive elections, strikes, assassinations, and paramilitary action.

VI.17 Italy: when Italy claimed Abyssinia (1934–1936), the Ethiopian emperor, Haile Selassie, appealed to the League of Nations. No help being offered, Italian tanks crushed the feeble resistance. Hugh intuits the 'abyss' in Abyssinia [UTV 252].

VI.18 Kegon Cataract: at Lake Chuzenji in Nikko National Park, Honshu; celebrated for its beauty. Misao Fujimura (1886–1903), a philosophy student rejected in love, wrote a farewell poem on a tree trunk before plunging to his death; others followed. Edwin Conger Hill's Columbia radio broadcast, syndicated for Hearst newspapers, was reprinted in *The Human Side of the News* (1934) [54–55]:

> SUICIDE SHRINES. In the Japanese conception, suicide is regarded as a noble gesture, sanctioned by the national code of honor. Young Japanese, weary of this world, have invariably sought romantic methods of leaving it. They wanted to die, but they wanted to die in beauty, with a beautiful gesture.
>
> For a long time Kegon Cataract, an almost vertical waterfall 260 feet high, was the shrine of the unhappy and self-doomed. Into that vortex hundreds cast themselves, and their bodies disappeared forever. When the authorities decided that the cataract had claimed enough victims, they closed all accesses with barbed wire.

VI.19 Oshima: largest of the Izu Islands, eighty miles south of Tokyo, dominated by the caldera of Mt. Mihara, into which (12 Feb. 1933) Kiyoko Matsumoto, a twenty-one-year old student, jumped [**#II.77**], starting a trend and tourist attraction. Nine-hundred forty-four people did likewise that year (authorities vainly erected barriers and banned one-way tickets). Hill continues:

> Shortly afterward candidates for suicide discovered the little volcanic island of Oshima, in the Pacific, just off Yokohama. Poets began to sing the praises of Oshima's beautiful maidens, its gorgeous red camellias, and its fire-breathing Mt. Mihara, eternally crowned with fire and smoke. In ever-greater numbers people flocked to the island, to plunge into the crater abyss and be cremated in incandescent lava. The jump of about seventeen hundred feet implied a painless death, with the flesh rising to heaven with the immortal soul.
>
> The poetic vision exercised an irresistible attraction on the sentimental maidens of Japan. Mt. Mihara began to devour them. The first butterfly to wing her way to the red glare of the volcano's crater, was Miss Kiyoko, a lovely society girl of Tokio. With a friend she climbed to the edge of the crater, wrote a charming farewell to life, and took the fatal plunge. Almost daily terrible scenes took place at the crater. A woman leaped with her baby in her arms. A man of eighty had himself carried to the brink in order that he could end his earthly career with his last strength. Young girls concluded death pacts with young students, and the couples hurled themselves together into the flaming furnace. Tourists flocking to Oshima Island, climbing the slopes covered

with azalea groves and then with lava and ashes, would see a young man or a young girl run to the brink, wave a hand, and leap from sight. The mountain would roar ominously, and a column of smoke would leap from the depths. A soul had passed.

The craze assumed such proportions that the government again had to intervene and deny access to the volcano. No less than 200 persons had sought and found death, since the beginning of the year, in the raging heart of Mt. Mihara. And now the suicidally disposed and the poets of the cult are seeking a new shrine which must combine beauty with terror. First a waterfall, then a volcano. One wonders what form it will take next, this shrine for the release of troubled souls.

VI.20 bodies falling into the volcano: in Liam O'Flaherty's *The Black Soul* (1924), the Stranger, shell-shocked by war, envisions "millions of dying men, worlds falling into pieces . . . the noise of the guns, millions of guns" [60–61]. Compare the ending of UTV [**#III.117**].

VI.21 ski-jumpers: Japanese suicides earlier suggested Norwegian ski-jumpers [**#II.77**].

VI.22 Nils Bruus: in *The Rector of Veilbye* (1829), by Steen Steensen Blicher (1782–1848). Bruus, a servant, disappears after arguing with his master, who is accused of murdering him; Rector Qvist cannot recall this, but facing compelling evidence confesses, and is sentenced to death. Twenty years later, Bruus returns.

VI.23 Antigua Bell rocks: uncharted. Bell Rock, off the Angus coast, Scotland, otherwise the Inchcape Rock, attracted many shipwrecks before the Bell Rock Lighthouse was built (1811). Antigua, named by Columbus for the *Virgen de la Antigua* in Seville Cathedral, and rich in pirate history, is the largest of the Leeward Islands.

VI.24 Custom House: a classical edifice, built 1828–1839, at Canning Place on the Old Dock, housing Post and Telegraph offices, the Mersey Docks, and Harbour Board. Bombed in 1941, it might have been renovated (the centre remained intact), but was demolished (1948).

VI.25 Leeward Isles: islands of the Lesser Antilles (leeward of the Windward Isles), where the Caribbean meets the Atlantic. They include Antigua [**#VI.23**] and Monserrat [**#I.19**].

VI.26 *Leslie Howard:* (1893–1943); English actor and Hollywood star of: *Berkeley Square* (1933), *Of Human Bondage* (1934), *The Scarlet Pimpernel* (1934), *The Petrified*

Forest (1936), and *Gone with the Wind* (1939). Having returned to England to support the war effort, he died in a plane from Lisbon shot down by the Luftwaffe.

VI.27 ***Outward Bound:*** a 1930 film starring Leslie Howard as an inebriate, with Helen Chandler and Douglas Fairbanks [**#XII.35**] as lovers who have committed suicide (gas); based on the 1923 play by Sutton Vane, about passengers on a fog-bound ship unaware they are dead and sailing to judgment. Lowry saw the play with his parents [Bowker 32]. The film was remade (1944) as *Between Two Worlds*; a phrase Sigbjørn presciently uses. Dana is "outward bound for hell" [U 53]; in 'June the 30th, 1934' a ship's bar [**#II.56**] reminds Firmin of the play, which also features in 'Sumptuous Armour' [P&S 41, 238]. Ethan and Jacqueline pick one another up shamelessly at a Toronto cinema showing it [OF 12]; they hear the question, "—but are we going to heaven, or hell?"; and the reply: "*But they are the same place, you see*" [**#VII.103**].

VI.28 creatures: "Maggy Mays", Liverpool's notorious prostitutes. Sigbjørn's "who could escape?" implies, amidst loftier sentiments, VD.

VI.29 samson posts: supporting cargo-loading booms or windlasses; compare 'West Hardaway' [P&S 26]. Like Philistine pillars, Lowry's derricks often collapse [**#IX.6**].

VI.30 ***Legs of Man:*** once opposite St. George's Hall in Lime Street, near the Empire Theatre; the *triskhelion* is the three-legged emblem of the Isle of Man [**#VI.39**; UTV 313].

VI.31 Bass in Bottles: brewed in Burton-on-Trent since 1777, Bass was the original Pale Ale; the red triangle and "Bass in Bottles" (not "draught") asserted its quality [**#XIII.34**].

VI.32 ***Caergwrle Ale:*** brewed until 1948 by Lassal & Sharman, in Caergwrle, North Wales [**#XII.27**]. The Consul, returning to Liverpool, recalls its aroma [UTV 131]; in 'Sumptuous Armour' Dick misses it [P&S 232]. Birkenhead's Dolphin Hotel offers a like menu: "do not offer cheques in payment, a refusal often gives offence . . . Caergwale Ales" ['Goya' 270].

VI.33 Cheesy Hammy Eggy: slices of ham on white bread, covered with grated cheese and grilled, with a fried egg on top; costing "1/9" (one shilling and ninepence).

VI.34 Futurist Theatre: a progressive Lime Street cinema, beside the smaller Scala [U 26], showing silent movies and early talkies [**#XII.35**]. In 'Sumptuous Armour', Fritz Lang's "German film called the Nibelungs" is "at the Futurist" [P&S 234].

VI.35 red cross on a white ground: the Cross of St. George [see **#VII.11**].

VI.36 Guantanamo: southeast Cuba, leased by the United States in perpetuity (1903) after the Spanish-American war; a coaling and naval station (not yet the disgrace it became). **Cienfuegos** is in southern Cuba.

VI.37 voyage to hell: in Rimbaud's *Drunken Boat* (1871), for *A Season in Hell* (1873); or "outward bound" [**#VI.27**]. Yet "song of iron" echoes the opening of Greig's 'Hjemme igjen' [Home again; **#VII.120**]: "Hjulene synger mot jernet" [the wheels sing against the iron]. For the "verse of idiot creaking", see **#V.40**.

VI.38 Maleboge: It. "evil ditches"; in the eighth circle of Dante's *Inferno*, ten concentric trenches, or *bolge*, in which are pouched seducers, panderers, simoniacs, sorcerers, barrators, hypocrites, sowers of discord, and falsifiers—likened by Hugh to journalists [UTV 100].

VI.39 Isle of Man: a Crown dependency in the Irish Sea, technically independent. Lowry, when asserting a dubious Manx ancestry over a specious Norwegian one, took pride in this (Cosnahan, in 'Elephant and Colosseum', is Manx). A regular ferry served Pier Head and **Castletown**, since 979 site of the *Tynwald*, or Manx parliament (in 1873, the capital and House of Keys relocated to Douglas).

VI.40 axes: Chekhov's *Cherry Orchard* (1904) reverberates to the distant sound of an axe, ending an era; **rotten wood** hosts the death-watch beetle [**#V.72**; **#V.130**].

VI.41 watery abyss: in Genesis 7:11, fountains of the deep break open, and waters of the abyss cover the face of the world. In Conrad's ***Typhoon*** (1902), Captain MacWhirr of the *Nan-Shan* summons his inner resources to endure the storm.

VI.42 break: Tennyson's lament for Arthur Hallam: "Break, break, break, / On thy cold gray stones, O Sea / And I would that my tongue could utter / The thoughts that arise in me." This invokes the epigraph from Auden, the ship going down [**#II.1**].

VI.43 *Baltimore Clipper*: where Redburn sups [**#V.65**; **#VI.54**]; 'respite' is Mumford's word for Melville's final years [**#IV.7**], a major theme of this chapter [**#VI.75**].

VI.44 giggling limericks: 'tis pity that writers like Lowry, whose prose is notoriously flowery, should be so dismissive of lore so permissive that eunuchs like us rise like kauri. Laruelle in the 1940 *Volcano* laments the degeneration of Orlac in the Hollywood remake, *Mad Love* (1935), to "a feeble-minded lout giggling limericks" [30].

VI.45 *Peleus*: a Blue Piper, built in Belfast (1900); reputed an unlucky ship, having stuck on the ways at launching, and collided with the *Marchioness* (1915). In 1931, she was sold, renamed the *Perseus*, then scrapped at Osaka. The *Oedipus Tyrannus* to which Hugh transfers likewise has "No refrigeration, only an icebox" [UTV 167]. When Lowry's ships hit the waves, "rolled all the sticks out of her" is a frequent refrain [**#XII.56**].

VI.46 *Achilles*: another Blue Piper, built in Greenock (1900); torpedoed off Ushant (1916), with five lives lost. Her successor was "laid down" in Greenock (1916); sold to the Admiralty (1941), she was soon scrapped (1948). Many ships were "laid up" (retired) in the Depression.

VI.47 put back three times: to reload the cargo [**#XII.54**]. "**City boats**" are those of the Ellerman Lines [**#XV.44**].

VI.48 Blue Peter: a signal flag, the letter 'P' [Fr. *partir*, "to leave"], blue with a rectangular white panel, flown when a ship is ready to depart.

VI.49 haunting shapes of conscience: like Eliot's "devil of the stairs" in *Ash-Wednesday*, Pascal's demon of doubt that is inseparable from the spirit of belief.

VI.50 Futurity broods on the ocean: from 'A Clock Striking at Midnight', a "quatorzain" (sonnet) by Thomas Love Beddoes (1803–1849), author of *Death's Jest-Book* (1850), whose sensibility Mumford likens to Melville [122]. The poem begins: "Futurity / Broods on the ocean, hatching 'neath her wing / Invisible to man, the century / That on its hundred feet, shall totter by . . . "

VI.51 future can change the past: the Consul ends his letter in the 1940 *Volcano* [26] with this Dunne-like sentiment [**#VII.3**]. A similar "dialogue" features in *Blue Voyage* [18].

VI.52 daubed: Masefield's *Dauber* (1913), a poem about a young artist at sea [U 50]: his paintings are mocked; but, rounding Cape Horn, having proved himself a man, he falls to his death from the shrouds.

VI.53 blocks: pulleys; two or more acting together constitute a "block and tackle".

VI.54 as Melville had written: Redburn describes the interior of 'The Baltimore Clipper' [**#V.65**] exactly thus. His head full of old abbeys, Lord Mayors, maypoles and fox hunters, a first reality check is the "confused uproar": ballad singers, bawling women, babies, and drunken sailors [*Redburn* XXVIII].

VI.55 Horsey: a sailor from *Ultramarine*.

VI.56 glycerine: a colourless, odourless viscous fluid soluble in water; because of its low freezing point (-37.8° C), used in compasses and the hydraulics of steering systems. Optimal efficiency is obtained with a 65% mixture of glycerol to water; anything else raises the freezing point dramatically.

VI.57 death ship: a "coffin-ship" [**#VII.99**], a decrepit vessel, over-insured, intended to founder [**#XII.54**]. Traven's *The Death Ship* (1934) savages the practice [**#VII.187**].

VI.58 shore bosun: in charge of wharf workers [**#XII.57**].

VI.59 White whale! White Sea!: in 'The Whiteness of the Whale' [*Moby-Dick* XLII], the blind malicious force of fate is manifest [**#I.Title**].

VI.60 old harpoon: when an old bull whale is killed [**#III.151**], a corroded harpoon is found imbedded in his flesh [*Moby-Dick* LXXXI].

VI.61 not wanted: Redburn's humiliations begin when he is unwanted for a watch by both the Chief and the Second Mate.

VI.62 BRUUS' SUICIDE: accepting his fate [**#VI.22**], with a grim pun on "leaving dock".

VI.63 breaking up: compare Hugh: "if our civilization were to sober up for a couple of days it'd die of remorse on the third" [*UTV* 117].

VI.64 suicide of shame: Liverpool's *Echo* ran no such headline for Paul Fitte [**#III.125**]; but Sigbjørn Wilderness recalls "Undergraduate Suicide of Shame" [*Mordida* 254, 380].

VI.65 which way would you go: Melville's "Whence came you, Hawthorne?" [**#IV.3**], blended with the prayer, what would Jesus do?

VI.66 Mother Earth: Ethan Brand's farewell before leaping into the furnace [see **#VI.73**]:

> O Mother Earth, who art no more my Mother, and into whose bosom this frame shall never be resolved! O mankind, whose brotherhood I have cast off, and trampled thy great heart beneath my feet! O stars of heaven, that shone on me of old, as if to light me onward and upward!—farewell all, and forever. Come, deadly element of Fire,—henceforth my familiar friend! Embrace me, as I do thee!

Sigbjørn hesitates at *brotherhood*. Compare the later epigraph [**#XVI.1**].

VI.67 wavering flag: Hawthorne's furnace as stokehold, an abode of trimmers [**#I.49**, **#II.69**], who, in Dante's *Inferno*, futilely pursue a wavering banner

[#V.125]. Ethan, by night, conjures a **fiend** from the furnace [#XVI.39], to discuss the Unpardonable Sin [#VI.73] (Sigbjørn's "familiar **friend**" assumes a maternal form).

VI.68 Norwegian flag: when fireman Anton is buried overboard, Narvik hauls back the flag that enwrapped him [*Ship Sails On* 88].

VI.69 Erik Brandt!: a surreal nocturnal encounter (Hawthorne liked solitary late rambles), fusing Melville and Hawthorne (*Ethan Brand*) with Erikson and Herman Bang (*Ida Brandt*).

VI.70 melancholy sandhills: the "bleak sands" of Southport, where Melville remarked to Hawthorne, during his 1856 Liverpool visit, that he had "made up his mind to be annihilated". Hawthorne concluded his account of that meeting: "It is strange how he persists—and has persisted ever since I knew him, and probably long before—in wandering to-and-fro over these deserts, as dismal and monotonous as the sand hills amid which we were sitting" [Mumford 275, 263; **#V.54**].

VI.71 hypos: Ishmael's affliction [*Moby-Dick* I]:

> Whenever I find myself growing grim about the mouth; whenever it is a damp, drizzly November in my soul; whenever I find myself involuntarily pausing before coffin warehouses, and bringing up the rear of every funeral I meet; and especially whenever my hypos get such an upper hand of me, that it requires a strong moral principle to prevent me from deliberately stepping into the street, and methodically knocking people's hats off—then, I account it high time to get to sea.

VI.72 Plotinus Plinlimmon: "embodiment of the ambiguities" [Mumford 147; **#IV.76**].

VI.73 the unpardonable sin!: the title on publication (1850) of Hawthorne's *Ethan Brand*, about a lime-burner who seeks that sin; but when asked about it can say only "an intellect that triumphed over the sense of brotherhood with man and reverence for God, and sacrificed everything to its mighty claims!" Its enormity is such that he leaps into his kiln [**#XI.9**; **#XVI.1**; **#XVI.40**]. His skeleton calcifies, but within its ribcage is a chunk like a human heart. Mumford (in his first edition) contended that Ethan's obsession was patterned on Melville, his language a parody of Ahab's, the book written "by way of warning" [145]. He argued that Hawthorne had committed the "unpardonable sin of friendship; he had failed to understand Melville's development, or to touch by sympathy and faith that part of Melville that was beyond his external reach" [146]. These fallacies structure Sigbjørn's epiphany.

VI.74 lees of my better being: Ishmael considers his likely death [*Moby-Dick* VII]; but "somehow" grows merry again (as Sigbjørn may):

> Methinks we have hugely mistaken this matter of Life and Death. Methinks that what I call my shadow here on earth is my true substance. Methinks that in looking at things spiritual, we are too much like oysters observing the sun through the water, and thinking that thick water the thinnest of air. Methinks my body is but the lees of my better being. In fact take my body who will, take it I say, it is not me.

VI.75 Healed of my hurt: facing the ocean (accepting his destiny), Sigbjørn cites Melville's poem to which he earlier alluded [**#V.20**]:

> Healed of my hurt, I laud the inhuman Sea—
> Yea, bless the Angels Four that there convene;
> For healed I am even by the pitiless breath
> Distilled in wholesome dew named rosmarine.

There are minor errors ('laud' for *bless*, 'sea' for *Sea*, 'Yes' for *Yea*, 'am I' for *I am*, 'ever' for *even*, and 'their' for *the*). The last of seven 'Pebbles', it offers brief insights into the sea, benedictions for the respite now possible. By ritualizing the 1856 meeting of Melville and Hawthorne, Sigbjørn has exorcised his hypos [**#VI.71**].

VI.76 rosmarine: *rosmarinus* ("sea-dew"); or rosemary, a distillate to restore physical and spiritual health. In Jonson's *Masque of Blackness* (1605), *Aethiop* in his final speech commends the nymphs:

> *You shall (when all things els do sleepe*
> *Saue your chaste thoughts), with reuerence, steepe*
> *Your bodies in that purer brine*
> *And wholesome dew, call'd* Ros-marine.

These words, decked in classical dignity, mask an obscenity, for the foam (Gk. ἀφρος) that generated Aphrodite rose from the castration of her father, Uranus. Lowry, following Melville, ignores this, but the masque unfolds at the end of Aiken's *Blue Voyage*, where Demarest (who wants to bite Faubion and awaits her knock) quotes the "wholesome dew called rosmarine" as he brushes his teeth, "with lips quaintly arched and an overflow of blood-streaked foam" [358].

CHAPTER VII

VII.1 tram circuit: three interlinked circles at Pier Head [**#V.106**; **#XIII.27**], since 1869 the heart of the Liverpool system. The network was expanded in 1897; buses, introduced in 1911, by 1928 served Pier Head. Trams ("Streamliners", "Baby Bogies") were crimson-lake and cream until 1933, when olive-green and cream ("Green Goddesses") was preferred.

VII.2 white city: the Mersey as a White Sea, raising the futility, as Huysmans might, of going anywhere [**#V.97**], let alone Archangel. This is a Hyperborean Atlantis, invested with the nameless white terror of *Moby-Dick* [XLII]: "Is it by its indefiniteness it shadows forth the heartless voids and immensities of the universe, and thus stabs us from behind with the thought of annihilation?" [**#V.54**; **#VI.70**]. In Mann's *Magic Mountain*, each snowflake, icily regular [480; **#II.47**], refracts the anti-organic order of death [*Mordida* 42, 331].

VII.3 fourth dimension: Sigbjørn's hope, mediated by Dunne's *An Experiment with Time*, that the past might be changed [**#VI.51**].

VII.4 cirrus: clouds, light and high; here, a veil of falling snow.

VII.5 Woodside: north of Birkenhead, a ferry and rail terminal to Liverpool. **Goree Piazzas** are warehouses near Pier Head [**#VI.15**]. The **Brocklebank dock**, or Canada Half-Tide Dock (1862), on the Liverpool side near the open sea, served the Elder Dempster line [**#XIII.29**] and Belfast ferries.

VII.6 Okee Chobee: Lake Okeechobee, Florida, head of the Everglades; its supernatural associations vague [Fort, *Book of the Damned* 127].

VII.7 Debacle of self: Sigbjørn has used this phrase to Erikson and his father [**#IV.27**; **#X.41**]. It now suggests "immolation" (self-sacrifice), lost souls leaping into volcanoes or furnaces [**#III.90**; **#VI.19**; **#VI.66–67**], seeking annihilation [**#V.54**; **#VI.70**; **#VII.2**].

VII.8 Calderstones . . . Mount Pleasant . . . Old Swan: suburban destinations [**#V.96**].

VII.9 'cabman's lift': as a cabbie decanting a comatose fare.

VII.10 rigid with gazing: in 'At the Bar' [*CP* #26], and *Ultramarine* [69], Pier Head derelicts clutch the rails, motionless (in heraldry, "at gaze"). Ships take the Saturday tide to avoid unlucky Fridays.

VII.11 Norwegian flag: for merchantmen, an indigo cross, outlined in white on a red field. Lowry describes the St George Cross [**#VI.35**], or Elder Dempster ensign [**#XIII.29**]. For the **Direction**, or *Director*, see **#IV.16**; **#IV.58**.

VII.12 Port Said: a fuelling station (1859) at the north entrance to the Suez Canal; **Bitter Lakes**: two lakes of concentrated salts in the Suez isthmus, used by the Canal: Great Bitter (fourteen miles) and Little Bitter (eight miles); **Bab-el-Mandeb**: Ar. "Gate of Tears", between the Red Sea and Indian Ocean [UTV 163]. See 'Peter Gaunt and the Canals' [CP #15].

VII.13 Penang: an island state in northwest Malaya; a coaling station. Dana goes ashore from the 'West Hardaway' [P&S 29]; or plays billiards in the Chinese quarter [U 62].

VII.14 such a day as this: given the bleakness, King Lear's "such a night as this" [III.iv.17], rather than the serenity of *The Merchant of Venice* [V.i.1].

VII.15 parallelogram: the *Philoctetes* [UTV 162] is a "fantastic mobile football field"; its two square "trankums" [166] resemble rugby goalposts.

VII.16 cathedral: Liverpool's Anglican Cathedral, St. James' Mount, finished in 1978; rising stolidly from the Mersey like a celestial warehouse [**#VII.126**], or Kafka's Castle [**#VII.106**]. The **apprentices** enact Ibsen's *The Master Builder*.

VII.17 clock: the Royal Liver Building [**#VI.14**] has two clock towers; their faces, twenty-five feet across, are the largest in Britain. Its illuminated dials and "jewelled finger" are visible (fog permitting) to mariners; and to Dana, from the ferry [U 141].

VII.18 *Titanic*: an Olympic-class White Star liner, largest of her class. Considered unsinkable [**#III.28**; **#III.63**], she hit an iceberg near midnight on 14 April 1912, on her maiden voyage, and sank with the loss of 1,517 of the 2,223 on board.

VII.19 *Vestris*: of the Lamport & Holt line, launched 16 May 1912; from 1922 chartered to Royal Mail, serving New York and Buenos Aires. Leaving Hoboken (10 Nov. 1928), she hit a storm. Water shipped through an open bunker caused a starboard list (Sigbjørn implies she was overloaded [**#VII.136**]). She was abandoned off Virginia, with 112 (of the 322 aboard) lives lost. Like the *Brynjaar*, her SOS was curiously delayed [**#V.74**].

VII.20 *Lusitania*: of the Cunard Line, torpedoed by a U-boat (7 May 1915) off Old Head of Kinsale, Ireland, with the loss of 1,198 of the 1,959 on board. Controversy raged, as she carried munitions, but her sinking brought the United States into the war.

VII.21 unvintageable: Homer's wine-dark sea, drawn from *Blue Voyage* for 'On Reading Redburn' [CP #65]: "unvintageable terrors".

VII.22 crucified: at the masthead, as in 'Imprisoned in a Liverpool of self' [CP #233].

VII.23 Sphinx . . . Jocasta . . . *Oedipus Tyrannus*: Oedipus, who solved the riddle of the Sphinx [**#IV.32**; **#IX.9**], became King of Thebes, and married his mother, Jocasta. Lowry's note on a letter from Jan, 3 May 1934 [NYPL 1:2, 34 verso], confirms that "only a woman" implies the older Charlotte Haldane.

VII.24 Café Cantante: flamenco cafés, their singing and dancing to the guitar the rage in Spain and Cuba (but not Liverpool). Lorca's 'Café cantante' (1921) recounts a flamenco dancer's dialogue with Death.

VII.25 blue girls . . . white ones: in *Christopher Rilke* [**#I.1**], a soldier at rest: "And to learn over again what women are. And how the white ones do and how the blue ones are" [25]. The 'Varsity' CB, noting "Rilke" [**#II.40**], adds: "a swaying in the summer winds that are in the tresses of warm women" [26].

VII.26 L.N.E.R.: London North Eastern Railways, linking the North-East and Scotland to the south; one of the "Big Four" created by the 1921 *Railway Act*. They also ran buses, double-decker "Liners".

VII.27 floating pier: "George's Landing Stage" at Pier Head, a long buoyant structure giving access (passengers, cars) to the Mersey and Isle of Man ferries, or larger liners.

VII.28 Woodside . . . Rock Ferry . . . Egremont: Liverpool ferries to **Woodside** [**#VII.5**] or **Rock Ferry** [**#IV.7**] began in the early 18th century; those to **Egremont** (north Birkenhead) in the 1830s. Dana and Janet avoid the Egremont Ferry [U 141].

VII.29 gantries: cranes, with hoists and overhead beams, fitted to a trolley on rails; used in shipbuilding and loading dockside vessels.

VII.30 *Herzogin Cecile*: a German four-masted barque (1902), after the Archduchess Cecile of Mecklenburg-Schwerin [**#XI.46**; **#XIII.26**]. 'Forest Path' [259] calls a celestial apparition of terrifying beauty "a whole blazing Birkenhead Brocklebank dockside of fiery Herzogin Ceciles". She ran the longer routes to Chile and Australia (**Walleroo** is on the Yorke Peninsula, South Australia) while sail was competitive against steam. On 25 April 1936, making for Ipswich, she grounded on Ham Stone Rock, and sank near Salcombe.

VII.31 'Rounding the horn': Eliot's 'Gerontion' (1920), cited approximately: "Gull against the wind, in the windy straits / Of Belle Isle, or running on the Horn, / White feathers in the snow, the Gulf claims".

VII.32 Futurist: the progressive cinema [**#VI.34**], showing *Outward Bound* [**#VI.27**]. The **Empire** opened 9 March 1925, Lime Street, replacing the Royal Alexandra Theatre and Opera House, with seating for 2,400. ***Crazy Week*** was a variety show devised by George Black (1931) for the London Palladium; its success inspired other Crazy Gang Shows.

VII.33 *Arcturion*: Melville's doomed whaler [**#XIII.25**]; '**toppling**' suggests Mississippi paddle-steamers [**#VII.41**].

VII.34 gladstone bags: after William Gladstone (1809–1898), British PM: portmanteaux separated by rigid frames into equal deep halves (casually, soft round leather bags, opening at the top). Compare *Blue Voyage* [2].

VII.35 *perpetuum mobile*: L. "perpetual motion"; one of D'Israeli's follies [**#X.27**].

VII.36 empty: as Tor's nameplate the night he died [**#III.4**].

VII.37 madness: *King Lear* [III.iv.11]: "O, that way madness lies; let me shun that."

VII.38 Siamese twins: like ChangandEng (1811–1874), conjoined twins born in Siam, who joined Barnum's circus. Another celebrated pair was/were Daisy and Violet Hilton, fused at the hip and buttocks. In America they learned to sing and dance, appearing in the movie *Freaks* (1932). In Lowry's film script, Siamese Twins unlock G. W. Pabst's *Secrets of the Soul* [*Tender* 164]; here, they mock the unity (and separation) of Sigbjørn and Nina [**#VII.54**].

VII.39 Pity that dare not approach: I. A. Richards, *Principles of Literary Criticism* (1924), an Aristotelian definition of tragedy: "Pity, the impulse to approach, and Terror, the impulse to retreat", brought into "a reconciliation which they find nowhere else" [245]. Their union is the catharsis that "gives its special character to Tragedy" [247]. Hugh, recalling the futile panorama of revolution, agrees [UTV 248].

VII.40 Faust: the Soldiers' Chorus from Gounod [**#VII.177; #VII.194**].

VII.41 bedizened: the 'Varsity' CB notes: "We sailed in a huge toppling steamer, bedizened & lacquered within like an imperial junk". In Melville's *The Confidence Man* [II], "The great ship-canal of Ving-King-Ching" is likened to the Mississippi, with "huge toppling steamers, bedizened and lacquered within like imperial junks."

VII.42 persiflage: frivolity, flippancy. *The Confidence Man* presents a coxcombical fellow, "full of smart persiflage" [XIII].

VII.43 cornucopias: horns of plenty: Zeus was raised on the milk of Amalthea, a she-goat whose horn he broke; in recompense, the Gods filled it with her wishes.

VII.44 pantry: the office of "Sparks", the wireless telegraph operator [**#XVI.8**].

VII.45 greasers: to lubricate the ship's machinery; **wipers** clean up after them.

VII.46 No Trust: cash only; the barbershop sign on the *Fidèle*, in *The Confidence Man*.

VII.47 necessarily mutable ends: unlike *necessarily immutable* ones (divine rectitude, determinist faith); the human condition as necessarily imperfect, but by virtue of that imperfection capable of attaining a state perfected and immutable. Sigbjørn turns the theological paradox into a socialist axiom.

VII.48 mystical vision: Sigbjørn's exorcism of his hypos [**#VI.71**; **#VI.75**].

VII.49 Novalis: Georg Philipp Friedrich Freiherr von Hardenberg (1772–1801); his "blue flower" was the emblem of German Romanticism. Lowry echoes Thomas Mann: "The revolutionary principle is simply the will toward the future, which Novalis called 'the really better world'" [for details, see **#X.29**; **#X.78**; **#X.100**]. For Novalis, this embraces Wagner's *Liebestod*; for Lowry, in 'Without the Nighted Wyvern' [CP #315], it conjures future taverns, where:

> There are no no trusts signs no no credit
> And apart from the unlimited beers
> We sit unhackled drunk and mad to edit
> Tracts of a really better land where man
> May drink a finer, ah, an undistilled wine . . .

VII.50 sealed orders: a mission revealed when instructions are opened, after departure. Sigbjørn has similar intimations in Norway [**#XVIII.19**].

VII.51 adaptive organism: in evolutionary biology, maintaining stability despite environmental change, if necessary modifying internal structures to cope. Whatever her source, Nina's "sociological tendencies" emerge; she uses "human status" in the technical sense of inclusive humanity that makes no distinction between race or culture, as opposed to the Aryan or Nordic ideal [**#VII.156**]. "[T]here is no peace" may echo *I Bring Not Peace*, by Charlotte Haldane, wife of the biologist, J. B. S., whose theories of mind and atomic matter were explored (*inter alia*) in *Possible Worlds* (1927).

VII.52 unbroken equilibrium: in *The Book of the Damned*, Fort comments [10], "All biologic phenomena act to adjust: there are no biologic actions other than adjustments. Adjustment is another name for equilibrium. Equilibrium is the Universal." For Nina, religion is an adaptive process by which the human organism achieves equilibrium, this finding its sociological expression in the Church.

VII.53 erotic immolation: the libido as a human furnace, with images of leaping into volcanoes or kilns (the desire for annihilation). Freud's *Beyond the Pleasure Principle* (1920) defines two basic instincts: *Eros*, the sexual drive and life force; and *Thanatos*, the impulse towards ultimate equilibrium, the homeostasis of death [**#X.78**].

VII.54 Chang and Chen: *Eng*, inexplicably, is renamed [**#VII.38**].

VII.55 Hotel Nazareth: Yvonne's labels ("here is your history") include "Hotel Nazareth Galilee" [UTV 67], where Jan stayed in 1934; but not **Schenectady**, New York, the Twins' destination.

VII.56 'A fat man with a steak and bottle': obscure; but typically Oxbridge witty trivia. Sigbjørn notes "Spender's Aristotle woman", but Stephen Spender (1909–1995), poet and indoor marxman, was no judge of Aphrodite.

VII.57 'going about and about': the mind tries thus to ascend the Hill, cragged and steep, where Truth stands [Donne 'Satyre III: On Religion'; **#IX.23**]; but Sigbjørn descends the spiral stair, to where it is hot and dark [**#VII.96**].

VII.58 elemental: for Paracelsus, a spiritual being (gnome, undine, sylph, or salamander), mirroring the four elements (earth, water, air, and fire) [**#VII.63**].

VII.59 build the Ark: as Noah did, in God's covenant [Genesis 6:9], to survive the deluge and rebuild the future [**#I.29**]; here, Sigbjørn's wish to integrate politics with the Godhead, whatever the socialist incongruity.

VII.60 Mother Carey's chicken: a storm petrel [**#V.75**]; like the spirit of God, brooding on the face of the waters [Genesis 1:12; **#VIII.33**].

VII.61 skunk: Genesis 7: clean beasts entered the Ark, in sevens; then the unclean, in pairs; but the skunk . . .

VII.62 divided against myself: Matthew 12:25: "every city or house divided against itself shall not stand"; as mediated by Lawrence: "We are divided in ourselves, against ourselves" [*American Literature* VII].

VII.63 elemental world: Lawrence insists: "Know the sea that is in your blood. The great elementals" [*American Literature* IX]. Sigbjørn's *elemental* assumes dialectical force [**#VII.58**], but like Chekhov's old woman [**#VII.74**] he is left with nothing.

VII.64 Great gates slammed in his brain: like those of Bellevue [*Maelstrom* 39; **#XI.12**]. A **shadow-play** uses screens and illumination to motivate images; Lowry intends the puppet theatre in Bellevue ("something that must have happened in another existence").

VII.65 windhover: Hopkins's falcon [**#XIII.17**], with the anguish of the "terrible sonnets".

VII.66 *Star Rover:* in this Jack London novel (1915), Darrell Standing, incarcerated in a strait jacket, survives by self-projecting into the astral regions.

VII.67 canalize: see 'Peter Gaunt and the Canals' [*CP* #15]: connecting things, rather than investing them with an irrelevant significance.

VII.68 *au grand sérieux:* Fr. "with profound seriousness"; as Lawrence said dismissively of Melville [*American Literature* XI].

VII.69 ships that pass: ... in the night, without recognition. Nina's "In the army" mocks Sigbjørn's sea-dogma. Liverpool transatlantic routes, except for the White Star Quebec–Montreal service, usually went south of Ireland, rather than via Belfast and Glasgow as Lowry's timing requires.

VII.70 *cracked church bell:* Lawrence's Melville cannot resist the sea: "He hears the horror of the cracked church bell, and goes back down to the shore, back into the ocean again . . . back to the elements" [*American Literature* X].

VII.71 drummond light: after its promoter, Captain Thomas Drummond (1826); an intense white light ("lime-light") as an oxyhydrogen flame renders quicklime incandescent.

VII.72 'as a little child again': Matthew 18:3: "Except ye be converted, and become as little children, ye shall not enter into the kingdom of heaven." Here, "travail of a rebirth" anticipates a more profound discussion of this theme [**#X.35**, and subsequent references].

VII.73 La bêtise est mon fort: Fr. "Stupidity is my strength"; twisting Paul Valéry's "La bêtise n'est pas mon fort", from *La Soirée avec Monsieur Teste* (1896), an "intolerable" text (laconic, ironic, solipsistic) for any serious socialist.

VII.74 Tchekov's old lady: 'In the Graveyard', where a shabby old actor (male) recalls one who robbed him of his faith and left him with nothing [**#XVIII.67**]. Lowry refers Aiken to 'Tchechov', who "wanders around graveyards thinking it is no go" [CL 1:321 (1940)].

VII.75 contradict myself: as Whitman's *Song of Myself*: "Do I contradict myself? Very well, I contradict myself."

VII.76 'noli me tangere': L. "Do not touch me": John 20:17, Christ to Mary Magdalene.

VII.77 Holy Grail: the vessel containing Christ's blood (*sang réal*); in Arthurian tradition, the holiest of symbols, attainable only by the purest of heart; in the Grail legend, used to cure the wounded King. Sigbjørn's political illness is diagnosed in chapter X: "we need first to see ourselves clearly, then change the social organization" [**#X.37**].

VII.78 Ricardo: David Ricardo (1772–1823), economist [**#XIII.18**], whose *Principles of Political Economy* (1817) defined the theory of rent and comparative advantage.

VII.79 guardian angel: Rilke's archetype, a "power for good" [**#II.23; #XIV.3**], that conditions the possibility of one's spiritual being (—Have some Chianti, Nina said).

VII.80 Chianti: red wine from the Chianti region, Tuscany, a bulbous bottle nestled in its woven straw container, or *fiasco* (Lowry ignores the potential pun). ***Orvieto*** is not *chianti* but a white wine from that Umbrian town.

VII.81 Yokohama: in Japan, where Hugh sees two ships in the "roads" (waiting to berth), turning with the tide, almost colliding but finally sliding by [UTV 165].

VII.82 phantasy of the unconscious: Lawrence's *Fantasia* (1921); equally wishing to make personal feelings the basis of any understanding of things outside the self [**#III.85**].

VII.83 strange remark: Dana overhears: "I hate those bloody toffs who come to sea for experience" [U 19]; and Hugh: "we've got a bastard duke on board" [UTV 159].

VII.84 yield himself to the angels: the dying words of Poe's Ligeia: "Man doth not yield himself to the angels, nor unto death utterly, save only through the weakness of his feeble will." Poe attributed this to Joseph Glanville (1636–1680), philosopher and clergyman.

VII.85 Selah: in the Psalms, a rhetorical conclusion [*Blue Voyage* 278].

VII.86 a gallant story: in Synge's sense, a *gallous* story (honourable, deluded, but with echoes of the *gallows*).

VII.87 windmills: fantasies (honourable, deluded), as Don Quixote battling giants.

VII.88 bullet . . . wave: the particle/wave duality, a quantum paradox, the wave informing Tennyson's "break, break, break" [**#VI.42**].

VII.89 kingdom of heaven: Luke 17:21: "the kingdom of God is within you"; the quantum paradox of an outer social order based on an inner spiritual principle [**#XVI.36**], which is simultaneously the mystery of the Fall.

VII.90 swims in the air: the Tao [**#II.39**] might resolve this paradox.

VII.91 Spinoza's sense: Baruch Spinoza (1632–1677), philosopher and lens-grinder [**#III.55**], short-circuited Cartesian dualism by affirming matter as a pantheistic extension of God; thus, a true substance (*natura naturans*) at once inside and outside. Might this flotsam suggest Eliot's "ordinary man" who falls in love, or "reads Spinoza" ['Metaphysical Poets', 1921]? Sadly, no.

VII.92 Snow: as in Joyce's 'The Dead', blotting distinctions between the living and dead.

VII.93 Alfred Gordon Pym: Lowry's usual error for Poe's *Narrative of Arthur Gordon Pym* (1838), which ends in the polar south, in a blinding vision of white. Pym comments in Chapter II, "My visions were of shipwreck and famine; of death or captivity among barbarian hordes; of a lifetime dragged out in sorrow and tears, upon some gray and desolate rock. . . " Pym avoids the fate of his fellows (killed by savages); but escaping by canoe is pulled into a cataract leading to a chasm surmounted by an immense white figure. Poe mentions neither **Land's End** (the SW tip of England), nor **Dead End** (New York City). Pym's desire to be "led captive by barbarian hordes, on some Arctic [*sic*] island of wilderness and snow, in a land desolate and unknown" was, Lowry claimed, Poe's admirable description of a hangover ['Work in Progress' 84–85].

VII.94 positivism: the philosophy of Auguste Comte (1798–1857), recognizing only the certainties of scientific analysis, excluding all supernatural, metaphysical and spiritual agencies, and maintaining that the sole criterion of knowledge is sense experience. The ***quack quack*** comes from *Blue Voyage* [188].

VII.95 stupid doggerel: rhyming 'coup-de-grâce' with Nina's earlier comment about the death of [his] merchant 'class'.

VII.96 spirals: in *The Ship Sails On* [167], fatal tendrils wind upwards to ensnare a life [**#III.51**]. The "stony ground" is Bethel [Genesis 28], where Jacob envisions a stairway between earth and heaven. Sigbjørn's "dark cavern" [**#XI.66**] opens into Dante's *Inferno*, spiralling downwards [**#VII.57**].

VII.97 coffin-ship: death-ships, poorly loaded, badly "trimmed" [**#VI.57**]).

VII.98 no faith: Lowry's 'Notes' [16] elaborate the Captain's view [**#IX.5**].

VII.99 plimsoll: the Plimsoll line, instituted by the *Merchant Shipping Act* (1894), marked the level to which a ship might safely be loaded; Samuel Plimsoll (1824–1893), "the sailors' friend", opposed putting "coffin-ships" to sea.

VII.100 captain's wife: a woman on board betokens misfortune; in dirty weather, therefore, she should be thrown overboard to lighten the ship.

VII.101 revive a corpse: as in *Finnegans Wake*, Joyce's revolution of the Word [**#III.82**].

VII.102 Midland Adelphi: the Britannia Adelphi [**#V.116**], previously the Midland; hence **penthouse bolsheviki**, superior indoor marxmanship [CP #317].

VII.103 outward bound for hell: "—but are we going to heaven, or hell?" [**#VI.27**].

VII.104 few are chosen: Matthew 22:14, of those called to the Kingdom of Heaven; as Sigbjørn will find, many are cold but few are frozen.

VII.105 Elks: the Benevolent and Protective Order of Elks (1868), an American fraternal order, in Lowry's day restricted to white adult male believers (Sigbjørn might qualify).

VII.106 aphorism: when K. approaches Kafka's Castle in the opening chapter, he is the only living soul, saving some children and their teacher [**#X.1**]. Kafka's *Aphorisms* appeared from 1917.

VII.107 little old one: the Old Adam within the fallen consciousness.

VII.108 oceanic feeling: in *Civilization and Its Discontents* [I], Freud states his inability to believe in God, replying to Romain Rolland, who, after reading *The Future of an Illusion*, said that religious sentiments derive from a "a sensation of 'eternity', a feeling as of something limitless, unbounded, something 'oceanic'" [**#II.9**]. Such views, said Freud, expressed by an honoured friend, put him in a difficult position: "I cannot discover this 'oceanic' feeling in myself." Nor can Dick Diver [*Tender* 65].

VII.109 Words, words, words: but devoid of action [*Hamlet* II.ii.192].

VII.110 Boddy Finch life jacket: of cotton cloth stuffed with kapok, with front-fastening tabs; invented by Finch Portman Ingram, and used on transatlantic liners [*Blue Voyage* 283; U 151]. After the *Vestris* disaster [**#VII.20**], a Convention for Safety of Life at Sea (1929) made life jackets compulsory for merchant marines, and required vessels to hold a *muster* (lifeboat drill) within twenty-four hours of departure.

VII.111 New Brighton: where Lowry was born (28 July 1909), at 'Warren Crest', 13 North Drive, on the Birkenhead side of the Mersey [**#VII.127**].

VII.112 Sculls: a galley-boy; a *scullion* [U 150], rather than one who rows.

VII.113 *io, io*: compare "Klio, klio" [*Blue Voyage* 304; **#VII.94**]; the flight foresees the cockle-pickers against the vermillion glare [**#IX.12**].

VII.114 God's blood: Faustus, in extremity, sees Christ's blood streaming in the firmament; one drop would save him [UTV 65].

VII.115 Lyonesse: in Arthurian legend, adjoining Cornwall; the home of Tristan.

VII.116 the flag, the cross: the Tarnmoor Line [**#VI.35**; **#VII.11**]; equally, the Christian cross and the banner over Dante's trimmers [**#II.69**], tormented with gadflies, hornets, and worms rather than Lowry's ice and fire.

VII.117 leaflet: presumably authentic (the White Star Line promoted itself thus).

VII.118 new found land: integrating, as in Jensen's *Long Journey* [**#II.92**], the Viking discovery of America with that of Columbus, and thus the voyages of Sigbjørn and Nina. **Leif Erikson** (c.970–1020), son of Erik the Red [**#I.18**] (and possible ancestor of William), was the first European to reach Newfoundland, five hundred years before Columbus in the ***Niña*** committed his indiscretion (1492).

VII.119 took her hand . . . leave paradise: compare the end of Milton's *Paradise Lost*: "They hand in hand with wand'ring steps and slow / Through *Eden* took thir solitary way."

VII.120 Norwegian poem: from the *Hotellerie du Pont St Prest* (1934) Lowry drafted a letter to Grieg [NYPL 2:30], recalling from 'Hjemme igjen' [Back home], the last poem of *Stene i Strømmen* [Stone in the Stream, 1925], poignant images of two lovers. Grieg's "to elskende kind mot kind" [two lovers cheek to cheek] are not sundered by sea and time; but Sigbjørn's "nights of the west are gloomy" approximates line 4: "Vestlandets eget mørke" [the Western Region's distinctive darkness]. Part V of *Ultramarine* (from "westward" to "yours and mine") ends with a faithful translation of most of the poem [172–73].

VII.121 human soul: Nina has not accepted Sigbjørn's sense of the human soul, but (a woman reading Aristotle?) can admit distinctions between its **form** and **substance.** This informs the image of **jetsam**, as material thrown overboard from the ship of the dying (as opposed to the immortal) soul. When the "log" (jetsam, *substance*) turns out to be a wooden leg (Ahab, *form*) a curious reconciliation follows.

VII.122 feed-pump: supplying fluid to a boiler, by a piston; the **injector** is the nozzle and valve through which it is pumped, to be converted into a high velocity jet of greater pressure than that within the boiler; "**bucking**" (violent jerking) occurs if air bubbles are sucked into the line. The ***water-tight bulkheads*** conform to new construction rules [**#III.28**].

VII.123 'aphorisming eclectic': Coleridge criticizes the corrosion of metaphysical thought in popular philosophy: "that corruption, introduced by certain immethodical aphorisming eclectics, who, dismissing not only all system, but all logical connection, pick and chose whatever is most plausible and showy" [*Biographia Literaria* XII.x].

VII.124 shawled in snow: Aiken's phrase [**#IV.33**], affirming the philosophical thrust: the concrete on one side (windward), and the elemental on the other (leeward).

VII.125 Overhead Railway: the "Dockers' Umbrella" [**#VI.10**].

VII.126 the day's evil: Matthew 6:34: "Sufficient unto the day is the evil thereof." This undercuts Sigbjørn's repeated images (cathedral as warehouse, Kafka's *Castle*, Ibsen's *Master Builder*) [**#VII.16**], his hope that he and Nina are building something solid.

VII.127 New Brighton tower: modelled on the Eiffel Tower; at 568 feet the tallest in the United Kingdom, with views of the Isle of Man, Lake District, and the Welsh mountains. Opening in 1900, it was neglected during WWI; the cost of steel forced closure (1919) and demolition (1921). In 'Ghostkeeper', *The Magnet* (1950) screens Lowry's birthplace [**#VII.111**]: "There's the cathedral! That's Seacombe Pier! That's New Brighton Pier! There used to be a tower only they knocked it down. That's the old prom—called the Ham and Egg Parade. Birkenhead Ales, my God" [P&S 217].

VII.128 bricks of straw: Exodus 5:16: "Ye shall no more give the people straw to make brick, as heretofore: let them go and gather straw for themselves." Nina misconstrues the metaphor (compare 'Three Little Pigs').

VII.129 wavered: like Dante's trimmers [**#I.49**; **#II.69**; **#III.54**].

VII.130 Turk's Head: an ornamental knot resembling a turban.

VII.131 marlin-spike: an iron tool, tapering to a point, to splice ropes (or open tins of condensed milk [U 21]); here, loosening the ship's "strings" (an easy *berth*) from "the wharf's gray womb" [**#VII.203**].

VII.132 Last Post!: the trumpet solo played when a soldier is buried; **Reveille**: to rouse laggards, who mutter after Irving Berlin's 'Oh! How I Hate to Get Up in the Morning' (Sigbjørn's line is of his own making):

> *Someday I'm going to murder the bugler,*
> *Someday they're going to find him dead;*
> *I'll amputate his reveille, and step upon it heavily,*
> *And spend the rest of my life in bed.*

VII.133 Heloise: less Abelard's castration than his enforced parting. The Consul reflects that Yvonne has been reading *something*, perhaps the letters of Heloise [UTV 346].

VII.134 unsuccessful attempt: compare John Lee [**#II.4**].

VII.135 *Zeitgeist*: Ger. "spirit of the age".

VII.136 Hoboken: a grim New Jersey port on the Hudson; compare 'A Poem of God's Mercy' [CP #93]. The *Vestris* left Hoboken on her final voyage [**#VII.19**].

VII.137 Tao: from Lao-tze's *Tao Te Ching* [XXV], via Ouspensky's *Tertium Organum* [290; **#XIII.I**; **#XVIII.1**].

VII.138 escape from yourself: the Consul asks a frustrated Yvonne: "What's the use of escaping," he drew the moral with complete seriousness, "from ourselves" [UTV 84].

VII.139 Spitzbergen: north of the White Sea [**#I.58**; **#XVII.16**].

VII.140 grandma's beaded bag: the "indispensable", a Victorian fancy; intimating an uncomfortable return to the womb.

VII.141 Lawrence: "dark forces", a paean to sexual freedom and revolution, are equally a step towards fascism, as in *The Plumed Serpent* (1926). Lawrence affirmed a deep mystical communication between primitive peoples, based on feelings within the sympathetic ganglia and **blood consciousness** rather than the rational faculties, which he distrusted. Sigbjørn's belief that he might have turned to the left, had he lived (Lawrence died in 1930), is specious.

VII.142 America: perceived by leftists as a battleground. In Traven's *Cotton Pickers* (1926), Gale (a "Wobbly") becomes a rebel and a revolutionary by his love of justice and desire to help the wretched.

VII.143 university fashion: 1930s Cambridge was a nursery for Soviet spies.

VII.144 Goering: Herman Goering (1893–1946), Commander of the Luftwaffe. Hitler's right-hand man, by 1936 he held economic control and was a byword for ruthlessness.

VII.145 Hedda Gabler: in Ibsen's 1890 drama, Hedda's ruthlessness (another 'H. G.'?) causes immense suffering, but triggers her suicide when she loses her power over others.

VII.146 imitation of Christ: less the devotional work by Thomas à Kempis than its informing principle, that a Christian's every moment enacts Christ's perfection.

VII.147 white Hawthorne: white blossom of the *may*, or hawthorn; echoing Melville's "whence came you, Hawthorne?" [**#IV.3**; **#VI.69**].

VII.148 my bonny: 'My bonny lies over the ocean'; compare Aiken: "My bonnie will surely die young . . . Oh, bring back my bonnie to me" [*Blue Voyage* 210].

VII.149 hurricane deck: the promenade atop a passenger liner.

VII.150 Eastham ferry: Eastham, south of Birkenhead, had operated a ferry since medieval times, but service declined in the 1840s with the railway, Woodside [**#VII.5**] taking most of the traffic. The last paddle-steamer crossed the Mersey in 1929.

VII.151 swastika: Skr. *svastika*, "auspicious"; an ancient Aryan emblem that under Hitler (who adopted it from the Thule Society) became the *Hakenkreuz*, signature of the Reich. There is no confirmed record of any German battleship having entered the Mersey.

VII.152 Old Ropery: central Liverpool, near James Street station; a "rope-walk" where yarn was spread to be twisted into rope [U 73].

VII.153 penny for my eyes: Guy Fawkes Day (5 November): "A penny for the guy"; but pennies traditionally cover the eyes at death.

VII.154 Zionist: one committed to the right of Jewish peoples to their homeland, realized when Israel was born after WWII. Melville visited the Holy Land in 1856. Sigbjørn blends into his Hawthorne fantasia that pilgrimage with Tor's long journey [**#II.92**]; **annihilated** expresses Melville's death-wish [**#V.54**; **#VI.70**].

VII.155 metallurgies: Ernst Henri's Foreword to *Hitler over Europe* (1934) gave Lowry his title for 'June the 30th, 1934', that "Night of the Long Knives" beginning phase two of National Socialism (Goodyear's dream of 'metal' would enter a revised *In Ballast* [**#I.2**]). Henri predicted a third phase: either Hitler's death and a socialist revolution, or a European conflagration. The ambiguity of 'with' (*for, against*) reflects Sigbjørn's ambivalence.

VII.156 apex of Nordic culture: the vision informing Nazi ideology. As Nina presciently notes, Norway's raw materials (wood, iron ore) would trigger a German invasion (1941); she would not, as Sigbjørn hopes, be spared. Nina defines the contradictions in reconciling Sigbjørn's Nordic ideal with the grimmer realities of Aryan ideology that found expression in Vidkun Quisling's "**program of salvation**" [Henri 152]: a "**Nordic League of Nations**" to embrace National Socialism and unite the Baltic in close alliance with the Reich. Lowry claimed that (like Grieg) he recognized the danger early; Henri made this possible.

VII.157 headache: Ishmael's "hypos" [**#VI.71**].

VII.158 Chinese white: a dull oil for painting waves. Southport's melancholy sandhills [**#V.54**; **#VI.70**] are far from the Mersey, but Lowry (who knew better) follows Mumford.

VII.159 lee side: Ahab says: "Leeward! the white whale goes that way; look to windward, then; the better if the bitterer quarter" [*Moby-Dick* CXXXV]. The dialectic of *leeward* (abstraction) and *windward* (reality) informs Lowry's chapter.

VII.160 the roar of the sea and the darkness: a coda to Chapter II of *The Ship Sails On* [26]. The title of a poem [*CP* #97]; another opens with the line [*CP* #105], it was also Lowry's choice for his selected sea-poems. 'West Hardaway' and Part 5 of *Ultramarine* end thus; and the words echo in 'June the 30th, 1934' [*P&S* 40; **#X.102**].

VII.161 Cape Horn: to round the Horn and bypass the Land of Fire was for Lowry (as Masefield) the ultimate test. As the Consul notes, Cape Horn has a bad habit of wagging its tail [UTV 47].

VII.162 spindrift: spume from cresting waves.

VII.163 astral world: Tor, from *au délà*, somehow registers *perpetuum mobile* [**#VII.35**].

VII.164 whiteness ... redness: the White Sea as the whiteness of the whale [**#I.Title**]; there lurks "an elusive something in the innermost idea of this hue, which strikes more of panic to the soul than that redness which affrights in blood" [*Moby-Dick* LXII].

VII.165 Red Star: the Soviet emblem of Revolution. For **Novalis**, see **#VII.49**.

VII.166 Cummings: e.e. cummings (1894–1962), American poet; Sigbjørn implies his 'next to of course god america i / love you' (1926). Cummings visited Russia in 1931, recording his disillusionment in *Eimi* (1933).

VII.167 Myers: F. W. H. Myers (1843–1901), English essayist and founder of the Psychical Research Society; his *Human Personality and Its Survival of Bodily Death* (1890) affirms "progressive moral evolution" and spiritual discovery [**#X.25**]. Compare 'Peter Gaunt and the Canals', where the vision of the "really better land" falters: "Under the bleak north star of his self-mistrust / He has read or not read about in Myers?" [*CP* 52].

VII.168 Heine: Heinrich Heine (1797–1856), German-Jewish poet of wit and elegance. His *Dichterliebe* (1840) were set by Schumann (Op. 48, #18): "Ich grolle nicht, und wenn das Herz auch bricht / Ewig verlor'nes Lieb" [I do not murmur, though my heart break, love eternally lost]. Lowry's source is Houston Peterson, *The Melody of Chaos* [242], with reference to Aiken's *Blue Voyage*; Demarest, thinking of the unattainable Cynthia, is "Something like Heine who was at his most brilliant when his heart was breaking."

VII.169 Hedda Gabler: having found Lövborg's manuscript, Tesman gives it to Hedda [**#VII.145**] for safety, putting both men into her power. Fittingly, it concerns social forces shaping civilization.

VII.170 steerage: cattle-class.

VII.171 charity: cynical ("Charity begins at home") and selfless: "Charity suffereth long, and is kind" [1 Corinthians 13:4]. For *no trust*, see **#III.46**.

VII.172 eternity to eternity: Psalm 90:2, "from eternity to eternity thou art God."

VII.173 Goodbye, old masthead: Ahab, launching the final pursuit, addresses his lost leg: "But good bye, good bye, old mast-head . . . Aye, minus a leg, that's all . . . good by, mast-head—keep a good eye upon the whale, the while I'm gone. We'll talk tomorrow, nay, to-night, when the white whale lies down there, tied by head and tail" [*Moby-Dick* CXXXV].

VII.174 Job: his sons destroyed, livestock taken, and servants slain, Job, alone, testifies to God's goodness [**#III.42**].

VII.175 Coendet: perhaps a corruption of Ger. "So endet".

VII.176 *Goby* Dick: a tropical tiddler; Lowry's pun to Whit Burnet [*CL* 1:154].

VII.177 Soldiers' Chorus: now identified [**#VII.44**; **#VII.194**].

VII.178 Bidston Hill: *mons veneris* of the eastern Wirral [**#IX.24**; **#XI.37**; **#XI.41**].

VII.179 devil: in Liam O'Flaherty's *Shame the Devil* (1934), Lowry noted, the devil hankers after "fame and the fruits of success and social respectability" [*CL* 1:151]. Yet 'The Devil was a Gentleman' [*CP* #40]: he "Dantesquely loved a woman, / She proved as cold as ice".

VII.180 dances . . . / In Sicily!: *Il ballo dei diavoli* [dance of the devils], on Easter Sunday at Prizzi, Sicily, when villagers dressed as devils dance through the streets collecting souls. Mt. Etna is reputedly an entrance to the underworld.

VII.181 Davy Jones: those drowned at sea enter Davy Jones's locker; but "two" Siamese Twins cannot fit into one trunk.

VII.182 Barbary Coast: Ar. *barbaria*, "to babble", an appropriate etymology [**#V.111**].

VII.183 shilankobozzle: presumably, on the booze.

VII.184 *Merther* Nature: a *lusus naturae*, or freak of Mother Nature. Compare Artemus Ward, faced with a huge bear, which loved him "as a mer-ther loves her che-ild" [*London Punch Letters* pt. 5.7]. Nina abused the word 'che-ild' a little earlier.

VII.185 Ivory Coast: another African shore; barbaric feet on the ivory tablets of the Law.

VII.186 Caesar Imperator . . . Capitalismus: Traven, *The Death Ship* [150]: "The modern gladiators are greeting you, O great Caesar, Caesar Augustus Capitalismus. Morituri te salutamus! The moribund are greeting you, great Imperator Caesar Augustus. We are ready to die for you; for you and for the glorious and most holy insurance." Hence, 'liquidated'.

VII.187 by crimes: one of Masefield's bolder oaths; here, the criminality of the "coffin-ship" [**#VI.57**; **#VIII.49**]. For glycerine, see **#VI.56**.

VII.188 ploody cargo: with **barium peroxide**: an oxidizing agent, a bleach; **carbolic acid**: phenyl alcohol, an antiseptic from coal oils; **napthaline**: a white crystalline byproduct of coal-tar distillation, a disinfectant; **fusel oil**: from fermentation, present in many alcohols.

VII.189 Eurydice!: Orpheus has lost his wife [**#III.53**].

VII.190 diapasoned: with just intervals in the Pythagorean scale; here, the length of the heart's octave (from 'doom' through 'Pang' to 'Break').

VII.191 ghost of schism: metaphysical disjunction: the Siamese twins (facing different ways) mock Sigbjørn's divided self.

VII.192 shark glides white: "The shark / Glides white through the phosphorous sea"; from Melville's 'Commemorative of Naval Victory' [Mumford 3, 210; **#II.32**; **#XV.43**]. Pedantic note: the only White Sea shark is the Greenland Grey.

VII.193 quadrant: an instrument to determine latitude; **gaff-topsail boots**, like Redburn's [**#III.141**]; **fustian:** bombast; a heavy fabric (cotton weft, linen warp), garb of the fool.

VII.194 Gounod: Charles-François Gounod (1818–1893), composer of *Faust* (1859). 'The Soldiers' Chorus' [**#VII.177**] is popularly rendered as "O Jemima, look at your Uncle Jim"; said Uncle ("riding on a bicycle, just you look at him") having a torrid time: "First he goes to the left, / And then he goes to the right, / And now he's gone completely out of sight." Sigbjørn might not relish the irony.

VII.195 a nice burg: from the *Titanic*'s galleys [**#VII.18**]; **bon voyage**, as famously uttered by Samuel Goldwyn to those farewelling him.

VII.196 Collision mats: rough ("fothered") squares of canvas and twine, to absorb impact.

VII.197 country of counterfeit architecture: England, as described by Francis Wey in *A Frenchman among the Victorians* (1936) [130]. 'Counterfeit architecture' is a technical term for projections painted to imitate marble.

VII.198 *Doom*: like the last stroke (Sigbjørn is running, it is twelve) on the night Tor died.

VII.199 cradle-song ... threnody of the sea: as Whitman's 'Out of the cradle endlessly rocking'.

VII.200 horror of opposites: Ouspensky's unity of opposites [*Tertium Organum* 242]; Blake's contraries, without which there is no progress; or Boehme's strife of opposites. Lawhill agonizes, "I am sent to save my father, to find my son, to heal the eternal horror of three, to resolve the immedicable horror of opposites" [*The Last Address* 104; **#II.67**].

VII.201 trembling in every mast: like Vigil Forget [**#V.77**].

VII.202 *Adam Cadmon*: archetypal Adam, or "primal man" of the Kabbalah or Blake; the esoteric *Idea* of Adam. Ouspensky explicitly invokes Adam Kadmon when imaging the soul as a liner [*Tertium Organum* XVII 202–03; **#XVIII.1**]. Hence Sigbjørn's sentiment: "let the ship be man"; with **factions**, like those phantoms of the Consul's fragmented being [**#IV.67**]; intimations of **molecular disaster** [*Blue Voyage* 288; **#III.122**]; and **terrible eyes**, seen again as Sigbjørn leaves home [**#XI.28**].

VII.203 gray womb: following earlier intimations of "berth" [**#VII.131**]

VII.204 anguish with the sea: Lowry noted: "My soul is breaking in anguish with the sea" [UBC 1:75]. Sigbjørn adds: "'The Sea rushing through your soul in great cold waves of anguish' is a wonderful end to a chapter"; this is "vascular remorse" [*Mordida* 42, 332].

CHAPTER VIII

VIII.1 [Epigraph] E. T. Brown: unidentified. Improbably, Thomas Edward ("T. E.") Brown (1830–1897), a Manx poet Lowry mentioned to Jimmy Craige [CL 2:781 (1956)]. A **surd** is an irrational number; **residual difference**, that between the statistical mean and an observed instance. The epigraph suggests Sigbjørn's troubled mind [**#VIII.4**], wherein obscure forces determine "momentous transition".

VIII.2 iron bridge: near the Caldy clubhouse [**#VIII.5**]; players descending Croft Drive passed under it, perhaps noting, as the marginalia to 'Sumptuous Armour' does: "Warning: Low Archway" [**#III.114**]. Lowry added "**Cheshire Lines 1840**", noting: "a railway bridge a century old" [UBC 11:12, 1]. Yet that rusted inscription is mysterious: '1840' is not obviously a date, as the West Kirby to Chester line was opened in 1866 by the London NW and Cheshire West Joint Railway—not the Cheshire Railway, which ran the central Wirral line (New Brighton to Chester) [**#VIII.62**].

VIII.3 first and ninth holes: the clubhouse faced the first tee and ninth green. The ninth (par 4,356 yards; now the sixth) was "The Donga", after an awkward fairway sluice with rushes and gorse; players either cleared it to reach the green, or laid up safe but short. Quaunahuac's *barranca* is an "immense intricate donga" [UTV 130]. Lowry's film script offers this setting: a single-line railway embankment left, water to the right [*Tender* 105].

VIII.4 the horrible to the commonplace: from Kipling's 'The Phantom Rickshaw' (1885): Jack Pansay, haunted by the spectre of Agnes Wessington (a past paramour), passes from sanity to madness.

VIII.5 club-house: a cottage built (1908) for £350, with a verandah on the playing side, a lounge with log fire, and a locker-room right (another added in 1925). Caldy was then a private club, its nine holes designed by Jack Morris, the Royal Liverpool professional [**#VIII.12**]. Construction was £50, but the land when bought from the Caldy Manor Estate in 1923 cost £7,000. Arthur Lowry was Club

Captain from 1920. The house, still named "The Nineteenth Hole", is now privately owned.

VIII.6 *The Golfer*: *Golf Illustrated*, a monthly edited from 1913 by Harold Hilton, of West Kirby, who won the British Amateur four times and the US Open (1911); an annual Harold Hilton Medal tournament commemorates his 1897 victory at Hoylake (his home club).

VIII.7 medal: unlike *matchplay* (holes won, lost, or halved), in a *medal* round strokes are tallied, the winner taking fewest. Caldy held monthly medals for the Dawpool and Dinn Cups.

VIII.8 three strokes: to win the hole, the Captain must beat Sigbjørn by four strokes (e.g., birdie to triple bogey); a win by three would halve; two or fewer, lose. Notes to 'Sumptuous Armour' say that when Arthur Lowry stopped playing his handicap went from sixteen to twenty, and next year would be twenty-four [UBC 11:12, 1].

VIII.9 Macleoran: Caldy had no Professional until J. H. Youds of Hoylake was appointed in 1936. Any import of Macleoran's name, or his refrain, "It's the way it is", is unknown.

VIII.10 eighteen holes: in 1929, the Estate [**#VIII.5**] offered the Club fifty acres to extend the course to eighteen holes. James Braid, golf course architect and five times Open winner, critiqued (for ten guineas) the proposal. Work began in 1930 with the new holes played in 1931. Lowry modifies this time frame.

VIII.11 fifth: Braid lengthened the third (392 to 490 yards); realigned the fourth, shortening it (220 to 185 yards); and complicated the fifth (later the fourteenth) by lengthening it (286 to 305 yards), turning the "straight run" into a dog-leg right [**#VIII.60**].

VIII.12 Royal Liverpool: members stress the 'Royal' [**#XIII.11**]; a links at Hoylake, north of Caldy; often home to the British Open. Its first is a slight dog-leg.

VIII.13 drink: the original clubhouse had no bar, but tea was ordered through a fireside hatch. Sunday play began after 12:30 p.m., with no refreshments available. A bar eventuated, with the first drinks served 5 August 1932.

VIII.14 golfballs: serving the obsolete: the **Dunlop 30** was a mass-produced rubber core. The **Chemico Bob**, made from 1910 by the Birmingham County Chemical Co. ("Chemico"), sold for one shilling (a "bob"). Russell Lowry recalled the **Zodiac Zone**, with its "pattern of stars and crescents" [UBC 14:30]. The Consul asks, "Who hunts my Zodiac Zone along the shore?" [UTV 203]; one appears (along the shore) in *October Ferry* [113]. **Repaints** are balls whitened for re-use (new ones were expensive).

VIII.15 Drake in Plymouth: Francis Drake was playing bowls on Plymouth Hoe (19 July 1588) when the Spanish Armada [**#VIII.93**] was sighted; there was time to finish the game, he insisted, and beat the Spaniards. Yet 'Not all of us were heroes' [CP #259]: the Poet, at Plymouth, has "played woods too long / On dark unshaven greens" [**#VIII.56**].

VIII.16 through a mist: echoing Bix Beiderbecke's piano solo, 'In a Mist'; recorded New York (9 Sept. 1927); repeated throughout Lowry's *Tender is the Night*.

VIII.17 well-deck: a small afterdeck, near the waterline.

VIII.18 innermost bulb: balls like the Zodiac Zone were machine-made, rubber strands wound about a soft core, within a hard shell; an advance on "gutties" and "featheries".

VIII.19 clubs: in 'Sumptuous Armour', Dick farewells his clubs: "iron, niblick, putter, mashie, brassie" [P&S 230].

niblick: with a wooden haft and metal blade, for chipping; roughly, a wedge.

mashie-iron: wooden-shafted; a middle iron [**#VIII.69**].

clock: otherwise, *cleek*, with a narrow face and little loft; for longer shots.

spoon: a wood with a concave face, for lofted shots; roughly, a #3 wood.

Braid-Mills putter: with an aluminium head; designed by James Braid [**#VIII.10**] for Sir James Mills's Standard Golf Co. (1890 to the 1930s).

jigger: like a niblick, with lesser loft; for longer chips.

VIII.20 re-teed: having disturbed his ball, the Captain (illegally) replaces it.

VIII.21 sliced, topped: hit high on the ball (*topped*) and sent right (*sliced*).

VIII.22 Pangloss: Candide's tutor [**#VIII.58**] believes, despite his evident misfortunes, in Leibniz's pre-established harmony, the doctrine that all is for the best.

VIII.23 Point of Ayr: the northeast corner of **Flintshire**, on the Welsh side of the estuary; a prevailing nor'-westerly enters the Dee off the Irish Sea. The Welsh mountains are visible from the Wirral; compare the Taskersons' vista [UTV 17].

VIII.24 Mostyn: an iron-working town across the Dee; the vermillion glow is from its steel furnaces. Compare the view from Dollarton across Burrard Inlet to the **[S]HELL** Refinery at Burnaby, Lowry's later emblem of hell **[#VIII.98; #XVI.43]**.

VIII.25 Irish Channel: the Irish Sea north and west of the Wirral; a busy shipping lane.

VIII.26 sands: when the tide ebbs in the Dee estuary, extensive mottled sands are exposed. The only water visible is mid-estuary; when the tide returns, the sands disappear.

VIII.27 Neston: a mining town on the Wirral side of the Dee. ***Parkgate***, downriver from Neston, was a shipyard active in the slave trade until the port silted. Edward King's long journey **[#VIII.95]** began in Parkgate, home to Lady Hamilton (and Russell Lowry). The father in 'Sumptuous Armour' says, "All on one side, like Parkgate" [P&S 231], meaning three pubs facing the river.

VIII.28 memory of Norway: leaving Kristiania, Grieg's *Mignon* passes Sivert's house, shining with fresh white paint.

VIII.29 second tee: par four, its 236 yards later extended to 330; an easier hole.

VIII.30 three-ball matches: three players compete **[#VIII.7]**, each result "matched" against the other two.

VIII.31 shirred: Pip's terror: "White squalls? white whale, shirr! shirr! Here have I heard all their chat just now, and the white whale—shirr! shirr!" [*Moby-Dick* XL].

VIII.32 natural hazards: inbounds obstacles, from which players must hit without grounding the club, or take a penalty from a designated drop; features of the terrain (trees, rocks), rather than 'water' or 'man-made' (bunkers).

VIII.33 face of the waters: Genesis 1:2, the wind like the spirit of God **[#VII.60]**, arousing, with the train, smoke, and evanescence of steam (from chapter I) the spirit of Tor.

VIII.34 single line: West Kirby to Chester **[#VIII.3]**; for golfers outward bound, to the left; compare 'Sumptuous Armour' [P&S 229].

VIII.35 Thurstaston: the next stop south; a Viking settlement mentioned in the Domesday Book as *Thurstanetone*, "town of Thorsteinn" **[#I.18]**; but assumed to be 'Thor's Stone', after a sandstone outcrop on Thurstaston Common. Lowry's jazz-musician might have become the Earl of Thurstaston (like 'Duke' Ellington, or 'Count' Basie) [*Maelstrom* 103].

VIII.36 socket: to "shank", or hit the ball with the neck ("socket") of the club, *slicing* it. As the wood is to larboard, the Captain must be left-handed.

VIII.37 mid-iron: for shots to the green rather than from the tee. This green is easily driven; the Captain's approach is short.

VIII.38 sheep: in the early 1920s, when Lowry played, sheep cropped the grass; this practice was abandoned, but reintroduced during WWII.

VIII.39 proper discharges: certification of completed voyages, in the Blue Book [**#XIII.30**].

VIII.40 privity: defining legal responsibility; crudely, if the master should have acted, he is at fault; if the owners have determined the conditions, they are. Lowry's film script asserts "the privity of the owner that is not yet the privity of the master" [*Tender* 172]. Lowry noted to Robert Giroux "a famous point in maritime law 'where the privity of the owner be not the privity of the master etc etc', the clause that the latter so rarely avails himself of even though entitled to" [*CL* 2:542 (1952)].

VIII.41 next tee: the third hole, the "Spinney", par five, 392 yards; both play this well.

VIII.42 all in all: Hamlet, of his father: "He was a man, take him for all in all, / I shall not look upon his like again" [I.ii.187–88].

VIII.43 pretty: the "fairway" (obsolete).

VIII.44 *Skibets reise fra Kristiania*: Erikson's novel [**#I.51**]; no such incident occurs in Grieg's original.

VIII.45 mutually assist: added to Sigbjørn's *hyrkontrakt* from the (British) 1894 Seamen's *Articles*. When Lowry joined the *Pyrrhus* an extra clause stated that firemen and sailors should "mutually assist each other in the general duties of the ship" [U 17; UTV 157]. Grieg notes the divide between seamen and firemen, between "two worlds on opposite sides of the alleyway, a boundless mutual contempt" [*Ship Sails On* 81]. When the *Mignon* hits a storm and Anton dies, firemen and seamen work strenuous double shifts; antipathy is briefly overcome, and Benjamin gains respect.

VIII.46 *Henrik Ibsen*: on which Grieg sailed to Cape Town and Australia (1921), returning via the Suez [**#IV.68**; **#XIV.29**]. This inspired *Rundt Kap det gode Haab* (1922) and *Skibet gaar videre* (1924) [**#I.51**]. She was built in Middlesbrough (1906) for Vilhelm Torkildsen (Bergen), and scrapped in 1952. The name, Sigbjørn Wilderness reflects, is profound, if only he knew what the implications were [UBC 9:5 355]. Lowry recounts discussing the writer 'Henry Gibson' with Grieg, to find that the subject was *Henrik Ibsen* [*CL* 1:110].

VIII.47 another war: a "nightmare" foreshadowed in 'June the 30th, 1934' [#VII.155].

VIII.48 elements: proclaiming "a sort a determinism about the fate of nations" (as in 'June the 30th, 1934'), the Consul enlists the periodical chart (and the esoteric) to reject intervention as useless [UTV 303–04].

VIII.49 Girdlestone: in Conan Doyle's *The Firm of Girdlestone* (1890), a father deceives his son over disastrous speculations; recovery ploys, such as sending out unseaworthy over-insured ships, cause greater disasters. In a late chapter, 'A Voyage in a Coffin-Ship', they flee in one of these; it founders, and in the ensuing chaos Ezra brutally kills his father.

VIII.50 senseless force: the malignant White Whale as Schopenhauer's doctrine of the Will [#III.20]: a blind, mindless force let "loose" [#IX.5], as opposed to Tor's sense of "accident" [#II.25] and whatever "power for good" [#II.23] Sigbjørn may be seeking. The Captain's next two shots illustrate the point.

VIII.51 periwinkles: courtesy of the Mad Fisherman of Worcester [#III.58].

VIII.52 without addressing: without having aligned his club against the ball. The Consul imagines his new Silver King "twinkling" on the green [UTV 203].

VIII.53 British Law: the *Merchant Shipping Act* (1894) limited owners' liability for maritime losses, protecting trade and allowing them to stay in business by insuring against risks, and restricting responsibility to loss or damage of cargo "carried on board".

VIII.54 matrix: the hole created by the ball [#III.96].

VIII.55 stymie: of a shot finishing between another ball and the hole.

VIII.56 walk unseen: Milton's 'Il Penseroso' [lines 65–66], a paean to poor putting: "And missing thee, I walk unseen / On the dry smooth-shaven green" [#VIII.15].

VIII.57 fourth: the 'Pond': par three, 220 yards (later shortened to 185), towards the railway.

VIII.58 cultivate our garden: recalling Tor's reference to Candide's final words [#III.69].

VIII.59 divot: turf hacked out as the shot is played ("gardening"), failure to replace it the unpardonable sin. The Consul is "Poet of the unreplaced turf" [UTV 203].

VIII.60 fifth: the new "Dog Leg" [**#VIII.11**]. The Captain (now right-handed) "pulls" his shot towards the embankment. His fear of slicing out of bounds (at Caldy) is excessive.

VIII.61 marguerites: Thomas à Kempis, *pretiosa margarita, a multis abscondita* [pretty marguerite, hidden from many], the soul's *Imitation of Christ* [XXXII.iv]; "hot and dark" was Sigbjørn's deistic sensation on the *Arcturion* [**#VII.57**].

VIII.62 asphaltic slag: tarry debris from coalmines. Lowry has invested Caldy with features of the West Cheshire course [**#VIII.2**]; the Cheshire Line adjacent to that *might* carry residue from the Cheshire mines, but neither it nor the West Kirby line would run fifty-six trucks. Further . . .

VIII.63 Llay Main: a mining town near Wrexham; in 'Sumptuous Armour', Dick passes south of Crewe "sixty-six trucks of asphaltic slag from Llay Main" [P&S 236–37], noting an "indefinable plangency" as each clicks by. "Where was Llay Main?" admits the problem.

VIII.64 Brueghel bird: as Pieter Brueghel the Younger's *Winter Landscape with a Bird Trap* (1565), an allegory of the ensnared soul. A black bird flies as Childe Roland nears the Dark Tower [**#VIII.83**].

VIII.65 Preston: whence the *Unsgaard* departs. Sigbjørn's curious ignorance (later qualified [**#XIII.54**]) accentuates "the road to the North" motif.

VIII.66 Norsk Konsulat: see **#V.59**.

VIII.67 watched: at the clubhouse a policeman awaits [**#IX.18**]; Jump is monitoring Sigbjørn [**#XII.32**]. Ghostly surveillance pervades Lowry's writing.

VIII.68 immaterial: punning on corporeality; the Captain's soul, not his fate, is immaterial. Compare Faustus, terrified by certain damnation.

VIII.69 full mashie: about ninety yards; a *mashie* [**#VIII.19**] is shorter than an iron, its swing constrained. Properly executed, it takes some turf.

VIII.70 banking the turf: building a capital green [**#IX.8**].

VIII.71 sixth: 286 (later, 335) yards, the "Estuary"; turning towards the clubhouse.

VIII.72 Gutties: solid rubber (*gutta percha*) horrors of limited velocity, however thwacked. Laruelle and "Joffrey" drive "some wretched gutta-percha golf balls" into the sea [UTV 17].

VIII.73 Silver Kings: quality balls, their coloured dots denoting different weights.

VIII.74 Harry Vardon: (1870–1937), Jersey, winner of six Opens; despite the Captain's assurance, never at Hoylake, though he won his fourth (Prestwick, 1903) with a gutty.

VIII.75 daisy-cutter: a shot that skims the ground.

VIII.76 serve the obsolete: Melville's 'The Stone Fleet: An Old Sailor's Lament' (1861) celebrates ships long gone: "they serve the obsolete" [**#XI.69**].

VIII.77 pot-bunker: small, deep, and round; easy to enter, hard to escape.

VIII.78 rabbit: in the 1940 *Volcano*, Hugh's brother Jack releases rabbits "with a mashie-niblick" [323], eliciting James Stephens's poem about a snared rabbit.

VIII.79 dormie: in matchplay, up by the number of holes to play, requiring but a half to win.

VIII.80 seventh: par five, the "Cliffs", 374 yards. Holes 8 and 9 are not played.

VIII.81 cliff: the last three holes followed the coast, along a clay cliff thirty feet high. Erosion was a concern; in 1937 a hole was abandoned when its tee fell into the estuary. The advice to drive left is odd (Lowry wants to get to the shore), as the "wood" aligns the distant railway embankment, with another fairway between.

VIII.82 Roman turret: there are no Roman remains here; Lowry perhaps mythologizes some ruined lime-kilns near the shore.

VIII.83 Childe Roland: Browning's 'Childe Roland to the Dark Tower Came' (1855); the title, from *King Lear*'s Mad Tom [III.iv.187], suggests a disturbed mind [*Blue Voyage* 208]. Sigbjørn registers a curious link to the ivory tower . . .

VIII.84 Roland Childe: I. A. Richards's *Practical Criticism* (1929) tested the critical acumen of Cambridge English majors, with predictable results. Sigbjørn cites lines 5–8 of Poem #12, Wilfred Rowland Childe's sonnet, 'Ivory Palaces' (1925).

VIII.85 *Lusitania*: outward bound; she was sunk on her return [**#VII.20**].

VIII.86 plunging freighter: compare the French collier [**#V.76**]; Sigbjørn often envisages such disasters.

VIII.87 quartermaster: the seaman responsible for practical navigation [**#XVI.5**].

VIII.88 log-wheel: a wheel at the stern to determine progress, as measured by a marker thrown astern, playing out a line knotted at regular intervals (hence "knots").

VIII.89 salvaged her: in the 1930s attempts were made, led by Simon Lake, to salvage the *Lusitania* [**#VII.20**], using a steel tube to set a chamber on its deck, from which divers would retrieve valuables. Lake's contract expired (1935) with little success; sporadic attempts have been made since.

VIII.90 minute lens: to imprint an "optogram" on the retina of a victim of murder: "The murderer's image in the eye of the murdered" [*Ulysses* VI]. When Harry [Henry?] Gibson's son, in Jules Verne's *The Kip Brothers* (1902), magnifies a photo of his father's eyes, two specks of light reveal his murderers. Maurice Renard in *The Hands of Orlac* (1921) calls this fantasy. The scene is an illegal anatomy lesson, the corpse supplied by "resurrection men".

VIII.91 twelve bones: of the skull: two of the *os frontis*; four each of the *os occipitis* and *ossa temporalis*; and the two *ossa parietalia*.

VIII.92 wolf: Webster's *The White Devil* [V.iv]: "But keep the wolf far thence, that's foe to men, / For with his nails he'll dig them up again"; equally, Eliot's parody of resurrection in *The Waste Land*, the corpse buried in the garden (a burden of guilt), dug up by the Dog.

VIII.93 Armada: galleons sent by Philip II of Spain to invade England (1588) [**#VIII.15**].

VIII.94 Pen-y-Pass: a col in Gwynedd, Snowdonia, atop the Llanberis Pass. In September 1933, Lowry and Jan, with Tom Forman, stayed at the **Gorphwysfa** Hotel ("primitive and damned cold"), the men rock climbing [*Inside* 27; **#XII.7**]. This provoked 'The walls of remorse are steep' [*CP* #75], recalling the death of Paul Fitte [**#III.125**]. **Penmaenmawr** (Welsh, "great stone hill") is a town on the North Wales coast; **Snowdon**, 3,560 feet, the highest peak in Wales; **Cader-Idris**, a mountain in Snowdonia National Park.

VIII.95 Hilbre: an island in the Dee estuary, accessible by foot (or donkey) from West Kirby [**#X.20**] at low tide. 'Sumptuous Armour' opens on this course, a freezing day with snow in the bunkers: "Out there, beyond Hilbre, Lycidas had drowned" [*P&S* 230]. Edward King's drowning off Hilbre (1637) inspired Milton's ***Lycidas***; Sigbjørn quotes its opening line.

VIII.96 such a son is drowned: Marston's *Antonio's Revenge* [V.ii.3], via *Blue Voyage* [303, 308], with Lowry's variant [*CP* #21]: "Rich happiness that such a son is crowned."

VIII.97 sand martins: small swallows, with soft brown heads and upper body, dark-brown banded chest and white below; they nest in holes dug into banks, sandy cliffs or gravel pits.

VIII.98 Mostyn furnaces: lasting intimations of hell [**#VIII.24**; **#XVI.43**], with the rote of the bleak, dark sea.

CHAPTER IX

IX.1 [Epigraph] W. H. Hudson: from 'El Ombú' [**#V.1**], in *Tales of the Pampas* [41]: the narrator beneath the tree recalls great sadness, and Donata's dead husband [**#V.50**]. For Lowry's changes, see the Textual Notes.

IX.2 sentiments: as Tennyson's 'Ulysses': "To seek, to strive, and never to yield"; cited (at school break-ups and the like) when Youth sets forth on Life's great Adventure.

IX.3 Boy's Brigade: founded in Glasgow by William Alexander Smith (1883), to reconcile discipline and manly activities with Christian values.

IX.4 Salvation Army: founded by General William Booth and his wife Catherine as the Christian Mission (1865), emphasizing street services, music, and care of the poor [**#V.26**].

IX.5 ***loose*:**

> Captain Hansen-Tarnmoor believes in the destruction of time, in eternal recurrence, simply in a notion that life is like a wave, that the tendencies of a previous life are strengthened in this one: but this also is based on no faith. The notions of punishment and reward, etc believed in by Sigbjørn, however, do not fit in: all he can say is if you turn back from the true path, whether God or damnation was at the end of it, you loose something nobody can arrest. ['Notes' 16]

Earlier intimated [**#V.84**; **#VIII.50**]. An allegory of the True Path [**#IX.27**] follows; Sigbjørn must be bold, despite invisible antagonists [**#XIV.48**].

IX.6 derrick crazily adrift: Grieg's storm scene [*Ship Sails On* 120] recurs in Lowry's poetry [*CP* #99, #105, #118]. Compare *Blue Voyage* [240].

IX.7 topping-lift: a line ("uphaul") from the masthead to the outward end of the boom, to support the mainsail when "topped", or hoisted. **Crosstrees** are horizontal masthead struts, anchoring topgallant shrouds: "Courage is not standing on the crosstrees / Checking the topping lift . . . " [*CP* #195].

IX.8 turf-cutters: men banking turf for nine new holes [**#VIII.70**], imaged like an Expressionist still. Drainage was a concern.

IX.9 riddle of the sphinx: *what goes on four legs in the morning, two legs at noon, and three legs in the evening?* Oedipus answered correctly: man, who crawls as a baby, then walks upright, and uses a ferrule in old age [**#IV.32**; **#VII.23**].

IX.10 extraordinary consideration: as the one-legged beggar to the legless one [UTV 341].

IX.11 dark skeleton: enhancing the Captain's sense of something *loosed* in the world [**#IX.5**]; later applied to the coal-chute [**#XV.32**].

IX.12 cockle fishers: the Dee estuary's extensive cockling beds are accessible at low tide; pollution and over-picking were a problem. The **vermillion glare** reflects the Mostyn furnaces [**#VIII.24**].

IX.13 Newton: Sir Isaac Newton (1643–1727) dismissed his achievements, saying however he might appear to the world, "to myself I seem to have been only like a boy playing on the sea-shore, and diverting myself in now and then finding a smoother pebble or a prettier shell than ordinary, whilst the great ocean of truth lay all undiscovered before me." Newton was Blake's spectre of rationalism, occluding the doors of perception; Blake wrote to Thomas Butt (22 Nov. 1802): "May God us keep / From Single vision & Newtons sleep."

IX.14 jagged circumference: the small headland adjacent to the ninth green.

IX.15 dark ocean: in his preface to *The Only Possible Ground* (1762), Kant says that to acknowledge that God exists one must "venture into the bottomless abyss of metaphysics", which proves "a dark ocean without shore and without lighthouses". For Sigbjørn, this is but the "beginning" of Kant's transcendental philosophy [**#III.55**]: because the *Ding an sich* is inaccessible to sensory perception in the phenomenal world, knowledge is partial, lacking a common absolute [**#II.33**] (as the subsequent miscommunication confirms).

IX.16 desolate heath: elemental, like that of *Macbeth*, or *King Lear*. The **spume of reality** suggests Yeats, 'Among School Children' (Stanza VI): "Plato thought nature but a spume that plays / Upon a ghostly paradigm of things ".

IX.17 putting green: a practice area near the first tee, the wire fence excluding sheep.

IX.18 policeman: surveillance, by a power of good [**#II.23**; **#VIII.67**; **#XII.32**].

IX.19 station: Caldy station, built 1909, the club contributing £250; back under the iron bridge [**#VIII.2**], and over Croft Drive. Many members came by train.

IX.20 Birkenhead: "Liverpool's bedroom": a dormitory town and industrial port; the main ferry terminal to Liverpool before the Mersey Tunnel (1886) [**#VI.4**]. The *Pyrrhus* departed from Birkenhead.

IX.21 iron bridge: Lowry repeats '1840' [**#VIII.3**].

IX.22 Fleet Lane: a cutting (since lost under landscaping) from Croft Drive to a bridleway (continuing Shore Lane); emerging where **King's Drive** winds up Caldy Hill. Young Lowry, free-wheeling down King's Drive, crashed at the "hair-pin bend" and gashed his right knee, leaving a diagonal scar that became (Margerie insisted) "a bullet wound suffered on his earlier trip to China" [P&S xii]. **Grange** is between West Kirby and Caldy on the A540, the "main road" to Chester.

IX.23 abandoned road: a circuitous route now barely identifiable, ascending Caldy Hill past the quarry [**#IX.25**], towards Fleck Lane and away from Inglewood, which is on the flat (the Captain lives on the hill). The topography has allegorical insistence [**#IX.29**]; to reach home (Truth) they must go (like Donne) "about and about" [**#VII.57**].

IX.24 red sandstone: much of the Wirral comprises two ridges of Triassic red sandstone: west (the Grange, Caldy and Thurstaston hills); and east (including Bidston Hill [**#VII.178**]). The Fender Valley between was scoured by an ancient glacier.

IX.25 donkey-engine: an auxiliary steam-powered winch used in mining or logging, or (at sea) to hoist sails, load cargo [*Blue Voyage* 6–7], and pump bilge-water [**#XVI.31**]. The debris (overturned trucks, flanged wheels) is the residua of a tramline taking sandstone from Caldy Hill to the shore; quarrying ceased in 1935.

IX.26 lights of Liverpool: visible from Grange Hill, but not from Caldy. The **lighthouse** is, perhaps, that on Hilbre; one of a network that dotted the Wirrall. Red (port) lamps are ships going out; green (starboard), those returning. **Thurstaston Hill** is an elevation of the western Wirral (298 feet), southeast of Caldy; part of Thurstaston Common and location of "Thor's Stone" [**#VIII.35**].

IX.27 true road: taken by Christian [**#IX.29**] from the Wicket Gate; "the way is narrow that leads to life" [Matthew 7:14]. For **foolish virgins**, see **#II.72**.

IX.28 'N.L.': surname unknown [**#II.36**]. New growth obscures such carvings.

IX.29 Christian's burden: in *Pilgrim's Progress* (1678), Christian meets Mr. Worldly Wiseman, who tells him to ease his burden by consulting Legality; but it seems heavier. He is relieved by finding the right way, straight and narrow, that leads to

Salvation and the Cross; whereupon the burden falls from his shoulders, tumbles into the Sepulchre, and disappears.

IX.30 new forms of relation: as Rilke said of Ibsen [*Malte Laurids Brigge* I], an ever more desperate search for visible correlations of the inwardly seen.

IX.31 waterfall: the forest path to Parián is similar [UTV XI]; Hugh in the 1940 *Volcano* "sees" Niagara thus [324].

IX.32 Skjaeggedalsfoss: a waterfall (525 feet) fifty miles east of Bergen, near Tysseda in the Hardanger Fjord. The 'Varsity' CB sets the scene: "near to them a little streams singing was quite swallowed up by the savagery of this tumult; & Sigbjorn thought of the waterfalls at home in Norway, some so slender that they seemed [*almost*] from far below mere frescoes on the rocks [*but with gathered impetus*] others fell roaring for a quarter of a mile from the summit to the shoulders of cliffs." From Robert McBride, *Norwegian Towns* (1923), of nearby Naerodal [64]; reworked by Lowry into almost the final form (his "cry of the sea" is not McBride's). From the next page [65] he copied: 'Skjaeggedalsfoss—three times the height of Niagara". This cataract illustrated a review of Edward Rashleigh's *Among the Waterfalls of the World* [*Country Life* (15 Feb. 1936, 167)], which Lowry may have seen.

IX.33 chain-breaker singlets: under-vests, originally worn in strong-man circus acts; **fireman's slippers** offer grip and insulation on a stokehold floor; tincture of **iodine**, potassium, or sodium iodide dissolved in ethanol and water, relieves grazes and burns.

IX.34 Birkenhead Park: a station on the Mersey Railway, before Birkenhead Central, where commuters could leave cars. Rail service to West Kirby began in 1938; hence, the narrator of 'Sumptuous Armour' is chauffeured [P&S 233], and Sigbjørn drives there.

IX.35 long journey: repeating the ex-sailor's ominous words [**#II.92**], the Norwegian scene [**#IX.32**] endorsing Jensen [**#X.73**].

CHAPTER X

X.1 [Epigraph] Franz Kafka: (1883–1924), Bohemian-Jewish author of *The Trial* (1925) and *The Castle* (1926) [**#VII.106**]. Lowry cites his 'Zürau Aphorisms' (1917–1919), trans. Edwin and Willa Muir, in 'Reflections on Sin, Pain, Hope, and the True Way' [#64 294].

X.2 trial by fire: guilt or innocence established by walking over hot coals or holding red-hot irons; with a nod towards Kafka's *Trial*.

X.3 'Hairy Ape': Eugene O'Neill's play, *The Hairy Ape* (1922). The brutish Yank, formerly content as a stoker, jumps ship when a rich girl calls him a "filthy beast". Seeking his identity, he is everywhere rejected until he meets his fatal imago in the Bronx Zoo gorilla. Lowry saw a Cambridge Festival Theatre production (Nov. 1928) [**#III.146**].

X.4 coal burner: a ship reliant on coal (not oil) to generate steam [**#XII.48**].

X.5 limper: from Sigbjørn's *hyrkontrakt* [**#V.56**]. Correctly (as Lowry surely knew), Nor. *lemper*, or *kullemper*, "coal-heaver". The error intimates *Oedipus*, "swell-foot" [**#III.16**]. See the Textual Notes.

X.6 flag: the whirling banner of Dante's *Inferno* [**#V.125**].

X.7 *forêts de symboles:* from Baudelaire's 'Correspondances' (1857), Nature a temple: man passes there through forests of symbols that watch him with esoteric glances. Swedenborg's *Heaven and Hell* #303] affirms a correspondence of the natural world with the spiritual; an a-causal force of coincidence within a serial universe, binding individuals and configurations in time and space, correlating by affinity and analogy. See the Textual Notes.

X.8 wings of folly: on which to fly high, then fall into the abyss of despair.

X.9 infantile: Freud's term for the first part (until age six) of sexuality, with oral, anal and genital phases before periods of latency, then puberty. Sigbjørn sets the theme: sea voyage as rebirth or regression (folly), or both. Lenin's *Left-Wing Communism: An Infantile Disorder* is invoked later, the political mirroring the psychoanalytical [**#X.86**].

X.10 Parnassien: Rimbaud declared (24 May 1870): "je serai Parnassien"; a symbolist poet publishing in *Le Parnasse contemporain*, home to the Parisian muses.

X.11 'sun's vintage': from the opening of *The Coming of Coal* (1922), by Robert Bruère: "During ages without number the shifting seas and the slow-moving mountains had pressed down the sun's vintage in the coal beds of the earth." Bruère affirms "the progress of the race toward brotherhood" [9] and "our own Nordic ancestors" [11]. Jan Gabrial was researching a story about coal mining [*Inside* 79]; coal as metaphor fuels Lowry's chapter.

X.12 heave ashes: to winch baskets of ashes to the deck, emptying them into the sea.

X.13 ssspang: with vague intimations (perhaps) of Tibetan mysticism, as in *The Teachings of Padmasambhava*, on the understanding of infinity [Guenther 70]. The falling coal is metaphysically that shifting in the bunkers, threatening the physical ship [**#VII.19**; **#X.14**].

X.14 underground railway: Freudian threats [**#III.50**] are explicit: the **crater** as womb, mine, vortex, and volcano [**#II.38**; **#VI.9**]. Sigbjørn departs on his **birthday**; hence rebirth [**#X.9**]. The **outward event** is the delivery, as opposed to conception (or infusion of the soul); hence, 'Outward Bound' [**#VI.27**] as an inward voyage to reintegrate the matrix. **Caesarian** (a tribute to Roman engineering) delivers two "babes" from the earth's womb.

X.15 Uncle Bjorg: who committed suicide [**#III.108**].

X.16 living reality: from Arthur Eaglestone, *A Pitman's Note Book* (1925), as Roger Dataller (*dataller*: a miner paid by the day): "The dream is wiped out for you immediately upon awakening, and remains (if it remains at all) as the frailest of phantasies. But with many an underground worker, such a subconscious adventure would be much more closely allied with the world of living reality" [104]. This won Eaglestone an Oxford scholarship. Lowry cites an excerpt, 'From a Miner's Journal': "the recognition that we are all falling . . . we see the slimy walls slip past, streaking upwards with the shadow of bars flung upon the brickwork. The air is whistling now, howling, shrieking . . . The four, straight, steel conductors roar . . . " [*Adelphi* I (1924), 713–14]. Lowry adds coal, shifting in the bunkers.

X.17 Versailles: the treaty ending WWI was signed in the Hall of Mirrors, Versailles. For Kant, if all knowledge is subjective, and knowledge of that equally so, *ad infinitum*, then consciousness (*apperception*) becomes an infinite hall of mirrors.

X.18 Nero: Claudius Augustus Germanicus (AD 37–68), Roman Emperor; a byword for tyranny. Allegedly, he fiddled as Rome burned (AD 64); or worse, he lit the fires to do so.

X.19 temporal towards co-extensive consistency: in *Essays on the Logic of Being* (1932), Francis Haserot argues that *co-extensive consistency* exists when propositions to which an individual may assent are non-contradictory [40ff]; but *temporal consistency*, partial or radical (either propositions or premises change), is unstable: "Dialectic is the movement of temporal towards co-extensive consistency. It is the process by which the elements of contradiction manifest or latent in a point of view are exposed and eliminated" [47].

X.20 artificial lake: West Kirby lies between Caldy and Hoylake, facing Hilbre [**#VIII.95**]; its Marine Lake was built (1899) for recreational boating. Laruelle sailed there in a twelve-footer managed expertly by Geoffrey [UTV 18].

X.21 first tack: each "tack" (change of direction when sailing into the wind) may be temporal (unstable), but the Captain's craft assumes co-extensive consistency [**#X.19**].

X.22 burgee: the triangular pennant of a yacht or boating club. *The Red Burgee* (1906) is a set of sea comedies by Robert Morley.

X.23 rigging the mainsail: releasing ties that hold the mainsail to the boom; clipping the halyard to the sail-head; letting it out until the sail is fully raised; then securing it to cleats at the bottom of the mast. To **trip the lug** is to raise a square sail (*lug*) attached to an obliquely hanging yard and raised by a *tripping-line* (attached to the topgallant yard).

X.24 supernatural . . . subnormal: the Consul, his world a projection of his inner self, asserts a correspondence between the subnormal and abnormally suspicious [UTV 34, 355; **#IV.67**]. Keyserling's *The Recovery of Truth* (1929) assumes "no strict line between external and internal phenomena: man is no less responsible for what befalls him than for what he does . . . Man encounters only occurrences allowed to his particular nature, since his unconscious conjures up the accidents that befall him" [113]. Coincidences occur to remind us that a supernatural order exists [OF 146].

X.25 metaphysical problems: L. H. Myers, *The Root and the Flower* (1935): "To ignore metaphysical problems is not to abolish them . . . every man who thinks at all is, willy-nilly, a metaphysician" [428]. Myers was the son of his father [**#VII.167**].

X.26 going somewhere: from temporal to coextensive consistency [**#X.19**]; **going about**: changing tack, typically around a marker or buoy.

X.27 D'Israeli: Isaac D'Israeli (1766–1848), bibliophile, whose *Curiosities of Literature* (1791–1823) enchant [**#V.17**]. The Captain cites 'The Six Follies of Science' [Bk. I]:

> Nothing is so capable of disordering the intellects as an intense application to any one of these six things: the Quadrature of the Circle [**#I.55**]; the Multiplication of the Cube; the Perpetual Motion [**#VII.35**]; the Philosophical Stone [**#I.55**]; Magic; and Judicial Astrology. In youth we may exercise our imagination on these curious topics, merely to convince us of their impossibility; but it shows a great defect in judgment to be occupied on them in an advanced age. "It is proper, however," Fontenelle remarks, "to apply one's

self to these inquiries; because we find, as we proceed, many valuable discoveries of which we were before ignorant."

X.28 Fontenelle: Bernard le Bovier de Fontenelle (1657–1757), encyclopaedist, polymath and defender of the Cartesian faith. Nephew of Corneille and friend of d'Alembert and Diderot, he attributed his longevity to strawberries.

X.29 will towards the future: Thomas Mann argues, "The whole thing depends on the attitude we take up, by temperament and intention, toward the past and the future. The revolutionary principle is simply the will towards the future, which Novalis called 'the really better world.'" ['Freud's Position' 178; **#VII.49**; **#X.100**].

X.30 vacancy of the imbecile: Charles Fort, *Lo!*: "the vacancy of the imbecile is the ideal of the scholar. I approve this, as harmless" [346].

X.31 Le Brun: D'Israeli's *Curiosities* [**#X.27**], 'Imitators' [Bk. I]:

> Le Brun, a Jesuit . . . was a Latin poet, and his themes were religious. He formed the extravagant project of substituting a *religious Virgil* and *Ovid* merely by adapting his works to their titles. His *Christian Virgil* consists, like the Pagan Virgil, of *Eclogues*, *Georgics*, and of an *Epic* of twelve books, with this difference, that devotional subjects are substituted for fabulous ones. His epic is the *Ignaciad*, or the pilgrimage of Saint Ignatius. His *Christian Ovid* is in the same taste; everything wears a new face. The *Epistles* are pious ones; the *Fasti* are the six days of creation; the *Elegies* are the lamentations of Jeremiah; a poem on *the Love of God* is substituted for the *Art of Love*; and the history of some *Conversions* supplies the place of the *Metamorphoses!* This Jesuit would, no doubt, have approved of *a family Shakespeare*.

Virgil (70–19 BCE) was a virtuous pagan, whose **Eclogues** and **Georgics** celebrate pastoral life; his ***Aeneid***, the founding of Rome, becomes the **Ignaciad**, a life of St. Ignatius of Loyola (1491–1556), founder of the Jesuits and pilgrim to the Holy Land (1523). **Ovid** (43 BCE–17 CE) was a black sheep: his **Epistles** record his exile to the Black Sea; **Fasti**, the origins of Roman festivals; **Elegies** (*Amores*), his love for the elusive Corinna (Jeremiah laments the destruction of Jerusalem and the Holy Temple); ***Metamorphoses***, transformations of gods and mortals; and the ***Art of Love*** (*Ars Amatoria*), how to find women, seduce them, and prevent others from stealing them (Sigbjørn forsakes this theme).

X.32 Dido and Aeneas: in Virgil's *Aeneid* [V], Juno's sudden storm sends Dido's courtiers to seek shelter, and hastens Dido and Aeneas to a cave where their love is consummated. Sigbjørn retells this as the crucifixion, the empty tomb on

Easter morn (the stone rolled from the cave); this is less D'Israeli than Aiken [*Blue Voyage* 305]. **Ulysses** and his men are trapped in the Cyclops's cave [**#V.147**], sealed with a large stone [*Odyssey* IX].

X.33 Kafka's dictum: "The Martyrs do not underestimate the body, they cause it to be elevated on the cross. In that they are at one with their enemies" ['Reflections' #30 285].

X.34 Substitution!: *displacement* or *sublimation*: for **Freud**, unconscious redirection of an impulse onto a more acceptable target, or symbolic substitute; a basic defence mechanism; **mental expression** is the psychic representation of instinct, experienced as phantasy.

X.35 technic of the transition: from Waldo David Frank's address to the International Congress of Writers for the Defence of Culture (Paris, June 21–25, 1935), published in 'The Writer's Part in Communism' [*Adelphi* 9–10 (1935)]. Frank insisted [260] that the process of political change must be organic: "By which I mean that *the whole of man*, heart and mind, subtlest sense and deepest intuition, as well as belly and loin, must partake of it—or it miscarries. The orthodox revolutionary creeds, which are the technic of the transition of this crucial hour, do not comprehend the whole man" [**#X.40**; **#X.44**; **#X.91**; **#XI.19**; **#XIV.2**].

X.36 praelectors: L. *praelegere*, "to announce"; public readers, promoting the matriculation and graduation of Cambridge scholars.

X.37 social habituations: Trigant Burrow claims, "the object that challenges our inquiry is nothing less than the entire background of our personal and social habituations" ['Autonomy of the I', *Psyche* 8 (1928), 37; or *Adelphi* 9–10 (1935), 311]. He discusses social neurosis and the structure of insanity: our medium is too much part of ourselves to become an object of our contemplation; we suffer from a collective neurosis; salvation lies in cooperation; we need first to see ourselves clearly, then change the social organization [**#VII.77**].

X.38 process of becoming: as the Tao [**#II.39**].

X.39 but doth strange: varying Ariel: "Nothing of him that doth change / But doth suffer a sea-change / Into something rich and strange" [*Tempest* I.ii.400–02]. See the Textual Notes.

X.40 travail of rebirth: Frank concludes 'The Writer's Part' by imaging the old world as an embryon "in travail", lacking the *knowing* to complete rebirth [264]. He had earlier stressed the need for *conscious* participation in the Whole:

"those who rise to rule in its travail of rebirth, are men in this crisis of transition" [*America Hispana* 253].

X.41 'debacle of self' . . . 'death of private grief': see **#IV.27**; **#VII.7**.

X.42 does not act: a Taoist maxim: he who knows but does not act knows imperfectly.

X.43 offensive corrupting organ: Matthew 8:19: "And if thine eye offend thee, pluck it out, and cast it from thee."

X.44 child . . . degeneration: Frank, 'Writer's Part' [259]: "The revolutionary hour in which we live is but the present phase . . . whereby man . . . will emerge into a conscious culture; even as the child at a certain physiologic stage must become adult or go down into degeneration." A later epigraph [**#XIV.2**]. See the Textual Notes.

X.45 close-hauled: with sails trimmed tightly and sailing close to the wind, to tack upwind; **boom-dodging**: ducking to avoid the *boom* (the spar extending the mainsail) as it swings to bring the yacht about [**#X.26**]; **bailing**: removing bilge-water. Sigbjørn's "**all set**" (ready to go about) continues the yachting metaphors.

X.46 mimic reflector: as the sea assumes its colour from the sky, but believes otherwise, so the moon thinks itself the only begetter of its pale fire. Compare the drunk who, told that the moon in the stream is a reflection, retorts: "Then how did I get up here?"

X.47 scions: from Lucien Maury, 'Strindberg's Confessions' [*Living Age* #310 (1921)], of influences to which an artist is subjected, his borrowings, originality and genius: "What is the part played by his predecessors and by his contemporaries? What share in his growth have the scions, snatched living from distant trees, and the wandering seeds blown here and there by the winds? What remains of the art itself when these accretions are taken away?" [79].

X.48 Athanasius: (293–373), Bishop of Alexandria, who disputed with Arius the doctrine that Christ is of substance different from His father. Banned and restored repeatedly, he inspired the expression, *Athanasius contra mundum*, "Athanasius against the world".

X.49 cloud: "Jerry" Kellett, *Whirligig of Taste* [**#III.25**; **#V.129**]: "A cloud no bigger than a human hand appears on the horizon, and in an hour or two the whole sky is changed, and with it our critical judgement" [127]. See 1 Kings 18:44: "Behold, there ariseth a little cloud out of the sea, like a man's hand"; that "little cloud" (*Dubliners*, *Ulysses*) promises relief.

X.50 purposelessness: Kant's synthetic "purposive purposelessness" of aesthetic objects, against the Captain's pragmatic phrasing.

X.51 utter tentativeness: words Lowry uses elsewhere [*CL* 1:216, 240]; compare Newton's paradox of the pebble and great ocean of truth [**#IX.13**].

X.52 every hair: Luke 12:17: "But even the very hairs of your head are all numbered. Fear not therefore: ye are of more value than many sparrows."

X.53 Dorotheus' statement: Lowry's 'Notes' read: "If we love God, then to the extent that we approach to Him through love of Him do we unite in love with our neighbours, and the closer our union with them, the closer our union with God also . . . Avva Dorotheus (VII century... M. D. Lodizhensky.)". Ouspensky's *Tertium Organum* [XXII 286] quotes M. V. [sic] Lodizhensky's *Superconsciousness and the Paths to its Attainment* (296), which records the "VII century" Greek Orthodox theologian, Dorotheus, as offering the mystical image of God as a circle and arguing that the further from its centre the more remote from one another we become.

X.54 ship's chandler: one who supplies ships; hence, "Ship's Swindler".

X.55 love one's neighbour: Matthew 22:39: "Thou shalt love thy neighbour as thyself" (the "golden rule"); and Kafka: "If you love your neighbour within the world you do no more and no less injustice than in loving yourself within the world" ['Reflections' #69 292].

X.56 father of Oedipus: Oedipus, son of Laius and Jocasta, was destined to kill his father and wed his mother. Exposed at birth, he was rescued by a shepherd and given to Polybus, king of Corinth, and his wife Merope. Belatedly enlightened, Oedipus blinds himself and is led by his daughter Antigone to Colonus. Lowry's confusion may reflect the prophecy that Troy would burn if a noble child born that day were not sacrificed; Paris, son of **Priam** (the king of Troy) was exposed but survived, to bring Troy to destruction. His putative paternity is reasserted in 'King Lear blinded Oedipus in a dream' [*CP* #71].

X.57 father surrogate: the son's need to devour his surrogate father, as Lowry to Aiken. Its "eternal recurrence" is Nietzschean [**#I.50**; **#III.103**].

X.58 leap the walls: of van Gogh's *Prison Courtyard* [**#III.102**].

X.59 richer, warmer life: perhaps (if "out of the pages of a book"), Compton Mackenzie, *The Early Life and Adventures of Sylvia Scarlett* (1918): "a richer, warmer life beyond these little houses" [115]; as a film (1935), it was a notorious flop.

X.60 secrets of the sea: Gérard de Nerval (1808–1855), French poet, promenaded Thibault, his pet lobster, on a blue silk ribbon, for lobsters did not bark and knew the secrets of the sea [Symons 72; *Blue Voyage* 148].

X.61 imaginative flight: as Schnizler's *Flight into Darkness* [**#XI.1**].

X.62 indefinitely postponed: Lewis Spence claims that if elements of the human body are brought into harmony with nature, then age and death might be "indefinitely postponed" [*Encyclopedia of Occultism*, 'Paracelsus' 687].

X.63 Ruge . . . Echtermayer: Arnold **Ruge** (1802–1880), German philosopher and political writer, founded with Ernst **Echtermayer** (1805–1844), philosopher and literary historian, the *Hallischen Jahrbücher für deutsche Kunst und Wissenschaft* (1837), to affirm Hegel's sense of society's progression towards freedom (it was suppressed in 1843), while criticizing his vision of history as closed to the future. As young Hegelians, they interrogated the Romantic (Catholic) impulse of their age from a liberal (Protestant) perspective, and in 1838 issued a 'Manifesto against Romanticism', defining it as a reactionary political movement with a subjectivity and internality that failed to confront reality.

X.64 German romantic school: the prevailing 19th-century aesthetic. Turning to medievalism for inspiration (Wagner, Novalis), it accepted the cult of an idealized age, informed by a neo-Catholic *mythos* (*Tannhäuser*). In 'Der Protestantismus und die Romantik' (1839), Ruge and Echtermayer discussed, from an intellectual Protestant perspective, a spiritual sickness that returned many Romantics from politics of emancipation to **Catholicism**. The Captain anticipates Georg Lukács (1953), who saw German Romanticism as marking the point in intellectual history where the German tradition separated from Europe and moved towards National Socialism.

X.65 utilitarian vocables: Carlyle, in *Sartor Resartus* (1831), mocked German Idealism as "a froth of Vocables" and Utilitarianism as "a kind of *Stomach*" [Part II].

X.66 vanity: see Ecclesiastes 1:2, 1:9 [**#IV.37**].

X.67 metaphysics: T. S. Eliot, in the final stanza of 'Whispers of Immortality', rejects Grishkin's pneumatic bliss:

> And even the Abstract Entities
> Circumambulate her charm;
> But our lot crawls between dry ribs
> To keep our metaphysics warm.

Lowry described Eliot thus [CL 1: 352]. In the 'Varsity' CB, Tor states, "I don't run into any danger of creeping into church to keep my inhibitions warm. I often think of dying."

X.68 Santayana: George Santayana (1863–1952), Spanish philosopher who taught at Harvard under William James, whose pragmatism he endorsed, warning Aiken and Eliot against the Abstract Entities. An "aesthetic Catholic" agnostic who cherished the Virgin ("God may be dead, but Mary is his mother"), he was relaxed about religion, as this unattributed (Aiken?) anecdote suggests. Dana recalls walking with his father (as Lowry with Aiken) through Harvard Yard: "What shall we talk of, Gene—Santayana?" [U 54].

X.69 crane on top: like Liverpool's unfinished cathedral [**#VII.16**].

X.70 brotherhood of man: a theme that will "rise again" in UTV, where Hugh agonizes about betraying Geoffrey, and the ideal of brotherhood.

X.71 swing right round: turn 180 degrees; **tip the lug:** set the sail in readiness [**#X.23**].

X.72 fire to ice: molecular catastrophe [**#III.122**]; an analogy that ignores essential differences between quantitative and qualitative changes. Also . . .

X.73 Jensen's book: *The Long Journey* (*Den Lange Rejse*, 1908–1922); a trilogy by Danish author, Johannes V. Jensen (1873–1950), reflecting his evolutionary views in a human drama from the pre-Ice Age to Columbus. Jensen won the Nobel Prize for Literature (1944). A. G. Chater's English translation appeared 1923–1924, Parts I and II entitled *Fire And Ice*; III to V, *The Cimbrians*; and VI to VIII, *Christopher Columbus*. Part I ('Fire') is set in primeval European forests, near a huge volcano. Fire glows on its summit and lava floods the slopes. Primitive man has worshipped the fire-god in terror; but a first great moment arrives: the emergence of a man of mind and will, a Prometheus who solves the riddle of fire and brings down a torch, lighting fires to deter predators. Observing the stars he infers *time*, the first abstract idea won from chaos. He steps toward civilized intercourse, discovering tenderness in sexual love. Dying a prophet's death at the hands of obtuse masses, he bequeaths a rich legacy. In Part II ('Ice'), the world has changed, the volcano extinct, the climate cooling. Defying the general migration south, one man faces north to confront hardship. Carl is an outlaw, avoided by others, whom he despises. Accepting the cold, he grows hardy and strong, and on a woman who shares his hardships he fathers the Nordic race. Rediscovering fire, he founds a new civilization. In *The Cimbrians*, another genius invents locomotion: wagons and boats driven by oar or sail. Men of the North, hearing the call, begin the long journey proper. Later books are set in historical times: the Cimbrians marching on Rome, Viking raids, and finally Columbus, who in the spirit of his Nordic ancestors discovers another New World.

X.74 wild animals: in 'The Forest Fire' [*Fire and Ice* I:iv], when the volcano Gunung Api erupts, wild beasts flee in panic; in 'Winter' [II:iii], great herds migrate south as the Ice Age begins (only the mammoth turns back). The **single youth** is Carl, who faces north to found the Nordic race; the **girl** is Mam, who shares his destiny. *In Ballast* might have ended thus, with Sigbjørn finding Birgit [**#XVIII.51**].

X.75 memory: the people of the North increase and prosper, but do not lose the visceral memory of their past world. *Fire and Ice* ends with a new generation awakening to that world: "Childhood, that is the Lost Country" [293]. **Eden** and the **Blessed Isles** are Lost Countries of the Hebraic and Hellenic peoples.

X.76 Vikings: Carl's descendants, the Ice People, meet the Seafarers; their union engenders the Danes, whose voyages are prompted by legends of a distant land. Others go south, to the Danube and Black Sea, planting their seed in warmer climes. In *The Cimbrians*, one branch migrates from Jutland to Gaul, threatening Rome. Defeated, their Nordic legacy lives on in the captured maiden, Vedis, and the sculptor, Cheiron, who will generate a new race.

X.77 stillness in the heart: Lawrence, the final sentiment of his poem, 'Nothing to Save': "now that all is lost, / But a tiny core of stillness in the heart / like the eye of a violet". Integrated with **murder**, as in De Quincey, whose 'Knocking on the Gate in Macbeth' recounts the retiring of the human heart and suspension of earthly passion [UTV 136]; and Poe's tell-tale heart [**#V.72**].

X.78 ego instincts are death instincts: in *Beyond the Pleasure Principle* (1920), Freud set the death-drive (*thanatos*) against the life-force (*eros*); **coal** and **fire**, which kindle this chapter, represent these basic qualities. The **rocky inanimate** is Freud's *thanatos* instinct, whereby organic life strives towards the pre-existent, returning to the mineral whence it originated; the "ancient inanimate quality" of coal is its correlative [**#X.11**]. Mann associates Freud's attraction to the mineral with Novalis's death-wish, through the latter's experience as a mining engineer ['Freud's Position' 195; **#VII.49**]; the Captain sets Norway (the rocky inanimate, return to the matrix) against Russia (sexual instincts, life).

X.79 mental hygiene: the Mental Hygiene movement was founded (1909) by Clifford W. Beers, whose experience of mental illness shaped *A Mind that Found Itself* (1913). Beers drew on Alfred Meyer (1866–1950), who believed mental disorders arose from interactions of individuals with their environments, in particular, traumatic early childhood experiences.

X.80 sexual: Freud's *Interpretation of Dreams* suggests that "hysterical identification" frequently expresses "sexual community", two lovers as "one" [**#IV.46**].

X.81 Roback and Macdougall: in *The Psychology of Character* (1927), Abraham Roback cites William Macdougall's 'Instinct and the Unconscious' (1919), 37: "The innate structure of the human mind comprises much more than the instinct alone . . . There are many facts which compel us to go further in the recognition of innate mental structure. . . " [604]. Roback (1890–1965), a Polish-born psychologist and philologist, taught at Harvard; Macdougall (1871–1938), a British social psychologist specializing on instinct [**#X.99**], visited Harvard (1920–1927). They did not collaborate.

X.82 speech: Charles Maurice de Talleyrand (1754–1838), diplomat: "*La parole nous a été donnée pour déguiser notre pensée*" [We were given speech to disguise our thoughts].

X.83 White: Andrew Dickson White (1832–1918), diplomat and historian, who co-founded Cornell University; his *History of the Warfare of Science with Theology* (1896) dismisses biblical sentiment as based on fatuous reasoning.

X.84 gybe: to change direction suddenly by swinging the sail across the boat, or inadvertently when sailing "close to the wind" [**#X.45**].

X.85 rival: Freud's repressed Oedipal Complex arose, he said, when his baby brother, Philip, displaced the father as little Siggie's rival for their mother's affections.

X.86 infantile: Lenin's *Left-Wing Communism: An Infantile Disorder* (1920) warned the Bolsheviks against total dictatorship of the proletariat [**#X.9**]. The Captain implies the imperialist state of childhood succumbing to other forces, but in danger of reinstatement.

X.87 omnipotence: in Freudian psychoanalysis, limitations that the reality principle places on the pleasure principle restrict the sense of omnipotence that the child has earlier assumed.

X.88 adjusted . . . environment: *polymorphous perversity*, whereby the embryo expresses freely its libido; outside the womb a hostile environment limits that pleasure, as the mother's ability to answer every need diminishes. The **padded cell** is a post-natal image of the womb.

X.89 great castration: self-inflicted impotence (Europe lost a generation of men); not the splendid legend of Pius IX removing genitalia from the Vatican statues (1857).

X.90 suicides practically cease: since in war aggression, particularly self-directed, finds other outlets. The Captain may follow Tor's example.

X.91 will towards the future: Mann, fired with Freudian dynamics [**#X.29**; **#X.78**; **#X.100**]. For the **whole of man**, see Frank's "technic of transition" [**#X.35**].

X.92 Tostrup-Hanson: the Underwriter [**#V.8**], checking the *Arcturion*.

X.93 sexuality: Freud's *Three Essays on the Theory of Sexuality* (1905) challenged views of sexuality as inherent fate determined by gender by arguing that all humans are born with a bisexual nature, sexuality manifesting itself in the evolutionary course of interaction with one's environment. The "certain myth" and its "reinstatement" is the return to the womb.

X.94 Plato's Symposium: where Aristophanes (having had a few) explains why lovers feel whole when they find their soulmates: humans were originally double, with three sexes: male-male, female-female, and androgynous; after Zeus, outraged by their perfidy, split them apart, the separated halves yearn to be complete again [**#III.105**].

X.95 Brihad-Aranyaka Upanishad: the Upanishads ("sitting at the feet") are the sacred Sanskrit texts of Vedic teaching. The *Birhad-Aranyaka Upanishad* (source of *The Waste Land*'s Thunder) is the oldest, pre-dating Buddhism and explaining individuality (*Atman*). Its fourth *Brahmana* tells how the Self, alone, feeling no delight, wished for a second and became two, husband (*pati*) and wife (*patni*), each half a shell.

X.96 St. Paul: Galatians 3:28: "There is neither Jew nor Greek, there is neither bond nor free, there is neither male nor female: for ye are all one in Christ Jesus."

X.97 Bernard Shaw: *Back to Methuselah* (1920) moves from 'In the Beginning' (4004 BC) to 'As Far As Thought Can Reach' (31,920 AD), where humanity has evolved to emerge, fully formed, from large eggs. Pygmalion fashions two primitives, male and female, from the 20th century, but they are destroyed. The Ancients inform the Children that mankind's destiny is to be bodiless immortal vortices of energy.

X.98 Caliban past: weighed by corporeality, like the monster of *The Tempest*. Demarest, a "gross Caliban" [*Blue Voyage* 332], tries to be an Ariel.

X.99 Roback: *The Psychology of Character* [**#X.81**] differentiates principles from instinctive drives: "while an instinctive expression is no more than a *particularization* of an act involving one's own self, the guiding principles which are under discussion represent *universalizations*, involving naturally also the individual who is acting, but directed toward humanity in general, of which this or that person appears as a case" [605].

X.100 ethical renunciation: Mann calls individual existence a supra-sensual act of the will, "a resolve to concentrate, limit and take shape, to assemble out of nothingness, to renounce freedom and infinity and all slumbering and weaving in spaceless and timeless night: an ethical resolve to be and to suffer" ['Sleep, Sweet Sleep' 274; **#X.29**]. He echoes Novalis: completion and perfection achieved for a voluntary renunciation of infinity [**#VII.49**; **#X.78**].

X.101 voices: Hugh, in the 1940 *Volcano*, calls past masters "ambassadors between life and death" [328]; and hears the Voice of the Dead saying to the Living: "Do yourself no harm, for we are *all* here" [335].

X.102 the roar of the sea and the wind: echoing Grieg [**#VII.160**], wind replacing darkness. In Hugh Walpole's *The Green Mirror* (1917), the wind creeps "round the house, trying the doors and windows" [390].

CHAPTER XI

XI.1 [Epigraph] Arthur Schnitzler: (1862–1931), Austrian writer known for his bleak analysis of the psyche. 'Ruth' gave Sigbjørn *Flight into Darkness* when he first visited Mexico [DATG 63]. The novel pursues the gathering dark forces in the mind, as "Robert —" fears he has murdered his wife and other women. The epigraph reflects the end of chapter VIII, when Robert visits at night the home of Dr Rolf; he desperately simulates normality as his inner world crumbles, then kills his brother and dies. See the Textual Notes.

XI.2 avalanche of coal: images of coal [**#X.11**; **#X.16**; **#XVIII.23**] intimate: Freudian trauma and a return to the mineral [**#X.78**]; *Holmenkollen* [**#I.54**]; refuelling [**#XV.32**]; and Poe's Antarctic/Arctic whiteout ("poised bears", perhaps bi-polar [**#VII.93**]).

XI.3 not as it had been: the ending of *Julian Grant* [**#I.2**; **#II.41**] enacts Julian's psychic state; compare the Consul in the Salón Ofélia [UTV X].

XI.4 scuttle: a small hatch set into the deck.

XI.5 renunciation of infinity: Thomas Mann reduced to the platitudes ("Words, words, words") of Polonius [**#VII.109**; **#X.100**].

XI.6 tennis-court: Inglewood had a tennis court. Compare: "A gust of wind moaned round the house with an eerie sound like a northerner prowling among the tennis nets in England, jingling the rings" [UTV 309–10; **#X.102**].

XI.7 sleigh-bells: compare "tinkle of sleigh bells" [U 118]; or Robert Frost, 'Hyla Brook', frogs "like ghost of sleigh bells in a ghost of snow". Hence . . .

XI.8 Erckmann-Chatrian: Émile Erckmann (1822–1899) and Alexandre Chatrian (1826–1890), French co-authors of ghost stories. Their play, *Le Juif polonais* (1867), translated by Leopold Lewis as *The Bells* (1871), was Sir Henry Irving's masterpiece. In Act II, as the northerly wind whistles about the house, sleigh bells at his daughter's wedding remind the innkeeper, Mathias, of a murder committed fifteen years ago; in Act III he confesses, and describes putting the body into his lime-kiln. Hence . . .

XI.9 Ethan Brand: who, having experienced the Unpardonable Sin, becomes a fiend and leaps into his lime-kiln [**#VI.73**]. The quotation is inexact [see the Textual Notes].

XI.10 Plenty of warnings: Charles Fort insists, "Often before disasters on this earth there have been appearances that were interpretable as warnings" [*Lo!* 787; **#III.64**].

XI.11 Zuyder Zee: the *Zuider Zee* [Southern Sea], Holland, opening to the North Sea; much reclaimed (see Goethe's *Faust*, Part II). Before the Zuyderzee Dam (1932) it was known for sudden storms. Freud likened analytic therapy to draining the Zuider Zee.

XI.12 dithering crack: like the Bellevue gates of *Maelstrom* [38]; a ship hitting the rocks. The "dithering crack of two boulders" [*Blue Voyage* 80] echoes in 'Economic Conference, 1934' [57]. For 'consummation', see **#III.60**; 'interpenetrate' is another cherished word.

XI.13 Otto Hurwitz: perhaps, a scion of the London-based Hurwitz Furs, or Aiken's "Hurwitz, the poet" [*Blue Voyage* 186]. Hamlet meets disaster at sea: "Up from my cabin, / My sea-gown scarf'd about me, in the dark" [V.2.12–13]; Otto Hurwitz meets the press.

XI.14 Baker Street fog: obscuring 221B, the London address of Sherlock Holmes. Conan Doyle nowhere uses the word 'pea-souper' (its sulphurous yellow-green colour); Holmes nowhere says, "**Elementary**, my dear Watson" (nor would he give it an esoteric inflection).

XI.15 warm up the car: the role of the *chauffeur*. **Exchange** is Tithebarn Street Station [**#V.3**; **#XI.68**], north of the Flags.

XI.16 'Fall of Icarus with Statue': perhaps, Brueghel's *Armed Three-Master with Daedalus and Icarus in the Sky* (1561), as an engraving is specified, though 'statue' remains obscure. Again, Brueghel is associated with *The Lighthouse Invites the Storm* [see **#V.43**].

XI.17 to fall with Icarus: as Lowry told Aiken [CL 1:80 (1930)]; repeated to Grieg [CL 1:105 (1931)]. Smith, a mediocrity, will die forgotten, unlike those who lie under "Icarian rocks" [*Blue Voyage* 293].

XI.18 Belawandellow: *Belawan*, Sumatra, busiest port of the Dutch East Indies; 'dellow' fouls *Deli*, its tributary river. Compare 'Belawen' [U 64], and 'Belawandelli' [U 138].

XI.19 'no facts can hurt it': Waldo Frank's 'Writer's Part', quoted by the Captain [**#X.35**; **#XIV.2**], affirms the "organic view" of revolutionary consciousness, implicit in every artist, however dissident, "with infallible continuity from the Egyptian sculptors and the Hebrew Prophets through the Patrists, through the builders of the Gothic, through the great sixteenth and seventeenth century founders of modern science" [261]. This persists (Frank insists) from Spinoza and Hegel to "the historical-prophetic vision of Karl Marx", despite resistance from "shallow empiricists" of the Enlightenment. ***Patrists*** are learned Church Fathers of the early Christian era; ***estuary*** is Sigbjørn's metaphor. Pedantic footnote: when this appeared in a **book** (*In the American Jungle*, 1937), *technic of transition* became "technique of transition" [281]; Sigbjørn is reading (Lowry is citing) the *Adelphi* essay.

XI.20 garden: hints of Marvell's 'The Garden' ("stumbling"); Eliot's *Waste Land* (hyacinths under winter snow); Wordsworth (daffodils); and Anne Beale's 'A Spring Morning' (1841), where "the nativity of Spring" encourages rebirth.

XI.21 Mapleson's farm: perhaps Marples Field [U 42], after Joseph Henry Marples, a Caldy farmer.

XI.22 tenor warnings: high-pitched sirens of ships befogged.

XI.23 gardener: Inglewood was tended by George Cook; on his death (1940) Lowry wrote 'Epitaph on our Gardener' [*CP* #208], "Who to the world's wickedness added naught."

X.24 dead reckoning: current location estimated from positions previously determined by regular calculations with compass and log; originally, "deduced reckoning".

XI.25 Vulcan: a tiny planet near the sun, invented to explain oddities in Mercury's orbit.

XI.26 great circle: an arc on a curved surface [**#V.85**].

XI.27 telegraph poles: Aiken's "threnody" [**#I.12**] as Tor's *Valse Triste* [**#III.109**].

XI.28 scattered eyes: compare the *Arcturion*'s departure [**#VII.202**]

XI.29 pall: a coffin carried to burial. From Melville's 'The Enthusiast': "Walk through the cloud to meet the pall, / Though light forsake thee, never fall / From fealty to light" [**#I.24**]. Lowry responded: "The pall is comfortable enough" [CP #22].

XI.30 double-declutched: Sigbjørn changes down into first without stripping the gearbox by twice engaging the clutch (into neutral, then first). Lowry, a dreadful driver, would have mangled this. **Starboard lights** are green.

XI.31 cross-roads: in chapter IX the Captain's house was on a hill [**#IX.23**]; these cross-roads (Caldy Road at Montgomery Hill) suggest leaving from Inglewood.

XI.32 Frankby: northeast of Caldy, identified by *The Farmer's Arms*. At the end of the straight, Frankby Road becomes **Greasby Road**, the *Coach and Horses* to the right. The identical route is taken in 'Sumptuous Armour' [P&S 232–33].

XI.33 Minerva: Roman goddess of wisdom, her emblem the owl. Lowry described the 1940 *Volcano* to Whit Burnett as emerging from Europe's unconscious, "an owl of Minerva flying at evening" [CL 1:337]. Arthur Lowry's Minerva was unlikely to hurtle by "like a shell"; compare the ending of 'June the 30th, 1934'.

XI.34 Red Sea: parting that the Israelites might escape their servitude [Exodus 13:17ff].

XI.35 Bromborough: near Port Sunlight, south of Birkenhead. The stop serves the West Kirby-Bromborough bus, its counterpart encountered head-on.

XI.36 Upton: near Birkenhead; Dana recalls a "slate-paved dairy" [U 42]. In 'Sumptuous Armour' a "blue Indian" motorcycle slants by [P&S 233].

XI.37 Bidston Hill: a high point (2,312 ft) on the Wirral [**#VII.178**]. Before the telegraph [**#XIII.3**], ships nearing Liverpool signalled their arrival via Bidston Hill. The **Observatory** was relocated (on local sandstone) from London's Waterloo Dock (1866); its observations served weather, time and tidal research.

It fired electronically, precisely on the hour, the "one o'clock gun" [**#V.147**] on the Mersey, near Morpeth Dock, Birkenhead.

XI.38 Port your helm: previously, to turn the wheel to starboard (right) and the ship to port (left) [**#III.31; #V.38**]. The Captain means the latter, for a car is not a ship, but Sigbjørn (in England, driving on the left) turns right, towards the oncoming bus. Similar ambiguities caused the *Brynnjaar* disaster. This is the basic reading, but things get complicated: Sigbjørn (we are told) instinctively spins the wheel *left*, then *right*: this implies, firstly, that he reacts according to the new regulations, and either (i) the bus is on the wrong side of the road, or (ii) the directions have been revised (by Jan?) to reflect North American conditions.

XI.39 jumps out of the way: compare the Captain's sentiment about a horse and house; or Tor, how a man stationed in one dimension may direct his life by another [**#III.34**].

XI.40 Noctorum: Ir. *Cnocc Tirim*, "Dry Hill"; now a Birkenhead suburb.

XI.41 Bidston Common: one hundred acres of heath and woodland sold (1900) by Lord Vyner for public use. **Bidston Hill** has an observatory, a lighthouse, mysterious rock carvings, and a **windmill**, present since 1596. The original was destroyed by fire in 1791, but the mill operated until 1875, when it was neglected until restored in 1927.

XI.42 silent: the Captain belatedly registers the implications [**#XI.38**].

XI.43 Oxton: a village, since 1877 part of Birkenhead.

XI.44 White Star: the name adopted when the Oceanic Steam Navigation Co., a Liverpool trans-Atlantic line, entered the American-based International Mercantile Marine (1902). Its "big four" were the *Celtic*, *Cedric*, *Baltic* and *Adriatic*, the ultimate in luxury before the *Titanic* [**#VII.18**] and *Britannic* [**#III.28**]. The Royal Mail Steam Packet Company bought the White Star Line in 1927 [**#V.99**], and in 1934 merged it with its rival, the Cunard Line.

XI.45 Seacombe . . . Egremont . . . Poulton . . . Liscard: districts of Wallasey, on the New Brighton side of the Mersey; the first two are ferry terminals.

XI.46 *Herzogin Cecile*: a barque of baroque beauty [**#VII.30**]; compare 'Sumptuous Armour': the "crosstrees of a windjammer" [P&S 233].

XI.47 reaches: straight sections of a river inlet between bends; here, inner docks where old ships are "laid up" and scrapped.

XI.48 Turner sunset: Joseph Turner (1775–1851), English artist whose extravagant sunsets and seascapes testify to God's sublime presence in a world denatured by man.

XI.49 Thalassa, thalassa: in Xenophon's *Anabasis*, troops marching through a hostile Asia Minor reach the Black Sea, crying: "The sea! The sea!" [*Blue Voyage* 3, 20, 289, 303]. Lowry uses this (Greek letters) in *La Mordida* [50].

XI.50 blew the horn twice: like Roland, hero of the 12th-century *Chanson*, whose slughorn defies 400,000 Saracens. This gesture (repeated) mocks Sigbjørn's aspirations [**#XIV.67**].

XI.51 Captain of a Line: commander of a battleship or frigate; but an Admiral assumes responsibility for engagements.

XI.52 Jacobsen: Jens Peter Jacobsen (1847–1885), novelist and biologist, controversially translated Darwin's *Origin of Species and Descent of Man* into Danish. His *Mogens and Other Stories* (1921) was praised by Rilke and admired by Lawrence.

XI.53 Tranmere-Woodside tramline: Britain's first tramline, from Woodside Ferry to Birkenhead Park (30 Aug. 1860), was horse-drawn, then extended and electrified; "the first street cars" appear in 'Sumptuous Armour' [P&S 235]. The Wirral Tramway line between Woodside Ferry and New Ferry (1877) approached Tranmere pier; it closed in 1934.

XI.54 Birkenhead Park: the first publicly funded UK civic park (1847), and model for New York's Central Park, advocating open spaces for public use to improve the workforce. It included grounds for cricket, football, archery, bowls, quoits, and rugby (the Birkenhead RUFC was founded in the 1880s).

XI.55 dropped a goal: in rugby union, to drop-kick the ball over the crossbar between the uprights, then scoring four points.

XI.56 Rock Ferry tram: Rock Ferry, south of Birkenhead Park [**#IV.7**]. It opened (1891) as a terminus of the Mersey network, with links to Hamilton Square and Liverpool. Trams surviving into Lowry's day were gone by 1937, overtaken by bus and train.

XI.57 Birkenhead Park Station: in **Duke Street**, opposite the Park (1888). An interchange between the Wirral (to West Kirby) and Mersey (to Liverpool) lines, it offered parking for commuters like Arthur Lowry.

XI.58 Futurist . . . '*Crazy Week at the Empire*': see **#VI.34** and **#VII.32**.

XI.59 Hamilton Square: on the Wirral Line, between Green Lane and James Street, last stop before the Mersey tunnel.

XI.60 Gaillard: Jules Gaillard, violin virtuoso, whose orchestra performed in the 1920s at Liverpool's La Scala theatre.

XI.61 Hippodrome: Ohmy's Grand Circus, Grange Road, became the Gaiety Music Hall (1888), then the Metropole (1898). Renovated (1908), it was acquired by Dennis J. Clarke, who renamed it (1916). Dana considers taking Janet there or to the Argyle [U 26]; both feature in 'Sumptuous Armour' [P&S 233]. Hugh imagines being sung there [UTV 164].

XI.62 Argyle: opened (1868) as the Argyle Music Hall, seating 800. Renamed the Prince of Wales theatre (1878), it soon reverted to the Argyle (and music hall) until destroyed in the September 1940 blitz.

XI.63 Brown's Bioscope: a fairground attraction, popular around WWI, with a stage where dancing girls entertained to an organ between short films, a forerunner of Variety shows. "Brown's Royal Bioscope" played at the Argyle until 1925.

XI.64 Liverpool Irish: twenty-two percent of Liverpool's population was Irish, the city a souk for many fleeing the Great Famine of the 1840s, a transit for those seeking seasonal work in Scotland, and a staging post to America. Specifically, the 64th Lancashire Rifle Volunteer Corps that fought the Boer War and in WWI; disbanded in 1922, they re-formed for WWII.

XI.65 under the water: the Mersey Railway Tunnel [**#VI.4**].

XI.66 dark cavern . . . Matrix: returning to the womb ("Inward Bound") [**#VII.96**]. Lowry's 'Strange Type' begins: "I wrote: In the dark cavern of our birth"; punning on 'matrix' as womb and a printer's case where leaden type is stored [CP #131; **#III.96**]. John Masefield's dedication of "C. L. M." to his mother strangely typified the "C. M. L." [Clarissa M. Lorenz] of *Blue Voyage* for Clarence Malcolm Lowry. Masefield begins: "In the dark womb where I began / My mother's life made me a man".

XI.67 James Street Station: the first Liverpool stop after the Mersey Tunnel [**#VI.4**]. The **Water Street** entrance to James Street station reaches the platform by a long tunnel (the "secret tunnels bored through gloomy buildings" of 'Goya the Obscure' [277]). Lifts from the James Street entrance serve the platform directly; Lowry's, erroneously, access the Water Street entrance. The DATG typescript recalls the long "foot subway" [UBC 9:22 624].

XI.68 Exchange: Sigbjørn will reiterate the name [**#V.3**] until the train departs.

XI.69 serve the obsolete: Melville's ancient ships [**#VIII.76**].

XI.70 all havens astern: Ishmael, starting from sleep, senses something wrong: "whatever swift, rushing thing I stood on was not so much bound to any haven ahead as rushing from all havens astern" [*Moby-Dick* XCVI]. Lawrence presages such doom [*American Literature* XI]. Compare Hugh's vertigo when swinging into St. Catharine's [UTV 176].

XI.71 thrumming: of Lowry's early ships: "*Te-thrum te -thrum: te-thrum te-thrum* . . . one heard the engines: the beating of its lonely heart. One . . . became startlingly conscious of the fact that one was all at sea; alone with the infinite; alone with God" [*Blue Voyage* 166].

XI.72 platform ticket: permitting access but no right to board trains or use services; allowing farewells while discouraging crowds. The Preston train departed Platform 3.

XI.73 inaudible phrases: in a surreal scene from Mann's *The Magic Mountain* [VII], Mynheer Peeperkorn speaks inaudibly before a tumultuous waterfall. Compare the two Mexicans, opening and shutting their mouths, their words drowned by the cascade [UTV 319]. Lowry noted in a draft of DATG: "mutely opening and closing his mouth, so that he might have been Mynheer Peepercorn [sic] before his suicide making his final inaudible oration" [UBC 9:3, 213, 217; *Mordida* [99]. The Captain is trying to tell Sigbjørn about the credit note, or bill of *exchange*, he can draw on in Oslo [**#XII.2**].

XI.74 special past: used by C. K. Ogden of *Basic English*, with reference to the perfective aspect of action ("I have departed", rather than the imperfect "I was departing"), where the participle is not an 'ed' structure but a *special past* form, as "I have *gone*".

XI.75 Fratricide: slaying one's brother, as Cain slew Abel. 'Murderer' and 'Fraticide' echo 'WHORE!' and 'MURDERER!' from the Festival Players [**#II.58**]; here, an effective curtain.

CHAPTER XII

XII.1 [Epigraph] spiritual quest: from Ouspensky, *Tertium Organum* (1923), of 'Man-in-Himself', his imperfect understanding of psychic existence and the noumenal self. Jailed within the phenomenal world, we mistake its reflections for the noumenal: "In this dwells the tragedy of our spiritual questings: *we do not know what we are searching for*" [XVI 196]. See Lowry's 'Notes' [21]; and (where it is cited more accurately) *La Mordida* [218].

XII.2 "What could happen?": Sigbjørn has a source of credit in Oslo [**#XI.73**; **#XII.33**].

XII.3 donkeyboiler: a large drum heated above a grate, an extra boiler in port. In *Blue Voyage*, one "universe" speaking to another prefers a pipe [18]. Again, cigarettes intimate the brevity of life [**#II.10**].

XII.4 "Bootle Cold Storage": Jan typed "Bottle Cold Storage", an ice Freudian slip. This is the depot at the Canada Dock, as the Ormskirk line goes south of **Bootle**. Compare "Nemesis, a pleasant ride" [UTV 189]. Bootle's springs long supplied Liverpool's water.

XII.5 sirens . . . fog: compare *Outward Bound* [**#VI.27**].

XII.6 Carnarvon Castle: a motte-and-bailey structure in Caernarfon, North Wales, above ancient Roman fortifications; rebuilt impressively over the centuries.

XII.7 Llanberis Pass: *Bwich Llanberis*, a traverse over **Pen-y-Pass** [**#VIII.94**] to the town of Llanberis, Snowdonia. The **Gorphwysfa Hotel**, at Pen-y-Pass in Snowdonia National park (later a Youth Hostel), was the obvious refuge for rock-climbers.

XII.8 Taffy: a ditty sung in the Marches (by the English) on St. Daffyd's day (March 1): "Taffy was a Welshman, Taffy was a thief / Taffy came to my house and stole a leg of beef."

XII.9 Haarfragre: Harald Haarfagre [sic], or "Finehair" (850–933), vowed not to cut his locks until he became first king of a united Norway. Despite this clear allusion, Lowry consistently spelled the name as *Haarfragre* [see the Textual Notes]. Captain Skaugen commanded the *Fagervik*, Lowry's ship [Bowker 124].

XII.10 Aintree: home of the Grand National, a handicap chase of four miles, 856 yards with thirty fences, on a Saturday early in April.

XII.11 Devil's Kitchen: *Twll Du*, "Black Hole", in Snowdonia National Park near Llanberis, named for the spray arising as moist air meets the rocks and condenses when forced upwards. The climb is better attempted in spiked boots ("nails") than canvas shoes ("rubbers"). In 'The walls of remorse are steep' [CP #75], Lowry recalls behind a gin-fog of lost Novembers climbing the Devil's Chimney, and hearing his friend (Tom Forman) boast, "I'd climb that rock again in sandshoes for sport, / And then in spikes for the glory of God!" He concludes that he had been given one chance: "And as well end that fall too at the end of a rope." The spectre is Paul Fitte [**#III.125**].

XII.12 eyes like stones: the empty sockets of Dante's damned [**#II.68**].

XII.13 Parson's Nose: a rock face at the *Clogwyn y Person Arête* ridge, North Wales, five miles southeast of Llanberis; after the indelicate avian *pygostyle*, offered to the visiting Reverend. Hugh recalls this note in the visitors' book: "Climbed the Parson's Nose . . . in twenty minutes. Found the rocks very easy"; to which some "immortal wag" had added: "Came down the Parson's Nose . . . in twenty seconds. Found the rocks very hard" [UTV 181]. Lowry's authority was I. A. Richards [note on UBC 30:10 TS 22].

XII.14 Poland: caught between Russian and Prussian expansionism, Poland had long desired independence, briefly succeeding after WWI. Joseph Conrad was born (1857) in Berdyczów, part of the Ukraine "owned" by Polish gentry, where the peasantry dreamt of liberation; his father, Apollo Korzeniowski, actively resisted Russian oppression, supporting both Poles and Ukrainians in their ambitions.

XII.15 problem of Wales: that of a would-be nation, its distinct language and culture threatened (as the Ukraine by Poland, or Poland by Russia) by a stronger neighbour.

XII.16 Prince of Wales: Edward VIII (abdicated 1936) was invested as Prince of Wales at Caernarfon Castle (1911).

XII.17 Peer Gynt: in Ibsen's 1867 play, *Peer*, after years of feckless wandering, peels an onion layer by layer, to find (like the self to which he has been sufficient) it has no centre.

XII.18 Midnight Sun: McBride's *Norwegian Towns*, subtitled *Vistas in the Land of the Midnight Sun*, discusses this phenomenon at length.

XII.19 Maghull: last station on the Preston line before the Lancashire county boundary.

XII.20 aeroplane: 'obscure' refutes "Airplane or aeroplane or just plain plane" [CP #106]; it watches over the next chapter.

XII.21 *Aftenposten*: Nor. 'The Evening Post'; Oslo's largest newspaper, founded 1860; despite its name, a morning issue with an evening edition [**#III.116**]. Conservative, it was between the wars bluntly anti-communist. The two Norwegian items must be from *Aftenposten*, yet neither incident has been identified. Curiously, on the morning of 11 Aug. 1931, the day Lowry left Preston, the English cargo ship *Ryburn*, from Rotterdam to the Kara Sea with steel, sank off Ålesund; and the second mate, who could not swim, was drowned. This featured in the Norwegian papers, but Lowry nowhere mentions it.

XII.22 ***Trelast damper . . . russiske sagbruk*:** Nor. "A timber-carrying ship aground in the Måløy tidal-stream. The ship was leaving but before she began the trip from Omega to Preston, as one can see, fully loaded with timber from the Russian sawmills. . . ." **Måløy** is a few hours north of Bergen; **Omega** (the last Greek letter) should be *Onega*, a timber port on the White Sea, eighty miles southwest of Archangel.

XII.23 Wigan: between Ormskirk and Manchester (now a borough of Greater Manchester); once a major mill town and coal-mining centre; even before Orwell's *Road to Wigan Pier* (1937), an emblem of depressed industrial urban life.

XII.24 Mississippi river boats: with paddle-wheels, toppling smokestacks, and confidence men [**#VII.41**; **#XII.28**].

XII.25 Ormskirk: ON *Omr's Kirk*, or "Serpent's Church", after Omr, its Viking founder; a market town midway between Liverpool and Preston.

XII.26 ***Skibet som mitt . . . Pa billedet*:** Nor. "The ship fully-loaded goes to sea . . . This is how the steamship 'Viets' looked, when she came into Kristiansand fjord after her terrible journey from Archangel. As the morning issue reported yesterday, the first mate was swept overboard as the storm raged most intensely. In the picture . . . " Kristiansand is in south Norway [**#IV.9**]; "morning issue" confirms *Afterposten*; but no record exists of any steamship called 'Viets'. Lowry's source for these shipping disasters remains a mystery.

XII.27 Melville's Caergwrle Ales: apparently, a local purveyor of these ales [**#VI.32**].

XII.28 Pegdog and Piddlededee: the *Pequod*, in *Moby-Dick*, and ("Fiddlededee") the *Fidèle*, of *The Confidence Man* [**#VII.41**]. After the modest success of *Typee* (1846) and *Omoo* (1847), Melville told Hawthorne (in a letter of June 1851) that he would "go down to posterity" as the "man who lived among the cannibals".

XII.29 football: rugby union: **three-quarters**: an outside back (*centre* or *wing*); **sold a dummy**: pretended to pass, diverting a would-be tackler, but retained the ball; **fullback**: the last defender should an opponent (here, the *three-quarter*) break through the line; **stand-off half**: one who "stands off" the scrum to receive the ball from the scrum-half (*half-back*); otherwise, the *first five-eighth*. A **try** is scored when a player crosses the opponents' goal line and grounds the ball. This was then worth three points, but if **converted** (into a '**goal**') two more: the ball is placed upright, in line with the touchdown, and kicked over the crossbar. Two **linesmen** go behind the posts; if this succeeds, they *raise their flags*; otherwise, they *flag it away*. The referee's **whistle** sounds like the emergency drill ("pipe") on a ship.

XII.30 Smith and Hermannsson: unknown (the latter form is Swedish). The "familiar" design is a post-horn, typifying Norwegian stamps since 1871; 'D.S' is *dampskip*, 'steamer'.

XII.31 Mecca cafes: Sigbjørn's destiny is woven about him [**#IV.38**; **#V.149**].

XII.32 Jump: introducing the theme, earlier intimated [**#VIII.67**], of shadowy surveillance; compare UTV, mysterious men in dark glasses. Lowry's sense of pursuit was not entirely paranoia, for telegraphs in the Liverpool Public Records Office confirm that Arthur Lowry paid an agent (Mexico, Los Angeles) to watch over his wayward son. This may have begun earlier, in England. Here, it implicates Sigbjørn in the "crime" of murder [**#XIV.8**].

XII.33 note to draw on: a letter of credit, guaranteeing bills submitted or moneys advanced.

XII.34 time bills: bills of exchange payable at a fixed maturity; unlike *sight bills* (payable when presented), they offer significant discounts. A **lien** gives legal rights over the cargo until debts are paid; **charterers** are investors who commission ships, retaining rights over the merchandise. Haarfragre reacts since Sigbjørn has implied that his ship is a *tramp*, with an irregular schedule and taking on goods wherever she can (by calling the *Pyrrhus* a tramp [*Liverpool Echo*, 12 May 1927], Lowry roused his shipmates' ire).

XII.35 *Douglas Fairbanks*: (1909–2000), the Hollywood heartthrob who played the lover in *Outward Bound* [**#VI.27**]; like 'Futurist' [**#VI.34**], the title now has immediacy.

XII.36 Christoforidas: Eleutherios Christoforidas, Captain of the Greek steamer, *Marpessa* (Buenos Aires to New York), walked off the ship with thirty-four of his forty-man crew, leaving her at the Staten Island quarantine station (Dec. 1935). Abandoned over the New Year, she dragged her anchor, scraped a tramp steamer, swung within inches of the government dock, and drifted with wind and tide about a bow anchor.

XII.37 fumitigated: i.e., *fumigated*, using gas to eliminate pestilence; compare *deratisation* (nautical), "to rid [a ship] of rats". **Quarantine** was originally "forty days" isolation of a ship, its crew or cargo, to contain infection.

XII.38 Croston: on the river Yarrow, near Preston.

XII.39 Kwantung Peninsula: occupied by Japan in the first Sino-Japanese war (1884–1895); returned to China by the European powers; then leased by Russia (1898), for a naval base at Port Arthur. After the Russo-Japanese war (1905), Japan assumed the lease, infiltrating **Manchukuo** [**#XII.44**] and retaining the territory until WWII ended. The ship passes: **Cape Esan**: a volcanic outcrop in southern Hokkaido, where the **Tsugaru Strait** (between Honshu and Hokkaido) meets the Pacific, its lofty cliffs densely forested; **Hakodate**: a port in southern Hokkaido; the **Sea of Japan**: as enclosed between the Asian mainland, Japan and Sakhalin; and **Korea**: the large peninsula, rounded en route to **Dairen**, separating the Sea of Japan from the Yellow Sea.

XII.40 Dairen: the major port of the Kwantung Peninsula: occupied by the British (1858); ceded to China (1880s); taken by the Japanese (1895); then Russia (1898); re-ceded to Japan after the Russo-Japanese war; and now in China. Dana is told, "Well, Hilliot, we'll be in Dairen this time next week" [U 175]. The *Pyrrhus*, taking this northerly route, left Yokahama (19 July 1927), arriving at Dairen (23 July), and leaving (28 July) for Tsingtao [*Pyrrhus* Logbook n.p.].

XII.41 *Oedipus Tyrannus*: the reborn *Pyrrhus* [**#III.16**]. In *Ultramarine*, the shore visit is in "Tsjang-Tsjang" (from Grieg's early poem, 'Skibslisten' [List of ships]), essentially Dairen with touches of Yokohama, Shanghai, Tsingtao, and Liverpool's Paradise Street.

XII.42 Socony: the Standard Oil Company of New York, headed by John D. Rockefeller and later called Mobil; similar oil tanks are seen in Tsingtao [U 28].

XII.43 hint of Russia: during their occupancy [**#XII.39**], the Russians poured millions of roubles (buildings, railways) into Dairen and fortified the harbour. After the Revolution, Dairen and nearby Port Arthur served the White Russian exodus. Haarfragre pronounces 'Dairen' the Russian way, as in *daln'y*, "distant" (Sigbjørn, in the Japanese manner) [U 180]. A seaman on the *Oedipus Tyrannus* insists: "Basra's—hotter—than—Dalny" [193].

XII.44 Manchukuo: the ancient Manchu state, now Manchuria, seized by Japan (1932). A puppet government was installed, from which Japan invaded China. Dana sees Manchuria a mile to port [U 22], which implies that (i) the *Oedipus Tyrranus* is heading north from Tsingtao, and (ii) somebody was confused, for Lowry's copy of the 1933 version says "the coast of China" with "*Manchuria*" written in [26]).

XII.45 spindle head: in a machine, where a driving-rod engages the cogs of a gear-box, so typically covered with grease; the ship (as "spindle") enters the filthy head (Dairen) [U 191]. This image also appears (Lake Charles, Louisiana) in Lowry's unpublished story, 'Tramps'.

XII.46 Leningrad: the Soviet name (from 1924) for St. Petersburg (or, post-1914, Petrograd); in every sense, the westernmost city of Russia. **White nights** are long summer days when the sun barely skirts the horizon; St. Petersburg is known for its White Nights festivals.

XII.47 built on a swamp: St. Petersburg, Peter the Great's window to the West, was built (1703) astride the **Neva**, which drains Lake Lagoda into the **Gulf of Finland** (the eastern arm of the Baltic), the river named from a Finnish word for *swamp*. It was Russia's capital from 1712 until the 1917 revolution, when governance reverted to Moscow. A complex of islands, swamps, and canals was gradually disciplined by the great granite blocks that define both city and river. Haarfragre's "too" implies the founding of Oslo on a swamp [**#IV.10**].

XII.48 oil-burner: compare Bruère's *The Coming of Coal* [**#X.11**]; **windbag** denotes a *windjammer*, or sailing ship.

XII.49 Cape Desolation: at the Magellan Channel, near the **Horn** [**#V.12**].

XII.50 boats: of eastern ports: ***orange boat***: typically, laden with fruit; ***balloon boat***: used in shallow bays, the uplift from its single spinnaker drawing little water; ***laundry boat***: used by *dhobis* [**#V.47**] to collect washing from ships docked. All three appear in *Ultramarine* [153] and 'Seductio ad Absurdum' [P&S 17].

XII.51 rightee: as to an illiterate Lascar or heathen Chinee, typically doing such work.

XII.52 Farington: a town four miles south of Preston.

XII.53 dark skater: see the Kafka epigraph [**#X.1**]; the deathly shadow is offset by that of the aeroplane, a power for good [**#II.23**; **#XII.20**].

XII.54 reload her: compare the death-ship [**#VI.57**].

XII.55 Ribble: running southwest through North Yorkshire and Lancashire to the Irish Sea; the northern boundary of ancient Mercia [**#XII.64**; **#XIII.54**].

XII.56 rolled all the sticks: in Kipling's 'A Tour of Inspection' (1901), Pyecroft steadies the ship: "Meet 'er! Meet 'er as she scends! You'll roll the sticks out of her if you don't." That is, the waves will break the masts. Sigbjørn Wilderness recalls a ship that "rolled all the sticks out of her", from Vladivostock to Archangel [*Mordida* 187; **#VI.45**].

XII.57 Marine Superintendent: responsible for maintenance of vessels in port, docking, loading and unloading of cargo, and hiring of personnel; the **Harbour Master** is responsible for general management of the port, safe navigation, and harbour security; the **shore bosun** commands the wharf workers [**#VI.58**].

XII.58 strains, and opens . . . upper works . . . coppers and grates: Haarfragre's tale, relocated to Archangel, derives from *The Naval Chronicle* 5 (Jan.–July 1801). W. J. Fletcher, 'The Last Voyage of the *Elizabeth*', tells how the ship, south of Mozambique (1764), was beset by gales and squalls, so "all the brick work of the coppers and grates fell down"; and "the ship strained and opened very much in her upper works" [264]. When the *Elizabeth* reached home (Spithead, via the Cape), she was a complete wreck, and had to be broken up.

XII.59 upper irons: wrought-iron bolts and braces that secure the rudderstock above the water line to the blade. Fletcher comments [265], "The upper pintle-iron of the rudder was broken". The rattletrap repairs to the broken rudder he calls a "steering machine" [267].

XII.60 frap it: to lash down, to strengthen the ship and prevent her from turning by passing ropes and cables beneath her. Fletcher notes [266], "We have most of us heard of frapping a ship. When St. Paul's ship was under-girded between Crete and Malta, the principle was the same; but few seamen of the present day have ever had occasion to resort to it." En route to Rome, Paul's ship was beset by a storm and wrecked on Malta. Fletcher alludes to Acts 27:17: "they used helps, undergirding the ship"; Haarfragre alludes to Fletcher.

XII.61 Flying Dutchman: a legendary ghost ship, fated never to make port [**#XIV.51**; **#XVI.17**]. Her master, Vanderdecken, doubling the Cape of Good Hope, found a contrary wind, but gambled his salvation on success, and was condemned to sail that course for all eternity, lest saved by a woman's devotion. Jensen affirms Columbus as his original: "*For it is the* Santa Maria *that is the phantom ship,* Columbus *is the restless skipper-soul who is condemned to sail the seas until the Day of Judgment*" [*Long Journey* III:xv; **#X.73**].

XII.62 isobars: connecting points of equal atmospheric pressure.

XII.63 race-horses: from the *Tao Te Ching* of Lao-tze, or *The Canon of Reason and Virtue* [XLVI.1], Moderating of Desire: "When the world possesses Reason, race horses are reserved for hauling dung. When the world is without Reason, war horses are bred in the common."

XII.64 Preston: administrative centre of north Lancashire, on the Ribble [**#XII.55**]; once a centre of textiles and shipping ("Proud Preston"), but as these declined, so too the city.

XII.65 Old Man: the Captain (the usual term). By **chinnings**, Haarfragre means *chin-wags*, casual chats; he struggles to say that officers and other ranks should not fraternize, as this jeopardizes discipline and respect. Compare Redburn's visit to Captain Riga [*Redburn* XIV].

CHAPTER XIII

XIII.1 [Epigraph] Tao: from Ouspensky's *Tertium Organum* [289], which draws on Annie Besant's *The Ancient Wisdom*, notes from which, including this, appear in 'Ordeal' [UBC 22:19 145]. The original is Lao-tzse, the *Tao Te Ching* [XXV]. It returns in Lowry's 'Work in Progress' [97] and 'Forest Path' [234–35; 282], the eternal ebbing of the tides. Lowry adds, from these sources ['Notes' 20]: "Tao is a square with no angles, a great sound which cannot be heard, a great image with no form" [*Tertium Organum* 290; **#VII.137**].

XIII.2 lone airman: the plane was earlier heard and its shadow seen [**#XII.20**]; it affirms that "power for good" watching over all [**#II.23**], yet suggests Yeats, 'An Irish Airman Foresees His Death' (1918). Lowry perhaps made this flight with Tom Forman.

XIII.3 telegraph stations: a signalling system, devised by Barnard Watson, using numerical coding: towers with three (later four) mobile arms relayed signals to the next station. The Liverpool Docks Trustees instituted the Holyhead to Liverpool line (1827), the relays as Lowry records. The distance was seventy-two miles; with stations five to twelve miles apart a signal to Liverpool might take less than a minute. Incoming ships could signal their owners, report problems, and arrange facilities. The line was replaced (1861) by an electric telegraph.

Holyhead: North Wales, west of Anglesey [**#XIII.7**], a ferry port to Ireland. The telegraph station, built for a local system (1810), was rebuilt (1841) on the north face of Holyhead Mountain.

Cefn Du: central Anglesey, near Llanryddlad; moved from an earlier station at *Carreglwyd* (1840).

Point Lynas: northeast Anglesey. The station was on the northern slope of *Mynydd Eilian*, above the Point with its distinctive lighthouse.

Puffin Island: *Priestholm*, an uninhabited island and wildlife sanctuary, east of Anglesey. The station, long disused, was at its northeast tip.

Great Ormes Head: a limestone headland at Llandudno. Built for the Admiralty, at what is now Telegraph Inn; a new station with twin towers replaced it in 1841.

Llysfaen: a village in Conwy, on Colwyn Bay. The station, now privately owned, was on *Mynydd Marion*.

Veryd: or *Foryd*, a town near Rhyl. This station was added to facilitate signals between Llysfaen and Voel Nant; it was moved (1841) when the railway needed the land. No trace remains.

Voel Nant: or *Foelnant*, between Prestatyn and Gronant, near the Dee estuary. The original 'Coastguard' or 'Telegraph', now privately owned, was replaced in 1841.

XIII.4 yesterday afternoon: when the Tarnmoors were golfing. The chapter offers many such perspectives (e.g., the "northeast March wind" from Norway [**#XI.6**]).

XIII.5 Sea birds: random cries: **Meev**, Jensen's gulls: "*Meev*, they say to each other as they fly; that means the day is blue, all is right with sea and sky" [*Long Journey* III:80]; ***quark***, the duck, yet anticipating the "*Three quarks*" of Joyce's seabirds [*Finnegans Wake* 383]; **klio**, the seagull's cry [*Blue Voyage* 304–10]; fading to ***io***, a nymph seduced by Zeus, changed into a heifer and tormented by a gad-fly.

XIII.6 Hilbre Island: in the Dee estuary. Edward King, Milton's **Lycidas**, drowned off Hilbre [**#VIII.95**]. The telegraph station was rebuilt in 1841, at the island's midpoint.

XIII.7 Anglesey: northwest Wales, separated from the mainland by the narrow Menai Strait. Milton's *Lycidas* promotes the common error, that King drowned off Anglesey.

XIII.8 red brick house: a perspective of house and road earlier befogged.

XIII.9 last station: Bidston Hill, whence signals were relayed to Liverpool [**#XI.37**]. Technically, the last station was Liverpool: originally, a lookout in Chapel Street; later, the tower of St. Nicholas Church; from 1856, the Tower Building in Water Street.

XIII.10 Crosville 'bus: the Crosville Motor Company, founded by George Crosland in 1906, ran Wirral services, including (from 1919) this, from New Ferry to Meols, via West Kirby and Hoylake. Janet awaits Dana at a Crosville bus stop [U 27].

XIII.11 Royal Liverpool: the *Telegraph* is the par-four fifth (424 yards) [**#VIII.12**].

XIII.12 Hoylake Promenade: from the ancient port of **Hoylake** (Hoyle Lake, a natural harbour), along the north Wirral coast to **Meols**, named for its dunes (ON *melr*). The **old forest** is a petrified wood between the two, at Dove Point, now virtually submerged. Laruelle recalls "an antediluvian forest with black stumps" [UTV 17]; here, there is no hint of Atlantis or the Flood, but Roman artifacts are found nearby.

XIII.13 Leasowe Castle: built (1593) by the fifth Earl of Derby. In the Civil War it fell into ruin ("Mockbeggar Hall"), but was renovated as a hotel. Its **Star Chamber**, named after the oak ceiling panels with bright stars (from the Old Exchequer Buildings) that convicts might contemplate when sentenced, features four great tapestries depicting the seasons.

XIII.14 Rock Point Fort: *Fort Perche Rock*, off New Brighton ("little Gibraltar of the Mersey"); a coastal battery built in Napoleonic times on Black Rock, once inaccessible at high tide, to protect Liverpool; now a museum, displaying *Titanic* and *Lusitania* memorabilia and photographs of the Blue Funnel Line. Thomas Kaye notes of the west front: "**six 32-pounders**, on cast-iron traversing platforms"; "**sixteen 32-pounders** [sic] on the surface of the fort, and two in casements of the towers"; adding: "Furnaces for heating **shot** are also constructed" [*Stranger* 282–83]. **Karl Marx** and **Queen Victoria** were born, respectively, in 1818 and 1819; **Napoleon** (against whom the shot might be heated) died in 1821. Kaye describes the nearby *Magazines*, where incoming vessels deposited powder and those outgoing replaced it [281]; these were not, as implied, within the Fort.

XIII.15 dowels and trenails: the Fort is built of Runcorn red sandstone; Lowry reinforces it with details from Kaye's description of the Lighthouse masonry [**#XIII.16**]: each stone "united to the one underneath by dowals, treenails & c., and the whole compacted together by a liquid cement of **puzzilani**, a volcanic material, from the neighbourhood of Mount Etna, which subsequently becomes harder, if possible, than the stone itself, thus cementing the whole together like a solid rock" [*Stranger* 284]. **Dowels** are round steel pins that strengthen masonry; ***trenails***, pegs of dry compressed timber that swells when moist for a tighter fit.

XIII.16 marble lighthouse: "Beyond the battery stands the Lighthouse, built of very hard and durable marble rock, from the island of Anglesey. This admirable structure rises about ninety feet above the level of the rock, and is surmounted by a lantern, which shows its light out to sea to a great distance" [*Stranger* 283–84]. It was operative from 1830.

XIII.17 windhover: a falcon [**#VII.65**], Lowry's rhythms suggesting its flight. Hopkins's heart had stirred for his bird in north Wales.

XIII.18 Ricardo: David Ricardo, economist [**#VII.78**]. As member in the Commons for Portarlington, an Irish pocket-borough, he opposed the protectionist Corn Laws. His Jewish name, shrill voice, and tolerance of any doctrine (anti-Christian or otherwise) initially won more attention than his arguments, but at his death Henry Brougham hailed his intelligence and integrity as triumphing over "untoward circumstances and alien natures" [Lawrence Taylor, 'David Ricardo', n.p.].

XIII.19 top of the tide: liners await the turn; the Mersey's tidal flow ranges from a neap of four meters to a spring tide exceeding ten.

XIII.20 Runcorn: an industrial town on the Cheshire side of the Mersey. The **Manchester Ship Canal** "forms a connexion between Manchester and the River Mersey at Runcorn; hence a direct communication was opened betwixt the two principal towns of the county of Lancashire" [Kaye 175]. A canal was built (1773) by Francis Egerton, Duke of Bridgewater; another (deeper, wider, thirty-six miles with complex locks) opened in 1894. Aiken somehow recalled from *In Ballast* a "drunken steamboat ride up the Manchester Canal from Liverpool to Manchester" [Bowker, *Lowry Remembered* 39].

XIII.21 *Leviathan*: the SPD *Leviathan*, a massive dredger, built by Cammell Laird & Co., Birkenhead (1909), for the Mersey Docks and Harbour Board; named for the sea monster of the Book of Job, as in Melville's prefatory "Extracts" to *Moby-Dick*. In *Omoo* (1847), she is an American whaler on which the narrator farewells paradise; a "luckless ship", launched "under some baleful star" [LXXXII]. Julien Green's *Dark Journey* was first *Léviathan* [**#XVIII.32**]. However, this "**other Leviathan**" is the German liner, *Vaterland*, launched April 1913 for the Atlantic service and impounded in Hoboken when WWI began. When the United States entered the war, she [he?] was acquisitioned as a troop carrier and renamed *Leviathan* ("Levi Nathan"), remaining in service until 1933.

XIII.22 graving-docks: dry docks, from which water is pumped during repairs. There are still some but once were many both sides of the Mersey. Those near Pier Head are the oldest features (from 1756) of the Liverpool Docks.

XIII.23 Greek timber ship: Lowry's *Dimitrios N. Boglazides* (a perfect pentameter); originally the German *Ingelfingen* (1908–1912), but in turn Danish (*Orissa*),

Russian (AZ) and British (*Maid of Corfu*). Bought by N. D. Bogiazides & Sons, she was renamed the *Dimitrios N. Bogiazides* [sic] (1924–1939). As the *Alba*, under the Panamanian flag (1939–1942), she was commandeered by the Germans; and as the *Aquila* sunk by British aircraft off Midtugulen, North Norway (8 Nov. 1944). An "old Greek bastard of a tramp steamer" [U 76], she brings timber from Archangel to Garston; reappearing in 'Goya the Obscure' and 'Hotel Room in Chartres': a ship with "stacks of timber from Archangel beside her" [P&S 23; **#V.93**]. In 'From Helsinki to Liverpool with Lumber' [CP #77] she steams down the Mersey; in 'Reflection to Windward' [CP #124] she rolls seaward tempestuously; and in Lowry's film script she arrives too late to rescue a doomed Dick Diver [*Tender* 239].

XIII.24 Geordie collier: coals from Newcastle.

XIII.25 ***Arcturion*****:** the doomed whaler of Melville's *Mardi* (1849) [**#III.29**], continuing the *Leviathan*'s voyage in *Omoo* [**#XIII.21**]. Named for *Arcturus* [L. "guardian of the bear"], the brightest star in the constellation Boötes, she meets with "disastar" near Kamchatka, sinking as her luminary disappears from the northwest horizon. Lowry added her name on the first draft margins; she features in 'China' and 'June the 30th, 1934'.

XIII.26 ***Direction*****:** or *Director* [**#IV.16**]; ***Herzogin Cecile*****:** a byword for beauty [**#VII.30**].

XIII.27 three rings: tramlines at Pier Head [**#V.106**; **#VII.1**]. Many trams were double-deckers; hence the "special altitude" of the apprentice, dreaming (like Dana) of distant ports.

XIII.28 Milk Street: upper and lower Milk Street, in Liverpool's Vauxhall district, housing an impoverished Irish population.

XIII.29 'My Old Man's a Fireman': a Liverpool ditty that inspired Lonnie Donegan's 'My Old Man's a Dustman' (1960):

> Oh, my old man's a fireman,
> And what d'you think of that?
> He wears gorblimey trousers
> An' a little gorblimey 'at.
> 'E wears a bloomin' choker
> Around 'is blinkin' throat,
> For my old man's a fireman
> In an Elder-Dempster boat.

Elder Dempster Lines (Colonial Buildings, Water Street) began as the African Steamship Company (1852), with contracts for the Belgian Congo (including munitions), and services to Ghana and Nigeria. Their flag, an embossed gold crown on a red George Cross on a white swallow-tailed field, resembles that of the Tarnmoor Line [**#VII.11**].

XIII.30 blue books: Blue Discharge Books record a seaman's service, listing signings and discharges, reliability and conduct; Sigbjørn Wilderness retains his [UBC 9:1, 98]. Compare the "green Norwegian discharge book" [**#V.59**].

XIII.31 *Mauretania*: sister ship to the Cunard's *Lusitania* [**#VII.20**]. The largest and fastest ship of her time, she won the Blue Riband on her maiden voyage (1907), and retained it for twenty-two years. Requisitioned as a troop and hospital ship during WWI, she returned to civilian duty, but when Cunard and White Star merged (1934) was deemed surplus to requirements.

XIII.32 Mallalieu: from Celtic and OE (*moel-hlaw*), one living on a bare hillside (thus, the depressed economy); a name not uncommon in the northern shires.

XIII.33 laws of average: used by insurers to neutralize liability (the unpredictability of the unit) by spreading risk (the virtual certainty of numbers).

XIII.34 Cotton Exchange: a fantasy, the Lutine Bell, tolling at Lloyd's when a ship is lost [**#II.89**], proclaiming bankruptcy among brokers [**#V.2**]: the rotting corpses of cotton porters [**#V.28**], demobilized after WWI yet a decade later still unemployed; and once-abstemious brokers, now broken, reduced to drinking draught. In the **Oyster Bar** (Tower Building, Water Street), Bass was better served in bottles [**#VI.31**].

XIII.35 rampant bulls: stock-market vagaries ("Bulls" and "Bears"), likened to street spectacles such as bullfights and [non-]dancing bears.

XIII.36 smash-and-grab: breaking windows and absconding with whatever.

XIII.37 root-hog-and-die philosophy: self-reliance, from the colonial practice of turning pigs loose to fend for themselves.

XIII.38 Mecca Cafe: compare the end of Chapter V [**#V.149**], a disturbing hint of 'war'.

XIII.39 *Speke*: in greater Liverpool, north of the Mersey and east of Runcorn; its airport, built 1930–1933, then the second busiest in the United Kingdom, with services to Croydon and Dublin (now the John Lennon Airport, its terminal roof proclaims: "Above us, only sky"). The name is "oddly evocative" of John Speke (1827–1864), who found the source of the Nile.

XIII.40 weaving sheds: long, single-storey buildings of the industrial era, built to facilitate power-loom weaving.

XIII.41 puddling furnaces: reverberatory furnaces in which cast iron becomes wrought iron or steel by "puddling": stirred by rods to oxidize the slag and remove impurities. **Retorts** are small furnaces, but "secret" and "mercury" intimate alchemical flasks.

XIII.42 roving: or *rolag*: a bundle of fibres ready for spinning; prepared by **carding**: combing raw wool with a wire brush to untangle and align the fibres in long strips.

XIII.43 Bolton . . . Blackburn . . . Accrington: having followed the **Ship Canal** inland, the pilot, now heading north, sees these quintessentially industrial towns.

XIII.44 Pennines: like the Mersey, the Ribble [**#XII.55**] rises within the Yorkshire Dales, in the *Pennines*, a low range separating Lancashire from Yorkshire.

XIII.45 high road: the ancient turnpike (1726), from Warrington (in Cheshire, at a Mersey crossing) to Preston via Wigan, later replaced by the M6; equally, the London–Liverpool road, also passing through Warrington.

XIII.46 Poseidon: Greek god of the ocean.

XIII.47 coke . . . sulphate of ammonia: industrial residua, once negligible, but increasingly valuable in the burgeoning plastics and fertilizer industries.

XIII.48 first steam tram: the first British tramway, laid by George Francis Train [!] in Birkenhead (August 1860), operated until 1901; but its trams were horse-drawn. Steam traction for tramways, demonstrated in Birmingham (1876), was introduced in Wantage (Oxfordshire) later that year.

XIII.49 Lancashire towns: St.Helens: a centre for mining, glassware, and brewing; **Culcheth**: six miles northeast of Warrington; **Flixton**: now absorbed by Greater Manchester; **Upholland**: five miles west of Wigan; **Newton-in-Makerfield**: northeast of St.Helens; **Oswaldthistle**: south of Blackburn (Hugh's aunt moved there from London [UTV 157]); **Maghull**: on the Preston line [**#XII.19**]; **Coppull**: near Chorley, once the centre of a **munitions** industry; **Leyland**: south of Preston, from 1896 the home of Leyland Motors.

XIII.50 Shap Fell: a Cumbrian quarry, noted for its pink granite, near the village of Shap; a notorious hazard (vicious bends, long climbs) on the A6 south from Scotland.

XIII.51 howitzers: artillery pieces, typically pointing upwards (like chimneys).

XIII.52 mine shafts: the South Lancashire Coalfield extends west to Wigan, presumably the town "dark with smoke" [**#XII.23**]. There are no mines beneath Preston.

XIII.53 one class to another: the uneasy alliance between proletariat and intelligentsia, united by their antipathy to the bourgeoisie.

XIII.54 Preston docks: extending (then) from the city to the Ribble estuary. From 1806 land was reclaimed, bends straightened, a new channel dug and lined with stone. They re-opened in 1892, servicing the timber trade; to attract larger ships the river was dredged and deepened between city and sea. This became unsustainable (the dockland is now a marina).

XIII.55 canal: the Lancaster Canal, accessing the north.

XIII.56 Alma Mater: L. "mother of the soul"; one's old school or university; the Ribble estuary as matrix, delivering the Industrial Giant. Lowry's landscape is the Lancastrian equivalent of Blake's giant Albion.

XIII.57 poverty grass: spare grasses (*Donthonia spicata, Aristida dichotoma*) that grow in sandy soils; the only sign of life near the barren scrapheap on Preston's wharves. Seen in *Maelstrom* from the Bellevue windows.

XIII.58 Susquehanna: the West Branch, arising in west Pennsylvania (an industrial region), joins the North Branch before reaching Chesapeake Bay.

XIII.59 Freckleton: a town, east of **St-Annes-on-the-Sea** (an Edwardian golfing resort), near the estuary where the Ribble forms the Irish Sea. For **Farington**, see **#XII.52**.

XIII.60 north: the ground beneath the plane (approaching the Pennines) assumes Nordic qualities, reflecting the thematic drive to the North.

CHAPTER XIV

XIV.1 [Epigraph 1] Christoforus: from Jensen, *The Long Journey* [3:48], with many minor errors [see the Textual Notes]. Christopher, patron saint of travellers, was a gentle giant who carried wayfarers on his back across a dangerous river; he took up a small child, revealed as Christ, the intolerable burden that constitutes the Christian's lot [**#X.73**]. Lowry lamented to Jan, of things weighing upon him (April 1934): "too bad if St Christopher had just sunk over his neck" [CL 1:145].

XIV.2 [Epigraph 2] Waldo Frank: earlier quoted by the Captain from the *Adelphi* 9–10 (1935) [259] [**#X.35**; **#X.44**]; for differences (one crucial), see the Textual Notes. Waldo David Frank (1899–1967), writer, social critic, and editor of Hart Crane's *Collected Poems*, treated American history as a visionary process of spiritual renewal impossible in the Old World. Lowry met him (1935) in New York and admired his socialist views [Bowker 194].

XIV.3 Christopher Burgess: like Christoforus [**#XIV.1**], he carries travellers.

XIV.4 diurnal attempts: temperature variations, from daytime highs to cool of night. Lancastrian winter-spring fogs arise as humid air moves north over the cold land.

XIV.5 mushroom: a driver who "pops up" occasionally; unlike **journeymen**, who work "by the day", the owner sharing the profit; or **flatraters**, on a fixed *per diem* ("float"), who retain the profits (or sustain the losses).

XIV.6 Dandy Dinmott: a small terrier (*Dandie Dinmott*) with a distinctive top-knot; after a character in Scott's *Guy Mannering* (1815), who owned six.

XIV.7 Agnes: her name (Gk. "sacred") continues the Christoforus motif.

XIV.8 Mr. Jump: authority (others jump at his command); Ishmael's "invisible police officer of the Fates, who has the constant surveillance of me, and secretly dogs me, and influences me in some unaccountable way" [*Moby-Dick* I]. This is "part of the grand programme of Providence that was drawn up a long time ago" [**#IX.18**; **#XII.32**; **#XV.29**].

XIV.9 'Father of mine': recited in 'Economic Conference, 1934', by a drunken taxi-man (Bill) to an American journalist (Bill), in a room full of curios [**#XIV.79**]:

> Father of mine awaken I pray thee to the truth,
> Two helps of egg and bacon are requisite for youth;
> And since thy little nipper needs more food than thee
> Deny thyself that kipper and hand it on to me.
> The meal no longer dull is, Dad, chuck across that toast,
> For at last my empty stomach says that I should rule the roast.
> Hunger must have its qualm allayed, beyond my wildest dream,
> Go slow there with the marmalade, let me scrape out the cream;
> Pile up my platter rather than thine, with chunks of pine,
> Because my need dear father, is greater far than thine. [52–53]

American Bill's objection to 'chunks of pine' is overridden: "Pineapple" [53].

XIV.10 Beardmore taxi: built by William Beardmore and Company (Paisley), 1919–1930 (thereafter London); known for sturdiness and comfort, it defined the UK taxi trade between the wars, and the shape of cabs to come.

XIV.11 Preston North Station: opened (1838) as the North Union Station; rebuilt (1880) with a long central platform. The Liverpool–Ormskirk service terminated at one of the bay platforms (10, 11, 12); that for Windermere (Lake District) departed from 3.

XIV.12 mackerel sky: cirrocumulus or altocumulus cloud in regular patterns, with blue sky between, resembling mackerel scales; a harbinger of storm. When formations break up, into small shoals, it becomes a **herring sky**.

XIV.13 cruising cab: one unlicensed for the "station rank", seeking street fares.

XIV.14 Fishergate: the main street [**#XV.9**] of Preston, running east–west past the station towards the Ribble and the Liverpool Road. **Lune Street** runs north off Fishergate.

XIV.15 wicket gate: a small gate set within a larger, keeping Mr. Badman from the wharves. In *Pilgrim's Progress*, Christian, seeking deliverance, passes through the Wicket Gate, to the path that is straight and narrow. Lowry called his Dollarton abode the Wicket Gate.

XIV.16 What did that mean: 'gard' (Nor. *gård*) is a yard or enclosure; 'uns' (Ger.) is us: *argal*, by garbology, *us guard* becomes "guardian" [**#V.57**; **#XIV.95**].

XIV.17 Adriatic boat: apparently, a boat (short and stubby) plying the Adriatic, between Brindisi [**#XIV.87**] and the Balkans. Possibly, the Liverpool-based *Adriatic*, reputed unlucky, which was broken up in Preston (1899), her fittings acquired by local hotels.

XIV.18 patent cartwheel hoops: iron strips to strengthen and protect cartwheel rims [*OF* 231–32]. These details derive from an advertisement at the back of William Dobson's *History of the Parliamentary Representation of Preston* (1868), for F. Mann & Co., of their Avenham Street warehouse:

> Where will be found the LARGEST STOCK IN PRESTON of Bar, Rod, Sheet, and Hoop Iron, Smiths' Circular and Long Bellows, Anvils, Patent Cart Wheel Hoops, all kinds of Steel, Springs for Conveyances, Rain Water Pipes, O.G. and plain Cutters, Heads, Shoes, Stop Ends, Red, White, and Orange Leads, Vermillion, Russian Blue Patent Dryers, Raw and Boiled Linseed and Moderator Lamp Oils, Turpentine, Arm Moulds, Warrington and Scotch made Bushes. [108]

XIV.19 cruet stands: of metal, ceramic, or glass, holding condiment containers. From the same advertisement, but for Mann's General Ironmongery Establishment, 113 Fishergate, Preston:

> Where can be had all kinds of House Furnishing Goods at reasonable prices, viz., Marble Mantels, Register and Sham Stoves, Fire Tiles, Iron Mantels, Fenders, Fire Irons, Coal Vases, Toilet Setts, Copper and Brass Kettles and Pans, Table and Dessert Knives (Rodgers and other celebrated makers),

> Electro-plated Spoons, Forks, Tea and Coffee Setts, nut Crackers, Cruet Stands, Toast Racks, Fish Knives, in cases &c., Metal Tea and Coffee Pots, Dish Covers, Japanned Wares, Brushes, Gas Chandeliers and Globes, with every requisite for furnishing. [108]

XIV.20 wringing machines: the ad continues: "Gas Pipes and Fittings, Emery, Glass and Emery Cloth, Washers, Files, Brass, Iron, and Copper Wire, Locks, Hinges, Nails, Screws, Roofing Felt, Wringing Machines, Chaff Cutters, Gunpowder, Shot, Caps, &c." It concludes: "SOLE AGENT FOR PATENT SECURE HANDLE, TABLE, AND DESSERT KNIVES, PATENT WATERFALL WASHING AND LAWN MOWING MACHINES."

XIV.21 hydrometers, saccharometers and thermometers: the next ad [109], for Messrs. Cartwright, Opticians, 22 Fishergate, Preston, offers: *Opera, Race, or Field Glasses, Hydrometers, Saccharometers, and Thermometers for Brewers', Publicans', and Distillers' uses.* A *hydrometer* measures specific gravity of the mash; a *saccharometer*, sugar; a *thermometer*, temperature [**#XV.28**].

XIV.22 seventy-six years ago: Dobson's first edition (1856) lacked the 1868 advertising [**#XIV.18**]; however, the date suggests a present of 1932.

XIV.23 mobile police: traffic police, a separate force that Christopher has encountered.

XIV.24 short-armed bastard: "short-arm parades" are VD inspections [U 28]; here, a misbegotten wanker. The Cambridge **brush-up** is Tor's suicide.

XIV.25 Scotland Yard: London Metropolitan Police, whose headquarters at 4 Whitehall Place backed onto Great Scotland Yard. Relocating to 10 Broadway (1890), *New Scotland Yard* persisted. The Preston office of the Lancashire Constabulary was on Lawson Street.

XIV.26 Docks Police: "exercising their powers only on dock premises, and handing over their prisoners after arrest to the Metropolitan or the City Police" [Somes, *English Policeman* 237], as Jump is tempted to do. The Preston dockside station was in nearby Watery Lane.

XIV.27 pensionable: as pension entitlements in the London Metropolitan and Home Counties constabularies were high, other agencies might not match them.

XIV.28 wire runners . . . bollard . . . bight . . . hawser: *wire runner*, a rope or cable, played out by a winch; *bollard*, a sturdy quayside post, to which mooring cables may be attached; *bight*, a loop in a cable to run around a bollard; *hawser*, a rope used in mooring.

XIV.29 sulphur dioxide: the "rotten eggs" (sulphurous coal) smell of industrial pollution; from the tank farm next to the dock.

XIV.30 Skowegian: derogation of God's finest; "Look at our Skowegians" [U 189]. Haarfragre's men objected to reloading the ballast recently unloaded.

XIV.31 Trelast: Nor. "timber" [**#XII.22**]; *Trelast Arms* is Lowry's construction.

XIV.32 good intentions: proverbially, paving the road to hell.

XIV.33: as Melville's Stone Fleet [**#VIII.76**; **#XI.69**].

XIV.34 'Bowker's celebrated Tic-pills': not a cure for biographical excess, but a patent medicine advertised in Dobson's *History* [**#XIV.18**]:

> THE MOST POPULAR REMEDY EXTANT. BOWKER'S CELEBRATED TIC PILLS, An Infallible Remedy for Tic-Doloreux or Face-Ache. These Pills have obtained a high reputation both in England and Abroad, as a cure for that dreadful malady Tic-Doloreux; and for all Neuralgic Affections of the Head and face. Being very minute they are easy to take. Price, 7½d. and 1s. 1½d. Per box. The large size sent post free direct from the Proprietor for 15 stamps. Prepared only by W. BOWKER, Dispensing Chemist, North Road, Preston. [117]

Tic-Doloreux, or *Trigemina neuralgia*, is a nervous disorder causing stabbing pains around the eye or lower face.

XIV.35 transom: a bar across the top of a door.

XIV.36 Johnson Avenue: in Jersey City. Correctly, *Johnston Avenue*, after John Taylor Johnston, Central Railroad president; part of it, renamed Audrey Zapp Drive, leads to the CNJ Passenger and Ferry Terminal, where Webb "decked" (landed).

XIV.37 dark: lights extinguished to discourage U-Boat attacks.

XIV.38 Webb: "this damn Bolshevik" in his proletariat cap vaguely suggests Sidney Webb, founder of the Fabian Society [**#XIV.84**].

XIV.39 'old and mild': otherwise *Granny* ('Old and Bitter' is *Mother-in-Law*).

XIV.40 legal opening time: 12 to 2:30 p.m., and 6:30 to 9:30 p.m. [**#II.51**], hours set as a wartime measure by the *Defence of the Realm Act* (August 1914).

XIV.41 shot: an unresolved mystery. Compare the language of the Bath Hotel [**#II.56**]: "*he ran like a bloody stoat*" against "*leaping like a bloody chamois*" (a small mountain deer noted for its agility). "*Lor lumme*": once, "Lord, love me."

XIV.42 out of work: the industrial North was hard-hit by the Depression; Sigbjørn, like Dana or Hugh, may be doing a good man out of a job.

XIV.43 sergeant: in deference to a constable when apprehended, or apprehensive. **McGlone** is not further identified.

XIV.44 *Ariadne Pandelis:* built (1910) as the *Boyne*, of the Hain Line, subsidiary of the British India and P&O companies, trading in the Mediterranean, West Indies, and Brazil. In 1930 she was sold to a Greek line, renamed, then destroyed by fire, and beached and abandoned on the Brazil coast (1936). Lowry wrote despairingly to Aiken (3 March 1940): "Ariadne N Pandelis and Herzogin Cecile in In Ballast went to the bottom a few weeks after I had written about them" [CL 1:297]; adding, "these here correspondences of the subnormal world with the abnormally suspicious are damned queer." These lost ships augment "the coincidence of Erikson" in the DATG typescript [UBC 9:1, 126].

XIV.45 Mussolini: Benito Mussolini (1883–1945), Fascist dictator whose trains ran on time.

XIV.46 slave: the refrain of 'Rule Britannia': "Britons never never never shall be slaves."

XIV.47 can't outrun: intimated earlier: "*oh fly your fate*" [**#II.58**].

XIV.48 on the mat: facing authority. The DATG typescript elaborates: "They know all about you, and they're just waiting for an opportunity to get you on the mat" [UBC 9:22, 693].

XIV.49 half seas over: sloshed.

XIV.50 dunnage: extraneous material securing cargo; here, Sigbjørn's seabag.

XIV.51 Vanderdecken: captain of the *Flying Dutchman*, who turned from the Cape, not the Horn [**#XII.61**]. Jensen imagines Darwin's *Beagle* meeting the Phantom Ship, frustrating the Captain's "obstinate attempt to force a passage south of Cape Horn" [*Long Journey* 3:244]. Thus, the theme of destiny: no turning back [**#IX.5**].

XIV.52 Rightly carried out: Jump cites the *Police Journal*, vol. 7 (1934):

> The duties given to the police these days make police work one of very great importance to the community. Rightly carried out it ensures that degree of ordered life for the State which is so necessary for steady progress, and without which serious and far-reaching troubles may result. The police service unquestionably affords an honourable career for men of ability and character, but even more than most other professions, it calls for something over and

> above the desire for an honourable profession; it contains a call for service, and should be approached from a high sense of duty. [304]

XIV.53 double fifteen: in the darts game 501, players may begin but must end with a double; fifteen is unpopular, sixteen the preferred choice.

XIV.54 Guinness: a pint of stout; *old*, **Old Ale**, a dark malty beer; ***mild and bitters***: a mixture of Mild (malty, lacking in hops) and Bitter (Pale Ale).

XIV.55 licensing laws: from Alwyn Somes, *The English Policeman* (1935) [224]: "Frequent visits must be made to public houses to see that they are properly conducted, and that the licensing laws are not infringed." PC Lowry [Somes 247] would agree.

XIV.56 tramps census: according to Somes, "Our friend the 'Bobby'" [224] must send to HQ "Periodical Returns" that include [227]: "Dates and hours of Petty Sessions, Annual Licensing Returns, Lapsed licences and those requiring confirmation, Undetected crimes, Tramp [sic] census, Tramps arrested for begging . . . "

XIV.57 floating engines: vessels or barges equipped to fight dockyard fires from the water. According to Somes, the (Thames) River Police should:

> scrutinize ships, tugs, barges, and wharves; examine and test the security of mooring ropes, look out for overloaded barges, and tugs with more than the regulation number of barges on tow . . . in the event of fire breaking out among the shipping or in the riverside premises, summon the floating engines, keep order while the firemen work, and render any assistance within their power for the saving of life or property. [235–36]

XIV.58 keep watch: given the wicket gate [**#XIV.15**], with Christian vigilance.

XIV.59 exception: without forfeiting his pension [**#XIV.27**].

XIV.60 John Jameson: an Irish whiskey [**#III.18**]; ***Old Hollander***, Gordon's Old Holland Gin [U 116].

XIV.61 force majeure: Fr. "greater force", beyond control, hinting at another order of reality [**#XVI.24**]; the **plane of the normal**, punning on 'aeroplane', invokes "another world", offset by the cuckoo-clock, the "real world" and business as usual after Opening Hour. Jump may be a **bonafide policeman**, but all present intuit that he is "high up", or an agent of a serial universe, Melville's invisible policeman [**#XIV.8**], whatever his "good faith".

XIV.62 Preston Station Restaurant: on the wide island between Platforms three and four. For its proposed role in the revised novel, see **#XVIII.69**.

XIV.63 choose life: Sigbjørn's dilemma—to retreat with his whiskey to the embryonic security of the bar or to face life—is dramatized in Lowry's different endings to *The Last Address* and *Swinging the Maelstrom*.

XIV.64 sandwichless bulbs: compare the waiting room in Noel Coward's *Still Life* (1936), filmed as *Brief Encounter* (1945), sandwiches in large round glass containers.

XIV.65 Bear's Paw: the old Bear's Paw Inn, 38 Church Street, Preston, Mine Host Ann Horsfield. A Liverpool pub thus named, 53 Lord Street, was destroyed in WWII by German bombing; Joe Passalique stands obscurely outside it ['Goya' 276]. **Three White Mice:** not located; Liverpool and/or Preston have never seen such a site in their life.

XIV.66 barons of beef: double sirloins, undivided, spitted for a banquet. In 'Economic Conference, 1934', taxi driver Bill imagines, in these precise words [52], a gang rolling up in full armour, chucking him a purse of gold, demanding to come in and dine.

XIV.67 What did that mean?: Sigbjørn unwittingly echoes Christopher [**#XIV.16**], now his guardian; Christopher sounds the horn twice, echoing him [**#XI.50**].

XIV.68 AALESUND: the *Unsgaard*'s "port of registry" [**#XVIII.2**].

XIV.69 Newfoundland: Ethan's brother, Gwyn, "wanting to go to Newfoundland, set out, because he couldn't find another ship, recklessly for Archangel" [*OF* 9; **#V.59**].

XIV.70 Fyrbøter: Nor. "fireman".

XIV.71 drag: a trimmer hauls ashes from the furnace to throw overboard.

XIV.72 buckshee: gratis; Persian *baksheesh*, a tip or gratuity.

XIV.73 Private: the lounge bar, where gentlemen might accompany women. There was often no connecting door, lest patrons of the one embarrass those of the other.

XIV.74 carburettor sauce: 'Economic Conference, 1934': "Ah. But they don't give you decarbonized plaice and carburettor sauce there, do they?" / "Pardon?" / "Not gasket of beef and upholstery pudding. I mean to say. They may do you well like, but you don't get Piston of Pork and Texaco sauce" [50]. The latter puns upon Tabasco Sauce.

XIV.75 carbolic acid: a disinfectant. Taxi-man Bill continues the gastronomy: "you don't get roast and mashed ball bearings, nuts, split-rings, and bolts, sweetheart and radiator custard, tyre lever grease, biscuits and cheese with two bottles of distilled water with a drain [sic] of carbolic thrown in" ['Economic Conference, 1934' 50].

XIV.76 word of a bloody lie: "I ain't telling you the word of a bloody lie" [U 136; 189].

XIV.77 in a poem: the poet is Don Gordon (1902–1989), Communist and revolutionary, whose 'Underground, 1935' invokes the Austrian civil war of February 1934 that ended Social Democracy. Towards the end of the poem, the poet reflects, "Yet they remember / The Karl Marx—the detonations still in ghostly Floridsdorf, / They build now, on their black base upward, on sturdier rock."

XIV.78 embrasures: narrow openings that permit weapons to be fired while affording protection; **pillboxes** (concrete guard posts for machine guns) reflect similar construction rules; **sallyports** are secure entries, in a fortification, that permit defenders to make sudden raids ("sallies") upon their attackers.

XIV.79 Ryde: a seaside resort on the Isle of Wight. The bric-a-brac is precisely that of taxi-man Bill's London apartment ['Economic Conference, 1934' 49–50], where another invitation to "kip" on the sofa is made; there, the "Present" is wrongly said to be from "Rye".

XIV.80 Daimler's: an independent British manufacturer of luxury cars, in Coventry, which purchased the Daimler name from the German company in 1896. 'Economic Conference, 1934' adds parenthetically: "(The taxicab was a Beardmore)" [50].

XIV.81 my garden: taxi-man Bill of 'Economic Conference, 1934' does likewise, telling American Bill about the "grapetree" and five dead cats, the affectionate poodle and three dead brothers ("three dead Hardys"); he does not mention a sister.

XIV.82 epidemic: Spanish influenza (1918–1920) caused more deaths than the War.

XIV.83 smash things: in 'Delirium in Vera Cruz' [CP #31], the poet, gazing into a mirror, obliterates his image. Christopher, awakening, wanted to break a window.

XIV.84 Webb's shop: the Charity Commission (1890) asked Manchester schoolmasters for "useful books for practical men" (*Robinson Crusoe* their example); Webb's endorsement of this Fabian principle reflects that campaign. This Webb is not the darts player [**#XIV.38**].

XIV.85 electric eye: as "eye test" suggests, the eye above the pharmacy advertises Messrs. Cartwright, Opticians [**#XIV.21**]. It seeks out Sigbjørn as the *Unsgaard* leaves Preston [**#XV.40**], affirming, for ward and guardian, *follow your intuition.*

XIV.86 copper kettles ... toilet seats: from F. Mann's LARGEST STOCK IN PRESTON of scrap iron [**#XIV.18–20**].

XIV.87 Brindisi: a major terminus on Italy's south Adriatic coast. Passengers from India might disembark here [U 180], continuing to London by train. Sigbjørn's hallucination about being scrapped recalls that Christopher was an Adriatic "seagull" [**#XIV.17**].

XIV.88 Empson: in the final chapter of William Empson's *Some Versions of Pastoral* (1935), '*Alice in Wonderland*: The Child as Swain', the Walrus and the Carpenter assume Wordsworthian grandeur and aridity: "the landscape defined by the tricks of facetiousness takes on the remote and staring beauty of the ideas of the insane" [293].

XIV.89 Accident alone: unlike a serial world where adverse orders interpenetrate, Jump's intercession on Sigbjørn's behalf intimates (necessarily) another order. The novel interrogates (to reject) the universe as the random play of accident [**#II.25; #III.19**].

XIV.90 royal babe: Princess Alexandra, second child of the Duchess of Kent, was born on Christmas Day, 1936; by then, the Lowrys were in Mexico. Jan may have added this later, as a detail "suggested in conversation" [Bowker 202].

XIV.91 economic student: like Karl Marx, exposing the causes leading to the collapse of capitalism; or, perhaps, a casualty of the 'Economic Conference' [**#XIV.9; #XIV.74**]. The celebrated Imperial Economic Conference was that in Ottawa (1932); Lowry may intend an echo of 'June the 30th, 1934'.

XIV.92 sirens called: the police presence is thus marked in *Outward Bound* [**#VI.27**].

XIV.93 trembling in every mast: a journey to oblivion [**#V.77**].

XIV.94 on the side of life: a Lawrentian catchphrase affirming rebirth; one that the upright Waldo Frank [**#XIV.2**] and a comatose Sigbjørn might equally endorse.

XIV.95 on his shoulder: as befitting a Christoforus, the final '*Unsgaard*' [**#XIV.16**] affirming his guardianship.

CHAPTER XV

XV.1 [Epigraph] Herman Melville: Ahab's words on the third day of the chase [*Moby-Dick* CXXXV]. See the Textual Notes.

XV.2 Once more: Benjamin arrives at the *Mignon*: a "young face" appears on the quay, stares up at the iron world, and wonders, "What is there inside this ship, what does she conceal?" [*Ship Sails On* 2]; in Cape Town, he returns to her: "Once more a young face paused on the quay in the darkness" [213; **#IV.28**].

XV.3 tally clerk: one who "tallies" goods loaded onto or from the ship.

XV.4 fiddley: the iron frame around the stoke-hole opening; hence, the hole itself, leading to the "little hell" below [U 23; **#XVI.32**].

XV.5 lever weight and fulcrum: compare *Ultramarine* [23]; 'West Hardaway' [P&S 25]; 'June the 30th, 1934' [P&S 44]; 'Forest Path' [225]. From J. D. Jerrold Kelley, 'In the Stoke-hole': "you marvel at the nicety with which lever, weight, and fulcrum work, opening and closing hidden mechanisms, and functioning with an exactness that dignifies the fraction of a second into an appreciable quantity" [Chadwick, *Ocean Steamships* 171].

XV.6 enclosed by his soul: Jung, 'Modern Man in Search of a Soul': "He is like a child, only half-born, enclosed in a dream-state within his own psyche and the world as it actually is . . . Psychic reality . . . awaits man's advance to the level of consciousness where he . . . recognises both as constituent elements of one psyche" [195–96].

XV.7 hawse-holes: holes in the hull through which *hawsers* (mooring ropes) are winched.

XV.8 Easter: as Goethe's Faust considers suicide, Easter bells recall him to life. Sigbjørn's birthday voyage begins this Sunday. Lowry frequently mentions the trembling aspen (from which the Cross was fashioned); here, the living wood defies a world of iron (the ship, the ballast on the wharf).

XV.9 Post Office: Fishergate Hill, not far from the docks; Sigbjørn walks from it towards town, going little further than the top of the hill. Preston has no *Main Street*, but **Fishergate**, serviced by trams, was effectively such [**#XIV.14**]. Compare the Consul's paralysis in the telegraph office [UTV 39].

XV.10 Candide: see **#VIII.58**.

XV.11 pregnant woman: another (ironic?) metaphor of rebirth; compare similar details at the outset of Rilke's *Malte Laurids Brigges*.

XV.12 middle watch: between midnight and 4 a.m.

XV.13 *Nel mezzo del cammin di nuestra vita:* It. "In the middle of the road of our life"; the first line of Dante's *Commedia divina*, with Spanish 'nuestra' [see the Textual Notes]. Preston is "Dante's original" because hope is abandoned: "*Per me si va ne la città dolente / per me si va ne l'etterno dolore* [*Inferno* III.1–2: "Through me you go to the grievous city, Through me you go to everlasting pain"]. Preston lies outside the great Lancashire coalfield that fuelled its industry, but Lowry believed there were mines below.

XV.14 *In la sua voluntade è nostra pace:* It. "In his will is our peace" [**#II.61**]. *Something*, working through Dante, returns Sigbjørn to the right path, which he almost loses (he must not miss the ship, which, he believes, has "sailed with the tide").

XV.15 Coeur de Lion: Richard I, "Lion-heart" (1157–1199), renown for his crusading valour, and for neglecting England while being valorous. Lancashire mining had barely begun, and Richard's Lancastrian contacts were fleeting; but Robert Galloway's *Annals of the Coal Trade* (1898) notes a charter granted Bishop Pudsey "by Richard I., Coeur de Lion", creating him Earl of Northumberland, to procure from his silver and iron mines "money for crusading purposes" [I:15]; this is Lowry's puddled source.

XV.16 Alexander: (356–323 BCE), King of Macedon, and mighty conqueror. Galloway notes: "the mineral begins to be heard of about the time of Alexander the Great" [*Annals* I.1].

XV.17 Theophrastus: (372–287 BCE). Galloway adds: "In his book about stones this author specifies earthy ones, found in Liguria in the north of Italy . . . and in Elis, in Greece, which kindled and burned in the very same manner as charcoal, and were used by smiths" [*Annals* I.1].

XV.18 mandrake: the genus *Mandragora*, growing at a tree where the semen of a hanged man has dripped into the earth; the plant thus conceived screams when extracted.

XV.19 igneous: L. *igneus*, "fire"; rock formed from the cooling of magma or lava; leaving **chimneys**, or narrow vertical fissures.

XV.20 magnetic to a star: Lowry's source is obscure. The phrase appears in Charles Eaton's poem, 'The Portal of the Trees', *University Review* 8 (U Kansas City, 1941), 155.

XV.21 marriage of heaven and hell: Blake's prophecy (1793) reflects Swedenborg's *Heaven and Hell*, its vision of an energized Hell ("energy is eternal delight") affirming the material world and physical desire equally as part of the divine order. In a draft of DATG, Lowry noted: "What is above is like that which is below" [UBC 22:19, 142; **#XVII.12**].

XV.22 Why the crusades?: because "Coeur de Lion" so determined [**#XV.15**].

XV.23 Virgil: Dante's guide through the Inferno [**#III.54**], as **Christopher** guards Sigbjørn; further manifesting that power for good watching over all. This despite the Medieval truism, *Media vita in morte sumus* [in the midst of life we are in death], presumably Sigbjørn's translation of Dante's "*nel mezzo . . . di nostra vita*" into Latin.

XV.24 hill: Fishergate Hill overlooks the docks rather than the town, but Lowry wants the Castle Hill connection.

XV.25 bright rails: Lowry ended a 1933 letter to Jan by saying he was "going down to the station to look at the bright railway line that saw you last" [CL 1:123]. Lawrence describes collieries and rusted iron, a railway like a harbour below, "bright rails" and the embankments of a level-crossing [*Women in Love* IX, 'Coal-dust'].

XV.26 Norwegian proverb: there is no such proverb (nor, traditionally, any pavements outside Christiania).

XV.27 fellow-seaman: not from *Ultramarine*. Compare the seaman in 'China' who spent his life plying from Lisbon to Liverpool, and retiring could only say of Lisbon, "The trams go faster there than in Liverpool" [P&S 49].

XV.28 go to France: beneath Dobson's advertisement for Messrs Cartwright (the optician with the electric eye, located in Dobson at 22 Fishergate) is another for W. France , at 117 Fishergate [*History* 109; **#XIV.21**; **#XIV.85**; **#XV.40**]:

> If you want a First-class SHOOTING BOOT, go to FRANCE!
> If you want a First-class DRESS BOOT, go to FRANCE!
> If you want a First-class RIDING BOOT, go to FRANCE!
> If you want a First-class WALKING BOOT, go to FRANCE!
>
> It is admitted by all that wear them, that FRANCE'S BOOTS are the Best in the TRADE.

Bowker's Tic pills are for neuralgia [**#XIV.34**]. Compare *October Ferry* [123]: "Preston, Lancashire, in 1939 . . . *If you want a good boot go to France*. And remedies for *That Most Excruciating and Painful Sickness of Man: Tic Doloreux*."

XV.29 policeman: officers of the Fates [**#XIV.8**] keep Sigbjørn on the right path.

XV.30 eternal pattern of three: Ouspensky's "Law of Three" (Affirming, Denying, Reconciling) manifests itself throughout his various writings [**#VII.200**].

XV.31 Christopher: Sigbjørn, as Christoforus, must "ferry himself over the stream".

XV.32 dark skeleton of iron: an escalated chute carrying coal from dockside tips to a ship's bunkers: "An immense dark skeleton of iron hung over the open bunkers, and out of it came an endless clattering belt of black stones. The dust whirled everywhere" [*Ship Sails On* 37]. To **warp away**, of a ship, is to change orientation by hauling on a hawser affixed to a bollard; here, to access the coal tips.

XV.33 dream: the avalanche of coal [**#XI.2**].

XV.34 Silverhjelm: a name noted in the 'Varsity' CB. Baron de Silverhjelm was Swedish Minister Plenipotentiary to England in the early 1800s. The hint of Mercury ("silver-helmet") induces Sigbjørn's sense of his role, hereafter, as plenipotentiary for Tor.

XV.35 before our time: as the *Mignon* from Cape Town [*Ship Sails On* 214]. Lowry left Preston 11 Aug. 1931, reaching Ålesund five days later [**#XVIII.2**].

XV.36 tuco, tuco: the *tuco-tuco*, "a small rodent with the habits of a mole" [Hudson, *Idle Days* 16–17].

XV.37 Tusen Tak: Nor. "Thank you."

XV.38 towards the Ribble: from what is now the marina, the docks offset from the river.

XV.39 gun: compare Liverpool's "one o'clock gun" [**#XI.37**].

XV.40 electric eye: Messrs Cartwright, Opticians [**#XIV.21**], featured two eyes behind lenses ("adapted to perfect vision") on their Fishergate sign; but not an electronic eye. Sigbjørn's chemist (*alchemist*) is conjured by the shopwindow's all-seeing eye [**#XIV.85**].

XV.41 metallurgy: 'There is a metallurgy of the mind' [CP #80]; or 'June the 30th, 1934' ('Metal'), the chthonic vision of a metallic world.

XV.42 perpetuum mobile . . . philosopher's stone: follies of science [**#X.27**].

XV.43 gliding: as Melville's white shark [**#II.32; #VII.192**]. Richard Goldstein felt his feral soul "gliding through existence on an unseen but coherent path" (*New Yorker* [1 Apr. 1974], 52); an anachronism excused by its esoteric pertinence.

XV.44 City boats: of the Ellerman Lines, founded in London (1892) by John Reeves Ellerman, trading to the Mediterranean; by absorbing small companies it expanded hugely. Ellerman ships typically featured 'City' in their names [**#VI.47**]: *City of Hong Kong* (Hull, 1924); *City of Paris* (Wallsend, 1921); however, *City of Warsaw* was not their vessel. In a draft of 'Sumptuous Armour', as "we" near Birkenhead, "Funnels appeared over sheds of the Ellerman line" [UBC 11:11, 8].

XV.45 silent as Charon's boat: Charon ferries dead souls across the Styx to Hades. In *The Ship Sails On*, as a Cape Town ferry crosses the harbour a child falls overboard and drowns; the ferry stops awhile then slowly advances, "silent as Charon's boat" [184]. Lowry used the phrase (1953) to Markson [CL 2:694; in SL 349, it admits quotation marks]; he would not have known that Grieg had reused the image in a 1925 review of Sutton Vane's *Til Ukjendt Havn* [Outward Bound] at the National Theatre [U.B. Ms 4° 2811 (*Aftenavis* n.d.)].

XV.46 deserts of Egypt and Arabia: imaginatively, entering the Red Sea [**#VII.12**].

XV.47 *Halvt*: *Fult*: *Sakte* . . . *Igjen*: Nor. "Half"; "Full"; "Slow" . . . "Again" [U 109].

XV.48 cluster lamps: large lamps lowered into the hold [UTV 49].

XV.49 pulpit: a raised platform jutting from the bow, used for soundings; **heaving the lead**: using a lead weight and knotted line to determine the depth beneath the ship [U 168].

XV.50 immigrants of old: Jensen's *Long Journey* [**#X.73**] infiltrates Sigbjørn's quest.

CHAPTER XVI

XVI.1 [Epigraph] Hawthorne: Ethan Brand's valediction as he leaps into the lime-kiln [**#VI.66**].

XVI.2 [Epigraph] Jonson: Lowry's blunder: in Marlowe's *Doctor Faustus*, Mephistopheles is himself his own hell, as in *Blue Voyage* [203]; in *Outward Bound*, Heaven and Hell are the same [**#VI.27**]. Lowry settles the reckoning in *La Mordida* [91; see the Textual Notes].

XVI.3 protractor: a semi-circular transparent instrument, to measure angles and degrees.

XVI.4 nine knots: nine nautical miles per hour, suited to a Jungian night-sea journey. A nautical mile equals a minute of latitude (1852 metres).

XVI.5 quartermaster: the experienced seaman who steers the ship and applies helm orders from the Captain or watchkeeper [**#XVI.9**], with added responsibility when either turns in.

XVI.6 Starboard your helm: turning the wheel to port, the ship to starboard; Haarfragre uses the older idiom [**#III.31**; **#XI.38**].

XVI.7 N-79-W: 'N' marks the leading course; '79-W' is degrees west of that meridian (line of longitude). The *Unsgaard* heads eleven degrees north of northwest, into the Irish Sea, before turning north to round Scotland; she should cross the path of the *Arcturion*, southwest from Glasgow.

XVI.8 Sparks: the invariable name of the wireless operator.

XVI.9 watch-keeper: responsible for recording speeds, distances, and changes of direction. The position must be entered by his relief before he turns in.

XVI.10 wireless watcher: a rating who relieves the wireless operator; trained to recognize a distress call, he reports it to the operator.

XVI.11 tank soundings: measuring liquid in tanks and boilers, checking for leakages and stability, refilling where necessary: responsibilities of the ship's carpenter [U 40].

XVI.12 stokehold floor: where trimmers unload barrows of coal (in rough weather, baskets) from the bunkers for the firemen. Benjamin notes the effects of the voyage: "each day had eaten a little farther in, and now it lay a long way off" [*Ship Sails On* 100]. The **fiddley** is the entrance to the stokehold [**#XV.4**].

XVI.13 oatmeal and water: for hydration; on the *Mignon*, lime juice is preferred.

XVI.14 slice: "the heavy iron rod that kept the sea of fire in order" [*Ship Sails On* 102]. To maintain a clean fire, firemen eliminated "clinkers" (incombustible lumps), raising them with the slice above the fire to be cracked apart or pulled out [U 23].

XVI.15 tramp: in Lowry's 'Notes' [18] (Appendix B) another "solitary tramp" appears.

XVI.16 screws: propellers; not making the gentle "thrum" of other voyages.

XVI.17 *Expectamus te*: L. "we are expecting you". From 'The Phantom Ship', F. S. Bassett's precursor to the Flying Dutchman [**#XII.61**]: "Falkenberg was a nobleman, who murdered his brother and his bride in a fit of passion, and was condemned therfor [*sic*] forever to wander toward the north. On arriving at the seashore, he found awaiting him a boat, with a man in it, who said, '*Expectamus te*'" [278].

XVI.18 *Signalisering . . . Kristiania 1901:* Nor. "Signalling rules must be closely followed. Women, children, passengers and disabled people should be put ashore before the ship's crew. Kristiania, 1901." These instructions appear in *Ultramarine* [55], in garbled form [see the Textual Notes].

XVI.19 Columbus: Lowry's 'Notes' [8] cite Jensen [*Long Journey* III:xii]: "Columbus completes the Northern migration and at the same time renders impossible Christianity as a terrestrial dream." Seeking a passage to the East, Columbus discovered America; in Jensen's words, he "went clean through all imaginary realities and came out with a new one" [III.ix].

XVI.20 Magnetic Mountain: in the *Arabian Nights* (Third Calendar), a mountain extracting the nails from nearby ships, Prince Agib's disintegrating when winds drive it nigh. Day Lewis dedicated a sequence by this name to Auden (1933), It begins: "Somewhere beyond the railheads / Of reason, south or north, / Lies a magnetic mountain / Riveting sky to earth" [Poem #3]; it draws iron vessels to their doom [**#I.37**]. He celebrates Magnitogorsk, "socialist city of steel" in the Urals, founded (1929) as the world's largest steel plant. Lowry told Aiken of a planned poetic series, entitled 'Iron and Steel' [CL 1:66 (1929)].

XVI.21 Daggoo: as the *Pequod* sinks, Tashtego, her fierce harpooner (the error is Lowry's), defiantly hammers a red burgee to the masthead; Sigbjørn affirms its revolutionary qualities.

XVI.22 'donkey's breakfast': a straw mattress [U 44].

XVI.23 samshaw: a Chinese spirit, distilled from rice or sorghum [U 188]; compare 'The Glory of the Sea' [*CP* #5]: "And live on samshaw, fleas and rice".

XVI.24 cinesthesia: the sensation of muscular movement; here identified with *cenesthesia*, subconscious feelings generated by the internal organs. From F. G. Crookshank's introduction to Blondel's *Troubled Conscience* [**#IV.1**]:

> when *repressed* cenesthesia persistently invades the sphere of normal consciousness, as, according to Blondel's hypothesis, is the case for the insane mind, then the patient, trying to express what he feels, finds his experience beyond the resources of his habitual linguistic reserve, and the cenesthesia taking on—as if by *force majeure*—some disorderly verbal expression, he becomes conscious of the antagonism between his experiences and the seized verbal symbolisms, and suffers from those feelings of disintegration [*sic*], disorder, and alienation that emotionally characterize the insane mind. [12]

For Blondel, "clear consciousness" may be carried by "cenesthesia" without deliberate awareness [51]; hence Sigbjørn (asleep) understands Chinese. Compare Chapter IV of Bergson's *Creative Evolution*, the cinematographical mind [**#III.55**].

XVI.25 Factory ships: mother ships, processing whales killed by other vessels.

XVI.26 'Oh, jolly is the gale': sung by Stubb [*Moby-Dick* CXIX], defying the storm that dismasts the *Pequod*.

XVI.27 Coffee time: *kaffeen*, a meal before the late watch [*Ship Sails On* 47].

XVI.28 Gustav: Grieg's self-righteous sailor [**#IV.66**]; his is the "new voice" in Sigbjørn's dream, insisting that "Jesus loves us" [*Ship Sails On* 85]. Like Gustav, Grieg was born in Bergen (1 Nov. 1902); hence Oscar's abusive "You **Bergener!**" [*Ship Sails On* 52; U 16].

XIV.29 Wilhelmsen: *Wlm. Wilhelmsen ASA*, a maritime group founded in 1861; by 1940 the largest Norwegian line. Its subsidiary, NAAL (Norway Africa & Australia Line), 1911, owned the *Henrik Ibsen*, on which Grieg sailed to Cape Town and Australia [**#VIII.46**].

XVI.30 Christ Jesus: see Luke 2: Lowry's "not every little Christ Jesus in the Temple can come running around cargo steamers" [U 131] echoes Aalesund: "You'd do better playing Christ Jesus in the temple instead of going to sea" [*Ship Sails On* 19].

XVI.31 Donkeymand: or "Donkeyman", responsible for boilers and auxiliary machinery [**#IX.25**]; listed among the crew [U 55]. In Lowry's 'Notes' and the DATG typescript he is Haarfragre's brother [UBC 9:5 346].

XVI.32 little hell: the stoke-hold [U 202].

XVI.33 outlines of the Cross: as in one (in turmoil) makes the sign of the Cross.

XVI.34 dread question: Ahab obsessively paces the *Pequod*'s bridge, hailing passing vessels, "Hast seen the White Whale?"

XVI.35 Pyramid of Cheops: Egypt's great pyramid, c.2580 BCE, its stifling passages and galleries ventilated by shafts, of mysterious astrological import to some.

XVI.36 Kingdom of Heaven: Matthew's phrasing (other gospels prefer "Kingdom of God") [**#VII.89**]. Lowry's 'Notes' record that the Kingdom of Heaven Columbus sought [**#XVI.19**] was the "bible's mystical abode, Paradise", but "he sought it on earth, not knowing it was rooted in his nature". Seeking the Indies, he finds the New World; it seems the Almighty, or somebody not as good, is playing with him [*Long Journey* III:xii; **#XVIII.62**].

XVI.37 Cipango: the palace of Cipango [Japan], with gold so abundant that its roof shone. From the *Travels* 3.2] of **Marco Polo** (1254–1324), who accompanied his father Niccolò and uncle Maffeo to the court of Kublai Khan. Returning to Venice in 1295, after twenty-four years, he told his tales to Rustigielo of Pisa, who made of them a sensation. Asked on his deathbed to retract his extravagances, he famously replied that he had told but half of what he had seen.

XVI.38 starting to peel: compare "The iron tools blistered his hands" [U 171], from Chadwick's *Ocean Steamships* [173], whence the stokehold imagery in that novel directly derives. **Six bells** end the third hour of the watch.

XVI.39 something similar: no such incident features in Grieg's novel, but during a storm, with watches short-handed, Benjamin labours as a trimmer.

XVI.40 fiend: conjured by Ethan Brand, standing erect with his arms on high [**#VI.66**], before plunging into the flames. Ethan's **unpardonable sin** [**#VI.73**] is here that of the Intelligentsia, thinking themselves above their comrades, the Proletariat.

XVI.41 paste of ashes: compare "pasty with ashes" [U 171], from Chadwick's *Ocean Steamships* [171].

XVI.42 without equivocation: Dana uses this phrase when "morally refrigerated", ready to be eaten by "a lustless Eskimo" [U 126]. He had hesitated before offering to climb the mast to rescue the 'mickey'; this underwhelmed the crew, but his later unequivocal willingness to dive into dangerous waters to rescue the bird wins acceptance. Lacking any chance of selfless heroism (unlike Dick Diver in Lowry's film script), Sigbjørn remains unredeemed.

XVI.43 Mostyn furnaces: a final, iterated image of hell [**#VIII.24**; **#VIII.98**]. The last, isolated sentence is typical of how Grieg (and hence Lowry) ends a chapter.

CHAPTER XVII

XVII.1 no boatswain: the bosun typically relays orders from bridge to crew. 6 a.m. is odd: the "morning watch" runs from 4 a.m. until 8 a.m.; new workers should not yet be "turning to".

XVII.2 forepeak: that part of the hold nearest the bow.

XVII.3 A. B.: Able-Bodied [Seaman].

XVII.4 soogie: Jap. *soje*, "cleaning"; a mixture of soap and caustic soda ("soogie-moogie"), for cleaning paintwork and woodwork [U 147].

XVII.5 companion ladder: by which officers access the quarterdeck.

XVII.6 beneath the tumult of Niagara: the Cave of the Winds, behind Niagara [UTV 286]. Disasters (conflagration, earthquake, flood, typhoon) are elemental (fire, earth, water, air).

XVII.7 frozen in the postures of the living: an 'Address' by L. M. Sargent to the Seaman's Bethel Temperance Society (Boston, 1833) exampled the *General Arnold*, which, its crew intoxicated, encountered an icy storm (26 Dec. 1778): "The men had crowded to the quarter deck, and even here they were obliged to pile together dead bodies, to make room for the living. Seventy dead bodies, frozen into all imaginable postures, were strewed over the deck . . . The bodies remained in the postures, in which they died, the features dreadfully distorted" [14]. Sigbjørn earlier used the phrase [**#III.26**]. The Consul pictures (after a necessary drink) "three hundred head of cattle, dead, frozen stiff in the posture of the living" [UTV 208–09].

XVII.8 four bells: halfway (two hours) through the watch.

XVII.9 fading coal: Shelley's image (*Defence of Poetry*, 1821) of the creative mind: "which some invisible influence, like an inconstant wind, awakes to transitory brightness."

XVII.10 holms: ON *holmr*, "small island".

XVII.11 companion pinnacle: another compass pointer, on the *companion*, or bridge.

XVII.12 correspondence: Swedenborg's marriage of heaven and hell: "What is above is like that which is below" [**#XV.21**]; within the subaqueous realm of consciousness. Compare Captain Tarnmoor's sense of Norway and the "rocky inanimate" [**#X.78**].

XVII.13 *Norskerennen*: the Norwegian trough, important for navigation; an elongated depression, between 50–95 km wide, reaching 700 m deep; created by fluvial erosion and glaciation. From *Oslofjorden* it follows the Skagerrak around southern Norway, then breaks north from about Ålesund towards the continental shelf, channelling the Norwegian Current (from the Baltic towards the Barents Sea).

XVII.14 Norwegian Sea: that part of the Atlantic, beyond the North Sea, between Norway and Greenland. **Aalesund** is the *Unsgaard*'s destination [**#XVIII.2**].

XVII.15 Oslo fjord: *Viken*, "the Bay"; a large inlet (not really a fjord) in southern Norway, leading to Oslo.

XVII.16 Spitzbergen: the largest and only permanently populated island of the Svalbard archipelago, between the Norwegian Sea and Arctic Ocean; once a whaling base, and still a source of mineral wealth. The 'Varsity' CB copies from McBride's *Norwegian Towns* [79ff] details of its mines and bleak beauties [**#VII.139**; **#IX.32**].

XVII.17 Finnmark: the largest, most northerly, least-populated county of Norway, bordering the Kola Peninsula. Nordahl Grieg sailed there (1923) on the hospital ship *Viking*, to begin *Skibet gaar videre* [**#XVIII.53**]; he spent much of 1929 there in virtual isolation.

XVII.18 North Cape: a steep cliff on Mager⌀ya, where the Norwegian Sea meets the Arctic Ocean; considered the northernmost point in Europe.

XVII.19 five bells: marking two and a half hours of the watch.

XVII.20 Blucher boots: knee-length rubber boots (Wellingtons) for slushy conditions; Norman, on the *Oedipus Tyrranus*, wears them [U 19]. Blücher was the Iron Duke's Prussian counterpart at Waterloo.

CHAPTER XVIII

XVIII.1 Man has much in common: Ouspensky's *Tertium Organum*, affirming that each 'I' contains many "little I's", invokes this image of house and ocean liner [XVII, 203; **#VII.203**]. This, he concludes, is "a fairly true presentment of a human being". Lowry agreed: "if you wanted the right image for the soul of a man, you should think of a liner at night" [*Tender* 172]. The Textual Notes record minor changes.

XVIII.2 Aalesund: Nor. "eel sound"; a fishing port in Norway's Sunnm⌀re region, on several islands between two fjords (*Valderhaugfjorden*, *Borgundfjorden*), ten hours (bus, boat) north of Bergen. The **port of registry**, recorded in a ship's documents, often differs from the home port escutcheoned on her stern [**#XIV.68**]. The *Fagervik*, out of Preston, diverted to Aalesund, arriving 16 August 1931. Lowry stayed two weeks, then caught a boat to Åndalsnes for the night train to Oslo. In the 'Varsity' CB, he added 'Aalesund' to a map of Arctic regions copied from McBride's *Norwegian Towns* [67]. Ålesund was to provide a full chapter; in the 'Pegasus' NB, Lowry outlined a schema: 1. "Approaching Aalesund"; 2. "In Aalesund"; 3. "In the Möre"; 4. "The Nina incident"; 5. "The Climb"; and 6. "The train journey".

XVIII.3 ancient nobles: *Møre og Romsdal* is a county in west central Norway, Ålesund its largest town. Møre traces its history from Rognvald Eysteinsson, Earl of Møre (fl. 870), whose lineage the *Heimskringla* recounts. Jorgenson mentions the "earls of Möre" [53, 63].

XVIII.4 foreganger: a line grafted to a harpoon, to which a longer rope is attached. The 'Notes' foregang Lowry's intention: by a "great series of coincidences" Tor (as Silverhjelm) and Erikson shape Sigbjørn's rebirth.

XVIII.5 principal character: Grieg's Aalesund, native of this town [**#IV.59**]; such naming is typical.

XVIII.6 "make fast to a treestump": to avoid wharf charges until her next task is determined. Bowker wrongly assumes that Ålesund has no deep harbour [125]. The "many little islands" suggest that the *Fagervik* berthed in *Borgundfjorden* (to the south [**#XVIII.2**]), perhaps at *Lilleholmen* [the Little Island], near the shore where a road led directly into town, more than a mile away. The *Oxenstjerna* is tied "stern-on to the stump of a tree" in Oslofjord [U 66].

XVIII.7 charter: Lowry's 'Notes' elaborate the conflicting telegrams; Sigbjørn meets the shipbroker in Oslo.

XVIII.8 the Møre: a stolid four-storey building at *Skaregate* 8, near the docks, no longer (since mid-century) a hotel; previously the *Phenix* (in 1904, Ålesund was devastated by fire).

XVIII.9 kaffistove: specifically, *Kaffistova* [the Coffee-Lounge], on *Notenesgata* at *Lorkenestorget* (long gone), near the Latin School [**#XVIII.12**].

XVIII.10 Carsten Walderhaug: Jan confirms that this teacher asked Lowry (9 May 1932) for a copy of *Ultramarine*, saying that he (a violinist) had started a little jazz band called 'Rumba' (a Cuban dance), playing "night clubs and the streets, with many jobs" ['Notes' 4]. His surname suggests the nearby fjord [**#XVIII.2**]. One Karsten Walderhaug won a local chess tournament shortly before Lowry arrived, and "Kr. Walderhaug" convened a meeting on the Icelandic fishing trade [*Sunnmøresposten* 24 Aug. 1931]. Walderhaug is the likely translator of the many sequences of Grieg's poetry that entered *Ultramarine* [**#VII.120**; **#V.40**; **#V.94**], as no English versions existed.

XVIII.11 China: Grieg reported (as Lowry sailed by) the civil war between the Kuomintang and Communists for Oslo's *Tidens Tegne*, publishing his essays as *Kinesiske Dage* (1927), which Walderhaug is reading. It gave Lowry his first look (not a cover-photo, but opposite page 96) at Grieg. The DATG typescript recalls the "coincidence" of "Kineske [*sic*] days in Aalesund" [UBC 9–22, 669]. Hugh's "Chinese days" were less productive [UTV 99].

XVIII.12 gymnasium: *Latinskolen*, or *Ålesund videregående skole*, on *Latinskolegata*; the oldest *gymnasium* in Ålesund (founded 1865). There is no record, at the school, in the Ålesund Museum Archives, or in Skjeldal's *biografi*, of Grieg either visiting Ålesund or reading his poetry there. However, *Norge i våre hjerter* [Norway in Our Hearts] (1929) had won many admirers (though some thought the title "pompøse"); following its success Grieg gave several readings, in the south, in Oslo (1 Feb. 1930) and in Stockholm [Skjeldal 139].

XVIII.13 newspaper clipping: presumably authentic, but unconfirmed. Norwegian papers often published such ephemera, signed by a Christian name only; but 'Nina' seems contrived [**#XVIII.16**]. Calling Grieg the "Håp for Norge" [**Hope of Norway**] implies his first anthology, *Rundt Kap det gode Håp* (1922).

XVIII.14 strike-bound: echoing Sigbjørn's dream [chapter XVI], what sailors do in port: "We go on strike for instance" (like the *Unsgaard*'s crew in Preston).

XVIII.15 coal tips: wharves for direct bunkering. Ålesund's *Bunkerstasjonen* occupied a headland into *Valderhaugfjorden*, northwest of the town; "on the Aalesund side" confuses, as the town faces two fjords, but Lowry intends the northern dockyards.

XVIII.16 Nina: one of Columbus's three ships, the *Niña* sails in Jensen's *Long Journey* [Part 3; **#X.73**]. The 'Nina' coincidence intrigues [**#II.36**], but it is massaged. In Lowry's 'Notes' [3], the collier is from Dantzig. A *D/S Nina*, built 1917, hailed from Oslo; but Lowry's vessel was the *Norna*, from Bergen and Danzig, sailing under the Polish flag and recently returned from the White Sea (*Bergens Tidende* 22 juli 1931: 2). Earlier the US *Lake Winthrop* (1918) and *Barbara* (1925), she was sold (1929) to C. A. J. Naess (Oslo), R. Bekmans (Riga), then the Norna *rederi* (D. Lexow, Danzig), who renamed her (thus, not affronting the Norse Goddess of Fate). Sigbjørn (unlike Lowry) could claim to be Norwegian, but providence protected him: the *Norna* was wrecked off Rørvik (16 Sept. 1931), and scrapped at Stavanger (1932). Had Lowry known this . . .

XVIII.17 Bygdø Allé: Grieg's "ultramodern" apartment was at 68 Bygdø Allé, third floor [Dahlie, 'Grieg Connection' 35]. The ground-floor restaurant is no longer there.

XVIII.18 shipping company: the *Fagervik* was operated by Nilson, Nyquist & Co., in the 1930s at *Lille Strandgate* 1, *Postboks* 161, *Oslo*. The 'Notes' [4] say *Raaokusgarten*; Lowry perhaps confused this with Grieg's publisher in *Rådhusgata* [**#IV.4**].

XVIII.19 sealed: Sigbjørn recalls his earlier intuition [**#VII.50**].

XVIII.20 smørbrød: an open sandwich on dark rye. Dana regrets not sitting "in a lunar park in Aalesund, holding hands or eating smorbrod" [U 69]. Ålesund has no Luna Park but Oslo had a restaurant by this name.

XVIII.21 Helgefjord: unidentified; earlier associated with his mother [**#III.76**].

XVIII.22 violin: their mother present in spirit, Tor played (and Sigbjørn slept) before he died [**#III.109**].

XVIII.23 coal crashing: as in Sigbjørn's dream [**#XI.2**], the Freudian matrix explicit.

XVIII.24 Cattegat . . . Skoane . . . Kullen: the *Kattegat*, between Denmark and Sweden; *Scania (Skåne)*, in southern Sweden; *Kullen*, a lighthouse, on the Kullaberg Peninsula at the mouth of the Öresund. Jensen explains the geography:

> the lands lie buried under snow, snow half-way up the stems in the woods, the earth everywhere hidden, a single white snowfield as far as the land extends, white shores along the Cattegat, white over in Skoane, on both sides of the Sound, Kullen looking like a headland of snow running out into the sea, the isles like isles of snow; and between all the buried coast-lines the sea open and black, reeking with frost, like gall; until the sounds too are closed with ice a fathom thick and the snow smooths out all the countries in one. [*Long Journey* III:33]

XVIII.25 *'freighted for the future'*: Jensen argues [III:xii] that Columbus [**#XVI.19**] has moved from history to mythology.

XVIII.26 Bimmonpolet: the *Vinmonopolet*, or 'Polet' [wine monopoly], founded (1922) to regulate alcohol sales by high prices and limited access. The DATG typescript further slurs matters: 'Pimmonpolet' [UBC 9:1, 349].

XVIII.27 Bygdø: or *Bygdøy*, on the Bygdø Peninsula, a short ferry ride from central Oslo, or, by *Bygdøy Allé*, as Lowry's pocket discovered, some miles ("20 or 30" is excessive) southwest. Its heritage centre hosts the Maritime and Viking Ship Museums. Bowker says that Lowry and Grieg visited the Viking Ship at Bygdø and dined "at the Röde Mölle" [127]; this is unlikely [**#XVIII.41, 49, 50**].

XVIII.28 deus ex machina: L. "god from the machine"; resolving narrative impasse by improbable coincidence. Christiansen as broker is responsible for the *Unsgaard*'s vicissitudes; hence, an appropriate agent for the ship of Lowry's wandering soul.

XVIII.29 'Cain' . . . 'Judas': still a concern [**#I.45; #III.45; #IV.74**].

XVIII.30 Biblioteket: *Universitetsbiblioteket i Oslo*, the University Library (1811), on *Karl Johans gate* in central Oslo; the national library until the University relocated (1989). Dana likens it to Harvard's Widener Library [U 54]. *Nasjonalbiblioteket* (110 *Henrik Ibsens gate*) opened in 1999; Grieg's papers are there.

XVIII.31 Tauchnitz edition: Bernard Tauchnitz, Leipzig, offered good literature in cheap paperbacks. Lowry took to Norway the Tauchnitz *Anthology of Modern English Poets*, ed. Levin L. Schücking (1931).

XVIII.32 *The Dark Journey*: the translation of Julien Green's *Léviathan* (1929) [**#II.26**; **#XIII.21**], about Paul Guéret's fatal obsession with a young laundress, Angèle. The DATG typescript recalls when "he" bought, fourteen years ago,

> not the first edition but a Tauchnitz, on the first dramatic occasion of his having met Gulbrandsen, and just after they had parted in the street, in the dark stormy tree-tossed Bygdo Alle in Oslo, in the little book-shop near the huge Biblioteket, stamped on since by how many Teutonic boots? What hint of that time, what message for the future, was there in that now? [UBC 9:1, 81]

The "little bookshop" is Tanum AS, *Karl Johans gate* 37, established (1928) when Johan Grundt Tanum annexed another operation; it became Oslo's largest. Lowry, like Sigbjørn Wilderness, took a first edition of Green's novel to Mexico (1946).

XVIII.33 a play of his: *Atlanterhavet* [The Atlantic], Grieg's four-act drama condemning capitalism and commercialism. Oslo's *Teaterchef*, another Christiansen, promised the new play by Christmas (*Aftenposten* 12 Aug. 1931); it opened 23 Jan. 1932 [**#XVIII.63**].

XVIII.34 Elizabethan dramatists: Grieg was not writing about the Elizabethan dramatists; this is Rupert Brooke's study [**#XVIII.46**], written while he was at King's.

XVIII.35 dramatisation: see **#V.87**.

XVIII.36 *you kill me*: Aiken's theme, the son's need to kill his spiritual father [**#V.70**]: "inevitably the son must 'destroy' the father, castrate or crucify him" [*Ushant* 239]. This exchange seems melodramatic.

XVIII.37 National Gallery: *Nasjonalgalleriet*, on *Universitetgata* 13, built 1882 and enlarged 1903–1907, housing 19th- and early 20th-century Norwegian paintings. Lowry sent Aiken 'The Shriek', a parody of Munch's lithograph, 'The Scream' (1893) [CL 1:111].

XVIII.38 Kristian IV's gate: named for a respected monarch (1577–1648); crossing *Universitetsgata* at *Nasjonalgalleriet*.

XVIII.39 Munch's pictures: a room at *Nasjonalgalleriet* is dedicated to Edvard Munch; this is another display, perhaps of works later (1963) housed in the Munch Museum (*Tøyengata* 53).

XVIII.40 Kataev's play: Valentin Petrovich Kataev (1897–1986), Russian novelist whose exposure of post-revolutionary society avoided Soviet censure. The play is *Rastratchiki* [The Embezzlers], a 1926 novel Kataev adapted (1928) at Stanislavski's request.

XVIII.41 Circus Revy: in Lowry's 'Notes' [12], "opposite the Holmenkollen" (the National Theatre T-*bane*); specifically, *Bestefarstomten*, then an open mound (now an enclosed ring-road) off *Stortingsgata* near *Slottsparken*, the Palace Park. Dana recalls: "the gallery at Revy Circus Globus. Do you remember? Vi [h]ar nu program for alle og [enhver] smak. Hand balances from a Springboart and Tumpling act! Morsomme Klovner! Akrobater! Balansekunstuere! Slangemennesker! Luftakrobater[!] Obs!. Popul[aer] billetpriser: Galleri kr. 1." [U 73; We have a new programme for all tastes . . . Springboard and Tumbling act! Funny clowns! Acrobats! Wire-walkers! Snakepeople! Trapeze artists! Look! . . . Popular ticket prices. Gallery 1 krone]. **Circus Globus** opened in Oslo (Wed. Sept. 9); it dates Lowry's meeting with Grieg as probably the 8th [see **#XVIII.49**]), when they were setting up. Performances were at 5 ("Circus") and 8:15 p.m. ("Circus og **Revy**" [Revue]), with prices from kr.1 to kr.3.50 (children half-price); it ran until the 21st, and was positively reviewed [*Aftenposten* 10 Sept. 1931], with director Leth Carstensen's trained horses particularly applauded. In 'On Reading Edmund Wilson's Remarks about Rimbaud' [CP #68], the poet joins a "Springboart & Tumplingakt"; in Wilson he joins a circus, travelling as an interpreter and barker to Scandinavia. Lowry's copy of *Ultramarine* notes in the margin: 'Rimbaud' [96].

XVIII.42 Kristiania Bokhandel: Danish publishers of *Skibet gaar videre* (1924); from 1925 Grieg dealt with its Norwegian affiliate, *Gyldendal Norsk Forlag* [**#IV.4**].

XVIII.43 fixed curve: unlike Grieg's opening "spiral" [**#III.51**].

XVIII.44 with the card: unlike Tor's empty nameplate [**#III.4**]. Later that year, Grieg paid a similar visit to Graham Greene; they became good friends.

XVIII.45 sinister fashion: Erikson is equally a destructive force [**#III.135**]; a "double" may be an "exact opposite".

XVIII.46 book about Rupert Brooke: in *De unge døde* [Youth died] (1932), Grieg discusses six poets: Keats, Shelly, Byron, Brooke, Sorley, and Owen [**#IV.50**].

Brooke's "stock" was "very low" because of the poetics revolution led at Cambridge by Richards and Leavis, the Georgians sinking as the Modernists rose, though many felt that Brooke "had something" the Squirearchy lacked. Grieg's title unwittingly echoes John Summerfield's *They Die Young* (1930), which Lowry admired. It was prophetic: Grieg died young, observing a bombing raid over Berlin (2 Dec. 1943).

XVIII.47 ***John Webster and the Elizabethan Drama*:** Brooke's Cambridge MA thesis, published posthumously (1916), sees Marston as a sinister precursor of Webster, and "one of the strangest figures" [76] of the age [**#IV.50**]. Lowry's "long letter" to Grieg [**#XVIII.49**] discusses this book in astounding detail; but one annihilated line calls Marston "that mysterious misanthrope, haunted by oblivion" [UB Oslo, 365b]. The "astounding detail" owes much to Houston Peterson's *The Melody of Chaos* (1931), a study of Aiken that Lowry presumably had with him: "It was Brooke who appreciated more than anyone before or since his day the far-reaching importance of John Marston, that mysterious misanthrope, haunted by oblivion, who revived the old tragedies of blood" [218]. Much of the "long letter" (even Eliot's Webster quatrains) derives verbatim from chapter XI of Peterson.

XVIII.48 Røde Mølle: Nor. "Red Mill", a popular *danserestaurant* in Oslo's theatre district, after the *Moulin Rouge* of Paris. Opening (1925) at the Tivoli Theatre, it was demolished in 1937 (others assumed the name). Dana proposes "mittag" there to Janet, under the geraniums [U 73]; see Lowry's letter to Jan [*CL* 1:129].

XVIII.49 long letter: from "Hotell Parkheimen, Drammensveien 2, 8.9.31"; discovered by Hallvard Dahlie (1987) in the Grieg collection at the University Library and edited by Sherrill Grace [*Swinging the Maelstrom* (1992), 43–51; *CL* 1:103–10]. Dahlie and Grace fail to note the debt to Peterson [**#XVIII.47**]. Lowry implies seeing Grieg "in the Red Mill", requests another meeting, and discusses Brooke's book, with its "skibet gaar videre" qualities and discovery of Marston. Brooke was (he argues) "*approaching a Keatsian predicament*" [**#IV.49**], for which war was a catharsis, just as Keats had seen in Chatterton's death the consummation of his own theories; and Brooke's neglect is accountable only as a casualty of the "whirligig of taste" [**#V.129**]. Lowry is reshaping *De unge døde*, even before it is written. Grieg replied nine days later (17 Sept.), rejecting the overture by saying he had to "work as hell . . . . As a fellow-writer I know you will understand and forgive" [Huntington, AIK 2574]. This suggests that Lowry was still in Oslo [**#IV.9**], but (despite Bowker's elaborate fantasia) that no further meeting had ensued.

XVIII.50 Viking ship: *Osebergskipet*, interred c.834, excavated (1904–1905) from a large burial mound at Oseberg (west of Oslo); the grave of an affluent woman. Earlier housed at the University, it went (1926) to the new Viking Ship Museum [**#XVIII.27**]. *Gokstadshipet*, the even more impressive sepulchre of a Viking chieftain (c.890) unearthed in Vestfold (1880), remained in the city (with the remains of *Tuneshipet*) until 1932. Lowry ends his "long letter" by recalling seeing the ship with Grieg, and suddenly finding "we were speaking in whispers"; but this contradicts his other accounts of their meeting. His invariable use of 'ship' (singular) suggests no awareness of the other longboats, in town; and Grieg was too busy to go to Bygdø [**#XVIII.49**]. Lowry told Jan he had visited Bygdø; this is indisputable ("200 years" echoes the curiously restricted dates (850–1050) of the glorious Viking age that the Museum admits), but on another day, alone. Dana recalls seeing with Janet "the Viking ship" [U 54]. Grace, trusting Dahlie, assumes he was with Grieg [*CL* 1:109]; but like Lowry's seeing Grieg at the Red Mill this "might have been imagination" [102].

XVIII.51 Birgit: her absence from Lowry's 'Notes' suggests that the potential love she embodies (Solveig to his Peer Gynt; no more tiresome Nina) reflects a revised ending, accentuating rebirth. Sivert's beloved in Grieg's novel is Birgit; but this does not explain Sigbjørn's white heat; and Grieg was then single. To invoke Chapter IV: "This represents the flaw, the injured nuance which . . . renders more perfect a pattern of destiny because we cannot see *all*." Lowry outlined to Markson a scene where Sigbjørn, at his mother's grave (*Vår Frelsers gravlund* in Oslo's Gamle Aker [U 72]), meets a girl and falls passionately in love. The feeling is returned, constituting his first experience of mature love [CL 2:427].

XVIII.52 Tostrupkjaelderen cafe: Dana suggests dinner with Janet, "modestly, at the Tostrupkjaelderen" [U 72], *Karl Johans gate* 25, opposite parliament. The "Cellar", after Jacob Tostrup (1806–1890), goldsmith [**#V.8**], was a famous bar and press club. Yet this setting is, unmistakably, Frognersaeteren Restaurant, with the spectacular views of *Oslofjorden* that Lowry described to Jan [**#II.78**].

XVIII.53 where *Skibets reise fra Kristiania* began: in Grieg's novel Kristiania is mentioned only casually, well into the book's blue waters [15]. Grieg began writing *Skibet* in Bossekop, Finnmark [Skjeldal 123; **#XVII.17**].

XVIII.54 Arctic . . . Cape Horn: ultimate tests [**#VII.161**]; a composed insert ['Notes' 15]. Lowry credits Hardy's *Woodlanders* [Ch. III] for showing that "lonely courses" form no "detached design" but are "part of the pattern in the great web of human doings then weaving in both hemispheres, from the White Sea to Cape Horn" [UBC 9:5, 377; 'Work in Progress' 98].

XVIII.55 Adam and Eve: Lowry's "conceit" appears in his 'Notes' [15].

XVIII.56 dreams and knowledge: in the first draft, Lowry links the opening vista [**#I.4**], on Castle Hill, with a proposed ending: "They stand, looking down on the world, through the world, while the ship passes, beyond their dreams & knowledge." In Aiken's 'The Bitter Love-song', from *The House of Dust* (1920): "Day after day, beyond our dreams and knowledge, / Presences swept, and over us streamed their shadows." Echoed in *Ultramarine* [27].

XVIII.57 communism: Lowry's 'Notes' [16] affirm the incommensurability of human and divine law; yet the body "should seek to move within the soul". Tor considers that all is accident and Captain Tarnmoor accepts eternal recurrence, life as a wave [**#IX.5**].

XVIII.58 Erikson believes in nothing: one of Grieg's maxims was "Hva vet vi?" [What do we know?; **#III.67**].

XVIII.59 ideal . . . real: sentiments recorded by Lowry ['Notes' 15–16]; their ambiguities might have developed had the ending been realized [**#I.33**].

XVIII.60 day of privacy: the "poet" may be Cecil Day Lewis [**#XVIII.66**], whose turning from privilege to Communism inflects *A Hope for Poetry* (1934).

XVIII.61 few in life are important: in Lowry's 'Notes' [17], Erikson suggests that Sigbjørn has discovered he is not a writer; this (to the non-Socialist) is more chilling.

XVIII.62 Fata Morgana: a mirage. Lowry's 'Notes' [8] quote Jensen [*Long Journey* III:xii]: in Columbus [**#XVI.19**; **#XVI.36**], "*the pagan yearning for Nature unites with Christianity's* fata Morgana—*and they perish together!*" The Erikson link is Jensen's sense of Columbus as a pawn in a larger game: the advent of the first modern man.

XVIII.63 Nationaltheatret: Nor. "The National Theatre" (Henrik Ibsen Theatre), Oslo [U 72]; since its opening (1 Sept. 1899), Norway's centre for dramatic arts. It staged Grieg's *Barabbas* in 1927, and *Atlanterhavet* in 1932 [**#XVIII.33**]. Grieg read from his new play here (11 Aug. 1931), even as Lowry entered that ocean.

XVIII.64 latest play: if Erikson's "latest play" is *Barabbas* [UTV 328], Sigbjørn's inscribed future defies irony. However, Sigbjørn Wilderness in the DATG typescript recalls "buying the play En Ung Manus", or *En ung manns Kjærlighet* [A Young Man's Love], also produced in 1927 though written earlier, about one "who cannot transcend his past" [UBC 9:5, 348].

XVIII.65 hanged man: Sigbjørn has experienced the suffering, if not the Truth [**#I.63**].

XVIII.66 an infant: Matthew 18:3: "unless you . . . become like children, you will not enter the kingdom of heaven" [**#VII.72**; **#XVI.36**]. Specifically (in the 'Varsity' CB), Day Lewis, the final stanza of *From Feathers to Iron* XIV:

> Our joy was but a gusty thing
> Without sinew or wit
> An infant flyaway; but now
> We make a man of it.

XVIII.67 Tchekov's old lady: "thinking it is no go" [**#VII.74**].

XVIII.68 depth-charge: Day Lewis, 'The Conflict', from *A Time to Dance* (1935), cited in the 'Varsity' CB. It begins: "I sang as one / Who on a tilting deck sings"; but the "land to be won" fades to impalpability, and the poem ends thus:

> The red advance of life
> Contracts pride, calls out the common blood,
> Beats song into a single blade,
> Makes a depth-charge of grief.
> Move then with new desires,
> For where we used to build and love
> In no man's land, and only ghosts can live
> Between two fires.

XVIII.69 How shall I live without my misery?: Lowry's 'Notes' record this twice, not as a planned finale [**#IV.24**], but following Erikson's comment (with no Birgit present) that he, Sigbjørn, has learned at least he is not a writer [**#XVIII.61**]. He can stand that, Sigbjørn says, but what will he do without his misery? Jan Gabrial said the book would end with this cry, "which epitomized those nightmare horrors Malc both fled and craved" [*Inside* 80]. 'In Le Havre' ends with the narrator accused: "You love only your own misery" [466]. Yet, as Lowry concluded in his 1931 letter to Grieg (acknowledging the unconscious desire for crucifixion), "misery is creation, and creation is love" [*CL* 1:105].

Accordingly, the 'Pegaso' NB proposes another ending, integrated with a new beginning [**#I.2**], and imitating Claude Houghton's *Julian Grant Loses His Way* (1933), whose protagonist awakens in the back room of a Paris café to find he has been all the while in hell: Sigbjørn wakes, "still at Station Restaurant" (Preston [**#XIV.62**], shaded into Montparnasse). He remains in a dream, and as he "watches cripples pass" sees his characters ("Christopher Burgess, Jump turns into gendarme") go by. Lowry invokes 'Hotel Room in Chartres' (where, after much turbulence, two lovers find each other); then meditates on "Going home to heart" (perhaps echoing Grieg), to find that sailors have no homes, that was the way of things. This is inconclusive, yet Lowry's revision might have enclosed the entire story within a dream of reconciliation, poised between a vision of new life and an awakening from a season in hell.

Bibliography

This bibliography has five parts: **A: Lowry** (published works); **B: Unpublished materials** (Lowry and others); **C. Works referring to *In Ballast to the White Sea*; D: Lowry's Sources** (specific texts or editions used in this compilation); and **E: Works quoted or discussed** (standard texts). Asterisks indicate works from Lowry's personal library.

A. Lowry: Published Works

The Cinema of Malcolm Lowry: A Scholarly Edition of Lowry's "Tender is the Night." Ed. Miguel Mota and Paul Tiessen. Vancouver: UBC Press, 1990. Cited as *Tender*.

The Collected Poetry of Malcolm Lowry. Ed. Kathleen Scherf, with explanatory annotation by Chris Ackerley. Vancouver: UBC Press, 1992. Cited as CP.

Dark as the Grave Wherein My Friend is Laid. Ed. Douglas Day and Margerie Lowry. Harmondsworth: Penguin, 1972. Cited as DATG.

"Economic Crisis, 1934." *Arena* 2 (Autumn 1949): 49–57.

"Goya the Obscure." *The Venture* 6 (June 1930): 270–78. Cited as 'Goya'.

Hear Us O Lord from Heaven Thy Dwelling Place. London: Cape, 1962. Stories cited by short title.

"In Le Havre." *Life and Letters* X (July 1954): 462–66.

The Last Address. In *Swinging the Maelstrom*, pp. 103–90 [below].

Lunar Caustic. Ed. Earle Birney and Margerie Lowry. London: Cape, 1965.

La Mordida: A Scholarly Edition. Ed. Patrick A. McCarthy. Athens & London: U of Georgia P, 1996. Cited as *Mordida*.

October Ferry to Gabriola. Ed. Margerie Lowry. New York & Cleveland: World Publishing Company, 1970. Cited as OF.

Psalms and Songs. Ed. Margerie Lowry. New York: New American Library, 1973. Including: "Seductio ad Absurdum" 3–18; "Hotel Room in Chartres" 19–24; "On Board the West Hardaway" 25–35; "June the 30th, 1934" 36–48; "China" 49–54; "Under the Volcano" 187–201; "Ghostkeeper" 202–27; and "Enter One in Sumptuous Armour" 228–49. Cited as P&S; stories cited by short title.

Selected Letters of Malcolm Lowry. Ed. Harvey Breit and Margerie Lowry. Philadelphia & New York: Lippincott, 1965. Cited as SL.

Swinging the Maelstrom: A Critical Edition. Ed. Victor Doyen and Miguel Mota, with annotations by Chris Ackerley. Ottawa: U Ottawa P [in association with EMiC], 2013. Cited as *Maelstrom*.

Sursum Corda! The Collected Letters of Malcolm Lowry. Ed. Sherrill Grace. 2 vols. Toronto: U of Toronto P, 1995, 1996. Cited as CL 1 and CL 2.

**Ultramarine*. London: Cape, 1933 [UBC 55].

Ultramarine. 1933. Rev. ed. Philadelphia & New York: Lippincott, 1962. Cited as U.

Under the Volcano. New York: Reynal & Hitchcock, 1947. Cited as UTV.

The 1940 Under the Volcano. Ed. Paul Tiessen and Miguel Mota. Waterloo, ON: Mlr Editions Canada, 1994. Cited as 1940 *Volcano*.

"Work in Progress: The Voyage that Never Ends." Ed. Paul Tiessen. *Malcolm Lowry Review* 21–22 (Fall 1987 & Spring 1988): 72–99. Cited as 'Work in Progress' [UBC 32:1] (1951).

B: Unpublished Works

(i) by Lowry (UBC Special Collections, unless otherwise specified)

"Dark as the Grave wherein my Friend is Laid." N.d. MS. UBC 8:3–19, British Columbia.

"Dark as the Grave wherein my Friend is Laid." N.d. TS. UBC 9:1–23, British Columbia.

"Enter One in Sumptuous Armour." N.d. TS (with marginalia relating to *In Ballast*). UBC 11:12, British Columbia. Cited as 'Sumptuous Armour'.

"In Ballast to the White Sea." N.d. MS (opening section). UBC 12:15, British Columbia. Cited as 'first draft'.

Letter to Nordahl Grieg. 8 Sept. 1931. MS. Nordahl Grieg Collection. Brevs nr. 365b. *Nasjonalbiblioteket*, UB Oslo. Ed. Hallvard Dahlie [below].

"The Ordeal of Sigbjørn Wilderness." N.d. MS UBC 22:19, British Columbia. Cited as 'Ordeal'.

"Pegaso" Notebook. N.d. UBC 12:14, British Columbia. This file also contains thirteen charred fragments of a later (early 1940s) revised typescript of *In Ballast to the White Sea*.

"Tramps." N.d. TS. UBC 25:9, British Columbia.

Ultramarine. N.d. Carbon TS of the revised text. UBC 25:10–15, British Columbia.

Ultramarine. 1929 MS. Conrad Aiken Papers. AIK 3381. Huntington Lib., San Marino.

"Varsity" Composition Book (with pencilled note on front cover, 'In Ballast to the White Sea'). N.d. MS. UBC 12:14, British Columbia. Cited as 'Varsity' CB; extracts noted as 'early draft'.

(ii) by others

Aiken, Conrad. Letter from "Harry" [Waters] to Malcolm Lowry. 15 March 1933. MS. Conrad Aiken Papers. AIK 2583. Huntington Lib., San Marino.

Grieg, Nordahl. Letter to Lowry. 17 Sept. 1931. MS. Conrad Aiken Papers. AIK 2574. Huntington Lib., San Marino.

——. Utklipp' (newspaper clippings by or about Nordahl Grieg). Nordahl Grieg Collection. *Nasjonalbiblioteket* UB Oslo, 4° 2811.

Lowry, Russell. N.d. In Lowry Family Fonds: Box-Files labelled "Documents of Importance" and "Russell Lowry on Family Matters." Comp. George Brandak. UBC Special Collections, British Columbia.

Pyrrhus Logbook. N.d. Maritime Archives and Library of the Merseyside Maritime Museum, Liverpool.

(iii) Jan Gabrial Papers (New York Public Library)

Gabrial, Jan. "Introductory Notes to *In Ballast to the White Sea*, by Malcolm Lowry." N.d. MS. Jan Gabrial Papers. Series iii, Box 2:6. New York Public Lib., New York. Cited as 'Notes'.

Lowry, Malcolm. *In Ballast to the White Sea*. N.d. TS. Ed. Jan Gabrial. Jan Gabrial Papers. Series iv, Box 3:1–6 (typescripts and fragments) and Box 4:1–4 (clean typescript).

——. "Letters from Lowry." N.d. MS. Jan Gabrial Papers. Series iv, Box 2–11. New York Public Lib., New York.

C. Works referring to *In Ballast to the White Sea*

Ackerley, C. J., and Lawrence J. Clipper. *A Companion to "Under the Volcano."* Vancouver: UBC Press, 1984.

Ackerley, C. J., and David Large. *A Hypertextual Companion to "Under the Volcano."* University of Otago. N.d. Web. Accessed 27 July 2014. <http://www.otago.ac.nz/englishlinguistics/english/lowry/index.html>.

Ackerley, C. J. "'And wholesome dew, call'd *Ros-Marine*': Malcolm Lowry, Herman Melville, Conrad Aiken, and Ben Jonson." *Cuadernos de Literatura Inglesa y Norteamericana* 13.1–2: 23–28.

——. "Personal Apocalypse: Malcolm Lowry's *In Ballast to the White Sea*." Backdoor Broadcasting Company. Academic Podcasts. N.p. N.d. [conference paper, U Bergen, 18 July 2012]. Web. Accessed 15 November 2013. <http://backdoorbroadcasting.net/2012/07/chris-ackerley-the-nordic-vision-of-malcolm-lowrys-in-ballast-to-the-white-sea/>.

Aiken, Conrad. *The Letters of Conrad Aiken and Malcolm Lowry 1929–1954*. Ed. Cynthia C. Sugars. Toronto: ECW Press, 1980. Cited as Aiken, *Letters*.

*——. *Ushant: An Essay*. New York: Duell, Sloan & Pearce; Boston: Little, Brown, 1952.

Asals, Frederick. *The Making of Malcolm Lowry's "Under the Volcano."* Athens & London: U of Georgia P, 1997.

Bowker, Gordon. *Pursued by Furies: A Life of Malcolm Lowry*. New York: St. Martin's P; London: HarperCollins, 1993. Cited as Bowker.

——, ed. *Malcolm Lowry Remembered*. London: Ariel, 1985.

Bradbrook, M. C. *Malcolm Lowry: His Art & Early Life: A Study in Transformation*. Cambridge: Cambridge UP, 1974.

Dahlie, Hallvard. "Lowry and the Grieg Connection." Grace, *Swinging the Maelstrom* 31–42

——. "Lowry's Debt to Nordahl Grieg." *Canadian Literature* 64 (Spring 1975): 41–51.

Day, Douglas. *Malcolm Lowry: A Biography*. New York: Oxford UP, 1973.

Dilnot, Colin. *Malcolm Lowry @ the Nineteenth Hole*. N.p. N.d. Web. Accessed 27 July 2014. <http://malcolmlowryatthe19thhole.blogspot.com/>.

——. *Gutted Arcades of the Past*. N.p. N.d. Web [website depicting Lowry's early life]. Accessed 27 July 2013. <http://guttedarcades.blogspot.co.uk/>.

Doyen, Victor. "Fighting the Albatross of Self: A Genetic Study of the Literary Work of Malcolm Lowry." Diss. Katholieke Universiteit te Leuven, 1973.

Gabrial, Jan. *Inside the Volcano: My Life with Malcolm Lowry*. New York: St. Martin's P, 2000.

Grace, Sherrill, ed. *Swinging the Maelstrom: New Perspectives on Malcolm Lowry*. Montreal & Kingston: McGill-Queen's UP, 1992.

——. "Nordahl Grieg, I greet you." Grace, *Swinging the Maelstrom* 43–51.

Kilgallin, Tony. *Lowry*. Erin, ON: Press Porcepic, 1973.

Lowry, Russell. "Clearing Up Some Problems." *Malcolm Lowry Review* 20–21 (Fall 1986 & Spring 1987): 100–01.

McCarthy, Patrick A. *Forests of Symbols: World, Text, and Self in Malcolm Lowry's Fiction*. Athens & London: U Georgia P, 1994.

McCarthy, Patrick A., and Chris Ackerley. "Annotating Malcolm Lowry's *In Ballast to the White Sea*." *Making Canada New: Editing, Modernism, and Digital Media*. Ed. Dean Irvine, Vanessa, Lent and Bart Vautour. Toronto: U Toronto P, forthcoming.

Skjeldal, Gudmund. *Diktaren i bombeflyet: ein biografi om Nordahl Grieg*. Oslo: Cappelen Damm, 2012.

D. Lowry's Sources

Aftenposten (Oslo). Issues from 1 July to 30 Sept. 1931.

Aiken, Conrad. *Blue Voyage*. New York: Scribner's, 1927.

Auden, W. H. *Poems*. London: Faber & Faber, 1930. Also, 2nd ed., rev. London: Faber & Faber, 1933.

Bang, Herman. *Denied a Country*. Trans. Marie Busch and A. G. Chater. New York & London: Knopf, 1927.

——. *Ida Brandt*. Trans. A. G. Chater. New York & London: Knopf, 1929.

Bassett, F. S. "The Phantom Ship." *Legends and Traditions of the Sea and Sailors*. Chicago & New York: Belford, Clarke, 1886. Rpt. in Joseph Lewis French, ed. *Great Sea Stories: Second Series*. New York: Brentanos, 1925. 276–301.

Beers, Clifford W. *A Mind that Found Itself: An Autobiography*. New York: Longmans, Green & Co., 1908.

Bennett, Arnold. *The Journal of Arnold Bennett*. Vol. 1. New York: Garden City, 1933.

Bergens Tidende (Bergen). Issues from 1 July to 30 Sept. 1931.

Bergman, Hjalmar. *God's Orchid*. Trans. E. Classen. New York: Knopf, 1924.

*Bergson, Henri. *Creative Evolution*. Trans. Arthur Mitchell. New York: Random House, 1944.

Blavatsky, Helena. *The Secret Doctrine: The Synthesis of Science, Religion, and Philosophy*. Cambridge: Cambridge UP, 1888.

Blicher, Steen Steensen. *The Rector of Veilbye*. 1829. Rpt. in Project Gutenberg. N.p. N.d. Web. 202–21. Accessed 13 April 2013. <http://www.gutenberg.org/catalog/world/readfile?fk_files=38430&pageno=202>.

Blondel, Charles Aimé Alfred. *The Troubled Conscience and the Insane Mind*. Ed. F. G. Crookshank. London: Kegan Paul, Trench, Trübner, 1928.

Brooke, Rupert. *John Webster and the Elizabethan Drama*. London: Sidgwick & Jackson, 1916.

Bruère, Robert Walter. *The Coming of Coal*. New York: Association P, 1922.

Burrow, Trigant. "The Autonomy of the 'I' from the Standpoint of Group Analysis." *Psyche* 8.3 (1928): 35–49.

Carmina Mariana. London: Burns & Gates, 1894.

Chadwick, French Ensor, et al. *Ocean Steamships: A Popular Account of their Construction, Development, Management and Appliances*. New York: Scribner's, 1891.

Chesterton, G. K. "The Racial Question and Politics." *Illustrated London News* 14 May 1910; rpt. in *Collected Works of G. K. Chesterton*. Vol. 28, *The Illustrated London News 1908–1910*. Ed. Lawrence J. Clipper. San Francisco: Ignatius Press, 526–29.

Conan Doyle, Sir Arthur. *The Firm of Girdlestone*. London: Chatto & Windus, 1890.

Constantine, Murray [Katharine Burdekin]. *Proud Man*. London: Boriswood, 1934.

Cornwell, Paul. "American Drama at the Cambridge Festival Theatre, 1928–1935." *The Eugene O'Neill Review* 27 (2005): 61–75.

Crane, Hart. *Collected Poetry*. Ed. Waldo David Frank. New York: Liveright, 1933.

Crosby, Harry. "Illustrations of Madness." *transition* 18 (Nov. 1929): 102–03.

Dante Alighieri. *Inferno*. Trans. Jefferson Butler Fletcher. New York: Macmillan, 1931.

Dataller, Roger [Arthur Archibald Eaglestone]. "From a Miner's Journal." *Adelphi* (Jan. 1924): 711–18.

——. *From a Pitman's Note Book*. London: Cape, 1925.

Day Lewis, Cecil. *Collected Poems 1929–1933* and *A Hope for Poetry*. New York: Random House, 1935.

De Hartog, Jan. *Captain Jan: A Story of Ocean Tugboats*. London: Cleaver-Hume P, 1952.
Dobson, William. *History of the Parliamentary Representation of Preston During the Last Hundred Years*. 1856. 2nd ed. (with additional backpages of advertising). Preston: W. & J. Dobson, Fishergate, 1868.
Dunne, J. W. *An Experiment with Time*. London: A. & C. Black, 1927.
Dunsany, Edward Lord. *The Last Book of Wonder*. London: Mathews, 1916.
Durant, Will. *The Story of Philosophy*. New York: Simon & Schuster, 1926.
Empson, William. *Some Versions of Pastoral*. London: Chatto & Windus, 1935.
Fielding, William J. *The Caveman within Us*. London: Kegan Paul, Trench, Trübner, 1922.
Fletcher, W. J. "The Last Voyage of the *Elizabeth*." *Naval Chronicle* 5 (Jan.–July 1801). Rpt. in *Macmillan's Magazine* vol. XC (May–Oct. 1904): 261–69.
Forster, E. M. "The Poetry of C. P. Cavafy." *Pharos and Pharillon*. London: Hogarth P, 1923. 91–97.
*Fort, Charles. *The Books of Charles Fort*. Ed. Tiffany Thayer. New York: Holt, 1941. Lowry used earlier separate editions, but references are to this collected edition from his personal library.
——. *The Outcast Manufacturers*. New York: Dodge & Co, 1909.
Frank, Waldo David. *America Hispana: A Portrait and a Prospect*. New York: Scribner's, 1931.
——. *In the American Jungle*. New York: Farrer & Rinehart, 1937.
——. "The Writer's Part in Communism." *Adelphi* 9–10 (1935), 258–64.
Freud, Sigmund. *The Standard Edition of the Complete Psychological Works of Sigmund Freud*. Ed. James Strachey, in collaboration with Anna Freud. 24 vols. London: Hogarth P & the Institute of Psychoanalysis, 1953–1974.
Galloway, Robert L. *Annals of Coal Mining and the Coal Trade*. 2 vols. London: Colliery Guardian Co. Ltd, 1898.
Gerbault, Alain. *The Fight of the "Firecrest"*. London: H. F. & G. Witherby, 1926.
Goldstein, Richard. "Adventure in an Age of Austerity." *New Yorker* 1 April 1974: 50–52.
Gordon, Don. *Collected Poems*. Ed. Fred Whitehead. Urbana & Chicago: U Illinois P, 2004.
Grasset, Joseph. *The Semi-Insane and the Semi-Responsible*. Trans. Smith Ely Jelliffe. New York: Funk & Wagnalls, 1907.
Green, Julien. *The Dark Journey*. Trans. Vyvyan Holland. New York: Harper & Bros., 1929.
Grieg, Nordahl. *Kinesiske Dage*. Oslo: Gyldendal, 1927.
——. *Rundt Kap det gode Haab. Oslo: Gyldendal, 1922.*
——. *The Ship Sails On*. Trans. A. G. Chater. New York: Knopf, 1927.
——. *Skibet gaar videre*. Oslo: Gyldendal, 1924.
——. *Stene i Strømmen*. Oslo: Gyldendal, 1924.
Guenther, Herbert V. *The Teachings of Padmasambhava*. Leiden: Brill, 1996.

Haldane, Charlotte. *I Bring Not Peace*. London: Chatto & Windus, 1932.

Haldane, J. B. S. *Possible Worlds and Other Essays*. London: Chatto & Windus, 1927.

Haserot, Francis S. *Essays on the Logic of Being*. New York: Macmillan, 1932.

Henri, Ernst. *Hitler over Europe*. New York: Simon & Schuster, 1934.

Hicks, Granville, et al., eds. *Proletarian Literature in the United States*. New York: International Publishers, 1935.

Hill, Edwin Conger. *The Human Side of the News*. New York: Black, 1934.

Hodgkin, E. C. "In Memoriam Emile Marmorstein 1909–1983." *Middle Eastern Studies* 20.2 (1984): 131–32.

Homer. *The Odyssey*. Trans. T. E. Shaw [T. E. Lawrence]. New York: Oxford UP, 1932. Reviewed in *Time* 28 Nov. 1932:51.

Houghton, Claude [Claude Houghton Oldfield]. *Julian Grant Loses His Way*. London: Heinemann, 1933.

Hudson, W. H. *Far Away and Long Ago*. London: Duckworth, 1918.

——. *Tales of the Pampas*. London: Knopf, 1916.

Huneker, James. *Egotists: A Book of Supermen*. New York: Scribner's, 1921.

Huysmans, J-K. *Against the Grain*. Introduction by Havelock Ellis, with a Preface (1903) by Huysmans. London: Three Sirens Press, 1931.

I Ching: Book of Changes. Trans. James Legge. *Sacred Books of the East*. Vol. 16. Oxford: Oxford UP, 1899.

Irving, Washington. "The Mutability of Literature." (1819.) *The Sketchbook of Geoffrey Crayon, Gent*. New York: Putnam, 1868.

Jackson, Charles. *The Lost Weekend*. London: Bodley Head, 1945.

*James, William. *The Varieties of Religious Experience*. New York: Random House, 1902.

Jensen, Johannes V. *The Long Journey*. Trans. A. G. Chater. New York: Knopf, 1933. [Includes *Fire and Ice* (1923), *The Cimbrians* (1924) and *Christopher Columbus* (1924), each novel separately paginated.]

Jorgenson, Theodore. *History of Norwegian Literature*. New York: Macmillan, 1933.

Joyce, James. "Haveth Childers Everywhere." *transition* 16/17. Rpt. London: Faber, 1931.

Jung, C. G. *Modern Man in Search of a Soul*. London: Kegan Paul, Trench, Trübner, 1933.

*Kafka, Franz. *The Castle*. Trans. Edwin & Willa Muir. New York: Knopf, 1941.

——. "Reflections on Sin, Pain, Hope and the True Way." *Zürau Aphorisms*, in *The Great Wall of China and Other Pieces*. Trans. Willa and Edwin Muir. London: Secker, 1933. 278–307.

Kaye, Thomas. *The Stranger in Liverpool, or, an Historical and Descriptive View of the Town of Liverpool and its Environs*. 10th ed. Liverpool: Thos. Kaye, 1833. Almost identical volumes were entitled *Picture of Liverpool* [below].

Kellet, E. E. *The Whirligig of Taste*. London: Hogarth Press [Hogarth Lectures #8], 1929.

Keyserling, Count Hermann. *The Recovery of Truth*. New York & London: Harper & Bros, 1929.

Kierkegaard, Søren. "A Personal Confession." Trans. Alexander Dru. *European Quarterly* 1.2 (Aug. 1934): 115–20.

Lao-tze. *Canon of Reason and Virtue*. Trans. D. T. Suzuki and Paul Carus. La Salle, IL: Open Court, 1913.

Larsen, Hanna Astrup. *Denmark's Best Stories: An Introduction to Danish Literature*. New York: Norton & Co., 1928.

Latham, R. G. *Norway and the Norwegians*. 2 vols. London: Bentley, 1840.

Lawrence, D. H. *Fantasia of the Unconscious and Psychoanalysis and the Unconscious*. London: Secker, 1923.

——. *Studies in Classic American Literature*. New York: Seltzer, 1923.

Leonard, William Ellery. *The Locomotive-God*. New York: The Century Co., 1927.

London, Jack. *The Star Rover*. New York: Macmillan, 1915.

Maeterlinck, Maurice. *Poems*. Trans. Bernard Miall. New York: Dodd, Mead, 1915.

——. *The Unknown Guest*. Trans. Bernard Miall. London: Dodd, Mead, 1913.

Mann, Thomas. "Freud's Position in the History of Modern Thought." *Past Masters and Other Essays*. Trans. H. T. Lowe-Porter. New York: Knopf, 1933. 167–98.

——. *The Magic Mountain*. Trans. H. T. Lowe-Porter. London: Secker, 1928.

——. "Sleep, Sweet Sleep." *Past Masters and Other Essays*. Trans. H. T. Lowe-Porter. New York: Knopf, 1933. 267–76.

——. *Tonio Kröger*. Trans. H. T. Lowe-Porter. London: Secker, 1930.

Masefield, John. *The Wanderer of Liverpool*. London: Macmillan, 1930.

Maury, Lucien. "Strindberg's Confessions." *The Living Age* #310 (July–Aug. 1921): 78–83.

McBride, Robert Medill. *Norwegian Towns and People: Vistas in the Land of the Midnight Sun*. New York: McBride & Co., 1924.

*Melville, Herman. *Moby Dick, or, The Whale*. 1851. Rpt. New York: Modern Library, n.d. [1950].

Menninger, Karl. *The Human Mind*. New York: Knopf, 1930.

Muir, Kenneth. "The Contemporary Novel." *European Quarterly* 1.2 (1934): 70–76.

——. "Oswald Spengler." *European Quarterly* 1.3 (Nov. 1934): 143–52.

Mumford, Lewis. *Herman Melville: A Study of his Life and Vision*. New York: Harcourt, Brace & World, 1929.

Myers, F. W. H. *Human Personality and Its Survival of Bodily Death*. London: Longmans, Green & Co., 1906.

Myers, L. H. *The Root and the Flower*. London: Cape, 1938 [four individual volumes published in the 1930s].

New York Times. Various issues, including 24 Apr. 1912 (*Titanic*) and 2 Feb. 1935 ("singing slayer").

Nietzsche, Friedrich. "Dawn: Thoughts on the Prejudices of Morality." Trans. J. M. Kennedy. London: George Allen & Unwin, 1881.

O'Flaherty, Liam. *The Black Soul*. London: Cape, 1924.

Ogden, C. K., and I. A. Richards. *The Meaning of Meaning: A Study of the Influence of Language upon Thought and of the Science of Symbolism*. London: Kegan Paul, 1923.

Olivero, Federico. *Rainer Maria Rilke: A Study of his Poetry and Mysticism*. Cambridge: Heffer & Sons, 1931.

Ouspensky, Peter. *A New Model of the Universe: Principles of the Psychological Method in its Application to Problems of Science, Religion and Art*. Trans. R. R. Merton with the author. New York: Knopf & London: Routledge, 1931.

——. *The Symbolism of the Tarot*. Trans. A. L. Pogossky. St. Petersburg: Trood, 1913.

——. *Tertium Organum: The Third Canon of Thought, a Key to the Enigmas of the World*. Trans. Nicholas Bessaraboff & Claude Bragdon. 2nd ed. London: Kegan Paul, Trench, Trübner, 1923.

Parker, Herschel. *Herman Melville: A Biography: Vol. 2, 1851–1891*. Baltimore: Johns Hopkins UP, 2002.

Peterson, Houston. *The Melody of Chaos*. London: Longmans, Green & Co., 1931.

The Picture of Liverpool, or, Stranger's Guide. 1805. New ed., enlarged. Liverpool: Jones & Wright, 1808. [This was Redburn's "Old Morocco".]

The Picture of Liverpool, or Stranger's Guide. 1805. 10th ed., rev. Liverpool: Taylor, 1834. [This edition (by Thomas Kaye, above) was used by Lowry.]

The Police Journal: A Review for the Police Forces of the Empire. Vol. 7. London: P. Allen & Co., 1934.

Powys, John Cowper. *The Meaning of Culture*. London: Cape, 1930.

Rascoe, Burton. *Titans of Literature*. New York: Putnam's, 1932.

Renard, Maurice. *The Hands of Orlac*. Trans. Florence Crewe-Jones. New York: Dutton, 1929.

Richards, I. A. *Practical Criticism*. London: Kegan Paul, Trench, Trübner, 1929.

——. *Principles of Literary Criticism*. London: Kegan Paul, Trench, Trübner, 1924.

Rilke, Rainer Maria. *The Tale of the Love and Death of Cornet Christopher Rilke*. Trans. M. D. Herter Norton. New York: Norton, 1932.

Roback, Abraham. *The Psychology of Character*. London: Routledge & Kegan Paul, 1927.

Roberts, Morley. *The Red Burgee: Sea Comedies*. London: Nash, 1906.

Robinson, E. A. *Amaranth*. New York: Macmillan, 1934.

Rogers, Stanley Reginald Harry. *The Atlantic*. New York: Crowell, 1930.

Roler, A. W. "The Wild-Animal Trapper and his Captives." *St. Nicholas: An Illustrated Magazine for Young Folks*. London: Warne, 37.2 (1909): 156–63.

Saltus, Edgar. *The Anatomy of Negation*. New York: Brentano's, [1886].

Sargent, L. M. "Address" [delivered before the Seamen's Bethel Temperance Society]. Boston: Ford & Damrell, 1833.

Schnitzler, Arthur. *Flight into Darkness*. Trans. William A. Drake. New York: Simon & Schuster, 1931.

Schopenhauer, Arthur. *The World as Will and Idea.* Trans. R. B. Haldane and J. Kemp. London: Kegan Paul, Trench, Trübner, 1896.

Schücking, Levin L., ed. *Anthology of Modern English Poets.* Leipzig: Tauchnitz, 1931.

Somes, Alwyn. *The English Policeman 1871–1935.* London: Allen & Unwin, 1935.

Spence, Lewis. *Encyclopedia of Occultism and Parapsychology.* New York: University Books [New Hyde Park], 1920.

Spengler, Oswald. *The Decline of the West.* Trans. C. F. Atkinson. London: Allen & Unwin, 1926–1929.

Sunnmøresposten (Ålesund). Issues from 1 July to 30 Sept. 1931.

Swedenborg, Emanuel. *Heaven and Hell: Things Heard and Seen.* Trans. James Hyde. London: Warne & Co., 1904.

Symons, Arthur. *The Symbolist Movement in Literature.* New York: Dutton, 1919.

Taylor, Lawrence. "Ricardo, David (1732–1823), of Gatcombe Park, Glos." *The History of Parliament: the House of Commons 1790–1820.* Ed. R. Thorne. Martlesham: Boydell & Brewer, 1986. Web. Accessed 27 July 2014. <http://www.historyofparliamentonline.org/volume/1790-1820/member/ricardo-david-1772-1823>.

Thomas, Edward. *A Literary Pilgrim in England.* London: Dodd, Mead, 1917.

Traven, B. *The Death Ship* [1926]. Trans. (by Traven) New York: Knopf, 1934.

Von Scholz, Wilhelm. *Der Wettlauf mit dem Schatten.* München: Müller, 1921.

Walpole, Sir Hugh. *The Green Mirror: A Quiet Story.* London: Grosset & Dunlap, 1917.

Ward, Artemus [Charles Farrar Browne]. "Science and Natural History." *The Complete Works of Artemus Ward.* Vol. 5. *London Punch Letters* 5.7, 1865. N.p. N.d. Web. Accessed 10 May 2013. <http://ebooks.gutenberg.us/WorldeBookLibrary.com/5ward.htm>.

Wey, Francis. *A Frenchman among the Victorians.* New Haven: Yale UP, 1936.

White, Andrew Dickson. *History of the Warfare of Science with Theology.* 2 vols. New York: Appleton & Co., 1896–1898.

Wybergh, W. *Prayer as Science.* London: Theosophical Publishing House, 1919.

Yeats, W. B. *Wheels and Butterflies.* London: Macmillan, 1934.

E. Works quoted or referred to (in the common domain, or where the version Lowry used is either unspecified or irrelevant; cited by chapter or part, stanza or line, rather than by page). Several authors also appear in section **D.**

Adamic, Louis. *Grandsons.*

Aiken, Conrad. "The Bitter Love Song"; *Great Circle;* "Landscape West of Eden"; "Literature in Massachussetts."

The Arabian Nights.

Arnold, Matthew. "Empedocles on Etna."

Artaud, Antonin. "Le Théâtre de la cruauté (manifeste)."

Auden, W. H. "Musée des beaux arts."
Bang, Herman. *Generations without Hope.*
Barrès, Maurice. *Le jardin de Bérénice; Sous l'oeil des barbares.*
Baudelaire, Charles. "Correspondances"; "Le Voyage."
Beale, Anne. "A Spring Morning."
Beddoes, Thomas Love. "A Clock Striking at Midnight"; *Death's Jest Book.*
Blake, William. "Letter to Thomas Butt"; "The Marriage of Heaven and Hell."
Breton, André. *La Révolution surréaliste.*
Browning, Robert. "Childe Roland to the Dark Tower Came."
Bullfinch, Thomas. *Mythology* [Appendix].
Bunyan, John. *Pilgrim's Progress.*
Carlyle, Thomas. "Mirabeau"; *Sartor Resartus.*
Chekhov, Anton. *The Cherry Orchard*; "In the Graveyard."
Clare, John. "Noon."
Coleridge, Samuel Taylor. *Biographia Literaria.*
Conrad, Joseph. *Typhoon.*
cummings, e.e. "next to of course god america i."
Cummins, Maria. *Haunted Hearts; The Lamplighter.*
Dante Alighieri. *The Divine Comedy.*
De Quincey, Thomas. "Knocking on the Gate in Macbeth."
Dickens, Charles. *David Copperfield; The Pickwick Papers.*
D'Israeli, Israel. *Curiosities of Literature.*
Donne, John. "Satyre III" ["On Religion"]; *Sermons* [#49].
Dostoevsky, Fyodor. *The Brothers Karamazov; Crime and Punishment; Poor Folk.*
Eaton, Charles Edward. "The Portal of the Trees."
Eliot, T. S. *Ash-Wednesday*; "Gerontion"; "The Love Song of J. Alfred Prufrock"; "The Metaphysical Poets"; *The Waste Land*; "Whispers of Immortality."
Erckmann, Émile, and Alexandre Chatrian. *Le Juif polonais*
Forster, E. M. *Howards End.*
Freud, Sigmund. *Beyond the Pleasure Principle; Civilization and Its Discontents; The Future of an Illusion; The Interpretation of Dreams; Three Essays on the Theory of Sexuality*; "The Uncanny"; "The Unconscious"; *Wit and Its Relation to the Unconscious.*
Frost, Robert. "Hyla Brook"; "West-running Brook."
Goethe, Johann Wolfgang von. *Faust.*
Grieg, Nordahl. *Atlanterhavet; De unge døde; En ung manns kjærlighet; Norge i våre hjerter.*
Grimm, Jacob and Wilhelm. "Hansel and Gretel."
Haggard, H. Rider. *She.*
Hardy, Thomas. "The Convergence of the Twain"; *The Woodlanders.*
Hawthorne, Nathaniel. *Ethan Brand; English Notebooks; Mosses from an Old Manse.*
Heine, Heinrich. *Dichterliede.*

Hemingway, Ernest. *The Sun Also Rises.*

Homer, *The Odyssey.*

Hopkins, Gerard Manley. "The Windhover."

Huxley, Aldous. "Farcical History of Richard Greenow."

Ibanez, Vicente Blasco. *La Bodega.*

Ibsen, Henrik. *Hedda Gabler*; *The Master Builder*; *Peer Gynt.*

Jacobsen, Jens Peter. "Mogens and Other Stories."

James, William. *Pragmatism*; *The Will to Believe.*

Jonson, Ben. *Masque of Blackness.*

Joyce, James. "The Dead"; *Finnegans Wake*; *A Portrait of the Artist*; *Ulysses.*

Kafka, Franz. *America.*

Kant, Immanuel. "The Only Possible Ground."

Kataev, Valentin Petrovich. *Rastratchiki* [The Embezzlers].

Kipling, Rudyard. "The Phantom Rickshaw"; "A Tour of Inspection."

Lawrence, D. H. "Nothing to Save"; *The Plumed Serpent*; "The Primrose Path"; *Women in Love.*

Lenin, Vladimir. *Left-Wing Communism: An Infantile Disorder.*

Mackenzie, Compton. *The Early Life and Adventures of Sylvia Scarlett.*

Marco Polo, *Travels.*

Marlowe, Christopher. *Doctor Faustus.*

Marston, John. *Antonio's Revenge.*

Marvel, Andrew. "The Garden."

Marx, Karl. *Communist Manifesto*; *Das Kapital.*

Masefield, John. "C. L. M."; *Dauber*; "Sea Fever."

Melville, Herman. "Bartleby"; "Benito Cereno"; *Billy Budd*; "Commemorative of Naval Victory"; *The Confidence Man*; *The Encantatas*; "The Enthusiast"; "Healed of my Hurt"; *Israel Potter*; *Mardi*; *Omoo*; *The Piazza Tales*; *Pierre*; *Redburn*; "The Stone Fleet: An Old Sailor's Lament"; *Typee.* (For *Moby Dick*, see section **D**.)

Milton, John. "Il Penseroso"; *Lycidas*; *Paradise Lost*; *Samson Agonistes* (Preface).

Newman, Cardinal John Henry. *Apologia Pro Vita Sua.*

O'Flaherty, Liam. *Shame the Devil.*

O'Neill, Eugene. *The Hairy Ape.*

Plato. *The Republic*; *Symposium.*

Poe, Edgar Allan. "Ligeia"; *Narrative of Arthur Gordon Pym*; "The Tell-Tale Heart."

Ricardo, David. *Principles of Political Economy.*

Rilke, Rainer Maria. *Malte Laurids Brigge.*

Rimbaud, Arthur. "The Drunken Boat"; "A Season in Hell."

Robinson, E. A. "Man against the Sky."

Ruge, Arnold, and Ernst Echtermayer. *Hallischen Jahrbücher für deutsche Kunst und Wissenschaft.*

Service, Robert. "It Is Later than You Think."
Shackleton, Ernest. *South.*
Shakespeare, William. *Hamlet*; *King Lear*; *Macbeth*; *Measure for Measure*; *The Merchant of Venice*; *Richard II*; *The Tempest.*
Shaw, Bernard. *Back to Methuselah*; *On the Rocks.*
Shelley, Percy Bysshe. *Prometheus Unbound.*
Sienkiewicz, Henryk. *The Lighthouse-Keeper*
Sophocles. *Antigone*; *Oedipus Tyrranus.*
Sturluson, Snorri. *Gulfaginning.*
Tennyson, Alfred Lord. "Break, Break, Break"; *In Memoriam*; "Ulysses."
Thomas à Kempis. *The Imitation of Christ.*
Thompson, James. *City of Dreadful Night.*
Traven, B. *The Cotton Pickers.*
Valéry, Paul. *La Soirée avec Monsieur Teste.*
Vane, Sutton. *Outward Bound* [play].
Verne, Jules. *20,000 Leagues under the Sea*; *The Kip Brothers.*
Virgil. *The Aeneid.*
Voltaire [François-Marie Arouet]. *Candide.*
Walpole, Hugh. *The Green Mirror.*
Webster, John. *The Duchess of Malfi*; *The White Devil.*
Whitman, Walt. "Out of the Cradle Endlessly Rocking"; "Passage to India"; *Song of Myself.*
Wordsworth, William. "Daffodils."
Xenophon. *Anabasis.*
Yeats, W. B. "Among School Children"; "An Irish Airman Foresees His Death."
Zola, Émile. *L'Assommoir* [Drunkard]; *La Débâcle* [The Debacle].

Textual Notes

The Jan Gabrial Papers at the Division of Manuscripts and Archives, New York Public Library, contain virtually all of the primary sources for this edition of *In Ballast to the White Sea* as well as related documents such as Jan Gabrial's notes on *In Ballast*. The collection includes two "complete" typescripts of this unfinished novel that Jan created in or around 1991, using a word processing program. The typescript in Box 3 is the earlier printout, and an attempt was made to correct errors in the later typescript, in Box 4. Even so, both typescripts include typing errors that I have tried to identify and correct in this edition. Except where I have indicated otherwise, all references in the following notes to Jan's 1991 typescript(s) are to the second, revised, typescript.

The collection includes photocopies of four complete chapters (I, II, IV, and XII), and a single page from another (XIV), in the 1936 typescript on which Jan based Chapters I through XVII of her 1991 version. This edition follows the 1936 text wherever it is available, with the exception of epigraphs (apart from IV, where one was later added in Jan's hand, there are no epigraphs for the 1936 chapters). The authority for the epigraphs is unclear, but I have no doubt that Lowry meant to include them. There are many differences between the 1936 and 1991 typescripts, sometimes because Jan spotted and corrected an error in the earlier text. In those cases I have accepted her judgment. What I have not retained are the many other changes she made in the text, which often amount to a rewriting of the novel. As Lowry's ex-wife, Jan was also his onetime typist, editor, and collaborator, so in editing the typescript she might well have believed she was carrying out Lowry's wish, stated in a 1936 will, "that she try, in her own time, to make something out of the inchoate notes for the novel I have left behind on the lines I have sometimes suggested in conversation with her" (Bowker 202). Whatever Lowry might have meant by this statement, the numerous changes Jan made in the phrasing, punctuation, and paragraphing of the 1936 typescript inevitably undermine any claim her typescript might have to represent the novel as Lowry wrote it. In many cases, I believe, those changes are improvements, but my purpose has not been to rewrite Lowry's book, only to represent it in the best possible light, preparing the text much as he might have wanted it to be prepared for submission to a publisher.[1]

Textual notes are generally limited to exceptions to the following principles of emendation:

1. Wherever possible, the 1936 typescript has been used as copy text except when there is good reason to do otherwise.

2. Likewise, the principles of the 1936 text have been applied to chapters for which we have only Jan's later typescripts. For example, dashes that are used to introduce dialogue should always come at the beginning of paragraphs, and the protagonist's name is Sigbjørn, as in 1936, Chapters I and II (with slashes inserted by hand), not Sigbjorn (as in 1991).

3. Obvious mechanical errors have been corrected, for example, a paragraph of dialogue without an introductory dash (in a chapter that uses dashes to introduce dialogue) or a typo such as "didmn't."

4. Underlining is represented by italics, and the use of italics for names of ships, titles of books, Norwegian passages, etc. has been regularized.

5. The typescripts' irregular punctuation has been emended in two ways: redundant punctuation, such as the use of both a comma and a dash (or a comma and an ellipsis) before and after a phrase, has been simplified, and the two-dot ellipses in the 1991 typescript have been treated either as periods or as full (three-dot) ellipses, whichever seems better in each case. However, I have not corrected Lowry's somewhat erratic use of commas unless failure to do so might pose a serious problem for readers: thus I have not inserted a comma after "Dandy Dinmott" in the sentence "Stooping, he fondled the ears of his cat, Dandy Dinmott with one hand while with the other he stroked his moustaches." In this case, the absence of a comma after the appositive (a frequent Lowryan practice) is unlikely to obscure the meaning of the sentence.

6. Lowry's dashes are represented in the typescripts by single hyphens. To avoid confusion I have distinguished between hyphens and dashes.

7. In the typescripts, the book's title and its author's name appear at the beginning of each chapter. This practice is more appropriate for an unpublished manuscript than for a published book, so I have deleted both name and title. I have regularized the placement and presentation of epigraphs.

8. Foreign words and phrases have been corrected except where errors in phrasing might seem deliberate or significant.

9. In most cases, I have regularized inconsistent spellings. However, the spelling of "whiskey" and "whisky" posed a problem: the first spelling is correct in a reference to an Irish whiskey (like John Jameson, in Chapter III) and the second in an advertisement for a brand of Scotch whisky (Dewar's, in Chapter V), but the 1991 typescript reverses both. The spelling has been regularized as "whiskey" (except for the Dewar's passage), partly because this is the more common

spelling in the typescript, partly because Lowry refers most often to Irish whiskey, and partly because it is the spelling I prefer. I have also changed the occasional typescript spelling "noone" to "no one" even though the odd spelling may be found in Lowry's letters (as in a 1951 letter to David Markson, CL 2:416). My own experience confirms Fowler's judgment that *no one* should never be combined into one word due to "the natural tendency to pronounce *noone* 'noon'" (H. W. Fowler. *A Dictionary of Modern English Usage*. 2nd ed. New York: Oxford UP, 1965. 174, 394.).

10. With some exceptions, misspelled names of real places have been corrected ("Greasby" rather than "Gresby" road; Voel Nant rather than Noel Vant). Reasons for exceptions are noted.

To facilitate the location of passages referred to in these notes, page numbers are followed by one (or occasionally more than one) of the letters a, b, c, d, indicating the top quarter of the page (a) and so forth. The letters are omitted when they are not needed (as for epigraphs); more than one letter is used when the passage begins in one section and continues into (or is repeated in) another.

NOTES FOR CHAPTER I:

Copy text: 1936 TS; epigraph from 1991 TS. The University of British Columbia's Lowry collection has the first two pages of Chapter I from the same 1936 typescript (UBC 12:15). Curiously, instead of drawing a slash through the "o" of Sigbjorn, to make the name Sigbjørn, as Lowry did on the NYPL copy, there is an umlaut over the "o," so that the name becomes Sigbjörn. Another difference is that the sentence "An armistice was signed in the spiritual hostilities between them" is not changed in the UBC version of the second page (see note on page 4(a) below). However, at the end of the same paragraph, in "obstructing the light, yes, existence itself," brackets have been drawn by hand around "light, yes" and "yes" has been crossed out.

p. 3: [Epigraph]: In the Norton translation of Rilke's *The Tale of the Love and Death of Cornet Christopher Rilke* this reads, "Perhaps we always nocturnally retrace the stretch we have won wearily in the foreign sun?" (11). As I note in the introduction, the substitution of "summer" for "foreign" might be attributed to eyeskip if Lowry (or Jan) copied this passage directly from the Rilke work, since "summer" appears twice in the following lines; but if it was copied from the notebook in which Lowry wrote this passage correctly (UBC 12:14, Varsity Composition Book [34]), "summer" cannot have been a mistake because the next lines were not copied into the notebook. I have treated "summer" as an intentional alteration, its memories playing against the winter background of the novel's opening scene.

p. 4(a): ceasing: The sentence originally read, "An armistice was signed in the spiritual hostilities between them." Lowry crossed out "in" and wrote "ceasing" above it; then, without crossing out "ceasing," he wrote "amidst?" (1936 2). Jan's 1991 TS (3) has "easing."

p. 4(d): harbour: The 1936 TS has "harbor" (3), the 1991 TS "harbour" (4). The latter is more consistent with Lowry's normal (although not invariable) practice.

p. 4(d): setting out: Thus in 1936 (3); but, probably having recognized Lowry's allusion to Yeats's "Among School Children," Jan changed the phrase to "setting forth" (1991 4). See the introduction and annotation.

p. 5(a): Dostoievsky: "Dostoevsky" in 1936 (3); "Dostoievsky" in 1991 (4). I have adopted the latter spelling which, although less common, is the one Lowry generally preferred, here and in other works (see, e.g., *La Mordida* 39, 47, 209) and letters.

p. 6(a): That smoke which is so evanescent: The mysterious 1991 reading, "That snake which is so evanescent" (6), resulted from Jan's misreading of the 1936 TS (5), on which "smoke" was mistyped as "smake," after which an "o" was typed heavily over the "a." The word still looks like either "smake" or "smoke," but it is not "snake."

p. 7(a): *doom, doom:* Not underlined in 1936 (6) or 1991 (8), but italicized here to be consistent with practice elsewhere, for example, 1936 page 24.

p. 7(c): replaced it: 1936 TS has "was replaced there" (7), but Jan's emendation (1991 9) makes far better sense.

p. 8(a): workers: In the 1936 TS (7) "masses" is crossed out and "workers" inserted by hand. Jan's 1991 TS (10) changes "the workers" to "the betterment of the working poor."

p. 8(a): —I feel fatal without that, Tor said: In 1936 (7) "said" is crossed out and "was saying" entered in Jan's hand; in 1991 (11) the reading is "was saying."

p. 8(a): *Skibets reise fra Kristiania:* The 1936 typescript has *Skibets Reise Fra Christiania*. There are two main problems with Lowry's titles for Erikson's novel, one of which involves earlier names of Oslo, which in 1624 King Christian IV renamed Christiania (after himself); the spelling was changed to Kristiania in 1877, but in 1925 the city once again became Oslo. Depending on when the action of *Skibets reise* is supposed to occur, the city could have any of those three names, and Lowry seems not to have decided whether Christiania or Kristiania would be best in this case, but he seems to have been inclined toward the latter (of the nine references to the title of Erikson's novel in the 1936 typescript, only this one uses Christiania). A second problem is that common nouns and prepositions are not capitalized in Norwegian and are not capitalized in titles of Norwegian works (except as the first word in a title), so neither *reise* nor *fra* should be capitalized in the title; yet both words are almost invariably capitalized in the typescripts. I have regularized the title of Erikson's novel to the form given here; otherwise I have let the Christiania/Kristiania inconsistency stand.

p. 8(b): at home in Norway: Jan's emendation (1991 11); the 1936 TS has a large blank space after "in" (8), possibly so a long name could be inserted.

p. 8(c): The absolute: In the 1936 TS (8), "Or the quadrature of the circle" has been crossed out and "Yes, or" added (in Jan's hand) before "the absolute," so that the emended text would read as in 1991 (11):

> —The philosopher's stone, perhaps. Yes, or the absolute.

There is also a second copy of 1936 page 8 (on the back of which Jan wrote the epigraph for Chapter IV) that does not have these changes. I have rejected Jan's emendations and restored the original 1936 reading.

p. 9(c): dancing gloomily: 1936 (10) has "consciously?" written in hand as a possible alternative to "gloomily."

NOTES FOR CHAPTER II:

Copy text: 1936 TS; epigraph from 1991 TS.

p. 11: [Epigraph]: Apart from the misspelling of "going" as "ging" (corrected here), the only deviation from the text of Auden's "Get there if you can" is the deletion of commas after "talking" and "town."

p. 11(b): —The sun would shrivel you: Originally "The sun" was "It"; emended in Lowry's hand in the 1936 TS (12).

p. 11(d): Magdalene College: The 1936 and 1991 TSS (13, 16) read "Magdalen College," confusing Cambridge's Magdalene with Oxford's Magdalen College.

p. 12(d): answers that: The 1936 reading (14) is "Nothing out of nowhere answers what"; the 1991 reading is the same, but the sentence ends with a question mark (18). The sentence does not appear to be a question, so "what" is almost certainly a typographical error for "that."

p. 13(bcd): The two brothers . . . from mind to mind—: Here and elsewhere in II, the 1991 phrasing is significantly different. That version of the passage concludes:

> Although the movement of the river they now watched was infinitely slow, it belonged, together with more formidable currents, to that ultimate fusion of waters, a universal cataract, pouring from mountains, coursing across broad fens to reach the bright certainty of the sea, as man stumbles along the parched and hostile craters of philosophy in search of what? the soul?
>
> But what was that? Something that flows through air, or swims in waters, and which moves imperceptibly from mind to mind— (20)

p. 14(b): Up there a light snaps off: This passage is extensively rewritten in the 1991 TS (21): it is divided into two paragraphs, and several lines from the 1936 TS (16–17) have been omitted. At the end of the paragraph, Lowry wrote "rots" above "drops," which I have taken for an emendation even though "drops" is not crossed out.

p. 16(b): Round Church: Not capitalized in either TS; capitalized here as a proper noun (a name rather than a description).

p. 16(c): Queens': Both 1936 (19) and 1991 (25) incorrectly refer to Queens' (plural possessive) College as Queen's (singular possessive).

p. 17(c): *In la sua voluntade è nostra pace*: The usual form of this phrase, in editions of Dante's *Paradiso*, is "E'n la sua volontade è nostra pace" ("And in his will is our peace": Par. 3.85). However, apart from the absence of an accent mark, the typescript reading "In la sua voluntade e nostra pace" (and again on 330) follows another way in which the phrase is sometimes quoted, so it has been allowed to stand with minimal emendation.

p. 18(d): aren't revolutionary: In 1936, "communists who aren't revolutionary" is typed, with "can't commune" written above "aren't revolutionary" (22). But the original phrase is not crossed out, and "can't commune" is written in Jan's hand, suggesting that she was trying out a phrasing to parallel "explorers who can't explore," "sailors who can't sail," and "stokers who can't stoke." In 1991 (29) Jan chose the original reading, and I have followed suit.

NOTES FOR CHAPTER III:

Copy text: 1991 TS.

p. 21: [Epigraph]: Auden's "Get there if you can" ends, "If we really want to live, we'd better start at once to try; / If we don't, it doesn't matter, but we'd better start to die."

p. 25(d): But what do you come back with from the sea?: In the 1991 TS this sentence begins a new line that has been inadvertently indented.

p. 30(b): Wormwood: Not capitalized in Jan's TS (51).

p. 31(a): Helgefjoss: Misspelled "Helge Fjoss" in the 1991 TS (53).

p. 34(c): —: The 1991 TS (59) reads:

> The needle respects all points of the compass alike.
>
> —
>
> It's wrong she had to die, Tor said finally.

In leaving the dash on a separate line and adding a new dash before "It's wrong" I have made two assumptions about this passage. First, that the isolated "—" was on a separate line in the 1936 typescript, where, as in *Under the Volcano*, it signified an unspoken, unphrased thought, or perhaps a place where words might have been spoken but were not. Second, that Jan either neglected to place a dash at the beginning of the next line or assumed that the existing dash was intended to introduce the next line, the separation of lines indicating a delay in Tor's response.

p. 35(c): But Drammensveien: 1991 TS (61) has "But the Drammens Vei." (*Drammensveien* is a single word that includes the definite article.) The word is printed correctly in the 1933 edition of *Ultramarine*; see annotation III.112.

p. 39(c): Peterhouse: "Peter House" in the 1991 TS (69).

p. 39: *Sing,song,hang,soon:* Thus in 1991 (69). Here, the bells strike in quick succession, but the words separate as the bells slow down.

p. 40(d): Go back, go back, go, back: I have retained the comma after the final "go," which distinguishes this passage from the otherwise identical one on page 39. Here, the comma has the effect of slowing down the line, as in a countdown to death.

p. 40(d): spinal cord: 1991 (72) has "spinal chord," which I have treated as a simple misspelling rather than a pun.

NOTES FOR CHAPTER IV:

Copy text: 1936 TS; epigraph handwritten on a separate page of the 1936 TS (probably much later) and typed in the 1991 TS.

p. 42: [Epigraph]: As indicated in the introduction, the epigraph is *not* the work of C. K. Ogden and I. A. Richards: it is excerpted from F. G. Crookshank's introduction to *The Troubled Conscience and the Insane Mind* by Charles Blondel. Crookshank prefaces his remarks by saying that he is using "the terminology of Messrs. Ogden and Richards (in the *Meaning of Meaning*)." The remainder of the epigraph differs from the passage in Crookshank's introduction only in minor ways (deletion of commas; roman type instead of italics for *referents*, *references*, and *symbolization*, words that Crookshank apparently derived from Ogden and Richards). I have retained the erroneous attribution because Lowry presumably wanted Ogden and Richards attached to the passage. See also the annotation.

p. 42(b): Forlag: Here and in the heading to letter (e) the 1936 TS has "Vorlag" (57, 61); the 1991 TS has "Verlag" here and "Vorlag" later, the first instance perhaps indicating Jan's attempt to correct what she might have thought was a misspelling of German *Verlag*, "publisher" (73, 78). I have used the Norwegian equivalent, *Forlag*, as Lowry did on an envelope he addressed to "Hr. Nordahl Grieg / c/o Glydendal Norsk Forlag / Oslo / Norge" (NYPL 2:11).

p. 43(c): ἄσκησις: Lowry inserted this word by hand into the 1936 typescript (59), using Greek characters rather than transliterating it as *áskēsis*, or, asceticism (religious self-discipline or self-denial). Lowry's Greek spelling is **ἀσκησις**, which incorporates the smooth breathing (but not the acute accent) over the alpha. I have corrected it to **ἄσκησις**. The 1991 text (75) reads, "I am now left as I was three years ago, before I ever went to sea at all, as most of my generation...with an unconquerable aspiration towards a completion, a fulfillment of present existence" (ellipsis in typescript). This passage is discussed at greater length in the introduction.

p. 44(d): [gap in TS]: My insertion. 1936 has a passage whited out between "message to" and "is a scroll" (61); 1991 has "whose message...is a scroll" (78).

p. 45(c): of which the sea was the symbol: Jan's emendation (1991 79) of the obviously wrong 1936 reading "or which was sea is [as?] the symbol" (62).

p. 45(d): heeling shadow: The 1936 TS originally read "healing shadow," with "healing" emended to "heeling"; the 1991 TS has "healing." However, Lowry surely intended "heeling" (careening), as in his poem "Outside was the roar of the sea," lines 13–14: "and the heeling shadow of albatross / seeking forever the ancient mariner" (*CP* 105).

p. 48(d): excused me from lectures: Both typescripts (1936 66; 1991 85) have "excused me lectures."

p. 50(b): characters' pilgrimage: 1936 has "characters" (68); 1991 has "character's" (87). The context makes it clear that Lowry intended a plural possessive noun.

NOTES FOR CHAPTER V:

Copy Text: 1991 TS.

p. 54: [Epigraph]: Slightly different in Hudson's *Tales of the Pampas*: "The peace did not last long; for when misfortune has singled out a man for its prey, it will follow him to the end, and he shall not escape from it though he mount up to the clouds like a falcon, or thrust himself deep down into the earth like the armadillo" (27).

p. 61(ab): *hyrkontrakt*. . . *Aasgaard!* . . . Norsk . . . *D/S Unsgaard*, Sigbjørn Tarnmoor, *limper*: Here and elsewhere, Lowry's Norwegian led to difficult decisions. *Hyrkontrakt* is wrong—it should be *hyre kontrakt*—but it always appears in this form and seems to be what Lowry preferred. It refers to a sailor's employment agreement. *Aasgaard* (*Aagard* in 1991 106) would be *Åsgård* now, but Lowry's use of an earlier spelling has been retained. However, "Norse Konsulat" has been corrected to "Norsk Konsulat." In the 1991 typescript Sigbjørn's ship is T.S. *Unsgaard*, but "T.S." makes no sense and has been emended to D/S (for *dampskib*, "steamship"). As the annotations (X.5) explain, *limper* appears to be a deliberate error (leading to an Oedipal reference); otherwise it would have been emended to *lemper*, short for *kullemper*, "coal passer" (see annotation X.5). I have changed Lowry's "*Skibets Reise*" to "*Skibets reise*" in parallel with editorial emendations of Erikson's title.

p. 63(a): And hands . . . on the rocks—: The paragraph is not indented in the 1991 TS but should be as an instance of interior monologue, like "Oh, lovely ship . . ." two paragraphs earlier.

p. 68(b): façade: Spelled without a cedilla in the 1991 TS, where there are no accent marks.

p. 69(b): isthmus of Manchester Street: 1991 (97) capitalizes "Isthmus," perhaps because Jan thought it was part of the street's name.

p. 69(d): the old world monstrously reduplicated: In the 1991 TS this reads, "the old world (itself?) monstrously reduplicated" (123).

p. 69(d): "Did you hear my brassy ferrule? You're going for a long journey.": Note the use of quotation marks to indicate remembered dialogue (from the end of Chapter II), whereas in this chapter, current discourse is indicated by a dash. Cf. note on pages 331–32.

p. 70(a): You may see: In the 1991 TS (123) this begins a new paragraph that is not introduced by a dash even though it clearly continues the Captain's speech. Because Jan often broke up what she apparently thought were overly long paragraphs, I suspect that is what she did here, and that she forgot to add the dash.

p. 73(a): that he feels: In 1991 (130) "that" is enclosed within parentheses, probably a provisional emendation by Jan that I agree is helpful.

NOTES FOR CHAPTER VI:

Copy Text: 1991 TS.

p. 75: [Epigraph]: Lowry eliminates much of Fort's punctuation (commas, hyphens, quotation marks around "be") but otherwise reproduces the passage faithfully.

p. 75(d): James Street: 1991 (133) has "Jane Street."

p. 76(b): clangour: Changed from "clangor" (1991 134) in keeping with the general preference for British spellings. Jan's typescript uses "clangour" for the only other instance of the word (1991 309).

p. 76(c): Liver Building: 1991 (135) has "Liver Buildings," but Lowry clearly intended the Royal Liver Building.

p. 76(d): when he realized: 1991 (135) has "when (he) realized." The parentheses probably point to a much-needed emendation.

p. 77(d): creatures for whom: Jan's emendation: "creatures (for) whom" (1991 137).

p. 78(a): idealopogy: Thus 1991 (137): possibly a typo for "ideology," more likely (in my view) a nonce word, perhaps intended to ridicule outworn ideologies.

p. 78(c): Caergwrle Ales: The 1991 TS has "Caer Gwrle Ales (138).

p. 78(c): Cheesy Hammy Eggy: In the 1991 TS (138) this gourmet dish is "Cheesey Hamey Eggs."

p. 80(d): trumpeting their wrongs aloud: Cf. "trumpeting their wrong(s) aloud" (1991 143).

p. 82(c): weakened: Cf. "weaken(ed)" (1991 146).

p. 84(b): Healed . . . rosmarine: A slightly misquoted version of Melville's brief poem "Healed of My Hurt" (see annotation).

NOTES FOR CHAPTER VII:

Copy text: 1991 TS. (VII and XVII are the only chapters without epigraphs.)

p. 86(b): fear at: Cf. "fear (at)" (1991 153).

p. 87(a): In his mind: Above this phrase Jan wrote "memory," probably indicating a possible emendation (155).

p. 87(b): blue girls. And . . . white ones are!: In 1991 (155), enclosed within handwritten square brackets; probably a phrase Jan considered deleting. See the annotations for this allusion to Rilke.

p. 87(b): down: The word "down" is used three times within a short passage (following "swiftly," "slipway," and "shakily"). Jan apparently wanted to eliminate the redundancy, since in 1991 the second and third instances of "down" are enclosed within handwritten parentheses and crossed out.

p. 87(c): back against the sky: In 1991 (156), "back" is placed within handwritten brackets but not crossed out.

p. 89(a): passenger liner: 1991 (159) has "passenger lining."

p. 90(a): Yes—did he see: This begins a new line in both 1991 TSS (161), but the line is not indented even though the previous line stops short of the right margin (the typescripts are fully justified). Either there was an unintended hard return after the last sentence in the first typescript, which went unnoticed when Jan prepared the second draft, or "Yes" should be indented. This passage comes so close to the end of a long paragraph that it seems reasonable to assume that the paragraph should continue.

p. 92(b): 'The New Chang and Chen, Schenectady, Hotel Nazareth, Galilee': The typescript has "'the new Chang and Chen, Schenectady, Hotel Nazareth,

Galilee'" here, but in three of the four subsequent references to this pair, "new" is capitalized, indicating (I think) that Lowry meant to treat it as part of a proper noun. In this instance only, the name and address are treated as a quotation from an address label, and it seems most likely that "the" should also be capitalized.

p. 100(a): **No, that's not right either....Anyway, even if he hadn't died, you would have destroyed him...No, I take that back too:** The 1991 TS (180–81) has a four-dot ellipsis after "either," indicating that the ellipsis comes at the end of a sentence, but only three dots after "him." The TS is inconsistent in this regard in other places as well. I have not attempted to regularize Lowry's (or Jan's) practice, in part because it is sometimes unclear whether or not the ellipsis ends a complete sentence.

p. 100(c): **no more than a flake:** Cf. 1991: "fluke" (182).

p. 100(d): **are most appearances:** In 1991 (182) Jan typed "our" (apparently the erroneous 1936 reading) followed by "(are)."

p. 101(d): **mow at him:** In 1991 "mow" is placed within typed parentheses, presumably because Jan thought it might be a mistake (184). The word reappears on page 128 (1991 235) in the same context: "The thought rises up to jeer and mow at me in everything I do."

p. 105(a): **another. *Io, io*:** The 1991 reading (191) is "another. *io, io*." I have preferred this emendation to the alternative ("another: *io, io*.") to avoid too close a repetition of the previous *io, io*.

p. 106(a): **the *Nina*:** Properly, Columbus's ship was the *Niña*, but I suspect Sigbjørn pronounces it "Nina."

p. 106(b): **—'Passengers who go. . .:** There is no quotation mark after the dash in the 1991 TS (193), but I have added one to make it clear that Sigbjørn is reading the leaflet that he began reading shortly before and continues in the following paragraph.

p. 121(d): **—Let go . . . :** This and the next line are underlined by hand in the first, but not the second, 1991 TS (223).

p. 122(a): **no longer had way on her, but:** In the 1991 TS. (223) the comma is an exclamation mark.

p. 122(a): **Arms that would have waved . . . :** In the 1991 TS, there are typed parentheses around "to the side in desperation" and "stoop" as well as handwritten brackets around "now all . . . their souls."

NOTES FOR CHAPTER VIII:

Copy text: 1991 TS.

p. 124: [Epigraph]: Neither E. T. Brown nor the source of this passage has been identified, but the series of terms suggests a reference to the impact on the world of apparently irrational, random, trivial elements.

p. 124(c): monthly medal: 1991 page 228 has "monthly model."

p. 127(a): Point of Ayr: 1991 (233) reads "point of air."

p. 127(b): Neston: 1991 (233) reads "Noston."

p. 128(b): jeer and mow: See note on page 101.

p. 129(b): preoccupied with: The line breaks off without punctuation (1991 237). Sigbjørn continues after he and his father play their shots.

p. 132(a): Norsk Konsulat: 1991 (242), "Norsk Consulat."

p. 133(c): Or Roland Childe: Lowry's slight alteration of Wilfred Rowland Childe's middle name has been allowed to stand, along with the suppression of his first name, since both enhance the intended play on Browning's (and Shakespeare's) Childe Roland. The text of the Childe poem in the typescript differs from that in Lowry's apparent source, Richards's *Practical Criticism*, in trivial ways but also in one major way, substituting "whose mantled wise imaginations" for "whose mantles' wise imaginations." The text has been corrected here.

NOTES FOR CHAPTER IX:

Copy text: 1991 TS.

p. 136: [Epigraph]: From Hudson's *Tales of the Pampas*, with significant changes in the parts indicated here by italics:

> To one who has lived long, there is *no house and no spot of ground*, overgrown with grass and weeds, *where a house once stood and where men have lived*, that is not equally sad. For this sadness is in us, in a memory of other days which follows us into all places. But for the child there is no past: he is born into the world light hearted like a bird; for him gladness is everywhere." (*Tales* 41; italics added)

p. 136(d): You loose on a world: For Lowry's gloss on this passage see page 16 of his "Notes," in Appendix B.

p. 139(b): '*Members only . . .* ': In the 1991 TS this passage is introduced by a hyphen (or dash), which if reproduced would suggest that it is dialogue. I have assumed that it is not.

NOTES FOR CHAPTER X:

Copy text: 1991 TS.

p. 142: [Epigraph]: The 1991 TS (260) changes the British spelling "practising," in the Muir translation of Kafka, to "practicing" and ends the quotation with a long ellipsis. In the printed text this epigraph is a complete, self-contained section ending with a period.

p. 142(b): *L'homme y passe à travers des forêts de symboles qui l'observent avec des regards familiers:* In 1991 (260), "L'homme qui passe a travers des forets de symbols qui l'observent avec des regards familiers." The absence of underlining and accent marks and the misspelling of *symboles* are typical features of the 1991 typescript that would normally be corrected without comment, but the substitution of *qui* (who) for *y* (there) could be regarded as the Captain's error. I suspect it was not, so I have restored Baudelaire's phrasing.

p. 144(d): D'Israeli: Spelled "Disraeli" in the typescript (265, 266), probably due to confusion with Isaac D'Israeli's son, Benjamin Disraeli.

p. 147(c): Nothing of us but doth strange: Thus in 1991 (270). I have let the phrasing stand although, given the Captain's response, it is quite possible that Lowry wrote "change" rather than "strange" (see the annotation).

p. 150(a): much contradictions of class: I have allowed this poor phrasing (from 1991 TS 275) to stand because it might be attributed to the character. It is also possible that "much" should be "many."

p. 153(a): It's interesting to wonder: 1991 (282) has "(Well) It's interesting to wonder."

p. 157(a): your new life: 1991 (290) reads, "your now life."

NOTES FOR CHAPTER XI:

Copy text: 1991 TS.

p. 159: [Epigraph]: Quoted from the translation of Schnitzler's *Flight into Darkness* (70) with a few alterations: "brightly" deleted from "the whole house was brightly lighted up"; "Fate" not capitalized; "outward" changed to "outer."

p. 160(b): 'From that time onwards Ethan Brand was a fiend.': Despite the quotation marks this is not a direct quote from Hawthorne's story. It might be an amplification of "Thus Ethan Brand became a fiend" (*Hawthorne's Short Stories*. Ed. Newton Arvin New York: Vintage Books, 1960. 326). The passage Lowry used as the epigraph for Chapter XVI comes shortly after this one in Hawthorne's story.

p. 162(a): 'Eventually . . . no facts can hurt it!': Here, single quotation marks signify silent reading (cf. the following note).

p. 164(c): 'A terrible, terrible thing. That's Captain . . . ': In the 1991 TS (302) this line is introduced by a dash, but the discourse two paragraphs later is enclosed within single quotation marks, to indicate that it is imagined or hypothetical discourse. Since the first line clearly begins the imagined discourse, I have punctuated it accordingly.

p. 169(a): emerged: The 1991 reading (311) is "immerged," whose meaning—plunged into or immersed—does not fit the context.

NOTES FOR CHAPTER XII:

Copy text: 1936 TS; epigraph from 1991 TS. There are two partial sets of unnumbered pages from the 1936 TS in NYPL 3:6 ("Fragments"), which together constitute a text for the entire chapter. (In these notes I have added my own page numbers for the 1936 TS.) The surviving 1936 pages for Chapters I, II, and IV, numbered 1–10, 12–25, and 58–72 respectively, might be from a single typescript (despite the absence of page 11), but the unnumbered pages of Chapter XII are more likely to have come from a different typescript. Apart from the epigraph, however, it was Jan Gabrial's source for the chapter in her 1991 typescripts.

From this chapter on, the typescripts use quotation marks rather than dashes for dialogue.

p. 170: [Epigraph]: Slightly different in Ouspensky's *Tertium Organum* (see the annotation).

p. 170(c): Zzzzt!: The 1936 TS (1) has a period, which Jan changed to an exclamation point in 1991 (312). I have accepted her emendation, which seems appropriate, but not her extension of the word to "Zzzssst."

p. 171(d): Haarfragre: In the 1936 TS of this chapter, spelled thus twenty-five out of twenty-seven times; the two exceptions ("Haafragre shrugged his shoulders," page 9; "Haardragre added as if to himself," page 12) are clearly typos.

Although Lowry might simply have misspelled "Haarfagre" (see the annotation), it is conceivable that he wanted to change the name slightly, as when, in *Under the Volcano*, the name of Dr. Vigil hints at Virgil. The error, if it is one, is almost certainly Lowry's rather than Jan's.

p. 172(a): what your father said—that something might happen: There is no dash here in the 1936 TS (4), but it is included in the 1991 TS (315) and is needed.

p. 172(a): "I climbed it once . . . ": In the 1936 TS (4) this is set off as a new paragraph, indicating a change of speakers from Haarfragre to Sigbjørn, but in 1991 (316) Jan treated it as a continuation of Haarfragre's comments. The line does not sound like Sigbjørn, so I have retained the emendation.

p. 173(a): He was a member . . . without a core!: There are two copies of this page (5) from the 1936 TS, one of which contains Lowry's handwritten correction of a typing error: "that luxury" is typed twice, the first instance being typed over and "the soul" written above. Also, "Oh Peer Gynt" is emended by hand to "Ah Peer Gynt." Jan must have seen these emendations, since her 1991 TS has "Ah" rather than "Oh," but she ignored the other, crucial change and instead wrote "but bordering luxury," a change with no basis in the earlier typescript. There is a third change in the 1936 TS: at some point, on the same page as the other changes, "that onion" was crossed out. It is not clear when that happened, but the change makes little sense.

p. 173(b): *Trelast damper* . . . : The Norwegian here has been extensively revised (1936 6, 7; 1991 318, 319).

p. 173(c): distant: Thus in 1991 (318); 1936 (6) has "distance."

p. 176(a): "That would have been bad." "That would be": This exchange was written in Lowry's hand on one copy of page 10 in the 1936 TS; it does not appear in the 1991 version.

p. 179(c): reined: Both 1936 (16) and 1991 (330) have "reigned."

NOTES FOR CHAPTER XIII:

Copy text: 1991 TS.

p. 181: [Epigraph]: Lowry's source, a list of "The Sayings of Lao-Tzŭ" in Ouspensky's *Tertium Organum* (289), reads: "Being Great, it passes on; passing on, it becomes remote; having become remote it returns." Either Lowry or Jan added the ellipsis, perhaps to reinforce the idea of continuity.

p. 181(a): Veryd to Voel Nant: "Veryd" might simply be an error for "Foryd," but it might be Lowry's quasi-phonetic recollection of the town's name. The typescript reading "Noel Vant," however, is probably an inadvertent spoonerism for Voel Nant.

p. 181(c): Anglesey: 1991 (333): "Anglesea."

p. 183(b): the Manchester Ship Canal: 1991 (336): "the Manchester ship-canal."

p. 186(cd): St.Helens: Spelled thus, without a space, both times in the 1991 TS (343) and often, although not invariably, in the city itself (see www.visitsthelens.com and www.sthelens.gov.uk).

NOTES FOR CHAPTER XIV:

Copy Text: 1991 TS except for the last half page of XIV.1, which is based on an unnumbered page from the 1936 TS collected, along with Chapter XII, in NYPL 3:6 ("Fragments"). The typescript's erratic use of quotation marks (generally, double quotation marks in VIV.1, single for much of XIV.2, and double again at the end of XIV.2) has not been corrected.

p. 190: XIV.1: XIV is the only chapter formally divided into sections, which in the 1991 TS are designated XIV and XIV.2.

p. 190: [Epigraph #1]: The epigraph in the 1991 TS deviates so much from the text of Jensen's *The Long Journey* (III:48) that I have corrected it throughout. With two typos corrected, the 1991 reading is:

> Christoforus then carried him over, but now for the first time found a burden that almost exceeded his powers. The little child was a marvellous child, it grew heavier and heavier, and the river swelled beneath him, and became doubly dark, it was as though the elements would swallow him. The child weighed him down, never before had anything been so heavy. Such is the weight of Life's germ and the time to come of which we have no knowledge. And yet it seemed that the burden itself sustained him else he would never have come across without straining himself. When at last he reached the opposite bank it was as though he had carried the whole world on his shoulders. (NYPL 4:4; unnumbered page inserted between 347 and 348)

p. 190: [Epigraph #2]: The passage as it appears in Frank's "The Writer's Part in Communism" reads as follows:

> The revolutionary hour in which we live is but the present phase of the process, centuries old and destined to outlast almost the memory of economic conflict, whereby man (not a privileged, exploiting class, but man as a whole) will emerge into a conscious culture; even as the child at a certain physiologic stage must become adult or go down into degeneration. The key of the present phase of the long process is economic; therefore the importance of the class struggle and the imperative of entering it on the side of the workers.

There are several differences between Frank's text and the epigraph that might be attributed to sloppy quotation: the typescript substitutes "hour at which" for Frank's "hour in which," "outlive" for "outlast," "degeneracy" for "degeneration," "long phase" for "long process." However, the striking phrase "so man stands at this hour" does not appear in either printing of Frank's article, suggesting that it might be Lowry's contribution to the epigraph, so I have allowed Lowry's phrasing to stand.

p. 191(ab): As a matter of fact . . . fares: I have taken the liberty of repunctuating this sentence in order to clarify it without changing phrasing or syntax. 1991 reads:

> As a matter of fact it was going to be a sort of holiday to him also since by an arrangement between the mushroom, or owner, drivers..of whom he was one..the journeymen and the flatraters,- that is, between those drivers hired by their cab-owners (who took half,) and those who virtually rented their cabs from the owners and took all, his fares had been limited to a percentage which he would exceed over Easter if he taxied anything like the normal number of fares. (349)

The sentence would be clearer if Lowry had written "among" rather than "between," for there are three parties to the agreement: (1) mushroom drivers, (2) journeymen drivers, and (3) flatrate drivers.

p. 193(b): with both misgivings and curiosity: 1991 (353) reads, "with both misgivings and with curiosity."

p. 195(a): *Johnson Avenue*: This should be Johnston Avenue (see annotation), but I have retained the TS reading (357) because it is possible that the error is Webb's.

p. 195(b): ......: The six periods indicate a long pause, hence an exception to the general policy of regularizing ellipses.

p. 199(d): was impelled: From here to the end of XIV.1 the copy text is the surviving fragment from the 1936 typescript.

p. 200(b): another world: Jan's 1991 TS ends XIV.1 with "another world" (367), omitting the last twelve words of the paragraph.

p. 201(c): filetted: Thus in 1991 (370).

p. 202(b): Fyrbøter: 1991 (371) reads "Fryboter."

p. 206(c): who he vaguely imagined: 1991 (380) has "whom," which I assume is Jan's mistake.

p. 208(d): royal babe: This reference to the birth of Princess Alexandra on December 25, 1936 cannot have been foreseen in the typescript that the Lowrys left with Jan's mother before they left for Mexico months earlier. See the introduction and annotation.

NOTES FOR CHAPTER XV:

Copy text: 1991 TS.

p. 210: [Epigraph]: The 1991 reading (387) is "Forehead to forehead I meet thee this time, Moby Dick!" The deletion of "third" is too great an error to go uncorrected, since it sets up the chapter's theme of recurrence (see my introduction).

p. 211(d): But now was he to return again?: 1991 (390) "now" might be a typo for "how," or it might be what Lowry intended.

p. 213(c): *Nel mezzo del cammin di nuestra vita:* *Nuestra*, Spanish for Italian *nostra* (our), is wrong, but in what way? At least three possibilities present themselves: (1) Lowry made a mistake. (2) Lowry wrote *nuestra* to call into question the second old man's apparent knowledge of Italian. (3) The second old man deliberately uses the wrong word, either as a joke or as a means of testing Sigbjørn's Italian. The following note indicates why I believe the last possibility is the most likely.

p. 213(d): *In la sua voluntade è nostra pace:* See note on page 17. The appearance of *nostra* here reinforces my view that *nuestra*, just a few lines earlier, is a deliberate error by the second old man even though the speaker this time is the first old man.

p. 214(b): 'Nobody's . . . going.': In this chapter, double quotation marks indicate current dialogue, single marks remembered discourse.

p. 215(a): Could that seaman, Frank, now be this conductor?: Placed inside parentheses in 1991 (397). I suspect Jan considered deleting the line but realized that that would require more extensive revisions of the following paragraphs.

p. 218(d): *Halvt: Fullt: Sakte*: In 1991, *Half: Fuld: Sagte* (404).

NOTES FOR CHAPTER XVI:

Copy text: 1991 TS.

p. 220: [Hawthorne epigraph]: In Hawthorne's story the passage is longer: "Come, deadly element of Fire, —henceforth my familiar friend! Embrace me, as I do thee!" (*Hawthorne's Short Stories* 327).

p. 220: ["Jonson" epigraph]: Given the importance of *The Tragical History of Doctor Faustus* in *Under the Volcano*, one would expect Lowry to remember that this famous line comes from that play by Christopher Marlowe. In *La Mordida* (91) Lowry again confused Marlowe and Jonson by referring to Marlowe as the author of *Sejanus his Fall*. Despite the erroneous attribution, the passage from *Doctor Faustus* is quoted accurately.

p. 220(a): meridians: 1991 (405) has "medians."

p. 221(c): *Signalisering . . . Kristiania* 1901: This appears to be a notice that Lowry copied down to use in *Ultramarine*, in the process making as many errors as in the garden sign of *Under the Volcano*. The 1991 TS reads:

> *Signaliseiring areglerne maa noies efterkommes.*
> *Kvinder, barn, passagerer, og hjaelpelose.*
> *Personer skal sendes iland for skibets*
> *Besetning Kristiania 1901...*

This transcription introduces misspellings, runs words together, and introduces a period between an adjective and the noun it modifies (*hjaelpelose. Personer* would mean "helpless [disabled]. People"). It deletes the period after *besetning* (crew), a word that somehow becomes capitalized, apparently because it comes at the beginning of a line.

p. 222(b): Daggoo: 1991 (409) has "Dagoo."

p. 222(d): cinesthesia: Thus in 1991 (410); probably a deliberate distortion of *cenesthesia*, from Crookshank's introduction to Blondel's *The Troubled Conscience and the Insane Mind* (10–11) (see the annotation).

p. 224(a): Wilhelmsen liner: 1991 (412) has "Williamson liner."

NOTES FOR CHAPTER XVII:

Copy text: 1991 TS. (VII and XVII are the only chapters without epigraphs.)

p. 229(b): immediately forward: In 1991 (422) "immediately" is enclosed within handwritten parentheses. Jan might have wanted to avoid repeating the word from the previous sentence.

p. 230(c): Norskerennen: In 1991 (424), "Norske Rende."

p. 230(cd): which ran . . . Oslo fjord: In 1991 (424), enclosed within parentheses and set off by a comma after "channel."

pp. 230(d)–231(a): from which . . . forepeak: In 1991 (425), enclosed within parentheses and set off by commas.

p. 232(a): remarked: In 1991 (427), followed by an ellipsis rather than a comma.

NOTES FOR CHAPTER XVIII:

Copy text: 1991 TS. This "chapter," unnumbered in the 1991 typescript, includes material from sources other than the 1936 typescript, in which the text probably ended with Chapter XVII. The text that follows is derived from writings by Lowry, among them—as discussed in the introduction—a conversation in a draft of Lowry's *Dark as the Grave* (UBC 9:5 345–52) in which Lowry's autobiographical character Sigbjørn Wilderness tells the story of his own obsession with a Norwegian novelist named William Erikson, especially his trip to Norway to meet Erikson. Jan relied on this draft for part of her "Notes for the Last Three Chapters of In Ballast," and in turn relied on those notes in constructing a text for the last chapter. This process raises important questions of editorial principle, since Lowry wrote the section of *Dark as the Grave* with other ends in mind, but it provides some indication of where he apparently planned to take his narrative. One possibility that Lowry entertained for *In Ballast*, after the fire, seems to have been to abandon it as a separate novel, instead having Sigbjørn give a lengthy summary of it in *Dark as the Grave*, to preserve it in another form. Unfortunately, the published *Dark as the Grave* omits most of that summary.

p. 233: [Epigraph]: In *Tertium Organum*, after saying that our relationships with other people lead us to contain within ourselves "an innumerable number of great and little I's," some of which "do not even know one another, just as men who live in the same house may not know one another," Ouspensky elaborates on the analogy: "it may be said that 'man' has much in common with *a house* filled with inhabitants the most diverse." The remainder of the epigraph is quoted correctly except that it reverses the terms "involuntarily and unconsciously." Jan also typed "centre" as "center."

p. 233(b): (The three closing chapters . . . chapter 18.): Jan's note.

p. 234(b): met by chance . . . Møre: In 1991 (430), enclosed within quotation marks as well as set off by commas (three in all, with one before and one after the closing parenthesis). Since there are no accent marks in the 1991 TS, "Møre" is of course spelled "More."

p. 235(b): smørbrød: 1991 (432): "smorbrodt." Virtually all of the Norwegian words in this chapter are typed incorrectly in the 1991 typescripts and have been corrected to the extent that that has been possible.

p. 236(a): *'Only he in whom the past is stored is freighted for the future.'*: Slightly misquoted from Jensen (III:xii), with "stored" in place of "stowed."

p. 236(a): he is in Oslo: In the second 1991 TS (NYPL 4:4 433) this page is followed by another that Jan inserted into the typescript, headed "for interest only: insert; pp. 433-434." The insert, published in this edition as Appendix A, consists of prefatory comments on the sources for the remainder of the typescript, derived "from the existing excerpts and fragments of outlines for the chapters which would have comprised chapters 19 and 20," followed by a transcription of part of a letter from Lowry. There are several differences between this transcription and the original letter from which it is excerpted (CL 1:129–30), starting with the opening of this part of the letter, which in Sherrill Grace's edition of the correspondence reads "Hells delight" rather than "Hello delight." Aside from a few exceptions, I have made no attempt to edit this letter, which was neither written nor inserted in the 1991 typescript with publication in mind.

p. 236(a): Bimmonpolet: Properly, this should be "Vinmonopolet," but the annotations treat it as a deliberate distortion.

p. 237(b): Biblioteket: In 1991, "the Biblioteket" or "the Bibliothecket" (436, 437), in which the definite article is redundant since *Biblioteket* means "the Library"; likewise, "the Nationaltheatret" (1991 437, 439, 443). In each case I have deleted the English definite article.

p. 237(c): Notes from Malcolm's outline for In Ballast: Jan's editorial insertion. From here to page 367, "(end of fragment..)," the text is typed directly from pages12–15 of Jan's "Notes for Last Three Chapters of In Ballast (from Malcolm Lowry)," NYPL 3:5.

p. 237(d): Kristian IV's gate: 1991 (437) has "Christian den 4 des gade."

p. 237(d): Springboart and Tumpling Act: Thus in the 1991 TS (437) and in "Notes" (12); likewise in *Ultramarine* (1933 ed. 96). More accurately named "Springboart & Tumplingakt" in Lowry's "On Reading Edmund Wilson's Remarks about Rimbaud" (CP #68).

p. 238(b): who he feels would know: 1991 (438), "whom" etc.

p. 239(b): Birgit: A new character in the novel apparently destined to be Sigbjørn's next love interest, replacing Nina and the woman that he meets in the post office and kisses on the tram in Chapter XV. She is not Erikson's wife: like Grieg at the time of Lowry's visit, he is a bachelor.

p. 240(ab): principle of destruction: In 1991 (442), "principal of destruction."

NOTE

1. Many of the editorial decisions that shaped this text were influenced by Chris Ackerley's annotations, especially those which, in earlier drafts, called attention to misspellings of place names and other errors in the manuscripts.

Appendices

The Jan Gabrial Papers at the New York Public Library include parts of the 1936 typescript of *In Ballast to the White Sea* on which Jan based her planned edition of the novel, as well as two printouts of her own typescript. Both of her 1991 typescripts end, as Jan said the novel would have ended, with Sigbjørn's exclamation, "How shall I live without my misery?" It is not clear that this was to be the conclusion to the novel, but it does seem to be an appropriate conclusion for the chapter.

For the most part, Jan's typescripts differ from one another only in that some of the errors in the earlier typescript are corrected in the later one. There are, however, two major differences between the two printouts. (1) Inserted between pages 433 and 434 of the second, revised, typescript (page 236 in this edition) is a typed, single-spaced page, headed "for interest only: insert; pp. 433–434," which is printed below as Appendix A. Jan's note helps to explain the repetition of some material in the text that follows, and part of the note corresponds to Letter #48 in the collected letters (CL 1:129–30), to which it should be compared. (2) The earlier version of her typescript is followed by a separately paginated, 21-page typescript entitled "Notes for Last Three Chapters of In Ballast (from Malcolm Lowry)." As I have indicated in the introduction, pages 1–4 and 9–11 of "Notes" are adapted from a draft of Lowry's later novel *Dark as the Grave Wherein My Friend Is Laid* that is held at the University of British Columbia (UBC 9:5 345–52); other parts are apparently based on materials that, like most of the 1936 typescript, have been lost or discarded.

Although the "Notes" typescript was Jan's primary source for the last part of *In Ballast to the White Sea*, it also includes several interesting passages that did not find their way into the typescript of the novel, or that appear there only in very different form. For that reason they are printed in Appendix B.

APPENDIX A

for interest only: insert; pp. 433-434

NOTE: The following notes are from the existing excerpts and fragments of outlines for the chapters which would have comprised chapters 19 and 20, including two versions of the final paragraph.

There are likewise two versions of his meeting with Grieg: the first one, written 1934–35, two to three years after it took place, is probably the more accurate; the second from notes written but not used, in DARK AS THE GRAVE (some twelve years later) presents their encounter in a more exuberant light.

I am including the pertinent portion of one of Malcolm's letters to me, written in July 1933, which is interesting because of the specific details he gives regarding Oslo; and also because of the odd reference to himself as "one of the best friends of Nordahl Grieg," and to me as his wife: at this point, in spite of our many crossing letters, our joint history was brief: we had known each other barely two days in Granada.

> Hello delight, I hope this gets you in Barcelona—
>
> Scandinavia? Well, I know only Norway, which is a spiritual home or something of your doppelganger and me and my doppelganger.
>
> If you go there, queer things will happen. I promise you that. In the first place, it's as full of ghosts as Spain is empty of them, and they'll all try to help you at once because they'll recognise you. If you go there, do as I tell you, and you won't become confused.
>
> I should spend two to three days in Oslo, and if you do go, go to the Rode Molle and drink sherry under the geraniums: go down the Holmenkollen from there, which is the Oslo Underground, just turn to the left at the Nationaltheatret—go down the *right* entrance, and when you see a tram come along with Frognersaeteren on its forehead, take it, pay 90 ore, I think it is, and go all the way.
>
> It will take you up a mountain which is just the best thing in the world, and there's a restaurant up there where they speak German for you. If you want a quiet and excellent restaurant in Oslo, Jacques Bagatelle on the Bygdo Alle is marvelous as I remember it. And I should visit Bygdo itself and see the Viking Ship and drink wine and look out on the fjord. By God I'll be there in spirit with you all right, all right, Jan.

If you say you are the wife of one of the best friends of Nordahl Grieg it might help: his address used to be 68 Bygdo Alle and *Skibet Gaar Videre* is his book from which my play is adapted.

Eine langer brief kommt sofort, aber Liebe kommt hiermit is the nicest thing anyone ever said and I say it back to you with an unending ache of love in my heart......Malcolm

You should of course try to see Bergen also, and if you ever take a train journey for God's sake do it in the daytime because the country's marvelous.

APPENDIX B

[Notes 4; prefaced by Jan's parenthetical comment]

(Note: the name of the 'teacher' was Carsten Walderhaug and he wrote Malc again May 9th, 1932, which letter I have, urging him to write, to send a copy of his book, and mentioning that he, a violinist, had now started a little 'Jazzband' called 'Rumba' and are playing the "night clubs and the streets, with many jobs.")

The conflicting messages relayed to Haarfragre seem to Sigbjørn to reflect his own strange irreconcilabilities, though he must not force significance where no significance exists, but feels Tor's presence.

[Notes 8; from Jensen, *The Long Journey*; see annotation **XVIII.62**]

(Columbus completes the Northern migration and at the same time renders impossible Christianity as a terrestrial dream. The Kingdom of Heaven he sought was the bible's mystical abode, Paradise; but then he sought it on earth. He knew not that it was rooted in his nature. He sails for the Indies, means Paradise, and finds the New World: doesn't it look as if the Almighty, or someone not as good, was playing a game with him.

In the person of Columbus the pagan yearning for nature's unity with Christianity's *Fata Morganas*...and they perish together. It might be said that Columbus, regarded as the hero of a tragedy of destiny.) [sic]

[Notes 16]

Sigbjørn believes in communism but also believes that the soul is going out on its journey in life to seek God. And believes in the incommensurability of human or divine law, but believes also that the body should seek to move within the soul.

Tor believes that there is no single, central, immortal soul. Quite, says Sigbjørn. I never thought that concept indestructible. But what about the multiform, external evolving or devolving 'soul' (call it what you will) that all is chance; his own faith is that if all things obey a simple—or complex—law of supply and demand... the mad fishmonger of Worcester, etc., etc. it is nihilistic.

Captain Hansen-Tarnmoor believes in the destruction of time, in eternal recurrence, simply in a notion that life is like a wave, that the tendencies of a previous life are strengthened in this one: but this also is based on no faith. The notions of punishment and reward, etcetera believed in by Sigbjørn, however, do not fit in: all he can say is if you turn back from the true path, whether God or damnation was at the end of it, you loose something nobody can arrest/

[Notes 17; from Harry Crosby, "Illustrations of Madness" 102]

FIRE: I have heard for days and nights on end the reverberations crashing in my head of all the skyscrapers and buildings of the world, the reverberation of the crashing of ships in the fogs at sea, the reverberation of the crashing of our thoughts on the cold floor of the brain.

[Notes 18–19]

the officers put away their white uniforms...

Ten days after making London she was off again to Oslo, then she hurried to Hamburg to pick up a cargo for Reykjavik in Iceland. And thus they passed the winter, running from one port to the next, no matter the fog, the gales, the snow, and the general beastliness of the weather.

After six months of this battering, attention to the ship itself became essential. On her hull and superstructure barely a square foot of paint was left. Her decks were corroded by salt. Her rails were twisted by the seas that had broken inboard. Only by ceaseless repairs could her engineers keep her going. The wheel itself carried marks from the ice and the wet and even the binoculars and sextants of the officers did not altogether escape.

We passed a solitary tramp about an hour ago, portside, a Norwegian. She was pretty low in the water and rusty in the bargain, and except for her q.m. and watch-keeper she was absolutely deserted. And there's one ship that the mighty bulk of the Star of the Seas has not swept out of existence.

A glare rent the darkness as a furnace door was opened. Coal dropped flaming to the floor-plates; a fireman kicked it away. The fiery mass inside the furnace hissed and sputtered as the man thrust in his rake. He turned to the coal, and with a deep grunt tearing his chest at each pitch he sent great shovelsful hurling through the opening. At length, with a blow from his shovel, he slammed the furnace door, let the shovel itself drop on the floor-plates, and wiped his forehead with the sweatrag he carried round his neck.

The cranks that rose and plunged like mechanical arms kept producing the slightest shock, yet in some way contributory to that hollow thump which was sensed throughout the ship as if it were the beating of a heart.

The atmosphere was stifling, humid, laden with steam and heavy with the smell of hot oil and grease. There was everywhere the sense of motion that Sigbjørn felt throughout his body and his head rang with the confused clamour of it all as he edged carefully by the whirling, plunging metal.

Contributors

Chris Ackerley's research area is modernism and his speciality is annotation, especially of the writings of Malcolm Lowry and Samuel Beckett. His first book (with Lawrence J. Clipper), *A Companion to Malcolm Lowry's Under the Volcano* (University of British Columbia Press, 1984), has become a standard reference. He updated this in a dedicated issue (Nos. 49–50) of *The Malcolm Lowry Review*, and in a website dedicated to *Under the Volcano*. His recent work centred on Samuel Beckett. He has co-authored (with S. E. Gontarski) *The Grove Companion to Samuel Beckett* (Grove Press, 2004), republished as *The Faber Companion to Samuel Beckett* (Faber and Faber, 2006) and has annotated Beckett's novels *Murphy* (Journal of Beckett Studies Books, 1998 and Edinburgh University Press, 2004) and *Watt* (Journal of Beckett Studies Books, 2006 and Edinburgh University Press, 2010). More recently (2012–2014) Ackerley won a prestigious research award from the Royal Society of New Zealand for a major study of the medieval and traditional roots of the modernist aesthetic.

Vik Doyen completed his MA thesis on Malcolm Lowry's *Under the Volcano* in 1968. He then studied at the University of Pennsylvania and did archival research in the Malcolm Lowry Collection at UBC for his doctoral dissertation *Fighting the Albatross of Self : A Genetic Study of the Literary Work of Malcolm Lowry* (Katholieke Universiteit te Leuven, 1973). In 1984 he returned to UBC for archival research on Lowry's *October Ferry to Gabriola* and published "From Innocent Story to Charon's Boat: Reading the *October Ferry* Mss," in Sherrill Grace's edition of *Swinging the Maelstrom: New Perspectives on Malcolm Lowry* (McGill-Queen's University Press, 1992). In 1987 he taught, together with Chris Ackerley, a UBC graduate seminar on the manuscripts of the Malcolm Lowry Collection. He also presented papers on Lowry at international conferences in Norwich (1978), Vancouver (1987 and 2009), Toronto (1997), Antwerp (2005) and Brighton (2007).

Patrick A. McCarthy is a professor of English at the University of Miami and editor of the *James Joyce Literary Supplement*. His publications on Malcolm Lowry include *Forests of Symbols: World, Text, and Self in Malcolm Lowry's Fiction* (University of Georgia Press, 1994); *Malcolm Lowry's "La Mordida": A Scholarly Edition*, ed. (University of Georgia Press, 1996); *Joyce/Lowry: Critical Perspectives*, co-ed. with Paul Tiessen (University Press of Kentucky, 1997); "Totality and Fragmentation in Lowry and Joyce," in *A Darkness That Murmured: Essays on Malcolm Lowry and the Twentieth Century*, ed. Frederick Asals and Paul Tiessen (University of Toronto Press, 2000); "Modernism's Swansong: Malcolm Lowry's *Under the Volcano*," in *A Companion to the British and Irish Novel 1945–2000*, ed. Brian Shaffer (Blackwell, 2005); and "*Under the Volcano*," in *The Literary Encyclopedia* (online).

Miguel Mota is an associate professor of English at the University of British Columbia in Vancouver. He has published on numerous 20th-century and contemporary writers and filmmakers, including Malcolm Lowry, Derek Jarman, Jeanette Winterson and Mike Leigh. With Paul Tiessen he has published *The Cinema of Malcolm Lowry* (University of British Columbia Press, 1990). With Chris Ackerley, Vik Doyen, Patrick McCarthy and Paul Tiessen, he is co-editing a trilogy of novels by Lowry, published by the University of Ottawa Press. Furthermore, he has produced a film documentary, *After Lowry* (2010), and his book on the status of screenplays in print culture is forthcoming from Manchester University Press.

Paul Tiessen, founding editor of the *Malcolm Lowry Newsletter* (1977–1984) and *The Malcolm Lowry Review* (1984–2002) and Professor Emeritus at Wilfrid Laurier University, has published scholarly articles and book chapters on Malcolm Lowry. Also, he wrote the Introduction for Lowry's and Margerie Lowry's *Notes on a Screenplay for F. Scott Fitzgerald's Tender is the Night* (Bruccoli Clark, 1976) and edited *The Letters of Malcolm Lowry and Gerald Noxon 1940–1952* (University of British Columbia Press, 1988) and *Apparently Incongruous Parts: The Worlds of Malcolm Lowry* (Scarecrow Press, 1990). He co-edited: *The Cinema of Malcolm Lowry: A Scholarly Edition of Lowry's 'Tender Is the Night'* (UBC Press, 1990; with Miguel Mota); *Joyce/Lowry: Critical Perspectives* (University Press of Kentucky, 1997; with Patrick A. McCarthy); and *A Darkness That Murmured: Essays on Malcolm Lowry and the Twentieth Century* (University of Toronto Press, 2000; with Frederick Asals).

Printed in October 2014
by Gauvin Press,
Gatineau, Québec